HUGH OF TWYNHAM

Michael Stannard

Natula Publications

ISBN 1 897 887 04 3 (hardback)
ISBN 1 897 887 05 1 (paperback)

Natula Publications
Briar Park Business Centre
11 Stour Road
Christchurch
Dorset
BH23 1PL

Cover illustration and line drawings by Peter Newman © 1993

The line drawings heading chapters 2, 3, 9, 10, 17 were inspired by the roundels from the new stained glass window in the Priory which was designed by Hugh Powell.

The drawing 'The Carpenter' is by kind permission of Brian Mead.

British Library Cataloguing-in-Publication Data.
A catalogue record for this book is available from the British Library.

Printed by Pardy & Son (Printers) Ltd., Ringwood, Hampshire.

Foreword

By The Right Honourable The Lord Digby, K.St.J.,
Lord Lieutenant of Dorset.

In this book you will find the story of the building of a great Priory church which, in 1994, celebrates the nine hundredth anniversary of its foundation. The building is unique in several ways. Not only is it the longest parish church in England, but because of its fame, it caused the town to change its name in the Middle Ages from the old Saxon 'Twynham' to the present name of 'Christchurch'. Though written as a work of fiction, the book is based on historical figures both national and local, draws heavily on recorded facts, and contains previously unpublished material, all of which helps to throw light on the life and times of the ordinary folk of the period.

My Saxon forbears would have been aware of the major events and conditions in the country during this period, and since my Norman ancestors arrived in this country at about the same time, though not in the same area, I found the tale particularly interesting. The book has also given me a better understanding of the everyday lives of people in the eleventh and twelfth centuries, and the important part played by the legends connected with this particular building, I recommend the book to those who seek inspiration from the past for their lives in the future.

DIGBY.
Patron, 1994 Christchurch Priory Festival.

To Jeanne

Preface

This is a work of fiction and should be judged as such. However, the story tells of the building of the longest parish church in England, which celebrates its 900th anniversary in 1994, is set against a background of well-documented historical fact, containing many real people whose names and actions are widely recorded. There are also well-known local legends included which, though their historical accuracy cannot be verified, have come to be accepted as true from constant repetition since time immemorial. Since it is accepted that there is some truth in the old saying 'there is no smoke without fire', it is more than likely that something similar to the legends actually took place.

The historical characters are real people, as are many of the lesser characters whose names are recorded in such documents as the Domesday Book and the ancient Town Charters. It is the familes living in the ancient burgh of Twynham – which we know as the town of Christchurch – who are fictional, though similar people probably did really exist and play the parts they have been given.

History books tend to give us the impression that life in the past consisted of little but battles, pillage and carnage, interspersed with plot and counter plot. Even during the 'anarchy' of Stephen's reign, the Wars of the Roses and, to a lesser extent, the Civil War of Charles I's reign, much of the country never became closely involved in the fighting. Perhaps their only involvement was when some troop horse or infantry stamped through their crops flattening them and spoiling their harvest. Indeed, some parts of the country never saw anything of the wars at all. Christchurch, or Twynham as it was then known, being separated from the seat of power at Winchester by the New Forest, would have been thus sheltered.

Ordinary people have always lived very ordinary lives for most of the time. It is only occasionally that people are thrown into the midst of great events and their lives become affected by them in ways that they could not at the time foresee, and humble folk become part of the wider historical picture that we can view. It is this concept, based on the building of the ancient Priory Church in Christchurch, that this book tries to portray.

Throughout the book I have mostly used modern place names which, though historically inaccurate, will enable the reader to identify the location of the various parts of the action. No doubt historians will readily substitute the ancient place names for their own satisfaction. There are a few exceptions, Sarum is used since its location is the ancient hill fort outside Salisbury, a town built almost a century after this tale ends. The Isle of Wight is referred to by its commonly known Roman name of Vectis. The ancient Royal Forest in Hampshire is called by its pre-Norman name of Andret, for only the parts added by the Conqueror could at that time be called "New". Christchurch has, of course, to be called Twynham, since it was only as a result of the great Priory Church being built that the town acquired its present name. For some centuries the town was commonly called Christchurch-Twynham, although it is interesting that by 1216 at the latest, a charter of William de Redvers, Earl of Devon, refers to his 'Manor at Christchurch'.

I have drawn on four main contemporary sources for much of the historical detail. They are: the Anglo-Saxon Chronicle, The Domesday Record, the Christchurch Cartulary, and the Durham Charters. The credit for any historical accuracy must be given to these and the many other sources that I have consulted. These are too numerous to list fully, but I must acknowledge the debt I owe to such people as Ralph Arnold, Frank Barlow, H. S. Bennett, Nancy Bradfield, Iris Brook, R. F. Cassady, H. H. E. Craster, H. A. Cronne, Nicholas Culpeper, Professor Barry Cunliffe, Taylor Dyson, F. W. Maitland, J. N. J. Myers, Roger C. Norris of the Durham Chapter Library, H. S. Offler, A. L. Poole, Jeremy Potter, Frederic Seebohm, R. W. Southern, Sir Frank and Lady Stenton, L. E. Tavener, and P. Vinogradoff. Locally, I am also indebted to John R. Forster, Michael Hodges, Arthur T. Lloyd, Ruth Lavender, Len Newman, David J. Stagg, Ken Tullett, Frank Tyhurst, Allen White, Austen Willson, and, of course, the Vicar and churchwardens of the Priory Church, Christchurch. The blame for any historical inaccuracy lies squarely at my door. In return I claim credit for any pleasure that this tale may give.

I also owe a great debt to Bryan Wilcox, for his encouragement and advice and painstaking proofreading, and, of course, to Jane Martin, who undertook to see the book through its birth pangs. Without the help of all these people the book would have been stillborn.

Christchurch, 1993.

Contents

Illustrations

The Burgh of Twynham

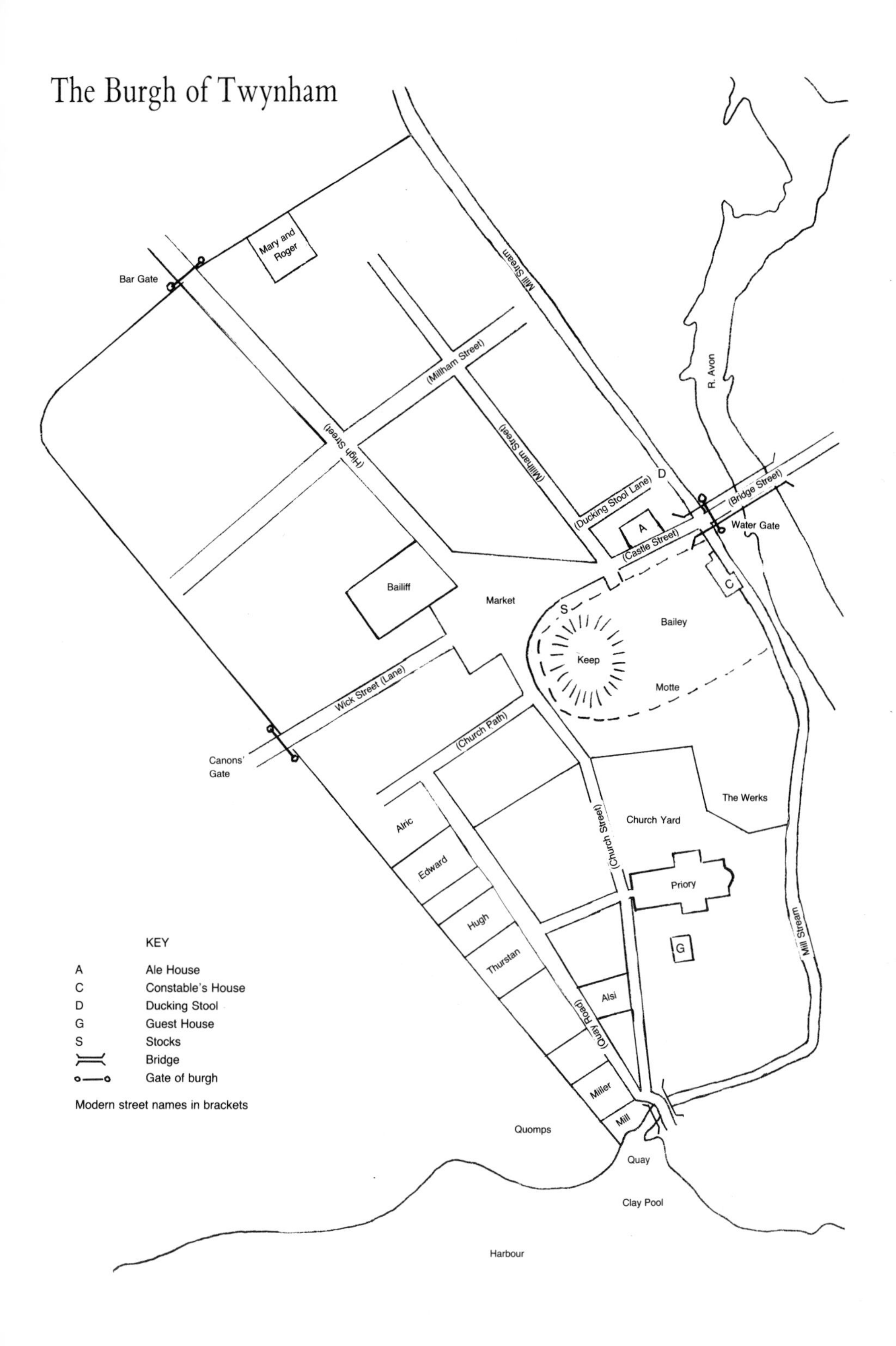

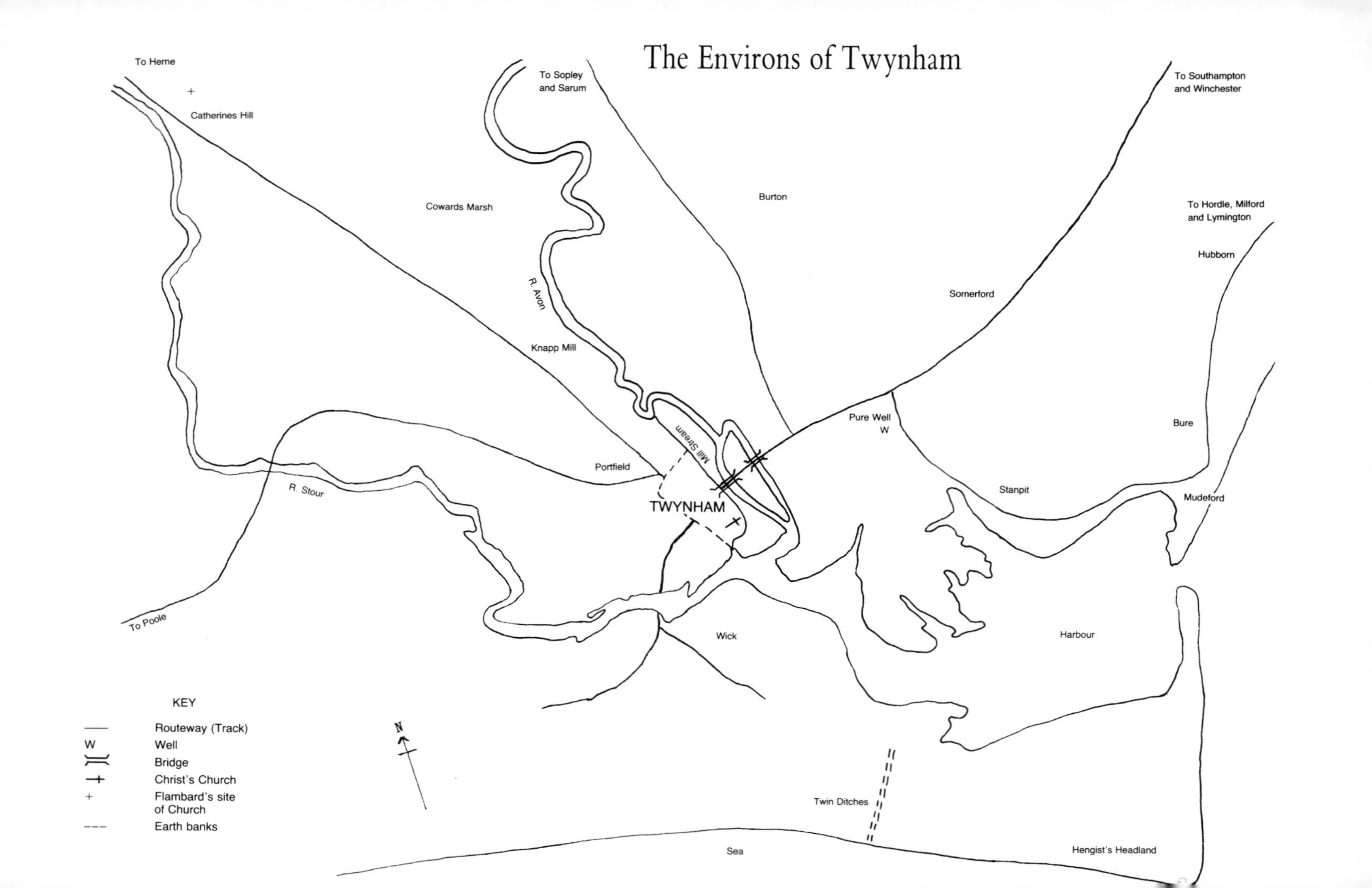

The Environs of Twynham
To Herne
Catherines Hill
To Sopley
and Sarum
Cowards Marsh
R. Avon
Knapp Mill
Burton
To Southampton
and Winchester
To Hordle, Milford
and Lymington
Hubborn
Somerford
Pure Well
W
Bure
Mill Stream
Portfield
R. Stour
TWYNHAM
Stanpit
Mudeford
To Poole
Wick
Harbour
Twin Ditches
Sea
Hengist's Headland
N
KEY
Routeway (Track)
W Well
Bridge
Christ's Church
Flambard's site
of Church
Earth banks

Chapter 1 1086

"Hugh, Hugh, what ails you lad? You should be up betimes today if you wish to see the King's Commissioners arrive. There is much to be done aiding your father at the mill before you can go to the bridge to watch for the Norman soldiers and those that come with them. Hugh, lad! Bestir your bones! Your brother and sister have broken their fast long since, and are already away about their business, so you had best look to your tasks."

My eyes were full of sleep and I had to knuckle them hard to bring myself fully awake. It was still dark in the cott, but I could see from the two piles of untidy bedding that my younger brother, Osbern, and Emma, the sister who was born between us, were indeed abroad. I sat up, and fumbling for my tunic, pulled it over my head. My breeches seemed to have gone astray, but I found them finally in a heap beside the narrow bed where Emma had been sleeping and struggled into them. They would soon be too small for me and Osbern would have them then. Our mother would then have to stitch me another pair, for despite her scolding she was kindly and cared well for us children.

Groping under the bed that Osbern and I shared, I found one shoe and eventually the other and pulled them hurriedly on. They were beginning to pinch my feet, for I seemed to be growing fast this year, and they also would soon be too small. Osbern would have these as well before many weeks were out, though they would not last him long, for I was hard on my clothes particularly when working with Father in our mill. I crawled out of our inner sleeping room to see Mother slicing a goodly hunk of bread from the loaf. On the table beside her was a crock which held honey, so I knew my belly would be full that day. Being the miller's son brought its advantages for we never lacked for flour to make bread, though sometimes, when the harvests were bad, it was little more than the sweepings from the floor.

"Here son, I've sweetened your bread, though it amazes me that I should, when you lie befuddled in your bed when the others are already about their business. They had no such favours from me."

She ruffled my hair and turned to busy herself with the cares of the house, and I smiled at her, for I knew that our mother cared for me, as the eldest of the three, perhaps a little more than the others. Though I had seen but fourteen summers, I was tall and strong for my age and could lift a full sack of corn for my father. It was hard working for him in the mill for he made small allowance for my youth, saying, rightly, that if I wished to learn a man's trade, then I must do the work of a man. Heaving sacks of corn had put hard muscles on me, so that the other boys held me in some respect for my strength, and because Father was a man of note in the burgh.

I munched my bread, scraping a dribble of the sweet honey from my chin where it was trying to escape. It was too good to lose any of it and Mother must have been in fine good humour to have treated me like this. Though our hives had done well last year, honey was never plentiful and had so many uses as our only sweetening that it was carefully guarded. Slaking my thirst from a clay beaker of water that stood in the corner of the room, I rubbed my mouth with the back of my hand to clean it before thanking Mother with a kiss on her plump cheek.

"Get along with you, your father will be angry with your lateness and I have no time for such foolery," she cried in mock anger, but I could see from her eyes that she was well pleased by my gesture.

It was but a few steps to the mill which stood at the end of its stream at the place where it fell into a pool beside the swift-flowing Stour. Only last week, Father had been explaining to me how our mill-stream, which had been dug by our ancient Saxon forebears so long ago, took its water from the steady flowing Avon river, yet emptied into the swift Stour near where the two rivers meet. He said it was because the ham, as it was then, had been built between the two rivers that it had become known as Twynham. He also said that later an ancient Saxon King, whose name he knew not, had caused the ham to have a defensive wall built around it, so that it became the strong burgh that it now is. One of the only three in the whole shire, along with Southampton and the King's seat at Winchester, he had boasted.

Casting a wary glance through the door of the mill to see if my father was by the millstones, I was relieved to hear the thud of corn sacks above the noise of the grinding stones. That meant that Father was busy in the room above, feeding corn into the hopper for grinding. Slipping quickly into the mill-house, I busied myself beside the trough where the ground flour collected, tidying up a few sacks that had fallen awry. Quickly dusting a little flour over my arms and face to make it seem that I had been hard at work for some time, I slipped across the mill floor and stumped with mock weariness up the ladder that led to the upper part of the mill where father was working.

"I've tidied up those fallen sacks, and seen that the flour was running freely into the trough. It will soon be full. Do you wish me to help you change it for an empty one or can you manage it by yourself?"

This I said to test him, for I knew he was a proud man and valued his strength and would not lightly ask for help with even the sternest loads. But he saw through my guile - had he not done the same with his own father? - and acknowledged my offer with a nod and a grin, and a twinkle in his eye that showed me that he knew my thoughts. I would be glad to be away as fast as possible to witness the excitement that the day should bring, but must first serve Father so long as he should have need of me.

"Ay," he said, "there is work a-plenty for today. Methinks we shall have several loads of corn to grind for Godric, for I saw him preparing his cart early and he said he was going to his store. He fears that the King's Commissioner will wish to bide with him next to the church and perhaps the soldiers too. Who knows how many days they will remain here, so that he will have many more mouths to feed beside the twenty-four canons - and they have appetite enough. There will be a full day's milling ahead of us, to be sure."

My face fell, for I knew that I could not leave my duty till all was finished and that if what Father said was true, then the angelus would have sounded before we were through. There would be no chance to see the soldiers arrive. I turned away lest father see my disappointment and started to hump the remaining sacks of grain towards the hopper head whence Father could feed them down to the grinding stones beneath. As I put down the third, I heard him laugh and felt his hand upon my shoulder.

"Nay, lad, I said it but to test you, to see if you were worthy of my trust. A miller must be trustworthy if he is to succeed, for the food of the burgh passes through his hands and he should not give the villeins short measure nor play them false with half-ground flour. My father Osric held this mill from the church as I do but the people of the burgh knew he ground good meal so came to him rather than the lord's mill when they could. In like manner they come to me, for my father taught me his art well. I will also teach you what I know, that you too may earn the respect of those who come to us, for one day this mill will be yours.

Finish stacking those sacks by the hopper head while I see to the flow of water on the wheel - I think I set the hatch boards a little wide for the flow of water we have this morning - and then you may be away. I know what you want to do, but keep a civil tongue in your head when the soldiers are near, for their swords are sharp though their heads be thick."

I looked up then, proud to be Oswald's son, for he was known throughout the burgh as a fair man whose word was good. He had the trust of Godric who was accepted as the head of the twenty-four canons who cared for the stone church and its nine chapels, though he held no fancy title such as it is said they use in the great burgh at Winchester. I toiled with a will, and before the sun was shining fully on the mill-wheel and noon was still an hour off, I had finished my tasks. I straightened my back to ease my aching muscles, for though I was used to the toil, I had worked fast to be finished the sooner. Father saw me and nodded with approval.

"Remember, Hugh," he said, "if you hold a carrot before an ass, he will walk for you and not heed the load upon his back. Beat him with a stick and he will not budge though you beat till he bleeds. It is so with a man: offer him a reward and he will work for you with a will. You have moved those sacks in half the time it would usually take. Mind the lesson and it will serve you well. Now away with you and see what is afoot this day, and keep your nose clean!"

I grinned and thanked him. I lingered only long enough to dust the flour from my clothes and limbs. Then, plunging my head and arms into the swirling mill-stream where it left the wheel, to cool my sweat and freshen my countenance, I hastened up the rise that led to the church and its surrounding nine chapels.

Approaching me was one leading Godric's cart which Father had mentioned earlier, now loaded with sacks of grain. Father was going to have plenty to do with me not there to help him raise the sacks to the upper floor. It crossed my mind that I should turn back to help him, for it was a task that needed two, but he had said I could go and no doubt the carter would be persuaded to help him, so I passed on.

Coming to the top of the rise, I slowed my pace to a walk since I did not wish to be seen to be hastening and excited. There were other boys heading the same way as I and it was good to see that they were running and some of them still had signs of their morning's work upon them. The miller's son must seem more aloof than other villein's sons, so they might think he need not toil, but could use his time as he wished.

Having passed through the churchyard, I entered the short street that led to the crossing at the middle of the burgh. Here I turned right-handed to descend the road that led to the nearer of the two bridges that crossed the first of the two parts of the River Avon. Upon this bridge, which was raised about an arm's length above the surrounding ground, stood Alwin the bailiff, with Godric beside him. Standing a little apart, though in front of the main group of villeins, was Alwin's wife Mary, distinguished in a newly brushed gown, her corn-coloured hair partly covered by its hood which was edged with a bright band of different coloured wools. Beside her were her two sons, Alric who is almost a year older than I though not as tall, and Alnoth who is but ten. On her other side stood Isabel their sister, her fair hair flowing down her shoulders and her light tunic held close around her slim waist by a blue girdle. Though two years my junior, she had a ready wit and winning smile which made her always welcome in our household. As I approached, she turned from her mother with whom she had been sharing a private joke, and smiled at me with her bright blue eyes. Was there ever a more truly Saxon maid, I thought.

"Oh Hugh, come and stand with us. The Normans are said to be approaching the further bridge and will soon be here. I think I can see the dust rising from the road yonder. My father and Godric are to welcome them and show them where they are to conduct their survey of all that is held in the burgh. I am to act as serving-wench to the Commissioner of my Lord the King. If I plead with Father, maybe he will permit you to act as page and help me."

My heart skipped a beat and I hoped that I hid my blushes. It was not for the favour that Isabel was showing me I told myself, but for the chance of being near the soldiers and examining their weapons and chain-mail. Such men-at-arms as we saw had little more than a leather gambeson, with perhaps a plastron to guard their chest from arrows or a direct sword-thrust. They said that the Norman helms were quite different from our Saxon ones which fitted like a bee-skep over the head. Soon I would know.

Isabel pulled at her mother's sleeve and, receiving a nodding smile from her, she moved over towards her father and slipped her arm through his. Waiting till he had finished his conversation with Godric, she spoke in her most winsome manner to him. Though I was out of earshot, I could guess what she was saying, for Alwin turned towards me looking me up and down. He seemed satisfied with what he saw and I was glad I had taken the trouble to brush the flour off my clothes and smooth down my long hair so that I did not look too unkempt. She must be a sweet-tongued wench I thought, for after a short time Alwin nodded to her and then turned and beckoned me to his side.

"Hugh," he said, "Do you think Oswald your father has knocked enough sense into your head for you to act as page to the Commissioner while he lodges in the burgh?"

"I trust so my Lord." A little flattery never came amiss. Though I knew he was not entitled to such a distinction, at a time like this to grant him a dignity that was not his would serve to raise his confidence in himself and his respect in the eyes of others.

"My father has always found me willing to do his bidding. If it pleases you sir, I trust that Godric will speak for me too since he has been schooling me these past twelve months when occasion allowed."

"Is this true, Master Godric? Is this young pup one of your flock? Tell me, does he follow you like a lamb or does he rather rootle round his sty like a hog and trample your pearls of wisdom underfoot?"

"More like a lamb than a hog, I fancy, though he shows signs of becoming the ram and marshalling the rest of the flock. He has his wits about him and can say his 'Pater Noster' and 'Ave Maria' without prompting. I was thinking he might soon be able to serve me at the Mass should I be short of one of the older boys."

"You hear what Master Godric says, Hugh. He seems to speak well of you but you have had little chance of temptation yet. You seem to be a well-set lad and my little Isabel will need assistance with the serving for she is but young yet. You may act as page to the Commissioner if you so wish and aid my Isabel in her duties. These Norman soldiers are not of our kin and they say that their manners are not ours either."

I dropped onto one knee before Alwin and said, "I hope you will find me trustworthy, sir, and as for Isabel, I would guard her with my life."

The colour had risen in Isabel's cheeks, and as I lifted my head her eyes caught mine and seemed to show pleasure. She quickly averted her gaze and, giving her father's arm a squeeze and offering him a quick smile of gratitude, she turned and moved back to her mother's side where I saw her tell her what had transpired. For my part, I stayed a little to one side of Alwin trying to calm my beating heart, for though I was pleased to be able to help Isabel, I was more gratified that I would be able to be close to the soldiers who were my main interest - or so I told myself.

There was a sudden murmur amongst those standing by the bridge and, all turning, we could see a small group of people coming over the further of the two bridges. I counted six men on foot, all of whom seemed to wear helmets, for the weak sun caught them on occasion and sent back shafts of light. Between them were two men on horseback. The foremost of the two had his hood close about his head and rode as if he were weary from a long journey or perhaps from age. The other, who was leading a pack animal on whose back were secured several bundles, appeared to be little more than a youth, for his hood was thrown back to reveal a beardless face. As they approached the bridge on which we stood, Alwin stepped forward to greet them. The party came to a halt and Godric, who came forward to stand beside the bailiff, raised his hand in blessing, saying as he did so, "Pax vobiscum."

"Et cum spiritu tuo," replied the elder horseman inclining his head, making the sign of the Cross as he did so. This done, he dismounted stiffly and, handing the reins of his horse to one of the soldiers, he moved forward to speak to Alwin.

"I bring greetings from my Lord the King, Master Bailiff. I am Gilbert the clerk, charged by King William to survey this part of his kingdom and render an account to him of all that it possesses in land and stock and men. He would also know what service each man owes to his lord."

"We had heard that you were coming from one who passed this way but two days gone. You are all welcome in our burgh. I trust you will lodge with me, and your scribe too. Godric here, who is the foremost of our priests, will house your soldiers beside the church, where the canons will care for them as they do other travellers. I have asked Godric to sup with us this night so that we may discuss with you how you wish to conduct your task tomorrow."

"You are kind, Bailiff, and your arrangements are good. Lead on to your house." Gilbert stretched himself. "Eh, I am weary from too much travel and care not overmuch for this horse. I will walk with you to stretch my legs and would then rest awhile before we talk." Turning to the other horseman he said, "Here Geoffrey, see to the horses and be sure that the parchments in those panniers are safely stored. Much time and effort has gone into their preparation and I would not have them mislaid."

"I will have them placed in a spare chest in my house if you wish and so they will be well guarded," answered Alwin.

"Come, Commissioner Gilbert, let us show you to our house," Mary said, stepping forward to greet him, "My daughter Isabel here will be your serving-wench, and bring you water that you may wash the dust of travel from you. Then perhaps you would take a cup of wine to refresh yourself before you rest."

As Alwin and Mary turned to lead Gilbert and his scribe to their house, Alwin called over his shoulder to me: "Hugh, do conduct the soldiers to the guest-house by the church and leave them in the hands of the canons. Speak with Ranulf that he may be sure they have clean straw in their pallets. If the soldiers have any special needs, come first to me with them, for we must be sure the King's men want for nothing that we can provide. When all is set, come to my house that you may aid Isabel with her tasks."

So Alwin led the way up the road with the young scribe Geoffrey bringing up the rear, leading the pack-horse with its precious bundles of parchments, while I led the six soldiers towards the dormitory which stood beside the refectory of the church. Had Alwin not told me, I would have taken these men, who were but poor common soldiers, to the almonry, and earned a beating for my error. I did not yet know how important was this survey the King had commanded.

As we neared the dormitory, Ranulf, the canon who kept the guest-house, came out and, greeting the soldiers, led them inside. I whispered Alwin's instruction to him and at Ranulf's bidding ran to fetch some fresh bundles of straw to add to what was already in the pallets. Meanwhile, Ranulf was producing blankets from a chest and checking to see that there was water in the jug beside the laver and clean towels. Candles already stood in the candlesticks on the table in the centre and there was wood beside the hearth, though I doubted they would need a fire so late in the spring. The soldiers, meanwhile, were ridding themselves of their armour, thinking themselves lucky to be so well housed. I was struck by the fact that all the soldiers were short-haired and clean-shaven, unlike we Saxons who prided ourselves on our thick locks which came down to our necks. Our Saxon beards made us look more manly compared to these youthful-looking Normans.

"Would you like me to clean your armour?" I asked one of the soldiers who seemed older than the others, and who by his bearing I took to be the one in charge of the rest.

"Ay lad, it could do with a shine, and there are a few rust spots on my helm that need attention. Here, catch this." and he threw me what looked like a handful of chain-mail. "You can burnish my helm and sword with that and make them gleam if you will."

I picked up his helm which was padded inside with cloth and straw. With his lack of hair, it was needed if he was not to end up with a sore head. Settling down beside the hearth, I set about rubbing his helm with the burnishing links he had thrown me. It was a more cunningly made helmet than our Saxon ones, being shaped to a point with rounded sides. It had a small neck-guard too which curled outwards and was fixed by flattened rivets, so that a man could look upwards without catching himself on the back of his neck. To the front was a nasal, formed in a 'V' to give it strength. It seemed a good helmet, offering better protection than our lighter and shorter Saxon helms. When I had finished burnishing it so that it caught the sun's rays, I tried it on. It fitted well enough, but the nasal made me squint and obscured my view. In close fighting it might well hamper the sight of an enemy.

I turned next to his sword, which was flat-bladed like ours, though not as heavy. Testing its edge, I found it sharp enough to deal a cruel blow, though I doubted whether it could sever a horse's head or a man's leg as they say our Saxon two-handed axe could. They say that King William's men suffered greatly at Senlac Field from those axes. I worked away at the blade of the sword till I was satisfied. Then I tried a few passes and strokes with it to see how it handled. The balance was good though I had not the skill to use it well.

"We must keep good guard while this fellow is with us or he will have us in pieces to feed the dogs," said the sword's owner to the others.

"Ay," replied another, "I'll keep my hauberk on while he is around", while a third grabbed his shield and hid behind it in mock terror. I reddened at this and put down the sword, and, turning to the shield, started to burnish its face with a will. It had seen service for there were several old dents in it where it had received blows from axe and sword, meant to dismember the owner. Its long kite shape seemed clumsy to me and the lower point kept hitting the ground as I moved it, but I am not over-tall yet and a man would fare better. I still prefer the circular shield our Saxon men use, with its big boss in the centre - a useful weapon in itself. When I had finished burnishing the shield to my satisfaction, I took it over to its owner, hoping for his approval.

"I have done my best sir, but it is hard to burnish where these dents are. Did you get them in battle?"

"That I did," he replied. "I was at Senlac Field these twenty years gone, though I was but a slip of a lad then. This shield served me well then as you can see, against the usurper Harold's housecarls. See this deep gash here? That was one of your great battleaxes. The blow knocked me flying and almost split the shield. Had it not been for the friend beside me who caught the axe-man with his sword just below his helm before he could recover from the blow he dealt me, it would have been me not him they buried. The blacksmith took some time to flatten out the worst of the damage in that shield, but what you can see reminds me to be ever watchful in the fray. I grant you this lad: you Saxons fight hard and long and it was only King William's cunning that let us win the field. But that is all long past and I have come to like you Saxons, though your winters are too wet and cold for my taste. Tell me lad, have you learnt to handle a sword yet?"

"A little, but we have small need of swords in these parts. I prefer a bow and we boys practise beside the church. There is a space on the shade side where the wind does not spoil the aim that is set aside for practice. I have split an apple at forty paces and can spit a coney on occasion if he runs straight. They make good eating."

"You'll not try for the King's deer in Andret, I trust, or it will be you that will be spitted!"

"No sir," I assured him earnestly, "I keep well clear of the King's forest."

Only too well did I know the penalty for taking the King's deer. A villein who held land with half a plough but a mile towards the forest at Stanpit had been caught with a haunch of freshly killed deer in his cottage and had his right hand severed for it. A one-handed ploughman is of little use and his family were near starving. It is a sore grudge our folk bear against these Normans, for though Andret had been a forest for King Harold, and the blessed Edward before him, neither had hunted there much and the forest laws had been sparingly enforced. Now William the Norman had turned men off their land where it bordered the old forest and added it to his great forest of Andret so that his deer could have more space to roam and he to hunt, though many still take small game at night when the verderers are abed. They often turn a blind eye, for men must eat and the King only chases the wild boar and stag.

"You have an old head on young shoulders lad. What is your name?"

"I am called Hugh, son of Oswald who has the mill by the church. And your name sir, that I may know you again?"

"They call me Belesme of St Lo, though it is many years since last I was there. I have followed Duke William since before he came to take this land as was his right. Now I have to travel with these five here to guard this Gilbert while he makes a record of all that is in this land. Others are doing likewise elsewhere in the realm so that it can all be collected in a great book at Winchester, where the King will see it. He would know what his kingdom has for him. Tomorrow we shall learn what there is here. Now leave us, Hugh, and ask Ranulf if we may have some food and drink, for it is a long time since we broke our fast."

Seeing that Belesme had no more need of me for the moment I hurried out and glancing into the refectory saw Ranulf and gave him the message. He grunted and mumbled something about his task being to feed the poor and travellers in need and not fill the bellies of lustful soldiers of an alien king. I stayed not to listen but hastened on to the hall where Alwin lived. Not for the first time, I noted how much bigger it was than our poor cott by the mill. I entered by the passage that separated the service rooms on the left from the main hall. As I turned the corner of the screen into the main hall, I could see Alwin and Godric seated at the table at the far end beyond the open fire in the middle of the hall, listening to Gilbert the clerk who seemed to be explaining something to them. Isabel, who was sitting on a stool a few paces away from them against the wall, glanced round as I entered and seeing me she hastened over to meet me.

"Where have you been? You were supposed to be page and help me with my tasks. I can see by father's look that he is displeased," she said.

"I have been with Belesme and the other soldiers, seeing to their comfort. I had to clean some of their armour and see that Ranulf tended to their needs of bedding and food," I answered in part truth. "Now I am here, what tasks have you for me?"

"Sit quiet by me for the moment. Mother is seeing to the cooking, and when she calls me we must serve the dishes. Meantime, pretend you have been here for some time when father notices you."

I moved to where her stool was set and settled myself beside it on the floor away from those at the table, half hidden by Isabel. After a little, Gilbert brought the conversation round to his task here.

"Yes, Alwin, I was with my Lord the King this midwinter last when he was at Gloucester. He had travelled much that year throughout all his lands. He had heard that Cnut, King of Denmark, had come to England to help Eorl Robert of Flanders lay claim to his lands in the north. The King, who was looking to his dukedom in Normandy at the time, hastened here with as large a force of riding men and foot from France and Brittany as ever had been seen in this land. It is said that there were more men than he brought with him to Senlac Field and sore trial they were to the land. The King sent them throughout the land to be fed by his vassals as best they might. The land by the coast where Eorl Robert and King Cnut would come ashore, King William caused to be laid waste, so there was nothing for them to take and no food to feed them when they should land. When Eorl Robert heard of this, he kept his men in Flanders, but King William's men remained here for a time. There was much grumbling amongst his vassals, so that William sent much of his force back to Brittany, though many still remained. Because the crops had been poor as you know, the hardship was the greater on our folk so that in some parts there was great unrest."

Alwin nodded sagely. "It is hard to blame them when the harvests are bad and such food as men have been able to gather is taken from them by foreign soldiers. I have heard that in places where the corn lay flat in the fields and sprouting in the ear from the wet, men have been reduced to eating acorns. When William laid a tax of seventy-two pence on each hide of land it was too much, so who could blame those who thought they might support Eorl Robert in his claim to this realm, for they said that Robert could not bear down on them more harshly than William. I am glad it all came to naught, for warring such as they have in Flanders and the Norman dukedom brings no profit to such men as us but only more hardship and sorrow."

"You speak wisely Alwin, and the King thinks much as you do too which is why he sent most of his force back across the sea whence they came."

"Surely his councillors must have told him how the crops had failed and how many beasts had died of hunger too?"

"No doubt they did, for when he reached Gloucester he held council with all the great men for five days. He asked why there was so little food in England when there should be plenty, for he feared that men were tricking him and hiding the crops because they disliked the soldiers and his harsh laws. Though no doubt there was some truth in what he said, he did not like to hear the true reasons. He held council with his clergy and bishops for three days too - though there were few enough of them as many sees are unfilled. The King proclaimed that men should travel through every shire to find out how many hides of land there are in each and who holds each hide and what dues each man pays. He wants to know what lands he himself owns and what is due to him from each piece and how many animals of whatever kind he has, and what service each man owes to him."

I saw Alwin shoot a quick glance at Godric at this.

"The King is asking so closely, that each man must say how many ploughs there are in lordship and how much meadow, woodland and pasture. He must know how many fish-ponds and mills there are and what each is worth. Each burgh and vill must say how many villeins, cottagers and slaves there are and also how many men are free and how many are freemen. Because our Lord the King has given much land to his lords and to the church, we are to ask in each place we go, who held the land before King William took it by right of conquest and lawful inheritance, and who had it from the King. Should land have been passed by death or inheritance or for some other reason, the King would know who holds the land now."

Gilbert paused to drink from his ale horn before continuing.

"You can see Alwin, that we have a great task before us. The more so as King William has commanded that the record be completed before he departs for his dukedom in Normandy at the end of this year. There is little time to complete such a great task and there are many commissioners like me who are travelling throughout the length and breadth of the land to do the King's bidding. All is to be collected at Winchester where it is to be written down in a great book."

Gilbert paused and sighed, and looked at Alwin and Godric who sat in thought for some time.

"Such a record has surely never been been made before," said Gilbert. "Can it really be done in so short a time? What if two men claim the same piece of land: who is to decide?"

"Ay, there's the rub," said Gilbert. "I would have to hear the claims of both men which they must back with good witness from their fellows. It does take time and men must take an oath that what they say is true. The burghs and vills in the Hundreds I have visited so far have given good testimony and the lands have been fairly listed. It has been said that by this book every man should know his right and not usurp another's."

"Maybe some good will come of it," said Godric, scratching his chin. "You may be sure that the King will know what he has and what he has taken and his Eorls likewise. But the common folk, what of them? Will their claims be good? There are men in this hundred whose land has been taken by the King to be part of his great forest of Andret. They can no longer graze it as they did and as their fathers did before them."

Gilbert's face hardened and his mouth set. "The King's forests are a special case," he said, "and not bound by the good and ancient laws of your old Saxon kings. Besides, there is land without the forests where men may graze their beasts. Would you begrudge the King his hunting? He has little enough time for sport with his two realms to rule."

"No, but I do begrudge him the right hand of one of my flock," muttered Godric under his breath as he turned away from Gilbert with an angry gesture. I caught the words but Gilbert missed them I think, for Godric had risen in his anger and stridden towards the fire in the middle of the hall. Seeing that things might go awry, I rose from my place beside Isabel and crossed to Gilbert saying, "I have done as you bid sir, and seen to the needs of Belesme and the other soldiers. They have clean bedding and Ranulf, the canon who cares for travellers, is preparing food for them. I stayed to burnish Belesme's armour or I would have been here before. Did I do right?"

Gilbert turned towards me, his thoughts broken in their train by my concern for his guard of soldiers, and his face softened into a smile.

"Ay lad, you did. Alwin, you have chosen me a good page I think who uses his head when he needs. If your fair daughter Isabel gives me as good care as our serving-wench, we shall do well and tomorrow's work will soon be done."

Alwin's glance lighted on me. I could see that he was pleased that Isabel found favour with Gilbert. As he came over to join Godric he passed me and whispered: "Well said Hugh. I feared that Godric would cross this Gilbert with his talk of Andret, but you have turned away the shaft for now."

Taking Godric by the arm to lead him back to the table, he whispered to him: "Guard your tongue on that score lest it is more than your hand that is severed." Turning to Gilbert he said as heartily as he could, "My throat is parched with much talking. Hugh, go fetch some ale that we may slake our throats before we sup. Gilbert, you will drink a horn with me I trust? By the smell of it our food is almost ready. Isabel my sweet, go speak with your mother and tell her we would eat now. Our friend Gilbert here has travelled far and must surely be famished."

As Isabel and I hastened about our duties, I heard Alwin ask Gilbert if he had heard the merry tale about Sifrid the swineherd. It is a good tale that always brings a belly-laugh and improves with each telling, so I hurried out to the serving room to fetch the ale. Before I could reach the room I felt a touch on my sleeve, and Isabel whispered, "Father was pleased that you turned Gilbert from wrath. We must walk with care these next days lest we cross Gilbert. Our lands may depend upon it though they should not. I will choose the choicest morsels to serve him with and do you be sure that he has the best horn to drink from."

"That I will and I will keep him well plied - but not too well lest his head be foul tomorrow and the work be undone." Then we parted, each to our allotted task.

The evening passed well enough and I kept Gilbert well plied with the best ale, taking my lead from Alwin who signed to me when to fill the horn and when to hold back. Isabel, for her part, softened his heart with demure smiles as she knelt before him with the best pieces for him to choose from. She did her task well, for he threw little but bare bones to the dogs that sat at his feet. The sweetmeats that Mary had prepared to end the feast found favour with Gilbert too. Sitting beside him, she kept him amused with light tales of this part of the land, stroking his arm the while and seeing to his every need and casting him sidelong glances, which seemed to flatter him. When Mary finally rose, saying that it was time to retire and taking Isabel with her, Alwin dismissed me too, having first ordered me to re-charge Gilbert's horn and his with ale and to leave a full flagon with them on the table; so I slipped away.

Outside, I took in a deep breath of fresh air. The hall, for all its height and that the window shutters had been thrown open, was smoky, and it was good to fill my lungs with the cool night air. There was a slight salty tang too as was customary when the wind was in its usual quarter from the south-west. Looking upwards, I could see the half-moon and a few stars showing through the drifting clouds. There was enough light for me to see my way and avoid the larger stones that lay about the ground. The smell of the marshes beyond the river fed into my brain as it cleared itself of the smoke of the hall and, as I grew accustomed to the quiet after the noisy chatter, I became aware of other more natural sounds: the night calls of birds and once the frightened cry of a small animal which had probably fallen prey to some night hunter.

I have always loved the quiet of the evening, particularly when the moon is up, so I strolled towards the Canons' Gate in the burgh wall. The gate was shut and barred for the night so I clambered up beside it to the top of the wall to gaze out over the marshland towards the river and beyond to where the open sea lay about a mile away. Below me, the land fell away from the wall to the reed-covered marshes that bordered the river. The breeze whispered through the reeds as their tops gently swayed.

There was a sudden cry and a frightened flutter of wings and a marsh bird took off out of the reeds to my left. I could not make out what it was for certain in the half-light. Not a wild duck for sure because the cry was wrong. Perhaps a coot or one of the many wading birds. It had escaped this time.

I confess that I had hunted wild duck in the marshes and raided their nests for eggs in the springtime. They were plentiful and though William the Norman held the lordship of the manor of Twynham, his steward had little regard to what occurred on the marsh-land. He preferred not to get his feet wet, so we boys were left undisturbed in our forays on the wild fowl - provided we kept quiet about it. We would not have had much success if we had not gone with stealth. Stalking wild duck requires much patience and great quietness.

I leant on the top of the wall to listen to the silence, trying to pick out the numerous sounds of wild fowl and night-hunting beasts. As my ears grew accustomed to the quiet my mind fell to wondering what Belesme of St Lo would have listened for if he had been standing where I was. Would he have tuned his ear to catch the stealthy approach of a man ready to make a sudden spring at him? How would we have fared if we had had to defend our burgh against him and his fellow Normans? Belesme looked a formidable foe, despite his kindly speech and manner, but his sword was sharp, as well I knew and he was skilled with it, I would wager,or he would not be here amongst us now. Would we have fallen into the same trap as the brave Saxon Fyrds at Senlac Field and rushed headlong from our safe defensive position in pursuit of the apparently fleeing Normans? The walls of our burgh seemed strong enough to keep out most attacking foes, though not as strong as the great twin ditches and banks that defended Hengist's headland across the river. It is said that in olden days before ever the Romans came to our land, this headland had a rich settlement of people and was a great trading port with the Normans' lands. It is hard to believe now for it is much overgrown and the banks and ditches have lost their steepness, but it still makes a wonderful place for us boys to play at fighting the Normans.

Picking up a small stone, I lobbed it from the top of the wall into the reeds below. There was a sudden angry quacking followed by a flurry of wings, and a duck took off towards the river and the marshland beyond. I marked the place it had come from as best as I could, meaning to return another evening to see if it was a nesting place. If I could snare the duck, Mother would be pleased to have it to add to our evening pottage. I doubt she would roast it on the spit, for the odour would carry too far and you can never be sure of prying eyes - or perhaps noses - and there is no point in giving my lord's steward reason to bring us before the Manor Court and perhaps risk a fine.

All else was quiet now except for the wind in the reeds. I had not realised that I had stayed so long on the wall and I was beginning to grow cold. I scrambled to my feet, turned, and slid down the inside of the bank and made my way back to Wick Street by which I had come. Then, turning soon to the right, I made my way slowly between the nine chapels and the burgh wall to our house. As I neared it, I could hear the muffled voices of Father and Mother as they busied themselves before retiring for the night. Lifting the latch, I entered and, because I knew Osbern and Emma would both already be abed, I shot the bolt quietly on the door, happy to be back in the homely warmth of our hearth.

"Where have you been this past hour?" growled Father. "We were beginning to grow anxious, for we felt sure Alwin must have finished his feast long since and would wish to be alone with Gilbert that he might ply him with good ale to sweeten him for the morrow. He would not wish for a stripling like you to be present then. We feared something might have gone amiss."

"I am sorry Father if I have angered you. I did not mean to, but the bailiff's house was over-hot and full of smoke, and I went and stood by the wall awhile to cool and clear my head. Much has happened today and I fell to daydreaming I fear."

"A fine time for such things when the moon has been up these past hours. Have a care son about night prowling. Those who do it are often thought to be mischief-making."

"Forgive me Father, I was foolish but many things were running though my mind."

"You fill your mind too much with matters that should not concern you, I think," Mother interposed. "To bed with you now and be careful not to wake the others as you go. We want you about earlier than you were today."

"What's that?" Father shot a questioning glance in my direction as I passed him.

"'Tis nothing," Mother hurriedly interrupted before I had a chance to speak.

"I kept Hugh a short time this morning to do an errand for me before he came to the mill and I want him to be sure to be early tomorrow to make up for the time he lost today."

I caught Mother's eye and gave her a grateful glance as I passed, which Father did not see as he had his back to me. Mother saw it and winked at me, and a quick smile flickered at the corner of her mouth.

"I doubt you will wake Osbern if his snores are any guide," she said, "but Emma sleeps lightly and is easily roused as you know. Go softly now and may the Blessed Mary keep you safe through the dark night."

"Good night Hugh, and may God keep you. Today has brought us new faces but tomorrow may show us what is in their minds. We shall need clear heads if we are to understand what is afoot. This survey for our Norman King needs careful handling, lest we find more is said than we mean. Tomorrow Hugh, keep your eyes skinned, your ears open, and your mouth shut."

"Fear not Father, I can play the' burgh Fool' when I have a mind."

I rolled my eyes, hung out my tongue, hunched my shoulders and shuffled out of the room with a foolish grin on my twisted face which made Father and Mother rock on their stools with laughter which they fought to keep silent lest they woke the others.

"Be off with you before the Devil fixes your face like that for ever," grinned Father. "We must be up at dawn tomorrow, for I would speak with the reeve early before good Master Gilbert, our great King's Commissioner, is about. I would hear what was said at dinner this evening and so, I think, would many others. If this Commissioner means to list all that we possess, we must be sure that we are agreed what we tell him. There are unresolved suits concerning land, and it were better that we settled these between ourselves rather than he should decide them. Good-night Hugh, and do not worry yourself about such things. They do not concern you yet."

With that, I crept into our sleeping room and, avoiding Osbern's snoring figure, I slipped out of my tunic, pulled off my breeches and slid beneath the rough cover. I heard Father and Mother moving about in the other room for a few moments, but before they had gone to their own small room I was in a dreamless sleep.

Chapter 2 1086

I woke to feel Osbern's knee in the small of my back. Rolling over, I gave him a great heave and sent him back to his own side of the bed.

"You little runt. Keep to your own quarters unless you want to find yourself sharing the sty with the other hogs at the bottom of the garden."

He grunted like the pig he is but never woke and huddled further down under the covers of our shared bed. I lay on my back for a while, thinking of the day ahead and what the Norman clerk Gilbert was going to write down about our burgh. I was worried lest it lead to these Normans wanting more taxes, or demanding that we serve in their wars, which were none of our concern. No doubt Father would be cautious in what he said, as would all the villagers and free men of the burgh.

Turning over on my other side, I looked at Emma where she slept in her separate narrow bed beside me. Her rich auburn hair fell about her face and one arm was thrown above her head, leaving one shoulder and most of one small rounded breast on view. Though but thirteen, she was already beginning to show the good looks of our mother and it would not be many years before she had a host of suitors, I thought. She was a good companion to me and hardy for a girl, and we understood each other well. Leaning over, I touched her arm gently and whispered:

"Wake up Emma, great things are afoot today, remember."

She started and sat up, resting her arms on the pillow behind her. Her long hair falling about her shoulders barely covered her young breasts.

"What is it?" she said. "You startled me. What is to do?"

"The Norman clerk Gilbert is here, and this day he is to make record of all the lands held in the burgh. Do you not remember? All men must be present when he makes the tally, and I would be there too to see what happens. You will come too, won't you Emma? Mother can surely spare you from your usual tasks this day, but I hope you will be dressed more seemly than you are now. You may be only thirteen but you have some shape to you and you will have all the serfs of the burgh sniffing round your tail 'ere long if you do not show more modesty. You will find yourself carrying more than you intend if you are not careful."

Emma raised her arms and thrust her hands through her hair above her head so that her full beauty was towards me. Then she twisted her body away and looked over her shoulder at me with downcast eyes.

"Why, do you think I am a wanton to be taken by any serf or slave? Remember I am the miller's daughter and intend to choose a freeman at least with his own lands. You are one to talk. Did I not hear that you were hanging round Isabel all yesterday like a dog on heat they said, and she but twelve? I must speak of it with Alric. No doubt he will knock some sense into your thick head - and dock your tail if need be!" Then with a sly smile she pulled the covers up to her chin in a show of modesty.

I reddened, disconcerted, for she had touched a raw place.

"I was but doing the bidding of her father, and no man lightly disobeys the bailiff. Besides, I had orders to help serve at his table and it was his choice that his daughter should act as serving-wench to the Norman."

"Hush, Hugh dear, I did but jest. Isabel is my friend and I would not have her hurt. I know you treat her like a sister." Then, drawing the covers up so that only her sparkling eyes were visible, she said, "Since I am to be so modest before you, you will please pass me my robe which is at the foot of my bed." She giggled, rocking back and forth in the bed.

With a snort, I reached down, gathered up the robe, bundled it into a ball and, as she sat up again, threw it at her head so that it caught her in the face. There was a squeal of alarm, followed by much muffled muttering until finally her head appeared through the neck hole of her robe. Then with a spring she was up and, stepping lightly off the bed onto the floor, she dropped me a mock curtsy and said, "Thank you Sir Knight," and skipped out of the room, shaking her auburn tresses as she went. You can never tell with Emma what she will do next, which is why I care for her so, even though she is my sister. I must guard her too, for she can be vulnerable and I mean no-one to take advantage of her if I am there to prevent it.

There was a grunt from the other side of my bed and Osbern stirred, rolled over onto his back, yawned, scratched his head, opened his eyes, and finally sat up. What a younger brother to be saddled with! Being yet but nine years old I suppose he must be suffered for a few years more.

"What were you two whispering and giggling about?" he asked as he rubbed the sleep out of his eyes. "You broke into my dream. I was just about to slay a huge Norman knight when you woke me up. Now I shall never know if I killed him or not".

"You will have your fill of Normans today if you can stir yourself enough. The soldiers I took up to the dormitory at the church last evening will all be standing around while the clerk Gilbert makes record of everything in the burgh on his parchments. Be sure to keep your mouth shut, lest you say things you might regret later. We do not know exactly what this Gilbert will note down, but I hear from both the bailiff and Father that the less we tell him the better it may be. No-one is keen to let the Normans know any more of our business than is necessary. They have a nasty habit of using it in ways we may not like."

With that, Osbern and I reached for our clothes and, hurriedly pulling them on, went out into the yard to douse our heads in the pail of water that stood by the door. Thus refreshed, we came back into the kitchen where Mother and Emma were already busy setting the bread and drinking pots on the table for us to break our fast.

"Did you sleep soundly, Hugh, after your service at table last night? Your father says that Alwin was pleased with you and marked how you tried to see that Gilbert the clerk was kept in good spirits. I hear that Isabel found favour in Gilbert's eyes too. She is a pretty girl for sure and seems to have a wise head on her shoulders for all her lack of years. I hear you made a good pair of lackeys."

Mother smiled at me as she said this and, catching the look in Emma's eyes, I felt myself colour, so turned quickly away to hide my confusion and muttered something about trying to do my best. As Mother turned her attention to Osbern, I heard Emma's whisper from behind me, "Here, lackey, pass me my drinking cup, and be sure not to slop it."

Picking up the cup which had the least in it and also the smallest piece of bread, I turned to Emma with a mock bow and said, "Certainly my lady, but surely such gentility should not eat so much."

As Emma's appetite is almost as large as mine despite her slight build, I felt I had levelled the score, which she acknowledged with a bob. Mother, knowing how we liked to tease each other, let it pass and turned her attention to Osbern to see that he was as tidy as you could expect him to be and had enough to fill his belly. There was some new cheese with the bread and we all ate heartily, for we were unsure when we might have our midday meal with all the events of the coming day.

Father rose, "It is time we went to the churchyard to hear what Gilbert has to say. Alwin has sent to summon all the men of the burgh to be present since all must state what they own. There will be no work in the fields this day nor at the mill. Hugh, Emma and Osbern, you may all come with me to see what takes place, but remember to keep quiet and utter not a word. I have discussed matters with Alwin and Godric and a few others and we have decided how to handle things. This Gilbert is a sly fellow by all accounts and little will escape him, so we shall need our wits about us if we are not to be trapped into saying more than we need."

"Yes, you may go with your father, Emma and Osbern. Keep close to them, Hugh, that nothing befall them in the crowd, for there will be many there and some idle hands looking for mischief. I shall not come - at least until I have finished the spinning I need for the new tunic I have promised you, Oswald."

With that the four of us went out of the kitchen, Father leading. As we walked up the slope from the mill to the churchyard, we could see others coming from the direction of the burgh, all heading the same way. As we neared the porch of the main church, we could see Godric busy getting tables and stools set where Gilbert could sit with Geoffrey, the beardless youth I had noticed yesterday. He was busy laying out parchments and quills and an inkhorn. Belesme of St Lo was there to one side with his five soldiers, but they seemed to have nothing much to do and were more interested in casting covetous eyes over the womenfolk who were gathering with their men. Judging by the grins and nudging elbows, it seemed that most of the remarks were bawdy, but they were in the Normans' own tongue so I could make little of them. Father raised his hand in greeting to Alwin who was already there, standing near to Godric and Gilbert. I saw that Alwin's two sons Alric and Alnoth and also Isabel were with him. Father turned to me.

"Hugh, I must go and talk with the bailiff. Go with Emma and Osbern and stand with Alric, Isabel and Alnoth. Be sure to keep together and guard your sister and Isabel well. There are too many idlers here for my liking. Tell Alric what I have said."

With that he was gone, making his way towards Alwin with whom he was soon in earnest conversation. We three edged our way through the press towards where Alric and the others were standing and when we joined them I gave Alric Father's message.

"Father said the same to me," he said. "Let us stand here, for we shall be able to hear every word that Gilbert says and with the soldiers but a few paces away we shall not be troubled by idlers. If the soldiers become too bawdy, you and I, Hugh, can put ourselves between them and Isabel and Emma."

"I can always speak to that older one. He is their leader and I polished his armour for him yesterday afternoon. He fought at Senlac, he says. He seems to have the others in check and I think might help me if I needed to ask him."

"I am not sure if I would trust any Norman," said Alric, "but it is nice to know that we could have a friend in the enemy camp."

There was a murmur of interest from the crowd. Turning, I saw that Gilbert had risen and was holding up his arms for silence. At that moment Belesme of St Lo also stepped forward and, striking his sword on his shield like a gong, shouted for all to keep silent.

"Men of the burgh of Twynham," he bellowed, "be it known that in Gloucester town last midwinter, Duke William of Normandy, your King, held council with his lords and has decreed that men should travel over all the land and visit each burgh and vill to discover how much land each man owns and what is its worth, and to whom each man owns his allegiance. You are to give account of the stock you have and all such matters as may be asked of you. Your Lord the King has sent Gilbert who stands here beside me, to be his clerk in this part of the land. He has come from Winchester that he may make a record of all that is told to him."

With that, Belesme stepped back a few paces and joined the other soldiers, pleased with himself at the impression he thought he had made on the assembled people. Gilbert now stepped forward and came round to the front of his table. Raising his hand in benediction, he made the sign of the Cross over us all and said, "Pax vobiscum".

There was a murmur of "Et cum spiritu tuo" from the crowd, led by Godric the priest.

"Men of Twynham," continued Gilbert, "you need have no fear. This command of your Lord the King is good. He does not wish to know what lands you own so that he may take them from you. He needs to know the worth of the lands in order to deal justly with it and those who use it, so that the service you owe to your Lords may be justly assessed, that you be not oppressed by false demands. It is well known to your King that much land has been taken by conquest and given to new lords since that day when your usurping King Harold was slain at Senlac Field. Other lands have been taken for the King's pleasure to enlarge his forest of Andret and still others have been sold or given in marriage portion. So that your Lord the King may deal justly in all things, he has called you all to bear witness before each other to say who owned what lands in the time of King Edward of blessed memory who owned it when King William gave it to those who did homage to him, and who owns it now. He would also know what was its worth in the time of King Edward, after Senlac, and now. In this way your King declares that every man will know his rightful possession and thus not usurp another's."

Here he paused for a little, and turning he went back behind the table again and sat down. "There is much detail to be noted," he said. "Come, let us make a start. Master Alwin, as bailiff of my Lord's lands tell us what he holds in this place."

"Sir," said Alwin, stepping forward and folding his hands before him in submission. "Our Lord the King holds much land in this hundred of Edgegate. Twynham itself is held by the King as it was by the blessed Edward. It has always answered for one virgate of land for as long as memory can recall. Is that not right Godric?" he said, turning to the priest.

"That is my recollection too, and I have been told that this has been so since Cnut ruled, though that is before my reckoning," replied Godric. Gilbert turned to his scribe and said, "Hand me that parchment at the bottom of the pile. Is there not a record of this that we have brought with us from Winchester? The scribes there took note from the King himself of much that he believed he owned. What does the parchment say on this matter?"

The scribe fumbled with the various parchments before him. Finally finding the one he required, he scanned through it till he came to the right section. "Ay, Master Gilbert, the King himself believes he holds the land that Alwin speaks of."

"That is good then. Pray continue master Alwin. How many ploughs are there?"

"Sir, by my reckoning there is land for thirteen ploughs though it is hard to gauge. There are two ploughs in lordship of that I am certain. Let me see, there are twenty-one villagers and also five smallholdings and these have eleven or twelve ploughs, I think. What say you Master Godric, is it eleven or twelve?"

"Let me see. You have sixteen oxen on my Lord's demesne, Alwin, which makes two ploughs . How many oxen think you were there last time they were gathered for a reckoning, ninety you say? Well eighty oxen would make ten ploughs, and another eight make an eleventh, and there are two over. That totals eleven ploughs between the villeins and bordars, but we had best make another reckoning when we question the villeins as to what land they hold."

"That would be wise, but what you say would seem to agree with what your Lord the King states. He has the burgh of Twynham in demesne as you say, for it belonged to Edward the King before him. It is therefore his by right of conquest. The land in the burgh is put at one virgate and it has two ploughs as you say. Geoffrey," said Gilbert turning to his scribe, "note that first on your parchment."

He turned to Godric and said, "It is the King's command that his land should be stated first. You say there are twenty-one villeins here. Let me see them."

With that, Belesme stepped forward again and, raising his voice for all to hear shouted, "You hear what Gilbert the clerk has said. Come forward all the villeins and stand in line before him so that he may see you. Come along now, we have not got all day. Line up in front of the table. Here, you men," he said, turning to the soldiers who were standing idly watching, "help me get these people in line so that I can count them."

There was much shuffling and pushing and not a little mumbling of discontent amongst these men of the burgh, for they had their pride as well as the land they farmed and did not care to be pushed about like cattle by these Norman ruffians. Eventually, they were all assembled in some sort of line and Belesme counted them up and found that there were twenty-one as Alwin had said.

"Are there any more villeins in this burgh?" asked Gilbert.

There was a general murmur of dissent and shaking of heads, which seemed to satisfy Gilbert.

"Now how much land does each one hold?" he asked.

A man stepped forward whom I recognised as Wulfric. He was well-known amongst us for being upright and honest, but also as one who feared not to speak his mind.

Looking Gilbert straight in the eye, he said, "Sir, I hold thirty-one acres which is put as one virgate, because a part of my land is of little use. The others here have all about the same, some a little more, some a little less, but not all the land is good, for some is near the King's forest and some near the river so is constantly too wet to grow a crop. It has always been agreed that each should be assessed as one virgate. You will find that in King Edward's time, when life was easier and crops better, we paid together by tale nineteen pounds. Since Duke William has become our King, some of our land has been taken by him into his Royal Forest of Andret and some have lost their lands. Now our lands are worth only ten pounds, but we have to pay by weight of twenty pence to the ounce and that comes to twelve pounds and ten shillings. It is said that the land now in the forest is valued at twelve pounds and ten shillings also. If you count up these two sums they come to much more than the nineteen pounds that was paid for all the land in the time of our blessed King Edward."

Wulfric paused and looked round at the others. Seeing them nodding in agreement, he went on.

" We have to let the King take the land he wants, but it seems to us that we have not only lost some of our land but are also paying more now for what is left to us. We like it not, Master Gilbert, for it means that we have to pay for the King's sport, and life is hard enough without that."

Wulfric stepped back into the line of villeins. There was a general murmur of assent and shuffling of feet as the villeins started to encourage each other to voice their discontent. Belesme, who had probably witnessed such scenes before, stepped forward and, loosening his sword in its scabbard in a warning gesture, cried, "Silence! Curb your tongues, or you may find you have none with which to speak."

Both Godric and Alwin stepped forward and held up their hands to quieten the villeins and prevent any more outbursts. They did not want the situation to turn ugly and cause Gilbert to make too hard a record of their holdings. Godric went up to Wulfric and laid his hands on his arms.

"Wulfric, Wulfric," he said in soothing tones. "We know how you feel. We all know that some of your land has been taken into the King's forest and that his deer come and eat your crops and that you are powerless to prevent it, but you have some good land, some of the best in the hundred. This is not a matter for Master Gilbert to decide. Let the matter rest and place it before the Manor Court if you so desire."

Turning to Gilbert he said, "Your pardon, Master Gilbert. Wulfric meant no harm. He was over-forthright in his speech. In your wisdom I pray you let the matter rest with us and we can hear it at the next Manor Court. It is not a matter for you to determine, who have enough worries making a tally of the worth of all the land."

Godric bent forward and I heard him whisper in Gilbert's ear, "I know this Wulfric. He is an honest man if somewhat hot-headed. I will speak with him later, and give him twenty 'Pater Nosters' and ten 'Ave Marias' as penance."

Gilbert nodded and I could see that his ruffled feathers were smoothed again. Even Belesme seemed to feel that the threat had passed. As for Wulfric, he looked chastened, though I was glad he had spoken out. These Normans are too free with our land which they regard as their own even when it has not been given to them.

Gilbert consulted with Geoffrey and then, looking up at the still waiting villeins, he said, "Do you all agree? Each of you holds a virgate or thereabouts?"

There was a general murmur of assent and Alwin added his voice, "Yes Master Gilbert that is so. These lands have been held since before the time of Edward our late King. Some indeed have been held since before Cnut ruled in like manner as the royal demesne". Gilbert nodded and, turning to his scribe Geoffrey, told him to note it down, which he did holding his tongue between his teeth in concentration as he did so.

"Who else holds land in Twynham? Are there any bordars?"

"Five," said Alwin. "Come forward those who are bordars and stand before Master Gilbert. These are the ones, but you had best question each as to how much land they hold for it differs with each one."

As Geoffrey found a spare piece of parchment on which he could make the tally, Gilbert asked, "How much land have you?"

"Five acres," said the first,

"I have fifteen but it is all poor land so that my crops yield barely as much as his five acres."

"That is your fault for not tilling it better," said another man. "My ten acres is next to yours and I get more from that than you do because I tend it properly. If you spent less time in the ale-house you could do better than me."

"Quiet Swein! We all know you for a braggart. You may not drink as much as Grim but you plough more wenches than furrows. I am surprised that you have the energy for both." Turning to Gilbert he said, "I have twelve acres, and Brand here has nine."

"How many ploughs do the villeins have and how many are there among the bordars?"

There was some muttering and counting of fingers. After consulting one or two of the others, Alwin said, "Master Gilbert, I find that we miscounted the oxen of the villeins, for some more have grown strong enough to be put to the plough .

They total 83, but two are sickly beasts and cannot plough. I doubt they will last out this month, so they are not to be counted. The bordars have 16 oxen between them though they have little enough to feed them on, so it still makes twelve ploughs between them all. Is that not so?"

A nodding of heads confirmed that it was so, and doing a quick count on my fingers I came to the same figure. Geoffrey solemnly noted this down on his parchment.

I nudged Alric gently and, when he turned towards me, whispered in his ear, "Your father and Godric are playing a cunning game. By seeming to be careful over small matters they may lull Gilbert into accepting that they will be careful over large things." He gave me a knowing smile and turned away feigning innocence and interest in what was being said.

"Now who else have we?" asked Gilbert. "Are there any serfs? What about radknights and coliberts? Are there any of them?"

"We have one serf and he works on my Lord the King's land. But there are four radknights and three coliberts. Come forward all of you and stand in order so that we may count you. They have two and a half ploughs between them I think, is that not so?"

Heads nodded.

"Now how much land does each of you own? Speak up, and tell Master Gilbert."

I felt a tug at my arm and turning, heard Alric whisper in my ear, "This Gilbert seems to want to know a great deal. Do you think it will mean we have to pay more taxes for these Norman's forays? Have you noticed that no one has mentioned the assarts some have. Perhaps this is the game you think they are playing. I am not going to remind them because ours is probably the biggest assart of them all. We must have about fourteen acres that we have cleared, and Swein, fool that he is, was nearly caught by his bragging for he has four acres cleared. No wonder he is seldom at home. The furrows he ploughs are in that field, though they say he will take any wench who will have him. Agmund is jealous of him because he has not tried to clear an assart himself and no wench will take him with his pock-marked face."

"What's that you are saying?" It was Belesme who spoke and I liked not his tone.

"It was nothing," I said hastily turning away from Alric. "My friend did but remark how clever the scribe was with his letters and I said I wished I had such skill."

Turning to Geoffrey who had looked up on hearing himself spoken of, I smiled at him and, bending over, pretended to examine his lettering with interest. I heard Alric let out a sigh and dug him in the side to warn him to be more careful in future.

"What have you just written? The script is clear but I have not learnt it yet," I asked the scribe, pointing to the last line of his script.

"That says 'The three coliberts hold 30 acres between them and the four radknights have 120 acres'. Let me see. That makes a total of 860 acres of tilled land. Master Gilbert" he said turning to the clerk beside him. "We have not enquired about meadowland and woodland yet."

"True. Indeed that is the next matter we must note down. Tell me Bailiff, what woodland is held?"

"None now Master Gilbert. All that there was in the time of Edward the King has been taken by Duke William into his great forest of Andret. It amounted to five virgates in all. Great hardship has come to some of our folk who have been turned off their land and have had to find other places to live. There were five villeins who suffered thus, each with a hide of land. It was a grievous loss for a burgh of this size, but that is the King's right and we have to suffer it. We have some meadowland, a hide by my reckoning, though it is not all in one parcel. How say you Godric, do I reckon right?"

"Let me see. It is 61 acres in full tally, so call it half a hide, yes."

"Note down 61 acres of meadowland, Geoffrey. That makes a total of 1,071 acres in the time of King Edward, but 921 now since the King has taken 150 acres into his forest. But the assessment of the land has been reduced from nineteen pounds to twelve pounds ten shillings in recognition of this. Do you agree, Bailiff?" asked Gilbert.

He thought for a moment, then nodded his agreement. I looked at Alric and our eyes sent the same message to each other. We would get little past this man for he was shrewd. No wonder the King had chosen him to make record of his lands. I could see that the same thought was passing through the minds of Alwin and Godric. We must be watchful.

"Now, have you a mill, and how many dwellings are there?"

"There are two mills, but one belongs to the canons as Master Godric will tell you. The mill I talk of is not in Edgegate but another part of the hundred called Shirley. It is one of the two at Winkton and pays five shillings, for it is but small and little used. Men prefer to use the canons' mill for it is in the burgh. There are 31 messuages in the burgh," continued Alwin, "though some are but sorry dwellings, and in sore need of repair for the thatch keeps out little rain. We had hoped that our Lord the King would grant us leave to use his straw to make repairs. Each dwelling has its garden where men try to scratch a few vegetables from the poor soil, but it is hard. There is space within the walls for more dwellings, but we have not the people either to build them or to live in them. Each man pays sixteen pence gavel tax for his messuage and many are hard-pressed to find such a sum."

"Come, Master Bailiff", said Gilbert with a wry smile. "You are not as poverty-stricken as you would make out if last night's dinner was aught to go by, and your ale is some of the best I have tasted for many months."

"Ah, sir, we did our best to honour the presence of Duke William's surveyor by offering him the best we had. It was right that we should kill the fatted calf," said Alwin making a bow as he spoke.

"You would cast me in the role of a Prodigal Son then?" chuckled Gilbert.

"Your pardon sir, you mistake my meaning. I was thinking more of a wedding feast, such as that at Cana in Galilee, though I would not cast you, a priest, as the bridegroom," and Alwin also smiled.

"You have a ready wit Master Bailiff, and I commend you for it," and Gilbert reached out and prodded Alwin in the stomach. "But we must continue. Have we listed all that concerns the land held by the King? If so then let us hear from you, Master Gilbert, the tally of the lands you and your canons of this church of the Holy Trinity hold. Geoffrey, mark a new heading on your sheet for the church's land. Now, Master Godric." And Gilbert leant back to listen.

"Sir, the canons hold five hides and a virgate in the vill and also a hide of land on the island of Vectis. You can see the island from the mouth of the two rivers. You cannot see our land from there because it is to the east of the chalk cliffs and the bay with the many-coloured sands. It is cared for by a priest on that island who visits us but seldom for he has much to occupy himself there. All this land has belonged to the church since before the memory of anyone. Some say that it was so even in the time of King Ethelred or King Edward the Martyr who ruled before him. We have 42 oxen that we can put to the plough, but two of these are old and will not last the year so that we have five ploughs in the demesne."

"Not so fast, Master Godric. Poor Geoffrey here must note this all down, and you run ahead of his quill."

Godric waited till Geoffrey has stopped writing and then continued, "There are eleven villeins on our land and thirteen bordars who have but eight oxen between them, and we have two serfs though we treat them well. Most of these people have to live in the six messuages in the burgh that belong to the church, though Alnod, one of the canons, lets some of them use two messuages that he has. He will tell you about them in a moment. The dwellings are poor and cramped though the land of some is larger than the others, for two of them pay two shillings and two pence and the other four pay two shillings and three pence. This makes a total of thirteen shillings and four pence. Then we have about a hide and a virgate of meadowland."

"Come, Master Godric, can you not be more exact than that? How many acres do you reckon to your meadowland?" asked Gilbert sharply. He was not going to let Godric escape with short tally, even if it was church land.

"Let me see." Godric put on a play of counting up his acres, though I was sure he knew to the nearest rod how much he had for he could be mean in his dealings when the fancy took him, for all his kindness.

"Ah yes, it must be, er, 108 acres. Yes that's it. We also have woodland for two swine only. Before King William's time we had more but the King took eight acres in that part of the hundred called Bovre to add to his great forest of Andret. I will say nothing of what the loss of that land has meant to the church. Our land is poor, for in the blessed Edward's time it was taxed at only six pounds. I fear King William reckons that it is now worth eight pounds." Godric sighed, though I doubt that it impressed Gilbert.

"But you have tithes, I think?" he asked.

"Yes for sure, though they do not always amount to much if the crops are poor. We have the whole tithe of the burgh of Twynham and one third of the Holdenhurst tithe. That land was held by Eorl Tostig, but King William holds it now, though Hugh de Port has received most of it from the King and it has never paid tax, though I know not why."

"And you have a mill I think," said Gilbert.

"Yes. The miller is Oswald here," said Godric, pointing to Father. "He pays thirty shillings a year for it. That mill grinds all our corn, and has done since before Edward the Martyr was King."

"Are there any other lands held by the church?"

"Oh yes. Alsi, come forward and tell Master Gilbert what land you hold," said Godric turning to one of the canons who was standing in the porch of the church. Fat little Alsi came waddling up, his red face shining with sweat.

"Yes, Master Gilbert, I held land from the blessed Edward at Bashley which is in Edgegate. I had a hide and three virgates then, but when King William came he took a hide away from me and put it into his forest of Andret so I only have three virgates left now. There is land for one plough, and I also hold sixteen acres of meadowland. One villein and one bordar work it for me and I have two serfs, though they are of little use. All my land was worth twenty shillings in the time of King Edward, and King William says it is still worth the same, though I do not know why when there is so much less. Oh, and I also have half of a small mill which is little used for it is only worth three shillings. I would grind more corn if I could. Much of what comes from my land I use for the poor of the burgh and for travellers. I think it was my flour that was used to make bread for your soldiers. I hope they found it to their liking." He stopped, out of breath, and looked about him for confirmation of what he had said.

"Thank you Alsi," said Godric. "He has spoken true, Master Gilbert. We use much of his flour for the poor. Alsi is always charitable. Alnod, you too hold some land I think. Is it not held from the King too, and was held from Edward before him? Alnod, Alnod, come forward and speak to Master Gilbert and tell him of your land."

Poor old Alnod, whom we youngsters often mocked for he was growing very deaf, turned and, putting a wrinkled hand behind his ear, said in his shaking voice, "My land; yes, yes, I do hold some land. Had it from the King; Edward that was. I well remember the day I got it. Had to do homage for it. Could get down on my knees easier in those days. What was I saying? Oh yes, land. Well I held it in parage with my cousin. Still do. I wonder what has happened to him? Haven't seen him for many years now. We held one and a half virgates from the King then. Still got the same amount now, too."

Alnod scratched his tonsure for a moment, while Gilbert waited for him to continue. At length he went on.

"We only have four oxen to work it, so we have to share the ploughing with a neighbour. Our two serfs do most of the work. Don't get much of a crop from it though. The ten and a half acres of meadowland are probably more use as we can graze sheep on it. There is a little mill too beside a stream though we only have a third part of it. What is it worth? Let me see: twenty-five pence I think."

He looked round him, seeking someone.

"Alsi, can you remember, what did I tell you my bit of mill was worth? Was it twenty-five pence? It was? I thought so. Yes. Oh, and I have two messuages in the burgh which I let some of the other villeins on the church's estate live in. There is not much room for them all in the other six houses. Terribly crowded when they have so many children. Don't know how they manage. Must see if I can't do something about it."

"Thank you, thank you, Alnod," said Godric, "That is all. Had you not better see to the altars. I think some of the tapers are burning low and should be changed." Heaving a sign of relief, he turned to Gilbert and explained that Alnod was a little vague nowadays. "But he is so kind to everyone and we all love him. He prays for us all, and of course, our Lord the King."

Gilbert gave a wry smile, puffing out his cheeks and scratching his chin in frustration, and grunted. No doubt he was used to dealing with the likes of Alnod, for much of what he needed to know about the old days would have to come from such people. Only they had long enough memories .

"Yes, yes", he said. "Now do any other priests hold land in this hundred?"

"There is Godwine, who has land almost two miles to the east of the burgh at Stanpit. Come forward Godwine, and tell us of your holdings," Godric called out.

I recognised him more by his size than his face for we seldom saw him in the burgh, but he is the biggest man I have ever seen. He must stand two yards and a hand's spread high and his shoulders are so broad that he has to turn sideways to enter some cottage doors. It is said that he can pull a plough better than a single ox and some would like to put him to the test, but he is a modest man despite his strength and holds back from such contests. I have seen him lift two full sacks of corn, one in each hand, and throw them both onto the top of a high laden cart together without so much as a breath of effort.

Once, I watched him carry a new millstone for Father fifty paces from the river to our mill without sweating, and then lower it so gently into place that it needed no adjustment afterwards. Yet he can be gentle too, and it is said that he has healing in his hands. He spends most of his time on his land and caring for the folk in Stanpit and Hoburne. They are surely fortunate to have such a man among them. He also visits those on the manor of Highcliffe, which has always been held by Bishop Walkelin of Winchester.

I could see Godwine moving forward through the crowd for he was head and shoulders above the others. He came up to the table and I noticed Gilbert give a small start of surprise when he looked up to see such a mountain before him.

Godwine cleared his throat and in his deep voice said, "Sir, I hold one estate in Stanpit, and Wislac holds the other. They are both of one hide and we have half a plough between us with one villein and a bordar each. We also have eight acres of meadow. We held the land first from King Edward and it was worth twenty shillings which we paid between us. When William came, he took it and gave it all to Hugh de Port, so we now hold our land from him. It is worth forty shillings now, but we have to pay sixty shillings. I think this is because we can graze sheep on the meadowland. There is more land in Stanpit that is used by the King's falconer Witro. He has a hide and his wife Adeline holds a virgate. She is well known for her charity in Stanpit and also Somerford. They say that she has helped restore the sight of several people using the waters from the pure well on the edge of the harbour there."

"Do you say that this woman Adeline works miracles? We have heard nothing of this in Winchester before." There was a sharpness in Gilbert's voice which caused all near him to look up with interest.

"We would not claim them as miracles," said Godwine, "for the church has never pronounced on them. But the well I speak of has been known in these parts since the days of the Romans. Its waters are of unusual purity and is in great demand for drinking in that area. It is much used for making ale of fine quality since it does not add its own flavour to the brew as so often happens. Your soldiers may have tasted some of it last evening, since Ranulf who cares for our visitors keeps a stock of it for the church's more honoured guests."

Belesme of St Lo leant forward and whispered in Gilbert's ear, " 'Tis true Master Gilbert. If that is what we were served last evening, it was some of the finest ale I have tasted in many a year - and I have some experience in these matters," he added with a grin.

Gilbert turned to Godric and said, "Perhaps I might be permitted to taste some too when we have finished here, but tell me more of these healings."

"Well sir," continued Godwine, "the falconer Witro's wife, Adeline, always uses the waters from that well to cleanse all wounds before she applies her healing balms, and the wounds seem to heal much faster than usual. Those who have a soreness of the eyes or whose sight is failing seem to get great comfort from bathing their eyes in the well water. Indeed, there are several people, both men and women, whose sight was failing and who after such ministrations can now see much more clearly. We do not claim that any have had their sight restored in the manner of Our Saviour, for that would indeed be miraculous, but only that they can see more clearly. It has been of great benefit particularly to those who have close work to do.

"I always try to use it myself for any cleansing I may do, since it seems to speed the healing process. Here, see this cut on my arm. I got that from a sharp thorn two days ago, and it went deep as you can see. As I was working in my fields, it was full of dirt for most of the day and it was angry, red and painful by evening before I could tend to it. But I washed it clean in water from that well by Stanpit. By morning I could no longer feel it and it was healing well. It needed no comfrey or other healing balm upon it."

Godwine showed Gilbert a deep cut on his left forearm which showed none of the usual signs of soreness in such hurts.

"Most interesting indeed," said Gilbert. "I shall visit this well on my way back to Winchester and perhaps take some of its waters with me."

I heard one of the soldiers who was standing close to me say to his neighbour: "And I know who will have to carry it too!"

"Now, let's get back to business," said Gilbert. "Hugh de Port holds much land in these parts, and I shall be seeing him later to hear from him about these holdings. Some of his land is held by others who live in this burgh, I think. Is that not so?"

Godwine spoke again. "Sir, the same Wislac who holds a hide at Stanpit also held a half hide at Ripley from King Edward as an alod. Now it is held from Hugh. You will find in that demesne there is but one plough and 8 acres of meadow. There used to be much woodland too but that has all gone into King William's forest, to our loss. Whereas it was worth twenty shillings in the time of King Edward, it is now only worth fifteen shillings. Then there is Ulvict the Huntsman who holds much land at Ripley too. He is not here today, being about his business in the forest where much of his land now is."

Godwine paused to allow Geoffrey to note this down, before continuing.

"Then there are the three hides and all the woodland which have been taken by the King, and is valued at five pounds. No doubt Hugh de Port will tell you of this himself when you see him. We have lost much land to the King's forest and though our Lord the King may do as he pleases in these matters and he has dealt fairly with us in many matters by lowering our dues, we would rather have the land, for without land to farm we cannot grow the food to feed our families or pay the King's taxes. Forgive me sir if I speak boldly, but I must speak true or I could not look my fellows in the eye with a clear conscience."

With that, Godwine bowed to Gilbert and stepped back a couple of paces. Gilbert looked at him carefully, sizing him up. Then a slow smile spread over his face.

"A bold man it is who will speak as you do, Master Godwine. Our Lord the King likes such as you who will speak honestly for the good of others and not be always seeking his own good. It would be a brave man who would argue with you and take matters to a fall, I am thinking. Here, Belesme of St Lo, would you try a bout with this man?"

"Not today, Master Gilbert. My knee is troubling me still with all this walking," and he put on a good act of a bad limp which he had not shown before. There was a ripple of mocking laughter not only from our own people but also from the soldiers, for Belesme would have been no match for Godwine and all present knew it.

"Let it pass then Belesme." said Gilbert, and turning to Godric he said, "This is an honest man who speaks the truth as he should, and I respect him for it."

With that, Godwine turned away and moved back among the crowd who were smiling and nudging each other, feeling that they had scored a point off the Normans on this occasion. For the general opinion seemed to be that Godwine could have taken on all six Norman soldiers single-handed and thrown them all into the nearby mill-stream before they had time to say "Pater Noster".

Gilbert looked about him, wondering how much more there was to be listed in this burgh. "Tell me Alwin" he said, "as bailiff can you name others who hold land in this area?"

"Surely Master Gilbert, but they are mostly great nobles whom we seldom see. Some indeed we have never seen though they take their dues from us regularly enough. The Eorl Roger of Shrewsbury holds two hides at Sway, and half a hide at Hinton, though Fulcoin holds it from him now, having taken it over from Ulvict these three years gone. There is other land held by Hugh de Port too. Herne he holds from Bishop Odo of Bayeux, the King's half- brother who gave it him, where there is a fishery besides, and also a hide at Knapp which has a mill worth twenty shillings and a fishery worth fifty pence. It yields good eels, but too much salmon which men grow tired of from too much eating. Most of the other land is held by the King himself. All of Holdenhurst he has, for he took it from the Eorl Tostig, King Harold's brother, after Senlac Field."

Alwin paused, and turning to Godric, held whispered converse with him before speaking again.

"Then there are thirteen villeins and three bordars who used to dwell on the land that is now in the King's forest. Many of these are near to starving, having no land from which to scratch a living. In King Edward's time that land was worth fourty-four pounds, but now it is worth only twenty-four pounds, though it has to pay twenty-five pounds at twenty pence to the ounce. What the King has taken into his forest is only valued at twelve pounds ten shillings, so the folk have a heavier burden to bear now; but I have no doubt you know of all this, Master Gilbert."

Gilbert looked up at him with displeasure. I doubt it was the first time he had heard such a tale of hardship wrought by this harsh new King, but Gilbert had to take such complaining on his broad shoulders and pretend not to notice. I could see him fidgeting in his seat nevertheless, for he seemed to have sympathy with those who were displaced. Perhaps it was good that we lived in the smaller burgh of Twynham, for they say that the Lord of Holdenhurst Manor lives in some style and takes as much as he can from his folk.

"Oh yes, then there is Winkton which Robert holds from Waleran the huntsman who holds it from the King. This too had been held by Eorl Tostig, who had it from King Edward as an alod. Now it pays geld for 3 hides and a virgate, though it had 7 hides before. There is land for 4 ploughs, with 1 ploughs in the demesne. The hall has the use of two mills, and each mill produces as many as 450 eels which are much sought after in these parts, but as you know, much land in this area is wild and of no use. You will travel over some of it on your way to the harbour of Poole. No-one lives on much of it for it will not support a crop and even the animals keep away from it as much as they can. It is too sandy and dry for most of them, though brocks and coneys find it easy for digging their burrows."

I pricked up my ears at this. I have never ventured as far as the port of Poole, but I like going after coneys; they are good sport. Brocks I care not for as sport, though I have lain and watched them sometimes playing near their sets in the springtime with their young when I have been near the edge of the forest. I nudged Alric and I whispered to him:

"We must go there soon and see what sport is to be had. I hope to have finished my new bow in a week or so and we can try it out."

He nodded and his eyes lit up at the thought of the sport we might have.

I felt a tug on my sleeve and, turning, saw Isabel and Emma beckoning to me to come away. I edged out of the crowd quietly to see what it was they wanted. When these two got together, some mischief usually followed. When we were all well clear of the throng, I went over to the wall round the churchyard and sat down on it, and the others joined me.

"Well, what is it?" I asked them.

"You remember hearing Godwine tell Master Gilbert about the healing powers of the Pure Well beside the harbour towards Stanpit and how interested he seemed to be. What do you say that we go down there with a flagon each and draw some out and bring it back to give to him? He said he wanted to take some back to Winchester with him. We could get enough for him and also the Bishop if he wanted. It could but stand us in good stead and might help him to be kindly towards us in his reckoning of our land holdings. He has made no mention of any assarts yet and it would be well to keep him sweet and not encourage him to enquire too closely. If the Bishop finds the waters as healing as Godwine says, then Goodwife Adeline may become as famous there as she is here." Emma's eyes sparkled as she said this, and Isabel looked at both of us and nodded in eager agreement.

"Oh yes," Isabel said, jumping off the wall. "Come on, Hugh. You go back to your house and fetch a flagon, and I will run back to ours and ask Mother for one, or two if she can spare them. Let's all meet at the bridge as soon as we can and go down there. We had best be careful though. Let's separate now and go our different ways, lest others see us and wonder what is afoot. I'll go first and you follow in a few moments."

With that she turned and sauntered away, stopping to pick some blades of grass which she proceeded to twist into a circlet for her hair as if that was the most important thing in her mind at that moment. My heart gave a leap of admiration at her cleverness. Turning, I saw Emma looking at me with amused eyes for she had noticed all. I reddened, and to hide my feelings I too got off the wall and started to move away, to be followed soon by the other two.

Chapter 3 1086

When we met again at the bridge, we all four had a large flagon.

"Best we hide them beneath our clothes," said Alric, "or someone will surely wonder what is afoot."

Alric and I stuffed our flagons under our tunics, while Isabel and Emma took off the shawls they were wearing and wrapped theirs in them tucking them under their arms making them look for all the world like a bundle of old clothes. This done, we crossed the bridge and set off to walk the mile to the well. The tide was low but because Father was not working the mill, the mill-stream which flows under the first arch of this bridge was hardly moving. As we crossed the second bridge I picked up a stone from the road and threw it into the reeds. There was a squawk and a flapping of wings as a pair of ducks took flight, quacking angrily as they gained height before circling away downstream towards the marshland that formed the inner edge of the harbour.

Isabel turned on me angrily. "Hugh, you craven wretch, look what you have done. You might have hurt one of them and they mean you no harm."

"How was I to know they were there?" I retorted, angry that she should upbraid me in front of the others, though I knew that she was right to do so for Father has taught us to care for all wildlife since it gives us our choicest food.

Emma put her arm through mine and, turning her smiling face up to me, said quietly, "Say you are sorry Hugh, and Isabel will forgive you."

I reddened again at this but did as she bid me, but I marked the spot where the birds had risen, meaning to come back later and see if perchance there was a nest nearby. It is a fair road that leads towards the place where the track from Mudeford crosses it on its way to Waleran the huntsman's hall at Winkton. At the crossing, we turned right-handed into Hugh de Port's land of Stanpit towards the well which is to the right of the track on the harbour's edge. As we passed Goodwife Adeline's cott, she came out carrying a bucket. She too was heading to the well, so we joined her wishing her "Good day".

"What brings you young folk out to these parts on such a day?" she asked.

"Methought you would be at the gathering of the burgh folk to hear what takes place at the reckoning of the land holdings for the King."

"We were, but most of the tally is now made and we are coming to the well for a purpose. Master Gilbert the King's clerk who is making the reckoning, was told of your cures and how the waters from the well can make eyes to see again sometimes. He showed a keen interest and means to take some of the water back with him to Winchester both for himself and the Bishop," said Alric. "Emma here thought we would gather the water for him and give it to him before he goes. It would please him I am thinking and might stand us in good stead with our masters."

"Ay, it might," replied the goodwife, "but there is no certainty that all will be cured. The waters have a cleansing property, I grant you, and will ease pain sometimes when a wound is cleaned with it, particularly if you use a cloth that has been kept wrapped in comfrey leaves. Here, take this piece of flaxen cloth and give it to this Master Gilbert with my blessings and tell him to use it when he bathes sore eyes particularly. Mark you well to tell him that it will not work miracles though it may ease aching eyes. How do you mean to carry the water?" she asked.

"In these flagons," Alric replied, pulling his out from under his tunic. "We have all brought one but hid them lest people asked what we were doing on such a day with these things. On the return it will be no matter for we can say what we mean to do should any ask, and no-one would gainsay us."

"It seems you have an old head on young shoulders," she said. "Is not your father Bailiff Alwin?" asked Goodwife Adeline. "And you young sir, are you not Oswald the miller's boy? Is his cough better? I told him to rinse his throat out with this well water at the end of the day these two weeks past, for he complained of a hoarseness. How fares he now?"

"My father said nothing to me of this but assuredly he has no cough now and it was troubling him somewhat, I know. I wondered that it should clear so quickly for it is a common hazard of millers. My mouth is always dry at the end of a day working with Father but I have thought little of it. I thank you for your kindness, Goodwife, and I will tell him of your enquiry," I said.

"Come here a moment lad," said Goodwife Adeline. "Let me see your eyes. They seem somewhat red. Do you rub them often?"

"Sometimes in the evening when I have been at the mill they trouble me with a pricking feeling. Often next morning they are slow to open too, but I am used to it and my eye is sharp enough to pick out a coney hidden in the grass."

"It will not be for ever," she said, "unless you take some care. Mark well what I say now. When you come from the mill, be sure to bathe your eyes well with a cloth soaked in this water and rinse them with it too. It will help to keep your sight keen and save the pricking you talk of. Here, put this small cloth in your pouch but keep it clean. It is best you wrap camomile leaves in it for they have healing properties too. You have brought four flagons with you. Then keep one for yourself when you return and give Master Gilbert but three. If he needs more, he can draw more for himself when he passes by on his way back to Winchester. Now may God go with you and mind what I have told you. Give my blessings to your father."

"My thanks to you Goodwife Adeline," I said. " Now we must draw up the water and carry it back to the burgh. Come on Alric, give me a hand and work the rope."

Then we set about filling the flagons from the well. First though, we filled Goodwife Adeline's bucket and at Isabel's bidding I carried it for her back to her cott. She bade me enter and showed me where to place it on the table by the window, near where she kept her herbs and remedies for simple ailments.

As I was going, Goodwife Adeline turned to me.

"Mark well the two lasses and keep them close. Two such budding flowers should be kept from harm and methinks that you have more than a passing interest in the bailiff's child. What is her name?"

"Isabel," I said, "and my sister is called Emma. They are good friends and Alric and I are close too."

I could not speak about Isabel but wondered how the goodwife had been able to read my thoughts when she answered, "She seems to have eyes only for you, but go carefully with her for she is a tender plant and would bruise easily."

She smiled at me, and I felt that she knew more than she was saying. Thanking her again for her kindness and promising that I would tell Father what she had said, I went out of her cott to find Alric and the two girls waiting for me by the gate. Alric was carrying my flagon as well as his own, and when he saw me he twitted me.

"Come on you lazy serf. Do you expect me to carry your load too? We cannot stand here all day while you gossip with the goodwife here, saving your presence lady," and he smiled at her.

"Be on your way then all of you, and remember me to your fathers. Tell Master Gilbert that if he wishes to call at my cott as he passes, I shall be glad to receive him and show him how to use the water to good effect." With that we bade her farewell, and set off back to the burgh.

It seemed a lot further going back, for the flagons were large and heavy to carry. I watched Isabel and noticed that she seemed to labour with hers after a while, so I moved close to her and put my hand into the flagon handle with hers to take the weight. She turned to me and smiled and sighed with relief at the easing of her burden. Thus we continued back crossing the two bridges and so up towards the church.

Before we reached there, we were met by Alnoth who called out, "Where have you all been? Father has been calling for you to come and serve Master Gilbert. The miller was angry that you were not there to help too, Hugh. Make all haste to the house and be sure to have a ready excuse when you arrive. I said that you had all been summoned on some urgent business but I doubt that it was believed."

"You did well," said Alric, "and spoke truer than you knew."

We all hurried to the bailiff's house. As we drew near, we could hear laughter which eased our minds.

"Give me your flagon, Hugh, and you Isabel give yours to Emma. We will hold them by the door while you slip in quietly and pretend that you have been in the house for some time. Use the rear door and so come into the hall from the kitchen. It may deceive them into thinking that you have been working there for some time."

Isabel and I did as Alric suggested. One of the bailiff's serfs was just going into the hall with a fresh flagon of ale, and as he passed us he said, "This Master Gilbert seems to be in a good humour but I think much of it is due to the bailiff's stories and his ale, for this is the second flagon I have refilled."

We heard no more of what he said for it was drowned by a great roar of laughter from the hall. Under cover of that, Isabel and I slipped quietly into the hall and, taking the refilled flagon from the serf, I carried it round behind where Master Gilbert was seated and refilled his beaker while he was turned away in converse with the bailiff. Quietly topping up the other beakers, I then moved back to stand behind the bailiff as if I had been there all the while. Isabel, meanwhile, had taken a dish of comfits from another of the servants and was offering it to her father. He took one without looking and continued with his tale which was at the expense of old Alnod the priest. He had fallen into the mill-stream beside the ducking stool when he was trying to persuade Martha the scold to cease her prattling and spreading of false tales. As she came up from the water for the second time, she had grabbed his sleeve and pulled him down with her into the pool. They both came up spluttering together, and a fish which had lodged in Alnod's cowl jumped out and slithered down inside his habit, to be caught at his waist by his girdle. Alnod's face, as he wriggled to get the fish free, for it was tickling his belly, reduced everyone to such a state that the reeve, who was holding the end of the ducking stool pole, let it slip so that Martha got an extra ducking and came up full of weed as well from having been left so long at the bottom of the pool. When the bailiff and Master Gilbert had recovered somewhat, they both drank deeply.

As I bent forward to refill their drinking horns, the bailiff noticed me and said, as he dried the tears of laughter from his eyes, "Ah, there you are. What kept you that you were not here to serve us as you were bidden?"

"We have been here the while, Father," said Isabel, offering the dish of comfits to him again. "You have been taking the comfits I have been offering you and I noticed that you chose your favourite ones too," she added with her winning smile. "But you are right, we were not here when you sat down and I crave your pardon and for Hugh too. We were about some business for Master Gilbert here which I trust he will find to his liking. We heard his interest in the healing properties of the Pure Well at Stanpit so Hugh and I have been there to draw some of its water for him so that Master Gilbert may take it back with him to Winchester. We have some flagons filled which Alric and Emma are guarding by the door for you. Shall I call them so that we may offer the water to Master Gilbert? We brought enough so that he could give some to my Lord the Bishop should he so desire."

Isabel paused to draw breath, a little frightened at her boldness.

"When we were at the well, we met the Goodwife Adeline whose works of charity you heard of this morning. She sent word that should Master Gilbert wish to call at her humble cott on his way back to Winchester, she would be most glad to tell him how she uses the water to best effect. She sent her blessings to you, Father, and also to you Oswald of the mill."

"'Tis true," I said, "and she showed me how to ease the pricking in my eyes when they are sore from the dust in the mill by bathing them with this cloth - see there is camomile wrapped in it too - and then soaked in the water. Do your eyes ever trouble you, Master Gilbert?" I asked. "For if they do you may gladly take this cloth she gave me for I think you need your eyes for reading more than I do."

I took the cloth out of my purse and offered it to the clerk. He looked at me with interest and taking the package, unwrapped it and examined it with care. Then, wrapping it all up again, he looked me straight in the eye.

"You have gone to some trouble for me and I thank you for it. I will take the cloth and if it proves good, I will remember you. You Isabel, you say you have fetched this water for me from this well? But the place is not in the burgh, I think. How far have you carried it?"

"A mile and more but others helped me. Shall I call them?" she asked. Smiling and turning, she beckoned to Alric and Emma to come forward from where they stood by the door. As they approached, Gilbert turned to me and said, "Bring me a dish that I may put some of this water in it now and bathe my eyes. They do trouble me at times and are somewhat sore now".

I hastened away to the kitchen to find a clean bowl and, bringing it back, offered it to Gilbert.

"Here, pour water in it while I unwrap this cloth that I may put all to the test."

So saying, he took the cloth, dipped it into the water and proceeded to bathe his eyes carefully one after the other. We all stood silently watching him. The water trickled down his cheeks making clean rivulets as it went so that his eyelids and cheeks became clear and no longer encrusted. We held our breath, hopeful that Goodwife Adeline's claims would be true for it was a gamble we took. After some minutes he finished. Then, squeezing the cloth dry before finally dabbing his face all over and blinking, he looked round about peering into different parts of the hall.

"By the Rood, Master Bailiff" he said, "'Tis true. I see more clearly than I have done for many a week and the soreness is eased somewhat too. I shall take some of this water with me when I leave."

Alwin's face broke into a smile of relief, for he too knew that if there had been no result then Gilbert would have felt he had been made to look a fool and it would have gone hard with all of us. As it was, we might all hope to have some profit, for Gilbert not only had the ear of the Bishop but also of the King, since it was to the King that this great record was to be given and to whom Gilbert would speak concerning the lands.

"I will send with you one who can show you where this goodwife lives, that you may talk with her and learn of her cures. There are many here who have good cause to be thankful to her," he said.

"May it please you sir," I said, "by your leave I will show Master Gilbert the well and Goodwife Adeline's cott too, for she so charged me."

"So be it," said Gilbert, and turning to Alwin: "Mark well this lad. He has done me a kindness which shall be remembered. Should he think to enter the priesthood then you should let me know. We could use such as he in Winchester." Turning to me he asked, "Boy, have you learnt to read?"

"But a few words only though I can recite the 'Pater Noster' and 'Ave Maria' without fault."

"That I can vouch for," put in Godric who sat nearby. "He learns fast and I have high hopes for him. He is trustworthy too - for his age."

"You hear what is said of you. Let it prove to be so. Your age, Hugh?"

"I am fourteen these past two months sir."

"You look older. Remember what I have said, Hugh. Always repay a kindness."

"Sir, I will," I replied, and made a small bow to him. "My father has always told me so too and our priest Godric bade us do the same in his sermon at Mass this last Sunday. He told us how Our Lord had said that we should not take an eye for an eye nor a tooth for a tooth but should turn the other cheek to our enemies and repay evil with kindness. He said it is in the fifth chapter of St Matthew's Gospel, and comes after the Beatitudes which he had been explaining to us. Have I remembered aright Master Godric?"

"My son, you do me credit." And he gave a laugh. "I thought not to have my sermons repeated back to me with such accuracy. Yes, you are quite right. We could make a priest of you yet, I am thinking." He turned to Gilbert and said, "I will keep this boy under my eye and instruct him as best I can, for he would seem to have head enough to become a priest."

"It is good that you should do so," said Gilbert, turning to Geoffrey the scribe, who was sitting at the far end of the table.

"Geoffrey, make you a note on your parchment there of this boy's name. It is Hugh and I would have his name given to the Abbot at Winchester as a likely candidate for the priesthood. Put down also that his father is Oswald the miller of the church's mill of this burgh". Turning to my father, he said, "Would you be content for your son to enter the priesthood, Master Miller, when he is of an age?"

"Sir," said my father, "you do me much honour. Our family has always tried to follow the teachings of the church and my son Hugh here seems to take them well to heart. I must confess that I had thought that he would serve the church here in this burgh if he were called. For the present, he works at my trade helping me in the mill. I can use his strength and he seems to have a knack of knowing how to set the millstones so that they grind smooth and fine. It is not every apprentice that can do so, as no doubt you know. I pray you, let him be for the moment until he is fully of age. In good time he may become one of our canons of this church of the Holy Trinity under the worthy Godric. The church could then profit both from his services and from his knowledge as an expert miller - should he so prove to be."

Gilbert looked thoughtful for a moment, casting his gaze first at me then at my father.

"Master Miller, you have spoken soundly. What you propose could benefit both the church and the burgh. We will leave it so for the moment and see how this young cub of yours shapes up. But look you, Hugh," he said, fixing me with his eye, though there seemed to be a smile in it, "think not that you can be idle just because some of your elders have spoken well of you. Remember also that it says in the Gospels: 'The labourer is worthy of his hire', so learn your trade well and also your letters and attend the Mass when you are bidden. We cannot all follow the example of our Lord the King and his lady the Queen, and build great churches to the honour and worship of God as they have done at Caen in their dukedom of Normandy, but we can offer our service to God and lead our lives as best we may. Each one of us has his part to play."

Gilbert turned to look first at Godric, and then at Alwin before going on to say "This burgh of Twynham has but a poor building for its church and the nine chapels that serve it are small and in need of repair. The offerings made to your church amount to little more than will keep your priests and allow them to serve the needs of travellers. There must be many of these because of your port and the trade that passes through it down the River Avon from Sarum and the countryside around it and what comes in from the King's land in the dukedom of Normandy. A burgh with such a trade, so near to the King's heart, should have a better place of worship more fitting to its importance. I will speak to His Majesty when I see him next and learn his will. He is keen to build great churches in this his new kingdom. He has plans well advanced for several already, though I doubt if any will be as fine as those he has built in Caen. They were to placate the Holy Father in Rome after William had married his cousin the Lady Matilda of Flanders. It was the softly-spoken Abbot Lanfranc who secured the lifting of the excommunication that had been placed on Duke William as he was then. We have much to thank him for."

Godric and Alwin exchanged surprised glances on hearing this. A new and magnificent church in this burgh. Who would pay for such a building and what changes would it bring about? Who could tell. In any case it was no concern of mine. Of greater moment to me was this talk of the priesthood. I was none too sure that that was what I wanted for my life. To help at the Mass yes, and to learn to read and write a little, but to lose the pleasures of sport with my friends was something else; and what of Isabel? If I remained in the burgh, I could still be a secular canon as father had suggested and she could be part of my life. To go to Winchester and enter the priesthood and perhaps an enclosed Order: that was something else and my spirit rebelled at it. I must keep my counsel I thought, and later, when all these matters had been put away with the passing of time, I would speak to Father. He seemed to understand my feelings and would surely guide me well.

Alwin sat up and cleared his throat as though to break the train of thought.

"Well, Master Gilbert, there are still some lands to record. Is it your wish that we continue to hear from those who hold them? I have given orders that all men who have not yet spoken to you be ready in the churchyard at two hours after noon. We should be able to hear them all before the angelus is struck. Would that be your wish? Then if you can spare the time, it would be our pleasure to have you dine with us again this evening."

"And on the morrow before you depart, it would do us great honour if you would join us in saying Mass before the altar of the Holy Trinity," added Godric.

"That will suit me well," answered Gilbert. "Now, let us to the churchyard once more and hear from those who have not yet spoken. I tell you truthfully, Master Alwin, this great collation of lands is a heavy burden on me but our Lord the King has so commanded and I must obey. It will enable him to raise his taxes with greater justice more especially in these parts where he has taken much land into his forest of Andret. Though many complain that they have been dispossessed of their lands, the King has let them settle elsewhere and means to lower the levy on those whose land is less. Let us be going then, and complete this work."

So saying, he rose and all followed his example and trooped out to return to the churchyard. Alwin's wife Mary caught my eye as I started to follow and beckoned me to her.

"Stay here, Hugh, and help Isabel and me clear the tables and prepare for the meal this evening. There is much to do for we must be sure to give Master Gilbert the best we can. He has influence in high places and some of the talk at table has great implications. Does the King mean to make this burgh a noble city? It seems unlikely but we know not what his thoughts may be. In the meantime we must play our part and make sure that such report as Gilbert may make is as favourable as possible. Tell me also, do you have a mind to be a priest as Master Gilbert suggested?"

There was more than a little interest in the question I thought, and Mary's face showed some concern as to the answer.

"I confess that I had not thought much about it. I had always thought that I would continue at the mill with Father. He has been teaching me the art and there is much to learn. I would learn to read and write too if I am able and Master Godric is helping me. To be a priest and perhaps leave the burgh for Winchester, or even to find myself sent to the great Abbey of Bec across the water, is something altogether different which has so far not crossed my mind. I doubt if I could live under its rules though I might be able to accept the life of a vanon here under Master Godric. He is strict but kind and understands how men feel. Besides," I added, "the love Mother and Father have for each other and the love they have shown me makes me feel that I would wish to follow their example and one day take a wife of my own. I doubt that the celibate life of a monk is for me and I would miss the company of Alric and my other friends more than I can say."

Mary's face softened into a smile.

"You should not be worrying over-much about such things yet," she said. "There is plenty of time to think about choosing a wife. You are right: I do not see you in a sombre habit with a tonsure. You have too much spirit and independence about you. Be on your guard lest it lead you astray, but seek to improve your knowledge as you can and crave the help of those who, like Godric, are willing to give it."

Mary turned and busied herself at the table.

"Now help me with these platters and then go to the cellar and draw more of our best ale that it may stand well before the evening meal. I must speak with my husband about wine too. When you have done that would you please go to our barn and fetch fresh rushes that we may put them on the floor. It may seem that we make much ado over this Gilbert but I feel that it will be to our advantage to humour him. To find that the burgh has to pay but one mark of silver less than we might have,will be worth all the care and hospitality we can give Master Gilbert and his scribe. Tell me, how do Belesme of St Lo and the other soldiers fare at the guest-house? Ranulf usually looks after the needs of his travellers well."

"They seemed to have what they required when I saw them last evening but I will go and enquire if there is anything else they have need of. I saw Ranulf giving them fresh straw in their beds and the meal smelt good. I will go and speak with Ranulf and tell him what you have said to me, if you wish."

"Yes, go to the guest-house and make sure that their every need is granted. Even these soldiers can aid our cause and we have a duty to care for our travellers of whatever sort." First I cleared the tables as I had been bidden and fetched fresh rushes. These I piled up outside the door while I raked up the old ones and the bones and other scraps which lay in them that the dogs had not found. All this I took outside and threw onto the heap at the bottom of the garden next to the pigsty where it could rot down . As I came back up to the house again, I passed by Mary's herb garden and stopped to gather a bunch of lavender and rosemary from the large bushes she had growing there. This I put on the high table and then went out to bring in the fresh rushes which I then spread out as evenly as I could over the earthen floor.

I was just finishing when Mary came back in from the kitchen, followed by Isabel who was carrying a pile of freshly cleansed platters which she set down on the high table. Seeing a pile of herbs already there, she was about to gather them up when I called to her.

"Stay your hand awhile.I was about to scatter those herbs on the rushes for they will give off a pleasant odour when they are trodden and will find favour with Gilbert. When I was with Goodwife Adeline this morning I noticed that her cott smelt pleasantly of herbs and saw that they lay on her floor too. She said that as you pass about the room you bruise the stems and the air is filled with the scent."

"'Tis a pleasant odour," replied Isabel. "I have some herbs in my pillow but we have never thought to put them on the floor."

"Maybe so," replied Mary, "but have a care with my herbs and use them not too freely for I have need of them for many purposes. Be not over-generous with others' goods. I would rather you had asked first before you gathered my lavender which I was keeping to extract a soothing oil."

"Mother, Hugh meant no harm, and only meant to please."

"I know, and he did well this time, but it might not have been so."

I felt abashed and hung my head. It is hard to do right all the time even though one's intentions are good.

"I am sorry if I displeased you," I said "but I meant only to help. We have lavender at home should you need it and for sure Mother would let you have some if I ask her."

"Take it not ill, Hugh. I know you meant well and I take it kindly. Besides I had not thought to put herbs on the floor myself and I am glad of the idea. I will keep it in mind for special guests in future. We will say nothing of it to our menfolk for they will not notice, but the odour will doubtless put them in a good humour. My thanks then, Hugh. Now be you gone to the guest-house as I bid you and see to the soldiers . If Ranulf has need of aught, come and tell me and I will see if we can provide. Come now Isabel, we still have much to prepare for this evening. I have in mind a special dish with salmon, for though it is common here, those in Winchester taste it but seldom and the way I prepare it finds favour even with those who often tire of it. It is the herbs I use - but it is not lavender, Hugh," she said with a twinkle in her eye.

So I turned and went about her bidding, no longer sore in mind.

As I passed through the market square, I glanced down to the left towards the bridges which crossed the mill-stream and the river. There was the massive figure of Godwine heading back towards his farm at Stanpit, leading a beast heavily laden with sacks of flour. He himself had another slung across his shoulders, but for all its weight it seemed he hardly noticed, and carried it with less effort than the beast. What a man he was and how the people of Stanpit loved him, for it was said that none who turned to him for help went away empty-handed.

There was still a small crowd in the churchyard, some of whom still had to be questioned about their lands and some who were using the opportunity to idle rather than work in the fields. Since the fields belonged to their lord, who could blame them? There was little benefit to them for their work. For Father it was different since the profit from the mill was his, and the assart we were bringing under crops was ours too. I could hear the noise of iron pots being scoured as I approached the guest-house kitchen, so went in there and found Ranulf as I expected, supervising the preparation of the evening meal. He turned as I came in, doing a quick calculation on his fingers.

"Hugh, we need more flour. Go to your father and ask him for another sack of that which he ground last week. It was particularly fine and white. It was some of the corn that came in from Holdenhurst as part of their tithe. There should be some left. It was marked with a tally of an 'H'," and he scratched the letter on the table top with the point of the knife he was holding. "You know the letter I think?"

I looked and recognised it.

"There should be one or two left," I said. "May I use your barrow to fetch it? It will be easier than carrying it on my shoulder, though I could manage it I am sure."

"What, use a barrow? Why, Godwine is carrying a double sack on his shoulders all the way back to Stanpit and it is but a few paces from the mill. Where are your muscles, lad!" he twitted me with a grin. "Yes, take it and be glad. You will find it behind the store-room door, and while you are there, please fetch me another string of onions and a bundle of dried sage that is hanging up near the window."

I did as I was bid and then went to the mill where Father was once again grinding corn. Giving him Ranulf's message, he helped me find the sack of flour we needed and I saw that it was one I had ground myself. Perhaps I did have some skill at grinding after all, though as yet Father had been unwilling to say so, no doubt for good reason. I loaded the sack onto the barrow and pushed it at a run back to the guest-house kitchen where I nearly sent poor Ranulf flying as I came fast through the door. He looked startled and stepped quickly out of my way as I headed for the corner where stood the bread trough. Heaving the sack off the barrow, I leant it against the wall, dusted down my smock and took a deep breath to recover.

Ranulf looked at me and grinned.

"You wasted little time over that task, Hugh. Methinks you must be anxious to be away. Hunting coneys with your friends perhaps? With the King's soldiers yet in the burgh, this might be foolish. They might do nothing themselves but tongues wag and we are too near to the forest to take risks. They might find you red-handed and it could be hard to persuade them that the blood did not come from one of the King's deer."

"I had no thought of coneys this time," I replied. "'Twas something else, but my thanks for the warning. One must be wary. Is there aught else that you require? Mistress Mary sent me to ask particularly, for she said that we should do all that we can to make sure that these men are well cared for, though they be but common Norman soldiers. She is preparing a special dish of salmon for Master Gilbert which she says he will not have tasted before. She said that they know little of that fish in Winchester though they must surely catch it in their River Test."

"No doubt they do, but it is of a different kind and does not taste the same. Certainly the way Mistress Mary prepares it will be something that they do not know. She uses special herbs and though I have asked her often she will not tell me which. It is her secret receipt. I thought to give them an eel pie for we had some come fresh from the stream at Sopley this afternoon, and a roasted haunch of pig. The flour you have brought I needed for some honey cakes which I have always found travellers like. Now do please check that the cask of ale that stands to the right of the others in the cellar is still well-filled. It is our best brew, made with the water from the well at Stanpit which Godric said we should use. Methinks we make much fuss over these visitors whom you call but common Norman soldiers. I think all is in order for this evening's meal, provided there is ale enough. See to it and let me know directly, Hugh."

I went and did as he had bid. I took the bung from the top of the cask. Dipping in the stick which stood by, I found that it was still three-quarters full, so drew off a half beaker to sample it. Certainly it had a finer taste than that we usually had at home but I am no expert on ale yet, though I would not admit as much to Alric. Replacing the bung and making sure the tap was well turned off, I returned to the kitchen and told Ranulf who was satisfied. As he had no further need of me, I returned to the bailiff's house to tell Mary that Ranulf had all he needed and also what he had said about her salmon dish. She smiled with pleasure for it was well-known in the burgh that Ranulf was no mean cook and that the canons fed well under his ministrations. She guarded her secrets too, just as he guarded his.

Then I went back to the mill in time to help Father stack the sacks of flour he had been grinding. That done, we checked the wheels and I greased the bearings which seemed a little dry. These last two months, since my fourteenth birthday, Father had left me to keep the machinery working smoothly. It can be a messy task, cleaning out the old grease that becomes filled with flour and dust, but if it is not done well the bearings can overheat and catch fire and the mill may then be lost. Father told me it happened at Throop Mill not many years gone. Such a disaster could ruin us so I take care with the task. A badly greased wheel can wear the bearings too and the flour will then not grind evenly, so any skill I may have at setting the stones can easily be put to naught.

At length all was done and Father was satisfied that we could leave the mill for the day. Before we left, he checked the sluices to make sure that water did not run to waste unnecessarily and that there was no weed or branches blocking the flow. Big branches could build up pressure on the sluice and if they were not cleared away could break it, causing the water to escape and the level to drop so that we could not work the mill. Although Father has constantly complained to Godric and also the bailiff some of the burgh folk continue to use the stream as a midden and we end up with the result. Today there was fortunately little to remove from around the mill sluice and the task was quickly done.

Leaving the mill, we walked the few paces to our house entering the garden gate that gave onto the path which led from the mill past the end of the church to the market square. Mother was busy feeding the few scrawny fowls that scrabbled in the dust by the pigsty for the grain sweepings she scattered for them. Hearing us come through the gate, she threw the rest of the grain and, picking up the bucket she had beside her, came towards us.

"Look," she said, "the fowls have started to lay again. We have four eggs today. If we have some tomorrow I shall be able to make a meal for us all with them which will be a change. I have gathered some pulses to put into the stew for this evening for Emma, Osbern and me, for no doubt you will be expected to be at the bailiff's house, Oswald, and Hugh will be serving there too, helping Isabel as he did yesterday."

"You are right, Maud. We have but an hour before we must be there so Hugh and I must bestir ourselves and wash off the dust from the mill, and Hugh, see to your hands and try to clean the grease from them. They are black from dealing with the bearings. You will need to clean them with some of Mother's decoction of fat and lye. Water alone will not serve, nor sand. Clean your nails too lad, if you are to serve at the bailiff's table. He was too busy to notice last evening but I vow Mary did and she would be displeased. Have you a clean tunic to put on?"

"Ay, Father. These hands of mine smell like a dung-heap," I said, sniffing them.

I went to find water to clean my hands as best I might. When I had scrubbed myself as clean as I could, I came back in to find Mother drawing out a clean tunic from the press. It was the one kept for high days and holidays, being made of Cotswold wool which a trader had brought down the River Avon from beyond Sarum, and was little worn. I put this on and adjusted the leather belt that went with it. I could not put on my old scrip for it was too worn, but Mother found a spare one of Father's that served. My hose were dusty but a good brushing with some birch twigs soon made them look clean and, having wiped over my shoes with a handful of grass dipped in the bucket of water and dried them on my old tunic while Mother was turned away, I reckoned my appearance was worthy of the office I had to perform. Before I could escape from the house, Mother seized me by the arm.

"Straighten your locks lad and make them lie down. You look to have come through a hedge backwards."

With that she applied her comb to my head, tugging out the tangles in my hair as best she could till my eyes watered with the stinging of it. At last it was done and she stood back to look at her handiwork.

"You'll pass muster," she said, "though you look more like a scullion than a page, but with luck Master Gilbert will not notice if your father and Alwin can keep him talking. So far as you may, let Isabel serve from before the table and you serve from behind. You can keep the beakers filled better that way, while she offers the dishes of food. Now be away. Your father is ready and sitting before the door waiting for you."

I found Father as she had said. He looked at me and nodded with approval and we set off to the bailiff's house. There, Father went straight into the hall where Alwin and Mary were already waiting, while I turned left into the kitchen behind the screen to attend to my duties. Isabel was already there making sure that the dishes of food were properly prepared. For my part, I looked to the wine and ale, making sure that the flagons were full.

The meal went well, and Gilbert praised Mary for her salmon dish which he said tasted better than any he had had before. I was able to snatch a little for myself between serving, and confess that I could not but agree with him. Isabel caught me and chided me for my greed but forgave me when I praised her mother's skill. When all were well satisfied and I had recharged the beakers yet again, Alwin called in some men of the burgh who were skilled at telling tales. One played the pipe, another beat time with the tambor, while a third joined with him in singing some of the old Saxon tales. This seemed to please Gilbert and I saw the scribe Geoffrey pull out a piece of parchment and his pen and write down some of the words of one song which took his fancy.

I sat the while against the wall beside the door leading to the kitchen, somewhat in the shadows, ready to do their bidding but otherwise unobserved. The talk was much of high politics and what our Lord the King would do. It seemed that he meant to sail again soon to his dukedom in Normandy, for his son Robert, whom Gilbert referred to as Curthose, was turning traitor on his father and joining with Philip the King of the French, to try to wrest much of the Norman dukedom from William.

"It seems that Curthose is not to be trusted," said Gilbert. "The King has managed to lock up his half-brother Odo the Bishop of Bayeux in a dungeon in Rouen and has stopped him from organising a rebellion in that realm, but his own son is if anything an even greater traitor. A man has a right to expect some loyalty from his family but it seems that these days even an oath of fealty counts for little. France's King Philip is but a poor fish on his own though he can claim fealty from the Norman Duke. Now the boot is on the other foot since it is Curthose who is making the running. King William will no doubt have to teach them both a lesson if he is to have peace in his realms. The taxes he raises from this country will be used to secure his throne in Normandy. Though he will use paid mercenaries to fight his battles and so save Englishmen being killed, no doubt there would be many here who would not be averse to fighting for him if there is booty to be had. They say that there is plenty of plunder to be had in the domains of the French King. Before I left on this latest journey, the King had sent out messengers to all his councillors and all people of any account who occupy land, to meet him in council at Sarum, where he means to test their loyalty by making them swear fealty and do homage to him. If he can manage this he can safely leave this land and sail to Normandy to secure his Dukedom and break Duke Robert's link with the French King."

Gilbert paused, and took a long pull at his ale horn before continuing.

"They say Robert is brave and almost as good a fighter as his father. He unhorsed his father at Christmas-tide back in '78 when the King tried to drive him from the French castle of Gerberoi near Beauvais. They say that Robert wounded his father in the arm, and though the arm has healed the heart has not and Robert may yet lose his Norman inheritance as his father swore at the time. Many thought the rift had healed when they both fought side by side to regain Robert's lands in Maine from the Count of Anjou in '83. More like it was a case of needs must when the devil drives. I would not be in Robert's boots, fat though they be, when William meets him, and though he may think he can drink his father under the table in an effort to make peace, I give him small chance."

Gilbert took a long pull at his ale horn, wiping his mouth with the back of his hand as he thought on this. Then he continued gravely.

"Nor can I see King William letting Robert succeed him to the English throne even though he is his eldest son. Few in this country would trust him and fewer still have seen him here in the south, though the men of Northumbria speak well of him for his defeat of the Scottish King Malcolm. It is said that the new castle he built on the River Tyne will stop those northern plunderers from coming south again. It is said too that Cnut of Norway means to cross the northern seas again to harry our land so that Robert's castle may prove its worth against another quarter. So William must be sure that his own kingdom is secure before he sails. Though the Norman dukedom may pass to Robert,my money is on the red-faced William to succeed to the English throne when his father dies. That is not likely for many a year yet, for the King is not yet sixty and as hale as a man half his age. He still rides a horse - and a woman - like a twenty-year- old and has proved his stamina on many of both. It is said that the red-faced William rides neither mares nor women, preferring stallions and boys. Such unnatural practices will not endear him to any kingdom I am thinking, so we must hope that the King lives to a great age. It cannot be gainsaid that he has done great things both for this realm and for his Norman dukedom. This great record of the land that we are now preparing is something that has never been attempted before, even in the times of Rome. What a man of unbounded energy he is. The only person who can really hold him is his Queen, though she be but half his height. She reaches barely to his chest, being but four feet and a couple of inches tall. It is from her that Robert Curthose gets his lack of inches."

There was a long silence when Gilbert had finished speaking, as the others thought over what he had said. This was all new to me too. To hear such matters of state discussed so freely opened my eyes to a world that was beyond my horizon as yet. No doubt the freely flowing ale had loosened tongues, but there was none to tell tales other than Godric, Father and the bailiff, all of whom would keep their counsel. There was much I would have to question Father about in due time, for it was men's talk I had overheard and they had forgotten my presence. I must choose my time carefully. Eventually Gilbert grunted, cleared his throat, stretched, and turned to the bailiff.

"Master Alwin, we have completed much this day and with your help and that of Godric here, we have accomplished what I feared might take two days. My thanks to you both. Would that every burgh was as helpful. I am weary now and there is still much to do tomorrow. 'Tis time for me to rest."

"It has been our pleasure to help you in your task, Master Gilbert. Men must speak true and do the King's bidding if the realm is to live in peace. Let me light you to your bed."

So saying, Alwin rose and taking a taper and lighting it from the torch that hung from the wall behind the table, led the way to the sleeping chamber beyond. Father and Godric rose stiffly to bid them 'good-night', and, when Gilbert had passed through the screen that divided the sleeping quarters from the rest of the hall, they too departed. I let them pass for they did not see me sitting in the shadows. I followed at a distance and when Godric parted from Father where the paths divided leading to the church and the mill, I quickened my pace and soon caught up with Father. He was deep in thought and did not hear me approach till I was almost beside him, so turned with a start when my foot kicked a pebble in the way. Seeing that it was but me, his manner relaxed.

"I thought you had been abed this last hour at least," he said.

"No, Father, I stayed to serve as I was bid, should anything have been needed. I sat in the shadows so was unobserved. Master Gilbert had much of interest to tell though its full import was beyond me. He seems to have the King's ear and knows what is afoot at Court. To rule lands as large as those the King controls must call for great power, the more so as one half is across the water. I hope we shall not have to pay too heavily for any sortie the King wishes to make against the French King. I wonder that our King troubles himself with his Norman dukedom when he has so much land in England. His wealth here must be far greater. If I was him I would let Robert be, provided he swore an oath of loyalty that he would not trouble me and would support me against the French King."

"It sounds simple lad, but kings are not like us. The more you have the more you want. Why do you think the Norman Duke came over to this country in '66 and fought us at Senlac Field unless it was to gain more land and spread his wings? To the great, power is everything and ambition knows no bounds. You need not worry your head about such things, and it were best you speak to no-one of what you have heard this evening. Leave it to those who wield the power. But hush and keep silent now for the others will be asleep in the house and we should not wake them. Go carefully to your bed and disturb not Emma and Osbern. Tomorrow we will both go early to the bailiff's house to see Master Gilbert on his way. You did well to bring that spring water for him and it seems to have done his eyes some good. I will see to it that you show him the way to Goodwife Adeline's cott if he is to pass that way."

With that, Father raised the latch on the door and we both passed silently into the house. Feeling my way into our bed-chamber, for there was little light from the moon, I could hear the measured breathing of Emma and Osbern, who were deep in sleep. Slipping out of my tunic and hose, I put them carefully on the bench and then eased myself beneath the covers so as not to wake Osbern. He grunted once and turned over but did not wake, and I knew no more till I was woken by the crowing of the cockerel in our garden.

At the middle of the morning, Father summoned me to go to the bailiff's house, for Gilbert was about to depart. On my way there I fell in with Belesme of St Lo and his soldiers who were heading in the same direction. By the looks of them they had eaten and drunk well last night and the heads of at least two of the soldiers were none too clear. Belesme himself looked sprightly enough but I guessed he could hold his liquor better than most.

"Ha, my young friend," he said seeing me. "You did a good job on my helm. See how it still shines from your burnishing."

He took it off his head and turned it in the sunlight so that it caught the rays, dazzling me at times.

"If you ever think to take up arms in the King's service, send me word for I could use your skills. I might even teach you to handle a sword as well as you say you can use a bow. How say you? Would you come with me? There could be a chance of much booty if we could fight the right campaign. It is said that the King means to cross to his dukedom in Normandy and confront the French King once more. If he does I shall be with him."

"My thanks sir," I replied. "Though I would welcome the chance yet I must serve my father at the mill for I am still bound to him."

This I knew he would accept, for an apprentice to leave his master before he had served his full time brought grave trouble. Nor was I sure that I relished the chance of such a life which would be full of risks. Booty there might be but hardship and wounds too. To leave a secure home and family was not something to be thrown away lightly. For a poor serf with no land and little chance of ever raising himself from his poverty, it would be a different matter. Should the King raise a levy, I could name several who would go willingly for the chance of risking all on a throw which might bring fortune - if it did not bring death.

Outside the bailiff's house there was already a small crowd gathered as Gilbert prepared to depart. As I came up with Belesme and the soldiers, Gilbert turned to me.

"Now Hugh, I understand that you will show me the way to Goodwife Adeline's cott. I mean to speak with her about some of her remedies before I visit the manor of Holdenhurst on my way to the vill of Poole. See I have your spring water strapped to this beast for I shall take it with me. One flagon is for my Lord the Bishop when we return to Winchester," and he patted the basket of the beast in question.

Belesme mumbled under his breath but I could not catch his words, though his meaning was clear enough. He thought little of such things and felt that if Gilbert collected too much on his way then there would be small chance of him being able to snatch a ride on the beast himself and save his feet. At last all was ready, and with the usual words of parting we set off towards Stanpit once more. Alwin, Godric and Father escorted us all as far as the bridge over the first part of the river, after which we continued on our way.

Goodwife Adeline was not in her cott when we arrived but a serf who was passing knew where she was and was sent to fetch her. She came hurrying and Gilbert went with her into her cott while we sat down in the sun. Feeling thirsty, I went to the well and fetched water for all the party. They all drank heartily and Belesme asked if this was what was in the flagons. I told him it was and he nodded approvingly. It tasted clear and cold and quenched a thirst well.

While we were waiting, we could see a horseman approaching. Belesme ordered one of the soldiers to stand and challenge him on his approach for such was the custom of the Normans. They let none pass but those they had questioned so that they kept some account of people's movements. The rider dismounted as he drew near and called to the soldier in his native French, whereupon Belesme rose and approached him. They conversed, and shortly Belesme went to the cott and called out to Gilbert who came out.

"Sir, there is a messenger here for you from Winchester. It seems that there is a change in your orders."

"Greetings, Master Gilbert, from our Lord the King," said the rider. "You know that he has commanded many of his nobles to meet with him at Sarum. He now sends me to command you to cease your journeying towards the west and go directly to Sarum that you may be present when he meets with them. You are to speak with each one when he has sworn his oath to the King, that you may make tally of all the lands each holds. In this way you will not need to travel to each man's burgh or manor but may collate the holdings in one place. The King says that they will be more likely to give a full account if he is there in person to hear what is said. Here is the message from the King himself. It is sealed with his ring as you can see and I have brought with me more parchments for you to use in making this tally, for you would not have enough with you."

He handed over a small scroll which Gilbert took. Opening it, he examined the seal to see that it was indeed that of the King. He nodded and bent his head to read what was written. Satisfied with what he saw, he turned to the rider.

"You were fortunate to meet with us for we were on our way to the manor of Holdenhurst. We would have taken another route but I wished to call at this cott for some remedies, else you would have missed us. Geoffrey, come here and load these new parchments onto that beast and give this man the flagons I have in the pannier. Wait while I gather up the herbs I have just purchased from the goodwife for I would have them all taken to my house in Winchester to wait for my return."

Gilbert turned to the rider, and giving him a basket which the goodwife had now brought out to him, said, "Take this with you and these flagons, and give them to my steward, telling him to keep them safe till my return. Tell him that nothing is to be touched till I come. Give these completed parchments to my scribes in Winchester and tell them that they are to be entered into the great book. The lands to which they refer are clearly stated so that they can continue with the work before I return. There is much to do if the King is to have all finished before he departs for his dukedom in Normandy. Give him my greetings, and tell him I go with all haste to meet him at Sarum and may be there before him."

The rider took his packages and strapped them to his horse. This done he mounted, saluted Gilbert, turned his horse and set off at a trot back along the road by which he had come. Belesme for his part looked pleased and adjusted the panniers so that he could ride the beast should he wish.

Gilbert turned to me and said. "Hugh, I would thank you for your kindness. Remember what I have said and if you come to Winchester, ask for me at the Abbey. The church can always use such as you."

Then he mounted his horse. "Pax vobiscum," he said, making the sign of the Cross, and wheeling his horse to the left, led his little party off towards Sarum.

Chapter 4 1087

The months passed and matters continued much as before in the burgh. Travellers passing through brought us news of happenings in the world outside but as yet few of them seemed to trouble us.

The great book of all the land holdings in the realm was finally completed in the middle of the year. Godric, who had been called to Winchester on some church business, saw it and on his return told us of it. He had read the entries concerning the burgh and they listed everything just as our people had said it.

As Godric said, "To be sure the King now knows who holds what land and how much it is worth so that he can tax folk accordingly, but it is to our advantage as well. He cannot now say we own more than we do and so tax us more than he should. There is also a record for all to see so that if any claim land and try to say that it is his, the record can be consulted and the proof is there. For it is recorded what each man owns now and who owned it in the time of the Confessor. Those who try to trick their neighbours with false testimony can more easily be found out. Be sure that much good will come of it. The great will find it harder to oppress the poor in these matters."

Word came that nearly all the great owners of land had gathered in answer to the King's command at Sarum and duly done homage and sworn their oaths of fealty. It was said that some were loath to so commit themselves but with others more powerful than they standing beside them they had little option but to comply. The King felt more safe thereafter, for though some might think of breaking their oath, they remembered how William had dealt with King Harold who had broken his solemn vow. That ended in death on Senlac Field and the loss of the whole country.

Soon afterwards, William crossed to his Norman dukedom again, taking with him a goodly force of both horse and foot. They said that he meant to drive westwards from his Norman lands towards Paris and into the Vexin where he meant to deal with the French King once and for all, for he had been raiding into the dukedom and ravaging the lands. A boat had sailed from the harbour to Caen, and several serfs, who felt that they had nothing to lose since they had nothing, joined it. Word came back occasionally. Two had been killed in the fighting and one had the good fortune to capture a French knight whom he had ransomed. He came back these three months gone and bought a hide of land towards the forest which he was now trying to farm.

One day towards the middle of September - it was a feast-day, I remember, which is why we were free - Alric, Isabel, Emma and I took a small boat and crossed the harbour to the great double ditch that spanned the western end of Hengist's headland. We often spent time there, for though it had been a thriving place in earlier times it was deserted now and little used. A few cattle were grazed there but it was a mile from our burgh by water and more than two by land, for there was no crossing place over the fast flowing Stour for some distance upstream where cattle could ford. We used to roam the headland, hunting and running down coneys. Lying in the shelter of the ditch between great earth banks out of the wind it was warm and if you kept still, you could watch the coneys and other animals at play. Birds, whose song filled the air were in abundance there. We often spent time searching idly through the remains of the dwellings of those who had once lived there, and had found all manner of things. Alric had picked up the blade of a sword once and taken it home where he had cleaned and re-handled it. Though it was more clumsy than the swords we now use, he was pleased with it and practised often till he was quick with its use. I had found a knife but it would not sharpen well till the smith in the burgh showed me how to temper the blade by heating it and then plunging it into water till it turned blue. I had then been able to put as keen an edge on it as any in the burgh. The metal seemed better than any found locally and the smith thought it must have come from across the sea.

Emma and Isabel were more interested in homely things. They had found several earthenware pots which were decorated with weird patterns round the rim. These they brought home and we used them to store food. Others in the burgh had similar pots but they were frequently broken as were all such vessels. They often found stone spindles too which they brought back to give to their friends. By putting a stick into the hole they could then spin wool. They made welcome gifts.

The day was warm and we had spent some time chasing coneys up and down the ditches till we were heated and out of breath.

"I am weary of this sport," said Alric, "I am going to cool off in the water. Who is coming with me?" he asked as he stripped off his tunic, shoes and hose.

I jumped to my feet and quickly followed, with Emma and Isabel doing likewise. All four of us stood naked for an instant and then with a whoop of joy ran down the ditch and across the beach into the sea. The waves were breaking high and buffeted us as we dived into the water. It struck cold as we went under and came up gasping. Emma's auburn hair fell about her shoulders and as she tossed her head, she scattered a sparkling shower in all directions. Alric leapt out of the water and, pouncing onto her, submerged her beneath the next wave. They came up spluttering together, laughing as they regained their breath.

I looked round seeking Isabel who is not so strong in the water as the rest of us. She was further out trying to breast the waves. The next instant she had vanished as a larger wave swept over her. With a cry of alarm, for the shore slopes steeply down at this place, I struck out towards where she had been. As I neared the place, I could see her pale hair and then a hand appeared above the surface only to sink below the waves again. Desperately I drove on towards the spot and, diving below the surface, groped round for some sign of her. At last my hand touched flesh. In anguish I felt about and once more found a limb. I grasped it firmly and pushed back towards the shore till finally getting both my hands round her slim body, I thrust her upwards above the surface. Next moment my feet struck firm ground and I was able to take a stride shorewards holding Isabel above the waves. She was choking and spluttering from the water she had swallowed.

As we neared the edge of the water, she put her arms round my neck clinging to me and sobbing, "Oh Hugh, you saved my life. I could not find the bottom when the wave broke over me and I was frightened I would drown."

I carried her up the beach into the shelter of the ditch between the two banks, the warmth of my body bringing back life into her cold skin as she clung to me. I calmed her fears and caressed her telling her that I had been watching her constantly. "I would not let any harm come to you, I care for you too much for that," I whispered.

Drawing her to me and enfolding her in my arms, I rocked her quietly to and fro murmuring soothing reassurances in her ear as I pressed my cheek gently against hers. Her gasping breath eased as she quietened and soon she was able to pull away sufficiently to look me in the face. With one hand she brushed her hair from her other cheek then stroked mine with the tips of still trembling fingers. Then she leant forward and kissed my cheek before burying her head in my shoulder with a deep sigh and a shudder that went through her whole body.

"Hugh, oh Hugh, what would I do without you? Hold me tight and never let me go. I owe you my life," she said, and another deep sigh shook her. I continued to stroke her hair as I clasped her close to me.

Eventually she calmed and, lifting her head once more, she smiled at me and kissed me gently again, saying, "How can I ever thank you or repay you? My life is in your hands."

She leant back on her heels then and taking my hands, placed hers between mine in an act of homage, and smiling at me she kissed my hands. Then she sighed again, withdrew her hands and rose to her feet and stood before me in all her naked beauty. Though I had seen her thus often enough before it was always in the company of others and usually my sister, for if the truth be told I regarded her much as a sister just as Alric was almost a brother to me. This latest happening had wrought a change in both of us for which I was not yet prepared and I could only gaze at her open-mouthed in wonder, for she was more comely than I had realised. Perhaps she read my thoughts, I do not rightly know, for she held out her hand and said,

"Come, we must rejoin the others, or they will wonder what has happened to us."

I gave her my hand and rose to my feet as she turned and led the way back towards the beach, to meet Alric and Emma running towards us with worried faces.

"What has happened?" cried Alric as he neared us. "We missed you in the waves and thought you had come to some harm."

"A wave overtook me and I lost my footing so that I was swept beneath the water. I could not find the ground and feared to drown," said Isabel. "But Hugh caught me up and held me above the water and brought me safe to land though I was choking for want of air. I think I owe him my life," she said, as she lowered her head at the remembrance of it all and I felt a shiver pass through her again. "But all is well again now."

She dropped my hand and turned towards Alric and Emma saying, "Come, I have had enough of the water for today. Let us dress and rest awhile and then return, but I would ask you to say nothing of all this to Mother or Father lest they become anxious which I would not wish. Nor would I want them to forbid us to come here. There is no real danger. It was just that I missed my footing. There is none to blame but me."

So saying, she started to run towards where we had left our garments and we three followed. Soon we were clothed again and as the sun was warm, we rested awhile. I was glad to feel the warmth on my skin and to see the colour return to Isabel's face.

Later, we climbed to the top of the embankment and looked out over the sea. The sun was moving towards the white rocks that formed the cliff to the left of the great harbour beyond Poole, so I reckoned that it must be nearing the time for Vespers. I cast my gaze back across the water towards the east, and saw a boat close in to the end of the headland as if it would enter our harbour. It was small but fast and not the usual type that brought trade to the burgh. By its shape it was Norman-built.

"Look," I said, "That boat is surely going to enter the harbour for it would not sail so near the headland else. I doubt the captain knows these waters or he would not have sailed so near to the rocks. How say you that we sail to the entrance and guide him in? If he does not know the channel within the harbour he may easily go aground. It would be good sport, and we may even get paid for our pains."

The others agreed, so we ran fast to where we had left the boat in a small bay in the harbour. The wind was from the south-west, its most usual quarter, so we made good speed towards the harbour entrance, arriving just as the boat cleared the narrow spit that guarded it. We hailed the boat and came alongside it, offering our services as pilot to the burgh. The captain was Norman but could speak some English and was glad enough of our assistance and, as I had thought, did not know the channels. The four of us clambered aboard and, securing our own boat by a rope to the stern of his craft, we set about guiding him up the two-mile-long channel that leads to the burgh. It is a winding way, for the rivers hug the sand spit before turning sharply to the right to follow the line of the headland. Often have I seen boats enter the harbour and head straight across to where they think the river comes from, only to run aground on the sand bar that lies across within the entrance. We pointed this out to the captain who was grateful and caused it to be marked upon his chart for he had not sailed this way before.

Once we were clearly in the channel we began to converse more freely with the captain.

"I bring sad tidings," he said. "Our Lord the King is dead and his son William the red-faced is proclaimed King in his stead. It is for this that I have been sent that all those who owe homage to the new King as they owed it to the old may go with all haste to London. For William means to be crowned in the Abbey of Westminster before the month is out. Hugh de Port I must see and Roger Eorl of Shrewsbury if he is in these parts. If not, then I must send messengers to him. Also the new King would have Richard de Redvers, Eorl of Devon told, so that he may be at his coronation. Another boat sailed with me from Honfleur but took a more easterly route to pass east of Vectis Isle that she might reach Southampton burgh and from there send riders to Winchester to warn them there. We sailed together for some while but parted mid-channel for I had been told to sail more to the west that I might catch the tides that would take me faster as I neared the coast. 'Tis likely that I have reached this coast before him."

We stood agog at this news. When last we heard of the newly dead King, it was that he deported himself like a man yet in his prime. Now he was struck down.

"How came this about?" Alric asked. "We heard that he was strong like an ox and suffered no illness. Was he slain in battle?"

"From a battle if not in one," came the cryptic reply. "You shall hear all when I meet the bailiff."

"That you can gladly do, for he is my father and I will take you to him as soon as we are landed," said Alric.

"Then it seems we are well met. Think you that he can provide horses too? For I have two men here who would ride throughout the west country to summon all who can to come to London for the crowning of the new King."

He called the two who were leaning on the rail watching the land pass by as we sailed up the river. As they came forward, one of them suddenly stopped and held out his hands towards me.

"By Our Lady," he cried, " it is the young cub who burnished my helm and was so keen to try my sword last time I was here. How goes it with you lad? You made a good job of it and it has not looked so bright since. You remember me don't you, Belesme of St Lo? I had charge of the soldiers then, when we were escort to the clerk Gilbert on the great tallying of all the lands."

"For sure I remember, but what brings you here now?" And I grasped his hand.

"Well, we went from you to Sarum for the great oath-taking. Master Gilbert was able to speak to those present and list their lands and his task was made easier thereby so that we finished before the time appointed. After that, I followed the King when he took his force to his dukedom to settle his account with the French King Philip. You know that our King's eldest son Robert held his father's lands in Normandy from the French King his liege lord. It seems that he turned against his father and did the bidding of his liege and started foraying into the Norman Vexin, so we had to go and teach them a lesson. I had some good fortune in the fighting and carried off enough booty which I was able to put to good account. Things came about as you shall hear presently and I think to settle down if I can find some land hereabouts, though it is not my native country. I got the chance of a passage at the King's expense and shall be able to ride through this part of the land on someone else's horse to see what I can find. I have done enough fighting for one lifetime and come away without too many scars, so here I am."

There was a cry from the prow of the vessel. All eyes turned forward as the captain hurried to give orders to prevent the ship running into the bank, for the river narrows suddenly at this point. He gave orders for the sails to be dropped and the boat to be brought forward by oar and pole until it reached the place where the two rivers join which we call the Clay Pool, near to our mill. The river is shallow and a pole easily reaches the bottom in most places.

As soon as we had tied up at the quay, which is just by our mill, Alric jumped ashore and the rest of us followed. Alric led the way up to his father's house. I told Emma to run to the mill and tell Father and ask him to come quickly to the bailiff's house. As we reached it Mary, who had heard the commotion outside, came out to see what was to do. Alric quickly explained who the travellers were and as we went inside Mary sent a servant to fetch Alwin, while Isabel was despatched to the kitchen to fetch ale and beakers and to see about preparing a meal. Father came soon followed by Alwin, and all were struck silent by the grave news the captain brought. When we had all finished eating, Alwin called for more ale to be set on the table, and leant forward.

"Now, Captain, tell us fully how these things came about for methinks they will affect us all before long."

"What I know for certain I will tell you. I was at Honfleur loading cargo when Belesme here brought the news and bade me sail at once. I had brought over some of the King's force some time earlier, and as you know he had marched against the French striking south and east burning and harrying as he went. From the reports that came through, there was little left in the countryside after he had passed and women and children were slaughtered or maimed as often as men. He met strong resistance at Mantes on the river Seine but eventually that place fell to his onslaught too. The King was in the thick of the final assault and in his rage he ordered that every building was to be torched. It was there that it happened."

"I was in the town that day," said Belesme, and all eyes turned on him. Taking a pull at his beaker first, he rested his elbows on the table before looking round at all of us.

"Yes, it was some of the thickest fighting I have been in since Senlac Field. As you say, William had had some trouble with the Manteois for they would not open their gates to him. His force was too strong for them, and to teach them and others a lesson he ordered the whole town to be torched and its people put to the sword. We had a fine time of it for there were rich pickings to be had for the taking. I had some good fortune, for I came across a gold merchant's house and found things worth the taking still, though others had been there before me. The merchant would not miss them, for though he was still in the house, his brains were spilt on the floor and his right hand had been severed - no doubt for the rings that had been on it. I filled my purse with what I could and then gathered other things into one of his cloaks I found and slung it over my shoulder."

Belesme paused and lifted his beaker to his lips to take a deep draught.

"It was difficult to see clearly, for the smoke and the heat of the fires was terrible, but as I was staggering back into the square I could hear shouting. Looking across to the far side I saw the King riding through the broken buildings waving his sword. There was a sudden roar and half a building collapsed around him. His horse reared up in fright and the King was thrown onto the pummel of his saddle and then to the ground amidst the fallen balks of timber that lay all round. Whether one pierced his belly I could not see, but so it seemed from the way he lay. The horse lashed out in terror and I think caught the King a glancing blow before galloping off. The King lay still and some who were near him tried to raise him. Seeing that he was badly injured, two of them ran off to fetch a litter on which to place him and carry him to safety while the third stayed with the King to guard him, for there were still a few Manteois roaming the streets trying to save what they could and flee. Seeing that there was little I could do I continued on my way and eventually reached Rouen, where I was able to trade my gains to good effect."

Again Belesme paused and took another long pull at his beaker, then wiped his mouth with the back of his hand.

"That night they brought the King back to Rouen, for he did not wish to remain in Mantes where those whom he had trounced could crow over his own downfall. But the noise and hubbub of that town was so great that he had himself moved to the quiet of the Priory of Saint-Gervais close by. Perhaps he knew even then that his hurt was mortal and he wished to be near priests who could shrive him. I followed him there and kept guard with others at the door of his chamber that night. Two of his sons, the red-faced William and Henry Beauclerc, were at his side as was also the Archbishop of Rouen. His eldest son Robert was not there, preferring the pleasures of the French King's Court perhaps and no doubt fearful of his father's wrath. All present felt that the King was dying, for though he had survived many wounds before, none had been so grave. The King knew it too, for his mind turned to disposing of his wealth and lands. First he gave orders that lavish alms should be distributed in recompense for the rivers of blood he said he had spilt in his lifetime. Particularly he named the priests of the town of Mantes, where he had finally fallen. He gave orders further that those whom he had imprisoned should be released. Someone asked if that were to include his own half-brother, Bishop Odo of Bayeux. He was silent for a time and grunted an unwilling 'Yes'."

I saw Alwin shoot a swift glance at Father as he said this.

"There was much talk of who would succeed to the dukedom of Normandy and also the throne of England. At first the King would have disowned his eldest son Robert completely but there were several present who had already done homage to him for their lands and sworn fealty to him at William's own behest, so that they were able to persuade him to confirm Robert in his title, but on the throne of England he would not be moved. Raising himself up with much pain onto one elbow, he shook his fist at those around him and said 'I name no man as my heir to the kingdom of England; instead I would entrust it to the eternal Creator to whom I belong and in whose hand are all things. For I did not come to possess such a dignity by hereditary right.' With that he sank back with a groan upon his pillows. This put those around him into a turmoil and there was much coming and going."

Belesme sat silent for a few moments, lost in his own thoughts.

"I slept fitfully for some few hours and when I woke it seemed that some decision had at last been made. The red-faced William was standing beside his father who was placing in his hand first the great sword of state of England and then the jewel-studded sceptre which always travelled with him in his chest. It seemed he had changed his mind and divided his lands between his two elder sons. Some of those round the bed seemed none too pleased but the full import of it all was beyond me. Then the King ordered letters to be written to Lanfranc at Canterbury, instructing him to crown his son William in St. Peter's Abbey at Westminster with all haste. This he sealed with his own ring and put into the hands of his son, telling him to fill his purse and be ready to ride with all speed for England. On this the red-faced William left, seemingly to take horse at once, but it turned out that he had only been to summon his friends to make ready with a large troop of horse for instant departure when the end should come, for he was back within the hour."

Again Belesme paused to drink, and then waited while Alwin refilled his beaker.

"While William was gone, the King slept a little and then roused himself once more, this time to speak to his youngest son Henry. There had been much talk as to what the King would bequeath him. He was no fighter, and had stood silent all the while, occasionally seeing to some matter of organisation. When the King did at last summon Henry it was to give him but five thousand pounds in silver, but no lands or titles other than those he already held. All were aghast save Henry himself. He merely smiled. Then with rasping breath, the King told Beauclerc that his life would be far more brilliant than either of his elder brothers and that he would outstrip them both in power, wealth and fame. At that Henry smiled again and, kneeling beside the bed, placed his own hands between those of his dying father's in homage and kissed them. No-one knew quite what to make of this and some suspected that there might be some secret treaty between them which none but they yet knew."

Belesme cleared his throat before continuing.

"Soon after, King William asked to be shriven and to receive the last rights, which the Archbishop of Rouen gave him, though it moved him greatly to do so. The sky was beginning to lighten when we heard the great bell from Rouen Abbey ringing. The King asked what it meant and was told that it was the hour of Prime, whereupon he said that he hoped the priests there would pray for his soul. After a while he commended his soul to the Blessed Virgin Mary, asking that she intercede for him for his many sins, and with a rattle in his throat, he died."

We sat in stunned silence while each man crossed himself and said his own prayer for the soul of the departed King. For my part I murmured "Agnus Dei, qui tollis peccata mundi, miserere nobis et dona nobis pacem" under my breath, for I could think of naught else but to pray for the forgiveness of all our sins and that we might have peace.

"That was not the end," went on Belesme after a while. "No sooner had the King breathed his last than pandemonium broke out. The red-faced William swept past me shouting to his friends to follow him to horse, meaning to ride forthwith for England as his father had bidden him. Several of those in the room followed him out, seizing such of the rich vessels as they could lay their hands on as they left. Those that remained followed that example and started to grab everything they could: vessels, plate, ornaments, linen, robes, even the clothes off the body which was tipped onto the floor in their haste to take the bed covers. I stood by helpless for there was nothing I could have done against such a pack of curs fighting as it seemed over a bone. It was only when the Prior came, having been hastily summoned from Prime by the Archbishop, that the three of us were able to restore some order and replace the body of the dead King on the bed and cover it as decently as we could with such garments as remained. The King's wounds were still plain to see and his swollen belly about to burst open, while his chest was still stained with blood which he had been coughing up from his internal hurts. Never do I wish to see such a sight again. How are the mighty fallen."

Belesme paused and rubbed his eyes as if to try to wipe out the memory, then continued. "Henry Beauclerc called me to him soon after. He told me that he had sent to Duke Robert at the French King's Court to come with all haste to see to his father's burial, giving orders that the body was to be carried with all reverence to Caen where it was to be interred in his own great abbey. Then he gave me messages to bring to England, that as many as could be reached were to make all haste to London to be present in St Peter's Abbey where Archbishop Lanfranc of Canterbury would crown William as the new King. He said that if Lanfranc crowned and annointed him there would be none in the land that would gainsay it. He gave me orders to leave at once and take ship from Honfleur, sailing to the west country. Others he sent by different routes. Stopping only to gather up my treasure, I took horse and came with all haste and craved a passage with the captain here, as you know."

"That I can vouch for," said the captain. " Also that William the red-faced took ship. They had ridden hard and came some hours before you did, Belesme. I would have carried them myself but they found a fleeter ship that was also ready to sail. Such was their haste that they did not take on all their horses for fear they miss the tide and Duke Robert, should he come after them, take them by force. They gave me orders to spread it about that they had sailed towards Vectis Isle meaning to come to land at Southampton, and from there go by horse to Winchester and there have William crowned. This I did, though I knew from the ship's master that in truth they were headed for Folkestone to the east whence they would ride to Canterbury where they meant to meet the Archbishop Lanfranc."

The captain scratched his beard before continuing.

" From there they intended to ride on to London gathering support as they went. William means to be crowned before the month is out. From what you say, if Duke Robert has to see to the burying of his father first he will be sore pressed to reach England before then, should he think to try to take the crown from his brother. Mayhap Henry Beauclerc was playing a deeper game than we thought in sending Duke Robert to attend to his father's burial. For had he wished to support his eldest brother he could have seen to the matter himself and even put obstacles in the way of William to stop him leaving. Who is to know? Be that as it may, I spread the tale as I was told. I kept a weather eye open during our crossing, but none came in pursuit to see if I was carrying William so it seems that he has got clean away and will have several days' advantage."

There was silence round the table for a while, and beakers were refilled. After a time I asked "What sort of king will red-faced William be?"

None answered directly, but eventually Belesme spoke again.

"In some ways much like his father," he said. "I have seen him in battle and he fights almost as bravely and his temper can be as fierce. He is keen on the chase too, so that I doubt not that we shall see him often in the forest. More often than his father most likely. They say that once he has set his mind to a thing nothing will change it. I saw some of his friends while I was at Rouen and it gave me cause to wonder. It is said that he never takes a woman and certainly I only saw men enter his bed-chamber. I also overheard Henry Beauclerc discussing some of William's friends. One in particular was often mentioned by name and always seemed to be at William's sleeve. A man called Ranulf known as Flambard. It seems he is little liked but has William's ear in all things. It is said he is over-ambitious and means to make his mark. I met him once. It must have been at Winchester when I was with Master Gilbert, for he was engaged on the great tally of lands too. He could not look you in the eye and was for ever hinting darkly on the deeds of others. He is Norman born, the son of some village priest. When he came over here I know not, nor how he came to the notice of our dead King, but he did and seemingly wormed his way into his good offices and so to the task of listing the land holdings. If what is said about him is true then he will be using what he has learnt to his own advantage. He is certainly one to watch. I saw him follow red-faced William out of the King's death chamber when they set off for Honfleur, so no doubt he will be with him now. Yes, he is one to watch - but not to trust."

"Well, we shall have to wait and see how things turn out. This burgh belonged to the King, so no doubt the new William will keep it - unless he is persuaded to give it to this Flambard," said Alwin with a sigh.

Again there was a long silence. Eventually, Father spoke.

"Alwin, what think you? This is but a small burgh and away from the centre of things. London is but a name to us and Winchester is a full day's journey by horse, and besides, the great forest of Andret separates us and few make the journey for fear they be taken and accused of poaching the King's deer. Sarum is almost as far, and who besides traders have travelled there either? It seems that we have more links with the Norman dukedom if the captain's presence here is anything to go by, and ships ply often between this harbour and the Norman shores. The dead King passed but twice through the burgh and tarried not, though you offered him food and shelter as I remember, Alwin. He was more keen to return to the chase. There was a particular large stag that he was hunting which had escaped him, and he was not the man to let a beast get the better of him. You have little trouble collecting the dues which you send regularly to the King's treasury. You said that Hugh de Port likewise sends what is due from Holdenhurst manor which is greater than what we have to provide. If we give this new King no trouble, do you think we shall be left in peace?"

Alwin shrugged and spread his hands.

"It may be so. We can but hope and try to do naught that will bring us to the notice of our new Lord. As for you Belesme, you are about the King's business are you no? Tomorrow you mean to depart in search of Hugh de Port and the others whom the King has summoned. We will help you in this all we can. You will need a horse, no doubt, and that can be provided. Money for your journey you say you already have from Henry Beauclerc. Is there aught else you need?"

"A horse yes, as you say, but I would leave my goods and purse with you while I am gone. They are too valuable to take with me riding alone. Though it has been the proud boast of the dead William that a man could ride the length of the realm with a purse of gold and fear that none would take it from him, yet I would not wish to put it to the test! May I then leave those things with you till my return? You remember that I shall also be looking for a place where I may settle and find some land and the contents of my purse are needed for that. It will be a hostage for the safe return of the horse," he added with a grin.

"Assuredly, though we have no need of hostages since we have no need to distrust you. I shall lodge your purse with Godric, the priest of our church. He has a more secure chest there than I have here and it will be safe with him, have no fear. Land, you say? You would seek a place where you may settle and till the soil? That will be a change for you after your life of soldiering. Will you not weary of it and long to return to the vigour of the fight?"

"No, not now. I have had my fill of fighting and having come out of it without too much hurt I am minded not to put it all at risk again. You can overplay your fortune. Henry Beauclerc has given me a chance, though it doubtless was not in his mind at the time, so I mean to grasp it with both hands. Much is changing now, and such a chance may not come again. Yes indeed, I mean to settle down and live in peace. My father held land in Normandy though he lost it many years ago, but I tilled it with him when I was a lad so know something of what needs to be done."

"Well, if that is what you have decided you could do worse than settle in this burgh. There is a hide of land at Somerford and a virgate a little nearer the forest too. Swein, who was the hayward some years ago, had it, but he was killed in the forest, caught by a wild boar that tore out his belly. Since then the land has lain fallow for there has been none who wished to till it. It is good land as I remember and yielded well. You could take it on if so you wished. Think on it. Before you leave tomorrow I can have someone show you where it is and if you see nothing that takes your fancy more as you travel, on your return I will see to it that you can take it over."

I leant forward, to catch Alwin's eye.

"If Father can spare me from the mill," I said, "I will gladly show Belesme the extent of the land. I know the place well."

"How say you, Oswald, can you spare this lad of yours to do me a service again? It seems that whenever our paths cross he does me some service." Belesme asked, and turning to Alwin he said, "I like this place, I must confess, and if I do not see anything that immediately takes my eye as I journey, I may well take up this offer."

With that, Father agreed and Alwin looked pleased too, for it would be to his advantage to have that land brought under the plough again. We all rose then, and each went to his own bed.

The next day I was early at the bailiff's house. I led Belesme out of the burgh and over the bridges and so down through Stanpit. He remarked that we had been that way before when last he was here and so we came to the Somerford estates. I showed him the fields which were running wild now and full of weed. He walked over them, pulling up clumps of weed and letting the earth trickle through his fingers as I had often seen men do to test it.

"Is there water here, Hugh?" he asked, and I showed him where the stream ran across the corner of the land. It was but a narrow stream but free- flowing and sparkling clear. Shading his eyes he looked around at all about him, seemingly well satisfied with all he saw.

"Yes, this will do very well. I think I need look no further. I will speak with Alwin. Have you not noticed, Hugh, how our lives often seem to be determined by chance? Chance brought me here back in '86 and brought you to clean my helm. Chance brought me from Henry Beauclerc to this place again and chance caused you to meet us when our ship entered the harbour. Chance again put this land my way so that I feel I must take it. Or is there some Higher Hand that shapes these things?"

He scratched his head as he thought, and I too wondered how these things fitted into the scheme of things and resolved to speak to Godric about it all when next I went to him to learn more of the Mass. Bidding Belesme farewell, I returned to the burgh, while he departed on his journey.

Chapter 5 1092

Five years have passed since that fateful day when Isabel nearly drowned and when we also learnt that William the Norman had died and been succeeded by his younger son, William the red-faced. Belesme set out on his journey to seek out those whom he had to summon to the crowning of the new King William, and came back within the month having done all that he was commanded. He spoke again with Alwin and it was agreed between them that Belesme should take over the hide, but not the virgate of land next to it, which I had shown him. As he said, a hide was enough for one man to cope with. If things went well he could always see about the virgate some time in the future.

On his journeying, he said that he had seen nothing that pleased him as much. Some land might seem better but there was not enough water; or if there was, then there was no burgh or vill near enough for him to sell his spare crops. In other cases, he said that the reputation of the lord was such that he would rather suffer the hardships of the worst campaigns he had fought in than be his subject. Besides, he said that he felt he was amongst friends at Twynham and at his time of life that meant much to him.

"I have had to have my wits about me all my life so far and have seldom been able to sleep without my sword close at hand, or at least a sharp knife. It is time I settled down where I can live at peace and in safety and perhaps take a wife. If I do, I will make sure that her tongue is not sharp. They do say that a woman's tongue can cut deeper than any sword so I would not change one peril for another! Mayhap I can find some complaisant wench in your burgh when I have proved my worth and tilled the soil for a year or two."

Just so it turned out. Belesme wooed Ediva, the daughter of Ernwi the villein who had a hide and ten acres under the plough and which he cultivated with all his family. At first Belesme lived in the old hut that Swein had used. It took him a week to get it watertight, for the thatch was rotten and there were holes in the walls. I gave him a hand, helping to carry the reeds, which we cut from the marshland next to the harbour and also helped him mix the earth and cow dung to make the daub to fill in holes in the walls. A smelly job to be sure, but once it is in place it dries hard and makes a snug enough dwelling.

Less than two years after he came, Belesme and Ediva were wed by Godric in the church. Godwine had hoped that they might be wed by him in his little chapel, . for he was the priest who cared for the souls in Stanpit and the few who lived at Somerford which lies next to it. However, Belesme said he wanted to be wed in the burgh where he had found his wife, his peace, and his friends. Being the man he is, Godwine agreed, and carried the couple's wedding gifts from Ernwi's house to Belesme and Ediva's new home by Somerford.

Within the year their firstborn, a daughter, arrived. Then early this year came a son. Belesme was delighted to have an heir at last and we all thought that he would call him Belesme too, but no, he insisted that he was to be called Hugh after me and that I should stand as godfather to the child. As he said, I was the first one to have done him a kindness in the burgh when I burnished his helm and sword. Mother and Father were pleased, for Belesme was proving himself to be a valuable member of the burgh. His experience of war and his knowledge of foreign lands and of some of the great men at the King's Court were all laid open to Alwin the bailiff and those who looked after the well running of the burgh. It was on Belesme's advice that the walls of the burgh had been looked at and, where needed, the stakes which topped the walls were replaced and the wall itself strengthened with stones. He also took in hand some of us young lads and taught us how to use the broad-sword and how to shoot straight with the bow, though I felt there was little he could teach me about the bow except how to make the arrow travel further. Soon there were none of my age who could outshoot me and few men in the burgh either, except for Belesme himself.

Thus it was that I spent part of my free time with Belesme, often accompanied by Alric. Emma, and Isabel too, spent much time in his house helping Ediva with my godson Hugh. They both said that I was not to be trusted with the babe for I was too ham-fisted for such a little mite and might do him harm with my clumsiness. If the truth be told they both enjoyed nursing the child and playing with him, though Emma tired of it all sooner than Isabel. She seemed to take naturally to the babe and Evida was always content to leave him with her if she had other tasks to do. As for Isabel, she seemed to glow with happiness when she was with the child and it seemed that she could charm him out of any ill humour or soothe any hurt he might suffer.

It was on the eve of the feast of the Holy Trinity of '92 that Alric, Alnoth and I were with Belesme. We had all gone to the edge of the King's forest to gather wood against the winter months. We had collected almost as much as we could carry or load onto the beast we had with us when we heard the sounds of the chase. Quickly we looked about us to see that we were not within the bounds of the forest. We were safe enough, for the bank that marked its boundary was more that fifty paces distant and there were still plenty of fallen branches between us and it, so we continued with our task. The noise of the hunt came nearer, and within minutes there was much crashing of branches and there appeared the hunting party. Seeing us, one of the horsemen detached himself from the group and rode over to us.

"You there. What are you doing gathering wood in the King's forest? Know you not that this land is for his use only?"

He turned in his saddle then and called to two of the huntsmen who were on foot.

"You two, bind these serfs and bring them to the King that he may deal with them as deserves the thieves that they are."

As the two huntsmen were finding ropes to do this man's bidding, Belesme looked closely at him, and gave a start.

"I know this man. It is Ranulf known as' Flambard'. His tongue is hot and he has put men to the torch before now. I met him last at Rouen in the Priory of Saint-Gervais, the night the first King William died. Leave this to me. I think I can handle it."

With that, Belesme stepped boldly towards this Flambard, and made a deep bow.

"My Lord Ranulf, known as Flambard, if I am not mistaken. Welcome to this humble burgh of Twynham."

"Who speaks my name?" cried the horseman, spinning his mount round with a savage tug at its bridle.

"I have not been in these parts before yet it seems my fame has gone before me. Stand forth you who dare to address me by my name and let me look at you."

Belesme took a couple of paces forwards and made another bow, though from his back it seemed that it was more mocking than genuine, but the horseman was not near enough to recognise the difference. He spoke in French, which I could not understand, and later told us what he had said.

"Your pardon my Lord, I am Belesme de St Lo. I fought with Duke William at Senlac and was with him as King at Mantes when he fell from his horse. I was the other side of the square and too far from him to go to his aid though I would gladly have done so. I was also one of those who guarded his door the night he died, may the Lord have mercy on his soul. It was then that I saw you. If I am not mistaken, after the King had died you left with his son William, he of the red face, to take horse to this kingdom which his father had given to him."

"What if I did? Should I have done otherwise? Have a care how you speak to me. Methinks that you are a deserter from the King's army."

He turned then to the two huntsmen who were standing ready with the ropes they had found.

"Bind these men fast. Did this man speak of the burgh called Twynham? Are we so near to it already? I had not thought to reach it till tomorrow. If it is near no doubt these serfs can lead us the shortest way. I have business with the bailiff and a letter to him from the King. We can put these dogs before the bailiff's court when we get there and he can deal with them as they deserve. Make sure they are well bound, we do not want to let them slip. Search them well and their beast too and cast around. No doubt you will find one of the King's deer somewhere near that they have just slaughtered. Have they blood upon them? If they have we could even have some sport now and sever their hands. It would make them lighter on their journey."

He laughed and gave us an evil glance so that I began to fear for my life. I saw Alric look towards Alnoth who had turned white with fear. The two huntsmen went to Belesme first, but as they tried to put the rope round him he shrugged them off and raised his left palm towards Flambard.

"My Lord, I have seen you elsewhere before too and have heard much of you and know your power. I was with you in Winchester these many years gone when you and I were both concerned with the gathering of the facts for the late King's great Domesday Book. I was with Gilbert the clerk and travelled with him in charge of his guard throughout all this part of the land. I am no traitor or deserter from the King's force. Would I have guarded his body else? Would Henry Beauclerc have entrusted me with orders to summon the new King's friends to his crowning at Westminster if I had been a traitor? If some of his friends did not attend his crowning that is naught to me. It was but my duty to do as I was ordered. You have no need to bind us nor will you find any deer's carcass here. We are without the forest boundary in any case. You can see the ditch behind you some fifty paces away. I saw you clear it when you came out of the trees. We are but gathering wood on the common land as is our right. I hold my land from the King as the bailiff will tell you. You say you have business with the bailiff of this burgh. Then we are all well met, for these two lads are his sons and they can lead you to him. This other lad is the miller's son and godfather to my son," he said pointing to me. "I have lived in this burgh these past five years and am wedded to the daughter of one of their villeins. I think you will find that the bailiff and the priest will both speak for me if you doubt my word."

Flambard's expression changed and he looked not a little discomfited. The huntsmen grinned at each other and made mocking gestures at Flambard which fortunately he could not see for they were behind him. He grunted and muttered a curse under his breath, seemingly none too pleased that he had been worsted. Then, turning his horse, he galloped off to where the rest of the party was still standing at the edge of the forest, while the two huntsmen shuffled off after him still giggling and mouthing obscenities at him. Belesme turned to us, looking serious.

"We must be careful. This man needs to be watched, the more so as he will think that we got the better of him, though it was his own fault. He has few friends though many no doubt profess friendship, and many enemies. Saw you how the huntsmen mocked him behind his back? Treat him with all the deference he thinks is his due and, Alric, never let Alnoth be alone with him. This man Ranulf cares not for women but has a liking for young boys and I'll warrant that there will be one or two with him in his party now. There is more than one reason for him being called Flambard - a flaming torch. It is said that that part of his body resembles one in size and colour. Hugh, when we get back to the burgh, tell your father to keep Osbern out of sight till this man has gone. It will be safer so. I will see the tanner on our return and ask him to cut leather pieces that you may all stuff them in your breeches so that should he try to fumble you he will be disappointed."

Alric and I looked in astonishment at each other and I could feel the colour rising in my face. Such things I had heard of, for boys will talk and boast, but all knew such acts to be unnatural and against the sight of God. Could the King have such a man as his friend I wondered? Then I remembered that Belesme had told us that the King himself cared not for women either. I prayed that such a King might never come to our burgh. The chink of a bridle and the sound of muttered voices woke me from these strange thoughts and I looked round to see Ranulf Flambard approaching once more, this time with his whole party as it seemed.

"Belesme, did you say your name was? I have sent a message to the King who is hunting still at a little distant, that I mean to go to Twynham burgh this night. The King himself will spend the night at Brockenhurst where I was to have joined him. The sport is better in that part of the forest he says. As I told you, I have business with the bailiff and also letters from the King to your priest, what did you say his name was? Godric, is it not? He holds much land I think." His lips curled up in that ugly grin we had seen before and I feared what this could mean.

"The priest does hold some land it is true, though as no doubt you have been told, it is used for the benefit of the poor not only in the burgh but in the hamlets that surround it. He is also well known for his charity towards travellers too. There are many such for much trade passes through this port. It cannot be said that the priest is either rich or idle but he is well loved. There is not a day passes without deeds of charity being done. Indeed if the truth be told, he makes trouble for himself by his generosity, for some of those who make claim on the hospitality of the church are good-for-nothings who could well fend for themselves, but Godric turns none from his door. He would go hungry himself rather than not feed a supplicant, and offer his own couch rather than deny a traveller shelter."

"The more fool him then," said Flambard. "But this Godric you speak of, he is not dean of the church, I think."

"Dean? That is not an office we know of in these parts, though I have heard speak of it at Winchester and other great churches. No, he is not 'dean' as you call it, but he is the head of the canons, and all men look to him for guidance in spiritual matters. Indeed he is of great assistance to the bailiff, for in the burgh we settle things by consent so far as possible. The bailiff, reeve, priest and hayward are the chief men to resolve matters, but others such as the miller by the church and the smith give their advice if called on. Indeed on occasion they have asked me to help in certain matters to do with the defence of the burgh which I have been glad to do."

"Well I must speak with this Godric for I have news for him from the King. You, Master Belesme, you seem to have set yourself up nicely in this burgh. What did that cost you I wonder?"

"Nothing my lord but the fair rent I pay for my land to my Lord the King. This you may discover from the bailiff whom you are anxious to see. Come, shall we lead you to him? It is an hour's journey by foot if we hasten. By your leave I will unburden this beast here of its load of wood and send this lad here with a message to the bailiff to prepare lodging and food for you all. How many are there in your party?"

"Six besides me, though they can be fed by this Godric you say is so generous. Yes, send this lad ahead and have food and lodging prepared for me. Have him tell the bailiff that I want his best dishes and only his best wine or it will go hard for him."

With that, Flambard turned his horse and rode back to his party, giving orders for some to return to the King at Brockenhurst while others, including two stripling youths who were mounted on light horses, were told to follow him. Belesme called Alnoth to him and while we were all busy unloading the wood from the beast, he whispered urgently in Alnoth's ear.

"Ride as quickly as you can to your father and tell him what has happened. Tell him that this man Ranulf called Flambard who is one of the King's favourites is coming with messages for him and will stay the night. Tell your mother to prepare her best food. Tell your father that it were best if he give over his own bed-chamber to this man for the night but to be sure to remove the most precious things first lest they not be found there in the morning. Tell him that it were best if he give orders that all youths hide till this man is gone. Then go to Godric and bid him have food and shelter prepared for six travellers, though it may be that those two striplings will be summoned to Flambard's chamber if he can find none of his choosing in the burgh."

Belesme cast a quick glance towards Flambard, to make sure that he was still out of earshot.

" Tell Godric too, that this man has letters for him from the King and it would be wise if he were to summon all the priests he can gather to the church for Mass tomorrow so that they may have the strength of numbers when they meet Flambard. When that is done go to Oswald at the mill and tell him what is afoot and tell him that I advise him to hide Osbern. If he can escape in time, say he should go to my house and Evida will look after him. If Oswald and your father think they can arrange it, have them send Emma and Isabel to Evida too. If they leave the burgh by the Bar Gate they can cross the river towards Burton and so keep well clear of the path we shall take. I shall take them by the more easterly track and delay them if I can to give you more time. Is that clear lad?"

Alnoth nodded, too scared to speak, and I could see his hands were trembling. He put on as brave a face as he could, for he knew that much depended on him getting the messages right and the preparations made. So he mounted quickly while Belesme laid an encouraging hand on his knee and gave him a cheering smile.

"Ride fast, Alnoth, and God go with you".

With a clatter of hooves he was gone and the rest of us turned to face Flambard and his party. We spent a few minutes piling up the wood we had gathered, to give Alnoth time to put as much distance as he could between us, for we did not want Flambard to see that we would not be taking the same track.

When Flambard seemed to be growing restless at the delay, Belesme stumbled and sat down heavily, nursing his foot and then started to take off his shoe muttering something about having trodden on a thorn. It was a good act and it was several minutes before he had examined his foot carefully enough to find what the trouble seemed to be and made a good show of removing the thorn and then replacing his shoe. At last he was ready and he got to his feet again with muttered apologies to Flambard for the accident.

We set off then, Belesme leading, but he walked with a noticeable limp so that I offered to support his arm to help him on his way.

"Thanks, Hugh," he said loudly enough for all to hear. "That eases the pain somewhat but we shall make but slow progress I fear. It was that thorn bush we gathered. I knew we should have left it where it was for they always cause trouble. Wait while I cut a stick from that young ash-plant beside the way so that I can walk with that."

He shot me a knowing glance and winked at me, confirming my suspicions, so I played along with him. I have never known the journey take so long.

As we approached the bridges over the river and mill-stream into the burgh, I could see that Alwin was already there with Father, Godric and half-a-dozen of the priests, Geoffrey the reeve, Roger the hayward, and several other of the more prosperous villeins. All were cleanly dressed I noticed and though none carried so much as a knife that was visible, they presented an impressive body though their demeanour was polite enough. As we crossed the bridge, Alwin stepped forward and made a deep bow to Flambard.

"You are most welcome to our burgh my Lord, and do us great honour by your visit. Had we known earlier that you were coming I would have provided a more fitting reception, but you are most welcome to spend the night in my hall and my wife is even now preparing such simple fare as we can provide which I hope will be to your liking. Since my house is but small, I have arranged for the rest of your party to stay with Godric in the guest-house of the church. Ranulf the priest is even now preparing food for them. If your friends would please go with the priests here they will see that their needs are cared for. I know that Godric has ordered that clean straw be put in the mattresses and that ale stands ready in the refectory. You, my Lord, if you would be pleased to accompany me to my house there is wine awaiting you. Give your horses to my son here and the other lad and they will see that they are properly stabled and fed."

"That will serve well, but my two pages will accompany me. I like them to eat with me and they know my needs. They always sleep in my chamber. I could not be without my guards even in such a safe place as your burgh," Flambard added as he put an arm round the shoulders of the taller of the two youths and began to stroke his hair.

"On the morrow I will speak with the priest Godric for I have letters for him from the King with matters that concern him and his church."

"My Lord," replied Godric, "today is the eve of the feast of the Holy Trinity to which our church is dedicated. Tomorrow is our great feast day and we celebrate a special High Mass at which all our priests participate. We process through the burgh first and offer prayers at each of the nine chapels before entering the church for Mass. All folk in the burgh will be present and it is our custom after the Mass is finished to distribute alms to all the poor folk of the burgh and as many as care to come from the outlying hamlets. None are ever turned away."

Godric coughed nervously before continuing.

"It is also the day when those who have received some special favour from Our Saviour during the past year come and bring offerings to their church in gratitude for the grace God has bestowed upon them. Though there have been no miracles wrought, many have been most blessedly healed. Belesme here has told me that he means to make some offering in gratitude for the birth of his son, is that not so Belesme? Though the King's business must be attended to, he would not have us see to it before we have celebrated Mass, I think. You, my Lord, will join with us in our festival, I trust, and share the Blessed Sacrament ? Your companions too if they are so minded. Should any need to make their confessions before receiving the sacrament, any of my fellow priests will most gladly hear them. For you my Lord, should you have anything to confess, it would be an honour for me hear it, either this evening or before you break your fast tomorrow."

Flambard looked somewhat taken aback. He could not easily refuse to attend such a High Mass, but if his reputation was anything to go by he would not easily go to confession, particularly to a strange priest and one for whom he had some news which might not be to the advantage of the church.

"I thank you for your kindness, Master Godric," he said. "I made my confession but a few days past so have no need of your services. I will gladly share your Mass and will be pleased to witness the generosity of your people. Afterwards I would speak with you and give you the letters from the King and tell you of his will. It would be best if all your priests were present for it concerns them all. Belesme, you say you have a son now? May he grow to be as strong as his father and serve his King as faithfully. Now, Master Bailiff, lead me to your house for I am dry with much talking. Come, Francois and Verlaine," he said turning to his two youths, "give your horses to these lads and follow me. You could drink a cup of wine I am thinking," and putting an arm round the shoulders of both, he nodded to Alwin to lead the way.

Father, Geoffrey , Roger and two or three others accompanied Alwin as they went to his house, for it seemed that they meant to hold together in mutual support. Godric looked worried by what he had heard and after giving instructions to some of the priests to summon all the others to his house after Vespers, he questioned me about what had happened on the edge of the forest. Alric and I told him all we could.

"Have no fear," said Godric, "Emma, Isabel, and Osbern are safely away with Alnoth and should have been with Evida this hour past. Belesme did well to delay your arrival for it gave us time to make preparations. Your father Alwin, moved quickly. We are fortunate to have such a man as he as our bailiff, and those who stood with him can be relied upon. I like not this letter from the King. It bodes ill for the church, for this red-faced William is not above being generous to his friends when others have to pay. Now take the horses and stable them as you have been bid, then both of you go to Evida's house for the night too. I will tell your fathers that you are safely away but Hugh, I would have you here for the Mass tomorrow to act as my server. You will be safe enough robed and afterwards you can attend me when this Flambard delivers his letters. Stay cowled and stand in the shadows if you can, but listen carefully to all that is said. I may not remember everything so I would have a witness to remind me later. Now go carefully. Pax vobiscum," he said, making the sign of the Cross over us.

Alric and I led the horses by a back way round to the stables behind Alwin's house. When we had seen them safely stalled and fed, we slipped out unobserved through the Canons' Gate and made our way round the outside of the burgh wall past the Bar Gate, and so to the mill-stream and river which we forded, following the same paths that Emma and Isabel had taken. We came at last to Belesme's house where we found them safe but anxiously waiting, with Osbern and Alnoth, while Evida nursed young Hugh on her lap. As we entered she gave a sigh of relief and, getting up, she handed the babe to Isabel.

"Is all well with Belesme?" she asked. "I have heard him speak often of Flambard and nothing I have heard makes me want to cross his path."

"Be easy in your mind," I said," Belesme is too old a campaigner to fall foul of such as he, for all his evil ways, but his visit will affect the whole burgh I think, though I know not how. Godric wishes me to serve him at the Mass tomorrow as I have often done before and afterwards to attend him when this Flambard meets with all the priests to give them the letters from the King. He has asked me to be his ears and act as witness to what takes place for he may not be able to remember it all, with all the worries that he may have. Have no fear. I shall be cowled and stay in the shadows and no man would dare to touch me on hallowed ground."

Isabel looked up at me and I could see fear in her eyes, so I went and sat beside her and put my arm round her to reassure her. She sighed and leant her head on my shoulder.

"Take care," she said. "From what Evida has told us, this man is evil and could do us all much harm."

"Alnoth and Osbern shall be safe enough here," I said, "for neither he nor any in his party know we are here. Alric will remain with you till they are gone, to guard you if need be. I can serve us all better by being with Godric as he has asked. Should any danger be likely then I shall know of it early and will be able to send you word. When we have eaten, it were best that we put out the fire and not light it again till they have all gone. We will drive the animals out of their pens and into Father's assart and pen them there tonight. It is further from the track that leads to the forest and so their noise will not be heard. This cott will then seem empty should they chance to pass near, though I doubt if Belesme will let them. He will offer to lead them back to the forest by the easiest path which you may be sure will be well away from as many habitations as possible," I said with a grin, to try to cheer them.

"Let us hope that you are right," said Evida as she set about preparing the meal for us all.

Leaving Isabel to mind young Hugh and help Evida with the meal, the five of us set off to round up all the stock and drive it to our assart. It took us some time and we had particular trouble with the chickens. Some we could not catch and had to leave until dark when they came home to roost. It was well dark by the time we had finished but there was enough of a moon to light us back to the darkened and silent cott. We made no sound as we slipped in through the door and were soon asleep.

On the morrow we were all astir betimes for none of us had slept peacefully. As soon as I had snatched a bite to eat, I slipped out and made my way carefully back, using the same tracks by which we had come. I did not enter by the Canons' Gate, but kept on outside the wall till I came to the mill-stream where it flows into the river. Here I was able to slip into the mill and from there across the way to our house, where I found both Father and Mother making ready in their best clothes for the procession before Mass. Mother gave a start on seeing me.

"What news have you? Is all well with Emma and the others?" she asked anxiously. "It is good that Osbern was not here for Flambard asked for Alnoth and was angry when he heard that he had been sent on an errand and might not be back before tomorrow. He would surely have wanted Osbern had he seen him, or any of the other boys come to that had they been there. Thanks to Belesme's warning we hid them all and the girls too, though from what we hear they would not have interested this beast. Such practices disgust me. What sort of a King do we have who can have such friends as this and even share his doings?"

"Calm yourself, Maud. We have to live with the times if we cannot change them, though we need not condone them," said Father, and turning to me he asked, "Is all well with Evida and the others? I promised to let Belesme know when we meet him in the procession before the Mass."

"Yes. They are safe but a little fearful. Alric has stayed with them to guard them in case of need and we drove the stock away to our assart and penned them there. We had some trouble with the fowls but got them all safely into the hut eventually. We thought it best if the cott should look deserted should any of Flambard's party pass that way. We put out the fire last night when we had eaten and Evida will not light it again until we are sure they have all gone. I must go soon, for Godric is expecting me as I am to serve him at the Mass and so must accompany him in the procession. How did matters go at supper last night?"

"None too well, though it could have been worse I suppose. Mary charmed this Flambard with her wit during the meal, turning the conversation away from dangerous topics whenever occasion arose, though I could see that it sickened her to see how he fondled that long-haired youth Verlaine, whom he insisted sat next to him throughout. Mary produced dishes fit for a king, but most of it was wasted on Flambard who took little notice of what he was eating. His eyes and ears seemed always to be elsewhere seemingly trying to pick up snatches of conversations from around the table which might be of use to him later. Alwin had warned all present to guard their tongues, not to drink too deep, but encourage the visitors to talk rather than talk themselves and so learn what they could about this man and also of the King. Alwin served his best wine which helped to loosen their tongues. Wisely, he did not ply Flambard too freely for we do not want him to be too over-hung today when he meets Godric and the rest of the priests. A foul temper can cause much trouble which is best avoided, for afterwards its effects are harder to undo."

Father drove his fist into the palm of his other hand.

"Alwin and Mary had to sleep in the children's small chamber, for theirs was given over to Flambard," he said angrily. "As was to be expected, he insisted that his two pages, as he calls them, slept in the same chamber to be on hand should he have need of anything in the night, as he put it. He sought to insult us all by saying that they were to guard him while he slept. Is he so fearful for his safety that he feels he needs guards in our burgh? If he feels thus threatened then perhaps we have good cause to mistrust him. I am worried about what news he brings for Godric but we shall know the worst soon enough. Hugh, you had best go now. Godric knows as much as we do about how things stand. Tell him that Alwin and I and several others will be present after the Mass to hear what Flambard has to say and to support him as best we can. I will go and find Belesme now and tell him the measures you have taken for the safety of Evida and put his mind at rest. Go now and keep your eyes skinned. Look for me in the crowd in case I need to pass a message to you. I am not so important in the burgh that I shall be watched too closely, so that I can do it better than Alwin or Belesme. Good luck, Hugh."

He turned then to help Mother who was fussing over her dress. I slipped out as I had come, making my way along beside the mill-stream for some way until I could climb the rise on which the church lay, between the stream and the rest of the burgh.

The procession passed off well enough. Most of the folk in the burgh and many from the outlying hamlets were there as was to be expected, though it was noticeable that there was hardly a youth or maiden to be seen in the crowd, but only young children and babes in arms. These were safe enough and if anything would serve as protection to the rest of us.

Godric celebrated the Mass with dignity and humility, but I noticed when he elevated the Host, Flambard was paying no attention but seemed utterly bored, no doubt wanting him to get it over with so that he could attend to the real purpose of his visit.

When the Mass was ended, those who had thank-offerings brought them to Godric as he stood before the altar where he received them, before handing them to other of the priests who then placed them on the altar. Godric then thanked those who had brought gifts and received them in the name of God, offering them up to His service. I was startled by a movement near me and glancing, saw Flambard throw up his hands in despair, or was it frustration, at the time all this seemed to be taking. As was the the custom on this day, the whole congregation them moved out into the church-yard making a great semicircle round the porch.

Godric stood in the entrance while the other twenty-four canons busied themselves bringing forward the tables on which were loaded the gifts of food and raiment which by custom have for many years always been given to those in need in the burgh. As usual there were some strangers too, for the charity of Godric was well known in the surrounding vills and many came to claim it. None were refused. I stood as Godric had told me, in the shadows of the porch, well hidden behind the group of canons, though I could see well enough, watching Flambard's every move. As more and more of the poor folk continued to come to receive of the church's bounty he seemed to become more angry. He muttered something to himself but I was too far to hear what he said. Eventually, when all had been satisfied, Godric lifted his hands and blessed the crowd and then turned and went back into the church.

Flambard immediately stepped forward crying, "Now, Master Godric, now that you have finished giving away your goods to these worthless serfs, can we get down to the business that brings me here? Here, you priests, fetch me a stool that I may rest my legs for I am weary with overmuch standing during your long Mass."

Several of the canons hurried away to fetch several seats on which Godric, Flambard and the others could sit, for it seemed that what he had to say would take some time. Then Flambard reached inside his scrip and produced a roll of parchment from which hung a large seal.

"See here," he said, "This is the will of our Lord the King. He has given me this church and all that belongs to it and has placed me at its head as dean. There is no dean here at the moment you say, and you Godric, are but a canon who serves the church like any other. From henceforth I say what will happen here and how the goods of the church shall be disposed. Let there be no more nonsense such as I have just witnessed. You do but encourage these serfs in idleness. Read it. It is set down for all to see. When you have read it, tell the bailiff that it is so."

There was a silence at his words, such as I have never heard before. Godric blanched and leaning forward took the parchment with a shaking hand.

"From our Lord the King you say? Then these are matters of great moment that should be properly attended to. Let us go into the church. Have seats set before the altar so that I may sit and read this paper carefully and our noble visitor may take his ease too."

Godric turned to the other priests who were gathered round him.

"Brothers, fetch as many seats as you can so that Alwin our bailiff, Geoffrey our reeve, and any other of our chief men may also sit and hear what is the King's command concerning this church, for I will read it out for all to hear. What the King's pleasure is for this church must bear on the burgh, for the burgh belongs to the King too; is that not so, Master Bailiff?"

"Most certainly Master Godric," said Alwin, "this burgh is the King's and belonged to his noble father before him, may God rest his soul. 'Tis all set down in the great Domesday Book as all here can bear witness."

He looked round at everyone and all nodded in agreement.

"The burgh may belong to the King now," growled Flambard, "but he has promised it to me and the charter is even now being drawn up, so you will soon do homage to me as your Lord. The King is too concerned with greater matters to have to concern himself with such a little burgh as this, so you will look to me in future."

"My Lord, we hear your words" said Alwin, "but we must surely wait for the King's command before we do you homage. We would not doubt your word for we all know that you have the ear of the King, but we are powerless without the writ of the King. Is that not so, Master Godric?"

"So I have always believed. My Lord Ranulf, if it is the King's will that this church be yours then we bid you welcome, but come, let us all sit while I read this parchment."

He sat down and motioned to the others to do likewise. When all were settled and with all eyes expectantly upon him he unrolled the parchment, first examining the seal, showing it to Alwin and some of the others so that they could see that it was indeed from the King.

"Have patience with me I beg you," Godric said. "It may take me some time to read."

There was a grunt of impatience from Flambard which all ignored. Godric read the parchment through carefully from beginning to end. At last he finished, and looked up.

"My Lord Ranulf, it is even as you have said. Our Lord the King gives you this church and appoints you as dean. This is not a term we have used here before but I understand that it means you are appointed over all of the canons and that we must in future do your bidding. We will serve you as we are able my Lord, though you must know that we serve our Lord Jesus Christ first in all things."

He looked round at the other canons to seek their agreement, and there was a general murmur of approval.

"The King says nothing here about the burgh. Master Alwin, would you read the parchment and see for yourself. Here, let me show you the place. The church itself and the nine chapels that adjoin it and also the houses of all the canons shall belong to my Lord Ranulf. Likewise the church lands at Herne, Burton, and Preston and elsewhere are given to him besides all gifts that may be bestowed upon the church. There is nothing here about the burgh."

Alwin followed Godric's finger as he slowly traced over the words of the parchment.

"You speak true Godric. There is nothing here about the burgh so we must await the King's pleasure. My Lord Ranulf, we will do you homage when our Lord the King so ordains but we cannot do so until that time. We would be traitors else and you would not have us be that, I warrant". He stuck his thumbs in his belt and, leaning forward from where he sat, stared with some defiance at Flambard.

Flambard tried to pass off this reverse.

"I am glad to hear that you wish not to be traitorous; I thought to warn you how things stand. The King trusts me in all things and I have told you I have his ear. It is but a matter of time before the charter granting me the burgh is ready. The church and all its lands however are mine now."

His voice came like a thunderclap, and he banged his fist down on the bench beside him so that all started at the sudden noise.

"Eh, what was that? All the church's lands? Does that mean the lands we own too?"

Old Alnod leant forward and put his hand behind his ear to hear better.

"Yes, Godric," added fat Alsi scratching his tonsure anxiously, "does that mean my three virgates and meadowland? All that I grow and all the beasts I rear are used to feed the sick and poor. How will they manage and who will feed them and the many travellers who pass through the burgh?"

Before Godric could reply, Flambard rose. "Enough of this. You tire my patience. I have seen too much already of how you treat the serfs in this burgh with your charity as you call it. No wonder there are so many vagabonds in this place. You encourage them to be idle. I am putting a stop to all this now. Master Bailiff: in future any who come begging for food and shelter shall be put in the stocks and then set to work on my lands. Is that clear? From what I have seen as I passed through there is but poor yield from the lands hereabouts. I have no doubt that with proper tilling more could be produced. See to it. I shall be sending a hayward of my own to look after these lands of the church which are now mine. He will want full account of all that is produced. The poor indeed! None need be poor if they do but work. Idle men deserve no food. Hungry men soon learn to mend their ways."

He strode towards the door of the church, but before he reached it Alwin had risen.

"Not so, my Lord. No man is put in the stocks or suffers any other punishment in this burgh unless he has first been tried before the Court of the burgh. It is the King's command which I think you would not have us disobey."

Flambard stopped in his tracks and turned to face us all. "Who dares to question me?" he bellowed. "Know you not that I have the ear of the King and could have you all thrown into prison?"

Flambard turned on his heel.

"Here, Verlaine, Francois, and the rest of you," he shouted. "I like not the smell of this place. To horse. Let us ride back to the King and join his sport. Methinks that when he has had his fill of hunting deer he may well hunt some in this burgh though they would make poor eating - except fat Alsi there. I'll warrant I could cut a few juicy steaks off his rump," and he stormed out of the church followed by the rest of his party.

Alwin and Godric looked at each other. None present dared speak at first for all were shocked that any man could act in such a manner in the House of God. At length Alwin spoke.

"Well, Godric, you seem to have a new master and I am threatened with one, but I think the burgh may yet be saved such a fate for there was much bluster in that man and the King is no fool, though he may have his favourites. He may wish to keep the burgh for himself for it guards the harbour and the two rivers and the trade routes to Sarum and beyond. Perhaps if we send to Bishop Walkelin at Winchester, he may help us. He knows how you use such wealth as the church has and how many are healed and cared for."

"Alwin, I thank you. You stood by me when I needed succour. I was trembling in my sandals. All that we have is used for the poor and needy and the sick, as you say. Perhaps we are over-generous to travellers sometimes, but is generosity a sin? We have not heard the last of this man. Did you note how angry he was when we gave alms as always to those who came after the Mass? I called to mind how Jesus reproved Judas when he thought it wasteful that the sinful woman should anoint Our Lord's feet with the precious ointment. Methinks that we may have another Judas coming in our midst now. We must continue to do as we have always done. Brothers, we must be strong. This Flambard may now be our lord and we may have to do him homage, but our first duty is still to God and then to the King. If we have to suffer for that then it is no more than the martyrs have done through the ages. If we are weak, he will be strong. We must hold together. Before we leave this place let us pray for strength and guidance that we may do what is right in the sight of God."

He turned then to face the altar and sank to his knees and crossed himself. All of us did likewise and each in his own way prayed. Eventually Godric rose and turned to us.

"Now go about your business and be of good cheer. We must do as we have always done. Pax Vobiscum."

As he made the sign of the Cross over us, each one of us crossed ourselves with bowed head murmuring as we did so "Et cum spiritu tuo". Then rising from our knees, we made our way back to our homes.

It was clear that Flambard had ridden straight off to rejoin the King, so Father asked Belesme to tell Emma and the others that it was safe to return. They were anxious to learn all that had befallen while they were with Evida. While we were recounting everything that had happened, there was a sudden commotion outside and hurried footsteps. Father and I went to the door and looking out saw Godric hurrying back towards the church. But he turned off and went to the little dwelling where Alsi lived between the church and our house.

"What is to do?"

"It is Alsi. He has been taken with a sickness and great pains in his chest. He cannot catch his breath and I fear for his life," Godric called out before he disappeared through the door into Alsi's dwelling.

"Stay here, Hugh. But I must go to him lest there is aught I can do of service. He has been ailing for some time. What that man Flambard said came as a great shock to him for he feels that he will no longer be able to care for the poor as he has always done. He has always worried about things and told me as we left the church that he thought Flambard's actions terribly unfair. I fear he may work himself up to such a pitch that he may have a seizure. No, wait Hugh: go to the infirmarer and see he knows what is afoot. He has physics which may help in such cases."

We both went our separate ways. Finding that the infirmarer had already been summoned, I slipped quietly back to Alsi's house and stood by the door. The little house was crowded but the voices were hushed so that I could hear poor Alsi's laboured breathing. He was greatly distressed and kept crying out.

"What shall I do? I have tried to care for those in greater need than I all my life. I have no need of my land myself but what it produces has eased the burden of those less fortunate than I. When I am gone and this Flambard takes my land for himself, think you he will care for those in need? How can he say they are idle folk? They do what they can, but how can a man till the soil if he has had his hand cut off? His wife cannot hold the plough, she has not the strength. Would he have them starve? Surely he has some heart. Godric, speak to the Bishop for me and tell him how things are. Oh my poor souls, how will they eat?"

He continued in this strain for some time, now and then wandering off into incomprehensible mutterings. Godric and the infirmarer tried to calm him but he seemed to grow more agitated. There was nothing I could do and I could not bear to hear his agony of soul at the injustice of his plight. So I left and came home.

Some time later as we were thinking about retiring for the night, we heard the sounds of singing and I caught the words "Requiem aeternum". Father came in then looking sad.

"It is over." he said. "Alsi's soul has returned to his Maker. He could not abide the thought of his lands being taken so that he could no longer feed the poor from them. This man Flambard has much to answer for. If he means to continue as he has started then there are many more who will be ground under his heel. Godric means to withstand him with all his power though I fear that may be little compared to the might of the King's favourite."

Father stood musing for a few moments.

"I watched the greed in Flambard's eye as those who brought gifts to church after Mass offered them to Godric. He liked it not when Godric kept them not for himself but offered them up on the altar that they might be rightly used. Godric thinks that Flambard will take Alsi's lands to enrich himself though he holds enough already. He is sending to the Bishop tomorrow to try to persuade him to grant the lands to another priest, so that the church may still have the benefit of them. Much will depend on whether the messenger can reach the Bishop before Flambard hears what has befallen this night and can so make his claim. Matters look bad but we must hope."

Father stood listening for a while.

"The priests are singing a requiem now as you can hear, and tomorrow there will be a full Requiem Mass. Alwin has declared tomorrow a day of mourning and rest that all may come to the church to take part. I warrant it will be over-full for there is scarcely a soul around that has not received much kindness from Alsi; may the Lord have mercy on his soul and grant him eternal rest. He has earned it more than most."

Father crossed himself. Much distressed, we retired to rest.

As Father had said, the church was full and the churchyard too, for all wished to bid farewell to Alsi. It would have done Flambard much good to see the sorrow in the eyes of so many. Those whom he had dubbed idle wastrels had been up betimes to dig his grave and prepare wreathes of wild flowers. Many voices choked with sorrow as they sang the familiar words. Afterwards, as many as could went onto Alsi's fields and gave a day's labour freely, for they knew that he would have liked that and it was a small token of thanks that they could give for his life's work amongst them.

It was but a week later that Flambard rode into the burgh again. This time he went straight to the church, summoning Godric to appear before him. The news spread like a fire through dry thatch and as many as could flocked into the churchyard to hear what would befall.

"Master Godric," cried Flambard not deigning to dismount. "I hear that one of the canons died but a few days ago. He had some land I think. It falls to me now by the charter I brought you when last I was here. Give me an exact reckoning of what the priest held and what it is worth now. I have had its value noted at the time of the great Domesday Book but would know if it produces more now than it did then. It is not uncommon for that to be so, I have found," he said with an ugly grin.

"Do not think that I mean to keep the revenues of this land for myself. No. Just as our late and glorious King William the Norman built a great church at Caen for the peace of his immortal soul, so I mean to build as great a church here that all men may remember me. It is for this that I shall need the revenues of the lands you have here, and I shall start with this old priest's holdings. You have too many canons here for your needs. Mark my words well. No more shall be appointed here while I live, and as any die so shall their lands fall to me. In the meantime, all the revenues shall come to me now. As I told you last time, you are making idle scum of these folk. It is time they learnt to work. In future any who come begging shall be set to work in my fields, nor will you feed them till they have done a full day's labour. My clerk shall visit you on quarter-days when you will render him a full tally of all that the lands produce. Seek not to hide anything from him for he will surely find it out. You know my wishes. Make sure they are attended to. I mean to build such a church that all men shall wonder at and I mean to build it here. I have a master mason already at work on the plans. When they are complete I shall come with him and mark out the site. There will be no time for idleness once I start to build. All shall work on the building, so see to it Master Godric that my lands bear well. It should please you I think, that I mean to use the profits for God's glory and build Him a House of Prayer, not a den of thieves."

He laughed then, thinking that he had turned the tables on Godric by quoting the Scriptures back at him. He tugged hard at the reins, spinning his horse round where it stood, making it rear onto its hind legs. Then with a shout he galloped off towards the bridge and so out of the burgh.

As he went, Godric said quietly, "You may pull down this church and build greater but have a care lest you lay up treasure for yourself only on earth and have none in Heaven. You would do well to study the Scriptures more carefully. Any man can cull a saying from them for his own advantage, but what does it profit him if the full meaning is different. He may fool himself but even the simple-minded will find the truth by God's Grace."

We all heard him and though I saw many troubled faces it seemed they all took comfort from what Godric had said. Alwin approached and laid his hand on Godric's arm.

"You are a brave man to resist this Ranulf Flambard. We must stand all together for I fear he means to have the burgh too, if he can persuade the King to give it him. I draw comfort that he came with but one charter. Had the matter been settled he would have brought two, and taken the burgh forthwith. For this reason it may be that the King is not yet decided and means to make Flambard prove himself first before the burgh is given too."

There was general agreement at this wise council and so we parted, each to his own affairs. Father and I went to the mill, there to busy ourselves with the present load of corn.

"See," said Father, "this is some of Alsi's corn. Bag it carefully and put it to one side. I mean to talk with Godric and Alwin for we must plan how we are to handle this matter. I like not the idea of letting this Flambard have the goods that have always been used for the needy. This church he plans to build: I warrant it will be some years before it takes shape and when it does it will be for his glory rather than God's. Meanwhile the poor are always with us."

He sighed and pulled the full sack away from the shute quickly fixing another in its place as the ground flour continued to pour from the grindstones. I put my hand into the falling flour to feel its texture. It was some of the finest, for Alsi used only the best seed. I called to mind Alsi's words: "Think not that you can feed the needy poorly. All God's people deserve that which you would set before the King."

Chapter 6 1092

The summer of '92 was one of the best that I could remember in my 20 years. Certainly the greybeards of the burgh said that there had been others that had been hotter or drier - but that was before the memory of a stripling like me, as they were always keen to point out. I took it in good part, for many had wiser heads on their shoulders than I and, as Father said, there was always something to be learnt even from the most seemingly dunderheaded greybeard. As he put it, they had managed to survive longer than most and that in itself was an achievement.

The crops were good in the fields and the corn particularly stood high and full-eared. August came, and all were busy gathering in the harvest. There was the usual grumbling when Alwin, as was his right as bailiff, claimed the several days work of every man to bring in the lord's harvest. But he treated us well and did not insist that all the demesne lands had to be cleared first. We well knew that his attitude was that the King had much land from which to take his harvest, and if he lost a little, then it would not hurt him. For the men of the burgh to lose a fine day's harvesting could make the difference between plenty and hunger in the winter months. As Father said, Alwin was no fool, for by letting men gather their own crops in fine weather too, they were more ready to gather the demesne harvest well, so that the fields were often left cleaner as a result. The grumbling had little substance and came for the most part from those who had little skill in caring for their crops and used their complaints as an excuse for making a poor showing of gathering their own harvest.

Emma, Osbern and I usually tried to work with Alric, Isabel and Alnoth, and some of the other lads often joined us. Sometimes their sisters would join our party too, but many of them were silly and spent too much time giggling and playing foolish games so that they were more of a hindrance than a help in clearing the fields.They were welcome enough at mealtimes and made a pleasant distraction from the back-breaking job of scything and gathering with their flirting and winsome looks. Often enough there was some tumbling amongst the sheaves of corn which gave good cover from the prying eyes of the rest of us.

It often seemed that Emma found it convenient to work near Alric and bind up the corn he was cutting. Alric said that it was because she worked at the same speed as he did so that there was always a clear space behind where he worked, but he coloured when he said it, and watching them, they seemed to be drawing close to each other. When it was time for a break they would sit together and share their food talking quietly the while, sharing confidences and quietly holding hands. There seemed to be a change coming over the usually irrepressible Emma. Seldom was she the centre of the group hatching up some game or prank now. It seemed she had eyes only in one direction. Should my suspicions prove well-founded then I would be happy for her. I imagined both Father and Mother would be well pleased for, after all, Alric was the elder son of the bailiff.

After we had all retired for the night at the end of the second week of the harvest and when I was sure that Osbern was asleep, I slid quietly from my bed and crept over to sit on Emma's couch. Her eyes were open and from the smile on her lips I could tell that she had some secret that she might wish to share. Laying my hand gently on her shoulder, I said, "You seem more than usually content this night. Is it something that you can share with your brother?"

She turned her eyes towards me and I could see that they glistened with the beginnings of a tear. Then sitting up she leant forward and threw her arms around my neck and buried her face in my hair, while her naked breasts pressed against my chest.

"Oh Hugh, Hugh," she whispered. "I think Alric would wed me. He has not yet asked me directly but these last two weeks that we have been gathering the harvest he has spent nearly all his time at my side. When I have fallen behind in binding the sheaves, he has ceased his scything and bent to help me. At mealtimes he has offered me food first and chosen always the choicest pieces to give me, and he is for ever saying the sweetest things to me. Never has he tumbled me in the sheaves as the other boys try to do and it is not shyness on his part, for I have seen him try his luck with other girls in earlier years. Think you that he means to woo me and wed me? Father would be agreeable I think and Alwin has always treated me kindly so might well agree to the match, though his position in the burgh as bailiff sets him above our family."

Then, unclasping her arms from me and leaning back, she shook her head and, raising her arms, passed her hands through her auburn tresses, and with her hands still behind her head but with lowered eyes she said, "Think you that I am comely enough for Alric ?"

I stared at her open mouthed. It was nothing strange for me to see her naked, for we shared the same chamber and when we swam together, as we frequently did, we always stripped to the skin and would afterwards lie in the sun to dry our bodies before slipping back into our garments. I had never before given much thought to her comeliness, but looking at her now in the half-light of the gathering dark with shadows falling across her, she did indeed seem most comely with her firm young breasts accentuated by her raised arms and her anxious face with its downcast eyes framed in her glowing hair. Then she lowered her arms and took my hands in hers and, looking anxiously into my eyes, asked me again almost pleading, "Tell me Hugh, do you see me as comely and am I right in thinking that Alric cares for me?"

By this time I had regained my composure.

"Emma, my darling sister," I whispered, "you seem to me to be the most beautiful girl in the whole world, though I have never thought to look on you in that light before. Till now you have always been my little sister and frequent companion but the way you look now would turn any man's head. As for Alric, he is my surest friend and I could not wish for you to wed a better man. I have seen how he looks at you and how this harvest he has been constantly at your side. You say that he has not sought to tumble you among the sheaves. This I take to be a sure sign that he cares greatly for you and would not wish to sully you. He boasts sometimes of his conquests but it is idle talk, I think, for that is not his true nature; I know him too well for that."

"Oh Hugh, you give me such hope. I do think I love him for I cannot put him from my mind."

I have little enough to offer him, for his father is higher than ours. Do you think he will agree to the match, and will Father be able to provide a suitable dowry for me? Oh Hugh, what shall I do if he cannot?"

"Calm your fears Emma," I whispered. "From what I know of Alric and from watching him these last weeks, he is more moon-struck than you, if that is possible. As for Alwin, he is not blind to his son's wishes and our two families have been friends for many years. Alwin trusts Father and respects his judgement. Do you not remember how he wanted Father by his side when Gilbert the clerk came to make the Domesday Register of the burgh, and again when that Ranulf Flambard came these few months past? I think both would be more than happy with the match and I am sure Father can raise the dowry for you."

"You have eased my mind so much, dear Hugh. I could not speak of it to any of the girls for they are all such blabbermouths that it would have been all over the burgh before the next cock-crow. Nor did I wish to trouble Mother with it for fear that if nothing were to come of it she would be upset and reproach Father if he could not raise the dowry. You and I have never had any secrets from each other, so I knew I could speak with you on it. Do you think Alric will speak to me soon? I think I shall die if he does not." and she heaved another deep sigh.

"You must be patient Emma. I will try to encourage Alric to speak soon if I get the chance, and when the opportunity comes, I will try to put in a good word for you with Alwin himself. When next we are in the mill I will see if I can bring the talk round so that I can let Father know your feelings, for Alric must come and speak with Father to claim your hand . In the meantime, drop hints to Mother that she may know how you feel. She will surely gladly encourage Father and she is a good friend to Mary. Oh Emma, I am so happy for you! We must try to bring this to pass if we can."

"What would I do without you, Hugh?"

Emma smiled at me again and then, taking my hands in hers once more, she put her head on one side and asked in hushed tones, "And what of you and Isabel? She is my closest friend you know, and she cares deeply for you, though she would be angry with me if she knew I had told you so. If my eyes do not deceive me, you feel for her almost as much as I feel for Alric. Why Hugh, I do believe you are blushing!"

Still holding my hands, she bent forward and brushed my cheek again with her lips.

"She would suit you well I am sure." she whispered in my ear. "We could even have a double wedding if our families agreed - or do I go too fast for you?"

I was too overcome to speak but I in my turn bent forward and, hiding my face in her hair, whispered, "Is it so obvious? For sure I care for Isabel and have looked on her as a sister these many years, though I have never sought to share my thoughts with her as I do with you. It began, I suppose, that day I rescued her from the sea when we swam off Hengist's headland. Indeed my feelings for her have grown to be much like yours for Alric, and her beauty and gentleness enchant me."

Emma pulled away from me and looking at me straight with a wicked twinkle in her eyes she said, "Why, Master Hugh! Just now you told me that you counted me the most beautiful girl in the whole world. Would you now rate Isabel's charms above mine and even say as much to my face? Shame on you ! I shall never trust your word anymore and shall tell Isabel as much too. You sit before me in my nakedness, a helpless innocent girl. You shall never see my charms again!"

With that she seized the edge of the covers on her bed and held them up to cover her chin. She could not hide the light in her eyes though and I could see that she teased. Recovering my composure I played along with her.

"My lady," I said bowing my head in mock humility, "How could you think such a thing when all the world knows that not even the Goddess Venus can hold a candle to you. Were Isabel to be in your presence, she would serve only to show how far your beauty exceeded hers."

"You are forgiven this once, boy. You may kiss my hand if you wish," she said haughtily as she slid a hand out from under the covers and held it limply for me to kiss.

As I took her hand in mine and raised it to my downcast lips, she whispered, "Shall I tell Isabel how low you rate her beauty?" and could not restrain her giggling.

We both felt that the tension was broken, for each of us had bared our innermost thoughts to the other. We both felt surer of ourselves for knowing how each other felt. Alric would soon press his suit I felt sure and I would help Emma in this so far as I was able. For myself, she had helped me to see where my true feelings lay, for until that moment I had not faced them as squarely as perhaps I should. Had I been taking Isabel too much for granted I wondered. I would look differently on her in future and try to see how she really felt about me. Thinking thus, I rose and, kissing Emma on the cheek as I often did, bid her 'Good-night' and slipped beneath my covers. I heard the rustle of her covers and her sigh of deep contentment as she settled down to sleep.

For my part, I took some time to calm my feelings. My thoughts were in a turmoil from what Emma had said. Then I called to mind what Goodwife Adeline had said when I talked with her in her house that time we went to fetch the pure well water down by Stanpit. She had likened Emma and Isabel to two budding flowers. Both had assuredly blossomed now. What was it she had said of Isabel? "She seems to have eyes only for you, but go carefully with her, for she is a tender plant and would bruise easily." I hoped I had not harmed her or been rough with her but I could not be sure. I was so used to Emma, who was stronger than many of the boys of her age, that I tended to treat all girls like her. I vowed to take more notice of her but likewise not to show it.

Till now my thoughts had not seriously turned towards weddings; there was so much still to learn and do that was too exciting to think of settling down. Nor was I certain that Father had taught me all that he knew of the miller's trade. Until I could count myself as a master miller I could not think of taking a wife. How would I be able to support her and my own family? With such thoughts as these tumbling through my head I eventually fell into a dream-filled sleep, in which I have to confess Isabel played a pleasant and leading part.

Next day being Sunday, there was no work in the demesne fields. After Mass, each man went to his own land to continue gathering his own harvest. Emma, Oswald and I went with Father to our assart where we had corn growing for the second year. This time it was wheat, after last year's barley, and the ears stood full on the tall straw.

"Cut the straw as long as possible this time, and Emma and Osbern, take care how you bind the sheaves," said Father, as we were sharpening our scythes.

"I have a mind to keep the straw for thatching as it is long and strong. We may not see the likes of this for a few years for we cannot expect such weather again yet awhile. It will save us having to use reeds from the river and good wheat-straw lasts better than poor reed. With more houses being built in the burgh there is less good reed to be had now."

He tested the edge of his scythe with his thumb as he spoke.

"When Mother comes with the meal at midday, Osbern, take a scythe as well, for we can do with a third cutter if we are to finish this crop today as I would like. For now, we must bind as we go, so work with Emma that we may keep a clean field. If you find time on your hands then it will assist us if you can clear the edges ahead of us too."

Seeing that Osbern looked downcast at being set the lowliest task, he added, "I do not doubt your skill with the scythe Osbern, but we must work as a team and each task depends on the other. To have the edges clear before your mother comes will help us to work faster later in the day. Besides, by then I may be tiring and we will need a third scythe to keep pace with the women's binding, for you know how fast Mother works and Emma can almost keep pace with her."

I saw Osbern's good humour return at this, and my admiration of Father's way of bringing the best out in people increased. We set to then and, as always, worked well as a team, each at his appointed task. Emma was quieter than usual and I could guess the reason why. Now and then she would catch my eye and we would exchange smiles, each happy with our own thoughts. Mine were of Isabel whom I could imagine toiling, as Emma was, with her brothers in her father's field.

We were all four grateful to see Mother approaching across the wasteland that lay between our assart and the track to the forest. It had been hot work, for the sun had been beating down from a cloudless sky. Good drying weather for the sheaves no doubt, but hard on the back. Gratefully we ate the bread and goat cheese that Mother had brought and quenched our thirst with the thin ale.

"I came out with Mary, who was carrying food for her family," said Mother. "They were making good progress in their field of barley. Seldom have I seen one work so fast as Alric. He has an easy action with his scythe that seems to cut much more with little effort. He was stripped to the waist and you could see his shining muscles rippling as he moved. Were I thirty years younger I could fall for such as he." Turning to Father she added "If you remember, Oswald, I did, for you were cutting corn in your father's field when first I saw you. You may be a master miller now but I warrant there are few who could scythe a field as well as you even now."

I was sitting next to Emma and I saw her check as she was about to take another bite of cheese. The colour rose in her cheeks and I gently squeezed her arm as we looked at each other with understanding glances.

"Isabel was binding sheaves with Alnoth," she went on, "and they were trying to keep pace with Alwin and Alric, though the speed at which they were working it was a hard job. They would be glad of Mary's help I am thinking. Poor Isabel had no gloves, so I lent her mine for her hands were sore from the thistles, though she made not a word of complaint. I had to press them upon her for she would not take them willingly saying that I would need them myself, but I insisted, telling her that at my age my hands were past caring for. She took them gratefully at last and I could see that they eased her pain. I can't think what Mary was doing sending the girl out to bind sheaves without gloves," she snorted.

It was my turn to colour now and I tried to hide it by taking a long pull at the ale flagon. I could not tell if Mother's anger was feigned or real until I saw her glance in my direction. As she looked away again, I thought I caught a small smile of pleasure cross her lips. She suspected more than she let me imagine and it seemed she was not displeased. I felt Emma squeeze my arm in return as once more we exchanged knowing glances.

We ate in silence for a while and then talk moved to other topics. Then we lay with our backs against the stooks of corn while Mother packed the remains of the meal into the basket again. When she had done, Father stood and stretched his arms wide and rubbed his back with his hands to ease his stiffening muscles.

"By the Rood," he said, "it is the same each year. I find muscles I did not know I had. Moving sacks of corn requires a different strength to swinging a scythe. Come then, Hugh, let us get back to work. Now Osbern, show us your muscles and take the lead cut while we follow behind and try to keep pace with you. Set a steady pace mind and do not rush it, for your mother and Emma have to bind after the three of us, and we want to leave a clean field behind us. I doubt if any will come this far to glean after us so we should try to leave nothing behind, though no doubt the fowls will find a few pickings."

With that he picked up his whetstone and began to put a fresh edge on his scythe blade. Then, testing it again with his thumb and nodding in satisfaction, he spat on his hands and moved over to take his stand behind Osbern. I came up behind him and to his right so that the three of us were then in line diagonally facing the uncut corn.

We continued thus for the rest of the day, stopping only occasionally to slake our thirsts from the ale flagon. With all five of us at the task the uncut field shrank with satisfying speed and the lines of stooks of sheaves grew likewise. By the height of the sun I took it to be between Vespers and Compline when we finally cut the last swathe and Mother and Emma put the last two sheaves into the final stooks. With sighs of relief from us all, we stood surveying our work. I watched Father counting the stooks and then he took two or three sample heads of wheat. Rubbing it between his palms, he first blew away the chaff and them smelt the grain, before examining the amount in his palm.

"If the weather can hold for the next few days and we have no rain," he said looking up at the sky, "we shall be able to cart this crop back to store by the end of the week. It is good we chose to plant emmer wheat rather than spelt, for the yield is heavier. By my reckoning we should have almost thirty bushels if all goes well. Come, let us gather our tools and make for home. We have had a good day and I thank you all for working so well."

Father shouldered his scythe, and the rest of us gathered our things together. As Mother was picking up the food basket, I bent and took the empty ale flagon from her, for an idea had formed in my mind. As we reached the place where the track we took met the road leading to Stanpit, I said to the others, "Do go on. I have an errand I must make first. It will not take long and I shall be home before the evening meal."

With that I turned to take the left-hand track and strode off whistling softly to myself. I soon came to the well at Stanpit and, having first drunk my fill of the sweet tasting sparkling water, I washed out the flagon carefully before filling it and fixing back the stopper. Then I went to seek out Goodwife Adeline. She was busy tending the herbs in her garden, and straightened up when she saw me.

"Good-day to you. It is Hugh the miller's son if I mistake not, and what brings you to my cott at the end of a day's harvesting. Naught ails your family I trust?"

"Thank you, Goodwife, they are indeed well. We have this moment finished cutting the wheat in our assart and they are returning home, weary but content, for it was a good day's work. I come not on their behalf but for another. Have you a salve to put on hands and arms made sore from harvesting? There is one whom I think suffers somewhat from the unaccustomed work, for the thistles are mighty keen this year and I fear she may be in some pain this night where they have torn her flesh. I am taking a flagon of well water to bathe the sores but no doubt one of your salves would be of more help. I will gladly pay you for it."

She looked keenly at me for a moment.

"I mind the last time you came for water from this well, it was for Gilbert the clerk at Domesday time. Your sister was with you and also a fair-haired maid, the daughter of Alwin the bailiff if memory serves me. A sweet lass whose eyes seemed always upon you. Nay, fear not to redden before me for she is worthy of your kindness. Tell me truthfully, for it will go no further, do you mean well by her? Such a gentle lass as her should not be lusted after."

My cheeks were indeed fiery and I had to lower my eyes before I could reply. "Have no fear for Isabel on my account. We have been companions since childhood and Emma my sister is her greatest friend. I think I do care for her more than I thought, and", I blurted out, "her brother Alric means to wed Emma, though he has not asked her yet."

"Gossip to that effect has reached my ears," she said, "and it would be a good match. Your families have been friends for long, I think. Come into my cott now, and I will seek out a soothing balm and a salve as you ask."

She busied herself amongst the jars and pots that stood upon shelves. At last she was finished and, turning, she put a jar into my hands.

"You have done well to come for clear water. Bid the lass wash the scratches and sores well in it and bathe out all dirt from any cuts first. Then let her smooth on this salve night and morning for five days, rubbing it in gently to any open places. If all is not healed by then come and see me again. What she does not use, let her keep by her for this salve has many healing properties, but mark well, tell her to keep it well covered at all times lest evil odours and other foul pestilence enter it. Go now with my blessing, and if you mean to woo her, do so gently for she is more tender than most. Nay lad, I will take no payment. They say the salve works better when it is freely given."

I mumbled my thanks, overcome by her kindness and insight. Some said that she had magical powers that came from the Devil but I felt that could only be spite and jealousy, for I had received only kindness from her and many were the folk whom she had healed of diverse ills. With a light heart I bade her farewell and set off back to the burgh, going straight to Alwin's house.

As I came in sight of it I could see Isabel sitting beside the door, bending over her hand which she was examining carefully. She looked up as I approached and put one finger in her mouth to suck it. Taking it out again, she smiled at me but there was hurt in her eyes.

"What brings you here, Hugh, after a full day harvesting? You have not eaten yet I think as you still have your scythe. Oh these thorns! There is one deep in my finger and another in my palm. I think they are May thorns that came up with the barley when I was binding close to the hedge at the edge of our field. Fool that I was I never took gloves with me, though your mother insisted that I use hers when she came by at midday. I have just finished pulling out the last of the thistles from my hands and arms. See, they are all red and scored."

She pulled up her sleeves to show me the angry scratches.

"But it is these thorns that trouble me most. I have tried to dig them out with one of Mother's fish-bone needles but it is difficult as they are in my right hand and I have to work with my left. Besides," she said lowering her glance, "I am not sure if I have the courage to dig deep enough, it hurts so."

I took her hand in mine. I could see the torn places where the thorns had entered and broken off deep in her palm which was red and swollen.

"May I try?" I asked. "I will be as gentle as I can."

She nodded as she held out her hand, closing her eyes and pursing her lips tight. As gently as I could I prised the thorns out, and though I could feel Isabel stiffen as the needle stung her, she made no sound. At last I was finished and I took her hand and sucked at the wounds to remove any poison that might still remain. Isabel let out a sigh of relief and smiling, kissed me on the cheek.

"Thank you," she said, "I am such a coward and it was really such a little hurt."

I mumbled that it was no matter.

"I have brought you something to heal the sores," I said. "I heard that you were working in the fields without gloves, so on my way home I filled this flagon with water from the pure well at Stanpit and called on Goodwife Adeline and she gave me a salve for you to put on the sores and cuts."

I explained how the goodwife said she should bathe and treat them. She thanked me again and, smiling, kissed me once more on the cheek. Stumbling to my feet I turned and made some excuse to hurry away, with somewhat bad grace I fear, and Isabel went inside the house, no doubt to tell her mother how she fared.

As I went, Swein the serf passed by with his burly numbskull friend Edric. I nodded a greeting to them but they merely mouthed some obscenities to each other behind their hands sniggering the while. I thought nothing of it for they were but common serfs and addle-brained at that, passing their time in the poorest alehouses or else the whorehouse. Nearing our house, I smelt dinner cooking so hurried in, famished after the day's harvesting.

The weather held as Father had hoped and we were able to carry the sheaves back to our store at the end of the week. It was growing dark as I led the beast that drew the cart laden with the last of the sheaves. I had just passed over the bridge into the burgh when there was a commotion beside me and, turning, I saw Swein stumble out of an ale-house that stood hard by. He fell to his knees and was followed by his usual companion Edric who was being helped on his way by the boot of the ale-house keeper.

"If you can't pay you need not come near my ale again," he shouted, shaking his fist at them both. "I get plenty of trade without bothering with the likes of you two. Now get you gone before I haul you both up before the reeve who no doubt would gladly throw you in the stocks."

He turned on his heel and went back in. I took no notice and proceeded on my way holding the beast's head, for I did not wish it frightened lest it bolt and upset the cart. Then out of the corner of my eye I saw the bulk of Edric lumbering towards me.

"What do you find so comical, Master Hugh? Can't a serf have a drink like any other? Anyway his ale is weak stuff and tastes bitter."

He wiped the back of his hand across his mouth as he swayed towards me. It was not the first draught of ale he had downed that day, I was sure.

"Will you buy me ale or do you drink only fine wines, you and your smart doxy? A pox on her and all her kind. Did I not see you kiss her hand before the bailiff's house these few days gone? I warrant she would lift her skirts for any man who cares to have her, and probably has. I'll tumble her myself next time her path crosses mine, and afterwards Swein, I'll hold her down for you. Does her pretty white skin go all the way way up? No doubt you have looked often enough, eh Hugh?"

He thrust his face close to mine and his foul breath caught in my throat. He knew not what he was saying with the drink on him. Laying my hand on his shoulder I said, "I have no quarrel with you, but speak not ill of a lady nor of things you know not of."

"What say you? Did I not see you kiss her hand feigning to be a knight? No man calls Edric a liar."

He swung a blow at my head but I dodged and it went wide. I still held the beast and so could not defend myself and, though it offended me, I thought to take the insult which was misplaced, for he would not remember by morning. Besides I had no wish for a fight. Edric however, was spoiling for someone to take on after being kicked from the ale-house and I was the first one to hand. He swung again at me and I tried to catch his arm to stop the blow which only angered him more, so I was forced to face him and meet his onslaught. I let the beast go and hoped it would not bolt in the confusion, and stood ready to receive his next rush. He came at me with both fists flailing, so I stepped aside and putting my foot out tripped him as he passed, so that he fell in the dust. He lay for a while but rose unsteadily to his feet before coming at me again more cautiously this time and with an evil glint in his eye. He was taller than I and more powerfully built but slower on his feet and it was said that he fought foul. Still hoping he might think better of it, I started to edge away but he came at me again flinging more insults and calling me a coward for not wishing to fight. I saw that some had come out of the ale-house to see what was afoot, so I called to one that I knew to go take the head of the beast and lead it on to our store.

As I did so, Edric rushed me again so that I had to stand to him and caught him a blow to his mouth which stopped him but only angered him more. Then he grappled with me, seizing me round the waist with his great arms as he tried to squeeze the breath out of me. I broke his hold and caught him a hard blow to the side of his head, but he swung back-handed at me, finding my eye with his fist so that I saw nothing but stars for a while. I stepped back a few paces to recover, hoping that he might now be satisfied with the hurt he had done me, but he would not desist.

"You'll not be able to straddle her again when I have finished with you," he growled.

Making a coarse gesture, he lashed out at my groin with his foot, but I caught it and turning it swiftly, unbalanced him and flung him on his face in the dust. Kneeling on his back, I put my hand in his hair and pulled back his head so that he could not move. I heard a cheer go up from those outside the ale-house and two or three came forward to help me hold Edric fast. Others brought rope to bind him and take him before the reeve. I dusted my tunic and rubbed my eye which was beginning to throb. One in the crowd spoke.

"I saw how he came at you, Hugh, and how you tried to calm him but he would have none of it. He has been spoiling for a fight this last hour. He is in Frankpledge, so let his fellows see to him. It is a wonder you did not throw him out of the ale-house before, Brand."

"I had a mind to," said the ale-house keeper, "but so long as he had money I was happy to take it from him. Had I thrown him into the street he would only have wandered elsewhere and tried to ravage some woman. Often times he is here and I keep him till he is so drunk that he falls down in a stupor then I throw him in with the animals to sleep it off and he is gone by morning. This time his money failed too soon. He can cool his heels in the stocks awhile. He met his match this time I warrant, though I would you had given him a better thrashing Hugh. He usually picks only those smaller than he but his eye was not clear today. Have no fear Hugh, there are enough here that will speak for you before the reeve should he enquire into this matter. You did but stand your ground though no doubt you were sorely provoked, and there are those here who will bear witness that he struck the first blow."

The ale-house keeper slapped me on the shoulder.

"Your eye will bear witness for you too, I am thinking," he said with a grin.

I thanked him and so went on my way home, feeling my eye the while. It would colour no doubt and I would be twitted for it that I could not defend myself from such a lout as Edric. I feared to tell all and hoped that none had heard Isabel's name mentioned, or I might be called a craven for not defending her name more bravely. Such thoughts hurt me more than the blow, for I would have none cast doubts on her purity.

As we ate our meal, Father said that Godric had asked all who could to help with the harvest of the priests' lands and especially those of the dead Alsi. It had for long been the custom in the burgh for those wishing to do penance for their sins to work in the church fields, particularly at ploughing and harvest time.

All knew that much of the crop was used to feed the poor and travellers and only what was needed was kept by the priests for themselves. It was said by some that priests grew fat and slothful on the produce of their ever-growing lands. No doubt this was true of some abbeys but I suspected that the stories were often put about by evil-minded souls who perhaps had to suffer greater penance for their grievous sins than they liked. In our burgh we saw little evidence of sloth and gluttony amongst the priests. It was said rather that Godric and his fellows were renowned for their charity almost to their own hurt. Thus it was that there were always plenty of willing hands to plough and harvest the church fields.

Next morning, Osbern and I went with several others to reap what had been Alsi's largest field. Godric was there to greet us and to give us the church's blessing on our work.

"Leave the first swathe uncut" he said, "and be not over-careful in binding the sheaves so that enough be left for the gleaners who will come after. I would not have them left empty-handed."

We set about our self-appointed tasks and made short work of the field, partly because we did not wish to spend too much time away from our own fields and partly from the feeling of satisfaction that we had in serving the church and helping the poor.

We were near the end when a cry came from one of those binding sheaves near the roadway. All stopped and looked up to see horsemen riding towards us; beside the leader walked Godric. As they approached, I could make out the features of the leader, Flambard, who from his gestures and countenance looked none too pleased.

"What means this slovenly working Master Godric?" he said. "See how these men have left a full swathe at the edge of the field uncut and see the armfuls of full-grained straw left ungathered. I will not have my lands so poorly managed. See to it Master Godric that the field is properly cleared or you will answer for it."

"By your leave, my Lord, we do but follow our normal custom in these fields and leave some corn for those who would come and glean afterwards."

"I'll have no gleaners in my fields, Master Godric" cried Flambard. "Have these men clean this field properly, and you serf," he pointed at me, "get you to the edge of the field and cut the swathe you have left standing."

Before I could frame my reply Godric had stepped forward, face set hard to confront Flambard.

"By your leave my Lord, you have not the right to order these men to do your bidding. They are giving their labour as they have these many years past for the benefit of their church and as penance for their sins. Nor are they serfs but free men. As you well know this burgh is held from our Lord the King, and to him only do they owe allegiance, and may appeal to his courts, and his itinerant justices. Is this not so my Lord Flambard?"

"It may be so but I will still have these fields of mine properly cleared and gathered. I like not to see such waste."

It was clear that Flambard was trying to cover his mistake by his continuing bluster, so Godric answered him again as smoothly as he could while trying to contain his anger.

"My Lord, there will be no waste. Do you not call to mind how it is written in the second chapter of the Book of Ruth, that Ruth who was herself a widow, and daughter-in-law to the widow Naomi who had been left desolate? How Ruth went to glean in the fields of Boaz? You will recall, my Lord, that not only did Boaz charge his reapers to give Ruth food and drink when she was in the fields and not to harm her, but also to let fall handfuls of grain near where she gleaned and even to leave whole sheaves for her that she might gather corn more easily. This they did so that they might not hurt her pride by too easy a gift, but make it easier for her to do what she needed for herself and her mother-in-law in their distress."

Godric waited to see if Flambard intended to reply, but it seemed that he was taken aback by such firmness.

"We do but try to follow that example for we too have widows in this burgh who are needy. They have their pride, and though they are willing enough to accept gifts, yet most prefer to feel that they have earned their bread. You, a Christian, would not have us be less generous than the Jew, Boaz, I trust. And you my Lord, would you in your plenty begrudge the poverty-stricken of this burgh?"

"Bandy not words with me, Priest. How can I be sure that those you speak of are not wastrels and idle rogues? I like not to see my goods go to waste and it seems that you are over-generous to those you think to help. By my reckoning there will be more than a sack of grain from what is left in this field. It is too much."

"How so my Lord? Do you not recall that in the same chapter it is recorded that Ruth beat out a bushel of grain from what she gleaned that day? She was but one and we have many. How then can you say that we leave too much? Besides, this field belonged to the priest Alsi, he who died but a few weeks past. We do but gather his crops and will put them to the same use as he would have done. He kept little for himself and gave the rest to the church for the relief of travellers and the sick. We priests gain nothing from it."

Flambard turned in his saddle and looked keenly at Godric. "Alsi's land you say? Since his death it is for me to say how this land is to be used and how the crops are disposed as set down in the King's charter to me, of which I spoke last time I was here. See to it, Master Priest, and have a full tally made of all the crops gathered from this Alsi's land. Have the harvest threshed as soon as maybe, for I mean to send ships to carry the grain to Southampton and thence by cart to Winchester, there to be ground to flour for the use of the King's Court when next he comes to that city. How say you now Master Godric? Would you deprive our Lord the King of his bread?" His lips twisted into an ugly smile.

"In his necessity, no; but you would make the King less than Boaz who was but a Lord like you, and a Jew to boot, if you would take Alsi's crops and forbid the gleaners to do what custom has allowed since before the time of Moses. Would you indeed cast the King in such a role?"

Flambard saw that he was trapped, for he grimaced and spun his horse round, digging his spurs cruelly into its flanks so that it reared up and took such skill as he had to control it. It seemed that he cared as little for his costly mount as he did for poor mortals. Though I could only admire Godric for his bravery in facing up to the man, I feared for his safety and that of the rest of us if we were to continue to cross his path. As Flambard rode off with the rest of his party, he turned once more in his saddle.

"Look to the harvest, Priest, and guard well the crops," he cried. "I will send ships in six weeks to carry all my grain to Southampton. My Steward will be with the boats and will expect you to give him a full tally. No mere priest shall better me."

With that he was gone and we all breathed the easier. Godric for his part sat down heavily on the nearest stook of corn and mopped his sweating brow. I could see that he trembled, for it takes more than usual courage to defy a man such as Flambard. Only his priesthood saved him from a beating, I think. As for the rest of us, we all wondered what might befall the burgh now that Flambard was claiming the church lands.

That evening, Godric summoned a meeting of all the men to consider the matter. Alwin, as bailiff, called for order that all might hear what Godric had to say. First he retold what had happened in the field with Flambard so that all might know the full story. He asked me if he had told it right and I affirmed that he had, adding that I thought Godric had been most brave in his defiance.

"You know that the King has now given to Flambard all the lands of the church of this burgh," Godric continued. " It seems that he intends also claiming the lands of the priests themselves - at least when they die. It is for this reason that he lays claim to Alsi's crops. I have spoken with Ranulf who cares for the guest-house. He tells me that he has need of all that has been harvested this day if he is to continue to provide food for travellers and others in need as he has in the past. I have spoken with Alwin too. As the King's bailiff, he says that he will hold the corn from the field we cut today in the King's store and that I may call on it to feed those whom we have fed in the past as need shall arise. The corn will be ground in the King's mill, not that of the church. I am sorry Oswald, but it is safer this way, for the King will then have the benefit of the grinding and thereby be less willing to back Flambard should he try to press his claim for the corn."

Father nodded in agreement. Though he could see the sound reasoning it would be a sore loss to him, for Alsi's corn took many days to grind and we were entitled to one sack in ten for our labour. It was also some of the best flour in the burgh. 'Only the best is good enough for God' had been Alsi's motto in life.

"For the rest of Alsi's land, I have agreed with Alwin that we shall send word to Flambard that we have no men to gather his harvest or work his fields. As you know those that tilled his fields did so in payment for land they had from him to work themselves. Those that wish may continue to work for their new lord,

Flambard. Those who like not what they have seen of him should speak to the bailiff. Alwin, would you like to say what is in your mind?"

"Thank you Godric. The King's lands in this manor are not fully tilled at present. I can offer land to those who would rather work for the King on the same terms as those that hold now on Alsi's land. Such a move would find favour with our Lord the King I am sure, for it will increase the profit from his estate. Those that would make the change should consult with Godric and me before Advent Sunday. Remember also that those who hold land of the King have the right to redress in his courts, for they will be immediately the King's men and can seek his justice. Though some may think they have cause to complain of some of the King's actions if they are aggrieved then the King will do right by them. For the rest of the harvest on Alsi's land, much may go to waste, is that not so Godric?"

"Indeed it is. It grieves me to see good corn rot in the fields but what cannot be gathered by those who still owe Alsi service will not be harvested. Perhaps though, part of each field may be cut and then carried. When that has happened it would seem that any who wish to glean may do so once the last sheaf has been cleared, as is the custom."

Godric smiled as he said this, and in the silence that followed, first Alwin, then Father and a few of the others started to smile and then laugh openly. I cudgelled my brain to see what amused them and finally called to mind what Godric had said about the time of gleaning. A man who left but one stook of corn standing in his field prevented those that would from gleaning. It was a ruse seldom used, and then only by the miserly who would then make sure that his own family cleared every last grain from the field. Such action brought him scant respect from the rest of the burgh. Once a field was cleared of all stooks, it was a sign that a man had taken his crop and those who wished could glean what was left, be it fallen straws or uncut corn, often near the hedgerows or pathways. It was this that Godric had bade us do when we worked Alsi's field this morning - leaving an uncut swathe round the edge of the field. He was now stretching this to its limit and perhaps beyond, but he seemed to be carrying Alwin and the others with him. In this way the needy of the burgh would gain and Flambard would be hard put to find fault, though it would be to his hurt.

"For the rest of the land belonging to the church," Godric continued, "the service that is owed remains the same. Likewise those that wish to do penance for their sins at harvest time and at ploughing may continue to do so. Alnod has his family who can manage his harvest with the aid of some of the other priests. And Godwine has always been able to carry his own harvest - on his own back if need be."

This brought a smile to many faces, for Godwine's strength was well known though he was gentle with it. Godwine himself looked sheepish, for though he secretly gloried in his great strength, he knew that to do so was a sin of pride. He heaved a sigh, knowing that he would have to say many Pater Nosters as penance. He looked round at the assembled company.

"If it is of help, I will gladly carry what the gleaners collect and stack it for them in their stores. If I may Godric, I would beg you to allow me to use one of the carts belonging to the church that I may carry the grain more quickly."

Godric nodded his agreement.

"If there is need of more than one cart," Alwin added, " I will provide one from my lord's demesne and a beast to pull it too. We must clear the fields as soon as maybe and have them gleaned too. Godric, how many days do you think it will take to harvest the rest of the lands of the church?"

"If all the priests work a full day, we should be able to finish within the week. The church must not forsake its Offices but I see no reason why every priest should attend all the services. I will arrange a rota so that one shall say the Offices for all for a day. The other priests shall be granted absolution from saying the Offices until the harvest is all gathered. Were they to be travelling a great distance they would have similar absolution, so it would seem right to grant it in this case too. What they do is for the good of the church and would seem to accord with the teachings of Christ."

There was a general murmur of agreement at this. One or two of the older priests looked a little taken aback at the thought of having to spend hot days toiling in the fields. Two of them were looking at their soft hands and I nudged Father and caught his eye. He saw it too and smiled quietly sharing my feelings. A priest could often find an excuse to avoid hard labour by saying that he had to say an Office or visit some sick person. Thus the plan was agreed and the gathering broke up, each going to his own home.

The weather held all the week and as Godric had hoped, all the church's fields were cleared by the Saturday evening. There was a great feeling of goodwill amongst all those who worked in the fields. The whole burgh felt united in preventing Flambard from taking what everyone regarded as belonging to the church - more especially as so many knew that they would benefit directly in time of need. There was also a feeling that for Flambard to take old Alsi's crops - he who had harmed no-one but had helped so many - was a sin against the church itself. So it was, that at High Mass on that Sunday, there was a mood almost of Harvest Thanksgiving that all the church's crops had been safely gathered and the fields cleared by those who wished to glean. It was said that none could remember when so much had been gleaned, and assuredly many of the poor of the burgh had their storehouses stacked to the roof so that they would be facing the coming winter well provided for.

With all the activity I had had little enough time to myself that week, but as I left the church after Mass I found myself walking near Isabel. Seeing me she smiled and came towards me, but I could tell that something troubled her for she kept her eyes downcast.

"See," she said, "my hand is quite healed now," and she held it out for me to see.

Then a frown crossed her brow and she lifted her hand to touch my eye which was still discoloured from the blow Edric had given me.

"Did you really suffer that on my account?" she asked. "Can you forgive me? I had no thought to bring trouble about your head. I fear that your eye still pains you, but I hear that Edric suffered a full day in the stocks as a result which may perhaps teach him a lesson, though I had rather it had not been necessary."

I put my hand over hers where it still stroked my face.

"It was nothing," I said. "He had too much drink in him at the time and like as not he knew not what he said, though he is a bully and foul-mouthed too. I had no wish to fight him and did but defend myself. I will let no man speak evil of you as he did."

I felt my gorge rise as I called to mind what he had said of Isabel so unjustly.

"Am I forgiven for the hurt I caused you?" she asked.

"There is nothing to forgive and I was glad to be able to ease your hand."

There was more I would have said but the words would not come in my confusion. Isabel pressed my arm and gave me a shy smile.

"You know there is nothing I would not do for you," I managed to blurt out.

We walked on in silence and I could feel her warmth flowing into my body. At the entrance to the churchyard she stopped and began to say something, but changed her mind and with a shake of her head she turned, bade me farewell and hurried away towards her house, leaving me to walk slowly back to our home wondering what she might have said.

That evening I went down to the mill-race to watch the sun setting over the hills. I loved to sit watching the rosy orb settling down over the white chalk of the distant cliffs and listen to the turbulent waters behind me. The cool evening breeze was blowing in my face, and I felt a great peace upon me. How many countless generations had watched the same scene, I wondered, and how many more would do so in the future? The sun, water and wind were timeless and ever-enduring and would still be there long after I was gone. Looking slightly left, I could see the two great ridges of the Twin Ditches of Hengist's headland and I pondered, not for the first time, on the fate of those who had lived there so long ago. That they had thrived there could be no doubt. It was known the Romans had used the shelter of the headland as a harbour for their ships, and other peoples before them had lived and farmed there in safety behind the two great ditches and banks. They had been wealthy too, for fine tools and ornaments had been found there in times gone by, so it was said, though I had seen nothing better than a broken dagger, but one never knew.

I heard a rustle behind me and, turning, saw Emma running towards me, her auburn hair streaming behind her and such excitement in her face.

"Oh Hugh," she panted, "You will never guess."

She threw her arms around my neck and buried her face in my tunic. Before I could ask her what was the matter she went on. "Alric wishes to wed me. He asked me this afternoon and is coming to see Father even now to seek his blessing. I am so excited. Father will say 'yes' won't he? I think I would die if he did not, I love Alric so." Emma looked up at me, and I could see tears glistening in the corners of her eyes.

"Hush, you ninny. Of course he will, for you know that you can twist Father round your little finger when you have a mind." I continued with a mock frown on my brow, "I cannot think why you want to trouble yourself with such a dunderhead as Alric. Did I not see him tumbling Godiva the hayward's daughter in the cornfield this very noontide?"

Emma looked sharply at me in alarm so that my heart softened.

"Nay, I jest. Alric has no eyes for Godiva, though it is not for want of trying on her part. He sees only you for sure and with good reason. You will make a handsome pair and if I have to lose my closest friend there is no-one I would rather see him wed than you, though no doubt you will lead him quite a dance. I only hope that he can curb your waywardness."

She started thumping my chest with her clenched fists.

"It is not so," she protested. "Am I really such a minx? I never know when you are serious, and my head is in such a whirl. Come, we must return to the house or Alric will be there before us. I had to see you first to tell you for we have never had any secrets."

She took my hand and started dragging me towards the house, skipping with excitement as she did so. My heart was full of happiness for her. I cannot say that her news came as a surprise to me any more than I suspected it would be to Father and Mother. As we entered Mother looked up.

"I see Emma has told you her news. We are so happy for her. She will make a fine wife for Alric for all her flighty ways."

"It will be good to join our two families," said Father. "I touched on the idea with Alwin these few weeks past, Emma, when I saw how things seemed to be standing between you and Alric, and he seemed content enough. It is a good match for you, daughter, and will give you a better standing in the burgh than I could give as a miller. The wife of the bailiff's son is someone to be counted and, if all goes well, there is no reason to think that Alric himself may not become bailiff in good time. What think you of that, my fine lady? Will you still speak to your poor father then?"

"How can you say such a thing!" cried Emma, as she rushed over to throw her arms around his neck and plant a great kiss on his cheek. "You and Mother are everything to me, and always will be."

Both Father and Mother smiled at this. It was true. They had always been thoughtful for all three of us even when they had to rebuke us, and we all knew that there was nothing we could not speak to them about and no aid they would not give if it lay within their power.

I heard footsteps outside and there was a knock at the door. Emma glanced excitedly at Mother and Father who nodded. Whereupon she rose, and first straightening her dress and then patting her hair somewhat back into place, she drew a deep breath before moving with a firm step towards the door. She hesitated with her hand upon the latch before lifting it. As she drew back the door, the colour rose in her cheeks and she stretched out her free hand to take Alric's and draw him into our house.

"Father, Mother," she said with sparkling eyes, "Alric has something he would speak with you about. May he come in and sit down please?"

Alric looked abashed so I hurried to fetch a stool for him to put him at his ease. He greeted us all and then thanked me.

"I have a message from Isabel for you, Hugh," he added as he sat down. "She hopes you will call to see her as she has something she would show you if you have the time."

Gladly I took my leave. Alric's business was with Father and I would be better out of the way in spite of our family closeness. I would hear all later that night I had no doubt. Besides I was glad of any excuse to see Isabel. The sun had not yet set as I made my way to the bailiff's house, wondering what Isabel had to show me. The door stood ajar, so I knocked and entered. As I did so, Isabel rose from her seat beside her mother and came towards me.

"I am so pleased that Alric would wed Emma," she said. "I have been trying these past weeks to persuade him to ask her but he would wait till he was sure that she would have him. Besides, he wanted to make sure that he could care for her and have some place where they could live, but I will let him tell you their plans. Come and sit with us, I have something to show you."

She took my hand and led me to the table where her parents sat. I greeted them as I drew up a stool beside them and Alwin offered me a horn of ale.

"Look what Father has given me," she said.

Bending down, she lifted up a small harp and she plucked one or two strings on it. Pure notes came from it which echoed softly round the hall. She handed me the instrument for me to see. Such instruments were not common, though I had seen a few before, mostly when travelling players had passed through the burgh.

"Try it," she said, "and see if you can make a tune".

Taking the harp carefully in my hands, I plucked gently at a few strings but the sounds I made were harsh and dull. I tried again thinking of the tunes the priests sang in church, but though I knew the sounds I could not get the harp to make them, so I handed the harp back to Isabel.

"I have not the art it seems. Please show me how to make a tune."

Taking the harp from me, she set it on her knee and, resting it against her shoulder, she began to pluck the strings with her fingers. First she drew out the chant that Godric used at Mass. Some of the notes were not right at first and she shook her head when they were wrong and went back and tried again. After a while she had the tune perfect. She quietened the strings with the palms of her hands.

"Do you like the sound?" she asked. "I am not skilled yet as you can hear, but I mean to try to learn. It makes it easier to sing too, for the pitch of the note when you pluck a string is always the same if you have the string right. Listen." she said and she sang a few notes and copied them on the harp. Her voice was pure, and with the sound of the harp seemed to make make a perfect blend of sound.

"That is beautiful," I exclaimed astonished, and I saw Alwin and Mary smile with pleasure. "When did you learn this art?"

"Father only gave me the harp today and I have spent most of the afternoon trying my hand at the notes. As you can hear I have much to learn but I hope to learn to play some of the songs the travelling minstrels sing. I have tried part of one already. Listen," she said.

With that, she plucked a few more notes and started to sing one of the best known lays, which told the story of an ancient Saxon King and his love for a Celtish princess. I had heard it oft-times before but it seemed to have a new magic when it came from the hands and voice of Isabel.

"She has the touch in her fingers I think," said Mary. "I thought she would have, for her voice has always been pure and sweet and she is always singing about the house. What think you, Hugh? Do you think she would make a troubadour?"

"I think they would be hard put to hold a taper to her, Mistress Mary," I replied. "It seems she has a natural skill. I like the sound more than I can say, but as you heard it is beyond my hands. They are too clumsy I think for such gentle playing as Isabel makes."

"They can be gentle too when you wish. You eased the thorns from my hand and caused me less pain than I did myself".

"Isabel told us of your kindness, Hugh, and that you earned a buffeting for your pains" said Mary. "I see your eye still bears witness to it. Alwin, is it not time that that lout Edric was taught a proper lesson? A day in the stocks means nothing to him, I fear. He is a bully and like all bullies a coward too. I can see no cause why he should be able to torment those weaker than himself, though he picked the wrong man when he tackled Hugh," she added with a smile. "Alwin can you not bring him before the next View of Frankpledge? The others in his tithing should hold him in check or answer for it at the next Hundred Court."

"I have a mind to do that and will speak to others about it this week, but let us not talk of such things. Hugh did not come for sympathy over his eye from us. I am sure Isabel has done all that is needed on that score.You like her playing, do you Hugh? I am glad of it for that harp cost me a fair few silver pence which I can hardly spare, particularly now that I shall have to help Alric," said Alwin with a smile. "You have heard, no doubt Hugh, that Alric means to wed your sister. What think you of that?"

"Yes, she gave me tidings this evening and she seemed overjoyed. There is no man I would rather see her wed. Alric has been my constant companion these many years as you know. We are a close family and I shall be sad when Emma leaves us, but she loves him to distraction so I must be happy for her."

"His mother and I are content too, aren't we Mary? Though it will be a sad day for us when Alric leaves. He will need land to work and a place to live and we must help him in that. A fist-full of silver pennies would not come amiss I am thinking, so we must see what we can do. What of you, Hugh? No doubt you will wed one day."

This took me aback and I felt Isabel draw in a sharp breath. My head was in a whirl as I fumbled for something to reply. I mumbled something about being busy with the harvest, besides working a full day at the mill.

"When I feel that I can care for a wife properly I shall gladly wed - if anyone will have me."

Out of the corner of my eye I could see Isabel's blush, and though her head was downcast, yet I thought I saw a faint smile touch her lips. Mary was smiling too and it seemed that Alwin's nod was of approval. To cover my confusion I asked Isabel if she could play another tune so that I could hear her harp again, so she bent her head to the instrument to take care with the notes. She tried a soft lullaby this time that I had heard her sing to Belesme's child, and after playing it once she tried it again, this time setting the words to it. I had not thought that music could be so sweet.

It had grown dark, so I finished my ale and bidding them all 'good-night', took my leave. I took time to return for there was much in my mind to ponder on. When at last I re-entered our home, the others were all abed, so I softly crept into our chamber. Before I could shed my clothes Emma sat up and whispered to me to come and sit on her bed.

"Father has given Alric and me his blessing," she said. "Alric means to work a hide of land on the demesne that is not presently farmed and he says that Alwin has told him that he can repair one of the cotts that lies empty against the western wall of the burgh near our mill. It is the cott where Ernwi the swineherd once lived. You remember, he was killed while driving boar in the forest for the King's hunt these seven years back. No man has lived there since so there will be much to do to repair the cott, but it will serve us well, for it is a good size and has about ten rods of land by it where we can keep fowls and grow pulses and other vegetables. Alric says that his father will give him a bag of silver pence to start him off. He will have to do service to the King for the hide of land but he will be the King's man and so can seek justice in his courts. Father said that may well be needful if this Flambard gains too much power in the burgh."

"Oh Emma, I am so happy for you. You know that I will help you and Alric repair the cott whenever I have time. There is much to do, for though the walls look sound, when I passed by it a few days back I saw that the roof needs new thatch, but we can manage that between us for sure. When do you think to wed?"

"We have not set a date yet and we must go speak to Godric. Perhaps it may be Whitsuntide or Midsummer Day, but there will be many months work before the cott will be ready. Besides I shall be loath to leave this house and you, dear Hugh. One day you will wed too no doubt and then you will know how I feel. Do not wait too long lest another come to claim Isabel. She cares deeply for you, you know and I would see you as happy with her as I shall be with Alric. Might we not both wed the same day? It would make me very happy if we did."

"Softly, softly, Emma, do not rush too headlong. What you suggest would indeed be wonderful but there is much for me to think about first. Nor am I sure that Father thinks that I know all the skills of a miller yet. I must be sure of that first and also see how I can find land to work, for I would not take a wife I could not properly care for, the more so as Isabel is more high-born than I. How could I ask her to wed me if I could not house and feed her as she has been accustomed?"

"Now who is the dunderhead? Isabel would come to you if you lived in a roofless hovel. You have but to ask her. Did she not send for you this very evening - and it was not solely to let Alric and me be with Mother and Father alone."

"She wished to show me the harp she has been newly given. She plays it sweetly and it matches her voice marvellously too."

"Simpleton that you are. That was only the excuse to have you near her. Did no-one talk of weddings?"

"For sure and I was much confused by it."

"There you are then. Mary and Alwin think highly of you I know. Alric has told me as much. You have only to ask her. I will help you if you like for I would have you share my happiness."

"Oh Emma, you are sweet, but leave it be a little while yet. My mind is too confused and I must speak with Father first on several matters."

I sighed deeply and, leaning over, gave Emma an affectionate hug. She smiled back at me and bid me 'good-night', and wriggling down under her covers, was soon asleep, dreaming no doubt of her man. As for me, I lay awake turning things over in my mind. Yes, I thought, I must speak with Father as soon as possible.

Chapter 7 1092–1093

A week passed before I found opportunity to talk with Father. Until all the harvest was gathered none had time for gossip. All helped to gather the crops while the weather held, working till they could see no more and then were too exhausted to do aught else but throw themselves on their beds and fall into a dreamless sleep, knowing that dawn would come all too soon and they would have to be up betimes to continue in the fields.

It was always a critical time, for though the land was mostly good and yielded well, to miss a day's work and find that on the morrow it rained so that the crop was perhaps spoiled, could make the difference between plenty and the fear of hunger. A hard day's rain could flatten a crop so that it could not dry but would sprout in the ear where it lay.

For those who had to work on the demesne for several days each week, the risk was even greater. They would drag themselves out to their own land at the end of a hard day gathering the lord's harvest and then set about cutting and stooking their own. Eyeing the corn stacks, it seemed that the harvest was heavier than usual and most men seemed well content, though there were some who found fault even if it was only that there was too much to carry.

Our assart had yielded better than Father had expected and we had a full thirty-five bushels of emmer wheat stacked in our store beside the mill. The straw had proved good for thatching too and this was now piled against the end of the house, ready for use before the winter came. Seldom a year passed that we did not have to look to a few holes in the thatch, for birds would pull out strands of it for their nests and, thus loosened, the winter winds would quickly pull it apart if we did not attend to it.

Father and I were standing by the Bar Gate one evening after closing up the mill, watching the last of the carts bring in the final sheaves of the harvest.

"We shall have a full year's milling I am thinking," he said, "even without old Alsi's crops. Alwin was cunning to say he would store them and have them ground in the King's mill. Though ours is the loss the burgh will gain and sometimes that is more important. We shall not go short of work, I am thinking, and our crop is good too. I mean to grind and sell as much as I can this year to increase my hoard of silver. I shall perhaps have need of it with Emma being wed soon. I shall need to send her to Alric with a goodly marriage portion. Alwin is helping Alric generously and I must do the same for Emma. You would wish me to do that for your sister, Hugh, wouldn't you?"

"For sure, Father. I love her well and will miss her sorely when she goes, but she will have a position to uphold in the burgh as the wife of the bailiff's son. I have told Alric that I will help him repair the cott that they are to live in when I have the time. It has been empty these many years and needs much repair. Do you think we could spare some of the long straw we kept for thatching this year - that is if you do not have another use for it? Otherwise I will cut reeds from the beds over by the Twin Ditches, but it will take longer. I think our wheat-straw would last as long as the reeds for it is good and long. I would not suggest it otherwise."

"That is kindly said, Hugh, and a most generous offer. Such help will be the most thoughtful gift you could devise for them and I am sure they will welcome it. Assuredly you may use some of our wheat-straw for their thatch. You will not need it all I think, for there may be other uses for the rest of it before too long."

"How so? Have you a mind to rethatch our house? It seems sound enough in the main at the moment, or have I missed some fault?"

"Nay lad. Our house will keep out the weather for a few years yet I hope. It is elsewhere that it may be needed."

Father paused awhile, and seemed deep in thought before he continued.

"Tell me, Hugh, have you given thought to your own future? I have been observing you these last months in the mill and there is little if anything that I can teach you more about the work. You can set the stones as well as any and, when you grind it becomes the finest flour and of even texture such that no-one could fault, so that it commands the best price of any that is sold. Ranulf at the guest-house remarked on it particularly the last time I took him a load of flour. You could run your own mill if there was one available and you would not lack for custom. I can safely leave you to run our mill should I be away."

Father smiled at me and I felt a tingle of pride at his words. It was good to hear him thus voice his confidence in me.

"Likewise you have learnt much from Belesme and others about tilling the land. You can plough a straight furrow and cut a good swathe at harvest- time so that those who bind can gather it easily into stooks. You have also learnt to handle beasts and treat them kindly so that they work the better."

He put his hand on my shoulder then.

"It is good to have you with us in the house but there are lads younger than you who have left home and wed and become their own masters so far as maybe, serving their lord for the land they till. Do not mistake me, Hugh, we would not have you leave but we would not wish you to feel that you must stay if there were good reason for you to depart. You are a powerful lad and kindly too and there are few girls in the burgh that would not have you for a husband were you to ask them I am thinking. Have you no thoughts on that score, seeing that your sister is to wed soon? Your mother and I would be glad to see you settled, though we would miss you sorely as we shall miss Emma, but these things must be."

Father looked at me and smiled, encouraging me to unburden what was in my mind.

"You speak too highly of my skill I think. Any I have, has come from your teaching, but I am glad you think I have learnt your skills aright. Your encouragement has been a great help to me, and your patience when I have been careless. Nor have you clouted me when I have erred as so many would have done. That has made the lessons you wished to teach me the more lasting, for I know I have often deserved a beating for my stupidity though you never gave me one."

"That is not my way, Hugh. Beat an ass and he will not move and may even turn on you. Hold a carrot before him and he will bear almost any burden, and I think that you are somewhat better than an ass."

He smiled at me again as he said this and I felt a glow of warmth towards him, for it was true that Father had always found a way to encourage me in what I did, teaching me through kindness and understanding. It was the same with all three of us. Emma, Osbern and I had much to be thankful for.

"You have eased my mind indeed, Father, and I have been meaning to speak with you for I was not sure how you regarded my skill at milling. Indeed I would wed one day, but I could not take a wife till I was sure that I could care for her as I would wish and feed and house her too without fear of hunger."

"Well lad, you have the skills to earn a living and I would gladly let you have the assart we have cleared. It must measure half a virgate I think and it yields well too. There is more land that you can clear beside it when you have the time."

"Father, you have worked so long to bring that land under the plough, can you really bear to give it to me? I am sure I should not take it. It is too generous a gift and more than I deserve."

"Think not of it, Hugh. I had always thought that it would come to you one day and I have had pleasure working on it knowing that it would one day be of use to you. Besides, you have done more than your share of clearing the land and working it. When the time comes, remember that it will be yours. Is there perhaps a maid that takes your fancy?"

"I think you know there is, Father, though I have not asked her yet and cannot be sure that her father would give us his blessing. It is Isabel, Alric's sister. Do you think Alwin would welcome my suit?"

"Rest easy on that score. I have thought for some time that your interest in Isabel was more than just a passing fancy. I did touch on the matter with Alwin a few weeks back and he seemed well content with the prospect. She is a sweet lass and it would seem that she has eyes for none but you. Alwin would be well content should you decide to ask her if she would wed you. He and I are good friends and have the same ideas on many things. To join our two families thus closer together would give him as much pleasure as it would me. It would gladden your mother's heart too and also Mary's, though she will be loath to lose such a daughter. Have you given thought to where you would live? With Emma gone, you could have your present chamber to yourselves, for Osbern could sleep in the main part of our house. There is space enough for him there."

"'Tis kind of you Father, but I think we should see if there is some cott we could find where we could set up our own home. Isabel has been used to some comfort and I would not wish her to live any worse than she does now if there is aught I can do to prevent it. When Alric said he was going to repair Ernwi's cott, I went to view it as you know, having offered to help him repair it. There is another empty cott between it and our mill. Though it is but one room, it is dry, and there are about ten rods of land which are enclosed by the remains of a fence which ends at the burgh wall. Cedric the red-haired who went to fight with Duke Robert, lived there, but it is said that he was killed these three years past, and none has lived there since. As it is part of the King's land, I thought to speak to Alwin about it, if he will let me have Isabel's hand. We could live there when I have put it in order."

I waited a while to gauge Father's feelings and saw him nod approval.

"I had a mind to suggest that instead of payment in silver, I would agree to keep the burgh wall in good repair from the cott to the mill. I know there is always difficulty keeping it in good repair, for folk see no reason to trouble themselves with such work when we are at peace. As Belesme often says, it is when you let your guard down that you are most easy to attack. He does not trust this Flambard. I thought that it might please Alwin to know that at least part of the wall would be secure, the more so as few live on that side of the burgh at the moment and it more open to attack from the river. How think you, would Alwin agree to such a plan? The work on the wall would take little time, I think, and it would save me the pence I would have to pay else."

"I know the cott. It is small but could be made greater in time and it seems sound enough, though no doubt there will be some repair needed. A little thatching too, I think, but we have straw enough for that, even after you have helped Alric with his cott. It was this I had in mind when first I spoke. I cannot speak for Alwin but to have part of the burgh wall kept in good repair and someone watching over it would seem to make good sense. Do you mean to speak to Isabel soon?"

"I think so, yes. I must first clear some thoughts in my mind, for it is a step not lightly taken and I would be certain first that I can care for her as I would wish."

"Then I shall prepare the way a little with Alwin if you like. Will you speak of this to your mother this evening? She would be mightily pleased, I feel sure. It will please her too that you mean to stay close to us if you can have the cott you speak of. Delay not too long in speaking with Isabel. I think she pines a little for you and who could blame her!"

With that he clapped me on the shoulder, grinning broadly.

"Come, Master Hugh, let us home. Great things have been decided today and a horn of ale would not come amiss."

He turned then and together we walked through the burgh to our house, both of us with a light step.

Mother was seeing to the fowls when we returned, so I gave her my news there. She seemed overjoyed and started talking of a double wedding. I tried to calm her saying that Isabel had not yet agreed, but she would have none of it. Father calmed her eventually and we entered the house to drink to the future. There were but the three of us, for Emma was elsewhere with Alric, and Osbern was with his friends practising with the bow. I was anxious not to say too much or commit myself until I had had time to think over what Father had offered. His generosity had overwhelmed me and it opened up new prospects for me. With almost a virgate of land to till I could now be sure that I could provide some comfort for Isabel. As soon as I could, I rose saying that I was weary and would get to bed, for there was much to be done on the morrow.

There was no time during the week following for aught but work. We were busy in the mill all day, and when the grinding was done there was still work gathering fruits and bringing in a late cutting of hay from some pasture to provide winter feed for our beasts. Not till Mass on Sunday did I have a chance to see Isabel. I found myself standing near her and as we left I asked if she could show me her harp again and perhaps teach me to bring a tune from it.

"After my first efforts I would not have anyone near enough to hear lest they mock me. Shall we take our boat and go over to the Twin Ditches? We shall be safe from mocking ears and there would only be you to chide my poor efforts. Tis still warm and the sun should shine for the rest of the day if the lack of cloud means anything. I will bring food too so that if you can be ready shortly, we can be away before noon."

Isabel's eyes lit up.

"Give me time that I may change my robe from Mass and I will meet you by the mill where your boat is tied."

She turned and hastened away. My heart gave a leap too and I hurried home to gather food and some fruits and a flagon and made haste to prepare the boat. I did not have to wait long before Isabel came past the mill carrying her harp wrapped carefully in a cloth, for she prized it greatly. We set off then, for the Twin Ditches where all six of us had so often before spent many happy hours.

Time passed all too quickly. Isabel showed me how to hold the harp and bade me place my hands over hers to get the feel of the instrument. I tried to follow her slender fingers with my clumsy ones but made a poor showing, I thought. My cheek rested against her hair which oft-times would blow across my face so that she had to brush it away, stroking my cheek as she did so. We ate our meal and then sat musing, while she plucked a string ocasionally and sang a few snatches of some ballads she knew.

At length, I placed my hands over hers and looked into her eyes.

"Isabel, how many years have we known each other now?"

"Why do you ask, Hugh? I cannot remember a time when I did not know you. It seems that you have always been there and my life has been the happier for it. You do not think to leave I trust? That would break my heart." she said looking worried.

"Nay, that is far from my mind, but I did wonder if you cared for me perhaps a little."

She laid down her harp then and put her hands in mine.

"Surely you know that I do. Have I not always shared my thoughts with you and am I not always happy to be with you? You have been more than a brother to me these many years."

She bent forward and kissed my cheek.

I felt my heart give a leap and could scarcely find the words I wished so much to utter. At length, I summoned up my courage and, taking both her hands in mine, I knelt before her.

"Isabel, my love, do you think that you could wed me? I cannot offer you great wealth but I would try to care for you in comfort and would guard you with my life."

Her eyes shone at this and there seemed to be a small tear in their corners.

"Oh Hugh, how could you doubt that I would have you? See, my hands are once more between yours. Do you not remember the day you saved me from the waves? Afterwards you brought me to this very spot and after I had recovered a little, I placed my hands between yours then, and did you homage. I swore to myself then that I would follow you and serve you wherever you led. Did you not realise what I did that day? My life has been yours ever since. You had but to ask. I have waited so long for this moment, hoping that it would come. I know you to be careful and that you do not lightly undertake any matter. That is why I love you so, because I know that you would never let me down. My fear was that you would not think me worthy of you. Yes, dearest Hugh, I will wed you whenever you wish; my Love and my Lord."

With that we fell into each other's arms too overcome to speak. At length, when we had both recovered our composure a little, we kissed gently, savouring the moment of our deep content.

"What a numbskull I have been not to have asked you before," I breathed, "but I was afraid you would not think me good enough to wed the daughter of the bailiff. You are a lass of some importance in the burgh and I am but the miller's son though we have been friends these many years. Now at least I know the miller's art in all its forms and could run a mill myself. Father has also said that he will give me our assart so that we would have land of our own. It is not over-large but there is land beside it that we could use in time."

"I never doubted that you could run a mill yourself. Father has often said that the flour you mill is the best in the burgh, and he would gladly have you run the demesne mill for him. Where would you have us live? There is room in our house I think if you like. I could speak to Father and Mother about it. I am sure they would agree."

"I had thought to find a cott of our own. There is one that lies empty between our mill and the one that Alric and Emma mean to have. It is not over-large being but one room, though we could add more to it in time. It is sound and dry and needs only a little repair. Could you live there, do you think?"

"Oh Hugh, that would be wonderful. A cott of our own, and near to Alric and Emma and both our families. Could I keep fowls there and grow sweet herbs too?"

"There are about ten rods of land round the cott, which go down to the burgh wall. There is ample space for fowls and anything you would grow. I must speak to your father about it first for it belongs to the King as it is in the burgh. I must seek his blessing too if we wish to wed. Do you think he will agree?"

"Ninny that you are! Have I not told you that he thinks highly of you. He is waiting for you to ask for me and he has been growing anxious that you tarried so long. Mother will be overjoyed too. But what of your father and mother? They will welcome me I hope, as we have welcomed Emma?"

"Indeed yes; I must confess that they have been keen that I should press my suit and Emma will be well pleased, I know."

"I know, for she has confided in me."

We sat awhile close, feeling our love flow between us. Where we were in the shelter between the two great banks, flowers grew in profusion even at this late season. I rose and started to gather white and yellow blooms and a few blue cornflowers and, weaving them together, bound them into a circlet. Isabel lay watching me propped up on one elbow, while she twisted grass stems in her fingers. When I was done I came and kneeling before her, first stroked her fair hair back from her face and then placed the circlet on her brow so that it held her tresses in place. She smiled at that and I was overcome by her serenity and beauty.

"I would make you my queen," I whispered.

Taking my fingers, she kissed their tips and said, "My love, you shall always be my king."

Thus we passed some time and eventually rose, and then hand in hand walked towards the open sea and climbed to the top of the inner bank. The sun beat down warm on our faces as we looked first left, past the high hill of Hengist's headland to the white rocks that stand off the end of Vectis Isle like upturned spears; and then round over the waters to where the white cliffs of Purbeck's land reach up, still with the sun upon them, before it moved round to set behind them. Gulls flew overhead and other sea birds, their cries the only sounds to be heard above the continual washing of the small waves on the pebble beach below us. We stood in silence and at peace wondering at the glories of the sea and land before us, content to be alone with each other. At last Isabel turned towards me and throwing her arms about my neck, rested her cheek against my chest, and breathed a deep sigh of contentment.

"Oh Hugh, my Love and my Life. Would that we could stay here for ever like this, just the two of us."

I gently raised her chin and looked into her eyes. They seemed to be an even clearer blue than the cornflowers I had woven into the circlet she still wore about her hair. Smiling, I pressed light kisses on her face and hair.

"I know," I murmured, "would that we could and I shall remember this day always. Our forbears lived in security and peace here since before the legions came from Rome. It has always been a place of magic to me. Let us promise each other that if ever troubles befall us that we need to resolve alone together, that we will come to this spot where we can be in peace with naught but the sea, the sky and the wind, to clear our minds and find the answers."

Isabel pressed me close, looking into my eyes.

"I promise," she whispered. " Nothing can come between us when we are here and we shall hide no secrets from each other."

She raised her lips to mine and kissed me long and tenderly as we held the moment so that it should be fixed for ever in our minds. Though we should make other vows in the church, these we had made to each other in this lonely place, with only the birds as witness, would be as firmly held for the rest of our lives. We kissed once more and then, hand in hand, retraced our steps to where we had rested. Gathering up the remains of our meal, Isabel carefully wrapping her harp in the cloth that protected it, we made our way slowly back to the boat and so returned to the burgh.

As we approached the place where we kept the boat, Isabel reached for my hand.

"Would you show me the cott where we might make our home?"

I led her past our mill by the path that led to the cott. The door was closed but she lifted the latch and stepped inside. Crossing the floor, she opened the shutter that covered one window, letting in more light. Then she looked around, taking in all that there was to be seen. Though it was small, it was still clean and dry.

"Why, it is perfect. Look," she said, going to the window once more, "there are herbs growing in the garden and a bramble too with ripe fruit. We can be happy here. I do hope Father will agree to us having it."

I took her hand once more, and going out we carefully closed the door and continued towards the bailiff's house. Mary was sitting before the door spinning a fleece on her small stone spindle. As we approached she put it aside, looking at us quizzically. Noticing our happiness, she welcomed us both.

"Alwin is in the garden, Hugh, if you wish to speak with him. Come, Isabel, sit by me a moment and help me with this spindle. It is the one you use and has not the same weight as mine so that I have not found the best speed to spin it yet."

I thanked her, grateful for the excuse and passed through the house to find Alwin tending his vegetables. He looked up as I approached.

"How goes it, Hugh? Has Isabel taught you to play her harp yet? I think she said you were keen to learn."

"I have little skill yet, Master Alwin, though she is a ready teacher."

I paused awhile, thinking how best to frame my words.

"If you have the time to spare, I would speak with you if I may."

"Why surely. Is it something of moment on which you would have my advice? I will do what I can."

"Not advice so much as permission. You know that Isabel and I have long been friends. In fact I cannot remember a time when we have not played together along with Emma, Alric and the others. I have given much thought to the matter and, if I may, I would wed Isabel and seek your blessing."

Alwin turned, looking at me full square and his face lit up in a broad smile. Then he clapped both his hands on my shoulders.

"Why, Hugh, most gladly will I do so. I was beginning to think that you would never ask. Isabel is a sweet girl and though Mary and I will be most loath to lose our only daughter, if we have to do so there is no man I would rather see her wed than you. With your sister Emma and Alric to wed as well, it seems that our two families are to be securely joined for the benefit of them both. I think your father will approve too, for he has spoken of it in general terms to me. It seems that you have decided to undertake more than learning the harp this day. Come, let us go and join Mary and Isabel and tell them the good news. This calls for a horn of wine too I think. Mary," he called as he led the way into the hall, "come and join us and bring Isabel too. We have great news. I am drawing wine, for we must celebrate."

Mary and Isabel came in then and Isabel flew to her father and flung her arms round his neck.

"Has he told you, Father? Hugh would wed me. You will give us your blessing won't you."

"Hush child, you take my breath away. Have I ever been able to refuse you anything? Most gladly will I give you both my blessing. You were made for each other, I think. My wonder is that you have taken so long to decide."

I saw that his eyes twinkled and thanked him inwardly that he was making light of it for me. Filling the horns he had brought, Alwin said, "We must drink a full toast to your great happiness."

I reached for Isabel's hand and held it tightly while she smiled at me.

"Now, Hugh, have you any plans yet of how you will live and where? After all, Isabel is the bailiff's daughter and will expect some comfort, no doubt," he jested, "or we could find room for you here if you desire."

"Father, I am no great lady to be pampered. I would live wherever Hugh desires, but he has some plans for us already I think, haven't you Hugh?"

"As for how we would live, I can continue at the mill with Father, or take one of my own if there were a place. Father says that he has taught me all he knows and that I know the skills almost as well as him. He has told me too that he will let me work our assart. It is nigh on half a virgate and yields well. As to where we would live, you are generous in your offer for us to live here with you but, if possible, Isabel would rather have a cott of our own. There is an empty cott between our mill and the place where Emma and Alric mean to live. It is small but has some rods of land round it and could be made bigger later if need be. It was the home of Cedric the red-haired, he that was killed while fighting for Duke Robert these three years back. It is dry still and needs some small repair only. Being in the burgh, I suppose it belongs to the King and so I must render payment to you for it. The land goes down to the burgh wall and I had in mind that I might do service instead. It is nigh on half a furlong from our mill to the cott. I would keep that part of the wall well repaired if I may have the cott. It is not always easy to find men to keep the walls repaired, so it seemed that this might be a help to you."

"Father, please say yes. Hugh showed me the cott as we were coming here, and it is perfect. It is clean and dry and there are herbs growing already in the land, and a bramble and other fruits."

Alwin exchanged glances with Mary and then looked at Isabel, his face creasing into a smile.

"What can I say against such pleading? It sounds a good bargain for the King. I know the cott, and it is well built, or it would have fallen into decay 'ere now. Your offer of repairing the burgh wall is good too, Hugh. It is something that I might persuade others to do. I must speak to Alric about it for his cott is hard by the one you speak of. It could be that between the pair of you, you could maintain the wall as far as the Canon's Gate. It is not much above a furlong I think. It would be good to know that the wall on that side was well cared for. Though we have no reason to fear attack at present, yet we must be ever watchful. Duke Robert might return one day and try to claim the throne from his brother, though I think that he would have little support, for all the red-headed William's faults."

He paused in thought for a moment.

"Have you thought when you would wed yet?"

"Not before we have had time to put the cott in order. Beside, I have already promised that I will help Alric and Emma repair their home and it is in need of new thatch. Father has said that we may use the straw we cut this year from our assart. It is straight and long and will last as long as the reeds we could cut from across the river. To use the straw will save time cutting and carrying the reeds. Nothing is settled yet I think, but do they not think to wed about Whitsuntide or perhaps midsummer?"

"They have said something to that effect," said Mary. "Isabel, have you any thoughts on that score?"

"If our cott can be ready in time, could we perhaps be wed the same day? It would be a great thing in the burgh, I think," said Isabel. "Besides, Emma is my greatest friend and it would please me greatly to be wed the same day as her. I think she would like it too."

She looked towards me questioning.

"Emma would surely like that," I said. "I think the work can be completed by then if all else can be arranged, but we must speak with Alric and Emma, and also Godric the priest."

Thus we made plans, which would have to be discussed with others before they could be made final. At length, I rose to take my leave. Though I was loath to leave Isabel, I was anxious to tell them at home my news. Isabel came with me to the door and we lingered a little outside before finally parting, with a promise that I would see her next evening when work was done at the mill. I hastened home then and found them all seated round the table. Great was their pleasure at my news and they heard our plans with interest.

"What! Two moon-faces in one family. We shall never get anything done now," teased Osbern, for which I caught him a cuff about his ear.

As we readied ourselves for bed, Emma came and sat beside me. "I am so happy for you, Hugh, and I know Isabel loves you dearly. If we can wed the same day, it would make it the happiest day in my life."

She gave me a warm hug, and we each slipped beneath the covers of our beds, my thoughts being with Isabel and hers with Alric.

It was a month or so later that two ships came up to the quay beside the mill and tied up. Father saw them approach first and remarked that he suspected them to be the ships Flambard said he would send to load the grain from Alsi's fields, and so it proved. The captain of the first, an uncouth Norman, strode up to the church and demanded Godric. He was away visiting Holdenhurst at the time, checking the tithe. Ranulf, who kept the guest-house, came out to see what was afoot when he heard the captain's voice raised.

"Pax vobiscum," he said, "Would you drink a mug of ale after your voyage?"

"There is no time for that. Where is Godric your priest? I have come with Flambard's orders to load the grain from the fields of Alsi the priest, which my master now owns. Show me where it is that I may have my men start loading it. There is no time to be lost, for your harbour is shallow and I would not find my ships stranded and have to wait for the next high tide. I know you have a strange double tide in these parts such as I have never seen elsewhere, which is why I came in as soon as there was water enough for my ships to clear the bar. Besides, it was easier to enter on the rising tide. I mean to leave before the second high tide falls away, so that there are not many hours for us to work. Look lively then, Priest, and show me where the grain is stored. Flambard himself will be here before the tide turns to see how much we have to load. He comes by horse from Winchester, I think."

Ranulf hurried along with the captain, explaining Godric's absence as he went. All morning the sailors went back and forth from the store to the ships loading the heavy sacks. Father and I watched them occasionally from the mill but we were too busy with our own work to pay them much attention.

It was some time after our midday meal that news came that Flambard had entered the burgh and the captain had met him. Later, I had to go to discuss some business with Geoffrey the reeve. As I entered the market square, I saw Flambard approach on his horse. His face showed his anger and he was berating the captain and Ranulf from the guest-house.

"What means this? You say there is not enough grain to fill more than the one ship? How so, since he has three virgates under the plough? Would you steal my corn, Priest? You shall answer for it in my court if so."

"My Lord, it is not so. There is some grain stored still at Bashley which no doubt you will claim but there are only two serfs and a villein and a bordar who work the land. It is not enough to gather in all his harvest."

"Then how did he fare in past years?"

"Other priests helped him and many men in the burgh received absolution for their sins by working on his land."

"Then why has this not happened this year too?"

"The priests have had work of their own to do, my Lord, and the men of the burgh have been busy with their own harvests which have been heavier than usual. Besides, many have been working more on the demesne for their Lord the King."

At that moment I spied an old bent woman entering the square pulling a small hand-cart loaded with sacks of grain, behind which struggled a small child who was trying to help push. It was old Meg, a poor widow whose man had died long since, and whose daughter had died in child-bed while the husband had been killed fighting , so that she was left to bring up the child herself . She scraped a bare living and it had been a great blessing to her that she had been able to gather so much by gleaning in the fields. Father had agreed to grind her corn on the morrow for there was a gap in our work for a few days. If I knew aught of Father he would charge her but half the usual amount for grinding, for we all helped Meg and those like her in their trouble when we could. Flambard saw the small procession out of the corner of his eye too. Tugging his horse savagely round, he rode towards her.

"Whose corn is that you carry? No hag like you can rightly have so much. You have stolen it, no doubt, and I warrant that came it from my fields too."

"Sir, it is honestly come by, I swear. I did glean it from Alsi's fields this harvest-time along with others. Any man will tell you 'tis the truth. Ask this priest Ranulf here. He will vouch for me."

"Alsi's fields you say. Then it is stolen indeed, for those fields are mine now and have been since the old fool died. Get you gone you hag before I ride you down."

Flambard dug his heels into his horse's flank to spur it at the old woman. Before the horse had taken but a step, there was a flash of yellow and gold and a woman's voice crying, "Hold. Would you ride down a defenceless widow who has done you no harm?"

Turning, I was astonished to see Isabel tugging at Flambard's reins, her face flushed and eyes flashing in anger.

"Let go my horse you Saxon whore," he bellowed, and aimed a blow at her head with his gloved fist. Her arms flew up to protect her head from the blow, but the horse shied away so that the blow went wide.

"Would you strike me then and you a priest? Saxon I am proud to be, but abuse me not. My father is bailiff of this burgh, and answers only to my Lord the King, as you will too if you harm this widow."

All in the square were stunned to silence. As for Isabel, she was shaking with anger. Ranulf was the first to recover.

"It is true what the widow says my Lord. She did truly glean this grain with others from Alsi's fields, as was her right. This you were told last time you were here if you recall. You would not deny that ancient right, I trust. If you take these sacks she will have no other food this winter and she and the child will likely die. Would you, a priest, have that upon your conscience? I pray you let her be for you have food enough and to spare, I'll warrant."

The raised voices had brought others to the square, including Godwine the huge priest. He strode forward with anger in his eyes that he seemed scarcely able to contain. Elbowing his way between Flambard, whose horse still hoofed the ground in some fright, and Ranulf his fellow priest, he made straight to where the widow Meg cowered, clutching her granddaughter to her. Telling them to seek sanctuary in the church, he picked up the handle of the cart. Turning, he glared in defiance at Flambard and strode off rapidly towards our mill with the cart and its sacks behind him, growling under his breath.

Alwin too had heard the commotion and had come out of his house to see what was amiss. Hearing Isabel's cry, and seeing her anger, he too strode forward, brows clouded with anger, to confront Flambard. I hurried to Isabel's side but not before Alwin had called out:

"How now, Master Flambard. What means this disturbance in our burgh? If you have aught to complain of speak your mind to me. You shall strike no-one unless you wish to answer for it before the Shire Court of my Lord the King. I will not have the peace disturbed here."

Flambard was visibly taken aback at such a show of fortitude and reined in his horse as best he might, for it was still inclined to prance and might well kick out in its fright and injure one of those who still stood near. He seemed to be an indifferent horseman. At length, he calmed the horse and himself too.

"Ah, Master Bailiff if I mistake not," he said, controlling his voice with difficulty. "There are matters that need explaining. I come to collect my corn as I promised and find there is scarce enough to fill one ship. Moreover, it seems that I am being robbed of wheat which is rightly mine by all the serfs and other wretches who laze about in this burgh of yours. What have you to say to that?"

"My Lord Flambard, you are mistaken I fear. When last you were here I told you that those who would glean might do so. Would you deny them this right on your land then? It would be against all custom if you did. Your crop was thin this year for there were few to gather it. The priests gathered what they could but the rest was left for the gleaners. No doubt they will heap blessings on your head. Besides, the demesne of the King required extra labour this year, that all might be gathered in for him. I hear that his needs are greater than before since he would feed those that go to fight with him. Would you deny your King?"

Flambard saw that he was trapped again and, having none to support him in the crowd but the captain of the ship who was on foot and unarmed, thought better than to risk pressing his poor claim. He turned his horse once more and began to ride back towards the quay, the captain at his side.

"Mark my words Master Bailiff, you have not heard the last of this, nor you, Priest. You say your name is Ranulf? So is mine and I shall not easily forget you. Tell that priest of yours Godric that I am dean of the church here now and it is I who say how the crops are to be disposed of. Henceforth you priests shall have no more than a fixed allowance. All else shall come to me. I shall send my clerk to make a tally of all that you have so that I may know more readily what is mine. You, Master Bailiff, mark well my words and see that that idle priest Godric understands what is my will, or it will be the worse for all of you."

With that he spurred his horse and clattered out of the square, the captain following and shaking his head as he went. It seemed he liked what he had seen as little as the rest of us.

Meanwhile, I had gained Isabel's side and putting my arm around her, held her close, for she still trembled. I was confounded, for I had never seen her in such a rage before, and the courage she had shown in confronting Flambard amazed me, as well as all others. By the time Flambard had left the square she was composed again, and smoothing down her yellow tunic beneath the blue girdle which held at her waist, she placed her hand upon my arm.

"I could not stand idly by and see that brute ride down poor Meg. What harm has she ever done to anyone? I was just coming out of our house to fetch some water when I saw Flambard spur his horse at her. I know not what came over me that I could run so fast, but I had to stop him and he would have thought nothing of his horse trampling the child underfoot too. He cannot properly control the beast, it seems. Oh Hugh, did I do wrong?"

"My dearest love, I caught but a glimpse of you as you flew in front of the horse and your courage amazed us all and put us all to shame. I was too slow to act. I feared for you too when I saw what you did, for this Flambard is overly powerful. It was good that your father came out when he did or it might have gone hard with you. I see that I must keep close by you and take good care of you if you are to play the heroine in this way."

I pressed her to me then and she smiled a little wanly.

"Come, let me take you to your house," I murmured.

"Please Hugh, if you will, I think I must sit awhile. He will not return, will he ?" she asked anxiously.

"Not for the moment, I think, but he will surely send his clerk as he has promised, then the priests will have troubles. This burgh is well-known for its charity and miracles, but if travellers and the poor cannot be fed then few will come."

Entering the bailiffs house, we found Mary busy in the kitchen for she had heard none of what had befallen. She looked startled to see Isabel so pale but I explained what had happened and apart from scolding her, more in fright than anger, Mary soon regained her composure. I left Isabel with her and continued on my interrupted errand.

The news of what had occurred spread like fire, and when Godric returned from Holdenhurst he called a council of all the chief men of the burgh to discuss how best to prepare ourselves against the arrival of Flambard's clerk. So plans were laid that the priests might still be able to dispense their charity. It was good that we had such a one as Godric to lead the priests. Though Flambard might be dean and therefore had authority over them all, yet if he were absent Godric could still manage things as before. Besides as he said, he could always appeal to the Bishop Walkelin at Winchester who, it seemed, had little love for Flambard.

The months slipped quickly by for there was more than usual to occupy my time. My promise to Alric had to be kept and it took all the free days I could find over that autumn and winter to help him put his cott in order.We rethatched the roof before the worst of the weather came, but it was February before we could look to the inside. The partitions between the main room of the house and the two small chambers had to be replaced for the wattle had rotted with the damp and age. We had to cut new hazel stems to weave into the wattle partitions. That was a skill neither Alric nor I had to any great extent and our first attempts proved useless, but we managed it at last.

When the wattles were in place, I left him to mix and apply the daub himself. He had an ample supply of earth and there was plenty of dung in the yard where the demesne beasts were stalled for the winter. It is a mucky task mixing daub, for the only way to make a good mix is to throw the dung into the clay pit, add sufficient water and then tread it thoroughly. That done, the stinking mix has to be applied by hand to the wattles. Though Alric is a good friend there was a limit to my friendship for him. To have to stink like a sty for days on end stretched matters too far. Alric agreed. He would refuse such a request from me likewise, he said, as he stood up to his knees in mud and dung with the horse-flies buzzing round his head. Every time he tried to brush them away with his hand he left another streak of filth across his cheek. I twitted him on this and he aimed a clod of stinking pig muck at my head grinning as he did so. I ducked in time and it went wide landing at the feet of Flambard's clerk who happened to be passing at that moment. He scowled at us.

Flambard had been true to his word and sent his clerk, one Francis by name, to supervise the running of the church lands. He brought a message with him from Flambard that no priest would be appointed to fill Alsi's place and that all the benefit from his lands would go to Flambard.We learnt from Godric that Francis was to limit the offerings that were made at the altars of several chapels. But we saw little sign of this and it seemed that Godric had been able to persuade Francis that if he were to do so there would be little benefit, for the men of the burgh would give less so that Flambard would gain no benefit either way.Francis saw the sense of this, for if the priests received less they could assist the poor and hungry less, so that Flambard would have to provide for them himself. In this way no-one would benefit, so a compromise was reached. Besides, much of the fame of the burgh came from its generosity to travellers and pilgrims who came on account of the various miracles that were said to be performed locally. Certainly many were healed of their ailments in ways that none seemed able to explain. Also Flambard's wealth from the church grew and there was increasing talk that his plans for a new and massive church in the burgh were well advanced.

Once my promise to Alric had been fulfilled, I was able to turn to the cott that Isabel and I were to have. She had not been idle and had cleared the land, persuading her young brother Alnoth to help her. Osbern had fallen under Isabel's spell too and had done his share of the clearing for which I was truly grateful, for there was much to do.

It was not until spring had come that we were able to start on the repairs that the cott needed. These turned out to be less than we feared at first, though there were a few holes in the walls where they had been poorly built in the first place. It was Alric's turn to chide me for I had to undergo the indignity of mixing the daub to fill the gaps. I was somewhat more sympathetic towards him when I had spent a whole day at the task and found that though I bathed thoroughly in the river, I could not rid myself of the odour for most of a week. By then it was time to repeat the task on the next part of the cott. So bad was the stink that I felt constrained to sleep not in our chamber but in the main room of the house, as far as I could be from the others. Emma twitted me by always holding a posy of herbs to her nose when I came near. Indeed it was necessary to have bunches of lavender and rosemary in the house to try to overcome the odour.

For the most part I was kept outside the house out of regard for the others. Everyone was glad when the task was completed. I could then kiss Isabel without her having to hold her nose. It made me understand how lepers must feel when Osbern offered me a bell one warm day when the stink was particularly strong, for none would willingly come near me.

Once the walls were firm, Isabel and I were able to paint them with limewash. I paid Osbern a silver penny to help carry and mix the lime and aid us with putting it on. By the time we had finished all three of us were so splashed with white that it was hard to recognise us. I thanked Osbern for his help.

"'Tis nothing,"he said. "Isabel deserves a well-found cott to live in and I could not have my brother dwell in a hovel with her. I did it for her sake."

Isabel leaned towards him and kissed him in thanks. Osbern looked discomfited. He mumbled something and shuffled his feet but I could see that he was pleased.

"Well, I will leave you lovelorn twain to yourselves. For myself, I shall strip and plunge into the water below the mill and rid myself of this mess. If whiteness means purity then there can surely not be a single sin amongst us three."

He turned and gathering up the buckets set off whistling. I looked at Isabel.

"We are in a sorry state as well. Shall we bathe and clean ourselves in the river? We can scale the wall at the end of our land with the ladder we have been using and then make our way through the reeds to the river. It is away from prying eyes too."

While I fetched the ladder Isabel gathered up our clean clothes, for we had been wearing little more than rags for the work we had been doing. Climbing the earth wall at the foot of our land, I placed the ladder against the timber palisade which surmounted it and helping Isabel up pulled the ladder up and dropped it over so that we might descend. It was little more than a hundred paces to the water's edge where it formed a small bay before curving round towards the quay. The sparse reeds screened us but allowed us to pass easily. Reaching the water's edge Isabel was the first to strip off her stained rags. Stepping lightly to the grassy bank she stood facing the sun, passing her hands through her flowing hair.

"How I love to feel the cool air on my skin after our sweating labour," she said as she drew in a deep breath, sighing contentedly.

As I gazed at her against the sun with her hair making a golden halo about her head, I was overcome by her beauty and purity in her nakedness. I felt my manhood stir and my desire for her near overwhelmed me. I knew her wish to enter our marriage bed a virgin so, putting aside such thoughts, I gazed at her awhile longer in love. At length she turned and held out her hand to me.

"Come," she said, "take my hand lest I miss my footing. We must find deep water where we may wash."

We stepped into the river together and both let out an unwilling gasp for it was fresher than we had thought. We helped each other to cleanse away the clinging lime rubbing our hair and bodies till all was clean. Thus refreshed, we clambered out and lay awhile drying our bodies in the warm sun, lazily watching a heron stalking its prey in the slowly moving water. Meantime we dressed and gathering up our lime-stained rags wandered back the way we had come hand-in-hand. As we descended the inside of the earth wall, I paused to examine some part-rotted posts that projected from the high weeds.

"Isabel," I said, "look, there was a hut here once, I think. See how the nettles grow. 'Tis a sure sign that there were fowls here for there are always nettles in profusion where they have been kept."

"Could we build a shelter for fowls here too? I would have some if I may for I shall need eggs in plenty for cooking."

"Surely. I have to repair some posts on the wall which are too weak and while I am about that I will cut others for a shelter for the fowls."

"Could you make another beside it for a sow too? I mean to have some sows and raise a litter or two as soon as maybe for they will provide us with better meat than most other we are like to come across. There will be no shortage of feed from the sweepings from the mill floor for both fowls and sows."

"You will have us eating better than Flambard's clerk, Francis. Take care we do not grow to his size too, glutton that he is."

I paced out the spot to see if there was space enough.

"We can house both fowls and sows easily enough, the more so if I make the shelter against the earth wall. It will mean less building and give them better shelter from wind and rain. How like a girl," I teased. "Just when you think that you have done all that she desires, she devises some further scheme. Will my trials never cease?"

She threw her arms around my neck.

"That is what a husband is for," she whispered in my ear, "to do a lady's bidding. Or do you not love me enough for that? Perhaps I shall not wed you after all."

"Then 'tis true," I played along with her, "I saw you looking lustfully at that

Francis yesterday; you would wed him then? You will need no silken cushion when you recline against his great bulk. Will my lady still deign to cast me a crust as she rides by on her milk-white palfrey?"

"I might, but only for the love I have for his sister Emma who shall be my serving-maid, and he would have to grovel at my feet first." She held me close then and whispered, "The very thought of that man makes me shudder. How many days still before we wed?"

"Ascension Day is but a week from now and Pentecost falls ten days later, so it is less than three weeks. I am so pleased that Emma and Alric are to be wed the same feast-day. It is hard to wait but there is still much to do. We must all four meet soon to see that we have all things planned."

We closed the door of our cott soon after and parted, each to our own houses.

The days till our joint wedding passed quickly enough and Pentecost, which came not till mid-June that year, was soon upon us. The burgh was full of gossip and jollity at the thought of a more than usually merry feast day. Alwin had promised that he would provide a young ox to be roasted in the market square that all might share in the feasting. Father was providing more than enough of the best wheat flour to make honey cakes and white loaves for everyone. The ale-taster had given the best brewers instructions that they must have their finest ale only, and no watering down, as was often their custom on feast-days, when men tended to drink more than was good for them, caring not what quality it was. News of the happening had spread it seems, for it was rumoured that mummers would be in the burgh for the feast, besides some who could play the pipe and tabor.

So it turned out to be. Emma and Alric, and Isabel and I were wed by Godric after High Mass at Pentecost, and there was scarce room for all who would see us joined. Emma wore a robe of green which made her auburn hair glow like fire. As for Isabel, she was attired in a long robe of palest blue, held at the waist by a golden girdle. In her flowing hair she had flowers, blue and yellow and white, so that I was overwhelmed by the sight of it when she entered the church on the arm of her father. Indeed there was a gasp which echoed round the whole church as they entered.

We made our vows, each to the other, as couples had done in this place these two hundred years and more, with almost the whole burgh as our witnesses.

Tables had been set up in the market square outside Alwin's house where all could sit and feast on the ox that roasted in the centre of the square. We sat amidst our two families, watching and enjoying it all. Many brought the four of us small gifts, something they had made perhaps or else something needful for our cott. Walter the falconer brought us each cunningly made snares for catching game birds without harming them, and Goodwife Adeline brought us each a basket of remedies. As she put her gift into my hands, she looked into my eyes.

"You have chosen well, Hugh. Some years ago I bade you treat her gently for she was but a tender plant then. Guard her well now for she knows not how to be unkind to any man. She has an inner strength you may yet be unaware of that you may find you can lean on in your hour of need. Keep these simple remedies by you and when you both have time, come to me and I will show you their best uses; and may the Lord bless you both with the children you desire."

We both thanked her for her gift and I noticed that Isabel put it close by her, resting her hand constantly upon it. So the day wore on. When all had eaten their fill, first the mummers came out and kept us all in a high state of mirth. Then there was dancing to the pipe and tabor, and as the light began to fade so torches were lit and set about the square. At length, when it was quite dark and the older folk began to drift away, the four of us rose, and to the raucous guffaws of our friends and other lads and girls, we made our ways to our two cotts. As we did so I noticed Mary and Mother slip away, and when at last we reached our door I knew why. For as I lifted our latch there shone a warm glow from within where they had lighted tapers to welcome us to our new home.

As we turned to face those who had accompanied us thus far, Isabel put up her hands to her hair and, drawing out some of the flowers that formed her circlet, she threw them into the air for them to be caught by the waiting girls. Then amid their cries of delight and shouts from the lads, we turned and entered our home together and closed the door. We stood awhile in silence till those outside drifted away, and peace and tranquillity settled upon us. Smiling, I took Isabel in my arms and we stood savouring the first moments of our future life together. Someone - I know not who - had strewn sweet smelling herbs about our bed and placed others upon the pillow. Tenderly I led Isabel to our marriage bed.

We were not the first to be abroad next day and there were many who had thick heads after the feasting. Emma and Alric too were long in appearing and were the butt of as much nudging and winking from our friends as we were.

Life soon settled down however, and we were busy enough. The work at the mill had to be done and I had to see to the assart Father had given me.

Chapter 8 1093

The first harvest after Isabel and I were wed was gathered before Flambard came to the burgh again. We imagined it was to make sure that the crops he claimed were safely in. However, he brought with him this time a stranger of middle years, who by his bearing seemed knowledgeable. This man had with him a spare horse in whose panniers were bundles of parchments. Summoning Alwin and the other chief men of the burgh, and calling Godric to fetch a table, Flambard had the stranger spread the parchments out for all to see.

"This is what I mean to build here," cried Flambard. "A church such as you have never seen before and the like of which does not exist in this land. I shall build it and it shall be my church for I shall be its dean, as I am dean of this wretched place now. It is for this that I require the silver I raise from your church lands. Will it not be magnificent? It will be the tallest church in the country and I mean it to be seen from miles around so that all who pass near may wonder at it. Now I need to find the best place to build it."

We were all too astonished to speak. Those that could understand the drawings on the parchments looked at them with awe. We could not tell how big it would be, but by its many arches it would far outstrip our present church. As for its height, it seemed to reach almost to the sky for it had no less than three sets of arches, one above the other. Flambard stood enjoying the effect he had on us, before sweeping up the parchments and thrusting them at his companion.

"This man is Odo of Bec. It is he who has drawn these plans and will oversee the building of my church. He has done like things in France but none so great as I intend to build, is that not right, Master Odo?"

Odo nodded in agreement and replied with an accent that was foreign to us as he rolled up the parchments and returned them to the panniers.

"Now, Master Odo, we must away and seek the best place to build my church. That hill that lies some two miles to the north-west seems to be the highest place. We will ride there and see if it will suit. I would have my church seen from the sea too, that mariners may steer by it and give thanks for my foresight in giving them a landmark. I care not to have my church set on such a lowly site as now you use. It would be an insult."

Thereupon he jumped into his saddle and clattered out of the churchyard, while Odo struggled to mount and follow after him. As for the rest of us, we were left dumb-struck. To have a new and magnificent church would be a wonderful thing and bring fame to the burgh and prosperity too, but what did Flambard mean about a new site? To build it upon the hill of Catherine, a good two miles outside the burgh where no-one lived and where no tracks went, seemed foolish and to spell disaster. Did he mean to move the whole burgh?

We did not have to wait long for the answer, for before evening, Flambard and Odo had returned. He rode straight through the Bar Gate on his mud-spattered horse and dismounted outside the Alwin's house, seemingly in high good humour.

"How now, Master Bailiff, a horn of wine if you please. I am dry from so much riding. The place I thought to build my church will do very well. I cast my eyes all round from the hilltop and could see for many miles. It was clear, and the King's forest stood out to the east, and the two rivers that run north were plain to see. Vectis Isle stands out and perhaps I can even see some of the church land I have there. I must check with my clerk when I return to Winchester. All to the south is the sea, and my church will be a better beacon than I had hoped for sailors who pass between Vectis rocks and those of Purbeck. It is magnificent. Who will be able to forget me now?"

He slapped his thigh with pleasure and drained his horn of wine in a single draught, grinning with pride and pleasure as he did so.

"Now, Odo, you must set about ordering stone and arranging for it to be carried up my hill. I want as much stone brought as possible before the winter comes and the tracks we shall have to make become impassable in the mud. The foundations can be dug once we cannot move stone. My ships will bring the stone to the quay and you, Bailiff, will see to it that men and carts are provided to carry it up the hill. How is it called? Catherine's hill do you say? My clerk will see to the payment of the men and it shall be by the full load so that it will not serve if they try to be idle. I know you Saxons of old, how you try to cheat us, but you will discover that Ranulf is not called Flambard for naught. I am a flaming torch which lights up all manner of idleness and schemes, so take heed. I mean to have this church built soon for I have yet other fish to fry. See to it, Bailiff, that you do not cross me. Odo, how soon do you think that you can have the first of the stone arriving?"

"That depends, my Lord. Is it to come from Vectis, Caen, or perhaps Chilmark? A month perhaps or six weeks maybe, depending on the wind and tides too and how much is already cut in the quarries. Rest assured I will see to it that there is no delay. Masons we shall not need till the spring, I think, when all the frosts have gone. These I will find for they must be men I know and trust for their skill. Who is to dig the foundations when the winter comes, my Lord? Do you wish me to use men of the burgh?"

"That would seem wise, for they will know the place well enough by then, having carted the stone, and it will mean that they are not standing idle, They can be switched from one task to the other as you think fit. I will leave those matters in your hands. As for the masons you require, we will speak more of that later. There is time enough for that."

Flambard turned once more to Alwin.

"Are my orders clear, Bailiff? You should have no difficulty in finding men enough, I'll warrant. There seem always to be plenty of idlers standing round whenever I come into this burgh. I wonder you prosper as you seem to do, so see to it that there are men enough for my needs."

With that Flambard turned on his heel, and vaulting into his saddle, spun his horse round and spurred forward.

"Expect the first shipload of stone within four weeks," he called over his shoulder. "Be sure to have enough men ready and be sure that they are all strong too, for the captain will want it unloaded before the next tide."

The speed with which all this had happened left everyone speechless and dumbfounded. There was much head-scratching amongst the men of the burgh. Some who found it hard to scrape a living, for their labour was poor and they themselves feckless, saw an opportunity to earn some pence, though no doubt they would spend them soon enough in the ale-houses. Others who cared not for the church, finding its rules fitted ill with their lives, for attending Mass meant less time spent in their fields, were content that Flambard's proposed church should be built two miles distant. They reasoned that they could not be expected to walk the four miles there and back to attend the Mass, so that they would count themselves excused. As Godric pointed out, Godwine the priest at Stanpit walked more than twice that distance to say Mass every week in the chapel near Bashley which had been Alsi's.

It was a few days later when Isabel and I were taking a stroll in the cool of the evening after our supper, that we stopped at Alwin's door. We entered as we heard voices and Isabel was keen to ask her mother's help on some dish she would prepare and of which she did not have the receipt. Entering, we found Father, Godric and Belesme sitting at the table with Alwin, seemingly deep in worried converse. While Isabel sought her mother, I joined them at the table. Their talk was about this new church and all it would mean to the burgh. I had taken but one pull at the pot of ale handed to me when Alric and Emma entered too, for they had been enjoying the evening air likewise. Drawing up a stool, Alric joined us, while Emma went to seek out Mary, who at that moment appeared with Isabel, bearing platters of honey cakes. Belesme was the first to greet her.

"Ah Mary, you know my weakness. I can never refuse your baking, and your honey cakes melt in the mouth."

The women joined us at the table. While we savoured Mary's delicacies Godric continued.

"This new church Flambard means to build will surely mean the end of our church here in the burgh. As I see it, we priests will have to move to Catherine's hill and build new dwellings there that we may serve the church, but who will come to it? No man lives upon the hill for good reason. There is no water there and it is open to the wind and rain, so that those that try to live there will be driven out by the cold and wet. No man in his right mind would think to dwell there, and no priest would last more than a winter before the ice entered his bones as he said the night-time Offices. Nor would any traveller seek shelter there for like reason. I would try to persuade the people to go there to the Mass, but many would find excuses. What of the sick, how could they reach the place? Simon our infirmarer would lose most of his patients in winter time, and even in summer many who would go to him to be treated for their ailments would find the two mile journey too far, even before they had climbed its height. I calculate it must be almost 200 feet above the rivers that flow each side of it. All that he tries to do would be brought to naught."

"What of the children?" enquired Mary, "they would find it hard to make such a journey too."

"There is no track up Catherine's hill as yet," said Belesme. "The road that leads from the Bar Gate to Herne passes by the foot of the hill where it runs close to the Stour river. To make a path for men to climb the hill would not be hard, but what of carrying the stone? That would need a gentle slope if oxen and carts are to mount it. The ground is soft if I remember right and would be turned to mire at the first rain and quickly become impassable, so that the oxen would slide back and the carts most likely spill their loads. It would seem that Flambard has made problems for himself that he did not reckon on."

"Odo thinks the ground may be firm enough to build upon when you are at the top," said Alwin, "but how big is this church to be? If I remember the plan aright, it would stretch across the whole hilltop if it faces the way all churches must. There would be a danger then that each end would fall. No-one knows how heavy such a building would be, and surely if the hill is made of gravel, it would slide beneath the weight so all the work would be wasted."

Heads nodded in agreement and we sat silent for a while, pondering the problems Flambard had set himself and the seeming stupidity of it all. Alwin refilled our ale-mugs, while we felt that life in the burgh was soon to be disturbed in a way that none of us wished. Indeed it crossed my mind that our burgh, which had stood for so long, might soon become a ruin, and a new one built in a far worse place, with none of its present advantages of defence and trade; and for what?

I felt Isabel stir beside me, and she looked round at the solemn men who sat about the table.

"For what purpose is this church to be built?" she asked. "Is it to the greater glory of God or the greater glory of Flambard, for he seems to be overbearingly proud and ambitious."

All heads turned towards her as she spoke, and several showed clearly that such a thought had not yet occurred to them. Godric was the first to speak.

"Isabel," he said, "I think that you have gone to the heart of the matter. We have been thinking about the difficulties of such a building, but you have sought to find its purpose. You are right. It would not seem to be for the greater glory of God. From Flambard's own mouth we heard that he chose that site for his church that all men might be able to see it and remember him as its builder. He seeks fame for himself and glory and power. It was to be his church, he said, not God's; and men were to give thanks to him, not to God."

"Such pride and ambition is surely against the will of God," said Father. "Alwin, did you not say that you thought the ends of the church might collapse off the edge of the hill for the gravel would slip? I call to mind something in the

Gospels about a house built on sand that suffered the same fate. Godric, can you place the passage for me?"

"It is in the seventh chapter of Matthew's Gospel, where Jesus talks about sure foundations for our faith. If we build wisely on the sure rock of our faith, then naught can harm us. But he went on to say that a house built on shifting sands and buffeted by the rain, winds and storms will surely fall. The parable is apt, and its lesson drawn from life. I think you are right. Such a church as Flambard means to build to his own glory will fall, since it will have neither the blessing of God nor earthly foundations to sustain it."

Several heads nodded in agreement.

"What then is to be done?" asked Alric. "Odo might listen to us, since we know the hill better than he does. He is but the builder, and though he is skilled at his craft, he lacks our local knowledge and no doubt would welcome our assistance. Alas, it is not he who gives the orders but Flambard. Can you see him listening to what we would tell him? Nothing that I have seen of that man yet leads me to think that we should get anything but abuse for our pains and accusations that we wished to frustrate his plans."

"You speak true, Alric. Flambard is not a man to heed others," said Belesme. "You recall that I have known this man for many years, and nothing that he has done has ever been for the good of anyone but himself. When he was travelling the land helping to compile the great Domesday Book, his eyes and ears were for ever open for the chance to gain land and other benefits for himself. I heard say that oft-times he would agree to enter less than the true worth of an estate if he were granted certain privileges himself, though I never talked with any who had actually entered into such a bargain. It is well known that whenever the King's edict goes forth to tax the land at a certain sum, where Flambard is, the sum is doubled. Who can say if all that is gathered reached the King's coffers? Have you priests not suffered at his hands too, Godric?"

"For sure. We only have an allowance now, rather than the full sum that is due to us. Our work is therefore much curtailed. If the sums that Flambard receives were to be used to build us a finer church in this burgh, to replace our poor building and its little chapels so that we could carry out our tasks better and help to bring about God's Kingdom, that would be a different matter."

"What are you saying then, Godric? Would you have Flambard build his church then?"

"Here in this burgh, yes, for this is where men have worshipped these last two hundred years and more. We are famed throughout much of the land for our healing and care of travellers, and to have a greater building where men can worship and where others can teach and learn would be a fine thing. There is space where the church now stands and also for a monastery where monks could spread their learning, and transcribe their books. That would indeed be for the glory of God. I claim no benefit from it, but would work hard to have such a building in the burgh. I would die content if I could see a great monastery built here, adding to the work already being done at Winchester. Such a plan is being prepared at Sarum too, I hear. It is in this way that we shall bring the Kingdom of God on this earth. For that I would work both day and night. That is God's will, I think."

All sat silent awhile, pondering on Godric's words. At length, Alwin spoke.

"If you feel that God's will is that such a church should be built here, then should we not all seek how we can bring it about? What are the words of the Pater Noster? 'Thy Kingdom come, Thy Will be done, as in Heaven so on Earth.' Is it not so? Godric, is this what you think should happen?"

"I cannot be sure yet," replied Godric thoughtfully. "I must think on it and pray. Yes, we must all pray. It is too easy to think that our wishes must be God's because it would suit our purposes, but at the moment I am inclined to think that this may be so. Let us meet in the church at this time in three days. That will give us time enough to search our hearts and minds so that we may be as certain as maybe before we act."

Isabel spoke quietly again:

"Godric, you joined Hugh and I, and Emma and Alric in marriage here but a few months ago, and baptised all four of us here when we were babes. You buried Alsi not many months before. You and the other priests say Mass daily here in our church and the chapels that surround it. You care for us all here, and travellers come from far to learn from you and to be healed. Are we not told that these things have continued here long since ? Was not the church built here because men could reach it by land as well as by sea and river, and because it is sheltered too? Men lived on Hengist's headland before they settled in this place, but when they wished to build their church it was here they came. We can only guess at their reasons, but would they not have been guided by the hand of God?"

"You speak what is in all our minds I think, Isabel, but let us consider it again in three days time. Speak not openly of it to any man till we have met again. In the meantime I and all my brother priests will lay the matter on the altar that we may have guidance. Do you all come to Compline on Saturday, after which we will decide what is to be done."

With this we all agreed and so went our separate ways with heavy hearts.

Saturday dawned fine, but we could not feel content with the burden that lay over us all. Isabel and I joined the others at Compline as Godric had requested. After the Office was finished, during which each of us prayed silently that we might decide aright, Godric stood in front of the altar facing us.

"We have spent these last three days in constant prayer. We did not ask that the church should remain here nor that it should be rebuilt on Catherine's hill. We asked for guidance as to where we priests should continue our work and how it should be carried on. We laid the matter on the altar with open minds, praying for guidance. This afternoon, after Vespers, all of us brothers met here and each one spoke as he felt he should. All felt that the church should be rebuilt in this place and that it should be as magnificent as may be, that the glory of God may be proclaimed to the world. One thought a school should be built, another a larger infirmary, that more might be healed. Others wished for a monastery where a great centre of learning could be established, and the writings of the saints could be studied, and copied for others to read, but all felt that it was the will of God that the church should remain in this burgh if we were best to do his work. Now, let each one of you speak his mind."

This we did, and there was not one dissenting voice. When the last of us had spoken there was a heavy silence, for we all knew that we were taking on a task the bounds of which we could not see.

Alwin was the first to speak.

"Godric, we have all prayed for guidance and it has been given us, but prayer alone will not keep the church from being built on Catherine's hill. Men must act. Because I felt that the decision would be what it is, I have tried to plan how we might accomplish it. We know that very soon Odo will start bringing stone here for the new church, for Flambard has ordered it to be carried up Catherine's hill before the winter rains make the track impassable for oxen and carts. The foundations are to be dug in the winter so that the building can begin as soon as the frosts have ended, for we know that frost spoils the wet mortar in new stonework so that it will not stand. My plan is this."

He eased himself on his stool, and leant his elbows on the table before him.

"The stone will come by ship to be unloaded at our quay. Though ships could take the stone up the Avon river towards Catherine's hill, the land beside the river is too marshy for loaded carts and they would sink in the mud. The Stour river flows too fast for laden ships to beat against the current, so the stone must be moved by land. Men will then load it on carts at the quay and take it by the road that leads out of the Bar Gate towards Herne. There is a new track to be laid to take a gentle slope to the top of Catherine's hill that the oxen can drag the carts upon. There the stone will be piled ready for the masons in the spring. I walked up there yesterday to survey the ground. Many trees have to be cut to clear the place where they are to build. This work can be done, but the trees should be stacked as a barrier to the west. We will say it is to keep the wind off the builders, but it will also prevent men seeing the slope of the hill towards the Stour. When work ceases each evening and the stone carriers have departed, we can act."

Alwin paused and looked round at all of us to make sure he had our close attention.

"We have carts too and oxen. We shall work at night to load the stone and bring it down the hill by the new track to where it joins the road to Herne. A short distance towards Herne along that road, the river passes close by. Here we shall load the stone into boats and take it down the fast river to the quay, where it will be unloaded. Others will then carry the stone in carts to our present churchyard where it can be neatly stacked. When men come the next day to start work or to pass the church, they will see the stone where we have laid it. We need say nothing, but men will wonder at what they see. Those who carry stone to Catherine's hill next day will find the place bare of stone where there should have been a goodly pile. They will no doubt bring back this tale and men will wonder at it. Men will soon begin to question what is afoot, and why. Some will perhaps see in it the hand of God, and perhaps in one sense it will be."

Alwin paused and looked around him to see if his plan found favour. Several heads began to nod slowly in agreement. I tried to think how many men would be needed to carry out the scheme. The same thought passed though other minds too.

"It is two miles and more from the quay to the top of Catherine's hill," I mused aloud, "and the journey will take an ox-cart upwards of an hour, for the last part will be up a new and poor track. Each cart can make but three journeys in a day, for the carts have to be loaded and unloaded and men must eat. There are few carts that can be used for such work and some of those may find themselves at a distant farm when they are needed. It is scarcely half a mile from the hill to the

River Stour and it is downhill too. Boats will travel faster than oxen and will glide silently to the quay. From the quay to the churchyard is little more than a hundred paces. It seems that the stone will return to the church in half the time it takes to reach the hill, but will not men discover what is happening and so all our plans be set at naught?"

"Leave that to me," said Belesme. "False tales can be quickly spread if started in the right quarter, and men should be encouraged to stay within their doors at night. If we have strangers in the burgh there would be cause enough for there to be a curfew placed. The reeve could see that it was enforced and the gates kept barred so that none would know what we were about. Alwin, your plan has merit. Let us make a tally of the carts and boats we have amongst us for they must all be for our use alone. They can be kept well hid until we need them. Men will quickly come to think that the stone returns to where the church now stands by some Divine Hand. If you Godric, do not enlighten them, they will be encouraged in their belief and the tale will spread."

"Isabel and I will spread the tale amongst our friends too," said Emma. "There may be other ways that we can help, for though we have not the strength of men, we have our wits which we may use."

Such talk continued, each offering help in one way or another. It was growing dark when we finally agreed to part, setting a date for meeting once more a week hence, at which time the fine details of the plan would be discussed. Each one was to consider some part of the general plan, but none was to speak to any but those who were then present.

When next we met, the plan was well rehearsed and each was given his allotted task.

It was well that we had planned when we did. Odo returned within the four weeks that Flambard had ordered, with news that the stone would start to come from Vectis Isle in three days' time. He had orders with him to use such carts and oxen as he could find. First he took such men as he could muster to carve the new track up Catherine's hill. They made good progress that day and Odo declared himself well satisfied with what had been achieved, though those who had laboured complained, for it was dry and dusty work. That night it rained and continued so for several days, so that those who toiled had something different to complain about. Odo was put out too, for the track he cut was through soft earth that quickly turned to mud and washed away. When the first ship tied up at the quay with its burden of stone it was still raining. There was much grumbling as it was humped onto the quay and left in a great pile to be taken away later by Odo's carts. There was much complaining too when they came to load the stone and little was moved that day.

The rain ceased during the afternoon but the carters looked a bedraggled lot as they finally returned to the burgh, glad enough to repair to the nearest ale-house where the sailors joined them. Godric had told the captain that the ship would be safe enough at the quay, so that the sailors could spend the night ashore rather than sleeping in cramped quarters in the ship. Some were keen to seek out the sort of company they did not have on board, so that we knew they would not be seen before Prime.

Those who were to load the stone on Catherine's hill had left long since to collect their carts and take them to the hill. As soon as they saw the last of the retreating carts making its way back to the burgh, they came from their hidden places and started up the new track to the top of the hill. There were seven of us: Father, Osbern and I, Alwin, Alric and Alnoth, and Belesme. With three carts to load, we were kept busy. As soon as one was loaded, two of us would take it down the new track, joining the old Herne road at the foot of the hill. There we turned right-handed and led the oxen for the length of about three furrows along the road till we came to the spot where the river runs close by. There the boats were tied, each with a priest in charge. The three of us then transferred the stone to the boat, making sure that it was well balanced before the priest cast off into midstream, and steered the boat in the swift current downstream till he came to the open pool beside the quay. There in the slacker water, he steered the boat towards the quay till a rope could be cast to him, which he quickly secured. Willing hands then drew him to the quay and made all fast. Other priests then busied themselves unloading the stone from the boat into small carts which were pulled the hundred paces to the churchyard. There the stone was unloaded and neatly stacked.

As soon as the boat was emptied, it was cast off and towed away upstream for a distance. There a horse was waiting to be harnessed to the boat, to draw it upstream to where the river met the road, ready for reloading. Isabel and Emma had charge of a horse each, for it needed the priest to stay in the boat to steer lest it became snagged with the bank, and also, if occasion arose, help row if the current became too strong for the horse. Meanwhile, the two who had brought the loaded cart down retraced their steps to fetch another load, passing the second cart on the way down as they did so. In this way we cleared the stone before midnight, though it was hard work and our hands suffered from it.

Finally, we smoothed over the place where the stone had been stacked, so that there was little trace of it ever having been there, and only the tracks of the carts were left. Well satisfied with our first night's work we returned to our homes, while those whose carts we had used took them to their hiding places and let their oxen loose in nearby fields to graze till the morrow.

The priests had worked well carting the stone to the churchyard, and Godwine's great strength had been put to particularly good use, for some of the stones were of considerable size and it was vital that they be lifted quietly so that none should hear what we were about. Mother and Mary had been posted by the gate leading from the churchyard to the market square to meet any who thought to pass that way and persuade them to return to their cotts. As the wife of the bailiff, Mary carried some authority which she was not afraid to use should need arise. The boats we used were finally towed upstream and hidden in the reeds ready for the next night, and the horses which Emma and Isabel had led were stalled.

All of us slept deeply after the night's exertions but were abroad as usual next day, for we did not wish to be seen to act strangely. News of how matters had progressed reached each of us before Terce. Soon afterwards came the first news from Catherine's hill. The carter who returned from the hill having deposited his first load, brought a muddled tale about not being able to find the stone he had taken the day before. He got short shrift from the sailors and others standing by, who mocked him for having drunk too deep. He was a simple soul and merely shook his head, mumbling to himself while he waited for the cart to be reloaded. When the second carter returned with a similar story, there was some murmuring amongst those who were unloading the ship, for they liked not the thought that their work was for naught.

It was when those at the quay were resting and eating their midday meal that one came from the churchyard with news that there was a great pile of stone stacked behind the church. This caused no little stir amongst those on the quay. They all rose, some with half-eaten victuals in their hand, to go and see if what they were told was true, for if it were not, then the teller of the tale would surely find himself in the river for trying to make fools of them all. They were joined by the captain who had heard news of the tale. When he saw for himself the pile of stone, he sent one of his sailors to fetch Godric.

"Tell me, Master Priest, what stone is this and how comes it here?"

"Why do you ask, Captain? It looks like a pile of stone to me. Is there something special about it that you ask?"

"This man says that these stones should be on Catherine's hill, for that is where they took them yesterday."

"I know naught of that. Can he be sure that they are the same stones, for I could not tell one from another. If they are as you say, then they have been put here for a purpose. Perhaps Odo has changed his mind and the church is to be built here after all. It would seem right, for men have worshipped here these last four hundred years and there seems no reason why they should seek another place when the burgh is here and all men know of this place."

Godric shrugged his shoulders and turned to go back to the church. The captain scratched his head, puzzled, but since his task was only to see the stone safely delivered to the quay and safely unloaded, he let the matter rest. Since his ship was now empty, he summoned his men and as the tide was rising he made haste to leave. Those that stood by the quay bade him safe voyage.

"Expect me again in three days," he called. "With the tides to watch through the narrows by Vectis Isle, it will take me that time to reach the harbour where I must load, and then return."

The next ship came to the quay within the hour, having entered on the same rising tide. Those who were to cart the stone to Catherine's hill were sitting by the quay waiting and soon set about their task, though with no great speed, for the stones were heavy. The work continued throughout the day and men soon forgot about the events of the morning. Indeed, many had not even learnt of it for they had been in their fields before any discovery was made.

The sailors of this ship for their part were anxious to be away as soon as maybe and gave some assistance with the unloading, so that by evening there was a large pile of stone on the quay still to be carried to the hill. Their ship being empty and since the second high tide had not yet run off, the captain hastily called to his men to embark. He slipped his mooring, and with considerable skill steered the ship into the main channel and was soon lost to sight round the turns in the river, though we could mark his progress by the mast-tops which pointed skywards above the reeds.

Alwin, Belesme, and Godric came soon after to the mill to plan the night's work. It was agreed to follow much the same plan as the previous night.

"We have a goodly pile of stone still on the quay," Belesme said. " How say you that while those who bring the stone down from the hill are beginning their work, Godric has his priests move part of that pile from the quay to the churchyard. That way it will only be necessary to offload the stone from the boats to the quay to rebuild the pile that is there now. It will speed the process."

Thus it was agreed, and the night's work proceeded apace. Though there was more to be carried from the hill, we all knew better how to accomplish our tasks, having learnt from our mistakes the previous night. Once more we completed our tasks by midnight, and as we made our way to our rest, it was good to see how the pile of stone was beginning to grow in the churchyard.

By next day idle gossip was beginning to spread. Most of those in the burgh now knew that for a second time the stone for the new church had returned to the churchyard. With Godric's help, and like comments from the other priests, men began to think that perhaps it was meant that the church should be rebuilt in the burgh. Mary, Mother, Emma and Isabel spent much time gossiping with the goodwives to good effect.

"How ever would we be able to walk the little ones to Mass if we had to go to Catherine's hill?" said one. "I am six months carrying my next child and to have to take my two other babes so far would be more than I could manage. Is my immortal soul to be dammed to everlasting hellfire should I die unshriven for lack of being able to reach the new church and confess my sins before I die?"

"My husband is sick of such a fever now," complained another, "that he cannot rise from his bed and take more than a few steps. How could he reach the infirmarer if he were on Catherine's hill. He can scarce reach the church now, and that is but a hundred paces from my cott."

"Did I not hear that the stone now in the churchyard is to be used to build a fine new infirmary next to our present church?" asked a third. "It will be much warmer than the present one that is only wattle and daub. The wind whistles cruelly under the thatch, so that any fire in the room is little use. That is what my man heard in the ale-house last night."

"I had it from Godiva, whose husband was carting stone to Catherine's hill, that it was all a mistake taking the stone up there. The church is to be the length of two furrows they say, and Godiva's husband says that if it is so big, it will stretch right over the hill and down the sides, so it cannot possibly be built up there. Godiva said her man was so angry at having to labour all that way with carts of stone for no purpose, he said if he is asked to take another load he will tip it into the harbour."

"Who would blame him? Who wants a church up on that hill? No-one lives there and there is no water either, so whoever said that it was to be built there must be a fool."

Several heads nodded in agreement.

"Then I can put a name to him. It is Flambard, that braggart who came here on his great horse that he could hardly handle. What would you expect from such as he. The other who was with him, Odo was his name, I think, he seemed to know more of building. When they were here last, I saw him looking at our church and its chapels, and he walked all round the churchyard. I reckon he was seeing how much space he had there for the new church."

"Did he not pace it out from one end to the other?"

"I think I saw him too, and then he went to look at his drawings again. No doubt he was seeing if there was space enough for it."

"I heard that there is to be a monastery built too, where monks can read their ancient books and copy them for others. My son says that a friend told him that Rodric the priest hopes to have a place in the new church that he can teach the children. It is time my son learnt his Pater Noster, so I hope that is true."

"All those boys need Rodric's firm hand, but he is kindly with it and the boys all love him."

"That is because he can shoot straight with the bow, and after their lessons he takes them all out to practise down by the mill-stream. Yes, a place where the children can be taught would be a good idea. The new church will assuredly be big enough for that."

Thus the gossip ran and spread quickly, each person adding more detail. Before the day was out some even said they knew how many monks there were to be, and who would come to say the first Mass in the finished church. Some said that it would be Bishop Walkelin of Winchester. Others said he was not great enough and that it would be the saintly Anselm of Canterbury.

The next ship arrived at the quay and that too was unloaded. Those who led the carts discussed matters with the sailors whenever they had time for a short rest. Some showed little interest, but others who had heard rumours from those on the other ships were more curious and questioned some of the men more closely. The tide had fallen too far for the ship to leave that evening, so once more the sailors took the chance to spend the night ashore in the ale-houses. Godric again promised to see that the ship was secure so that all the crew could sample the pleasures that the burgh had to offer. Their purses were mostly empty when they returned to their ship next day and the ale-house keepers were well content. It seemed that the doxies of the burgh had been well employed too, and no man had been abroad that night but those of our party and the priests.

Once more we laboured at our appointed tasks. All the stone that had been so laboriously taken to the top of Catherine's hill that day found its way back, with our help, by track and water to the quay. There the priests silently took it from the boats, and as silently trudged with it to the churchyard, where it was added to the ever growing pile. It was exhausting work for all of us and we could scarce drag ourselves to our beds when it was finished. Indeed, had it not been for Godwine's great strength, we would have been at it for an extra hour. But Godwine, who had stripped off his priest's habit and worked only in his breeches, was tireless. He used the big cart that we had at the mill for moving sacks of corn and flour, and putting himself between the shafts where there would be our ox, he pulled it, piled high with stone, up the slope to the churchyard all night, his great muscles straining and bulging under the weight.

I slept late next day and Isabel had to rouse me from my slumbers. I awoke, to feel Isabel's soft hands stroking my chest and her lips kissing my cheek as she murmured endearments in my ear. Such sweet rousing made it all the harder to leave our bed, so I responded to her in like manner for a while. At length, she raised herself on one elbow so that her charms were more fully displayed, and leaning over me and smiling, kissed me softly again before throwing back the covers and rising to stretch her arms high in the air as she loved to do, and shake out her long fair tresses, before she bent to seek out her garments. For a while I lay wondering yet again at her slim beauty, before I too rose and hurriedly dressed. While I was clearing my head in a pail of water which stood beside the hearth, she was preparing our meal of bread flavoured with honey. She brought milk which she had freshly drawn from the goat we now kept in a shelter down by the wall.

Unwillingly, I left her when we had broken our fast, and embracing her as I always did before I left to go to the mill, I kissed her yet again, feeling her loving warmth.

We had not done above an hour's milling when there was a commotion from the direction of the quay, which we heard above the noise of the grinding wheels.

" Go and see what is afoot," said Father. "The next ship has docked I think, for I saw its masts approaching half an hour ago. Perhaps there is more trouble about the stone."

Dusting my smock clean as I went, I looked to see what was happening. There on the quay stood Odo. With him stood the captain, the same one who had first brought the stone. Odo seemed to be in a rage, for his voice was raised and he was waving his arms about as he faced a group of men. I saw Godric behind him, approaching in haste from the church. As he drew near, Odo turned and saw him.

"Now, Master Priest, what is this I hear? They tell me that the stone I ordered to be brought has been stacked in the churchyard. Did not Flambard say that this new church was to be built on Catherine's hill? Were not his orders that the stone should be carried there now so that it would be ready for the building to start as soon as the frosts are out of the ground, by which time men will have dug the foundations? What means this then?"

"Master Odo, your instructions were quite clear. All heard Flambard say that his great new church was to be built on Catherine's hill. We also heard you say that the stone was to be carried there with all speed. This we have done. Each shipload that has arrived has been taken that very day by cart to the hill and placed where you yourself ordered. Indeed, we cut a new track for the carts, for the hill would be too steep for oxen else. Ask these men who hold the carts here if this is not so."

There were several murmurs of assent from those who stood around.

"Then how is it that the stone is in the churchyard?"

"Master Odo, this is indeed a great wonder. Each morning when we have come to the quay through the churchyard, we have seen that the stone has been where you see it now. The first day we took little notice, thinking that it was but the remains of the shipload from the day before, but when the first carter returned from the hill to say that all the stone that had been taken up there the day before was gone, we began to wonder. The next day the same thing happened, and so it has been each day. Every day men have taken full carts of stone up Catherine's hill as you ordered, and each morning we find it where you see it now - in the churchyard."

Godric folded his hands in front of him.

"I have consulted with my other priests, and it seems to us all that perhaps it is the will of God that this great new church should not be built on Catherine's hill, but that it is meant to be built here in the burgh. This is a weighty matter for us, for it would mean that our present church and all its nine chapels would have to be pulled down. We would find that hard to bear, but if it is the will of God then so be it. We will continue with our prayer and ministry somehow while the work is progressing."

Odo scowled in disbelief.

"Find me a horse," he said, "and fetch the King's bailiff and also the reeve. We will ride to Catherine's hill that I may see for myself if what you say is true."

Godric turned to me and sent me to fetch horses, and call Alwin and the reeve. This I did, passing the mill on the way to tell Father quickly what was afoot. When we were all assembled, Odo and Alwin mounted their horses while the rest of us set off on foot to accompany them. As we went, we passed carts entering the Bar Gate and Odo stopped to ask the men what they knew. Each one told the same story, though with his own embellishments, and each one said that they were beginning to think that this great church was not meant to be built on Catherine's hill but should be built in the burgh. Each man had his own reasons which he gave, often unasked, and Odo became more silent as we progressed.

When we neared the place where the new track began, Alwin explained how it had been cut and how many men had been needed to complete the work quickly so that Odo's orders would not be delayed. At the top of the hill Odo rode to where he had given orders for the stone to be piled. There he saw but a smooth empty space bare of all trees or shrubs, and no trace of a single stone. Scowling deeply, he looked around him and then rode off towards the edge of the hill. He continued to criss-cross the top of the hill searching for any sign of the stone that should by now be a small hill of its own. Eventually, he rode slowly back to where the rest of us were standing. Alwin was the first to speak.

"Master Odo, this great church that is to be built, is it to have a monastery with it? It would seem that it should be so, for there will need to be many priests and they must lodge close so that they can say their Offices. How large will it be? I would pace it out if I may, to see how much land will be needed."

Odo looked at him shrewdly.

"Come with me," he said, and dismounting, led the way to the edge of the hill.

"I have talked with Flambard since last I was here, and he has told me what he needs. Yes, there must be a monastery, and it is to be a great one too for Flambard means his church to be more famous than any other in the land. Let us pace out the ground and I will show you the extent of the buildings."

First Odo walked several paces in from the edge of the hill and then picking up a fallen stick, thrust it in the ground. Next he looked up at the sun to find his bearings, before starting to pace out across the top of the hill, counting as he went. As he neared the other side, he began to slow, but still continued pacing and counting. Eventually, when he was almost at the edge where the land fell sharply away to the valley below, he stopped and dug in his heel to make a mark. Then he cast round for another stick and stuck that in the ground before looking about him. Next he walked some distance along the edge of the near cliff, taking in the lie of the land. Retracing his steps, he called for a digging implement. Someone brought him a spade with which he started to dig into the ground, throwing up the soft sandy earth till he had made a hole some four hand-spans deep. Breathing deeply from his exertions, he leant on the handle of the spade, and looked at Alwin.

"Tell me, you know this place well enough. Is there stone beneath this hill? I noted the track you had cut as we came up it, and it seemed to me that there was nothing but gravel here underfoot. When I looked down the far side towards the River Avon, it seemed that it was the same. How say you?"

"No man has dug deep on this hill, for no-one lives here. It would seem that you speak true, that it is but gravel and sand. No man lives upon the hill because there is no water here. Were there stone or clay, the water would be trapped upon it, but it is not so. Were men to live here, they would have to draw their water from the rivers and carry it each day up here for their needs. Such a task would seem impossible."

Odo nodded gravely, and heaved a deep sigh. Then once more he strode over to the edges of the hill, this time going both east, south and west. Once more he paced out the distance across the hill from east to west, and he then returned to where the rest of us were gathered. He looked about him as if to make sure that all the details of the hill were firmly fixed in his mind. Finally, he seemed to come to some decision. "We will return," he said. Then mounting his horse and pulling on the reins, he turned towards the track that led down to the road. As we rejoined the road, Odo paused, looking to the right.

"Where does this road lead, Alwin?"

"To Herne and Sopley beyond," he replied, seemingly showing scant interest. "There is little in either place but a mill, a small manor and a few cotts. William, son of Stour, holds Sopley as an alod, but my Lord the King has four hides from the manor which are now put into the forest with all the woodland. What was worth ten pounds in the blessed King Edward's time, is now worth no more than two pounds ten shillings. It is a place of little worth, the more so as our burgh grows for the benefit of the King."

Odo grunted as he continued to gaze up the road, then spurred his horse forward in the direction he was looking. The rest of us stood still, not wanting him to go too far up the road lest he come across the place where we loaded the stone into the boats. After he had walked his horse about fifty paces and finding that he was alone, for none had followed him,Odo reined in his horse and, turning it, made his way back to join us. He was too far from us to hear the collective sighs of relief that escaped all our lips. We returned in almost total silence, for though at first Alwin and Godric tried to point out matters of interest to him, Odo seemed not to wish to talk, so we all fell silent.

Two loaded carts passed us as we made our way back, and Odo noted the stone they carried. Both carters told him they were heading for the hill and both, when questioned, said they could not understand why the church was to be built there.

"Master Bailiff, I would lodge with you tonight if I may," Odo said as we entered the burgh. "I wish to spend the day seeing the stone unloaded and taken up Catherine's hill and I need to consult my drawings too. They are with the captain in the ship at the moment. Have them brought to your house if you will."

The day passed, and I returned to the mill and helped Father complete the day's grinding, and then reset the stones for the next day. As we were finishing, Emma hurried in, somewhat breathless.

"Odo wishes to confer with Godric and the reeve, and the captain is to join them when they dine with Alwin. I am to help Mary with serving, but Alric will probably be able to escape. Odo is sleeping at Alwin's house, and the captain has been persuaded to do so too. All the sailors are to be ashore as usual in the ale-houses. Alwin has told the reeve to put on a curfew so that no man may be abroad, and Godric has promised the captain that his ship will be safe under the protection of the priests. You will be short-handed this night for moving the stone, but Alwin says that with him, Godric and the reeve closeted with Odo and the captain, any suspicions they may have about how the stone comes to be in the churchyard may well be stilled. Will you be able to complete the task do you think?"

Father and I looked at each other.

"It will be hard, and we shall have to work longer, but we must succeed. We must leave for the hill as soon as maybe and start loading the boats. Tell Osbern to slip out and make his way to the hill as soon as possible taking Alnoth with him, and to collect the carts as they go from where they are secreted. Emma, thank Alwin for his message. I have no doubt that he will ply his guests with his best ale in good measure. Do you think that Godric can add his weight to the curfew with the threat of a heavy penance for any who break it?"

"I will tell him what you say, Father," said Emma before slipping out to hurry back to Alwin's house.

"Hugh, ask Mother if she will please go with Isabel this time to guide one of the horses that pulls the boats back upstream to where we load them. If they go together as soon as possible along the river bank, Isabel can show Mother the best track to follow. We shall be short-handed, but we dare not ask anyone else to help lest they fail to keep their mouths shut. There are enough who know our plan as it is, but neither of our two families will breathe a word nor will any of the priests whom Godric has placed under a vow of silence, and Belesme is trustworthy. Even the reeve has not been told. It is best that he remain ignorant so that he can play his part the better and in innocence. Go now, Hugh, and warn Mother and Isabel. See if you can send a message to Belesme too. I will see Godric and ask if we may have one of the priests to help us load the carts on the hill. Rodric would be best if he can be spared."

Looking first to see that there was no-one about near the mill, I slipped out quietly and walked, innocently I hoped, to Mother's house where I delivered the message and bade her see Isabel as soon as possible so that they could make their own plans.

As soon as we could Father, Osbern, Alnoth and I set off for the hill by various routes. I slipped over the wall at the end of our land and joined the road some distance outside the Bar Gate. Ahead of me I could see Alnoth, and looking back after a short time I saw Father in company with the young priest Rodric approaching across the Port Field. Each of us continued on our separate ways, for we had no desire to draw attention to ourselves by appearing to be together. Father and Rodric could well have been walking to the mill at Herne had anyone been curious enough to enquire. As I climbed the hill, I saw Osbern approaching from Ogber fields, where the cart he had charge of was secreted with its oxen. Alnoth appeared soon afterwards from the nearby marshlands of Cowards, and we made our way to the top of the hill and set about loading the first of the carts.

When the cart was laden, Osbern set off down the track to turn right-handed onto the Herne road and so to the place where the river passed close to the road, where the boat should be waiting. I went with him, for with only the priest in the boat and himself, the loading of the boat would have taken too long. It was no easy task to lift the heavy stones from the cart and take them down the steep bank and place them into the small boat, but we managed well enough. As soon as it was fully laden, the priest pushed off from the bank, guiding the boat into the swift current with his steering oar. Soon he was lost to our view, even though we looked for him as we climbed the track up the hill again for the next load.

We continued through the evening and far into the night. There was little moon but enough to give us light to see what we did. I prayed fervently that there was enough light for the priests in the boats to steer a safe course downstream to the quay. Should one of the boats run ashore on the river bank, all might be lost. Fortunately the priests who had charge of the boats had done the journey ever since we started and so knew the river's course well. Provided they kept to the centre of the stream where the current was fastest, they would have little problem and their journey would be quickest. When finally we had completed our task, and once more smoothed over the place where the stone had been stacked, so that it looked as if none had been there, the night was far spent. Wearily we made our way back to the burgh, Alnoth and Osbern first returning their carts and oxen to their hidden places.

As I slipped over the wall at the foot of our land and crept silently to our cott, I could hear the sounds of the priests saying Matins, the first of their Offices for the day. It must be almost three in the morning, I thought, for they were roused at two in time to prepare themselves for that Office. It crossed my mind that the priests had a harder life than I thought, having to say so many Offices during the day. No wonder they retired to bed so early at seven in the evening, and we had been keeping them from their beds all night humping stone to the churchyard!

I silently lifted the catch on our door and slipped inside our cott. Stripping off my clothes, I slipped quietly beneath the covers to feel Isabel's warmth, for she was already abed and deeply sleeping. She stirred as I snuggled close to her, and whispered something that I could not catch, before stretching out an arm to hold me. I kissed her lightly and felt her smile, for I could not see her in the darkness, and heard her contented sigh. Almost at once I too was in a deep exhausted sleep.

Next day the ship sailed as soon as the tide was high enough for it to leave the quay, and another ship arrived. News came with the first carter who returned from Catherine's hill that once more the stone they had taken up the hill the previous day was gone. On hearing the news, Odo sent for Godric and went with him to the churchyard, where once more they found the stone piled high. Both men stood looking at the growing pile, Godric remaining silent for he did not wish to be the first to speak. At length Odo spoke.

"There is some mystery here that I do not fully understand, and there are other matters that trouble me too that I must think on. You say that each day that men take stone to the hill it returns here? I have spent my life building great churches and often have found it necessary to make some change in the plans, because it seems that some Power that is greater than me, dictates what is to be. When I have heeded that Power, it seems that the work has gone well. If I have ignored it, then disaster has often struck, though I could not explain why from the way of building. You are a man of God, Godric, can you explain it?"

Godric turned and looked Odo in the eyes.

"It is not given to men always to know the will of God. Sometimes He works in mysterious ways, and uses men for His purposes in ways they do not understand. Maybe this is one such occasion. We are all in His hands and must try to do His work as seems most fit."

Odo nodded gravely. "I feel that too, but there are other matters that trouble me too that I must think on. Leave me now. I have much to ponder on. I stay with the bailiff still, and would hope that we may talk more this evening after we have eaten. I value Alwin's opinion and the three of us may perhaps be able to resolve my problems. Till this evening then."

Odo turned away and walked to the end of the churchyard. There he stood looking around him. He spent much of the rest of the morning there, pacing to and fro and casting his eye from side to side. At one time he went into the church and down the steps that led to the large crypt that lay beneath it. He called for Godric to join him and explain so far as he could what he knew of its building. Then he returned to the quay to see how the unloading of the stone from the ship was progressing. Finally, he returned, head bent and deep in thought, to Alwin's house.

That evening, Odo, Alwin, and Godric dined alone, with only Mary to serve them. When they had finished and were seated with full horns of ale beside them, Odo leant his elbows comfortably on the table. "Godric, when we were on Catherine's hill yesterday I examined the site carefully. No doubt you saw how I paced out the size of the top of the hill. Last night after we had all retired, I examined the drawings I have with me of what Flambard wishes me to build, and checked its size. It is as I thought. He now wishes the church and its monastery buildings to be so big that there is not room enough for them all on the hilltop. So the church cannot therefore be built where he wishes. He will be angry, no doubt, but you cannot build near the edge of a hill, much less if it is on soft earth. By my reckoning I can only build the church of the size he wishes here where the present church now stands. If I am to build a monastery too as he says he wishes, then any church on the hill would have to be very small in order to make room for the other buildings round it. This smaller church could not be as high, or it would look out of keeping. Besides, it would not stand if it were too high and not long enough. Then as you say Alwin, there is no water on that hill, so that they would have to carry it daily from the rivers. Even the shortest distance would be almost half a mile. That will make the building even more burdensome, for all the water for the building work will have to be carried too, and great amounts would be needed for the mortar and plaster-work. That would mean using many more men. I have paced out the space where the present church stands too, and examined the church itself and its crypt. There is space enough for a church as big as Flambard has planned and it could be as high as he wishes. I can also gain extra height if I build a tower upon it so that it would still stand out as he wants, and be seen from far."

Odo turned and faced Godric.

"You showed me the crypt this morning. It seems that the floor is solid ground and indeed you say that there is rock beneath. That would be good, for it will make the sure base that I would need for such a tall church. The sand on Catherine's hill worried me, I must confess. I had thought that it would be but a shallow layer but it seems that there is nothing solid on which to build on that hill. I will make no decision till I have slept on it, though I confess that it seems to me that the church is not meant to be built on that hill but should be where your present building is. I shall look for a sign. If tomorrow I find that the stone has once more returned to the churchyard, then I shall be persuaded that it is meant to be built there. If the stone is still upon the hill tomorrow, then I shall know that my doubts are groundless and that Flambard's wishes must be fulfilled, however hard that may seem to be. What say you to that, Master Godric?"

Godric sat silent for some time, considering what had been said, and how he should reply.

"Master Odo, your knowledge of how and where you can build is far greater than mine but I think what you have said makes great sense. For myself, I shall be content to leave the matter in God's hands. I have prayed long and earnestly with all the priests for guidance in this matter. No doubt you have too. Whatever you decide will, I am sure, have God's blessing. For our part, we will abide by your decision and work with you to bring about this great new church and its monastery. It will enable us to continue the work we try to do here and increase it. That is the purpose of all our lives. It is no matter to us whether the church brings fame to the builder. It will be God's house, not Flambard's. You, Master Odo, will surely use your great skills to raise a building that will glorify God through its beauty, whatever size it may be. If our present buildings have to be destroyed to achieve this, then so be it. We will work with you in that aim."

Alwin nodded in agreement.

"Our church is well known far and wide for the works of healing and the teaching that our priests give. If your new church enlarges this work, then surely it must be right. Master Odo, let us indeed await the sign you seek. It is a weighty matter for us as well as you, so we must all be sure."

There the subject was allowed to rest, and talk moved to other matters, for Odo had much to tell about his travels in other parts of the realm and also the dukedom of Normandy. So interesting was he, that it was nearing the hour of Matins before those round the table rose to go to their beds.

As for the rest of us, we knew nothing of what was being discussed, for we were hard at work moving the day's stone from the hill back to the churchyard. Short-handed as we were, it took us till well past midnight before we had completed all that had to be done, and we could once more creep exhausted to our beds.

The next day we were busy in the mill and it was nearing the time when men rested at midday to eat their victuals when a message came that Odo had returned from Catherine's hill. Father bade me leave work and make some excuse to go to the churchyard to hear what was being said. Others had the same notion too for there were several gathered near the great pile of stone. Odo was speaking as I came within earshot.

"It seems that the sign I looked for has been granted. Once more the stone has been returned to this churchyard. That it is the same stone there can be no doubt, for yesterday I marked many of the stones with a cross. See here and here, you can see the marks still. There can be no doubt."

We all peered to see the marks he had made. They were plain enough and there were many of them all similar, so that all were convinced.

"I said last evening, if that happened yet again, then I would take it as proof that the stone was meant to remain here and the church was to be built on this spot; so be it. I must now seek out Flambard and tell him all that has occurred here. I shall also explain to him that the church of the size he wanted could not be built on the hill in any case. Perhaps that will pacify him, though I doubt it. Once he sets his mind to something there is little that will turn him from it. In the meantime, I will give orders that no more stone is to be shipped here until Flambard's decision is known. It will be pointless continuing to take stone to the hill and there is no room for it on the quay. Those ships that are already on their way here should unload what they bring and let it be added to this pile here in the churchyard."

He sighed deeply as he pointed to stones by which he stood.

"This is indeed a mystery to me, but I am convinced that it is meant to be. Godric, I do not relish the thought of telling Flambard, but needs must. See to the unloading for me for I must away to Winchester to see if I can find Flambard, though I fear that he is elsewhere. I heard it said that he has gone to Ely, where many churches now stand empty and their lands have been seized by some of the barons and even the Bishop himself, and they have taken the fees to themselves. It is rumoured that Flambard means to take them to his own use now. If that is so, he may have more profitable matters to interest him so that he will not be too careful about this place. Let us hope so, for it will make my task easier if it is."

He sighed and turning, walked with Alwin back to his house. I saw him no more, but returned to the mill to recount what I had heard. Father smiled as I told him.

"It is well." he said.

That evening we all gathered quietly in Alwin's house to discuss the events of the past week. Though we were all well pleased with the turn of events, it was a solemn gathering for none could be certain how Flambard would react. Nor could we say anything of our part to any man. Finally Godric spoke.

"I have given deep thought to what we have done, for it is not a light thing to try to change the course of events, but I am convinced that we have done right. No church could have stood on Catherine's hill, and to have tried to build it there would have wasted great effort. As Isabel said, this is where our ancestors felt drawn to build and worship, teach and heal. What we should do is try to carry on that task more effectively if we can. The glory is not ours, nor would we wish it to be, but the benefit will be for all men. I must think carefully how I can explain what has occurred to the folk at Mass on Sunday. Rumour is rife so we must turn it in the right way. Men need to know that what has happened is meant to be. They will readily accept it I think, for many are angry at the thought of the new church being built so far distant and I have heard none say that he was pleased that the church was to leave the burgh."

Over the next few days, three more ships came to the quay, and their loads were taken to be added to the growing mound of stone in the churchyard. All seemed pleased, if only because they no longer had to trudge the weary track up to the hill. We were all glad that our lives could return to normal, and that once more we could have a full night's sleep. We waited for Odo to return and, as is the way of things, men soon forgot that their lives had so nearly been turned upside down. As for the mound of stone, it became a favourite playground for chidren who used it as a castle in their mock battles of Saxons against Normans.

Chapter 9 1093–1094

The year continued in its usual pattern after Odo left, and the events of the days when he was in the burgh soon became but a memory. Only the children noticed any difference, and that was because they now had such an excellent castle on which to play. It was not long before they had re-arranged some of the smaller stones to make an enclosure to defend in their mock battles, and their excited cries could be heard as far as the market square. Rodric the priest, whose task it was to try to teach them their 'Pater Noster' and 'Ave Maria', and other parts of the Mass, found that they became willing pupils once he helped them organise their games somewhat. He was adept with a bow and also the sling, and he taught the boys particularly these skills, being careful to instruct them how to stalk game silently too.

His instruction was not all destructive, for he said that one should only kill for food. He taught them to recognise different animals and to know which were rearing young and so should be left unharmed.

On occasion I found Isabel with them, for she had a way with small animals which seemed to come to her without fear. It was her quiet movements and gentle touch that gave them courage to approach her, and it was nothing unusual to see her holding in her hands some small creature which she had found when she was walking outside the burgh, while the group of children with Rodric crouched round her as they quietly examined it to make out its tiny features. Then, when they had learnt what they could, Isabel would sometimes give the creature to Rodric, and he would go with her to release the animal back into the wild near where she had found it, so that he would know where he might find others later. In this way, it became not unusual for me to find children round our cott when I came from the mill at the ending of the day.

As the year drew on, we had much to do on our assart. Where the wheat had been harvested, there was ploughing to be done, and I spent such hours as I could spare from the mill behind the ard plough that was pulled by the ox team. It was usually possible to collect the oxen when I needed them since much of the work I did was in the late afternoon when most others had finished for the day. Belesme helped us greatly since he had some oxen of his own, that we could use. When the ground had been gone over again to harrow it smooth with the wood and flint harrow, Isabel took care of the sowing. That year she broadcast emmer wheat in one part and a good barley seed in another part. When the seed had been scattered, I fixed a brushwood harrow behind our single ox and drew it over the land to cover the seed before the birds could find too much of it. Often, when we had finished in the field we would call at Belesme's cott and pass some time with him and Ediva and their babes. He taught me many tricks to help make a good harvest for which I was truly grateful.

Isabel also spent much time in the land round our cott. I had cleared the brambles and other wild growth from it so that she could plant herbs and grow such vegetables as she needed. Though it had been too late to plant many things in this our first year, she managed to harvest more than I had hoped of beans and fat-hen, which she dried for later use.

The shelter that we had found by the wall was now repaired and held our young sow which we hoped would litter in the spring. Beside it was another shelter that housed our fowls which were giving us a few eggs. There was food enough for them all from the sweepings from the mill, so that they would last the winter through. Our goat we tethered to a post, where it could not reach our growing crops, though it had space enough to roam and find food for itself. Often we turned it loose on the common to feed and fetched it back at evening, so that we could milk it again in the morning. Thus our days were spent in making our home and growing what we could on our land.

Winter came and went, and in the darkened evenings Isabel would spin on her drop-spindle the wool she had bartered for eggs, or for cheeses that she made from the goat's milk. She also used her mother's loom to make cloth that she would later turn into new garments for both of us. Though it was a simple loom, she could weave cloth four hand-spans wide which made garments without too many seams. She smiled when I remarked on the fineness of the cloth.

"The secret lies in the fineness of the spinning. It is a skill my mother taught me, though I cannot spin as well as her, but this will serve well enough for us, I think. Our clothes need to be strong so they need not be too fine, though I shall try to make some finer cloth for a robe later if I can find the time."

Throughout the winter, when it was not too cold and the ground was not frosted, I spent such time as I could clearing more land beside our assart to enlarge it, for we wished to grow more wheat and barley that we could sell. There were several trees that had to be felled. and these we brought back to store and season, for they would be useful later if we wished to enlarge our cott. There were also some hazel bushes on the land I cleared, and these I cut to make wattle fences round our garden. The roots I left, for they were all in a clump and would grow again for our use in future. The lop and top we brought back to store for kindling and to keep our hearth fire burning.

Spring was well advanced before we saw Odo again. It must have been a week after Easter, which fell on 9th April that year, for the crops were growing well in the fields but no hay had been gathered yet. He arrived on horseback with two others and an extra horse burdened with panniers which seemed to contain mainly parchments. The three of them went straight to Alwin's house and we soon heard how matters were to be, for a meeting was called of the chief men to hear the news.

When all were gathered in Alwin's hall, and with Odo seated between his two companions, Alwin rose and commanded silence so that Odo could tell us how things stood. All eyes turned then to Odo.

"Since last I was here, I have had to travel far and wide. Ranulf Flambard was not in Winchester as I had hoped, but was said to be away in the east by the town of Ely where he was settling some disputes over land claimed by the church and certain barons. It seems it was resolved to the satisfaction of neither party, for most of the land Flambard took to himself. I found that there was grave disquiet in the town over his actions when I arrived. One I spoke to had been in Canterbury last year when the blessed Anselm had at last been enthroned as Archbishop. It seems that at the feast that followed, this Ranulf had burst in like a bum-bailiff at a wedding feast, demanding all manner of lands and monies for himself. Though he be by profession a priest, yet he is in fact but a tax collector, and the most infamous prince of tax collectors to boot. Well is he known as Flambard on account of his cruelty which is like a devouring flame."

There were many grim faces at this news, for some feared that matters might be resolved in like manner here should a dispute arise. All that we heard of Flambard seemed to show his greed and lust for power.

"But Flambard was no longer at Ely when I arrived," continued Odo. "He had gone north to Durham where there were more disputes concerning lands at Ross near Holy Island. Bishop William Carilef of Durham claimed they had been taken from him by Robert, Eorl of Northumbria, some years before with the King's blessing. So I followed Flambard northwards and found that he was in Durham with Bishop Carilef. Not many months earlier, this same Carilef had started building a great new church at Durham. Many were greatly angered and distressed, for he first had to destroy the Holy Shrine of Cuthbert their saint, the protector of sea birds. There was a noble celebration when the work started I was told, for Malcolm the King of the Scots, he who had himself slain the tyrant Macbeth some years before, was among those who witnessed the laying of the first stone. It seems that this church at Durham is to be even bigger than Flambard had planned for this burgh, and that it will be almost a castle too. I sensed jealousy in his demeanour as he studied the plans, that another had thought to build greater than him."

"Then what is planned for Durham must indeed be huge," said Alwin.

"Indeed so," replied Odo. "While I was there, a Charter came from the King restoring the lands at Ross to the Bishop. Some said that Flambard received great benefit from the Bishop for the part he played. I saw an agreement was made, in which it may well be that Flambard played his part, that while Carilef was to build the church, the monks would build the monastery. Who can say which man will then be the greater?"

"Many weeks passed before I could speak to Flambard" continued Odo, "for he was always abroad searching out lands and churches to which men laid various claims. The north of this realm is a turbulent place for sure, and in spite of the present friendliness of the Scots King Malcolm, there is ever present the danger of attack by the Scots who live even further to the north beyond the great wall built by Hadrian the Roman. From all I heard, Flambard indeed made settlements of many rival claims, as he was empowered to do by the King as his Justiciar, and which will no doubt be confirmed later by the King's charter. It was said that in all but the simplest cases Flambard benefited himself greatly from the winning party. There can be no doubt that this Flambard is clever and one of the most powerful men in the realm, though whether he deals justly with all men, many would question."

"Rightly so by all accounts."

Odo first nodded in agreement, then shook his head, seemingly concerned by what he had seen and told.

"When at last I could gain Flambard's ear, I told as best I could all that has befallen here, and how it seemed not possible to build the great church he desired on the hill he had chosen. He seemed preoccupied with other matters and it was hard to arouse his interest. We were standing near the place where they were starting to raise the stones for this great church, and though I pressed him for his decision and explained matters a second time, his mind seemed to be elsewhere, for he continually let his glance fall on the works before him."

" At length, he said, 'Do what you will. Build the church as large as you can, where you think best. You know the plan and shape I desire. See to it and be sure to build a monastery beside it that monks may work to spread learning and the Gospels. There are lands enough belonging to the present church at Twynham, and you shall have everything that I receive from the Dorsetshire manor of Alfpuddle which the King gave me at Christmas-tide. With the other money that I shall send, you will be able to buy stone and hire the men you need. I leave the building in your hands, for you have the skill to do it I am sure. Send me an account of how the works progress each year at Advent time. By then the work of the year will be complete, and stone-laying ceased for the winter. If any changes need to be made at that time, I will tell you. When I am in Winchester I will visit you at Twynham if I have the time. For the rest, see you to it, and trouble me not further. I have matters of greater moment to see to. With that, he turned on his heel and strode away, leaving me open-mouthed."

"Who would not have been struck dumb by such news?" remarked Alwin. "What did you do then?"

"Next day I called on his Chief Exchequer Clerk to see what monies Flambard had said should be allowed me. From him I obtained a charter to draw on Flambard's purse in Winchester up to an amount each year. That done, I returned to my lodgings and set about calculating what I could build and thinking who could help me in the work, for I needed an expert mason and skilled carpenter amongst others to oversee the work. The men I needed I knew of, but they had to be persuaded to come, for they were working elsewhere. They are the two men who came with me today. Edward the mason, and Thurstan the carpenter."

He turned to each of these two men in turn. They rose so that all could see them and they both smiled as if they were pleased to be amongst us. Both were of middle age, and by their countenance seemed experienced and accustomed to being obeyed, though there was no sign of arrogance in their faces. When both had seated themselves again, Odo continued.

"We can count ourselves most fortunate that these men have been prepared to come to build the church here. Both of them have great experience and are masters of their crafts. I know of no mason who can better design an arch or carve a capitol than Edward. He has worked on churches both in Normandy and this realm. Likewise, Thurstan: his skill with wood is greater than any other I know, and he is also expert in making pulleys and other machines to raise the stone and timbers as the work grows higher. With two such men to guide the work, we shall be able to raise a building that will be a fitting glory to God, where men may come to worship Him and learn of His goodness and mercy, find tranquillity in their trouble, and where the work of healing for which the present church is already known, may continue to grow."

There was a long silence when Odo finished speaking. All felt that his words marked a turning point in the life of the burgh, for a great new church was to be built here after all. This would mean the destruction of our present church and its nine chapels. How would the priests continue to celebrate the Mass while the building was in progress if they had no church? When eventually the new building was completed, perhaps the burgh would become famous and a great seat of learning and healing. Who could tell? In the meantime many men would come to live and work here, so that our present peace and tranquil lives might well be greatly disturbed. Would there not be many opportunities for trade and betterment for those living here now? There was so much to ponder over, for all our lives would be touched. Like thoughts were passing through the minds of the others too, I felt sure. It was Alwin who broke the heavy silence.

"Well, Master Odo, you bring us momentous tidings to be sure. It would seem that it is the will of God that this great building that Flambard wishes to have, should be built here in the burgh, where men have worshipped for so many centuries. So be it. No doubt you will wish to talk long with Godric our main priest about the exact site for the church and the other buildings. I imagine you will be looking for a great many men to help in the building. I regret that we have no skilled masons or carpenters here, and no doubt you will be hiring those whom you already know to be skilled at their crafts. We do have many strong men who can be hired for the numerous tasks of digging and carting. Some will be clever enough to be trained in some of the crafts you will need. I would ask of you that if you can, you take on such of our folk as you are able as apprentices in the several crafts. This is our burgh and we are proud of it. There are few who would not wish to have a hand in shaping its new form and have the chance of being able to say, when all is done, 'I helped to build that.' We Saxons do not boast over-much, but we are proud of what we do."

There were several murmurs of assent at this and Odo turned to Alwin and Godric.

"You have spoken well and I thank you for it. Indeed there is much to discuss with Godric here, for I have a mind to build the new church round the main church you have here. In this way the worship that has been going on, - for four hundred years do you say? - will continue even while we are building, and, when all is finished, the heart of the new building will be the old one. As for men to work, indeed there will be need for a great many, far more than you have in the burgh, but I agree that any who live here and wish to work, provided they are honest and able, will be hired. I will speak to Master Edward and Master Thurstan here, and see how they feel about taking some of your young men as apprentices. This must be their decision, for they are the masters of their trades, and they decide who can be trained and join their Lodges, as they call them. How say you, Edward? What are your rules of your craft in this matter?"

All eyes turned towards Edward the mason.

"Our craft is ancient as you know. It dates back to ancient Egypt, and it is also recorded that King Solomon, when he was building his temple at Jerusalem, used many masons. We have our secrets, like all crafts, which only those who join us may learn. Those who enter as apprentices we train to use such tools as the rule, the gavel and chisel, so that they may roughly shape the stone before it is passed to their more skilled fellow craftsmen. There is much training even at this first stage, for stone needs to be cut aright if it is to be strong in the building. Nor does all stone behave in the same way. Some flakes, others crumble, some weathers quickly in the wind and rain if wrongly set, yet will withstand all the elements if set aright. Other stone will withstand anything, but is so hard to fashion that it is seldom used since it blunts the tools too quickly. Other stone again will polish and shine, and so add glory to a building."

"We have stone that is quarried near here," said Alwin. "Will some of it be of use, do you think?"

"I cannot tell till I have seen it, for there are many kinds. Each type has its special uses, and I plan to use many sorts here, some of which can only be worked by experts. Those who pass through their apprenticeship successfully may join us as fellows in our craft. They, with their greater skill, are taught to use such tools as levels so that the stones may lie even one upon the other. There is also the plumb-rule they need to master, so that when they build a wall, it will stand upright upon its base, and lean to neither side. They must also master the use of the square, and know how to make one, so that when they reach the corner of a building, it will be an exact right-angle. In this way, they will be able to make a building that is firm upon its base, strong in its walls, and regular in its appearance, so that all its parts will combine into one whole, perfect in its parts, a credit to the builder, and a glory to our Creator."

"How long does it take to learn these skills?" I asked.

"Many years I fear, and some never seem to master them all. A few there are, and I am accounted as one, who in time become master masons. We learn to work with yet other and more delicate tools. To us falls the task of drawing out the plan of the building, first on a board in small scale, and then on the ground, so that the labourers may know where to dig foundations. For this we need to acquire skill in the use of the compasses so that we can measure each part accurately, and compare it with other parts. Likewise we need to practise with the straight-edge and pencil so that we can draw our plan. Later, we learn to transfer this in full size to the ground."

Edward paused again and looked round on the rest of us before he continued, for he was touching on things that lay close to his heart.

"Much of the skill of a master mason lies in being able to see in his mind what he wishes to build, and then draw it upon the parchment and board. Many years are needed to gain such skills, and indeed few there are that achieve them. Other masters of the craft develop different skills, such as the ability to carve stone into beautiful shapes. There is one I know who is gifted in this skill, whom I shall try to persuade to come here to help beautify this building."

"Pray God he will be willing to come, that what we build may be a worthy offering," Godric said, crossing himself.

"Will you be able to use any of our people?"

"Yes, Master Alwin. If any man in this burgh wishes to help in the building of this great church, provided he works honestly and with a pure heart, for this is God's work, I will take him. Those who think they have the skills I have talked of may try to become apprentices. I make no promise that they will succeed. That will be for them to prove and for the masters of the craft to decide. All I can promise is that the work will be hard and the training strict and long. Those that do succeed will walk tall as you say, knowing that they will have given of themselves to make something much greater than themselves that will survive long after they are gone."

Edward ceased speaking then, but his gaze was fixed. He seemed to be seeing something that we could not, for he stood still for some time staring before him, with a light that seemed to shine from his eyes as though he saw a vision. Perhaps he did, and perhaps it was the great building that he was here to create which he saw in his mind's eye. Who can tell? At length, he resumed his seat, while we pondered all that he had said.

It was Godric who spoke next. "Yes, I think there will be some in this burgh who would wish to learn the craft of mason. I can call to mind several who could well have the skills they need in their hands." He thought for a moment. "Tell us, Master Odo, what of those who work with wood? Is their skill as great? Perhaps Master Thurstan can tell us."

All eyes turned towards where Thurstan sat, next to Odo. "Well, Thurstan," said Odo, "how do you rate the skills of your craft? Tell us, that those who are here may judge if there are some who could learn it too."

Thurstan rose in his turn and looked around at all of us, and then down at his hands which he spread out before him.

"My craft is ancient too. Perhaps older even than the mason's craft, for men used wood before they learnt to make tools that could work stone. It is certain that men worked with wood in ancient Egypt, and it is recorded in the Scriptures that when Solomon wished to build his temple at Jerusalem he sent to Hiram, the King of Tyre, to seek from him timbers from the great cedar trees of Lebanon. He also had palm trees and olive trees sent to use in different parts of the temple."

"It is indeed written thus in the fifth, sixth and seventh chapters of the first Book of the Kings, where the building of that great temple is described," murmured Godric. "There are many types of trees mentioned, each with its own use."

"That is so," continued Thurstan, "and my craft will use all kinds of wood, for each is best suited for one purpose. Those who would learn the craft must first become apprentices too, like the masons, and learn about the types of wood and the tools needed to cut down trees, such as the axe and saw. They must learn how best to cut a tree that it does little damage to itself in falling, or to its neighbours. They need to learn to trim the branches to make best use of them, and then how to to load the great timbers to carry them to where they are needed. This means learning the use of pulleys, for their weight may be so great that they cannot be lifted by even a hundred men."

"Where would you find such trees?" Alwin asked. "I doubt if I have ever seen such, even in Andret."

"They are rare indeed, and I may have to find some almost as big for the roof of this church, but no apprentice would be allowed to work on them. Those who can pass these tests and join their fellows in our craft must then learn how to cut timber to the right shape, using the strength of the grain of the wood to help them. They learn to shape the wood to the size that is needed, and how to join two pieces so that they will be as one and lose no strength. They also need to learn the art of setting one piece against another, that they may form an arch or span a roof that will be of such strength that it will take great weight. Likewise they need to make great hoists with which stone and balks of timber may be raised to great heights. Others learn to make the shapes of arches out of wood, so that the masons may build their stone about it. If their work is not perfect, then the stone arch will fall when the wooden frame is taken away and the work will be spoilt."

"Yes Thurstan," said Edward. "our two crafts work closely together in many things."

"As with your masons, few there are who can make more progress and so become master carpenters. The skills are great and few find it in their hands, however hard they try. I count myself blessed that such skill has been granted me, after many years. To us falls the tasks of making fine work such as doorways and the doors to fit them, and also chairs and tables and other things to furnish the building. This needs a thorough knowledge of how to joint the wood with strength. To others again, and this is an art that has escaped me though I have toiled long hours at it, is given the art of carving figures and designs in wood, much as Edward says his most skilled masons do in stone. Few there are who have this touch in their hands. All these skills and gifts will be needed here if we are to make a building worthy of the purpose it is to fulfil."

Thurstan paused, and I thought how each craft had its own skills which were so hardly learnt.

"Yes, Master Godric, we shall have need of many carpenters, and if there are any whom you think would be willing to learn the skills, then I will take them as apprentices. Be assured that they will have to work hard, and like those who would be masons, must be of a pure heart. I too can make no promise that all those who wish to try will succeed. It is for the master of each carpenters' lodge to decide if the apprentice has the skill we look for when he comes to make his test pieces."

Once more there was a silence, as all those around the table took in what had been said. Looking at Thurstan, it seemed that he too had a light shining from his eyes, as though he were seeing some great vision.

Finally, Alwin spoke again. "Master Odo, we have heard much of great interest this evening. There are men here who could well learn the skills of which we have been told. Others who do not have those skills may yet be willing to help labour, for there is not over-much work for all who live here. We should call the burgh together as soon as maybe, so that you and Edward and Thurstan may explain everything that you have told us here.''

Alwin thought for a moment, and then looked at those around him, to be sure that they agreed with him, before he continued.

"There may be other tasks that will need to be done which others may think they have the skill to undertake. Make a tally of all that you will need, so that when the burgh comes together they may know all of what is required. Then each man can make up his own mind if he is willing to play a part. Some will want no part and others will be fully stretched with their own labour, but I think all men should have the chance if they so wish. Indeed, it may be that some of the women may be able to add their skills to the work too, not at the crafts you have described but with cooking and caring for those who come to work here from elsewhere. When we know how many there are here who are willing to work, then you can calculate how many more will have to come from outside. They will need to be housed too. The reeve, Godric and I will gather the whole burgh together in the churchyard in three days' time and you can set out your plans then. Will that be time enough for you to make your plans? If there is anything you need to know in the meantime, then come and see one of us and we will give you the answers if we can.''

Odo looked at Edward and Thurstan who both nodded in agreement.

"So be it,'' he said. "We will come together as you say in three days' time. In the meantime, Edward, Thurstan and I will consult and make a tally of what we think we shall need.''

There was a general murmur of assent at this, and we all rose and went our separate ways. Father and I left together discussing things as we walked. When I reached the door of our cott, I left him and entered to find Isabel to tell her all that I had heard. She sat listening carefully. When I had finished she rose, and going to the window that faced our land and the burgh wall, she looked out, deep in thought. I joined her leaning my elbows on the sill.

"Hugh,'' she said, "We are growing some good vegetables in our land and the fowls yield more eggs than we can eat, so that I have some to sell as you know. I can manage the garden easily enough, now it is dug for me. There is spare land beyond our fence that is wild now. It looks to be about a rod wide which would make it the same size of what we now have. If you spoke to Father, do you think we could take it over and add it to our garden? You would have to pay him rent for it, or perhaps do service by keeping a little more of the wall in repair.''

She looked at the land on the far side of our fence, surveying the brambles that covered it.

"If we could clear the land and you could dig it, I could grow more vegetables and increase our stock of fowls. Perhaps have a second sow and another goat. With all the extra men who will come to live and work in the burgh on this great church, there will be a great demand for food. I could easily manage the extra land and stock, and what produce we have spare I could sell each day in the market place. I think we should act quickly if we are to do so at all, for others will think the same way and may ask for the land before we do.''

I looked at Isabel surprised. She had always been thoughtful and seemed to have the knack of going to the core of a scheme.

"Come," I said. "Let us go and pace out the land and see how big it is and what it is like. If the earth is as good as our present garden, it will be easy enough to till."

We went out and examined the place. It had never been used for habitation so far as I could tell. Fetching a spade, I tried it in the ground and turned over a few spits. It was good soil, though packed hard from want of use. We walked together round the space and paced it out. Like our plot, it was about ten rods long to the burgh wall, and about one rod wide, so that it would indeed be the same size as what we already had.

I looked at Isabel who was standing with a questioning gaze in her eyes. Knowing her as I did, I felt sure that she had already thought out how she would tend the extra land, for she never did anything lightly. Once more I walked down to the wall and looked back towards our cott. We should have to move the fence but that could be easily done. To have this extra land would be a great advantage and would bring us considerable profit if all went well. Returning to where Isabel stood, I took her in my arms and could not refrain from kissing her.

"My love, you are for ever thinking how we may prosper. This plan is good. Come, let us both go now to see your father and put it to him. I think I know what his answer will be, for I have never known him be able to refuse you anything."

"Am I so spoilt that I always have my way?" she asked, smiling. Then she lowered her eyes in mock humility, before nibbling my ear which she knew I could never resist. Holding her close I whispered,

"It is hard not to spoil you, but no, you only ask for what you have thought about and really think is needed. Let us go and see your father and see if he will agree."

We left our cott and walked, hand in hand as we always did, to the bailiff's house, where we found him busy with matters concerning the demesne. When at last he was free, Isabel explained what was in our minds. Alwin sat thinking about it for a while.

"Let us go and look at the land and see how it fits in with other plots around it. The idea is sound, and I have some other thoughts too."

Isabel looked at her father questioningly but said nothing. Taking my hand as we rose, she squeezed it knowingly. We went past our cott and then onto the land we were thinking of cultivating. Alwin walked over it and beyond, searching for something. He called for a spade, which I fetched him, and he then started clearing away some of the brambles and overgrowth.

"Here it is," he said at last. "I thought I remembered it. Many years ago, before you were born, there was a dwelling here, but it has fallen down long since. It belongs to the King, as most of the burgh does, but has been derelict these past thirty years. It was poorly built, so soon fell into decay when it became empty. I forget who lived here. The land was two rods wide and also went as far as the wall. Why don't you take the whole plot? It may seem more than you need, but there are going to be men coming here who will need somewhere to live while this church is built. Men like Edward and Thurstan who will bring their wives and need a comfortable cott in which to live."

Alwin came and stood by Isabel, and I saw his mouth crease into a smile.

"Isabel, how say you? Would you like to hold a messuage yourself from the King? It is worth little in its present state so the payment would be small, but you could rebuild the cott and then let it for a much larger sum. Besides, there would only be need to put half the land with the cott, so that you could still have the other half for yourselves to cultivate. I have a bag of silver put by and would gladly pay for the rebuilding of the cott for you. Nay, you overwhelm me! You will kill your father with your kisses. Save some for your poor husband."

Isabel had rushed to him and thrown her arms round his neck and was smothering him with her embrace, as tears of gratitude glistened in her eyes.

"Before you came this morning I talked with Alric and Emma too. There is another plot further along the wall that has likewise been derelict for longer than anyone can remember. I am doing the same for them, so do not think that you have twisted me round your little finger quite so easily - though I think you could if you tried," he added as he smiled at his daughter. "I had always meant to give you both something that you could use when you wed, but waited for the right time to see what would benefit you most. Besides, it will please the King to know that he will have more from the burgh, so do not think that I am doing this only for you two. It will be to my advantage as well."

He grinned, but I knew that he was only trying to cover his pleasure at Isabel's delight, for it was indeed a most generous gift. As soon as Isabel released her father, I seized his hand in grateful thanks.

"Do you really mean this?" I gasped. "This is really much more than we deserve. How can I ever repay you?"

"Care for this lovely girl you have wed, and that will be thanks enough for me," he murmured, overwhelmed by our combined gratitude.

"Now if you agree with my plan, we must make haste to rebuild the cott so that it will be ready when it is needed. I have some timber that can be used for the main structure, and I think you have some too which you brought back from your assart. Between us we should have more than enough, for I must also provide some for Alric too. I shall see to the hiring of men to help with the building, so that the work may be complete before they are needed for work on the new church."

Alwin continued to inspect the land, pulling brambles aside to see what lay beneath.

"After you left this morning's meeting, I spoke with both Edward and Thurstan to see what they intended to do about finding a place to live. Both said they wished to bring their wives here, so that they may live in some comfort during the years that they will be here. It was that which gave me the idea of rebuilding the cotts, for there are no empty places that they could have at present. You and Alric had the last two when you wed. I think there will be several more places built, though not all will be as large as we shall build, for the needs of others may be less. If we build the cott to measure a rod long and wide and a rod high at the centre, it will serve well. I have kept two timbers by especially for such a purpose to make the central poles to hold the roof at its peak. They are good oak and have been well seasoned so will last as long as you are alive and longer. Now I must leave you and see about arranging things. I am sure you two have plenty to do and plan."

Then he left us to return to his own house. As for Isabel and I, we were overcome with excitement, and spent the next half hour walking round the new plot, planning how we could use it and where we would site the cott. Later, we went to the mill and told Father and Mother, who were both delighted and offered such help as they could. While we were discussing our good fortune, Emma and Alric came in with their like news, so that we all celebrated together. Osbern came in soon afterwards.

"Would you like me to give you a hand with the work? I am quite good with an axe and saw, and could help with the timber-work if you like, after I have finished work each day."

We thanked him heartily. It seemed that we really were fortunate with our families.

That afternoon when work was finished at the mill, Isabel and I went to Alwin's house. There he drew up the charter needed for Isabel to take on the plot of land. Godric, Simon the infirmarer, and Rodric who taught the children, all witnessed the deed, and also the like deed for Alric and Emma.

The land was now ours to use. We gave the parchment to Alwin to keep for us in his great chest, for we had no safe place where we could guard it. Then Isabel and I went to claim her new holding and we staked it out while her father and Godric looked on, so that none could say afterwards that we had taken more than we should or claimed what was not ours by right. Then I set about moving the fence so that it enclosed the whole of the new plot.

For the moment, I was content to leave no boundary between our land and the new piece. That could come later when we had built the cott, and we wished to divide the rod of land that would go with it from the extra rod we would add to our land. One rod's width was sufficient for a cott to grow vegetables for a family, as we knew, so that the place we built would find ready takers.

With two rods for ourselves, we would be able to grow plenty to sell, and keep stock enough and to spare too. It was growing dark before Isabel, who had been helping me move the fence, suggested that it was time to eat. While she prepared the meal I finished the section of fence that I was working on.

While we ate, Isabel said, "I am going to speak to Edward and Thurstan when we have finished. They are staying with Father, so it is a good chance to find out which of them would like to have my new house when it is built. I mean to ask them if there is anything they would like in the building of it. It makes little difference to us, but if we can build it as they would like then it will make them more keen to have it. Besides, they are both expert at building and may have some new ideas that would make it a better place."

We found them both sitting over horns of ale with Alwin and Mary, so we joined them at the table. The talk was about how many men would be coming to work in the burgh.

"Where will you two live?" Isabel asked.

Thurstan was the first to answer.

"I have been speaking to your father, for I would hope to bring my wife to live with me here. We shall be here for several years and I would not wish to be away from her for so long, as you can well imagine. Is there an empty cott in the burgh that we could take? I have had no chance to look around yet, but perhaps your father knows of one."

"I fear not, but Father can perhaps say better than I. Would you be willing to take a new cott if one were built? One in which you could have a hand in the planning perhaps?"

Thurstan looked critically at her as she said this.

"Is there a new cott being built here now? Indeed that would be great good fortune, for it will be fresh and dry and I would know that the roof is sound. Yes, I would like such a place. Could you show it me tomorrow do you think?"

"That would not be easy," I said, " but I can show you where it will be. It is to be built next to our cott. Alwin has just arranged for Isabel to have the land next to our cott, and the charter was drawn up and witnessed today. We mean to start building a cott as soon as the design is fixed. If you like the idea, you can have a hand in the planning of it. Perhaps you have some new ideas on how best to make it comfortable, which we could use. Does the idea please you?"

"Such an offer I have never had before and it seems impossible to refuse. Tomorrow we will look at the place, and if you mean what you say I will gladly help in the design. It will not make it any more costly. There are some things that they do in other parts of the realm which I have not seen here, but which you may find useful."

Isabel looked at me for reassurance. Her father nodded his approval, and it seemed to me that what was being proposed made good sense.

"Shall we call for you after Prime tomorrow?" I suggested.

Thurstan looked pleased at this. "I will be ready. We can then view the plot and discuss matters further."

"What of you, Edward?" asked Alwin. "Have you any plans of where to live while you are here?"

"I have a wife and family that I would like to have with me. Is there any place that I could take for us all to live? It need not be over-large, but I have three small children so we should need room for them. What can you suggest?"

"Speak to my son Alric, for he may be able to help you, I think. He too has a plot of land on which he means to build a cott. Perhaps he would be willing for you to take it. Would you like me to send for him that you may ask him about it?"

I rose then. "We must depart," I said, " for there is much that we must do. Isabel and I will pass Alric's house and ask him if he can call on you here and speak with you this evening, if you wish."

We left the others, and as we went, Isabel said, "I think Thurstan may be able to help us greatly in the design of the cott. If it looks good, Alric can copy it too. We must tell him what is afoot so that he can have his reply ready when he sees Edward. To have two such people ready to take the places we can build is fortune that comes to few. It will be better that we build as well as we can, using such ideas of Thurstan as we may, so that the payment they will make may be the greater."

We found Alric and Emma at their cott and put the plan to them. They welcomed the idea, and we discussed the sort of cotts we should build before Alric left to see Edward as we had promised.

Next day. just as Prime was ending, we met Thurstan and took him to the ground next to our cott.

"We mean to add half the land to our garden, but the rest is a rod wide, and goes as far as the burgh wall as ours does. Will that be large enough for you, do you think? It is ten rods long by my reckoning." said Isabel.

Thurstan cast a critical eye over the land and paced it out, looking at our cott as he did so.

"Your cott is a rod square it seems, and has its roof held up by a single post in the middle I think. If I show you how to build with no central post so that the whole floor is clear, would you build that way?"

"Would it be strong enough? Surely the roof would fall in."

Thurstan took a stick and drew the end of a cott in the earth. Then he drew another plan of the side of the cott, showing the wall and the roof above it. He pointed to the first drawing.

"Do you see these timbers? They form the end of the cott. The two upright posts form the corners and the sloping ones form the end of the roof. This cross timber sits on the top of the corner posts and holds them together and also prevents the roof trusses from spreading. There is another at the far end and one in the middle and the ridge of the roof is supported by all three of the frames. This is a much stronger way of building, and also allows you to build bigger. What do you think of it?"

We looked at the drawings in the earth and then at our cott. It was troublesome having a post in the middle of the cott for one was always having to walk round it, though it was useful to hang things from.

"How thick do the timbers need to be?"

"No thicker than those in your cott, and the roof timbers can be a little thinner for they are not as long. They are easier to find, for smaller trees can be used."

"What do you think Isabel, shall we try this new design? Thurstan knows what he is talking about and has used it successfully before it seems."

"If you are happy, I am." she replied, and turning to Thurstan added, "If we build as you suggest, will you show us how to join the timbers, and also be sure to take the cott when it is finished?"

"That I promise," he said. "Here is my hand on it."

We both took his hand and the deal was struck. Then we three walked to Alwin's yard to look over the timber he had stacked. While he was making his choice, Isabel fetched her father and the timbers were selected. Most important were the four corner posts and two central uprights. Next, Thurstan chose the six main roof trusses and the two ridge poles. It was not necessary to have one long pole for the ridge for the two halves could be supported on the central truss. This made them easier to find, for each one had only to be about three yards long. With the timber chosen, and Alwin satisfied that we had not taken all his best timber - for he needed some for Alric's cott too - we returned to where the cott was to be built.

"Where do you intend the cott to be?" asked Thurstan.

Isabel went to the furthest corner of the land, and stood there.

"Here is the corner, and it should spread out from this point."

Thurstan came across to her, and putting a stick in the ground, tied a thin rope to it, which he took from his purse. He unravelled it as he walked slowly towards our cott. When he came to the end of the rope, he called for another stick and tied the end of the rope to it and thrust it into the ground, making sure that it was lined up with the front of our cott.

"There," he said, "that gives us the line for the front; now we have to fix the position of the sides. Do you know how to make sure that the cott comes out exactly square? I'll show you."

He took his thin rope again, and I noticed that it had several knots in it near one end.

"See," he said, "these knots are all the same distance apart. You make a mark that is three knots from the corner post along the line I have marked out towards your cott. Next, I draw a line that is four knots from the corner post, but along the side of the land. Now for the interesting part," he said smiling at us. "We go to the first mark I made, that was three knots from the corner, and stretch the rope five knots away from it towards the line that I made four knots from the corner. Look, I can make a line that will cross the other line. Now if I go back and stretch the rope from the corner through the place where these two lines cross, I will have a corner that is exactly right and square. Now we have the second corner fixed. We do the same thing again to find the third one, and then the fourth. If it comes out right, we should find that the fourth corner is exactly where I marked out the end of the first line."

He did as he said, and when he had finished, we went to where he had stretched the rope and looked at his lines. They indeed formed a perfect square and the last corner fell exactly on the place he had marked for the end of the first wall. I had often wondered how it was possible to make an exact square. Most cotts were about right but it was guesswork, and there were often problems when cutting poles, for they seemed to have to be slightly different lengths. I scratched my head, trying to puzzle out how he had done it.

"It is a trick we use much in building," Thurstan said. "They say it was known to the Greeks of old. They used many aids to calculating, which are a great help to a builder or carpenter. The important thing is to make sure that the knots are exactly the same distance apart from each other, and always to stretch the rope taut in the same way. If you fail in this, then the corners will not be exact. Your cott will now be a perfect square and be the stronger for it. Next we need to dig holes for the corner posts and two central poles. If the ground is firm, go down four hand-spans or a yard at least, and then place as large a stone as you can find under where the post is to stand. This will prevent it sinking into the ground. If the ground is soft, then you will have to dig until you find firm ground. Then you can fill the hole with stones to make a solid base, until it is about three hand-spans deep. Then it is ready for the corner post."

Over the next few days, we cleared the ground for the floor of the cott and dug the six holes for the main posts. Then we brought all the main timbers to the site and arranged them as Thurstan directed. He showed us how to cut the poles so that they sat neatly on each other, resting on a notch so that they would not slip, and how to fix the poles together with pegs so that they were firm. The whole shape of the end of the cott was now lying on the ground, with the base of the poles resting on the edge of the holes.

We then arranged the poles that would make the other end of the cott, and the centre arch. Next we cut the poles that would form the tops of the side walls, and also the ridge of the roof. These only needed to be three yards long, for they would be supported by the centre arch in the middle of the cott. I thought the poles that would form the tops of the end walls and span the middle of the cott seemed too thin for their length, which was a full rod, and bent easily when I lifted one end. I saw Thurstan watching me as I tried one of them.

"I know what you are thinking," he said. "Those long poles will not be strong enough for their work. We have some more poles to fit in yet. See here: we place another pole beneath the timber that forms the top of the end wall, four feet from each corner. This will hold the long pole steady. Likewise we place another short pole above it to help support the end of the roof, one on each side. We do the same with the centre arch, so the longest span with no support is only eight feet. The poles are quite strong enough to bear that strain and the slope of the roof is well supported. This cott that will be much stronger than most of those in the burgh. Often in my travels I have seen cotts that have been blown down by a strong gale for want of sound building. I'll warrant that this one will stand firm even though the poles we use are each one thinner than you might think necessary. It is the way each timber is bound to its neighbour that gives the whole strength."

We set about cutting the extra poles as Thurstan suggested, and found that there were plenty of such light timbers to choose from. It was always the great heavy timbers that were hard to find.

Then with the aid of Father, Osbern and a few others, we raised the main frame of the new cott. When it was up, there was much talk about it, for its shape was different to those normally built. Several men tried thrusting at the upright poles to see if they could shift them for they seemed flimsy, but were disappointed when they found they stood firm. Others tried hanging from the timbers that formed the tops of the walls, but they too took the weight and did not bend, for they had their supports too.

There was much gossip in the ale-houses afterwards and all had to agree that this man, who claimed to be a master carpenter, certainly knew his trade. For our part, we now had to fill in the walls with wattles and then apply the daub - stinking task that it would be as we already knew - and then cover the roof poles with thatch. It would be some weeks before all that was completed.

Meantime, Edward, the master mason, had been busy in the churchyard. Now it was decided where the great new church was to be built, he had to make his exact plan of its site. This he discussed carefully with Godric, who was greatly concerned how he and the other priests were to be able to continue to say Mass during the building works, for it was supposed that the present church and chapels were to be destroyed to make room for the new church.

"You have a fair church here already, built of stone with a crypt below it," Edward said. "There are also two smaller stone chapels, each with its own crypt. I have looked at the plan I made first and it seems to me that I can keep part of what is built in stone and use it in the new church. You say you fear for the souls of the people here if they cannot come to Mass. Would it suffice if they could come to the crypt to hear Mass? It would be covered from the rain and has small windows through which light can enter."

Godric considered carefully before replying.

"It would not be ideal, but we could manage in the short-term, but there is a further problem. All priests must say Mass daily, and there are twenty-two of them besides me now that Alsi is dead, God rest his soul. With only one altar in the church crypt, they would find it hard to find time for each to say his Mass. At present, with our church and nine chapels, two or three have to share one altar. I am not sure how matters would lie."

"Though I shall have to destroy the two stone chapels, I mean to leave their crypts, so that there would be three altars for you to use. Would that suffice?"

Godric considered this for a while, counting on his fingers as he did so.

"It could be done I think. Some of the priests may be able to use one or other of the small chapels at Stanpit, Sopley or Herne. If it is the will of God, then we shall find a way. But do you really mean to leave us the crypts, and can you find a way to have them in this new church?"

"I have been looking at the plan Odo drew, and it will be possible."

Edward took the roll of parchment he had under his arm and spread it out on the ground for Godric to examine.

"I have marked the position of the church and two stone chapels, here, here, and here. Now, do you see these lines? They show the outer walls of the church with its two transepts to the north and south, and these lines inside show the line of pillars that will support the main roof."

Edward pointed out each feature as he talked.

"Do you see how I have placed the two stone chapels inside the two transepts? In this way I can use them and keep their crypts. Now look at the inner line of pillars. See how they stretch beyond the nave and the crossing of the church towards the east. That is where the present church stands. I mean to set the new high altar in almost the same position as your present one, perhaps a little further to the east. I can keep the crypt of your present church and it will help to raise the high altar above the rest of the new church, so that all who come to Mass may see it better."

He looked towards the little church which had for so long been the centre of the burgh.

"The church itself I cannot use because it is too small and narrow, and besides, I mean to have great pillars where you now have small walls. We shall have to dig down beside the crypt to make the foundations for the pillars. It will be best if we leave the outside walls until that is done because it will make it easier to move stone and other things round the site if the outer part of the ground is left undisturbed. The two stone chapels can be left untouched for some time. That will mean you will have those chapels and their crypts to use for saying Mass. I can see how important this will be for you. I must carry the folk with me for many of them will be working on the building."

Godric nodded in approval.

"You are careful in your planning, Edward. If you can indeed build as you have explained, then you will carry the priests and most other men with you . When you are ready to call for labourers let me know, and I will speak to the people. I think it can be arranged that there should be a special Mass to which all should come. There may be a suitable feast-day that can be used. Pentecost is not many weeks hence. It will be my intention to explain the purpose of the new church and how it will benefit the burgh, and what part each man can play in its building. Those that come to Confession I can encourage to atone for their sins by helping with the building in some way. When I show them how you are intending to use the three crypts of their present buildings and also let them continue to worship in the two stone chapels, at least for the time being, they will see that all the old is not to be swept away, so that their traditions and background will remain. This will be a great comfort to many of them."

He spread his arms wide, as if to encompass the whole site.

"After all, men have worshipped on this site for over four hundred years now. To wipe that away as of no consequence would be a grievous loss and cause much upset in the burgh. As you rightly say, if you did that, you would not carry the people with you, so that the building would suffer and the spirit of the place go out of it. Much of what we try to do here would then be lost. Alwin the bailiff feels the same I know, and will help all he can to make sure that your ideas and plans are understood. Now, will you show me on the ground where the various parts of this new church are to stand? I find your drawings hard to follow, for I am not trained in their interpretation."

Edward rolled up his parchments, and tucking them under his arm led the way round the churchyard, stopping periodically to point out where each part of this great new building would stand.

While they were thus engaged, Alwin approached on his way to the quay, so he joined them that he too might learn the full extent of the proposed building. By the time Edward had finished explaining his plans, both Godric and Alwin were dumbfounded.

"Is it really to be so large?" they asked, "It will hold everyone in the burgh many times over."

"That may be so now, but when it is built there will be many more priests needed to care for it, and there will also be a monastery attached to it if I understand Flambard's wishes correctly. Besides, there will be many people coming to live here while the church is being built, and if they like the burgh and there is land available for them to plough, many of them will wish to remain. Others will come to trade and will also need to live here. I have seen it happen before elsewhere in the realm and also in the dukedom of Normandy. When a great building like this is raised, men flock to live near it for a multitude of reasons."

A worried frown crossed Edward's brow as he turned to Godric.

"You may find that you have the care of twice the number of souls before too many years are out, and that even this great new church is filled. Remember, Winchester is not far distant, and the King keeps his Treasury there. Besides he is ever fond of hunting, and his best forest is in Andret which lies between Winchester and here. The fame of this place will surely spread. It is likely that the King will need a castle built here too before too long, for that seems to be his common practice nowadays."

Alwin looked at Edward, startled. "Why, does he fear an attack?"

"Not necessarily, but he wishes to have his burghs well defended, so that those who are loyal to him can hold the land for him against any who might think to rebel. There have been uprisings in the Welsh Marches, not for the first, nor, I suspect, the last time. Many of the barons elsewhere are groaning under the taxes and gifts he levies on them and would rebel if they felt strong enough to do so. Even his brother, Robert Curthose, who has the dukedom of Normandy now, is not to be trusted I hear. William is only seeking to secure his crown in this realm by making sure that his friends are in secure strongholds. A castle here would simply ensure that a rebellious baron could not easily take the place and so deprive the King of its revenues. At present there would be little enough to take, I think, so that it would not be worth the risk so near to Winchester. When the new church is built and this place becomes more important, then the gain could well be worth the risk."

He shrugged his shoulders.

"Nothing of this is certain yet. I speak only of what I have seen and what I have heard of the ways of William. Since we three shall be working closely together for some years, it seems good to share my thoughts with you. I would hold no secrets from you."

As the three of them continued to discuss the plans, Odo joined them.

"Now that Edward has measured out the ground and seen how the various parts will fit and you know what is intended, I must settle down and make the master plan from which we shall work. This will need a large table which I shall cover with plaster on which I shall engrave the plan in scale. It is a difficult but vital task, for once it is done it fixes for ever the position of every part of the building. It is from that plan that the church will be built and to which the masons and carpenters and all the other master craftsmen will refer. It will be housed in a shed from which Edward will control the building works, for once the plan is settled my part is almost done. It is Edward who will see to the building of the church, aided by Thurstan."

Odo looked confidently at the pair of them and smiled.

"I shall visit the burgh occasionally or if Edward finds he has a problem he cannot solve - which I doubt for he is a most expert mason. I looked at the whole site with him, and we have decided that the best place for the shed will be beyond the east end of the new church, towards the mill-stream. There is space there too for the lodge from which the masons will work. There is also space enough for the stone to be brought for the men to shape and carve. Besides, it is sheltered from the main winds by the slope of the ground, so that it will be a better place for craftsmen to work."

The four of them walked over to the area Odo had mentioned, where he thrust a stick into the ground.

"This is where the shed will be. Alwin, have you timber to build it from?"

"There should be sufficient in my yard, I think, though you know that I need some for the two cotts that Alric and Isabel are to build for Edward and Thurstan. Come and see, but first let us mark out the exact site for your shed and pace out the size so that I may know better what timber you will need."

"I think you know that I have offered to help Isabel with the design of her cott," said Thurstan, "and will do the same for Alric too if he wishes, so I know what timbers they will be needing. Let us see what you have and I will choose what I need, if I may. Payment will be settled by Flambard as will all the expenses of this church. While the shed is being built, I will have time to see to the frame of the cott Isabel is to build for me."

Thus the shed came to be built, and the huge table to hold the plan; also the main lodge for the masons, and another for Thurstan and his carpenters. The days went by and Odo departed as he said, while interest grew amongst us all, with rumour playing its full part about how the church was to be built and how many would be needed in the building. Those who were not afraid to do an honest day's toil made themselves known to Edward and Thurstan, thinking that they would earn good steady wages. Some were taken on at once, where they were known to be reliable; others were told to wait until the plans were fully known. None were sent away empty-handed, but none were promised an easy or idle time either. Interest grew with rumour, and more became keen to have a hand in the great work. Both Godric and Alwin helped to encourage the interest, without holding out false hopes.

May 18th, which was Pentecost, was fast approaching, when Godric announced that there was to be special High Mass to celebrate the start of work on the great new church. The whole burgh was summoned to be present that day, for it was likely to prove a most important day in the lives of everyone. Godric said that at the Mass he intended to ask for God's blessing on the work about to be undertaken, so that it might prosper in the way that it should. Those who wished to take part in the work should come to Confession and be shriven, that they might better be prepared to take their part in the work. All twenty-three priests would be in their chapels from Vespers until it began to grow dark, so that none could say that they had not had the chance to confess. The plans of the new church would then be unveiled and explained, and details of how many men would be needed. Great was the excitement.

Pentecost dawned fine. Isabel and I had been to Confession with the rest of both our families the evening before, so that we woke with easy hearts. As she sat up in the bed beside me and stretched her arms wide, yawning as she did so to shake the sleep from her mind, I could not help but wonder, as I did every time I saw her, at her beauty and comeliness, with her corn coloured hair flowing free round her shoulders and her startling blue eyes. She smiled at me when she saw that I was awake, and bent to kiss me tenderly, brushing my eyes with her lips.

"Come, Hugh my love, we must stir ourselves if we are not to be late. It is long since the cock first crowed, and before we go to Mass I have food to prepare for the feast we are to have this night."

She rose then with her usual grace, and reaching for her robe, quickly dressed, before going out to fetch fresh milk from our goat. By the time she returned, I too was dressed and had sluiced my head and arms in the pail of water that stood beside the hearth and set the platters and beakers on our table, ready with the bread and a piece of cheese. High Mass was at noon, so that we should have the four hours fast, laid down by the church, between our meal and Mass. We ate our simple meal, happy in each other's company, and still warm in our love for each other.

When we had finished, I settled to making more of the wattles that we needed for the walls of the cott that we were building for Thurstan next to ours. There were still several to make, and not all were the same size. Some had to house windows, and others were needed to make the small partitions he wanted added from the outer wall to the upright pole that went to support the roof purlins at the middle arch. Though these were only four foot wide, they provided some shelter and privacy and were a new idea to me. They had merit I thought, and I kept them in mind for our own cott later.

As soon as the bell started to toll to summon us all to Mass, I left what I was doing to wash and change into a clean tunic and hose. Because it was a feast-day and there was the special Mass, I put on my newest tunic with its embroidered hem of coloured wools. I fastened it with my best tooled-leather belt with its burnished buckle, and added my new scrip that Isabel had given me to celebrate my birthday. Isabel for her part had on a fine yellow coloured woollen robe which she gathered at the waist with a deep blue girdle. Her head and shoulders were covered by a linen hood and scarf of the same blue as her eyes, and the scarf was held at the shoulder by a brooch that I had given her likewise on her birthday. She smiled at me modestly, for the robe was new.

"Do you like the colour?" she asked, "It is a dye from crocus flowers I have not used before, but I needed a soft colour for this robe."

I held her hands, then made her turn round, that I could see the full effect. Then I folded the hood back a little so that her pale hair could be seen framing her lovely face.

"My love, I doubt there is a lady at the King's Court that could hold a taper to you. May I take your arm, as we go to Mass? I shall be proud to do so."

As we entered the churchyard, I noticed that some of the priests were standing beside wooden crosses placed in the ground in several places. The first we came to was Sifrid.

"What do you here with this cross? Are you not taking part in the Mass?" I asked.

"Assuredly," he answered, "but twelve of us must first stand by these crosses to make sure that none are moved, for they mark the corners of the new church. Edward has placed us here having measured out the building early this morning. He means to tell the congregation about it at the end of Mass. Once everyone is assembled, we shall be joining Godric for the celebration of the Mass at the high altar."

We made our way into the church, and found places next to Mother, Father and Osbern, and beside Isabel's family, with Emma standing beside Alric. When it came to the part where the Epistle is read, Rodric first read in Latin from the second chapter of the Acts of the Apostles, and then afterwards told the Pentecost story of the tongues of fire descending on the disciples in the upper room, and how they all began to speak in other languages. Then Godric read the Gospel for the day, and afterwards spoke to us.

"Today we celebrate a very special Mass. Not only is this the feast of Pentecost, of which Rodric has already told you, but this is the day when we start to build the great new church in this burgh. I say 'we' because there is a part for everyone to play in the building, provided he is of a pure heart."

He looked round on the assembled folk then to see that he had their close attention.

"We mean to build on sure foundations too. That is why when first it was suggested that the church should be on Catherine's hill, it was found that it was not to be. God moves in mysterious ways that we do not always understand. Do you remember what it says in the seventh chapter of Matthew's Gospel? Christ tells us there that if we listen to what He says, it is like building a house on a rock, so that when the rain descends, the floods come, and the winds blow and beat upon the house, it falls not, because it is founded upon a rock. This church will stand here because beneath this ground there is rock, and we shall dig down to build the foundations on that rock. Had we built on Catherine's hill, we should have been like the man who did not listen to the sayings of Jesus. Our faith likewise must be built on a sure rock foundation, just as St Peter was the rock on which the Holy church was built."

There was much nodding of heads at this, for the Gospel story was well known. Godric looked round at all those who were gathered in the church, many of whom then bowed their heads in silent prayer.

"Afterwards, we shall go in procession round the gist of the new building. Edward here has already marked the outside corners of the building with crosses, beside each of which one of the priests was standing as you came this morning. As we make our progress round the gist, we shall consecrate all the land that lies within it, for it is to be holy ground. Thereafter, let no man swear or utter a profanity within that boundary on pain of severe penance. If this is to be Christ's church, then let each man hallow it."

He spread wide his arms to encompass us all, so that we might know that none should be excluded.

"When the procession is completed we shall return to the church, where Edward will tell you of his plans and also say how many he will need to help him build the church. Let no man feel he has not the talent for the work. Whatever skill he has it can be used, though it be but the strength of his arm. None that are honest need fear to offer their service. Alwin the bailiff has said that some boon-work can be rendered on the building of the church too. Let us therefore pray for God's help with the building."

All present listened to Godric's ringing tones in awed silence. So the Mass proceeded to its end. Then, as Godric had said, we moved in solemn procession, led by the priests who chanted as we went, round the boundary of where the church was to stand, pausing at each of the twelve corners of the cross-shaped building. As we stood at each corner, the priest who stood by the cross planted in the ground, took a spade and solemnly dug out a turf to mark the spot and show that the work had begun. The perambulation complete, everyone returned to the church, where Edward then addressed us as we stood in excited and curious silence.

"People of this burgh of Twynham. I speak to you this day with the consent of Godric your priest, Geoffrey your reeve, and Alwin the bailiff of my Lord the King's demesne. You have all heard and seen how Ranulf called Flambard wished to build a mighty church on Catherine's hill. You all know that powers mightier than he seemed to decree that the church should not be built on that hill, but here in this place where you have always worshiped. Flambard has now given Odo authority to make the plans for such a church, and to bring the best stone that can be found, and hire such labour as may be needed. Flambard also gave authority to pay fair wages to all that are hired, provided the work they do is good."

This brought a general murmur of approval and much nodding of heads.

"Odo and I have looked carefully at the land," continued Edward, "and he has drawn plans which are now in the shed that has been built near to the mill-stream. Those that wish, may see this plan later."

Edward looked slowly round at everyone before he continued.

"People of Twynham, be assured that this will be the greatest work ever done here. It will take many years to complete, and need more men than there are in this place to build it. As you know, Odo has now departed, for the King needs his skills to design other great churches in his realm. Though he will return from time to time to see how the work progresses, the main work of building he has now entrusted to me."

He paused again, as many turned to discuss this with their neighbours, seemingly disappointed that Odo would not be in here all the time.

"Skilled craftsmen will be needed too," continued Edward, "such as I doubt can be found in this burgh, for such men can only be found in the great towns where magnificent abbeys have already been built, and where their skills have been put to use. Such craftsmen Odo will send to come and help me here, but there are many other skills that you have amongst you that I shall need. There are also some amongst you who may have skills of which you know not. These I need to find, for I shall need masons, and carvers in stone; carpenters and workers in wood; and plasterers and workers in mortar. Later there will be need of workers in metal and glass. All these will need to be craftsmen skilled in their trades. Those that think that they may have skills in their hands should come forward and offer themselves. If they seem to have the ability, then the master craftsman will take them as apprentices and train them in the skills and arts of his trade. They will learn all that he has to teach, and so in time become masters themselves in their own right. This is not something that any should undertake lightly, for the apprenticeship is long and arduous, and only those of a firm mind and a pure heart will succeed. Those who would accept the challenge may speak with me, or Thurstan the carpenter, during this week when we can tell you more. Next Sunday, after Mass, we will both be by the lodge where the plans are kept. Those that wish can come forward then so that we may see if there is a place for you as an apprentice."

Edward was forced to cease speaking for a while, as there was much chatter about who might wish to put themselves forward.

"There are many more folk needed. Any who wish to dig, or cart stone, or labour in other ways will be welcome. As many as come forward, provided they will do an honest day's work for an fair day's wages, will be used. Not till I know how many there are in the burgh who will work here, will I know how many others I need to find from elsewhere. Since this is your burgh, I will use such labour as you can provide first, so let none say that he did not have the chance to work on this great church in your own burgh. As you have heard, Alwin the bailiff of the King's demesne has agreed that certain days of boon-work that you owe to the King may be given to the church. In this way all who dwell here should be able to play their part in the building. Later, when the church is finished, we may hope to add a monastery where the word of God may be studied and spread, and the works of healing, for which this place is already well known, may prosper."

Edward stepped back then beside Godric, who pronounced a final blessing on us all, before dismissing us with the customary "Pax vobiscum" to which we replied with a heartfelt "Et cum spirito tuo".

As Isabel and I walked slowly back with the rest of our families, I noticed that Osbern was close beside me.

"Hugh," he said in low tones, "I would talk with you. May I come with you to your cott now?"

When we were within and seated at our table, Osbern looked at me with a worried expression on his usually clear face.

"Hugh, I have been thinking much of late. You are now a master of your trade and will have the mill when Father is no longer able to work it. I know something of the work and we three work well together, but I shall never have the mill and so be my own master as you will be. If I were not there, do you think that you could manage the mill on your own, perhaps with a little hired labour in busy times? If you can, then I would dearly like to become a master of a craft myself. You know I have helped you with the building of the cott for Thurstan, and have watched how he handles timber. I have tried my hand at making joints in wood and have had some success. After hearing Edward speak today, I am thinking that I might seek to become an apprentice to Thurstan, if he will have me." He hesitated before continuing. "First I must know if you can manage the mill by yourself, for I would not leave Father else."

I thought this over for a while. Isabel, who had been busying herself preparing food, came and sat beside me and smiled at Osbern and took his hand in hers.

"You are ever thoughtful," she said. "Your father is blessed indeed to have two such sons. "

"It is right that each man should have the chance to be his own master if he so wishes." I said, thinking aloud. " I can provide such help for father as he needs now and still have time for my assart. Your going would not cause him hardship, though he would miss your company. He would be happy, I think, to see you apprenticed to Thurstan, the more so if you proved that you had skill in your hands."

I sat thinking a while, wondering how best to help Osbern in his desire.

"Speak to Father about it as soon as you may, so that he has time to give the matter proper thought before next Sunday, for that is when you must see Thurstan and offer yourself to him. I will speak with Father too,for he will have to give his blessing, and agree to your being bound to Thurstan, for you are still not of age. We live in exciting times, and it would be good to have a hand in the building of this great new church. Would that I had some skill that I could use, but I only know how to set the stones and grind corn."

"Setting the millstones as you do is a great art, and even your father cannot do it so well as he has often told you." Isabel stroked my fingers as she spoke. "Do not decry yourself."

Osbern rose then and bidding us farewell, went back to the mill-house, where he would speak to Father. Isabel came and sat beside me.

"Osbern would make a fine carpenter I think. He has a feel for timber. Have you noticed that he never takes the first piece of wood but always examines it to see if it is right for his needs? I saw some of the joints he made for the windows in the new cott. The last one he did was almost as good as those that Thurstan made himself. There is little doubt he will take him as an apprentice. I do hope he does, for it would be the making of Osbern. I wonder what my young brother Alnoth will do? There could be a chance for him too if he set his mind to it."

I loved Isabel for her thoughtfulness. It was always someone else she was concerned for. I remembered when Adeline had bade me take care of her and I swore again to myself that none should ever hurt her if I was near to defend her.

Chapter 10 1094

We were busy all next day, grinding corn for Ranulf at the guest-house. There is so much noise in the mill when the wheels are turning that there was no occasion when I could speak to Osbern to find out what Father had thought of his plan. Not until we had stilled the wheels for the day and were clearing the floor did I have a chance to ask Osbern how things had gone.

"Father considered the matter carefully and praised me for my desire to be my own man, but he would not finally give his blessing till he has spoken with you, to see if you will agree too. As he said, the mill is a family concern, and the head of the family should have such assistance as he needs from others in the household. He would not have you left short-handed when he can no longer work. If you really meant what you said yesterday, will you speak to Father soon, so that I may know that all is well? I would speak with Thurstan as soon as maybe if Father agrees, for there will be others who would be apprentices, and I mean to be the first if I can."

"Then I will speak with Father as soon as we have finished here."

I hastened to complete the tasks that remained, but before I had done, Father came down from the corn-loft above, where he had been arranging sacks for the morrow's work. He leant against the great wheel in the centre of the mill and folded his arms.

"Hugh, how many men do you think could run this mill? There is more work than when I was a lad helping my father. Then the two of us managed well enough. Now that the new church is to be built, I can foresee that there will be more mouths to feed, and so more corn to be ground. What say you?"

I ceased what I was doing, and rested my back against the wall before answering him.

"When first I started work, there was only you here, for grandfather had died some years before. You managed well enough, though it was hard I have no doubt, even if there was less to be done. With the three of us, the work is easy, so that we were able to clear our assart and enlarge it again last year. I have also had time to dig the land beside our cott, and help with the building of the new cott that Isabel will let to Thurstan. I think there is work for no more than two here, and even then they would have time to spare for much of the year. You are thinking about Osbern no doubt."

"He spoke to me last evening, saying that he would learn the carpenter's skills, if I would agree to it. He has a mind to be apprenticed to Thurstan after hearing Edward speak yesterday. I told him it would be harder than here in the mill, for the rules would be strict and it would not be his father that cuffed him when he was careless."

He smiled then, for I could not remember an occasion that Father had ever cuffed us, though he had often had need to speak roughly to us with good reason, for our boyish idleness.

"Could you run this mill without help, when I am too old to work?"

"That day is many years hence, but yes, I think I could, though there might be need of some hired labour to hump the sacks occasionally. I would be glad for Osbern to learn new skills and he has a way with wood. Isabel said yesterday that she had noticed how he had fashioned some of the window frames for the new cott nearly as well as Thurstan himself. He has skilled hands, and perhaps is wasted here in the mill now. You and I can easily manage here if he were to leave, and I could still find time for our assart."

"Then it is settled. I wanted to speak to you first to see how you felt, though I had little doubt what your answer would be. You have always considered your brother, which is kind of you. From what you say it would seem that Isabel will be content too. I will tell Osbern that he may do as he desires, and give him my blessing too. Come, let us finish here and go and find Osbern. He is probably with his mother. Besides, we must find Thurstan and speak to him as soon as maybe, for I must give him my consent for Osbern to be his apprentice. He has to be bound for seven years while he learns his craft. It is a long time, but he has the spirit to keep to the binding, I think."

Thus it was that Osbern came to be bound to Thurstan. I was sad, as was Father, to lose him from the mill, for we had worked well together and his good humour had often lightened the frequent drudgery of the work. Before the week was out, I heard from Alric that his young brother Alnoth was to be apprenticed to Edward as a mason. Alric shook his head when he told me, fearing that he would not be able to keep to the strict rules of the masons' lodge, and keep their secrets which were even more strictly enforced than the carpenters. Yet I was glad for him, for there was little prospect for him in the burgh otherwise. If he could become a skilled mason and even a master himself, there would always be work for him and an honoured place in any town where there were great buildings rising. If Edward's words were true, there would be plenty of such places.

Before the week was out, two master masons and a master carpenter had arrived, sent by Odo to help Edward and Thurstan organise the work that was soon to start. After Mass the next Sunday, as Edward had requested, we went with Osbern to the lodge near the mill-stream, where Thurstan stood. Alnoth was already standing with Alwin and Alric at the door of Edward's lodge, along with others who also wished to be admitted as apprentices to their crafts.

One at a time they entered the lodges with their fathers and sponsors to take their binding oaths. We stood silent outside, for only masters in the craft were allowed to witness the ceremony of binding along with the sponsor of the new apprentice. There were seven of them all together, four masons and three carpenters. Others had wished to be admitted but had not been thought suitable.

Edward himself had not been idle during the week. Now that the master plan was complete, he had been showing it and explaining it daily to those who were interested, after men returned from the fields. The cott we were building for him was progressing well, and there was no need for him to give any more help or advice. Instead, he busied himself with sticks and lines, marking out the ground where the foundations for the great pillars were to be built. At first there was much confusion, for the lines he marked were many feet inside the corners where the crosses stood, until he explained that those crosses marked the corners of the outside walls of the church. These would be in the form of a cross with a transept on each side which would enclose the two small stone chapels, one on each side, and a wide passage or aisle running the whole length of the church outside the great pillars.

"These aisles are needed to give support to the roof," Edward explained. "Though the pillars will be strong, the roof will be so wide that its weight may thrust them apart unless the weight is spread outside them. The outer walls will have buttresses in them where each pillar stands, so that the weight of the roof will be spread from the pillars across the sloping roof of the aisle to the buttress. In this way the pillars will be supported. See," he continued, pointing to our present church, "I have kept my word. The present church stands within the pillars we shall build. Though we shall have to take down the church when we come to build the pillars there, we shall use the stone of it to form the new pillars, so your church will remain, if in a different form. The crypt that lies beneath it will remain too, and can always be used even while we are building."

One afternoon when we had finished early at the mill, I watched Edward as he measured the ground to mark out where they should dig the foundations. He stood at the crossing in the middle of the church, holding a rod in one hand and a line and sticks in the other.

"See," he said, "The foundations of these four great pillars at the crossing need to be a full rod wide, and that is the width of the trench we shall have to dig. Because those pillars will have to support the roof of the crossing and the tower that will be above it, they will have to be wider than the rest of the pillars. I estimate that an extra foot will be enough. They will also be longer - four yards long - whereas the other pillars need only be eight feet in length. The foundations must still be twice as wide as the pillars themselves, to support the great weight above them."

I looked at the ground, and could see what he meant.

"The space between the pillars is to be three yards, and each pillar will measure eight feet at its base. Since the foundations need to be twice the size of the pillars, so we shall have to dig out all the ground between them to make the foundations. There will be a massive trench the whole length of the nave up to the crossing, and another from the other end of the crossing to the east end of the church. Since the crossing is almost eight yards across, and the foundations of the pillars extend but four feet all round them, there will be five yards in the centre that can be left. This will make it easier for moving about inside the building while work is progressing."

Edward paused for a moment before starting to walk towards the eastern end of the church.

"Come and see what is planned at the east end, past where the main altar is to stand. There is to be a rounded apse which I am about to mark out. You can help me if you like."

I followed him to the end of the church and watched while he stretched a line between the two corners of the end of the wall. Then he took a second line, measured the same length, folded it in half, and drove a stick into the ground where the half-way mark cut the first line to mark its centre point. Taking his second line again, he bade me hold one end of it to the stick he had placed at the centre while he measured out the distance he needed on the line. He then tied this line to another stick and, starting at the end wall of the church, drew a complete half-circle. Edward then stood back and looked at it critically.

"Yes," he said, "That looks right. There is the apse for the east end of the church. Now all I need to do is draw two more lines to show the extent of the foundations. Do you like the look of it, Hugh?"

I got up and walked over to where he stood, and examined the shapes he had drawn on the ground, trying to imagine how it would look when it was built. It was hard, for I was not used to seeing plans or even the shapes of buildings drawn out on the ground, but I began to see how the building would look.

"It seems enormous to me, but I can see the various parts now. I like the apse at the end too. Tell me, our present church seems to be right in the middle of where you will want to have the main altar. Do you mean this to be so?"

"Yes indeed. Your present church is the centre of the worship in the burgh, and I wanted that to continue, so I have planned to have the high altar set in the middle of where the church now stands. That way men can feel that they are continuing to worship God on the same site where they have always prayed. Though we shall have to take down the present church, we shall reuse the old stones for they are good, and the crypt will remain undisturbed beneath. In this way, the prayer and worship that was started here by St Birinus, four hundred years ago and more, will continue as it has in the past. I hope men will feel that I am right to do this."

I pondered all this for a while, thinking about all those who had worshipped here for so many generations.

"I am sure you are right, and by doing this you will carry most men with you. Godric is well liked as you know, and if it is thought that you are trying to do what is best for him and the other priests too and leave us the heart of what was here before, then men will help you. I will do so myself so far as I am able, though with my work at the mill and our assart to farm I shall have little enough time to spare. What time I have I will gladly use to help build and I will encourage others to do so. You know that my young brother Osbern is now apprenticed to Thurstan, and Isabel's brother is your apprentice too. It seems this church is touching the lives of all our families."

"I have found in other places where I have built that this is often the case. Perhaps it is inevitable with a building of such magnitude that is to be the centre of life here. I mean to see that the apprentices that Thurstan and I have taken on learn as much of our respective skills as it is in our power to teach them. This realm needs expert craftsmen, for the King means to make it secure and famous for its buildings. There are many castles being built too, as I have told you. In a few days' time, I shall be asking for the burgh to be called together again so that I can see how many there are who want to help with the work. The first task will be digging the foundations, and that will take many weeks."

We continued talking, while Edward marked out more lines on the ground, until the light began to fade. Then he folded up his parchments and returned with them to his lodge where he kept all his plans and tools. For my part, I made my way home to Isabel.

True to his word, as he had promised when he spoke to us all after Mass the previous Sunday, Edward called a great meeting of all the folk, to offer work to all those who were prepared to do it. Some there were who were too idle, preferring hunger and poverty to the exertions of a day's labouring. The usual vagabonds knew that the priests would never turn them away empty without a crust of bread and a mug of weak ale, caring nothing for the low opinion others had of them. There will always be some such folk. For the rest, having thought over Edward's words and his promise of good wages, those who had time to spare and strength to use were willing enough to offer themselves for hire.

"There is much earth to be moved," Edward told them. "You can see from the lines that I have drawn on the ground how wide the trenches are to be. They are also to be deep. Exactly how deep I cannot yet say, but by my reckoning they will need to be a full rod and a half deep. That means that four men standing on each other's shoulders at the bottom of the trench, would still not be above the ground."

There was a gasp as he said this. Edward continued.

"We shall need carts and barrows too, and pulleys to lift the earth from the bottom of the trenches as they grow deeper. Those that have a cart or barrow, I will hire. Those who have but themselves need not fear, for I shall have other carts made for them to use. Likewise, those who have oxen I will hire, and for those who do not, I will find beasts that they can use."

A voice was heard in the crowd.

"Where will you put all this earth that you dig out? Like as not, it will fill the harbour if you put it there or do you mean to make a mountain of it?. Did not Godric say something about faith moving mountains at Mass a few Sundays ago? Perhaps he will do it for you."

There was some subdued laughter at this, for the speaker was seen to be a scrawny man who often mocked the priests and what they did. Edward merely smiled at the man.

"It is a good question and I have the answer for you. Faith you need to have for sure, but for this task strength is more important."

This brought renewed laughter, for it was seen that Edward had got the better of the speaker.

"I mean to pile the earth we dig into a great mound - a mountain if you like - on the ground between the church and the road from the bridge that leads to the market square. It stretches down to the mill-stream and the ground is clear there.

The earth that is piled up will form the mound on which a castle may be built. This burgh only has a timber wall set on an earth bank above a ditch to defend it. The King is causing castles and keeps to be built throughout his realm so that those who are loyal to him may live in safety from those who wish to break his peace. You can do the King and yourselves service by building up this mound, for when he comes to have his castle built he will need such a mound on which to place it. If there were no mound then he would make you build one, so it will save you labour if you do it now."

Several heads nodded at the sense of this. Others, worried at the thought of an attack, pressed Edward further on the matter.

"I mean not to alarm you," he said. "There is no fear of an attack that I know of, but some of the barons support the King's brothers more that they do the King himself, and there is always a risk of such things happening. It is wise therefore to look to your defences at all times."

Edward waited a while to see if others had questions to put to him. Then, seeing that all seemed content with what they had heard, he spread his arms wide and looked round on all who stood gathered there.

"Now who will come forward and offer himself for hire to work on this great task? The wages will be fair and are the same as the bailiff now pays to those who work on the demesne. This work will last for many years too, so that those who are hired need not fear that they will be cast aside quickly. I can use any who come forward. If there are not sufficient, and I doubt there will be, then I shall fetch others from elsewhere to work. They will have to live here, and there will be shelters built where they may lodge, between the mill-stream and where the mound is to be built, but first I would hire all who are willing from the burgh."

There was a general murmur of approval, and men began to move towards where Edward stood to offer themselves. First one or two and then a few more until there was a fair crowd, for the matter had been well discussed in the ale-houses all week. It took some time for Edward to sort out those who came forward. Some he passed to Thurstan, and others to one or other of the master craftsmen. The names of all were written down and what they could do. Also whether they had carts or beasts that could be hired. By the time all had been listed Edward looked weary, for he had needed to do much explaining of what each task was and to hear what each man could offer. When at last he was through, he mopped his brow and heaved a great sigh, before consulting with the others who had been helping him.

"By my reckoning we shall still need twenty-five more men and six more carts if we are to move the work forward with the speed I would like. What do you think, Thurstan?"

He cast his eye down the list he had before him and then looked at those held by the others before replying.

"I agree. We shall need at least that number, maybe more, but let us start with those we have and send for twenty extra first. It is best that we do not have idle hands for they will cause trouble. When those who are here have settled into the work and the extra twenty are working well with them, then we can send for more men if we need them. Besides, we still have to build shelters where these extra men can lodge. It will take my carpenters some days to have them ready, so there is no need for them to be called yet."

This was agreed. There was much drinking in the ale-houses that night to celebrate the prospect of sure wages, and many of those who came to start the work had thick heads that first day, though they cleared quickly enough with the hard digging they were called upon to do.

By the end of a couple of weeks, the outline of the foundations had been dug, so that it was clear for all to see where this great building was to stand. Earth was beginning to pile up on the site where Edward said that the great mound should be for the castle keep he had talked of. Other men now came to the burgh to work, some from Southampton, others from Winchester, and still more from inland towards Sarum. Most were ragged and thin-looking when they arrived, for few of them had had work but had been trying to scrape a living from small fields which bore poor crops. News of regular work and good wages had spread fast, so that in no time there were more men than Edward could use, and some had to be sent away empty-handed. However Godric, from the kindness of his heart, and because he would never have it said that he turned any away with an empty belly, fed all who came, before sending them on their further journeying in search of work.

At first there was some trouble, for those who came from outside needed somewhere to lodge and the shelters were not all ready. However the weather was kind and there was little rain, so that those who had to sleep in the open to start with suffered no more than they had done on their journey, sleeping under the hedgerows and the stars. Food was provided for them as part of their wages, for Edward said he would get more work out them if they did not have to take time to prepare and cook their meals. They were better fed too, for Godric arranged that Ranulf, the priest in charge of the guest-house, should take over the supervision of main meals in his kitchen.

Rodric, too, was relieved of some of his other duties, so that he could help Ranulf, particularly with preparing and serving the food. With his experience of teaching the children, he found the task much to his liking and soon found himself entering into animated discussions with the men after their meal was ended. Many had interesting tales to tell, sometimes of hardship, sometimes of fighting, and at other times of kindness shown to them along the way. Rodric would always draw out some lesson from each tale, so that gradually the men grew to see that the world was not against them in their poverty, which was often of their own making. He told them of the local customs, and also something of the land round about, where fish might be caught and coneys snared, though only for food and not for cruel sport.

The men would listen to him talk while they ate, and most saw reason in what he said. The ale-houses fared well too from the extra throats, which were dry enough from the dusty work of moving dry earth. There was little drunkenness, for Edward had made it plain that any who were unfit to work from the excesses of the previous night could leave, and gladly be replaced by others who still came seeking work, having heard from travellers that the building had started. The shelters for the men soon took shape on the land between the growing earth mound and the mill-stream. They were set out in a neat row with a few rods of land attached to each, for there was space enough. Those who had come from outside to work became part of the burgh, for all were working towards the same end of building the great new church.

Work at the mill increased too, for there were more mouths to feed. Not only were there the twenty men from outside, who were now working at digging and carting earth from the deepening foundations, but there were also the masons and carpenters and other craftsmen sent by Odo who had set up their lodges near the mill-stream. All the grain that came from the church's lands was needed. This year there was no thought of sending any of it away to Winchester and Southampton as Flambard had done last year. There was also less time than I had hoped for work on our assart, so that I found myself returning from it when it was growing dark, even in high summer. But I was healthy, and it made a change to be in the clean air of the fields, and away from the dust of the mill.

Isabel and Emma put their heads together and devised a scheme for their mutual profit. It grew out of Ranulf's feeding the men who worked at the digging. Though he provided the main meal,there was a sore need for lighter refreshment at other times of the day. This the two girls began to provide. Isabel, who was the better cook, made honey cakes and small breads, which she would slice in two and fill with the goat's-milk cheese she made. When we had eggs to spare from our fowls, she would boil these too, and sell them with slices from the large loaves she also baked. To all these she added herbs for flavouring which she picked from our garden, varying them daily so that one never knew what the taste would be.

Emma, who had some skill at making cordials from wild fruits and flowers, set her hand to that, and flavoured the water she drew from the river so that it was in great demand as the weather grew warmer with the onset of high summer. These things they would take to the churchyard about midday and an hour before Vespers, having found that these were the times when there was the greatest need. Though their baskets were heavy-laden when they set out, they were always empty on their return and their purses full.

Those who were hard at work, came soon to look for the arrival of the pair of them. By the time the harvest was in, their noonday visit became known as 'Emma-time', whereas their pre-Vespers visit took the name 'Isa-time'. Their wares were in demand from the craftsmen too, so that the two of them became accepted as part of the work force.

By the time all the harvest was gathered and the fields cleaned by the gleaners, part of the foundations were dug to their full depth. This varied somewhat, as there was found a layer of hard ironstone in certain places. This, Edward said was the firmest base he could wish for, and there was no need to dig down further. Where the stone was missing, the digging had to continue so that it was almost two rods deep in some parts. The carpenters set up stout poles across the trench from which they fixed pulleys so that they could draw up the full baskets of earth on ropes from those who were digging below. These they swung to the side, where they were emptied into carts to be taken to the growing mound of earth towards the mill-stream. There seemed to be a never-ending succession of carts going backwards and forwards and a constant stream of laden baskets being raised from the depths below. As I stood beside the great trench one Sunday after we came from Mass, I tried to compare it with our cott.

Isabel, do you realise that if we were to pick up our cott and put it into this trench, its walls would only just touch the sides and the top of the roof would still be below the level of the ground?"

She looked at me in amazement, before going to the end of the trench and pacing it out. Then she cast her eye down to the bottom, trying to calculate its depth.

"For sure, it is even as you say. There is space enough in our cott for us. How many men could live in this great trench? To think that every basket of earth has been raised by a man and carried away, and they have not completed half the digging yet. It is indeed a great task that we are attempting. May we have the strength to finish it."

"How many baskets of food have you taken to feed the men, and how many extra sacks of corn have been ground so far? It seems that we shall have need of everything that can be grown here and more besides, to feed the extra mouths we now have. Flambard will have no need to send his corn away from the church's lands that he now has, for it will all be needed here. Rather, he will be bringing corn from his own lands on Vectis Isle to make up the shortfall. Anything we can grow on our assart will be needed too. It is good that we enlarged it last year, for our profit will be the greater. Likewise our work at the mill. Father and I will be kept hard at it with the extra grinding, particularly now that Osbern is no longer helping us. He has skills in his hands that I envy but I do not begrudge him the chance to learn his craft."

Isabel smiled at me as she took my hands in hers. "These hands of yours are skilled too. You know there is none in the burgh that can set a millstone as well as you and they are gentle, too, when you wish it."

She stroked her cheek with my palm as she said it, with a none-too-modest twinkle in her eyes. I took her hand then and kissed it, and putting my arm round her slim waist, hugged her affectionately. So we went towards our cott.

That evening, Isabel and I had our evening meal with Mother and Father in their cott beside the mill. Talk afterwards was much on the progress of the digging, for the foundations were taking such shape as all could begin to understand.

"Soon they will need to start laying the stone in the bottom of the trenches they have dug," Father commented as he took a long pull at his ale-mug. "They will be carrying the stone from Vectis Isle no doubt as they did before, but it would seem to me that they have a ready supply of good hard stone lying on the shore the far side of Hengist's headland. Edward was saying that where they have found the red ironstone at the base of the trenches, they could not have a firmer foundation. I am thinking that the stones on Hengist shore are the same stone, so that he could well use them as a base. There is no need to quarry them, for they lie on the sand and need only be gathered where they lie. I will speak to him about it when next I see him. Besides, if he can use them, then we could bring them here in our own boats. It would not be the first time we had carried stone in them, I am thinking."

He grinned, remembering how we had brought the stone down the Stour river from Catherine's hill when Flambard wanted to build his church up there. We all smiled too, for our secret was still secure with those who had taken part in the enterprise, and it seemed that it had turned out well for the burgh.

I was turning over in my mind the thought that we could use our boat for the work to our profit, when we heard voices without, and Emma and Alric came bursting in full of excitement.

"Oh Mother, I just had to come and tell you as soon as I was sure. I am with child. There is no doubt about it. I thought it might be so a few days ago, but Alric and I have just been to see Goodwife Adeline, who says that it is so indeed, though the babe is only just started. I cannot believe that there is another life growing within me. Did you feel the same when you were carrying us?"

"Yes, for sure I did at first," Mother replied, "and I am so pleased for you both. We had been wondering how soon it would be before one of you brought us such news."

She cast her happy smile over Isabel and I, as well as Emma and Alric. Isabel blushed slightly and lowered her gaze, before rising to cross the room to give Emma a sisterly kiss and add her good wishes.

"This is the best tidings I have had all week. I am so pleased for you. You must take care now, or I shall have to speak to my brother Alric firmly to make sure that you do," she teased.

I rose, and slapping Alric on the shoulder, grinned broadly.

"This calls for a mug of ale I think. Mind you take care of my sister from now on, or I shall break the ale-mug about your head."

I thrust the brimming mug that Father had just filled into his hand and bade him down it at one draught like the man he had shown himself to be. Alric took the mug with a wide grin, and did as I had bidden.

We all continued talking over Emma's great news till Alric said that they should go and tell his parents. At this, Mother rose and took Emma in her arms again.

"It was good of you to come and tell us first. We take it very kindly, but truly you should go now and tell Alwin and Mary before they retire for the night. I would not have them think that we kept the news from them till the morrow. Look after yourself, child, and God bless you both," and she kissed both Emma and Alric, as they left.

As she came back to sit at the table, Mother wiped a tear from her eye as she took Father's hand.

"I have longed for a grandchild these many years and now it seems that my wish is to be granted. Perhaps we may even have more than one."

It had crossed my mind that Isabel was perhaps sorrowing that she was not herself with child, as she had spoken little during the evening. I decided that I would try to comfort her if that was so, for she was such a gentle creature that I would not have her hurt by Emma's pleasure.

After a little while I rose, and suggested to Isabel that we should be leaving, making the excuse that I had to be early at the mill next day. We walked back to our cott hand-in-hand at first, till Isabel put her arm round my waist and hugged me close. I responded, thinking to give her comfort, and she smiled warmly up at me.

Arriving at our cott, we walked in the garden for a while and stood on the bank that formed the base of the town wall, looking out over the reeds and the river beyond to where the sun had set. Isabel remained silent, and I could not find words that would suit my purpose to comfort her if she were distressed, so I contented myself by holding her close and she seemed to respond with warmth. At length, she looked up into my eyes and then kissed me for a long time.

"Come, it is time for bed," she said. Then she led me by the hand back to our cott.

Once inside, Isabel closed and barred the door as we always did and then opened the window that looked out over our garden towards the burgh wall. Meanwhile, I was slipping out of my garments and was soon beneath the covers. Isabel busied herself beside the hearth for a few moments before she too began to loosen the girdle around her waist that held in her robe, which showed her trim figure to such advantage. Then, with her back towards me, she slipped her robe over her head and, discarding her other garments, she turned towards where I lay propped up on one elbow. Thrusting her hands through her fair hair as she loved to do, and then tossing her head to shake out her long tresses, she stepped lightly towards me, holding out her hands to me with a shy smile as she did so.

"Hugh, my love," she whispered as she bent to kiss me, and then knelt on the bed beside me. "Would you like us to have a child too?"

Sitting up, I took her in my arms and stroked her naked body, then placed one hand upon her breast, feeling my manhood stir as I did so.

"God willing, and if it would give you comfort, it would give me pleasure too, but it may be that for some reason we have to wait a while. Who can tell in these matters? I have seen how you care for Belesme and Ediva's child when we visit them, and know how good a mother you would be. No doubt in God's good time we shall be granted the blessing of a child. Fret not yourself over the lack of one," I continued in mock jest, "and thank the saints that you will not have your sleep disturbed by a mewling and puking brat yet awhile. Let Emma enjoy those pleasures for us. Besides, she will soon lose her figure, though she is plump enough as it is. I would rather have your comely shape to gaze upon, though I confess your beauty drives me half-crazed with desire."

With that I took her hands in mine and spread her arms wide, that I might gaze my fill on her rare loveliness, and also perhaps bring cheer to what I took to be her distress.

Still kneeling before me, she smiled coyly and dropped her eyes, and then took one of my hands and placed it on her belly.

"Hugh, I too am with child, and have been these past three months, for I have missed the third of my moon-time courses now. I too visited Goodwife Adeline yesterday while you were at the mill and she did confirm what I felt I already knew. I was only waiting for the chance to tell you, but we have been so busy lately that there was not a convenient moment for such news. I had meant to tell you before we went to sup with your parents this evening, but lacked the courage at the last moment. Then, when Emma came in with her glad news, I could not tell them about myself and so spoil her moment of pleasure, though it would have pleased your mother to hear our tidings. We can speak to her tomorrow and maybe fill her cup with gladness then."

I shook my head in disbelief at what she was saying. With both hands, I gently caressed her belly, thinking as I did so that a new life which I had helped to start was growing within her. Then enfolding her in my arms, I held her close and hid my face in her hair, for I could feel tears of happiness pricking behind my eyes.

"I thought that you were grieving that you did not carry a child," I murmured, "when all the while you held the secret within you. My love and my new life, I am so happy for you. I have often said that you were born to be a mother and care for others."

I moved so that I could look at her radiant face.

" Now come you to bed, that I may hold you both, and tomorrow we shall tell Mother and Father, and also your parents. I cannot wait to see their joy at this twofold news. Isabel my love, ours will be the first born of the two babes. Do you think your father will mind that you will forestall his eldest son?"

"Surely not. He will be overjoyed to hear that he is to have two grand-children so close together. As for Emma, it will be a comfort to both of us that we are with child, so that we can help each other when we find the child grows large within us."

She turned towards me and stroked my chest with one finger as a frown crossed her brow.

"Besides, it will be nice to have someone to confide in when my time draws near, for I confess that I somewhat fear the time of birth, even though women say it is a natural thing. Emma is always so cheerful and full of commonsense, and we two have never had any secrets. Why, we even discussed what sort of husbands you and Alric would make, before you both asked to wed us!"

She giggled and rolled over onto her belly.

Pulling back the covers, I lightly slapped her shapely rump.

"What!" I cried in mock rage, "is nothing sacred! Would you two compare our manly prowess like common strumpets? What have I wedded then?"

She turned towards me, and rose to her knees again.

"My Lord, your wife humbly craves your pardon."

Leaning over me so that her locks encompassed my head, she laid soft kisses on my brow . Then she lay down beside me and looked deep into my eyes, as only she knew how.

I woke late after the excitement of the previous night and had to hasten over breaking my fast if I was not to be late at the mill. Before I left, I enjoined Isabel to have a care over what she did and not to tire herself. She chided me for being a fussing mother hen, but I noted that she took heed of what I said, for instead of carrying a full pail of water into the house, she emptied half of it away.

Father noticed my cheerful mood as soon as I arrived.

"Good morrow, Hugh, you seem in fine fettle this morning. Is the news your sister brought us last evening so cheering that it puts a lightness in your step? Your mother is more than glad, for she has been craving a grandchild ever since you all wed."

"'Tis something like that," I said, not wishing to give Isabel's secret away, and busied myself with seeing that the millstones were well set for the morning's milling, for we were to grind barley that day. The work kept us both occupied till the midday meal when we were glad to take a rest.

When at last Father raised the hatch boards to cut off the water from the great wheel so that it came to a halt in the stream and grinding ceased, we both straightened our backs and stretched to ease our aching limbs. No matter how used we were to the work, it was always hard and continuous, and it came as a blessed relief when we could stop for a while and take a rest. A mill is a hard taskmaster. So long as the wheel is turning the stones, the grinding continues and the corn must be fed steadily between the stones or the edges, which take so long to dress, are quickly lost. Then the runner-stone has to be raised, and both it and the fixed bed-stone have to be be re-dressed, and hours of milling time are lost. As Father stepped outside to wash off the dust from his face and arms before settling down beside the mill-stream to eat his meal, I made my excuses, saying that I needed to give Isabel a message, and slipped quickly away. I was anxious to see that she was not overtaxing herself, now that I knew she was carrying our child. Besides, I was so excited by the news that I could not keep my mind from thinking of her and wished to be beside her every moment of the day, were this possible.

Hurrying to our cott, I could hear her singing a soft lullaby, and I was pleased to see her sitting just inside the door with the sun shining on her lovely hair. She had her back towards me so that I came up behind her unobserved. Placing my hands over her eyes, I kissed her lightly on her neck. She smiled, and turned her lips towards me, offering them to mine, and so we remained awhile lost in each other. At length, she moved her head away, smiling into my eyes.

"What brings you home in the middle of the day, Hugh? 'Tis a pleasant surprise. You have not forgotten the food I prepared for you, by chance?"

"No. I felt I had to see you, both of you, for I could not put your news out of my mind this morning. I wanted to be sure that you were not over-taxing yourself now that you carry our child. I was glad to see as I left this morning that you carried but half a pail of water into the cott. Be sure that you carry no more than that from now on, for they say that lifting heavy weights can cause you to lose a child. I will try to remember to bring in such water as you may need before I leave each morning, but do promise to remind me if I forget."

Isabel reached up and took my face in her hands.

"I am not a sickly maid you know, but I will try to do as you bid. It is not every husband that thinks of such things, and it is good of you to do so," and she rewarded me with a smiling kiss.

Looking beyond her, I saw that she was was setting up her loom.

"What are you going to make? Do we need more clothes already?"

"It is not for us, but the babe. I am going to weave the finest cloth I can to make a swaddling cloth for him. See, I have some specially fine thread that I have been spinning these past weeks when no-one was about, and before I was certain that the babe was within me."

She picked up a skein of the finest thread and held it out for me to see.

"I have almost finished threading up the warp now, for I shall only need about twice as much as I can reach with both arms spread. Then tomorrow I hope to start weaving the weft. With the fineness of the cloth, it needs more threads than usual in both warp and weft. I must take great care with the weaving, for the thread being so fine it can more easily part, though I have used the longest staple I could find. It is some I had from sheep that dear old Alnod, God rest his soul, had on his acres at Barton. They have the longest wool of any I have seen in this region, and it is so soft. Here, feel it for yourself."

She held out a handful of raw wool for me to handle. It was indeed soft, and as I teased out a few single strands, I marvelled at their length.

"Such a fleece must surely be costly."

"A little more than I would normally pay for sure, but it will save money for the cloth will last longer. I hope the swaddling cloth I mean to make will be used for all our children."

"How many is that to be?"

"Would you be content with eight?" she asked with a shy smile.

I threw up my hands in mock horror.

"No more than eight? I had hoped to have at least a round dozen, so that they can keep us in comfort in our old age."

"That would suit me well enough," Isabel replied, "though it will mean building a larger house for them - unless you mean to sleep in the garden yourself, or would you put out the sow from her stall by the wall?"

We both burst out laughing, and I picked her up and pressed her to me gently. Releasing her, I asked, "Do you really want so many children?"

"I think not," she replied , "but I do love them, and would gladly have more than one - if that would please my lord." With that she dropped me a curtsy.

I took her by the hand again and lifted her up so that I could gaze into her eyes.

"I never know when you are serious or jesting. It would be good if we could have more than one child, and not all boys either for I would not have you breed a line of soldiers. The little maids could stay to help you in the cott, though if they turn out to have your looks they would soon be swept off their feet by some handsome lad - a freeman at least or perhaps the lord of some manor."

"I am glad you would like maidens as well as sons. Maybe God will grant us both in time, and that they may grow up in a peaceful land. At least they will live in the shadow of a great church and perhaps receive some blessing from that. We must try to rear them aright."

We stood in silence for a few moments, but were roused from our thoughts by a voice without.

"Is anyone at home? Isabel, are you there? I have come to borrow some sweet herbs, for I have used all mine for the present."

Her mother knocked at the cott door and lifted the latch.

"Why, both of you at home at this time. Is there anything amiss?" she asked looking worried.

Isabel crossed quickly, and threw one arm round her mother's neck before reaching out her hand to take mine.

"Everything is very well, Mother, is that not so, Hugh? I am with child too. I told Hugh last night after we heard that Alric and Emma were to have a child. Hugh simply came back to see that I was all right. We were coming to see you and Father this evening after Hugh had finished at the mill. I said nothing of it yesterday for I did not wish to spoil Emma's joy."

Mary's face lit up with pleasure.

"Oh my sweet. I am so pleased for you and Hugh. Let me look at you. How long have you been carrying the child? I had noticed that there has been a new radiance in you these last few weeks."

"I have missed my moon-time courses for the third time now, and yesterday I visited Goodwife Adeline and she confirmed what I already knew. We would have told you last evening, but Emma was so full of joy that we did not wish to take it from her. Is Father at home now? If he is we would like to tell him too."

"No, he will not be back till near sundown. He has had to ride to Holdenhurst to see Hugh de Port to arrange for more grain to be brought to feed those who work on the building. He will be so pleased. Will you come and eat with us this evening when he returns? I will promise not to tell him first, though I shall be sorely tempted. To think of it, two grandchildren promised so close together. Was ever a woman so blessed!"

With that she embraced her daughter and kissed her warmly and then wiped away a tear of pleasure from the corner of her eye.

"How are you feeling? Have you any sickness?"

"None as yet, but do not be too concerned on my account. Hugh here has promised to make me be careful. Why, he has even forbidden me to carry more than half a pail of water, and has offered to do even that for me. I shall become like one of the fine ladies at the King's Court with no more to do than sit about and do fine needle-work. See, I have started already on some weaving. I set up the loom this morning, and mean to make a fine swaddling cloth for the child."

She showed Mary the partly threaded loom. Mary cast an expert and approving eye over the loom, nodding as she did so.

"Well I have taught you to weave, if nothing else. This is particularly fine wool you have spun too. Does it come from old Alnod's sheep? I thought as much, for there is none finer in these parts. We must try to buy one of his lambs and breed from her, for I would not have the strain lost. Such wool is always much sought after. Hugh, have you told your mother and father the news yet? I am sure they will be as pleased as I am."

"I was waiting till Isabel told you first, but we mean to give them the tidings this evening too. We must tell Emma and Alric. I think our child will be born some weeks before Emma's, so she may be disappointed when she hears. Isabel, you are her closest friend. Do you think you could see her this afternoon and explain?"

"Surely, I need to ask her advice on something so can tell her then. Now, what were the herbs you came for, Mother, and I will see if I have them."

"I need some fresh thyme and fennel, and if you have some rosemary, too, I would be pleased. I have them dried, but for the dish of fish I am preparing it is better if they are fresh, and I have used up all that was growing in my garden."

Isabel and her mother went out into the garden to find what was needed. I took my chance to leave them to their women's talk, while I hastened back to Father, who was just finishing his meal beside the mill-stream.

"There you are," he called as I approached. "Is anything amiss that you hurried away before you ate? Here, have some of this that your mother put up for me."

He passed me a hunk of fresh bread and a slice of soft creamy goat's cheese. I stuffed a large piece into my mouth so that I could not reply even had I wished to, for I feared that I would not be able to keep my counsel if he started questioning me further. The cheese was good as always, for Mother had a special method of hanging it which brought out its flavour, and was well known for it.

As soon as I had finished, we returned to the mill and continued the grinding until all was done. Then we stacked the full sacks of flour, ready for them to be collected and taken to the the bakehouse where Ranulf would make the bread for those who toiled in the digging. I returned to our cott to find Isabel once more spinning her fine wool, for she had completed the warp, which now stood ready to receive the weft. She laid her spindle carefully aside as I entered, and we went hand-in-hand to my old home. As we entered, Mother looked up, and seeing us so, put her hands to her cheeks and quickly called to Father to come in from the garden.

"What brings you here?" she asked as Father entered the house.

"I am with child too," said Isabel, "and our child should be born some weeks before Emma's I think."

Mother gave a small cry of pleasure and enfolded Isabel in her ample arms, while Father clapped me on both shoulders.

"That is why you seemed so light of step this morning, and why you rushed off at noontime. I thought there was something afoot. Well done lad. This calls for another celebration."

He swept up several beakers, and went to fill them with his best ale.

"Now, let us drink a bumper to you both, and my second grandchild. To think that I hear that I am to be a grandfather twice over in less than a day."

He downed his beaker in one draught while I shuffled my feet and murmured something, not knowing quite how to reply, but glad at their pleasure.

As soon as we could, we took our leave and made our way to Isabel's old home. I felt her sigh deeply, for she felt somewhat overwhelmed by it all, so I took her arm and squeezed it. She smiled up at me, grateful for my understanding.

Mary was busy in the kitchen preparing the dish of fish she had told us about, so I left Isabel with her quietly while I waited till Alwin should return. It was but a few minutes before he came in, brushing the dust from his clothes after his long ride. He greeted me warmly as ever, and Mary and Isabel too when they came in. Isabel went over and put her arms round his neck as I had seen her do so often when she was a little girl.

"Father," she said, "I too am with child. Are you pleased for me?"

A broad smile spread over Alwin's face, as he looked first at Isabel and then at Mary and me.

"You have filled my cup of happiness to the brim. When Emma told us of her coming child, I feared that perhaps you might not be able to bear one, and I was sad for you, knowing how you love children. Now my joy is complete. When is this to be?"

"Some weeks before Emma, I think, so ours will be your first grandchild. I said nothing when Emma gave us her news, not wishing to take from her happiness, but when I told her today, she was overjoyed."

"Well, Hugh, this calls for a celebration, and mind how you care for this daughter of mine."

He grinned broadly and, rising, went out to find a flagon of his best wine that we might all drink a toast.

It was a merry supper. Isabel relaxed so that by the time we left, none too late, she was her easy smiling self once more as we walked slowly back to our cott. Before entering, we stood awhile in the garden facing where the sun had gone down and feeling the soft breeze on our faces, while she rested her head on my shoulder contentedly.

At length, she turned. "Come," she said, and led the way inside.

When we had stripped and slipped beneath the covers, I laid my hand gently on her belly, wondering at the new life that was growing there. Smiling, Isabel placed her hand over mine, thinking no doubt the same thoughts as me. Then, snuggling down against me, she sighed in deep contentment and was quickly asleep.

Chapter 11 1094

It was a few days later, while Father and I were eating the fresh baked bread and goat's milk cheese which Mother had brought in to us and clearing our throats of the dust with long draughts of small ale, that Father brought up again his idea of using the ironstone on Hengist's headland shore.

"You remember a few nights ago, just before Emma came in with the news of her coming babe, I was talking about stone for the foundations of the new church? I remember you told me that Edward was planning to use the stone from the little church to build some of the pillars, but he is going to need a great stock of stone to build the foundations before he ever reaches the walls above ground. I was looking at the size of the trenches that he has to fill and it seems to me that he will need a whole quarry just for the works below ground. The nearest quarry is on Vectis, and since he may well need all that can be quarried there for the walls and pillars, he will have to find another quarry for the foundations. Perhaps he will use stone from Alban's headland, or even Portland, but the distance grows greater all the time. Last time I was on Hengist's headland on the seaward side, I remarked on the quantity of ironstone boulders lying on the sand."

Father put down the ale flagon and turned to me questioningly.

"What think you, Hugh? Could we load them into our small boats at low tide, say, and let the boats float off at high tide, and then sail them round to the quay by the mill? They could be easily unloaded there and carried in carts the few paces to the foundations. We could bring nigh on a dozen boats round in the time it would take to bring one from Vectis Isle. This would make the task much less costly."

A slow smile spread across Father's face as he looked at me to see if I saw which way his thoughts were running.

"Besides, if we handle the boats ourselves the profit comes to us in the burgh rather than the sailors who would come from Vectis. Since Edward would not have to buy the stone from the quarries, whichever one he used, it would save him much silver. Though Flambard can call on monies from many sources, if he could save a handsome sum it would suit all our purposes. What think you? If we asked for double a master mariner's wages for each man, would that be fair to cover the hire of the boats as well? Remember that it is needful to have a pilot to show the way into our harbour and avoid the sand-bars that are constantly moving at the entrance. Though we local folk know their position, others do not. How often have we seen those who try to enter the swift flowing Run without a pilot end up aground? Then they have to call for aid to be dragged off again, to the harm of their craft and delay of a missed tide."

Taking another pull at the ale flagon and then breaking off another mouthful of crusty bread, I thought this over for a while. A master mariner could earn half as much again as a labourer, so that it seemed that each man would be paid three times the wage of a day labourer but we would have to provide our own boats which could well suffer damage from their heavy loads. There had been much repair work done on our boats after we moved the stone from Catherine's hill, which cost us dear in time and timber, though the result proved worthwhile.

With three or four men to help load the stone into the boat and one to sail her, and perhaps five boats to carry the stone, we would need no more than ten men at most. With that, we could have a constant supply of stone brought round, so that those loading would have little time to sit on the sand and wait for the next boat to come for loading. It would be the same at the quay, where Edward's men with their carts would be used to carry the stone to the open trenches.

How many boats would be needed if they had to come from Vectis or even further afield? They would be larger and need a bigger crew and take longer to unload, and surely more than the five boats I reckoned would be required if a constant supply of stone was to be brought, since much time would be spent on the journey at sea. Picking up a stick that lay handy, I roughly sketched the shape of the harbour, headland and quay in the dust on the floor.

"See, Father, we would gather the stone from the beach here, carry it in five boats, and have it unloaded at the quay here. I estimate that we will need no more than ten men."

I put crosses in the dust where each would work, and drew shapes to show the boats on their journey round the headland.

"It is a day's sailing from Vectis and back, so that each boat from there could only do one journey each day, while each of our boats could do how many? Six, do you think? It would depend on the tides of course, but then the boats coming from Vectis or Portland would have to watch the tides too. I think we could ask for more and Edward would be willing to pay, for he trusts us to do an honest job, but I think what you suggest is fair. There is no sense in asking for too much and causing Edward to lose faith in us. In any case, there is more to life than riches in this world. We are helping to build a great church, so if we can store up treasure in Heaven, as Godric is always telling us, then we shall help to save our souls."

Father studied my drawing in the dust and nodded thoughtfully.

"Yes, you reason well, Hugh. Come, let us go and see if we can find Edward now and put the idea to him. No doubt he will be in his lodge at this time, so it will be a good time to speak to him. Let me explain the idea and then you can show him how you think it could be put into practice."

He rose, and dusting off his apron and then his breeches, led the way through, past the deep trenches of the great foundations to where Edward had his lodge down towards the mill-stream. Edward was indeed there, finishing his own meal. He welcomed us inside and listened carefully to what Father had to tell him. Nodding thoughtfully, he asked a few searching questions about the sort of stone, its size and how much there was.

"What you say has merit, but before I make a final decision I would like to view the stone myself and test it. Can we go to Hengist's headland now?"

"Surely," I replied, "the tide is not yet out, and we can take a boat across the harbour and then walk through between the headland and the double ditches to the beach. You can then see for yourself the full extent of the stone that lies on the shore."

Rising then, he picked up the tools he required and, calling to one of the other master masons, told him that he would be gone about two hours. Any problems that he could not solve himself should await his return.

We took a boat and crossed the harbour. We were soon on the beach the far side of the headland. Crunching over the soft sand, we turned left and made our way along the beach, under the cliffs of the headland. At first the beach consisted of little but sand and shingle with the occasional branch or log mixed with other flotsam that had been washed up by past storms. As we progressed, so we began to find boulders of red ironstone, and the further we went the more thickly were they strewn about the sand. Edward cast his critical eye over them and stopping occasionally, tested them with his gavel to see if they split or shattered under his blows. They seemed to withstand his attentions, showing little in the way of marks, though small sections tended to chip off. Then he tried with chisel and gavel to see if he could shape them. This was more effective, but from the effort he had to put in it seemed that they would need great force if they were to be brought into any regular shape. After a while, Edward straightened up and, putting his gavel and chisel away in his scrip, turned his gaze on Father.

"This stone is very hard," he mused, "and would not crush under whatever weight was put on it. Nor is it easy to shape so that it would be of little use in the walls of the church. For the foundations which will be below ground and need not be exactly shaped on the outside, this will do very well. By the looks of it there is more than enough here for our needs, though some of the boulders are far too large and heavy for men to lift. If we were to use those we should need pulleys to raise them into the boats, and would your boats be able to take the weight? How skilful are the men you would use for the work? If they did not handle the pulleys right, they could easily drop the great stones through the bottom of the boats, and they would then be useless. What think you of that?"

"How big are the stones you require? I had not thought to carry the largest boulders for the reasons you rightly give."

"The best size for my purpose would be the size of stone we use for building the walls. They should be about the length of my foot or a little more. That would mean that a builder could lift them himself unaided and position the stone exactly without undue strain."

Father nodded. "That is the size I hoped you would say, since that also means that one man could load the stones into the boat unaided and off-load them at the quay in like manner. I think we can find enough stones of that size, for the shore stretches for about six furlongs along this side and a further two furlongs round the end of the headland, where the stones lie even thicker on the sand. Come, let us continue our way and see if you think there will be enough."

The three of us continued to trudge through the boulder-littered shingle, with Edward constantly casting about to examine fresh stones to see if they were all of the same quality. He seemed satisfied enough, for he nodded frequently to himself.

After we had gone about three furlongs, Edward stopped and, looking about him, gathered up several sticks from the flotsam that littered the beach. These he placed at regular intervals, ten paces apart to form squares. Then he set about counting the number of stones which lay on the beach in each square and noting the figure on a piece of parchment he drew from his scrip.

Father and I sat and watched while he did this, for we were in some doubt as to the meaning of it. When Edward had counted all the stones in all the squares he had marked out he came and sat beside us, and scratching his head, began to work things out. I was pleased to see that he used his fingers as I do to help him with his calculations. Father noted this too, and, nudging me in the ribs, he gave me sly wink, meaning to say that for all his great knowledge, even Edward had need of simple aids in his calculations. It made me feel that perhaps I was not so stupid as I sometimes felt and I drew comfort from the thought. At last Edward seemed satisfied with his reckonings, for he turned to us.

"Oswald, I think you have solved a difficulty for me. I have been working out how much stone there is on this beach that I could use. If, as you tell me, there is the same amount all along the shore as there is here, and it stretches as far as you say, then there will be more than enough for the foundations. It will be easier to use this stone than fetch other from the Vectis quarries or from Alban's headland. You say that you could find men and boats to bring the stone to the quay near the building works? How many boats would you need? How much would the men need in payment and what if your boats are damaged? I could not pay for the repairs, since it might lead to carelessness by your men, I am thinking. How say you?"

" Yes, our men would use their own boats and not ask you to repair them, unless the damage were caused by storms say, when you wanted stone fetched at a time that we thought not prudent, for we know the seas well here and how storms can come up suddenly. Likewise, fogs and mists suddenly come upon you when it has been clear only a few minutes before. You must trust us to bring the stone when, from our knowledge, we think it safe."

"You make it sound as if the seas are full of dangers we landsmen know not of. The sea looks calm enough today. Can it really change so soon?"

"Look yonder to the right," replied Father, pointing towards Alban's headland. "Do you see that dark line of cloud, and how the wind moves upon the water, causing it to change colour seemingly, though it is but the movement of the surface? Shortly, there will be a squall here, with turbulent winds that could toss an unwary boat about, though it would cause no harm to those who know how to handle it. By the time we have walked to the end of the headland it will be upon us and you will see the change for yourself. It will not rain, I think, though the wind will change both in force and direction. Such things are as much second nature to us as the knowledge of stone is to you."

Edward nodded and, scrambling to his feet, started to walk towards the end of the headland. He was so intent on looking at the stones on the beach, stopping to examine some every now and then, that when the squall came it caught him by surprise, so that it blew his tunic up about his head. As he pushed it back down again and readjusted his belt, he laughed.

"You did indeed speak truly when you said the winds could rise suddenly. Had I been in a boat just now, I would have been in a sorry state and like as not you would have seen me no more, for I would have been wrecked. I agree to your conditions. The stone will only be fetched when you are content that it is safe. We have not decided on payment yet, nor how many men and boats you think would be required. What think you, Oswald?"

Father looked at me and then back at Edward.

"Hugh and I have talked this over and we think we would need about ten or twelve men and five boats. That way we could keep a constant supply of stone coming to the quay. Because our boats draw less than the ones that bring the stone from Vectis Isle, we could use more time when the tide is not so full and so have more boats coming than you have now. They would hold less so that each would be unloaded more quickly and it would make for a more even flow of stone coming to the site. Would that suit you better?"

Father moved the sand with his foot, wondering how to broach the most important part of the proposal. Then he scratched his ear.

"As for payment, you now have to pay the crews of the boats that come from Vectis, including the master mariners and the captains, besides the men who quarry the stone and take it to the ships. How many men is that? Many more than we propose. We would need twelve at the most, all of whom are as good sailors as any on the ships you use. Would you pay them double a master mariner's wage? Does that sound a fair bargain to you? It will be far less men than you now need to quarry and bring the stone and the cost would be less."

Edward sat down on a large boulder and, drawing out writing materials from his scrip, he began to do some calculations, scratching his head the while, and muttering to himself. At length, he finished and, folding up his parchment, he looked Father full in the face.

"That is a fair bargain. To be honest with you, I would have paid more, for I shall be saving much silver, but if you are content then so am I."

"Hugh and I considered that you might, but as he said, there is more to life than silver and we shall make a good profit ourselves. Besides, as Hugh said to me when we discussed it, we are helping to build a great church, and shall we not then lay up treasure for ourselves in Heaven?"

Edward nodded approvingly.

"Hugh, you would seem to have a wise head on such young shoulders. I wish there were more like him that I could trust, Oswald. Come, I have seen all I need here. Look, this is the best size of stone to bring, but they could be as large as that one, but no smaller than that one over there."

He pointed out three stones.

"When we get back to the double ditches we will make three piles of suitable stones so that your men may know the range of size that will suit best. Now, how soon can you start bringing in the stone, Oswald? Part of the foundation trenches are now complete and we can start building the stonework at the bottom within the week I think. I am anxious to have stone laid in the bottom of the trenches as soon as possible, for there is always the danger of the sides of the trench falling in if there is much rain. Then the work would have to be repaired which would waste time and effort. Could you have your men ready in five days, Oswald?" Father considered this for a few moments before replying, and then turned to me.

"Well, Hugh, what do you think? We have our boat, and Alwin has his, and there are the others we have used. I can count nine that would be suitable, so that we could always be sure of five at least. You know how to use a boat and so does Alric. Then there are Ernwi, Wulfric, Swein and Cedric, who would all help with the loading, I think. That makes six at a first count and there are sure to be others who will be willing to work for what we are prepared to pay for their hire. Am I right, Hugh?"

Doing a quick count on my fingers, I ran through those in the burgh whom I would gladly work with and was able to add a further handful to those Father had already named.

"Yes," I replied, "we can find enough men to do the work, but I would like a week to make the necessary arrangements, for some of those whom we would like to use may have work of their own to do in their fields. Let us say that we will have the full number of men and boats ready to start on Monday week. In the meantime we can make a start with our boat and Alric's and a couple of helpers to see how it will work out. We have to determine how long it takes to load a boat and sail it round to the quay, so that we can plan to use the men to best advantage."

"That will suit very well," said Edward, "for I have to make arrangements with the ships that are presently bringing stone from Vectis. Much of it is still rough and unshaped, for I had thought to use it for the foundations. What we have now can certainly be so used, but I will now send word to the quarries that in future all the stone should be roughly dressed before it is shipped here. That way we will have less waste stone brought. The apprentices have plenty of rough stone to work upon, and in future the part-dressed stone will be ready for the more expert workmen to square up, ready for the walls and pillars. In this way I can see that we shall be fully occupied during the winter months when sometimes building has to stop. They tell me that sometimes there is little frost here in the winter, so that we may be able to continue building the foundations almost without ceasing. In other places where I have built it has been much colder and we have had to cease work for much of the winter so the work has taken much longer."

Thus it was agreed, and we set about making our return. At the end of the headland nearest the double ditches, Edward stopped, and casting around, made three piles of stones as he had said, the centre pile being the ideal size and the other two piles being the smallest and largest sizes that he reckoned would be usable. When he had finished, he pointed them out to Father.

"There; when your men come, show them these piles and explain to them what I need. Then we shall do very well."

We made our way back to our boat, and recrossed the harbour. With the aid of the brisk breeze that was blowing, we were soon back at the quay, where Edward climbed out.

"Handling a boat is something I have never learnt and I can see that it takes some skill to make it move where you want. It is good to be able to use the wind to move it along and not have to rely on men working the oars. That is hard work, particularly when the tide or current is against you."

That evening after we had all supped, Father talked with Alwin, and I went to see Alric to put the matter to him. When the four of us had agreed the best plan, we called together such men as we felt would be best suited to the work and arranged for their hire. There was no shortage of takers, for the payment we offered was good in spite of the risk of damage to the boats. Over the next few days, Alric and I made the first trial run to see how long the journey took and to find out any difficulties there might be with loading the boats on the beach. We were well satisfied with the result, and all was ready for the full work to begin on the following Monday as we had arranged.

The red ironstones soon began to pile up, first at the quay and then on the edge of the great trenches that had been dug for the foundations of the pillars which were to support the main height of the church and its roof. Meanwhile, Edward's men were busy preparing the huge quantities of mortar that would be necessary to bind the stones together and make them solid. In a few weeks, enough was assembled for the building work to start and the first stones were ready to be lowered to the bottom of the deep trenches.

Two days before the first stones were due to be laid, Edward went to see Godric.

"In two days' time we start to build and lay the first stones of the foundations. This is no ordinary building, but a great church which should be to the glory of God. It seems fitting, therefore, that we should mark the start by calling on God to bless the work, just as we did when we marked out the boundaries of the building before the digging of the foundations started. Would you say Mass for us all and ask for God's blessing on the work and then help me to lay the first stone, that all men may see what is the purpose of the work?"

"You have thought wisely, Edward. I will gladly say Mass and we will walk in procession round the whole site once more to show all men the meaning of the work. This is the more important because some in the burgh say that you mean to destroy their old church with your new one. I have told them that this is not so. Though you will pull down our present small stone church, you mean to reuse the stones in the new one, and you have promised that the crypt will remain. Can you have some stones taken from our present little church, so that we can lay them with the ironstones from Hengist's headland at the foot of the foundations tomorrow? In that way, men will see that their church continues, if in a different shape, and the malcontents may be quietened."

Edward nodded thoughtfully. "That can be arranged. I shall need to start taking down the old church quite soon in any case. Leave the matter with me. I will see that several stones are loosened so that they can be easily removed. Then, when the procession comes to the place, I will have the stones taken from the church and carried to the edge of the foundations, there to be lowered into the trench where you and I can lay them firmly in place."

The word was spread through the burgh that a High Mass was to be said at the foundations so that the work of building might be blessed. All were summoned to attend and there were few who did not, for it meant a few hours relief from some back-breaking work. Godric led the procession, with Edward and Thurstan walking one on each side of him. Behind then came the rest of the canons, each one carrying a taper. Next came Alwin, Father and the other chief men, and then all who were involved in the work. Finally came the rest of the folk and their families. Isabel and I managed to find a good position to stand near the eastern end of the old church. As the procession neared us, it came to a halt and Edward stepped forward. Taking a gavel and chisel from his scrip, he knelt down and with a few blows loosened a stone at the corner of the building. This he lifted up to show to all present and proclaimed in a loud voice:

"This stone, which I have taken from your old church, is to be the first to be laid in the new church. I call upon Godric your priest to bless it, that it may lie, hallowed in its spot as a mark that your church here shall continue."

There was a murmur of approval as Godric lifted his hand in blessing on the stone. Thurstan then stepped forward and, taking a ladder which was resting against the end of the church, he set it up against the end wall. This he climbed, while the whole crowd watched wondering what was afoot. Reaching the top of the ladder, Thurstan took from his belt a saw which he raised above his head. His left hand he placed on the stem of the cross which rose from the ridge of the roof of the church. Turning so that he faced the crowd below, Thurstan addressed them:

"This cross, which has stood at the end of the church for as long as men can remember, I will now remove. It will be carried with the stone that Edward has taken from the wall of the old church and placed likewise in the foundations of the new church. Together they will ensure that the building where you have offered your prayers these last hundreds of years will not be lost but will continue, though in a different and greater form."

This said, Thurstan took his saw and cut through the stem of the cross. Then, with great reverence, holding the cross above his head, he descended the ladder and went to join Edward and Godric at the head of the procession. At Godric's signal, the canons burst into the singing of the 'Jubilate Deo' and the whole procession moved to where there were ladders set against the edge of the foundation trenches. While Godric, Edward and Thurstan carefully descended the ladders followed by four of the younger canons, the rest of the crowd gathered round the edge to watch. Reaching the base of the trench, the seven of them moved to the east end of the trench, with Edward going to the left side and Thurstan to the right, each accompanied by two of the young canons. I noticed that there was a pile of stones placed at these two corners.

When all were in place, and with Godric standing between the two groups, he lifted up his arms towards Heaven, and in a loud voice that all could hear, called down God's blessing on the great work of building that was about to begin. Then, turning first to Edward and then Thurstan, he pronounced a blessing on the stone and the cross that each carried. Each in turn then proceeded to lay their charge on the ground and, assisted by the two young canons, they laid stones over the cross and the stone from the old church and buried them, setting new stones over each and fixing them firmly with the mortar that lay in a pile beside where they stood. When this was completed, Edward, Thurstan and the four canons rejoined Godric in the middle of the trench and the seven of them all cried out together:

"May the work that we have this day begun be continued to God's glory. May those who work here do so in the sure knowledge that they will lay up treasure for themselves in Heaven. We have come not to destroy but to create. May prayers continue to rise here daily and may God's work continue and increase in this place that its fame may spread and men may continue to find comfort and healing here."

Godric turned and, lifting up his face so that he could look directly at the crowd that was gathered at the edge of the deep trench, he spread his arms wide again, and spoke in a strong voice:

"This will be the House of God, Christ's church. Hear now the words of the Psalmist King David; 'Except the Lord build the house, they labour in vain that build it.'"

He paused awhile, and turning round to face those that stood behind him, repeated the same words so that all present might be sure to hear. Then he pointed to the solid rock at the base of the trench where he was standing, and cried out again.

"We have dug deep and laid the foundations upon rock, so that when the storms come and the winds blow and floods arise, this church will not be shaken, for it is founded upon rock. This was Christ's promise, and He will not fail us."

Godric then turned and, followed by Edward and Thurstan and the four young priests, walked to each of the four corners of the deep foundation trenches and there made the sign of the Cross and pronounced a blessing. This done, he returned to the foot of the ladder and slowly climbed up to rejoin the rest of the crowd. Here he took up his position at the head of the procession and turned to face all present. We all remained silent, waiting for him to speak again.

"What manner of man should come to worship here?" he asked. "I will tell you. The answer is written in the fifteenth psalm, which we have often sung. Do you remember how it begins? 'The man of blameless life, who does what is right and speaks the truth from his heart.' We will now walk in procession round where this great church is to stand and we shall sing the fifteenth psalm to remind us how we should lead our lives."

This we then did. It passed through the minds of many that were present that we were witnessing the start of something that was far greater than anything that had happened to any of us before and that would continue long after we were but dust. As we walked slowly round the edge of the deep trenches, I felt for Isabel's hand and took it in mine. She looked into my eyes, and I could tell that similar thoughts were passing through her mind too. She put her free hand to her belly and I wondered whether the child growing there would see the great church completed. Somehow I doubted it, for there was so much to build, but was that important? What really mattered was that it was being built, and that it would influence all those connected with it, hopefully for good. Times would change too and the needs of the church would change with the times, so that if it was to fulfil its task, the church would have to change too. We could only pray that those who did the building would be worthy of their calling.

At last the procession was ended, and with a final blessing, Godric dismissed us to go about our various lives. As Isabel and I walked slowly back towards our cott we were joined by Alwin and Mary, Father and Mother. All were in sombre mood, for they, like us, felt that something momentous had happened. Mary asked us all to join her at her house to eat, for both Edward and Thurstan were to come too, so we made our way to the hall where we found Emma and Alric already waiting.

It was a sober feast, for the mood of the day had touched all of us. There was none who did not look into the future, thinking how all this would affect the burgh. Until now, most had thought only about the increased trade and prosperity that would come. Now that the first stones had been laid and the link with the old church so strongly established, our minds turned to deeper matters: how the fame of the church might attract pilgrims from distant parts who would bring fresh knowledge. Who could tell what the future might hold? Alwin turned to Thurstan as we sat eating.

"It was good that you took down the cross from our present church and placed it beneath the new one. At first I feared that some might try to prevent you, not understanding what you intended, but when you laid the cross on the rock at the foot of the trench, it gave all men a feeling that their church, which they treasure deeply, would not be spoiled but would form part of this great new building, so giving them a sense of continuing into the future. I shall not live to see it completed and perhaps Alric and Isabel will not either, or even my unborn grandchildren. One day it will be completed, and it is enough for us that we have seen the beginning."

Thurstan nodded gravely. "You have understood what Edward and I were trying to do. We have not come to destroy though your little church, which is not the first to be built here, must come down to make way for the greater building we have started. The prayer that has risen from this place these last four hundred years will not cease because a few stones are removed to a different place. Who knows? In years to come what we build now may be reshaped by those who come after us to suit the needs of some future time. We can only try to answer the needs of the moment as best we can. The rest is in the hands of God."

Mary put her hand over Alwin's and whispered, "Amen to that."

There was a long silence. Eventually Father spoke.

"How long do you think it will take to build the foundations up to ground level, Edward?"

"Much depends upon the weather. Now that the harvest is gathered and safely stored, there are more men who can spare time to carry stone. I am thinking that I shall keep the ships coming from Vectis, so that we may have as much stone as possible to continue building until the frosts come. Have no fear, Oswald, we shall need all the stone you can bring from Hengist's headland, for what comes from Vectis will be stored until we need it for the walls. I will only use some for the foundations so that we can make faster progress now. I prefer to lay plans well in advance so that we shall not be held up for want of building stone if the frosts keep off. When do you think they will begin?"

Alwin and Father looked at each other and shrugged.

"Who can tell. Some years we have little if any frost, for the sea keeps us warm, and if the winds keep in the south and west we find the land stays soft. If the wind blows chill from the north, then we may have ice on the harbour and snow to block the roads. There is no rule about these things and each year is different."

"Then let us hope that the wind stays southerly for I would fill as much of the trenches as possible before the winter rains come. That can cause the walls to collapse. It is a danger that I would avoid, if possible, for men have been known to lose their lives buried under the earth from a collapsed trench, and the work of digging has to be done again. It is for that reason that I am going to put timbers across the trenches at intervals to keep the sides in place. Alwin, can you find me more men tomorrow to help speed up the work? It will be for a short time only, but if there are any who are idle now I will take them on and so make as much progress as I can."

Next day, this was proclaimed in the square before the bailiff's hall. Several men came forward, spurred on in part by the events of yesterday and in part by the thought of earning good silver.

As the foundations began to take shape, we brought as much ironstone as we could from the headland. There were always men waiting to unload it at the quay and take it to the builders who toiled at the foot of the great trenches. Such stone as had already come from Vectis was mixed with what we brought, and so the walls began to rise. Great heaps of mortar were mixed constantly and lowered to the builders too.

When I could snatch a few moments, I peered over the edge of the trenches to see how the builders worked. At first, they built up a solid wall from the bedrock, filling the whole width of the trench. Many days went by while this work was in progress and in spite of the numbers of men involved, the walls seemed to rise very slowly. We were hard put to keep pace with the builders for they seemed to need a huge amount of stone. It was indeed fortunate that there was already a good store of it to hand, and had it not been for Edward's wisdom in keeping the supply coming from Vectis, the work would have slowed.

Edward, or one of the master masons, inspected each load of stone that arrived, dividing it into what was the right shape for use at once and putting to one side that which needed dressing before it could be used. This was taken to the masons' lodges where it was piled ready to be dressed by the apprentices with their gavels and chisels. When they had roughly squared the stone, it was returned to the building site to be lowered with the rest of the stone to the builders. Huge mounds of chippings began to rise beside the apprentices. These were also carted to the edge of the trenches, there to be piled for what purpose I knew not at the time. The stone dust was likewise gathered and taken to where men were mixing the mortar, for it was an essential part of the mix. Nothing seemed to be wasted.

Days passed and grew into weeks and this work continued. It must have been about Advent time, when the foundations had risen from the bedrock by more than the height of a man, that I noticed a change in the way the builders were working. Now, instead of building the wall solid for the whole width of the trench, they were building two separate walls, each about the thickness of a yard and each one set against the edge of the trench, leaving the space between them empty. The inner surface of each thin wall was left jagged and uneven. This they had done for the height of a yard. Seeing one of the masons passing, I asked him why this was.

"That is because Edward is satisfied that we now have a firm base on which to build. From now on the work will rise faster, for we shall fill the space between the two walls in the trench with rubble and mortar. That is why we have been piling these great mounds of chippings against the edge of the trenches. There is much misshapen stone that is too small to be cut into blocks or 'ashlar' as we call it. That too will be used to fill the space between the two walls. When it is mixed with mortar, it sets firm and solid so that it will never crush or break. Because the inner edges of the two walls are left so jagged, the rubble and mortar will bind tight to make a solid bond. Had we left a straight inner edge to the walls, there would be a danger that they would split away under the great weight that they will be carrying, so that the pillars might move and the whole building collapse. I have heard that such things have happened elsewhere and many years of labour have been lost. We shall continue in this way until we reach ground level."

He cast his eye down the trench and seemed to be measuring something.

"Very soon, we shall start to step in the foundations so that the wall will become narrower, for we shall not be building the pillars as wide as you see the foundations now. There is no need, but the pillars must be set on a wide base to spread the great load that they have to bear. The pillars will only be half as wide as you see the foundations now, but, set on the wide base they have, they will never move. You may think that pillars could bear any weight, but I saw one church where they did not build as we are doing and it fell during a great storm. The weight of the walls and the roof caused the pillars to sink into the ground and all was destroyed. Wise men learn by their mistakes and Edward is the wisest I have met. He will make few mistakes, you may be sure."

As he went on his way I looked at the work and saw what he meant. The next day began the work of filling the space between the two thin walls. This indeed made the work faster for there was no need to set each stone on its proper base as had been done for the outer walls. However, the masons made sure that all the crevices between the uneven stones were well filled with the stone chippings and mortar mix. Though the piles of stone and chippings began to decrease, it took many more days for the space between the walls to be filled.

I noticed now that each evening, after the builders had finished their work and before they went back to their lodges for their evening meal, they covered their work with bundles of reeds and branches. I taxed Edward over this when next I saw him for it seemed wasted effort, since they had to remove the reeds again before they started work the next day. He smiled before replying.

"Little escapes you, Hugh. There is good reason for what they do. Now that the time of frost is approaching I have ordered that all new work should be covered at the end of the day. Then, if there should be a frost in the night, the work will be protected from the cold. In this way it will harden properly. Otherwise, the frost would break up the new work and it would be of no use and have to be done again. Each morning, I inspect the previous day's work to see that all is firm and solid. If it is not, then the men have to break it open again. So far, all has been well, but as the winter comes on we have to take extra care. These rushes will keep out a light frost and so let us work for more days before we have to stop.

The more we can do now the less chance will there be of the sides of the trenches collapsing."

He looked along the length of the trench, considering the work that had been done so far.

"Next week, we shall begin to step in the walls by the thickness of a block of stone. This we shall do several times until the walls are the thickness of the base of the pillars that will rise from them; though the pillars will not be started till next year, I think. There is still much to do before we reach that stage. It is sometimes said, Hugh, that there is as much of a building below ground as above it. When you build such a great church as this, it is better to be safe and not sorry. This church will last for evermore, I hope, and I would not have those that come after me say that the builder skimped his work. This is to be Christ's church, so we men must give only of our best."

As he continued his tour checking each part of the work, I began to see some part of the vision he had of the great church he was building. He seemed to be inspired by what he was helping to create. Many of those who were working on the building seemed to be touched by the same spirit. It crossed my mind that I had heard little swearing, which was common enough amongst the serfs, and no blasphemy. Both had been forbidden, I knew, but that there should seemingly be none even when Edward's back was turned surprised me. Perhaps something greater than any of us realised was happening.

I walked back with Edward to his now completed cott which stood next to ours. As we neared it, Isabel came from our door showing clear signs of the babe within her. Edward smiled as he greeted her, enquiring how she fared.

"Well enough, and it is good that my robe is so full or I would have to think of setting in more cloth at the sides. I find it more becoming to wear no sash now."

She adjusted the full folds of her robe so that they fell about her in such a way that they hid her growing shape.

"Enough of me. How fares my young brother Alnoth with his apprentices-hip? It is six months now that he has been learning his craft. Does he show any aptitude? I have asked him but he says little, having us believe that what he does is secret, though I suspect that it is more modesty than secrecy that keeps him silent. By the looks of him when he passes by on his way home at the end of the day, he is kept busy enough, for he is always covered with stone dust. Has he any skill do you think?"

"It is hard to tell at this stage for it will be several years before he masters all the arts. So far, he seems to be the most skilful of those whom we apprenticed. The blocks of ashlar he handles come out nearer to a perfect square than those made by any of the others and that is the first test of a mason. His eye is true too. Maybe in another six months we shall think of letting the best of the apprentices take the second step and become fellows in the craft, and Alnoth could be numbered amongst those we choose. Say nothing to him of this lest it go to his head and he thinks that he is better than he is. Encourage him to keep at his work though, and to show you what he can do. There is nothing secret in what he does yet. The mysteries come later. At present he is becoming skilled in the use of the simple tools. The real test comes when he thinks to progress to carving stone."

We parted then and he turned to his own door, calling to his wife Godiva who hurried to greet him.

Isabel took my arm and led me into the garden to see what roots still lay in the ground that we could eat. We had harvested and dried a fair quantity of food from the land and I hoped that there would be sufficient to last us till the new growth started in the springtime. We continued on down to the shelter where the two swine lived against the burgh wall. They looked well, as they rootled amongst the scratchings that we fed them. There would be enough to feed one through the winter but the other must be slaughtered to provide meat. I scratched the hog between the ears, thinking that it would make good eating for it was fat about its rump and had good shoulders too. Isabel read my thoughts. "When you mean to slay him, let me know that I may be elsewhere. I care not to hear his death throes, though you will do it quickly, I know."

I pressed her arm, understanding how she felt. Though but a beast, it had grown to know us and now would turn towards us if we called. I promised I would do as she asked. Then we looked in the shelter next to it where the fowls lived when they were not abroad, hoping to find some eggs. There were four which Isabel put into a fold of her gown. At this time of year we could expect few and savoured those we had. Most of those we collected were used to make cakes and other foods for those who laboured at the building. It provided us with welcome extra silver which we put aside for the babe's arrival. Then we returned to our hearth, which I stacked with more timber to make a better blaze, for the air was growing chill.

"The first frosts may soon be upon us, I think. I must look to our wood pile. Tomorrow I will take the cart towards the forest and gather what I can by hook and crook along the way. I do not mean you to be chilled this winter, carrying our babe. I will speak with Belesme and see if he can help me bring in extra logs, for there is much fallen timber near his land and at the edge of the forest."

This I did and with Belesme's help brought in a goodly pile of timber which I stacked against the northern wall of the cott where it would be dry, away from the usual winds. We would be sure now of winter warmth. I also filled in the spaces between the walls and the roof of the cott to keep out the winds on the other three sides. The cott might be more smoke- filled, but I deemed it better to be warm and smoked than cold. Besides, as Isabel said, it would help cure the meat of the hog better.

Sometimes Belesme brought news of how things fared in the King's dukedom of Normandy, for some of those he had soldiered with would come to see him if they were travelling in these parts. It seems that the King had much trouble with his brother, Duke Robert, who was aided by the King of France, so that William had to go there to fight him. It was said that William prevailed, for the latest report was that William intended to be in London for Christmas.

"As long as he does not come into these parts, I shall be content," Belesme said. "I heard news that the men of Wales are rising against the Normans too, and the Scots have risen and killed Duncan their king, so that we shall most likely be left in peace, for William will have more than enough to occupy him and have little time to come here to hunt the stag in Andret."

With this we agreed. It seemed that Flambard too was fully occupied raising money to pay for William's army, so that Edward and Thurstan would be left to continue their building works without his hindrance.

"William raises money in many ways," said Belesme. "The twenty thousand men William had commanded should be sent to help him in his dukedom, gathered in Dover town ready to take ship to Normandy when the winds might be favourable. However, it seems that William, partly by guile and partly by fighting with the force he already had with him, managed to gain his ends without having to use the men gathered at Dover. He therefore sent word that they were to return to their homes. But Flambard was at Dover too, and he said that each man had to give back to the King half a pound of silver which they would have taken with them. This they did and were glad enough to be able to return to their homes, for they would still be in time to gather in their harvest which would be of more value to them than any money they might have lost. I heard from one that I knew in the old days who said that he doubted how much of the ten thousand pounds of silver would reach the King's coffers. Much would go no further than Flambard's chests, he thought."

I rubbed my chin thoughtfully on hearing this.

"It seems that Flambard serves his own purposes as much as those of his king. Most of the tales that we hear seem to tell the same story, how his wealth increases daily. When he takes lands and money from the great and powerful it concerns us little. It is a different matter when the poor are made to pay. I have heard too that he took large sums from some of the Bishops, particularly in the north, so that they could regain some of the lands that had been taken from them."

"True enough," replied Belesme, "though some of the bishops have money and to spare for they do little for their flock. I hear that in Durham the Bishop has to help fight the Scots and keep them at bay, so he at least may earn his keep, even though he may do little to save men's souls. Bishops seem prepared to leave that to the poor priests."

"We do well enough with Godric," I said, "and if some of the silver that Flambard has from the great lords comes here to help pay for the building of our new church I shall be content. The events that seem to trouble the King pass us by for the most part and I am glad that it should be so."

Belesme nodded in agreement, for he was happy enough to farm his land and care for Ediva, his wife, and his children.

Matters continued thus, and the weeks passed. Christmas came and was celebrated as we had always done, though there was scarce room enough for all inside the church when the High Mass was said, with all the extra folk that now lived in the burgh.

Chapter 12 1095

Winter came and went, and the work of building the foundations was able to start again. It had ceased during the frost time but towards the end of Lent Edward ordered the masons to start laying the stones in the trenches again. Men had not been idle. The masons had used the time to cut and shape stone that would be used for the pillars that would soon begin to rise above the ground. This was a time-consuming task, for it had to be done most carefully or the pillars would not be straight and even. A huge pile of stone chippings began to grow and this, with the stone dust, was carefully saved, for it was of great use in the making of the mortar on which each stone was to be laid.

Easter came unseasonably early that year, falling on March 25th, so that there were few wild flowers with which to decorate the church for the great festival. Rodric had been in Winchester at the time of the festival and brought back news from the King for he held his Court there at that time.

"The King was greatly put out by the poor decoration of the great church there, for the celebration of the Resurrection of our Saviour, and upbraided the bishop and the dean in heated words."

"How did the bishop like that?" I asked.

"He was most put out," Rodric replied, "and put the blame on the unseasonable weather and the early time of the year. He tried to excuse himself by saying that there were no flowers blooming so early, but that he had made the best showing he could with greenery and early leaves. The King was not to be pacified, and gave the bishop a purse of silver marks, saying, 'Let me never have to come to Mass at one of the church's main festivals where the church is not brightly decked with flowers, even if you have to send to foreign lands to buy them. Why, I hear that in the Holy Land around Jerusalem flowers grow all the year. Send there for some of those plants and have them grown here that our church may be well decked to glorify our Saviour.'

The bishop pocketed the marks with a bow, promising to do as the King had bid. I then saw Ranulf Flambard, who was standing close to the King, whisper something in his ear. After a moment's thought, the King nodded and called for his scribe and bade him write as he dictated. Next day, I happened to be passing the scribe, who was busy engrossing a parchment, and asked him what the King had ordered to be written down. It seems that Flambard had persuaded the King to grant some land which he holds at Stanpit to the church here to provide more money for the building. What this really means is that Flambard has the land, but he can use the money it raises to pay for more stone. I told Godric of this yesterday and he was pleased."

"It seems easy to have what you want when you are a King," I said. "Who would have thought that William minded so much about how a church looks. Perhaps he fears for his immortal soul and is trying to buy his way past Saint Peter."

"Speak not so of your King," Rodric rebuked me. "Is it not written 'Let him who is without sin cast the first stone'? Such a slander deserves ten 'Ave Marias' to be said kneeling before the altar. Were today not All Fools Day, your penance would have been the greater," he added with a smile.

I acknowledged my fault, and being free at the time, went to the church to say my penance, adding two more, one for Isabel and one for the coming babe. As I came out, I heard a commotion and saw Witro the falconer and his wife Adeline, who live at Stanpit, arguing heatedly with Godric.

"By what right does the King think he can give away my lands?" Witro shouted. "My father held the hide at Stanpit in the blessed Edward's time, and I had it from him. Adeline had her virgate from her father as you well know. We told Gilbert the clerk so when he came to make the record these eight years past. Is it not written down in the great Book of Domesday?"

"Calm yourselves," said Godric. "It is even as you say. The land which the King has given to Flambard for the church here is not yours but the two hides next to your land. I questioned the messenger who brought the news and he had it from the scribe who wrote the charter. He was not clear at first which land was being granted so went to the Great Book to make sure. Your lands are secure. It seems that the record has its uses and has made it clear that the land you claim is really yours, so put your minds at rest and give thanks that it is so."

Witro grunted, not sure that he could believe all that Godric had told him. Adeline nudged him in the ribs.

"You always were over-hasty. Now you have made us both look foolish. Forgive us Godric. We did not mean to doubt the King's word, but the tale we had said differently, and it seemed that we were to have our lands taken from us. It would not be the first time such a thing had happened, as you well know, so one cannot be too careful."

"You were right to be anxious," said Godric, "even though you may have been over-hasty."

"Do not think that we are ungrateful," Adeline replied. "We have no children, as you know, and when we die we mean to give our lands to the church, that a Mass may be said for our souls. Say nothing of this to anyone or they may think us boastful and trying to act like our betters."

"That would be indeed generous if you really mean to give the church so much," replied Godric. "I will keep such knowledge close and tell no-one. Do not think that you must be bound by what you have just said. Times may change and you have many years left to you both on this earth, I hope. You have always been generous towards the church in the past, and I remember you often in my prayers that God may look kindly upon you both."

I slipped quietly away then, resolved to tell no-one what I had heard, for it was surely a matter between Witro and Godric alone. I had reason enough to be grateful to Witro, for he had sometimes shown me how to flight a falcon, though I had never yet been able to make it bring me back a quarry. So I went on my way, and as I passed our cott, I looked in to see how Isabel fared, for her time was drawing close when our babe should be born. No more than two weeks she thought, and I knew she sometimes became anxious if left alone for too long. I found her busy finishing a garment for the coming babe. Seeing her thus occupied, I went happily on my way.

That evening, as Isabel and I were sitting by our hearth, she busy with more garments for the babe and I working at repairing our flint harrow for the assart, there was a knock at our door and Osbern entered. He stood in the doorway smiling and seemingly uncertain. I rose to make him welcome while Isabel bade him come and sit by her, but Osbern stood, scratching his ear.

"I have made something which may be of use for the babe," he said. "It is outside. Shall I bring it in?"

Putting her work aside, Isabel rose and came towards him, hands outstretched.

"There was no need, but you are most kind. May we see what it is?"

Osbern grinned and, turning, went outside again to return at once carrying what looked like a chest in his arms. This he placed on the floor before us.

"It is a cradle for the babe," he said. "I have been working on it these past weeks after I have finished each day at the carpenters' lodge. See, the corners are fixed with joints so that they will hold firm and I have put curved timbers under the feet so that you may rock the babe to sleep. That was Thurstan's idea. He helped me with the design and showed me how to make the joints that would hold best."

"This is truly beautiful," cried Isabel, and she bent down to examine the cradle more closely, before rocking it gently back and forth.

"We shall be assured of peaceful nights now, for I shall have the cradle next to me, and if the babe wakes in the night I shall be able to rock him to sleep without rising or waking Hugh."

I bent to examine the cradle too.

"Why, you have carved creatures on the corner posts! See, Isabel, here is a coney and here a duck and look, a fish. See how he has carved the scales. Is this not a hound too?"

Isabel and I ran our fingers over the carvings, marvelling how beautifully fashioned and smooth they were, while Osbern looked on with pleasure showing in his face. Isabel rose then and went to him and hugged him.

"This is the most beautiful thing I have ever seen," she said. "It must have taken many hours of labour. Where did you learn such skills? Did Thurstan teach you this too?"

"No. It is something that I find that I can do. When I have a piece of wood in my hands I look at it to see what it says to me. Sometimes I can see birds or animals in the grain of the wood and then, if I take a sharp knife, I carve the wood until the animal appears. That is what I have done on the cradle. See, the grain in this piece looks like the fur of a coney, so I had only to shape it. The wood did the rest for me."

He stroked his hand over the head and back of the little figure, as he would with a live coney to calm it. We examined the other creatures he had carved, marvelling at the lifelike forms he had made. Such a gift was rare indeed and no doubt Thurstan had been quick to seize on it and encourage Osbern in his skill.

"I am making another for Emma too, though say nothing of it to her yet for it is not finished and I would have it as a surprise for her."

"We will keep your secret and in the meantime hide this lovely thing you have made for us until hers is finished lest she become envious of us," said Isabel. "I would not have this spoil our friendship, particularly at this time."

We sat awhile. Isabel and I kept rocking the cradle back and forth and passing our hands over the little carvings, while Osbern told us of his work in the carpenters' lodge, how he was learning to make the various joints that hold wood together and how to fix two pieces so that they form as one and have no loss of strength. He showed us how this was done on our window frames and the door posts, and then picked up one of our stools which had always been loose about its legs. He explained how it could be made better if it were properly jointed. We laughed at his enthusiasm but thanked him too, for he promised that when he had the time he would make our stools more secure, so that there would be no danger of them falling apart which sometimes happened.

"Thurstan will make a master carpenter of you yet," I teased him.

Osbern looked at me with serious eyes.

"That I aim to be one day, God willing, though I still have much to learn."

Soon afterwards, Osbern rose and bade us good-night. He seemed to have grown in stature since he had started to learn his craft and there was something about him now that bode well for the future.

Isabel's time approached and passed by several days, so that we both became anxious that the babe was not born. I visited Goodwife Adeline in her cott by the Pure Well to seek her advice. She came with me to see Isabel, and examined her.

"Have no fear. Some babes come early and some are late. A few days will be no matter and the child will be more sturdy when it arrives. I think it will be born within the next two days, for it has dropped well in her belly now. When her pains begin be sure to send for me at once that I may be with her at the time of birth. She is a slender girl and so may have more trouble giving birth than your sister Emma. I have simples that can ease her pains if need be and I will bring these with me when the time comes. Have no fear, all will be well."

We were both much comforted by that and thanked her for her kindness. I promised to send to her as soon her pains started, and so it was. I had been asleep only a short time that night and it was still fully dark when I was woken by a cry from Isabel. She sat up and clutched her belly with one hand while with the other she sought my hand to give her courage.

Still befuddled by sleep, I turned to her to see what was amiss.

"The babe has started," she cried. "The pains have been coming this last hour."

The news cleared my head instantly, and I sat up.

"Stay calm," I said. "I will go and rouse your mother that she may come to be with you. Then I will go to Goodwife Adeline, for so she bade me."

First I lit a taper from the embers that still glowed in the hearth so that Isabel might have some light to drive away her fears. Then, quickly donning my breeches and tunic and giving Isabel a reassuring kiss, I hurried to the bailiff's house to rouse her mother. As I approached the door, I saw that there was a light within and wondered if aught was amiss. My knock was answered at once by Mary who opened it and appeared already dressed.

"Has the babe started?" she asked. "I thought as much, for a mother knows such things. Isabel was restless all day yesterday so I slept fully dressed, knowing that you would come for me as soon as it was necessary. Wait while I tell Alwin and I will come with you."

She hurried away to their sleeping quarters and I heard muffled voices, quickly followed by both Mary and Alwin appearing.

"So you are about to make me a grandfather," Alwin said. "This will be a proud day for both of us, I think. Now, Mary, be you gone and care for that daughter of mine. Hugh, this is women's work. Will you stay with me and keep me company in our waiting?"

"You are kind, but I must go to Goodwife Adeline, for so she bade me when the time came. She said she would help Mary at the birth, for she has great knowledge of such matters. I will go with Mary back to our cott first and then be on my way to fetch the goodwife."

Mary had meanwhile gathered up a bundle that stood by the door. Then we hurried back to our cott, to find Isabel anxiously awaiting our return. She was overjoyed to see her mother who went to her to comfort her in her pains. Leaving the two of them together, I hastened as fast as I could to Stanpit and arrived breathless at the goodwife's cott. My knock was quickly answered and she bade me enter while she gathered up her basket with such things as she said were needful. Then together we hastened back to the burgh, entering by the gate at the bridge over the river, which the gate-keeper had opened earlier to let me to pass out, and who was watching for my return in the half-light of the gathering dawn.

We made all haste to our cott, and as we neared the door I heard Isabel's cry of anguish, as another pain stabbed through her.

"Have no fear, Hugh. Women in labour need to cry out to bear the pain and help the child into this world, but I have simples here that can ease her travail."

We both entered the cott and Isabel held out her hand to me to comfort her. Meanwhile, Goodwife Adeline was examining her to see how she fared. She questioned Mary shortly before going to her basket and, taking out a small flagon poured out some of its liquid into a beaker.

"Drink this cordial, Isabel. It is a concoction of dittany mixed with pennyroyal that will ease your travail. It is much used in such cases."

Isabel took the beaker and drank it gratefully, then lay back exhausted. She gave me a wan smile while she felt for my hand.

"Oh Hugh, I am such a coward to complain so. I am sure other women manage much better than I to bear pain."

We sat for a time. It seemed that the drink had calmed Isabel and eased her pains, for the colour had come back a little into her cheeks.

As it began to grow light, Isabel spoke to me again.

"Hugh, will you go and see if Emma is abroad yet. She made me promise that I would send for her when my time came for she wanted to be with me. I would like her here if she is awake."

I hastened to the cott where Alric and Emma lived and found them already about. As soon as she heard the news, Emma dropped what she was doing and rushed to our cott. Alric called after her to be careful, for she had not many weeks to go before she would be delivered but she seemed not to hear and continued as fast as she could to be with her closest friend. Alric, for his part asked if there was anything that was needed.

"You are kind, but it seems that it is women's work and they have all that they need."

"What of you?" Alric asked. "You could sink a mug of ale at this time."

He went to where the cask stood and filled a beaker to the brim and I drank it gratefully, realising that I had been abroad for some hours. Then he handed me a hunk of bread and a wedge of cheese which I wolfed down greedily, for I was famished after my early journeying. When I had finished, I thanked him, and he placed a friendly hand on my shoulder as I went on my way.

"My thanks to you, Alric. Fear not, it will be your turn soon and I will do the same for you then you may be sure. There is little we men can do at such a time but wait and pray and hope that nothing goes amiss. Isabel is in the best hands with your mother and Goodwife Adeline to help her and Emma to comfort her."

I left him, and after calling at Father's house to tell them, I returned to our cott where I stood outside the door, not wishing to be in the way.

The hours dragged leaden-footed on and still I waited. Now and then, Mary or Adeline would come out to fetch something, and twice they bade me fetch clean water from the river where it flowed fast and put it on the hearth to boil. Once Mary bade me run to her hall and fetch a bottle that contained a concoction of camomile flowers beaten and mixed with gill. She said the goodwife needed it to soothe Isabel and bathe her skin, for she was growing feverish and it had many cooling properties. Noon passed and still I waited, my anguish growing with every gasping cry that Isabel uttered, for it seemed the babe was loath to enter the world.

At length, there was a great cry followed by a soft moaning, then the cry of an infant. Hearing the soft voices of Mary and Adeline, I could scarce contain my anxiety, but trusted that they would summon me as soon as they could.

I heard footsteps approach the door and the latch was lifted. I stood transfixed to the spot as Mary, smiling, held out her hand to me and said, "Come". Hardly daring to breathe, I entered our cott and looked towards our bed, where I saw Goodwife Adeline place a small bundle into Isabel's arms. She nestled the bundle against her breast, and lifting the cloth that hid what was within, bent her head over it with a loving smile. Then she gently stroked the tiny form, and turning her head towards where her mother and I stood beside the doorway, smiled wanly at me.

"Hugh, my love, we have a daughter. I am sorry that I did not bear a son for you. Can you forgive me?"

Stepping softly to the bed, I knelt beside Isabel as she gently lifted the covering from the babe that I might gaze upon it. I could scarce make out its tiny features through the tears that came to my eyes, but saw that the babe had hair the same colour as Isabel's.

"She has your colour hair," I said stroking it gently, " and if she grows to be as comely as you I could not ask for anything more. I care not to have a son if I have a daughter such as this babe. Did you suffer too much in bearing her? Your cries nearly tore me apart in my anguish. I would not have you suffer so again."

Isabel held out her hand to take mine.

"The pain is no more than a memory now, soon to be forgotten. Are you content with your daughter?"

She put the tip of her finger to the babe's lips and immediately the child began to suck.

"See, she is hungry already. Do you think that I have produced a glutton?"

Mary moved closer then, and moving apart Isabel's garments, placed the child to her breast.

"She is keen to suckle already. That is good. She will grow into a sturdy child, I think."

I stayed, still kneeling beside Isabel as she fed our babe, while Mary and Adeline stood beside the bed, smiling at her. I felt a hand on my shoulder and looking up saw Emma smiling down at me.

"You will make a good father. I trust Alric will be as kind to me as you are to Isabel. I was glad to be with her when she was delivered of the babe and to hold her hand and help her." Turning to Isabel, she said, "I shall be better able to manage when my time comes, now that I have been with you. It is good that we can share such times together."

Turning to Emma, Isabel murmured, "You gave me the courage I needed when the pains were sore. I hope I can do the same for you when your time comes."

There was a movement behind me, and Goodwife Adeline came forward quietly.

"Now it is time for you to leave Hugh, and Emma too. I have things to attend to with Isabel for she has had a hard time with the child. Mary, if you will stay and help me, we must do what we can so that Isabel is not too much weakened. Have no fear, Hugh, you will soon be able to return to be with them both. First though, fetch me more water from the stream and put it to heat upon the fire. Fill another pail too and place it nearby that I may use it as need be."

She hustled Emma and I out of the cott and I picked up two empty pails and went as I was bidden to the stream to fill them with clear flowing water. These I carried quickly to our cott where Adeline thanked me.

"Now grind up this sage and wormwood in this bowl for me Hugh, but be sure to lose none of the juices. I would use it to staunch Isabel's bleeding."

I sat beside the door and worked at the herbs as I was bidden, glad to be of some use. When I was done, I tapped lightly on the door and Adeline came to answer. Examining what I had done, she nodded approvingly.

"That will do well. I shall soak this new lamb's wool in it, and make a compress of it to place over the wound. Look not so worried Hugh. It is often thus when women bear children, and Isabel should be none the worse for it in a few days when she heals. I will show Mary how to bathe her with soothing remedies. She must keep to her bed for some days, for the less she moves the quicker will she heal. You have a fair daughter and no mistake, Hugh. She will have the looks of her mother, I think."

She looked across to where Isabel lay resting in our bed.

"You should leave us soon for a while and go about your work. When you return this evening, Isabel will be more rested and have need of your company. I will show you then how to use the simples I have prepared. Besides the sage and wormwood, I shall boil roots of comfrey in some wine, for that decoction has many healing properties too."

I sat beside the bed where Isabel lay with one arm round the babe, which slept. She seemed sleepy too, perhaps from a draught of distilled pennyroyal and other herbs that Adeline had given her. Kissing her gently, I left her and made my way first to the church, where I knelt to offer a heartfelt prayer for the safe delivery of the child. As I was about to leave, Godric entered and, hearing my great news, sank to his knees beside me to join his thanksgiving with mine.

"It is always a wonderful thing when a new member of our flock is born," he said. "May the child be blessed with health and learn to know our Saviour."

He gave me his blessing then and we both went about our business, I to the mill, where Father was anxiously waiting to hear how things were.

"You have a lovely granddaughter," I told him. "She is sleeping now with Isabel who is weary too, for she suffered much in bringing the babe into this world, I think. Goodwife Adeline says that all will be well if she rests now. There is naught for us to do at the moment, but I would cease work early this evening, if I may, to be with Isabel and see to her needs then."

Father grinned at me, and put his arm on my shoulder.

"I well remember the night that you were born, and so know what you are feeling. We shall keep you busy this day to take your mind off your worries and so the day will pass the quicker. We should have finished all that needs to be done before the angelus sounds. When your mother comes at noon time, I will tell her to prepare a broth for Isabel and you for the evening meal if you like, though I have no doubt that Mary will prepare something too. Now, to work. We have barley to grind today so see you to the setting of the stones for that, while I haul the first sacks to the head of the chute overhead."

The day passed, and we ground the full load of sacks that waited for us. So much did we grind, that at one point the wheels began to heat and I had to call to Father to stop the mill so that I could clean the dust from the bearings and grease them again. It was a filthy task and none too easy, for one of the bearings was deep inside the mill and I could only reach it by lying full length and stretching my arm to its fullest extent between the shafts. When I was done, I was covered with old grease and dust and smelt foul. Father twitted me and sent me to clean up with heated water and soapwort. Thus cleansed, I was better fitted to return to our cott to see Isabel and the babe once more.

"Oh Hugh, it is good to have you here now that I am rested. I was frightened lest something happened and I lose the child, but Goodwife Adeline had such soothing cordials that my fears left me and I was able to bear the pains, though they were fierce at times. Emma was such a comfort too and gave me the strength not to cry out too loud. I did not wish to frighten her knowing that she has to undergo what I have so soon. All that is past now, and we have a fine babe, though I am sorry for you that it is not a son," and she looked wistfully at me.

"There will be time enough for that," she added smiling. "You said once that you wanted ten children, I think."

"You know I jested then" I said. "For now I am more than content with my lovely wife and sweet babe. Who would wish for more than that?"

We sat awhile, and then I busied myself about the cott, doing what seemed needful to make the place more comfortable and seeing that those things that Isabel might need during the night were close at hand. Mary came in after we had eaten our meal to see that all was in order, and bade me call her if there was aught Isabel needed during the night. Then, when she had put the babe to her breast to feed once more, we settled down to sleep.

The days went past quickly and the simples and herbs that Adeline had distilled worked, for Isabel was about again sooner than I had thought.

It was less than two weeks later that I came home to hear her playing softly on her harp and singing a lullaby to the babe which lay in the cradle that Osbern had made for us. As I entered, Isabel laid the harp on one side and, seeing that the babe was now sleeping, she rose to greet me.

"The child has been feverish but has quietened now. I think it is nothing, but we must take care. Do you think we should ask Goodwife Adeline if there is aught we should do?"

I bent over the cradle to examine the tiny face which seemed flushed but peaceful. Not knowing what to do, I yet wished to calm Isabel's fears.

"I will go to her, and ask if she has anything to give the child. It may be nothing but we should ask I think."

Hastening to Goodwife Adeline's cott at Stanpit, I found her busy preparing some cordials. When she heard my concern, she put aside what she was doing and came at once.

"Now you are beginning to learn what it is like to be a father," she said. "It is a task that is never ended. All children have fevers but most of them quickly pass. Some I can cure though others are beyond the knowledge of even the wisest healer. Isabel cares well for your babe so that I have little fear for the child, but I will come nevertheless. One thing that you must needs be careful about: use only the clearest water for the babe and be sure to keep all flies and insects from her eyes and mouth, for it is thought that such things carry evil humours that may cause the child harm."

When we came to the cott, we found that Mary was with Isabel.

"I was passing by so called to see how my grandchild fared," she said. "Hearing that she had been feverish I stayed till you returned. How think you Adeline, is the babe sickly?"

Adeline took the child in her arms and unwrapped her swaddling clothes, feeling her small body.

"It is nothing but a little colic and should soon pass," she said at length. " If the child should become over-heated so that you think she has a burning fever, bathe her with this soothing lotion which will cool her. I have known it be of great use with other babes. For now, keep her well wrapped and away from the night odours and distempers, particularly those that come from the marshlands near the river. If she sleeps soundly, that is the best cure of all. Mary, you have the usual decoctions, I think, and know how to use them, but if there are others you need, come to me and I will see what I can find."

I thanked her for her kindness, and as she was about to leave I pressed upon her a basket of eggs for her trouble.

"You have no need," she said. "It is a sad world if one cannot help a neighbour in time of need."

Isabel insisted that she take them, so thanking us warmly the goodwife went on her way.

As I closed the cott door, I turned to Isabel.

"Our child is not yet named, nor has she been received into the church by baptism. It would be a terrible thing if some calamity befell her and she be taken from us without the blessing of baptism so that her immortal soul would be for ever dammed through our neglect. When she was sickly this morning I blamed myself for not having been to see Godric to ask him to receive the babe into the church. Should we not go to Godric now and speak to him? We are agreed on her name."

"You are right. We should have spoken to Godric before this, but there has been so much to do that it has slipped my mind. Come, let us go to him at once and see if he will baptise our little Martha after Mass this Sunday."

We found Godric busy preparing the vessels for a Mass. After he had questioned us about those who would stand for the child as godparents to see that she was brought up in the ways of the church, he agreed to accept her into the church if we presented her after Mass the following Sunday.

Thus it came about, and our babe became known as Martha to all the congregation who welcomed her, while Isabel and I breathed easier knowing that we had done what we could to save our child's soul.

It was a month later, when coming back from working on our assart near the forest for a full day, Isabel greeted me with the news that Emma had been delivered of a boy about two hours after noon.

"The babe arrived so quickly that there was no time to send for Goodwife Adeline. It was fortunate that I was sitting with Emma when her pains began - I was helping her with some garments she had not finished for the babe - so that I was able to run quickly to your mother and fetch her. I sent one of Father's serfs to run to Stanpit and fetch Adeline too, but Emma forestalled us and the babe arrived so soon that there was scarce time to make preparations for it. By the time Adeline came, for the serf had to search for her not finding her at her cott, Emma was already suckling the babe. He is a lusty fellow, with a cry that can be heard in the square! Emma will have her hands full feeding him I think. I am so pleased for her that she has a son for I know she dearly wanted one. You are an uncle now, Hugh, as well as a father. Emma said to tell you to go to her as soon as you returned from the assart so that she can share her joy with you."

Waiting only to dust my clothes from the toils of the day, I ran to Emma's cott and knocking lightly, slipped in to find Emma with the babe cradled in her arms and asleep, with Alric sitting beside them. Emma held out her free hand to me, bidding me to come close to see the child. He seemed sturdy enough from what little I knew of babes.

"You were always in a hurry and full of surprises," I twitted her. "What, could you not wait for Goodwife Adeline to come, but had to do things almost on your own?"

"I had Mother here and Isabel with me to give me courage. Look not so concerned, Hugh. Besides I wanted to have the child before Alric returned from Sopley where he had to go this afternoon. He does fuss me so. Don't you my love?" she said holding out her hand to Alric and smiling.

"Anyway, I was tired of being so misshapen, and longed to be slim again like Isabel."

"You never did have Isabel's figure," I grinned at her. "At least you will now be able to enter your cott sideways."

We all laughed then, for it has always been a matter of jest between the two girls that Isabel was so slender while Emma was the more buxom.

I was happy for my sister, and knew that she and Isabel would help each other in raising their children, for our two families were very close.

Some weeks later, as I was walking with Isabel, Emma and Alric through the churchyard, we stopped to look at the building works. Much progress had been made since the builders had been able to start again after the winter frosts. The foundations for the great pillars that would hold up the roof were completed for more than half their length, and the base of some of the pillars had been set out at the eastern end and also where the crossing would be in the middle of the church. I noticed that these four pillars were larger than the others, for they would have to take the extra weight of the tower that was to rise above them. Men had also started to dig out the trenches that would make the foundations for the outside walls of the church. These were to be some distance outside the pillars, so that there was a space of almost the span of a man's two arms spread wide, between the two trenches.

"See," said Alric, "these new trenches require less labour, for the earth from them is being used to fill up the outside of the trenches where the pillars stand. No wonder the mound of earth towards the mill-steam by the town bridge is not growing at the moment. All the earth is being used here."

"It is for the moment," I replied, "but you can see that they have filled in beside the stone foundations for the whole of the eastern end and hardly dug any of the outer trenches yet. There will be plenty more earth to be carried to the mound, I think. Did not Edward say that the mound would one day be used as a stronghold for the burgh? It will need to have a stockade on top of it when the time comes if it is to serve any useful purpose."

"True" said Alric. " It is before the memory of anyone living in the burgh now that there was an attack on this place, and that was beaten off by those who defended our wooden wall that tops the defences, so Father has told me. That is why he was pleased to let you and I, Hugh, take on the repairs needed to the wall from the mill to the Canons' Gate. As he says, a stout defence soon becomes known and trouble-makers try elsewhere for easier spoils. "It is easy for men to become careless when times are peaceful, and before long the walls fall into disrepair because men see not the need for them. That is when danger is most likely to occur. Father told me only last week that he had had to speak to Geoffrey the reeve to make sure that some of the timbers near to the Bar Gate were replaced, for they had become rotten. Geoffrey was loath to do anything, for he would lose men working on his own land, till Father said that the King would hear of it if nothing was done within the month. The work is almost completed now. I am glad, for it would be little use you and I keeping our part of the burgh's defences secure if there were a gaping hole elsewhere where men could rush in. What need would there be for the gates then? Thieves could come and go at will, and slaves escape and so gain their freedom if they could remain at large for a year and a day."

The work progressed all that year, and much of the next, until finally the foundations of the whole church, both for the pillars and for the outer walls with their transepts to the north and south, were dug out. Stone also was laid in them and brought up to the level of the surrounding ground. Now the full shape of the whole church could be seen and news began to spread of its great size, so that travellers began to come to see the works and marvel at them, for few had ever seen so large a building. The shape of the pillars was clear too, for the stones that would form their bases were in place. Some marvelled that they were square, thinking that would have been round like the trunks of great trees.

"This need not be so," Edward told those who questioned him on it. "Odo tells me that the great cathedral that he is helping Flambard build at Durham has rounded pillars, and that he is carving them with intricate patterns, each pair different from its neighbour, but Odo has decided that here he will use a different form. Though the base of each pillar will be square, the columns as they rise will take different shapes, so that they will seem to be several slender columns held together around a central square pillar. In this way they will seem to be taller, for the slender columns will carry your eye up to the top and you will not be aware of the great mass of stone that forms it. Odo says it is an idea that he has seen used in Normandy in the great abbey that Duke William had built at Caen in '59 in fulfilment of his vow to the Pope, - Nicholas it was then."

Edward picked up a stick, and began to draw lines in the dust.

"The slender columns that are grouped around the central mass lighten the whole structure and cast interesting shadows along its length. See, I have drawn them roughly to show what I mean. At the crossing where the transepts meet and above which rises the tower, the pillars rise to the full height of the triforium, so that one's eye is taken heavenward for an immense distance. It is this that Odo wishes to create again here. It seems that Flambard cared not for the idea and it was he who insisted that the pillars up in Durham should be round. One who has seen them says that they seem squat, though their massive size give the impression of immense strength. It would seem that there is little chance of that church falling down as happens in other places."

Those who stood by and heard Edward explain what he was about, nodded in wonder. Among them was Alnoth.

"Now I know where the rounded stones I have been working on for so long are to go," he exclaimed. "They are to form one of the columns of the pillars. I must check again to see that the top and bottom surfaces are exactly flat and at a right-angle to the rounded front, or the pillar will lean and perhaps fall. When first I was learning to square stones, it seemed that it mattered little if they were not exactly right for they were all below ground, and each one held to its neighbour. Now it will be different. If these pillars are not true, they will fall apart and perhaps the whole building collapse."

"Very true," said Edward. "You can see now that each man has his part to play, and if any fails then he can endanger the work of all the others. That is why I check each day's work so carefully, to see that all is well."

"Since you made me a fellow in your craft, I have never ceased to learn some new thing each day, and yet there is much that I still do not understand. Though I can now cut a stone fairly true, the mysteries of setting an angle on a stone, other than a right-angle, are still beyond me, though I hope to master them in time. I have tried to follow what some of the other craftsmen do, but the trick escapes me."

"Well, Alnoth, you are a bright enough lad and your work is clean. I have good reports of you from some of the master masons. Keep at your work and in six months time I will teach you, and some of the other craftsmen who may be skilful enough, the secret you wish to learn. For now, you have still plenty of other skills that you need to learn, as I think you know. The mason's craft, like that of the carpenter which Thurstan controls here, cannot be learnt in a few months. Both he and I were seven years and upwards learning what we now know, and there are others in the realm who have greater skills than either of us will ever have. Sometimes it seems that the finest skills are granted only as a gift from Heaven."

Alnoth nodded gravely at Edward's humble words, for though he was greatly revered by all in the burgh, it impressed us all that he could admit that even he had not mastered all the skills of his craft.

Edward left us then and we continued on our way. As we passed the place where the great central pillars were to be, I stopped and picked up one of the stones that lay beside where it was to be set. I had not thought to examine the stone closely before, but after hearing Edward speak I took a closer look. Its surface was smooth to the touch so that it scarcely roughened my hand, nor could I see any marks where the mason's chisel had worked it. As I turned the stone over, I marvelled to see how straight were the edges and how square the corners. Peering closely, I looked for the grain of it such as one finds in wood, but could find none.

I called to Alnoth, "Is this one of the stones you have wrought?"

He came close, and examined the stone.

"No, I think not. I cannot yet make so fine a finish as this."

"How do you square the corners so well?" I asked him.

He shook his head.

"That is one of the secrets of our craft that I may tell to none that are not admitted. I have tools to help me which you have seen, but how they are used I may not divulge. This I can say: the stone we use works easier than some other kinds, for it has no grain. Edward says that this stone will last many centuries and will neither crush under a great weight nor scarcely weather in wind or frost. It is the same type of stone that William used for his great abbey at Caen, though it comes from a different quarry."

He picked up a stone and rubbed the surface with his hand which he then held out to me.

"See how clean it is. No dust comes off when you rub it, yet it works easily with a chisel so that any marks can be removed. It can be carved too. When I was last in Edward's lodge examining the plans, I saw that he had a half-finished carving of a man's head on a shelf behind where he sits. I did not have time to examine it closely, but the features were clear and the surface smooth. I cannot be sure, but it seemed to resemble Godric. Say nothing of this to anyone yet for I doubt if many know that Edward is carving it. Maybe he means to place the head in the church, perhaps on one of the pillars at its top. Edward says that when carvings of angels are made for the great churches that are being built, they often use the face of the master builder or the abbot or some such man. If my guess is right, it would be good to have Godric's face for all time in our new church, for he has done much for this burgh."

We promised to keep Alnoth's secret to ourselves. I too ran my hand over the surface of the stone then and found that it was still clean as he said.

"How do you cut the stone to the size that you need?" I asked him. "It is not like the stones on Hengist's headland, which are of all sizes, so that we can pick up only the ones we need. This stone comes from a quarry you say, so must be broken out of the solid rock."

"That is something I can tell you," he said. "The great pieces are first cut with a rough saw at the quarry so that they are of a size that can be handled by two men. They are fairly flat at top and bottom so that they can be loaded tight into the ships that bring them here from Vectis. What we take off the stones when we shape them for our purposes, can be used either in the mortar to fix one stone upon another, or as rubble to fill the space between the smooth outer shell of the pillars and walls. You saw how we did that when the foundations were being laid, so nothing is wasted. This work is exciting and never a day passes without me learning some new skill. I would not boast, but it thrills me to think that I am taking a small part in building something that will still be standing far into the future when we are all long gone."

Isabel laid her hand on her brother's arm.

"I think often how the building of this new church touches all our lives in so many ways. It seems to be making many strive to work better than they have done in the past. Father says that there is more contentment in the burgh since the work started, for there is a great common purpose now, and Godric says he has given fewer penances since foul language was forbidden on the site."

It was true. Few swore on the site, feeling perhaps that it was already hallowed ground.

Chapter 13 1095–1096

It was not many weeks after the feast of Pentecost, which fell early that year in the middle of May, that the weather turned foul. The rains came and fell almost daily without ceasing right through the summer and into harvest time, so that the crops lay sodden in the fields and could hardly be gathered. Indeed much was lost, for the grain sprouted in the ear where it lay on the ground. Such grain as could be cut took many days to dry in the stooks, and it was mostly poor stuff.

Our assart yielded scarely half the normal crop, and Alwin said that the King's demesne fared no better. The clerk, whom Ranulf Flambard sent to make a tally of the crops gathered from his lands which had formerly belonged to the church, trembled when he saw how poor a crop he would have to report to his master.

"I fear Flambard's anger when I tell him how little has been harvested. He will no doubt accuse me of treachery and having sold much of it to my own profit. Though I can tell him that others have fared as badly, he knows little of husbandry and will likely not believe me. He grows more arrogant each year, and now that red-faced William uses him as his Chief Justiciar, though he has not been appointed as such, there are few who can hold him. It seems that he has a free reign to plunder and pull down and destroy any man's goods, if it is for the benefit of the King's exchequer. From what I have seen, not all that Flambard raises goes to the right quarter, and the great chest where Flambard keeps his own wealth is now so full that he has ordered another to be made. Perhaps I should not be discussing these matters, but I can only speak as I find."

He heaved a great sigh as he rolled up his parchments before putting them away in the pannier that rested on his horse's flank. Then, bidding Godric farewell, he mounted, and rode disconsolately out of the burgh.

That Christmas-tide there was much excitement, for news came from Winchester, and was indeed spread throughout every church in the land, that the Pope - Urban by name - had preached a great sermon in the Abbey of Clermont, near the southern border of Duke Robert's Norman lands. Godric broke the tidings to us after Mass on Christ's birthday.

"I have here a trumpet call from the Pope himself," he said. "He calls on all good Christians to cease fighting amongst themselves and to take up arms and make war against the heathens who have taken the city of Jerusalem and other parts of the Holy Lands and are denying pilgrims who wish to visit the Holy Sepulchre.

"We all know that there is little strife in this part of the land, but it seems that Duke Robert in Normandy is constantly at war with his neighbours. It is also said that there is much fighting in the west and north against the wild Scottish and Welsh tribes. It is the Pope's earnest wish that these wars should cease and men should turn their valour to re-capturing the Holy Places. Such men as answer the call will be assured of a place in Heaven should they suffer death in the attempt. Those that return will be pardoned of any sins they may have committed, however grievous. Thus it is written," and he held aloft the parchment he was holding for all to see.

There was a murmur of interest, and several of the gossips of the burgh could be seen whispering to each other and looking at some of the well-known trouble-makers to see if any would take up the offer. During the months that followed, several men did leave to join the Crusade, as it was called. Many said that they went more for the hope of booty, or because of the poor harvest of the previous year which had led to much hunger rather than to save their immortal souls.

For the rest of us, life became harsher. William had no intention of joining the Crusade himself, for he had too much on his hands keeping this island under his control. We heard that more of his barons were growing increasingly unruly. However his brother, Robert Curthose, wished to leave his Norman dukedom to take an army to the Holy places. Alwin broke the news to us all when he called everyone together in the churchyard.

"The King, like all men, wishes to save his immortal soul, but says that he cannot leave our land to the depredations of his unruly barons. Few men in this realm are able to leave their homes and go on such a journey either, though any who do will be assured of a place in the Heavenly Kingdom, we are told. He has, however, agreed to raise the money to pay for the army that his brother Robert is to lead out of Normandy. The King's coffers do not hold so large a sum, but he knows that all Christian men would wish to do their part in regaining the Holy places from the Infidel, so that our pilgrims can once more travel in peace to those lands where our Lord Jesus Christ once trod. The King has therefore decreed that a special tax is to be levied of four shillings for every hide of land to help pay for this noble army. William himself has agreed to take the money and hand it to his brother in his dukedom so that all men may know that he is not keeping it for himself."

There was much grumbling when folk heard this, for the taxes were heavy enough already.

"How am I to find the pence required of me when the harvest has been so poor?" complained one man. "When I have paid my tithe to the church as I am bound to do, there will be little enough left for me to feed my wife and three children; they are half starved as it is."

There was a sob somewhere behind us and, turning, I saw old Meg, the widow whom Flambard had so abused before for gleaning in Alsi's fields. She had her hands to her face which held a look of anguish.

"What ails you?" I said, moving to her side to hold her, for I feared that she might fall.

"Where shall I find a silver penny? I have no land to grow a crop and live by what I can glean and grow in my garden, and that is little enough this year with the wet. My child is in rags and there is scarce enough fuel gathered to last us through the winter. If it were not for the kindness of the priests we should have starved long since."

She let out another great sob so that others who stood near looked with sympathy on her, though there was little enough anyone could offer her. It was indeed a dismal prospect for many folk. Seeing the mood of those gathered round him, Alwin turned to Geoffrey the reeve, and Godric, who stood beside him, and held hurried converse with them.

"Calm yourselves," he said, raising his hands for silence. "I will speak with the King's clerks at Winchester and see what can be done. We shall find a way to raise the sum the King demands as we have always done in the past."

"Not if you have to deal with that Flambard," came an angry cry from the crowd, and there was a general murmur of agreement.

"Flambard is not the only man who can be spoken to," replied Alwin. "There are others that I know who will give me a more sympathetic hearing, and Godric is well known to some near to the King too. Between us we may be able to ease the burden set upon us. From what I have heard, the King may be hard put to it to raise what he needs from us poor folk since the harvest has been so scant, so that he may have to squeeze his barons harder."

"He may find that hard in some cases, for some of them are so fat that he could scarce get his arms round them. At least they would not be able to run away if once he caught them."

There was much laughter at this and the humour of the crowd returned, for all men trusted Alwin and Godric to do their best for them.

Alwin's endeavours bore fruit. The sum the burgh was called upon to produce was somewhat reduced and those in most need, like old Meg, were spared.

It was in the autumn that we heard how William had delivered the money to his brother. The captain of a ship which had brought wine into the harbour, whence much of it was to be taken to Sarum for the Bishop, brought us the tale. I was standing near him at the quay while he was watching his cargo being unloaded.

"That King William of ours is cunning and no mistake. You know he has paid for his brother's army to go to the Holy Lands. I was in Rouen loading cargo when he arrived. The ship he came in was so heavy-laden that I wondered it had not foundered on the voyage. Sixty-seven barrels, each one full of silver coins it carried. I would not believe there were so many until I had counted them for myself. I asked the captain of the ship that brought them how much it amounted to. 'Ten thousand marks,' he said. 'A King's ransom more like,' I replied, but he said, 'Not so. It is only a loan for five years, at the end of which time Robert has to pay the sum back. Robert is giving the whole of the Norman dukedom to

William as a pledge for those five years, in earnest of his intent to return the money.'

That set me thinking, for I know something of William's cunning ways. He has long coveted the dukedom, and who is to say that Robert will return from the Holy Lands? It is said that maybe half of those who travel there as pilgrims fail to return, whether because they fall in with robbers or other evil men on the way, or because they fall sick of some terrible disease that those heathens are said to spread, I know not. So it may well be that William will not need to hand back the dukedom. Even if Robert does return, who is to say that William will lightly give up what he has held for five years. He will have defended it more strongly by then too. Mark my words, the dukedom of Normandy will now be added to the kingdom of England, you see if it is not," and he nodded sagely.

"Either way it will matter little to us I think, unless it means that he is less in this kingdom and these parts than he is now." I said. "He spends little enough time at Winchester except at Christmas-tide, when we hear of him hunting the stag in his great forest of Andret. He has not visited this burgh yet for which we must be thankful, for such a visit would be over-costly and would surely lead to troubles. We have enough to concern us dealing with his close friend Ranulf Flambard, who now owns all the church lands here, and is building the great new church. That is what all this stone is for."

"I had thought it must be for a stronghold in the burgh," replied the captain, "for William is building such things in many places. If you have dealings with Flambard, you will have trouble enough without a visit from the King. If he is still close to William in five years time, and if Robert can find the ten thousand marks to return to William, you may be sure that they will have to pass Flambard's door first, and who can tell how many of them will go any further?"

"One thing is sure: we shall never see any of it back. Our chief concern is to be left in peace to till the ground, and for me to mill the corn that others grow. I have a wife and child and perhaps another soon to come and will gladly leave fighting to others. We have good priests here and the King's bailiff is fair in his dealings, so that we are mostly content with our lot. Though we may not prosper as some other burghs do, yet we do not starve, though this last year's harvest left many near to it. There is little spare this year to trade with such as you for the goods you carry; some woollen cloth perhaps, and reeds for thatching, but no wheaten flour. I fear that your French wine is too costly for us; we leave that for the wealthy nobles. Besides, we prefer that produced at Beaulieu."

"I feared as much. It is the same in many places where I have traded this last year. Much rain has spoiled the harvest. I had hoped that here, where it is often drier, you might have been more fortunate, for your fine flour is well known. Are you the miller for the church? It is to him that I have been told to speak, for it is his flour that is said to be the best.

I knew not that our mill was so well known, though travellers had often spoken highly of our bread. I had always thought that it was old Alsi's corn, God rest his soul, that made our bread so good.

"My father holds the mill for the church, but I help him with the grinding."

"Then lead me to him, for I would speak with him for the future. In the meantime, if you have any woollen cloth let me see it, for I must find a cargo before I leave. Reeds for thatching, you say? I have not carried such before, but good reed is needed in other ports I visit, the more so this year since in this wet so much has rotted on the roofs. If they are strong I could load them if I can find nothing else. Though the profit may be small, it is better than none and will at least pay for my crew. Times grow no easier, I fear."

I led the captain to Father at the mill. While they were discussing matters, I hurried home to Isabel and gathered up two lengths of cloth she had woven and which we had meant to trade at the next fair. These the captain took in exchange for silver and some spices, cinnamon and cloves particularly, and some few peppers. I also took him a bundle of reeds that we had standing beside our cott. These he examined closely.

"How much of this reed have you? If there is enough to fill half my hold, I will take them, for I know a vill where I may sell them."

"Come with me and I will show you."

I led him first to our cott and then to Alwin's barn, where he had a great stack of reed that had been gathered the previous year from the banks beside the harbour near where the two rivers meet, against the time when they would be needed. While he was examining the reeds, I fetched Alwin himself, and between the three of us we struck a bargain, for the captain gladly took the reed. He paid silver for ours, and Alwin traded some for a little wine and the rest for silver. The captain departed, well content, having seen to the despatch of the rest of his cargo of wine to Sarum, promising to return again when next he was in our waters.

That evening, when I returned to Isabel in our cott, she had prepared a stew of coney, but flavoured it with a pinch of the spices we had from the captain. Never had I eaten such a tasty meal, and it pleased her greatly when I told her so. After we had finished, Alwin joined us in fine humour.

"Isabel, my sweet, this husband of yours is turning into a good trader. He brought me that sea captain, who gladly took from me the huge pile of reeds we have had this last year, paying me in silver. We can gather plenty more when we need them. I also had from him a few flasks of some of the finest wine I have tasted in many a year. How did you fare?"

"We sold him the two bolts of cloth I had woven for the next fair, and Hugh made a better price than we would have got then. The captain added some spices too, which he seemed to value little, but see what taste they have added to this stew."

Isabel took a ladle and dipped into the pot which still stood beside the fire and gave it to her father. He sniffed it first before tasting, nodding with approval.

"You must tell your mother how you made this, for I would have her do likewise. It has a subtle flavour that is new, but keep the receipt secret, that we may impress our next important visitors. To have a new dish to put before them can lead to much profit. How are you, my sweet? The child you carry, does it trouble you with sickness still?"

"Little enough, God be praised, but that is because Hugh helps me more than most husbands."

Alwin clapped me on the shoulder.

"I have always been glad that you wed my Isabel, for I knew that she would be safe in your hands. I would not have let you wed her else."

Alwin went to the window and looked out on the steadily falling rain.

"This foul weather, is it never going to end? The crops in the demesne fields do not grow, and half of them have been washed away in the floods. How fares your assart, Hugh? It is higher land there, and perhaps drier for that."

"We suffer much as you do and shall be lucky to gather enough to feed ourselves, where even last year we had a few bushels that we could sell. It is good that we have a few swine, for they can rootle in the land and feed themselves. The roots and pulses that we grow in the garden are poor too so we may fare less well than we did last winter. I would not sell any grain or flour to the captain, though he pressed me for it, lest we find that we have not enough to eat later."

I looked out of the door towards where the church was being built.

"There is little work being done on the building either, and the remaining trenches fall in whenever they are dug out because the ground is so soft. Edward says that even the masons are hard put to set their stones right sometimes, for the rain washes out the mortar before it is set, so that they have to be relaid."

"Edward tells me that half of those he is using to dig the foundations will have no work soon. There will be more hungry mouths to feed and less with which to pay. You can be sure that Flambard will not keep idle hands. Rather he will turn them out to fend for themselves as best they can. There is little we can do but hope that he does not visit us again too soon. While he is absent, Edward can keep paying the men something, though even his monies are running low. We have had hard times before and survived and I have little doubt we will do so again."

Fate decreed that the rest of the year should be even worse and it seemed that even the sun had deserted us, for it hardly showed its face.

Winter came early and was bitter cold, so that the harbour was frozen over as few could remember it before. No ship could enter for many months and it was only a few weeks before Easter when the last of the ice melted.

There was little celebration that Christmas-tide, for each day it seemed that another died of cold or hunger as the famine gripped the land. Men could scarce leave their cotts for the cold and wind, which blew icy from the east, chilling through to the very bones. Wood grew short for kindling, for men had not the strength to venture forth to bring more in from the edge of the forest. It became a common thing to find some poor soul dead where he lay huddled in his bed with a covering of snow that had blown in under the roof, so that he seemed to have his burial shroud already upon him. Nor could they be buried, for none could break open the ground for the frost, so that the corpses had to lie beside the church covered with stones to keep off the preying dogs till the thaw finally came.

Isabel and I suffered less than some, for I had made our cott as secure as I could, filling up any hole there might be between the roof and the walls with straw. Little Martha lived in her cradle beside the small fire we were able to keep alight, and at night she slept with us, so that we all helped to keep each other warm.

I was much concerned for Isabel herself, now that she was carrying our second child. As her belly swelled, so did I have to persuade her to stay within the cott out of the chilling wind and snow and keep as warm as she could. It concerned me to see her hands so chapped and raw and her face so drawn, for the child within her seemed to be draining much of the strength from her. As Isabel's time approached I grew anxious, for we both feared to bring a child into the world at such a time.

At length, after Easter the sun returned, and when Isabel was delivered of a son we could give thanks for our survival and for the new child, though he was a poor weakly thing who seemed to cry constantly, with Isabel scarce able to feed him.

The child was not two weeks old when we took him to be baptised on Rogation Day, for he seemed so sickly that we did not wish to wait the extra days till Ascension.

"He should be called Hugh, after you," Isabel insisted, and to please her I agreed.

The child grew little in strength as the weather warmed and seemed much troubled with his breathing. All Goodwife Adeline's simples and cures seemed to have no effect, and she could only shake her head over the child and tell us to keep him warm and fed. Isabel spent much time tending him and singing lullabies to him with her harp, so that I grew to know and love the melodies.

Pentecost was two weeks past when I came back one evening having spent all day tending our assart trying to sow a late crop of wheat that would have been in the ground some months back but for the harsh winter. There was a strange quietness at the cott. No sound came from within and it seemed that the fire was out for there was no smoke. Hastening to our door, I entered to see Isabel crouched upon the floor silently rocking back and forth holding the babe close to her breast. As I came towards her, she lifted her head and turned her tear-stained and anguished face towards me.

"Oh Hugh, the babe is taken from us. He seemed a little easier when you left this morning, but after I had fed him this noontime he seemed to sleep fitfully. I lulled him to sleep with my harp, and then sat beside him. I must have fallen asleep myself, for when I woke this past hour and looked into the cradle, he was still. When I put my hand to his face to see how he was, I found that he was cold and breathed no more. I blame myself for not having held him at the last, to comfort him at his departing. He never knew the joy and warmth of summer and I feel my heart has gone cold too."

Folding Isabel and the babe in my arms, I rocked them gently to and fro to comfort them while tears streamed from my eyes. Such a little child, and so great an anguish, I feared that Isabel's heart might break. At length, she calmed enough for me to run to fetch Mary to come to sit with her while I sought out Godric to come and pray with us for the child's departed soul. Then we buried our son, to lie with all those who had died in that terrible winter.

For a time it seemed that we had been forsaken. As the weeks passed, and we saw how others who had suffered loss like us managed to bear up, we took comfort, aided by Emma and Alric and our parents.

By Lammas, time, that great healer, had brought us comfort and as the summer grew warmer so did Isabel regain her calm. She was greatly aided by little Martha's cheerfulness, for the child seemed always to be merry and laughing, so that it was hard not to share her mirth. Always there fell a shadow across Isabel's brow whenever someone talked of a babe, so that I dreaded her meeting with others who were nursing babes.

At length, one Sunday when it was bright sunshine and the sky cloudless with hardly a breath of wind, after we had returned from Mass, Isabel persuaded Emma to care for Martha, while we took a boat and crossed the harbour to Hengist's headland. There we could be in peace with only the birds and the small waves for company. Leading me by the hand, she took me to that same place where I had laid her when I took her from the waves that had so nearly drowned her. It was in that same place that she had agreed to wed me. As we neared the spot, I felt Isabel relax and she leant her head upon my shoulder as we walked. Finally we stopped, and sinking to the ground together, she let out a deep sigh before turning and burying her head in my chest.

"Hugh, my love, this is the spot where we promised to come if ever troubles overwhelmed us. We should have come here long since, for I cannot cease from grieving for our lost child. He was our first son and I was so proud to have born him for you. When he died, I felt that I had robbed you of something that was not mine to take. I do not know how to make amends, for had I not slept, perhaps the child would not have died."

She looked up at me then, while the tears coursed down her cheeks, so that I felt my heart would break for her agony of spirit.

Holding her close, I murmured, "There was nothing that you could have done to save the child. Even Goodwife Adeline had no remedies that would save him. Sometimes these things must be, and we have to learn to live with them. As Godric said when he laid the child in the earth, 'God calls some to his Kingdom before others, for reasons that we cannot know.' None could have shown more care than you in tending the babe, and it saddened me to see how you grieved for him. Comfort yourself that he did not suffer as some do, and that we have our Martha still. Who knows? If you so wish we could have other babes later. For now, it is enough for me to have you and Martha. Do not reproach yourself, for I do not, nor could I. I know of no-one who cares so much for children as you."

Isabel looked into my eyes as I spoke to see if I could really mean what I said to her, for it seemed that she still wished to doubt my words. At length, she raised her hands and stroked my face and finally set her lips to mine. Then, wiping her eyes with her soft fingers, she smiled wanly.

"You are right; I have been thinking only of my own grief, forgetting that you too have lost your first son, while we still have a daughter to cherish. Forgive me for my thoughtlessness, my Love and my Life. You saved me from the waves once; now once more you have given me new life. Help me to put this sadness from my mind so that I may raise our child and others that we shall surely have, in joy and gladness."

I stood before her then, and raising her by both hands led her to the top of the inner bank so that we could look out to sea and across to the white cliffs far to the west. The warm breeze blew on our faces, making Isabel's golden hair stream out behind her. She breathed deeply in and I saw her face relax, as she stretched up her arms wide above her head in that gesture of freedom that she so loved. Finally, she turned towards me and put her arms about my neck.

"You have brought me back to life, dear Hugh," she murmured. "Now I feel I can face the world once more. What is it about this place that brings me such peace?"

She looked around her again at the earthworks that spread out on either side of us.

"Here men lived for centuries, protected by these great earth banks. Few came to disturb them and they found contentment with the sea and sky just as we do. Here I can renew my spirit. Come, let us return, and put this sadness behind us. You have helped me to live again."

I felt her relax, and she turned to smile at me. I looked deep into her eyes and saw that they were once more clear and that the pain of the past months had gone. It felt as though a great burden had been lifted from me too, for I had not known how to help Isabel in her grief. Though I too had been affected by little Hugh's death, the burden of caring for the sickly child had fallen on her, and she blamed herself for his death. Now at last she seemed to have accepted it, though I knew that the scar on her soul would never completely heal - nor would I ever be able to completely forget. But we could pick up the threads of our lives again, and once more live.

Holding her close, I stroked her hair.

"You have brought me to life again as well, for your grief, which I did not know how to ease, was like to have killed me too. I could not find the words to tell you before. Here we can bare our souls. Come my love, we can return now with an easy mind. Little Martha needs us, and she should have brothers and sisters to play with too."

"You are right. I feel I could bear another child now."

Isabel turned then, and taking my hand, stepped lightly down the steep bank, humming a favourite lullaby as she went. Loosing the boat, we sailed back and as we went Isabel held my hand while we planned our life anew.

It seemed that life still held trials for us. For within a week, the weather turned foul again, and the rain returned and with it a cold wind, so that once more the harvest was ruined and famine stalked the land where only hunger had been before. The heavy tax that William had required all men to pay so that his brother Robert could lead his crusading army left many with nothing to buy corn when their own crop failed. Nor could they feed their stock, for much of the hay had been ruined too, being mildewed in the stacks so that the beasts would not eat it.

There were so many beasts slaughtered or dead from lack of food that winter that there were scarce enough to pull half the ploughs the next spring, so that much land was left untilled once more. Had it not been for the store that Father had in his barn and some that Alwin was able to let us use, we should have been hard put to keep alive. We caught fish whenever we could and grew heartily sick of salmon during the months that they came up the rivers, but they kept us and many others from starving. It was fortunate that a number of the more idle serfs had gone to follow Duke Robert on his Crusade, so that there were fewer mouths to feed and those that were left were prepared to work hard.

All work ceased again on the building of the church. The foundations could not be completed in the wet, and indeed some of the trenches began to fill from their collapsing sides. Edward was compelled to lay off most of those who worked on the building, keeping only the skilled masons and carpenters to continue with their work as best they might, against the time when building could start once again.

Within a few months, Isabel found that she was with child once more, so that I needed to take greater care of her, for we did not wish to lose another babe. The winter was not so bitter, and though we all suffered from the damp with constant coughs and sneezing, by the time she was delivered of another girl, whom we called Ruth, Pentecost had once more passed and it was warm again.

Some weeks before, at Easter-tide, the King had been in Winchester. Flambard took the opportunity to visit the burgh with Odo his master builder to see how his church was progressing. He was in a towering rage when he saw that Edward had not completed more of the building.

"How is it, Master Edward, that you do not carry out my orders? These walls should be rising much faster than I can see them. Do you think that I will pay for men to sit around idle when I have given clear orders for what work is to be done? The church I am building in the north at Durham is far greater than this and is progressing faster. If they can build as I command, why cannot you?"

"My Lord, we build as fast as we can, but it was not possible to dig the foundations because of the rain. No sooner had we dug a trench than its sides collapsed with the wet. Several men were almost buried in the falls and it is only by God's grace that we have not suffered the loss of lives. I cannot order men to risk their lives on such work. We have made as fast progress as is possible. If you will let me hire more men, I can now raise the walls faster, though it will require skilled men for the task."

"Make no such excuses to me. I care not if a few men are lost in the building, so long as it is raised quickly. I mean to have all completed within five years and will brook no delays. Look you to it, Master Edward, if you wish to continue in this place. There are plenty of others who will willingly do my bidding."

"What, my Lord?" cried Odo, turning on Flambard with eyes flashing. "Would you gainsay the words of Christ Himself, when He said that even the sparrows of the air are known to Him and could not fall without His knowledge? Would you lightly let men die building a house for Him? Not so, my Lord! Such a thing I will not permit where I am master builder. Edward was right to cease work when there was too much danger. I would have given such orders myself had I been here. I trust Master Edward to do right, and there is none who can carry out the work as well as he. I have looked at his walls and there is nothing that I can fault. They are straight and even and the joints are all well set. You will not find a better master mason in the kingdom, though the one who is building the church at Durham runs him close."

Flambard was taken aback by such a rebuke, and his hand went to his sword. There were too many standing close for him to strike Odo, and he knew that he had been once more shown to be wrong. He turned on his heel, and strode away to cool his anger, leaving soon after.

Meanwhile, Odo continued his inspection of the work thus far, and spent many hours with Edward in his lodge over the next few days discussing the details of how the work should progress. For those who worked on the building, Odo's words came as a comfort, for they knew Edward to be a fair master who treated them well. To hear it said by such as Odo in defiance of Flambard gave them courage and they worked the better for the knowledge.

It happened that Isabel and I were standing beside her brother Alnoth next day when he was working on one of the stones that would form part of a pillar being raised in the aisle of the church. As he worked away with his chisel and heavy wooden maul to smooth the rounded surface, sending flakes of stone flying, to add to the pile that was steadily growing at his feet, Odo and Edward came by and they too stopped and watched Alnoth awhile.

"This man seems to have the makings of a master craftsman one day, Edward," said Odo, bending forward to test the surface of the stone with his thumb. "Most men strike too hard with the maul, so that the stone tends to chip and chunks fly off leaving a rough surface that has to be reworked. This man has mastered the art of striking gently, which is quicker in the long run, and brings a far smoother surface. See how even his curve is. Tell me lad, how do you gauge the curve of the stone? Have you a template?"

Laying down his tools carefully, Alnoth reached behind him and produced a wooden arc, which he held up for Odo to inspect.

"This is what I use, sir. It was made for me by Osbern, the brother of Hugh here, who works with the carpenters. I showed him what I needed and he made it for me. See, I have several of different shapes, depending on where the stone has to go. This one here is perhaps the most useful."

He held up an oddly shaped piece of wood cut with several angles, which formed both a square and a round.

"This I use to form the stones that make up the sides of the pillars so that it all binds well together. I found that if I set the rounded part of the pillar separate, it would often fall away from the rest and so not bind in properly. With this shape, I can make sure that the whole pillar is bound to itself. Is that not what you told me?" said Alnoth, turning to Edward for confirmation of what he had said.

Edward smiled and nodded in agreement, pleased that his apprentice had learnt so well.

"Very true," he said. "I am using the shape of the pillars that I saw in the great abbey at Caen. Though the stones are more difficult to cut and build, it makes the pillars seem more slender and tall. I have seen rounded pillars at Tewkesbury and other places, such as you have ordered at Durham, which seem heavy. This irregular shape adds interest to the building and lightens the heavy mass of stone. Do you not agree? Where the pillars start to curve inwards to form the arches, I mean to have carved capitals on which the arch will rest, but the inner face of the pillar will continue upwards as a double slender column to the full height of the triforium. There will be carved capitals on top of them to take the great roof beams that will be needed to carry the roof across the centre aisle. It will be necessary to have one such beam resting upon each of the pillars.

I have men searching in the King's forest of Andret for trees that are stout enough to form such beams. Ranulf Flambard has persuaded the King to allow him to fell such timber as he will need for this church of his. There is no other timber that would be suitable nearer than the woodlands of Clarendon, and that is thirty miles distant near Sarum. Only a few have been found so far, for they have to be of great length and size. Some of the trees should be arriving soon, I hope, for they will need to season for several years before they can be cut and raised into position. Though they are Thurstan's responsibility, he and I work closely together in all things. He says that only the best oak of the forest woodlands will be good enough, and such trees are hard to find for they must be many hundred years old, he says, before they reach sufficient size for our purposes."

Odo nodded approvingly.

"You seem to have matters well controlled," he said. "There is more to building a church than cutting stone. Have you talked with Thurstan about making the templates for the arches and the supporting frames round which the stone will be laid?"

"Not yet, for they will not be needed before next year, I think. I would speak with you soon about the shape of the capitals for the pillars. I thought to have them decorated with carving and scroll work and would like your ideas on their design. Come with me to my lodge and I will show you some designs I have been experimenting with."

As the two of them moved away towards Edward's lodge, I heard Edward add, "There are two of the master masons who are skilled in carving and one of them can even represent a man's face in stone. I would not speak of it before him, but I know that the fellow we have been just been speaking with, Alnoth the bailiff's younger boy, has surprising skill for one so new to the craft. I have seen some of his work, and he too seems to have the beginnings of the carver's art. You saw how he handled the stone and his tools. I have seen some of his attempts at carving and like what I have seen, though he keeps them hidden and does not know that I have seen them."

He moved out of earshot then, so I could not hear what else he said. Isabel had heard too, and looked at me with bright eyes, but I put a finger to my lips enjoining silence. She nodded, and turning quickly to Alnoth, asked him to show her how he worked the stone to take his mind off what he might have heard. For his part, Alnoth was only too pleased to show her how he made an even curve on the stone, concentrating on his work as he did so, for it was clear that he found great satisfaction in it. For us, it was a revelation to see how under his guiding hands a rough piece of stone took on an ordered shape, and we could imagine how it would fit into the pillar he was working on. When at last he was finished, he carefully put his chisel and maul into pockets in his apron and, dusting off the chippings from it, he rose and called to another who was working beside him.

"Here, Sifrid, help me put this stone into the carrying stretcher, that I may take it to its proper place on the pillar. I would test to see if it fits as it should."

The two of them carefully lifted the stone, which was as much as the two of them could carry, and placed it onto one of the wooden stretchers that stood against the wall of the lodge. Then, standing one at each end, they bent down and took hold of the carrying handles and, at Alnoth's command, both lifted the stretcher together and began to walk slowly towards the church. Isabel and I followed until we all came to the pillar which Alnoth was working on and which already stood more than the height of a man. Beside it stood a platform, onto which Alnoth and Sifrid with my help raised the stone with much heaving and grunting. It was mighty heavy, and we had to lift the stone to the height of our chests to place it on the platform.

Then Alnoth and Sifrid clambered up to stand beside the stone and, getting a good purchase on it with their hands, heaved it up onto the top of the stone that had last been laid. We watched as they carefully shifted the new stone from side to side until it was positioned to their liking. Then Alnoth bent down and, picking up a plumb-rule, he carefully tried it against the edges of the stone he had just positioned to see if it fitted exactly with the stone that lay beneath it. This he did most critically, and seemed not to be fully satisfied, for he set down the plumb-rule, and fetching the maul and chisel from his pockets, began to work carefully on one part of the stone. Meanwhile, Sifrid sat down on the platform, with his legs dangling, swinging them to and fro and whistling, seemingly glad to be able to leave off from his work with good excuse.

"Would you sit still please, Sifrid, you are shaking the platform, so that I cannot strike the chisel accurately. There is a small blemish on the stone that I must remove before it will sit as it should, and with your swinging I may strike the wrong place."

Sifrid turned to look where Alnoth was working and screwed up his eyes to see.

"Where?" he asked, "I can see nothing. You are over-fussy Alnoth. The stone fits snug enough, and if it does not, you can always cover the place with mortar so that none can see."

"That is the difference between us," replied Alnoth.

He gave a few more light taps with his maul to the head of the chisel, and then ran his hand over the place to test it.

"There, that is better. Had I not taken off that piece, it could have been seen from below and would have cast a small shadow. I would have seen it every time I came into the church, and felt ashamed."

"No-one else would notice," Sifrid replied, "so I cannot see that it would matter. You make too much work for yourself."

"Not so. Nothing can be too much work if it is to be for God's glory. This is His House we are building, and even our finest work is scarce good enough for that. Pass me the plumb-rule again please, that I may test the stone once more. Yes, that is good. It fits well now. Help me lift it off again and then we can fix it with mortar."

Sifrid rose to his feet with a grunt and did as he was bid, and between them they first laid an even layer of mortar on the top of the stone that was already set and then carefully placed the new stone in its proper place. After much careful adjustment to make certain that the stone was not only exactly in line with the one below it, but also that it was level, Alnoth declared himself satisfied and, gathering up his tools, he jumped down to join us where we stood at the base of the pillar.

"Will you take the stretcher back to the lodge please, Sifrid. I wish to show my sister something of this work."

With a grunt, Sifrid hoisted the timber stretcher onto his shoulder and went off whistling.

"He is a good lad, but a bit careless with his work sometimes," Alnoth said as he led us to the centre of the church.

"I think he is too hasty, for he tends to hit the stone too hard and so knocks off more than he should and spoils what would otherwise be a good piece. I have tried to show him how to work stone gently, but he seems not to have the patience and does not always listen to his master either, and has earned himself many a beating as a result. I have saved him a few too, by putting right what he has done wrong when no-one is looking, for I like him. He is a cheerful fellow and means no harm."

When we had reached the great central pillar, Alnoth squatted down beside it.

"Now, cast your eyes down these pillars. Do you see how they all line up exactly? Each one is set in the same line. Now lift your eye up till it is in line with the top of the furthest pillar. Do you see that each one in between is still exactly in line. That means that each pillar is properly upright. Edward showed me how you can test it. It is quite simple. See."

He clambered up onto the top of the platform that stood against the pillar. Reaching into his pocket, he drew out a ball of fine twine and unravelled it till he came to the centre, where lay a small lump of lead.

"All you have to do is drop this lead weight down to the base of the pillar, so. Now I lift it gently, so that it is just not touching the base, and hold it the thickness of my little finger away from the stone. Isabel, will you steady the lead weight so that it no longer moves. When it is still, let me know and tell me how far away from the pillar the twine stands. It should be the thickness of your finger. Check to see if it is the same distance all the way up. Is it so?"

Isabel did as she was bidden, moving slowly so as not to disturb the weight.

"Why, it is exactly so," she cried in delight. "Did you have a hand in this pillar?"

"No, this one was built under Edward's directions, but I stood nearby to learn and see how he did it. This is what Edward calls the master pillar, since all the others are measured and checked from this one. That is why it is so important to be certain that this one is correct, and why I watched so carefully to see how he built it. Perhaps one day I may be a master builder myself, and then I shall need to know how this is done."

Alnoth looked serious as he spoke, and Isabel and I exchanged glances remembering what we had heard pass between Odo and Edward. Isabel put her arm through Alnoth's.

"From what you have shown us, it would seem that your wishes might come true one day, though there is much still to learn no doubt. I had no idea what skill was needed. I watched while Thurstan was building our house, how he made the joints of the timber so carefully. It seems that working in stone is even more difficult. Are there others as skilled as you?"

"Surely. All the master masons are far more skilled than I, and some of the apprentices too, I suspect, though I have seen little of their work, for each team works on its own."

"You are too modest of your skill Alnoth," I said, clapping him on the shoulder. "I watched the way you worked when you laid that stone and have seen how others do. It seemed that you took greater care than they and the pillar you are working on feels better to the touch."

We parted then, and Alnoth returned to his lodge to work on another stone, while Isabel and I made our way to our cott.

"I marked what passed between Odo and Edward," Isabel said as we went, "and I have seen some of Alnoth's carvings. They are most lifelike, and rank with Osbern's carvings in wood. I think this church will flower with the likes of those two working on it. Do you call to mind what Alnoth said about only the best being good enough for the church?"

I thought long about what Isabel had said of Osbern and Alnoth's work. Certainly, if the beautifully carved cradle that Osbern had made for our babes, and the care I had seen Alnoth take with the stone were any guide, then the example they would set others would be the best. Though I was but a humble miller, they might both become masters in their crafts and bring renown to the burgh through their skill. Perhaps even Flambard might come to realise that this church he was building for his own glory might have a higher purpose. It certainly seemed that each time he tried to gain his own ends, something stood in his way and turned the event around. Some Power, greater than him, seemed to be taking a hand in the building.

It could not have been more than two weeks later that we heard that poor old Alnod the priest, whom we had often cruelly mocked as youngsters, was taken with a seizure and died. He had been ailing for some years so had been able to do little except say his Offices. The whole burgh mourned his passing, for he was a kindly soul who had lived his life entirely in the service of others, so that many felt a pang of guilt when they remembered how they had sometimes treated him.

He was scarcely cold in the ground before a messenger came from Flambard claiming all Alnod's lands at Barton for himself, since all the church lands were now his. This amounted to a virgate and a half of good land, and almost eleven acres of meadow, besides a third of the mill at Barton. He also claimed the two messuages that Alnod had held in the burgh. One of these housed six of the other priests, for since many of their cotts had been destroyed to make room for the new church they had needed to find somewhere else to live. Alnod had moved out the villeins who had been living there with their families into an empty hovel which he had repaired at his own cost.

Flambard it seemed had other ideas.

"The priests who live in Alnod's messuage will pay their rent to Flambard in future," the messenger said. "See, it is all written here."

He showed Godric the scroll which bore Flambard's seal. As Godric examined it carefully, his brow furrowed with worry.

"Why, their rent is fixed at all they receive in altar fees. How are they to live?"

"That is no concern of mine," replied the messenger. "If you do not like it, you had better speak to Flambard about it."

He smirked, for he well knew what answer Flambard would give. Mounting his horse again, he spun it round on its hind legs and clattered off towards the bridge.

"I must speak with Bishop Walkelin at Winchester about this, for the priests will both starve and be unable to help the poor if this comes about."

Godric doubled up with a wracking cough as he spoke. At last he regained his breath and wiped away the tears of exhaustion from his eyes.

"This cough gets no better, and I have had it since last winter. I have tried everything to ease it and even Goodwife Adeline's infusions of hyssop honey, rue and of pennyroyal leaves are little help, though the marshmallow roots she boiled with honey have eased my throat. Enough of my ailments; they are as nothing to the sufferings I foresee for the other priests if matters are not put right."

The following day Godric set out to Winchester, though Alwin and others tried to dissuade him for the weather was still chill and the wind blew hard from the north. It was nearly three weeks before he returned. Nor would he have done so had not a kindly traveller picked him up where he lay beside the road, exhausted from his travels and his fruitless mission. It was several days before he was well enough to speak and give his news and by then he was coughing blood.

"It was a week before I could see the Bishop, and he could do nothing for Flambard was sitting beside him at the time. As a last resort, I sought audience with the King himself, since he is lord of the burgh. I had to wait almost another two weeks before that could be granted and by then Flambard had poisoned that ear too, so that there was no hope to be had from that quarter either."

He gasped in pain as another fit of coughing wracked his body.

"There is no hope for it, I fear. All Alnod's lands pass to Flambard, and what they produce will be used to pay for the church. The six priests who live in his messuage will have scarcely enough to feed themselves when they have paid their rent. I cannot think that this is right, but what can we do when such powers are ranged against us? I begin to wonder if the building of this church is indeed God's will, so many of our folk now seem to be suffering from it."

Simon the infirmarer, who was kneeling beside Godric's bed, bathed his brow with a cooling cloth soaked in a decoction of wood sage.

"The fault lies not in the building of the church, but he who has commanded it to be built. It seems that he is possessed by the Devil himself. The efforts of all of us, from Odo, Edward and Thurstan down to the humblest serf who clears away the rubbish, are hindered by Flambard's ambition to build greater than any before him, for his own glory. I heard from a monk who had journeyed south from Durham that the church Flambard is building there is far greater than this one. It seems that the man is obsessed with power and building memorials to himself. Though he tries to make out that they are to God's glory, there are few who believe him, and it is we who suffer for it."

Godric laid his hand on Simon's arm.

"Peace, Simon. Speak ill of no-one, for you will have to answer for it at the Last Day. I cannot find it in me to think that God will allow such a thing to happen. We must trust in His wisdom, though we may not understand it. All will come right in the end, have no fear. I may not be with you much longer, so you Simon, and the other priests who remain, must try to continue your work as you have in the past."

Godric gasped for breath again as he was seized by another bout of coughing which shook his whole weakened frame.

We left him then, and I called on Father to tell him what had occurred. He shook his head gravely.

"He is worn out by all the burdens he has had to carry. To stand up as he has done to that man Ranulf is enough to tax any man to extinction. Rightly is he called Flambard, for he seems to be an all-consuming flame that none can resist.

We can only hope that when his time comes he will himself be consumed by the fires of Hell."

"As for Godric," I added, "he surely will find a place with the angels, for his work here on our behalf has been tireless."

It was Rodric who brought us the news two days later that Godric had breathed his last. Though many had been expecting it, few could believe that the man who had so valiantly stood against all who tried to hinder God's will would be no longer there to guide and help us. There was scarcely a dry eye in the burgh as the priests laid the corpse that had once been Godric to rest in the deep earth. No work was done that day on the building, nor for three days afterwards, and there was not a man who did not have some tale to tell of kindness or staunch help that he had received from Godric. The gap he left in all our lives left many wondering how we would manage to resist the forces that seemed to be ranged against us.

As Isabel said, while we sat by our hearth that night, "By his example, he gave us all the courage to stand up for what we knew to be right, and we must continue to do so now he is gone. We must not fail him."

Chapter 14 1100

Four years have passed since Godric the priest was taken from us. During that time, two sons had been born to us, whom we named Oswald after Father, and Simon. Emma likewise was blessed with two more babes, and both Osbern and Alnoth took true Saxon girls to wife. Osbern wedded Adela the daughter of Wulfric, who held three virgates towards Sopley, and Alnoth took Matilda, Geoffrey the reeve's fair daughter.

At times it seemed that God had deserted us, for the weather was foul with over-much rain and the crops poor. Nor were we spared by the King, who levied even heavier taxes on everyone to pay for his wars to drive out the Scots and the fierce Welsh tribes, and to have castles built to keep them both at bay. There was little peace in his Norman dukedom either, which he said cost him much in money and men, though it seemed that it was the folk in the burghs and vills who provided most of both.

We saw little of Flambard, which brought us some relief, for he was too busy seeing to his great church at Durham and building a strong castle and tower for William in London beside the river to protect that town from the marauding Danes and others of like temper.

Work on our great church proceeded slowly, since Flambard was slow to send Odo the funds to pay for the work. Often times, Edward had to lay men off, so that many were near to starving, for the priests had nothing to give them, since all they had was taken by Flambard. Death was frequent in the burgh too, and the number of priests themselves greatly reduced, till there were less than half of their original twenty-four left.

Last year, which was the final year of the old century, brought two events. At Pentecost, the King was once more at Westminster, just outside his town of London. There he held Court in his newly completed great hall and he gave to Flambard the bishopric of Durham, which he had long coveted. With all the other high offices he already held, besides many other abbeys, we hoped that Flambard might forget about our small burgh which could surely not hold a taper to such places as Durham or London.

Shortly afterwards, at Martinmas, there was such a flooding in of the sea that much of the burgh lay under the water. Had it not been for the wall which lay at the foot of our garden, our cott would have suffered. Father's house suffered greatly, with part of its walls washed out, so that it only stayed upright because of the corner posts. Our mill being stone-built survived unharmed, though standing as it does on the edge of the harbour it was submerged so that only the upper floor was above the water. As Father said with a wry smile, at least it flushed out all the rats from their holes and gave the mill a better cleaning than it had had for many years. That may have been so, but it certainly gave me plenty of work clearing out the mud and rubbish afterwards, and everything had to be stripped right down and cleaned. Removing the mud and grease from the shafts and bearings was a stinking task and I smelt like a midden for a week afterwards.

Many who lived on the lower ground in the burgh lost all they had, and much of the grain that was stored in barns was spoilt by the water, so that there was famine once more. The fields near to the rivers were lost to view for many days and most of the beasts that had been feeding on them were washed away and drowned. For weeks afterwards men kept finding the rotting carcasses of their beasts which then had to be buried.

Belesme, who lived further inland and on somewhat higher ground, was saved, and so was our assart, so that we were able to harvest what we had sown and save our beasts. Those at Stanpit lost much of what they had, including Goodwife Adeline, whose simples and herbs were largely ruined and lost in the flood waters. It was some weeks before the pure well could be used again, for the salt water had entered it and made it foul.

No man could give a reason for such a flood, the like of which none could remember before. However, it was noticed that it was the first day of the new moon; many blamed the heathen gods for the disaster. Such travellers as came brought news of like flooding from all round the coast, where the land lay low, so that there was equal grievous loss suffered by some of the greatest in the land.

Even the King's family did not escape hardship at this time. News came to us from a monk of the priory at Lewes, who passed through on his way to Sarum, that one of Duke Robert's bastard sons who had been hunting in the forest of Andret at its eastern edge was slain by an arrow of a careless huntsman. He had then fled to the Lewes priory where he had sought sanctuary and become a monk. It seemed that the forest of Andret was fateful to the King, for William's elder brother Richard had been crushed against a tree and killed during the Conqueror's reign.

Lammas-tide came, and Isabel and I had been busy gathering our corn on our assart. We had stopped by Belesme's cott to see how his harvest fared, when there was the sound of hurrying hooves. Belesme glanced anxiously up and moved to take his sword from where he kept it above the door. Drawing it from its sheath, he stepped behind the door, at the same time signing to Isabel and his wife Ediva to gather up the children and hide in the inner room. I stood beside the door latch with my sickle, the only weapon I could lay my hand on, raised above my head. We heard the horse slow and finally stop and the rider dismount, then the sound of footsteps coming towards the door. There was a hammering followed by a hoarse cry, "Open, for the love of God."

Belesme and I looked at each other questioningly, wondering who would make such a request. Some fugitive no doubt, but to call on God's name in such a manner made us uneasy.

"Who stands there, and what is your business?" Belesme growled. "We are armed so have a care. You have called on God's name, so stand back from the door and lay down your arms if you come in peace."

We heard the sound of retreating footsteps, followed by the clatter of steel landing on the stones in the ground.

"I have done as you said and come in peace to seek your aid," said the stranger outside. "I mean you no harm."

Belesme's brow clouded.

"I know that voice," he whispered. "I cannot place it yet, but it is surely Norman."

He raised his voice. "What is your name, Norman? Speak, as you value your life," Belesme called out.

"I am Walter Tirell, Count of Poix. In the name of God open up while there is yet time."

At that, Belesme stepped to the door and, lifting the latch, slowly opened it, peering cautiously out as he did so.

"My Lord, it is indeed you. I recognised your voice but could not place it at first. My name is Belesme of St Lo, and I remember you last in Normandy. Enter my home. You seem in need of shelter and it were best that we hide your horse too. Hugh, lead the horse into the shed behind the cott and tether it where it may not be seen. Give the beast hay to eat, that it may be quiet."

By the time I had done as he bid and returned to the cott, the stranger was seated with his back against the wall, gulping down great draughts of ale from a mug that Belesme had given him. At last he finished, and putting the mug down on the table before him, wiped his mouth with the back of his hand, then let out a deep sigh.

"It is well that I have met you, Belesme. The last time we met was at the priory outside Rouen when Duke William lay dying. You stood by the door, if I remember rightly, and Henry Beauclerc sent you to take word of William's death to this land, to summon the barons to the present William's crowning. I had to stay with the red-faced one to keep him safe and have been near him ever since. I need your help now as never before. The King is slain!" he gasped out, "and I must flee the country as soon as maybe, for my life will be forfeit else. It was a most unlucky shot. An accident, I swear it."

He leant forward and covered his face with his hands as if trying to blot out some terrible sight from his eyes. Thus he sat for a long while, scarcely breathing, so that neither of us dared speak to him. At length, he seemed to regain his composure, for he lowered his hands to his knees and let out a deep sigh that shook his whole body.

"I have done a terrible thing, but I swear before God that it was an accident."

A look of agony passed across his face, and he looked pleadingly at Belesme.

"You believe me, don't you?" he cried.

"My Lord, I have no cause to doubt your word, but as yet you have not told us what occurred."

Walter Tirell sighed again.

"You are right," he said. "You must hear the whole story if you are to trust me. Yesterday was the feast of Saint Peter's Chains as you know, when the 'grease time' for hunting the fat red stags starts. William was in high good humour at the thought of the coming sport and had pressed his brother Henry Beauclerc to be with him on the hunt, also Robert FitzHaimo and William of Breteuil. Henry, Eorl of Warwick, was with us and Simon of Northampton and one or two others whom I cannot remember. He had also persuaded William Giffard to join the party. Having just been promised the bishopric of Winchester, Giffard could hardly refuse, though by the look on his face the thought of hunting close to the King terrified him. Though he sits a good horse, he cannot hit a barn at twenty paces with an arrow and he feared to look foolish before his King. The thought of having to rise before dawn to join the chase went ill with his usual comfortable life too. However he need not have worried, because we did not set off till after we had eaten at midday.

It seems that a monk from some French monastery who knew Robert FitzHaimo had roused him during the night to tell him of a vision he had seen, which deeply concerned the King's safety. I know not what it was, but FitzHaimo and others were sufficiently concerned to make them persuade the King not to leave for the chase until after the sun had passed its zenith. Though the King paid heed to their warnings, it put him in a foul mood, as you may imagine. He spent the hours of waiting dealing with affairs of state, complaining all the while that the wine he had drunk the previous night had been tainted and the food sour. If the truth be known he had indulged himself too freely as was his custom, and his head was paying the price, but I must not speak ill of the dead - though it is hard to believe that the King is no more." He shook his head again, and paused deep in thought.

Seeing that the stranger was seated between Belesme and I, Ediva and Isabel had meanwhile crept silently back into the room, having left the children to play quietly in the inner room. They listened to what Tirell had to tell.

"You say the King is dead?" asked Ediva.

"Then may the Lord have mercy on his soul," murmured Isabel, and they both crossed themselves.

"Amen to that," murmured Tirell, as he likewise crossed himself.

"We were preparing to mount and the King was drawing on his boots, when a blacksmith who lived locally, no doubt hoping to find favour with the King, approached him and, kneeling, presented him with six fine arrows. The King accepted them and examined the points approvingly. Then he turned towards where I stood a few yards off and called me to him. 'Here, my Lord of Poix,' he said, using for some reason my title rather than my name. 'Take two of these fine arrows for yourself. It is only right that the deadliest shot should have the sharpest arrows.' Then, turning to one of his household, he told him to give the blacksmith three gold pieces, joking to those who stood round him that with such fine barbs he was certain to bring down whatever he hit, even if the place he hit was not mortal.

We had mounted and were just moving off when a dusty monk arrived bearing a letter from Abbot Serlo of Gloucester, which he urged the King to read without delay since it concerned the King's own health, he said. Vexed at being further kept from his sport, William tore open the parchment quickly and cast his eye over its contents. 'What is this?' he growled, 'another dreaming monk, this time foretelling my early death as a punishment for my ill-treatment of the church? Why, Walter Giffard, have I not this very day given you the see of Winchester, and this monk dares to say that I ill-use the church. Does he take me for an Englishman to be put off my sport and business because some old woman has sneezed or had a dream? Not me,' and he burst out laughing. Then, turning to me, he said, 'Walter, you do justice in this matter'. For my sins I replied, 'I will indeed my Lord,' may God forgive me for it. Then the King set his spurs to his horse and galloped off towards the forest with the rest of us trailing behind him."

"Did the King kill his stag?" I asked, for I had heard that it always put him in a good humour if he made a clean kill.

"Would he had done so, lad," Tirell said, "for I would not then be fleeing for my life. We had all scattered into the thickets which the huntsmen had chosen as the most likely place for the stag to pass. The King called me to his side and bade me stand close to him. This I did, and placed myself behind a large oak some yards from him with the trunk hiding me from where I judged the stag would approach, and also from the King who was to one side of me. He had said that I was to shoot after him, but not to do so until I heard his whistle, for he might loose a second arrow if more than one stag passed by. He can loose an arrow quicker than almost any man I know, so I notched one of the new arrows the King had given me and waited. It is my custom always to test an arrow for its flight first before I put it to use, for each smith's barbs fly differently, but there was not time for that today."

He ceased speaking, and cast a fearful glance towards where his quiver stood against the wall.

"At length, a fine-headed stag came into view. Twelve points it had, and I was pleased that the King should have so fine a quarry in his sight. I stood ready as the stag approached, hoping that it would take a line towards the King. The great beast was almost passing between us when the King loosed his arrow, but his aim was high and he missed, though it frightened the stag which darted forward. I heard the King whistle, so knew he wished me to shoot. Because the tree obscured my view, I stepped forward and loosed my arrow quickly as the beast sped past. I blame myself for aiming high too, though it may have been the barb that made us both shoot high. The arrow only grazed the stag's shoulder."

He groaned and smote one hand against the other and shook his head in the agony of his distress.

"How could I know that the King himself had also stepped forward to be ready to take a second shot at the retreating stag if I were to miss, for he too had been behind a tree. I watched the beast drive onwards, and then turned to where I thought the King was standing, expecting to see him loose his second arrow, but he was not there. Instead, he lay on his back, with my fateful arrow which he himself had given me, sunk deep in his chest. Dropping my bow, I ran to him and raised his head to give him succour but it was too late. The shaft had pierced his heart and he was already dead. He had uttered no sound as he fell and did not even die with repentance on his lips. Making the sign of the Cross over the body, I committed his soul to God as best I might in a few words, lest his soul fly from his body un-shriven."

Once more he paused and I saw tears course down his cheeks as in anguish he crossed himself several times.

"Looking quickly about me, I could see no-one else, for that part of the forest had many close thickets and the others were all well hidden. So gathering up my bow, I hastened to where I had left my horse tied and, loosening it, mounted quickly. Then I shouted, 'Look to the King! He is yonder, between the two great oaks by that thicket. Look to the King!' and I pointed. Immediately others of our party appeared from where they had been hidden and made towards the spot I had pointed out. As they ran towards where the King lay, I called out, 'I go to seek aid.' and set my spurs to my horse's flanks, and set off eastwards before taking a wide sweep to the south-west, to head towards the coast, for I wished to put as much distance between me and them before they discovered what had occurred, and turn to accuse me."

We all sat dumbfounded at the tale, scarce able to believe that it could be true. Belesme was the first to recover.

"There are many in the land who will bless you for what you have done, my Lord, for the red-faced William has dealt harshly with the realm and cost it dear in both men and money. Your account of what you say occurred rings true to my ears, but by your hasty flight many will read it differently and hold you to account."

The rest of us nodded in agreement.

"My Lord," I said, "The King is not the first to die in such manner in the forest of Andret, for only a few months back we heard that a bastard son of Duke Robert was killed in like manner. The man who shot that fateful arrow has sought sanctuary in the priory of Lewes. What will you do now? There is no like priory here, only a half-built church. Nor could you reach the abbey in Winchester unharmed, for word of what has happened will have reached there before you. Could you not ride to Sarum and seek sanctuary there?"

"I doubt that I would be welcome there, for the Bishop is too close to the Court. Besides I do not fancy the thought of spending the rest of my days in a hair shirt on my knees in a cold cell. I have lands in France and mean to flee there if I can find a ship to carry me. You have a harbour at Twynham, I think, which trades with France. Is there a ship there now that I could safely take passage on? I would pay the captain well."

"The only vessel at the quay when we left this morning was one that brought stone from the quarries on Vectis Isle," I said. "Such a boat would not be suitable since it would only take you back nearer to Winchester, for it passes through the narrows by Hurst Point. Besides, your presence would be noted, for there is nowhere to hide on such a ship and the crew would surely talk. No trading craft from France is expected for another week. Your best chance is to take horse to Poole, where there are ships of all kinds. It is further to the west and less likely to have heard what has occurred. It would not take you many hours to reach that harbour, even avoiding the paths. If you ride due west you will approach the harbour from the north, but you will have to swim your horse across the two rivers, Avon and Stour. The first should be no trouble, but the second flows fast, so you had best take care."

Walter Tirell nodded. "My thanks for your advice. That is the course I will follow, but I think it best to hide up till the morrow. Belesme, may I pass the night here in your cott? I was not observed coming, so there should be no danger. It is much to ask, but my life is at stake."

"My Lord, we have both been soldiers, and faced death many times. I can place no blame on you for what you did. Indeed, from what you say, the King himself bade you do justice for him, though he meant it not in the way that turned out. I fear now for my wife and children, should any come in pursuit and find you here."

Turning to me, Belesme added, "Hugh, take Ediva and the children with you when you leave. They will be safe with you in the burgh, and no-one will think to question it, for all know that our families are friends and stay with each other often."

I rose to go, while Ediva and Isabel went to gather up the children.

Tirell groaned again. "My soul is tormented by what I have done. Is there a priest living near that I may make my confession and be shriven? I fear to die with such heavy guilt upon me."

"There is one who lives at Stanpit," I said, " which is on the road we have to take to reach the burgh. He will hear your confession and give you such help as he can. Shall I send him to you? He knows this cott well. You cannot mistake him for he stands two yards and a hand span high and is built like an ox, but a man of great kindness. There is on-one in the burgh that I would rather seek aid from. Is that not so, Belesme?"

"True, he has helped us before - that time when Flambard wished to build his church on Catherine's hill."

Belesme grinned as he remembered how we had brought the stone down from the hill each night, and how Godwine had carried huge boulders from the quay to the present site of the church as though they were but a bundle of faggots. "Then bid him come here with all haste if you will, so that he may shrive me before I sleep, for I could not rest this night with such a heavy burden on my soul."

Tirell turned to where he had laid his bow and quiver and, reaching inside it, drew out one arrow, which he held up for us to see.

"This is the fellow to the shaft that struck the King. Little did the blacksmith who made the barbs know what would befall when he fashioned them in his forge. I cannot keep this thing, for it is tainted."

He took it then in both hands and snapped the shaft across his knee with one blow and then held out both pieces to me.

"Take them Hugh, and give them to the priest when you speak to him, and ask him what penance I should submit to for this terrible deed. Now be gone, and take this terrible thing from me, for the very sight of it puts me in mortal terror. Tell this to the priest too, so that he may know my agony of spirit."

He thrust into his scrip and took out a handful of silver which he pressed into my hand.

"Here, take this for your pains. It were best if you say nothing of all you have heard until news comes from Winchester which will be soon enough, for we shall have a new king now. Duke Robert is in Normandy I hear, on his way back from the Holy Places where he covered himself with great glory. It is said that he has at last taken a young and pretty wife too, which is the cause of his so long dallying. No doubt he will now make all haste to return to claim the kingdom as the eldest son of the Conqueror. There are plenty who will rally to him who felt that he should have been King rather than red-faced William. Now go with all speed to the priest, and go in peace."

Dropping the silver into my scrip, I took the two pieces of the broken arrow and wrapped it with my sickle in a cloth that it might not be seen. Then, calling to Ediva and Isabel to bring the children, we all left.

"I will come to you at your cott tomorrow," said Belesme, "when I have seen my Lord of Poix safely on his way to Poole. Go quickly and bid Godwine for me to come with all speed by the back-ways, so that he be not seen. All of you guard your tongues, for none of us must be linked with today's events."

Turning to Ediva, he kissed her.

"Keep the children close, and let Hugh alone speak to Godwine, so that they may have nothing to prattle about to their friends. Now go quickly."

He raised the latch of the door, and peering out to see that there was no-one about, beckoned to us all to leave.

We made our way to Stanpit, with the children running about us and playing as they always did, so that the few we met on the road thought nothing of it. Those we passed enquired as to our harvest and we gave them a true account of what we had cut and asked them in their turn how they fared. Ediva and Isabel played their parts well so that none suspected the heavy burden we carried.

As we approached Godwine's small cott, Isabel turned to me.

"We will leave you here and go on to Goodwife Adeline's cott, for I would buy some salve from her for my hands. They always suffer at harvest-time, as I think you have cause to remember. Do you recall the blow you received in the eye the year you sought to wed me?"

I called to mind how I had had to ward off that great oaf who had lashed out at me when he was full of ale those years back, and how it had helped to make me decide to seek Isabel's hand. We parted where the two tracks forked and I turned away to Godwine's cott. He opened to my first knocking and welcomed me in with some surprise.

"What brings you here, Hugh? Is one of your family sickly? Sit you down, and tell me, that I may know how I can help."

He brought up a stool and placed it beside him near the hearth.

"We are all well, Master Godwine, and it is not for myself that have come to you for aid, but a stranger whose need is greater than I can say. He is with Belesme now at his cott, and bids you hasten to him if you will. He bade me give you this."

I fumbled with the cloth to remove the two halves of the arrow that Walter Tirell have given me and placed them in Godwine's hands. He looked closely at them for a while, and turned a puzzled gaze towards me.

"What does this mean? This was as fine an arrow as I have ever seen. How came it to be broken? Has someone died from it? I think not, for it is clean, and looks never to have been used."

"Not from this arrow, but its fellow. The King is dead, shot by an unlucky accident it would seem while hunting the stag in his forest. The man who did it, Walter Tirell, Count of Poix, fled the scene as soon as he knew what he had done, though he sent others to see to the King's body before he took to horse. We were with Belesme in his cott, when the man arrived, anguished and seeking shelter. He has sent me to beg you to go to him so that he may confess his sin and seek forgiveness, and be shriven. He could not bare the sight of the arrow, whose fellow had killed the King, so he broke it and sent it to you so that he may know you when you come. He asked what penance he should undergo, for he is distraught and truly penitent it seems."

I recounted the whole story to Godwine, whose look became more grave as I told him the full horror of what had happened. When at last I had finished, I enjoined silence on Godwine till the matter was widely known, as Walter Tirell had bidden me. Godwine rose then, and putting his stole and other things that he might need in his scrip, and taking up the staff he always carried when he was abroad, he put his hand on my shoulder.

"It is a heavy burden you are carrying for this man, Hugh. I will take it upon myself now and go to him. Speak to no man of this, and try to avoid being questioned about it lest you let slip more than you should. I shall pray for you, that you may have strength. Now I must go to this wretched man and give him such aid as I am able and consider his penance, which he says he so richly deserves. If he is already as penitent as you say, then there is yet hope for him. Go now on your way with God. Pax vobiscum." He made the sign of the Cross over me before moving to open the door and setting out for Belesme's cott.

As I watched him go, I felt a weight lift from my shoulders at his words of comfort. Seeing his great figure striding so confidently away, I felt that if any could help Tirell, Godwine could. I too turned, and made my way to Goodwife Adeline's cott, where I found the others, while the goodwife had our little Martha on her knee so that she could tend her palms, which were bleeding.

"She was running ahead of us to reach the goodwife first, and tripped and fell, grazing her hands as you can see," Isabel explained.

"It is nothing, but I need to clean the cuts and remove the grit that has entered the skin or the place will fester," Adeline said looking up from the child's hand she was bathing.

"There my pretty one, that will do well enough I think. You should take more care. I shall still be here tomorrow you know; there was no need to rush so."

"I wanted to be first because the others said that you might give the first one a honey cake," murmured Martha, wiping the remains of a tear from her stained cheek.

"So that was it! Well, let us look and see if we can find one, and perhaps one for the others too."

She busied herself amongst her jars and pots, and came back with her hands held out and her fists closed.

"Which one would you choose?" she asked. Martha pointed to one fist, and when Adeline opened it she let out a squeal of delight.

"Is this for me?" she asked, as she looked at the honeyed sweetmeat that lay in the open palm. Adeline nodded gravely at the child, who stretched out her hand

and carefully took the morsel. Then, going to Isabel, she broke it in two and gave one half to her mother.

"You can share it with me if you like."

Isabel took the morsel with a happy smile and, lifting Martha onto her own knee, hugged her, saying to Adeline, "She is always like that. Whatever she has, she always wants to share with others."

"I think she gets her thoughtfulness from you. Now let me look for the salve you asked me for. I always find people need it at harvest time, for the thorns and thistles are hard on women's hands so I make sure I have plenty by me at this time of year."

As she busied herself putting the salve into a pot, Isabel went to her.

"Have you any of that decoction of camomile, ground ivy and yarrow that you gave me two years back. A poultice of it quickly cleared an angry abscess Hugh had when he cut himself while cleaning the bearings on the mill-wheel, and I would have some more by me in case of need again."

Adeline reached down a jar from the top shelf and ladled some of its contents into another pot, before giving it to Isabel, who took it gladly.

"I will send you a basket of eggs tomorrow. Now, children, are we all ready, for it is high time we returned home. The angelus sounded some time ago I think, and if we wait much longer it will be dark and they will close the gate, then what should we do?"

With that we left Goodwife Adeline and continued back, with the children running on ahead, as usual. When they were out of earshot, I told Ediva and Isabel what had transpired at Godwine's cott, and they too were grateful that he had taken our burden on his broad shoulders.

The following day, some hours after we had eaten our midday meal, Belesme came to the mill. He made some excuse for me to leave Father for a while, so that he could tell me how things stood.

"Godwine came none too soon, for I thought Tirell might be taken with a seizure, he was so distraught. After he had talked with him for some time, he became calmer. I left them together, for it seemed that it was a matter between them alone. When I returned, Godwine was ready to depart and Tirell was himself again, though his eyes were red from weeping. 'I have confessed to Godwine as best I may,' he declared, ' and he has shriven me. As penance I must carry the two parts of the broken arrow with me for as long as I live to remind me of the dreadful deed. I must pray for the King's soul daily, for as he says, the King died without repentance, for which I must carry the blame. He has promised that he will never speak to anyone of the matter, for it was in the confessional that he heard it.' Tirell made me swear you and Isabel and also Ediva to silence, and this I did on the Cross.

There the matter will rest, and none shall ever hear of it again from the lips of any of us. This morning, before it was light, I set him on his way towards Poole, giving him instructions of the best tracks to take and where to cross the rivers. If fortune goes with him, he should find a captain ready to take him across the water before news of what has occurred can reach the port. Horsemen will be sent eastwards to London, and north to Sarum, but not to Poole I fancy, so he should be away before any can think to prevent him."

"None have come here so far and they would come here before they went to Poole. Come, let us go to our cott, and find Ediva and your children. They have been busy helping Isabel in the garden which will have kept them happy."

They were not there as I had expected, and Belesme looked worried till we heard the cries of young laughter. We made our way to the wall at the bottom of the garden, and found a ladder placed against it.

"They will be playing in the sand at the edge of the river," I said.

Climbing up, we looked over the wall, where we saw them all happily splashing in the shallows while Isabel and Ediva sat and watched them. Ediva looked up, pleased to see Belesme again, and anxiously enquired how things were. When he had told them both all he had recounted to me and sworn them both to secrecy, he called to his brood. Reluctantly, they climbed back over the wall and so returned to their cott.

Nearly two weeks passed before we had certain news of the King's death. There had been vague and wild rumours which most men put down to wishful thinking, for there were many who wished the King dead for the evil he had brought on the land. It was Alwin who brought the news when he returned from a journey to Winchester on the King's business concerning the crops from the demesne. On his return, he first summoned the chief men to his hall to give them the news, and then called the whole burgh together to tell them. When we were all assembled in the churchyard, he called for silence.

"Men of Twynham, I have great news. King William the red-faced is dead. Killed on the second day of Lammas-tide. It seems he was shot in the breast by an arrow while hunting in his great forest and died instantly, before any could reach him."

A small cheer went up at this, for there were few amongst us who loved the King. Alwin quietened it at once with an angry gesture, for as bailiff of the King's demesne, he could not have it thought that he was pleased by the event.

"It is not known for sure who committed this foul deed," he continued when all was once more quiet, "but it seems that Walter Tirell, the Count of Poix who was close to him on the chase, has fled, having been the first to raise the alarm. Some say that it was an accident, while some say that this Tirell or some other, murdered the King. Nothing is known for certain, but be assured that those near to the King mean to find out. However, now we have a new King."

"What, is Robert to be King of this island as well as Duke of Normandy like his father before him?" called out a voice from the crowd.

"Not so," replied Alwin. "The new King is Henry Beauclerc, the youngest of the Conqueror's sons. He has already been crowned at Westminster, outside London. When I was in Winchester, I heard that on William's death, Henry Beauclerc took horse with all speed to London, and there had himself crowned by Maurice, the bishop of that city, amidst great rejoicing, for he promised before the altar at Westminster to put down all the injustices that were done in his brother's time. All the great nobles who were present bowed the knee to him and swore oaths to be his vassals. It is said that he has sent for the blessed Anselm to return from the monastery in Auvergne where he has been living since William sent him away, to take his proper place at Canterbury and once more to be our archbishop.

He has also promised to fill the many empty sees, and in particular the northern archbishop's place at York."

There was much excited murmuring amongst the folk gathered in the market place at this startling news. When it had quietened, Alwin continued.

"Let us hope that this will mean that we can once more continue building this great church here. You can be sure that when I am called to do homage to the new King Henry I shall press him to let Edward and Thurstan continue with all speed with the work and to take on all those who have been set aside from the building works these last months. I can promise you nothing in this matter, but rest assured that I will do my best on your behalf. Tomorrow, Rodric will say a Requiem Mass for the soul of William our dead King, after which he will offer prayers for Henry Beauclerc, to whom we owe homage, not only as King but also as lord of this burgh. The rest of the day will be a holiday."

There was a general cheer at this, and the crowd began to shout and dance and throw their caps in the air with cries of "Long live King Henry".

That evening, Alwin gathered Mother and Father, Isabel and I, and also Alric and Emma, Osbern and Alnoth and their wives, into his hall.

"I did not tell the people all that I have heard," he began when we were all seated, "for it was not seemly. William had made no plans as to who was to succeed him, for he had no reason to fear such an early death. It was generally thought that Duke Robert would succeed to the crown, as was shouted in the crowd this afternoon, but Henry Beauclerc acted with great speed. I was able to speak with some who had been in the party that fateful day. It seems that as soon as Henry saw that William was dead, he leapt to his horse and, calling to his close followers, galloped with all speed to Winchester, leaving the body of the dead King where it lay on the ground. There it lay for some hours, until some passing woodman came across it and seeing by the clothes that it was a man of note, loaded it onto a cart and brought it to Winchester, where the soldiers guarding the King's Court immediately threw him in a dungeon thinking that he had done the deed himself. It was not till Henry Beauclerc was told that the man was released and sent on his way, pacified with a purse of silver, so that he ended up with his hoped-for reward."

"I would not have been in his shoes for a purse of gold, knowing how those Norman soldiers treat us," said Alric, with which we all agreed.

"Anyway, the first thing Henry did on entering the palace at Winchester, was to go to the Treasurer, William of Breteuil, and demand that he deliver the royal treasure chests into his care. De Breteuil is an old friend of Duke Robert's, and having paid him homage and done him fealty, said he could not do as Henry wished. It seems that he reminded Henry that Robert was the elder, and so had a better claim to the crown than him, added to which, he said that Robert had toiled for years as a Crusader in the service of God, and God was now restoring to him not only his own dukedom, but also his father's crown, which he would no doubt claim as soon as he landed within the month with his new wife. Seemingly such arguments carried little weight with Henry, for he countered them by saying that though Robert might be the elder, he was born a foreigner and only the son of a Norman duke, whereas he, Henry, was English born, and the son of an English king, and he drew his sword to be sure that de Breteuil understood his arguments.

Whether the sword, Henry's friends or his arguments won the day I cannot be sure, but suffice it to say that de Breteuil handed over the royal treasure to Henry there and then."

"That was indeed a swift move," I said.

"So swift," added Alric, "that some might think that it was already planned."

This set us all thinking for a while till Alwin continued.

"With his funds secure, Henry summoned all the barons and bishops and other leading men who were then at Winchester to a council and made his claim to the crown, adding that in any case Duke Robert's whereabouts was not known, nor his intentions. Since he had so long delayed his return from the Holy Places, there was no reason to assume that he would return quickly now - particularly as he had just married a beautiful wife. Though many would have rallied to Robert had he been in the country, his absence weakened their position. Besides, Henry won over the support of such bishops as were there by first confirming William's appointment that morning of William Giffard as Bishop of Winchester. Then he promised to invite Anselm to return at once to Canterbury and also to fill all the vacant sees forthwith. This swung the council in his favour, and they agreed that Maurice, Bishop of London, should crown Henry King at Westminster."

"Well, certainly Henry has secured his throne for the moment," said Father, while the rest of us nodded in agreement.

"Later," contined Alwin, "I heard it said that Gundulf of Rochester was none too pleased, thinking that he was senior to Maurice and should have been given the task, but he was too distant and had no authority in London. Henry ordered the council's agreement to be transcribed at once and witnessed by the most senior of those present, and within the hour he was on horseback again with his closest followers, heading for London, and had himself crowned three days later. He moved fast to forestall Robert."

"From what you have told us," mused Father, "it seems that Henry moved so fast that if he had not planned the deed himself at least he had laid plans to sieze the throne should the occasion arise. It can be said that he did nothing that William had not done before when the first William died at Rouen."

"Perhaps what happened in the forest was no accident, for William had many enemies," added Alric, "though I would not have any in this hall repeat that I said so."

"Such thoughts have crossed many minds I think, and will cross many more before the year is out," said Alwin, "but it is best that we keep such thoughts to ourselves."

"What of Ranulf Flambard?" asked Alric. "Whose side did he take?"

"I was told that he kept his counsel close to the very end and then went with the majority in supporting Henry, though if his face was any guide, he was far from pleased. As Bishop of Durham, and because of the many offices he holds, his voice would have been heeded closely. He is a quick thinker, and when Henry played the Englishman against Robert's Norman descent and absence, he guessed who the folk in the realm would follow. I think he was right, though it will cost him dear, for he will lose many of the rich abbeys he has robbed these past years, where they have had no Abbot. At all events, he rode with Henry to London to be near him at his crowning."

This gave us much to think on. For a while no-one spoke, all of us wondering how these events would affect our lives. At length, as if he could read our thoughts, Alwin said quietly,

"We shall have a new lord here, but I doubt if it will change things much. We have seen little enough of our last two lords, and the only change was when red-faced William gave our church to Flambard. Now he is too busy with his church at Durham. Odo may have some difficulty for a while finding money for the building, though perhaps if Henry wishes to please his English subjects, he may wish to use some of the royal treasure to help build some of the present churches. Who can tell? Time alone will give us the answer.

My greatest fear is that Duke Robert may try to stake his claim by force, in which case we may see the sort of ravaging and pillage that the Norman dukedom has suffered. We should look to our defences, I think. Hugh, Alric, are your parts of the burgh wall in good repair? I will speak to the reeve about the remainder of the wall, and it would be best that we all practised a little with our bows and swords."

"We should see that the gates are properly closed each night and that sentries are posted so that we are not surprised," I added. "I doubt Duke Robert would land this far west, but it would be wise if we set a watch on Hengist's headland to warn us of any approaching fleet. One man would be enough, and by day only, for no-one who does not know the sand-bars would dare enter the Run at night."

"Well said, Hugh," said Alwin. "A few wise precautions may save a lot of lives, though let us hope that it will not come to bloodshed."

We continued discussing matters for a while longer, then returned with sober hearts to our own cotts. On the way, Alric and I first went out through the Canons' Gate to inspect the section of wall which stretched from there down to the mill, which we had to keep in good repair as the service we owed for our land and cotts. I marked a few places where small repairs should be made, resolving to attend to them on the morrow. Before Isabel and I retired to rest for the night, we went down to the end of the garden against the wall, and I picked up the ladder which we kept there.

"We should keep this in the cott in future, I think. It would be too easy for an enemy to scale the wall if we leave it by the sow's sty."

As Isabel tended the children in their bed and tucked little Simon securely into his cradle, she whispered over them, "God grant that they may grow up in peace as we have done and be spared the ravages of war amongst our own people."

Next day, Alwin and Geoffrey the reeve made inspection of the whole length of the burgh walls. Several places were found to be weak and orders were given for the earth bank to be strengthened and the stakes which were driven into its top were to be sharpened and replaced with new ones where they were showing signs of rot. Thurstan was called upon to provide carpenters from amongst those who were working for him on the church, and he found timbers for the work too. Several of these I used for the places I needed to strengthen.

Edward was also prevailed upon to provide rough stone, such as he could not use, which was stored on the towers above the gates ready to be hurled down on any who might try to rush the gates. When these precautions had been taken we all felt more secure, the more so when Alwin sent word by one who was travelling to Winchester to let it be known in the market place and in the ears of those near to the King's Court that the burgh was well protected and could withstand attack.

"It does no harm to put it about that we are a well-defended place," said Alwin. "It will discourage any who might think to take advantage of the troubled times that may soon come."

The moon had not run a full course before there was a cry, one noontime, from the gate that a body of horsemen could be seen approaching from Stanpit. At first there was fear that the dreaded attack was about to take place, but those with more sober heads saw that there were others on the road who showed no fear, and no glint of armour could be seen from the horsemen, who were approaching at a walk.

Alwin and Geoffrey, with Rodric and a few others, went to the gate to meet the party, who seemed to be of some importance. As they approached, one man who by his bearing and dress seemed to carry most authority, rode forward.

"I am Richard de Redvers, and bring greetings from my Lord Henry Beauclerc, newly crowned at Westminster, King of this realm."

He dismounted, and giving his reins to a page, stepped forward and held out a parchment which he offered to Alwin.

"You would seem to be the bailiff of this burgh, so it is right that you should know by what authority I come. Great things have happened these past weeks. The King, of his bounty, has granted me this burgh, and I have done homage to him for it, so that you now owe fealty to me first rather than the King. I would tell you also that the King has imprisoned Ranulf known as Flambard in his tower at London - the same tower that this Flambard was himself building for the King. King Henry has also stripped Flambard of all his lands and offices for the evil he has done these many years, and has given to me this church and all its lands which Flambard held before. See it is all written in this charter."

He handed a scroll of parchment to Alwin, who, too taken aback by what he had just heard, took it in silence. Carefully unrolling it, he examined the names written at its foot before motioning Geoffrey and Rodric to read it with him. There was a stunned silence amongst all who stood at the gate until at last Alwin looked up from his reading.

"It is even as you have said, my Lord. We bid you welcome and, when we have assembled the whole burgh and explained matters to them, we will do you homage as is our duty. For the moment, will it please you to come to my hall and take some refreshment before you inspect your new domain? There is much that I and the priests would like to question you about, though such matters can wait until you are rested."

Richard inclined his head in agreement and the whole party moved off towards Alwin's hall. Meanwhile, the news spread like fire through stubble, so that before they had reached the market square, there was already a large crowd gathered. Mary came to the door of her hall, looking a little flustered, having just issued orders for food and drink to be prepared for the burgh's new lord. Dropping him a curtsy, she welcomed him and escorted him within.

It was an hour later that Isabel and I, standing with the others in the crowd in the market square, watched as our new lord came out with Alwin, Geoffrey and Rodric. Seeing the expectant crowd, Richard de Redvers lifted his hands to command silence.

"Good people" he cried. "As no doubt you have heard, I am your new lord, for our new King has granted me this burgh of Twynham together with its church. Have no fear, for I mean to do right by you, and have come to see what the King has granted me. This place has an honoured name and has existed since before any can remember. I mean it to prosper as it did in the past. In Winchester, I heard tell that you have newly repaired its walls and defences, which pleases me greatly. More; I have heard of the great church that is being built here and wish to see how it progresses, for it seems that it should be completed with all speed. I shall now view your burgh, and when I have satisfied myself with all there is to be seen I will speak with you again. For the moment, go about your business in peace, but return an hour after the angelus has sounded."

There was a general murmur of approval and excitement as people began to move away, discussing in groups what all this would mean. I borrowed a horse from Alwin and rode with all speed to tell Belesme the news, stopping at Stanpit to see Godwine and Witro begging them to give the news to any others they could reach.

When everyone was once more gathered in the market square, which was now so crowded with all those who had come in from their fields that some could scarcely breathe, Richard de Redvers mounted his horse so that all could see him, while Alwin and the others stood beside him.

"Men of Twynham," he began. "You will have already heard why I have come. I have now walked through the burgh and seen its walls which look stout enough now that you have repaired them. I see there is a great motte of earth raised less than a bow-shot from the mill-stream where the bridge crosses it. On this I mean to raise a wooden keep to defend the burgh should any enemy of the King wish to wrest it from me, for such evil men may well be abroad before too long. I have spoken with Thurstan, the master carpenter of the church, and he will set men to work on this at once. As for your new church, I have spoken with your priests, and also Edward the master mason, for I wish work to proceed with all haste towards its completion."

He waited for the excited murmurs to quieten before continuing, for there were many who for long had had no work and now saw the chance to earn a living again.

"You have already heard that the King has stripped Flambard of this church and all its lands and given them to me. Flambard is no longer dean of this place, and Rodric tells me that there is no-one who is the head amongst the priests. I mean to set that right, and appoint a new dean, to whom I will then give all the lands which before-time belonged to the church. There is land at Bosley, much land at Stanpit and Hoburne, and more land at Hampton near Winkton. The churches at Hordle and Boldre, and the chapels at Milford, Brockenhurst, Holdenhurst and Sopley, with all their tithes and lands will also belong to the dean when he is appointed, besides other lands on Vectis Isle and elsewhere.

I have no need of those lands and it were better that they were put to proper use for the glory of God. I have spoken with Edward and Thurstan, and told them to use such men as they require for the building of the church, for the crops and tithes of the lands that are due to the church should be enough to pay for the work. I am told that many of your priests have died and there are scarce enough to say the Offices and pray for the souls of the departed. On my return to Winchester, I shall speak to Walter Giffard, newly appointed by the King to be the bishop in Winchester, so that between us we may appoint a new dean to be in charge of this church, and also find some new priests to help in the work of caring for the souls of those that live here."

Richard de Redvers paused awhile to allow what he had said to sink in to those who listened to him, then he continued:

"I have other greater lands that I must see to, so that I shall not live amongst you. Alwin who has been bailiff here these many years and served the King faithfully, will continue in that office and render to me a full account each year. I mean this burgh to prosper, and so it shall with your help and under my guidance. To celebrate the King's goodness in granting me this burgh and its church, I have commanded that tomorrow shall be a holiday, and an ox shall be roasted in the square and ale provided from my demesne. Now, good people, God's blessing be upon you, and go about your business in peace."

There was a roar of approval from the crowd and caps were thrown in the air, while many tried to press forward to touch de Redvers' coat in thankfulness for his words. There were many who felt that for the first time in many months they would not go hungry now that they had the prospect of good work again, either on the church or the new keep that was to be built.

I turned to Isabel and shielded her from the press as we made our way back to our cott.

"This is good news indeed," she said. "We are rid of Flambard at last. I suppose I should not wish him ill, but he has caused all of us much hurt over the years and he has not made Edward and Thurstan's tasks any easier by his constant demands and by taking so much of the goods and benefits to himself which rightly belonged to the church."

"It seems that Henry Beauclerc means to right the many wrongs that have troubled this land during William's time. To have locked Flambard up in his tower in London was indeed a strong move that should act as a warning to others who may wish to cross his path. Let us hope that by so doing he has forestalled any who might wish to support Duke Robert, for I dearly wish to live in peace. If we can have more priests, perhaps Rodric will be able to spend more time teaching the children; they all need his guidance. Little Martha will soon be able to say her 'Pater Noster'. She is bright as a button and copies everything you say, I have noticed."

Isabel turned and smiled at me.

"I have tried to teach her a few things and she is quick to learn. She picked up my sewing needle the other day and was trying to copy my stitches with it on a scrap of cloth she had found. While she worked, she said snatches of the 'Ave Maria' to herself - though most of the time her tongue was so firmly stuck between her teeth in concentration that there was little time for speech. She is a bonny child. I would be loath to lose her to a convent when she grows, though she would be acceptable, I think."

"There is time enough to think of that, and I agree that I would rather she stayed in the burgh and wed and raised her own family. Though priests and nuns are needed in plenty, there is need also of God-fearing families living normal lives. If she can follow your example, then I think she will earn her place in Heaven as well as any nun."

I gave Isabel's arm a squeeze as I said this.

"You do me too much honour," she murmured. "I try to do only what I feel is right and what my own mother taught me. To consider the needs of others is not so strange, and leads to better understanding and avoids quarrels. The peace in the burgh owes as much to my parents and yours as to the priests, I think, particularly now that there are so few of them left. We need those that de Redvers has promised us, and let us pray that he sends a strong man to lead them and one who will do right by all men. From what Father has said, too many of the bishops and abbots are more concerned with their own comfort and wealth to care for the souls of ordinary folk. We need someone like old Godric, may his soul rest in peace, rather than Flambard."

"Take not too much of the burgh's burdens upon your own shoulders," I said. " We shall get by, I have no doubt, for there are many who feel as you do, which is why the ducking stool and stocks are used so rarely. It is good too that the tithing men have long seen to it that the men in their Frankpledge keep a watchful eye on each other to their mutual benefit, and step in early to stop trouble before it becomes serious. After that lout blacked my eye, the men of his tithing took him to task and saw to it that he worked hard and was kept out of the ale-houses for some weeks, which taught him the lesson he needed far better than any thrashing I might have given him. Edward and Thurstan use a firm hand on those they employ too, and the example they set is followed by more men than one might suppose."

"Let us see what Father is doing to prepare for tomorrow's feast. It should be a merry time. Should I take my harp do you think, to help with the singing?"

We found Alwin and Mary busy with the preparations for the morrow, seeing to the gathering of logs for the fire on which the ox was to be roasted, and preparing herbs and honey cakes and great pots of vegetables. Leaving Isabel to help her mother, I returned to the mill where Father was busy grinding extra flour, for Ranulf of the guest-house had sent word that several extra sacks of flour were needed to make bread for the feast.

The feast day dawned fine and there was much excitement at the extra day free of work. Much ale was drunk throughout the day, and by the time evening came there were a few sore heads. None were so drunk that they could not find their way to the square before Alwin's hall where the fire was glowing red and already roasting the great ox that willing hands kept constantly turning on the spit.

Throughout the afternoon there were constant calls to try the meat to see if it was done. Richard de Redvers spent much time talking with those who stood round, twitting them for their greed and shaking his head in mock seriousness that it would be many hours yet before the feast could start. When at last it was fully cooked, de Redvers drew a jewelled knife from his belt and with a great flourish cut the first slice, and holding it aloft, stuffed it into his mouth, while a hush came over all who stood around. Slowly, de Redvers chewed on the meat, first with a frown on his face as if the meat was not to his liking, and then, bursting into a great grin, he raised both his hands high above his head, and cried out, "This ox is the finest I have tasted in many a year. Master Alwin, you have done us all proud. Let the feast begin."

With that a great cheer went up from all who were in the square, and people began to press forward to those who were beginning to carve huge slices from the sides of the ox with sharp knives. As they handed them out to those who stood closest with outstretched platters and bowls, there were many cries of "God bless you my Lord", and "May the saints heap blessings on your family" and such-like prayers. Martha stood wide-eyed while little Ruth was jumping up and down in glee as she stood beside us holding Isabel's free hand. She was cradling our youngest, Simon, in her other arm, while I held little Oswald on my shoulder so that he could see all that went on.

"Do you think there will be any left for me?" he whispered in my ear.

"Have no fear," I replied. "It is the biggest ox of any that Alwin has, and there will be more than enough to go round, even with your big appetite."

He grinned at me, for we were always saying how much he ate. Rubbing his little hands together and smacking his lips, he said, "When I am a man, I shall eat a whole ox all by myself," and we all laughed.

So the feast continued, with every person having all that they could eat and plenty of ale to wash it down. Some there were who would have eaten, and more particularly, drunk themselves into a stupor, but Alwin had spoken with the priests, Geoffrey, Father and one or two of the others who were standing by the barrels of ale. Those who were known to take more than they could hold found that their ale mugs were filled less often, and then from watered ale, which in their present state they were unable to notice.

As Alwin said, "We should not abuse the generosity of our new lord, though the cost of the feast will not concern him. Better that he should think well of the burgh now, that he may treat us well in future, than that he should find us a pack of drunken louts that he would not think twice to treat harshly next time he is out of humour."

When at last all had finished eating, and the sky had darkened with the setting of the sun, men and women and whole families began to gather round the dying embers, sitting on the ground conversing idly with their neighbours. Then one began to play on his pipes, and another put well-known words to the tune. Others began to join in the chorus, while some were content to sit and listen, replete as they had not been for many a month.

After a while, when there was a pause in the singing as a song came to an end, Alric, who was sitting near us, called out, "Isabel, would you give us a song from your harp?"

"Yes, do please," cried Emma, the light of the fire shining on her auburn locks which she had let fall round her shoulders.

"I know you have your harp by you. Will you give us 'Parsley, sage, rosemary and thyme'? Alric and Hugh can sing the men's part, and you and I can take the women's, with everyone joining in the chorus."

Isabel looked towards me, questioning. She was too modest to have offered to sing herself, but was pleased that Emma should have suggested it.

"Will you sing with me, Hugh, if I play the notes?"

I nodded, beckoning to Emma and Alric to come and sit by us.

Settling the children round us, Isabel took up her harp and began to tune it carefully. Voices stilled, for all knew that Isabel sang most tunefully and held her in some respect as the daughter of the bailiff. Then, plucking a few soft notes, she nodded to Alric and me, so that we might begin.

"Can you make me a cambric shirt?" we sang, and the rest of the men sitting round followed with the chorus, "Parsley, sage, rosemary and thyme".

When it came to the last verse Isabel sang the whole melody alone, gazing deep into my eyes.

"When you have done and finished your work,
Parsley, sage, rosemary and thyme,
Then come to me for your cambric shirt,
And you shall be a true lover of mine."

A deep hush fell on all gathered round the embers as the last notes faded into the air. There were many eyes where tears glistened, for Isabel had sung most sweetly. At length, Richard de Redvers, who was seated close by us with Alwin and Mary, cleared his throat to hide his emotion, and leant forward.

"Never have I heard singing so sweet. It is not a song I have heard before. Whence comes it?"

"It is an old Saxon melody, my Lord, that has been handed down from our forefathers. My mother taught it me when I was a child at her knee, is that not so, Mother?"

"Why to be sure, though I never sang it so well my Lord, and I do not have Isabel's cunning in my fingers to play the harp as she does."

De Redvers nodded. "We have songs in Normandy but they are of a different temper. They tell too much of passionate love. Your songs tell of the love that comes of giving, each to the other. There is suffering too, I think, for nothing worthwhile comes easy in this world."

We sat in silence for a while, then de Redvers asked, "Will you give us another of your Saxon songs? I find them strangely restful."

Again Isabel bent her head to her harp and called forth another haunting melody, setting to it the words of another of our ancient songs. As she sang quietly, some of those nearest to her joined in. humming the tune softly to remind themselves of it while listening to the words she sang.

When the song was ended, de Redvers leant forward and spoke quietly to Isabel.

"Would you teach some of those songs to my wife when next I am in these parts? I would that she could learn them and sing them to me when I am troubled. I am Norman born and bred, but I find many of your Saxon ways to my liking."

"It would be a great honour, my Lord, but you must forgive any faults I make in the playing, for I am not schooled in the art and have only learnt to pick out the tunes by ear."

"You are too modest I think, for you have more cunning in your fingers than any troubadour I have heard these last ten years. Besides, as I have said, the songs you sing give me more pleasure than theirs."

Finally the feast drew to a close and folk slowly began to drift away to their cotts, bidding each other "Good-night" and calling out a blessing on de Redvers as they went. Little Oswald and Simon had dropped into a dreamless sleep, replete with overmuch food. Even Martha and Ruth could scarce keep their eyes open despite all the excitement of the scene. We too then slipped away, to tuck the children into their cradle and bed. I stood gazing down at their sleeping forms, then stripped my garments from me. Isabel did likewise, and coming to stand beside me, took me by the hand and led me first to the open window that gave onto the garden and the river beyond. There we stood naked for a while, gazing at the stars that shone brightly overhead.

"What can they see, do you suppose?" she asked, resting her head on my shoulder. "Do you think they know what the future holds for us? If we could ask a boon of them, for my part it would be that there be peace for our little ones in the realm with our new king, and prosperity in the burgh from our new lord."

"Amen to that," I replied.

She turned to me then and enfolded me in her arms, pressing her lips against mine while I stroked her corn-coloured hair. Then she raised her head and whispered "Come," and with soft steps led me by the hand to our bed.

Chapter 15 1100–1102

I woke next day to find Isabel still lying in my arms, her corn-coloured hair framing her head which nestled above my heart. As I stroked her tresses away from her cheek, she murmured under her breath then turned her lips towards me seeking mine. As I bent my head to hers, she dreamily opened her eyes and sighed in deep contentment. Thus we lay a while, savouring the joys of each other's bodies, till finally she roused herself, and raising herself on one elbow, she looked to where the children still lay sleeping peacefully.

Drawing back the covers, she rose and stretched herself, turning to face me as she did so while I gazed with delight as always at the full beauty of her naked body. Then, bending over me, she kissed me once more before turning to pick up her under-tunic which lay where she had left it the night before on a stool at the foot of the bed. As she raised her arms to pull the tunic over her head, I marvelled at the firmness of her still youthful body even after bearing our five children, and a lump came to my throat when I thought of the babe Hugh that had died and whose loss I felt sure still grieved Isabel.

The lines of sorrow round her eyes that had appeared after the child died would never leave her face, but some inner strength seemed to have possessed her soul to give her a calmness which I knew she used to help others in time of adversity, taking their suffering upon herself and easing their spirits. I felt deeply grateful that such a lovely creature should have consented to share her life with me, a humble miller's son.

Rising hastily from our bed, to hide my emotions, I dressed quickly then took Isabel in my arms again.

"It is time we enlarged this cott so that the children can have their own sleeping room. Martha is growing quickly. Besides," I continued, "it would be more seemly if we had our own chamber, do you not think?"

Isabel eyes smiled though she tried to keep a solemn face.

"Why Hugh, we do but act naturally, do we not?"

Then raising her face to kiss me again she continued, "You are right, my love. I had thought to mention it to you myself. How do you plan to make the cott larger?"

"Do you remember when Thurstan built his cott how he showed us that it was possible to make an upper chamber at one end? I have studied his cott next to ours, and I think it will be possible for us to do likewise. I mean to speak to him and ask if he will help us to plan the work. Osbern would help with the building, I am sure, for he is skilled now in the carpenter's art. It would be good if we could undertake the work before the winter. There is yet time when the harvest has been gathered from our assart and the silver we raise from selling our corn will more than pay for the timbers we need."

"Will you speak to Thurstan soon, then? I will speak with Father to see if he has any timbers that we can use; there is a great stack still in his yard. He may be able to sell us some, for it will be well seasoned and strong for our purpose."

Sounds came from our sleeping chamber then as the children began to rouse, so we hastened to greet them. While Isabel saw to their dressing, I busied myself with clearing my head in a pail of water and then setting the table for us to break our fast.

It was not till an hour after Sext that Father and I finished the milling for the day and we were able to eat our midday meal. When we had done, I set off to go to our assart where there was still much to do. Making my way up over the open ground to the south of the new church and in by the door which stood in the sunny corner of the south transept, I came out by the small door on the east side of the opposite transept, to take the path that led to the bridge. As I neared the great mound of earth piled up from the foundations, I glanced up to see Edward and Thurstan standing at its top. Seeing me, Edward called to me to join them.

"Can you spare a few minutes to help us, Hugh? We need three pairs of hands for what we are about."

I climbed up to join them and Thurstan explained their purpose.

"You recall that our new lord, Richard de Redvers, said that he wished to have a keep built here to add to the defence of the burgh? Edward and I are seeing how this can best be done and we are measuring the ground to see what size it can be. Here, Hugh, take this twine and stand with it at this point."

He dug his heel into the ground at a spot about two yards in from the edge of the slope of the mound. Then he walked to the far end of the mound, and after speaking with Edward, placed him in a similar position.

"Now we must make our square angles. Do you know how this is done, Hugh?"

I nodded and, taking another length of twine from Thurstan, measured out five exact arm's lengths on it, placing a knot at each one. Then I checked them to see that none differed from the others before holding up the knotted twine to Thurstan.

"See, I have measured the five equal lengths that we need. Do you not remember how you showed me the method when you were laying out the plan of your cott on the ground next to ours some years back? I have remembered it ever since. Three lengths down the first side, then four on the second side, taken from the same corner, and five from the end of the first three lengths, to cut the mark on the squared side. Is that right?"

Thurstan grinned as he looked towards Edward. "It seems he has remembered well what I have taught him, just like his young brother Osbern. I wish others had as ready a wit. Some I have to tell each time what to do."

"It is the same with my young masons," said Edward. "Few there are that will carry out a task rightly after only one telling. It is a pleasure when one finds such."

It gave me pleasure to hear such uncalled-for praise, and the three of us set about marking out the site for the keep. After several false starts, Thurstan and Edward at last fixed the size and shape which they thought would serve their purpose.

"We cannot build too near the edge of the slope or the earth will break away and the walls collapse. Nor must we allow too great a space at the foot of the wall or an attacker can gain a foothold there with too much room to wield their weapons and perhaps raise ladders. Two full paces between the base of the walls and the edge of the slope should meet the case. That will give us a space within the keep of three rods wide and two and a half rods deep."

"How high are the walls to be, and will there be any shelter within?" I asked, for like most people I knew nothing of such buildings.

"How say you, Thurstan?" said Edward. "Have you timbers to make the walls four arm's lengths high? That will mean timbers of near a rod in length, for they must be well set in the ground."

"We have enough, though some that we must use I have put to one side for use on the church roof. No doubt I can find others in time for that, for I fear there is still much work to be done before I can roof the church. As for shelter Hugh, yes indeed, there will be a guard house built against the back wall where men could sleep and eat in time of need. Also a store, for should the burgh be attacked, the keep must last out a siege, so it will need food and water, which must be kept in barrels."

"Why are the walls to be so high?" I asked. "The walls of the burgh are scarce the height of a man, so that he can see to shoot an arrow over when he stands upon the earth wall beneath."

"So they are, Hugh," said Edward, "but the keep needs all the height it can have. The strongest ones have a platform above a man's height inside the wall on which a bowman can stand to shoot down on those who try a foray against the walls. We shall build one such here, and the platform will add strength to the walls, for the posts that hold the inner edge of the platform will brace the outer wall. Besides, the platform will give shelter to those who may have to live within in time of siege."

"The extra height will give the bowman a better shot at any trying to cross the river and mill-stream too. It is only eighty paces from here to the mill-stream so that they would be an easy target."

Edward grinned at me.

"Well said, Hugh, we will make a soldier of you yet. Besides, the keep will serve as a watch-tower too, for you can see clearly for a good distance. See how the bridges over both parts of the river are open to us, and beyond, the Pure Well cotts stand out. Look to the right: across the marshes lie the few hovels and cotts that are Stanpit, and the water of the harbour is clear beyond that. When the keep is built, you should be able to see the harbour entrance too, for it is not above a mile and a half from here and there is nothing to hide it but a few trees on the marshes."

"De Redvers will soon have those cut down if it will mean a more open view. I will speak to him and claim the timber too, for we could use it," said Thurstan. "Look to the left: the view is clear over the meadows to the river and beyond. They are lush pastures to be sure, but marshy too when it rains and the river floods; and there is the Bar Gate; and there beyond lies Catherine's hill. Fool that Flambard was to try to build his great church there. It was wise that he heeded for once the signs sent from God that he should not build up there. It is about the only time that I have known him take such heed and it served him well. We are well rid of him at all events."

I smiled inwardly to hear Edward and Thurstan talking in this manner. They did not know the true facts, nor would they ever hear them from my lips.

When at last they were satisfied with the plan they had marked out on the ground, we all descended the mound and Thurstan thanked me for my help.

"We must seek out de Redvers first to make sure the plan meets with his approval before we start to build," said Edward.

As they turned to go, I took Thurstan by the sleeve. "Master Thurstan, I have been meaning to ask a favour of you."

"Say on Hugh. I will meet it if I can."

"Our cott is over-small now with our growing brood of children, and I would make it larger. When you built yours, I remember you showed me how you would make an upper chamber. Would you help me to make one in our cott? I would hope to extend the length of the cott to one side, and make an upper chamber over it which Isabel could use as her bower and could serve also as our sleeping chamber. Our children could then use our present sleeping room for themselves."

Thurstan took my hand.

"Why assuredly. I know how it is with so many children running about, A woman has nowhere that she can call her own. Besides," he said with a grin, as he slapped me on the shoulder, "there are times when a man and woman would be alone without prying eyes, is that not so, Hugh?"

Thus it was that with Thurstan's guiding hand that we planned the enlargement of our cott. Alwin provided the main timbers for it - well seasoned oak posts they were - which we paid for in corn from our assart. With Osbern to help cut the timber so that it was properly jointed, we raised an extra bay to the cott, with an upper and a lower room.

It took less time than I had feared, for we had many willing hands to help with weaving the osiers for the wattle that formed the walls. Mixing the daub was a stinking task as usual, the more so as the children were too eager to help and caused more hindrance than help, but how could we stop them from enjoying themselves, for they felt they were helping to build their house too. We set windows in the walls where they would give most light within, setting wooden shutters to keep out wind and rain, and, by raising wattle hurdles within the cott which we also covered with daub, we were able to divide the lower chamber into several parts so that we had extra rooms for the girls as well as the two boys, and a new store-room besides. Osbern also made us a new table and some extra stools, and for our birthdays he made us each a chair, both with arm rests.

"With such luxury, we shall soon be rivals to our lord Richard de Redvers," said Isabel, as she thanked Osbern for his fine gifts.

Meantime, work on the keep progressed apace, and the walls soon rose to the design that Edward and Thurstan had suggested and which de Redvers had approved. Before winter set in, it was completed with its inner platform and shelter and a watch-tower at one corner, raised even higher than the walls. It proved to be even as Edward had said, for from the watch-tower there was a clear view to the entrance of the harbour, where none could enter without our knowing.

As Alwin said, when he climbed the tower to see, "There will be time enough to gather folk together should any try to approach by water, even if they do manage to enter the harbour safely and avoid the sand bars. Likewise, any who come by land can be seen from afar, the more so now that some of the trees have been felled between the burgh and the cotts by Pure Well."

Advent season was approaching when next de Redvers came. He sent word ahead of him that he wished to take a View of Frankpledge. All men of the burgh were assembled then in their tithings, with their tithing man at their head, on the clear open ground below the new keep where our new lord planned to inspect and question them. The women folk stood to one side, interested in what would take place, but taking no part. The priests and those who worked on the demesne stood apart too, for priests formed no part of the Frankpledge because of their calling and the demesne men answered directly to the Lord of the Manor. In the time of William, that had meant the King himself, but now they looked to de Redvers. Clambering half way up the earth mound of the new keep, so that all could see and hear him clearly, he addressed the demesne men first.

"You men who work on my demesne are now in my Mainpast, working for me and eating my bread. Till now you have been the King's men and answered to him. Now that he has granted me this burgh, and its demesne, you must answer to me and in my court for any crimes you may commit. Because I have great lands and can come seldom here, I am appointing Alwin the bailiff to act in my stead. He will act much as the shire reeve does, overseeing my court, and in my absence take the View of Frankpledge twice a year. All men and boys above the age of twelve are in surety-ship, in Frankpledge, and I can see that you stand in your tithings now. I hear from Alwin my bailiff that it is some years since any had to raise the hue and cry and follow a malefactor who had fled, and that in all cases since the time of the Conqueror the tithing was able to capture the man and bring him back to justice, so that you were not at mercy before the court, and so did not have to pay the fine yourselves. You were wise to save yourselves that burden and I commend you for it."

There was a murmur of approval amongst the crowd, and much nodding of heads, for it is no little thing for ten men to have to find the fine of a mark for even a minor malefactor. Far better to catch the fellow and make him pay for his own misdeeds.

"Looking round, I can see that some of the tithings have shrunk and others grown too large since last a View of Frankpledge was taken, which Alwin tells me is some years ago. This I shall now set right. Master Bailiff, and you, Geoffrey the reeve, come with me. I have spoken with the wisest heads in the burgh and between us we have chosen some new men to be tithing men where they are needed, whether because some are now too old, though they have served well in the past, or because there is need for more now that there are more living in the burgh."

The three of them passed amongst the crowd, joining some small groups of men and dividing others that were over-large. When they came to where I stood, Alwin spoke to de Redvers, and pointed to me.

"This is one of whom we spoke."

De Redvers stopped before me, sizing me up before speaking. "What is your name, lad?"

"Hugh, the miller's son."

"You look to have a good head on your shoulders and some muscle too, I'll be bound. Will you fight?"

"Not if it can be avoided, but if needs must, I can give an account of myself."

"Well said, lad. I like your spirit. Keep out of trouble if you can, but meet it head on if you must. You are just the man I need to head a tithing. Will you do the job? Men will follow you I think. They would be fools not to if the size of your fist is any guide."

"My Lord, you do me an honour. If you think I am suitable, I will gladly be a tithing man."

"Good. You men there. Here is your new tithing man. That is settled then. Now, Alwin, we need two more and you said your own son might serve. Where is he standing?"

The three of them passed on to the next group and were lost to my view.

The View of Frankpledge continued till all was complete. Then de Redvers clambered once more half-way up the mound of the keep, and spoke to us all again.

"Men of Twynham, you are now in your new tithings and some of you have new tithing men. I have chosen them and they are all good men. Take heed of what they say and help them to keep the peace here. Go to their aid when they call upon you, particularly when they raise the hue and cry, so that should a malefactor flee you can pursue him at once and bring him back to face his accusers. Even though he may be a friend, it is your duty to produce him before the court. As his friend, you may then wish to stand bail for his appearance before the King's Justice, but that is not part of your Frankpledge, only what you may feel you owe him as a friend. Be warned: should he fail to appear in due time, then you will find yourselves at mercy before the court and have to pay a fine of half a mark. Think long before you put friendship to the test, for you will find its value is eighty pence, which is no small sum to find."

De Redvers turned then to where the men of his demesne were standing.

"You men of my demesne who are in my Mainpast, you will answer to my bailiff, Alwin, as he will answer to me. He has treated you fairly in the past and will do so in the future, I have no doubt. My justice is the King's justice, for I have pledged fealty to him and have bent my knee before him and placed my hands between his in homage for the lands I have from him. I owe the King service as you owe service to me. That is the way of things."

De Redvers paused then and looked about him to see how his words had been received. Alwin and Geoffrey were nodding in approval, and the priests likewise. I had little doubt that de Redvers had spoken to them before-hand, and had their approval. Though there were a few grumbles, they seemed to come only from those who would always complain, for de Redvers' words changed little. Then he raised his glance, seeming to be searching for someone in the crowd.

"Where is Belesme of St Lo?"

Heads turned, seeking him, and then a cry came from one side of the crowd.

"Here he is," and another called "Why, what has he done?"

There was a movement in the crowd as Belesme made his way forward to the base of the earth motte on which de Redvers stood. As he came, he looked confident enough and seemed to be reassuring those around him that there was nothing to fear. De Redvers beckoned to him to come and stand beside him.

"You all know Belesme of St Lo who has lived amongst you a dozen years now. You see this keep which I have had newly built on its motte? It will act as a sure defence to the burgh should any try to take it. Henry Beauclerc, our new King, is continuing red-faced William's design to build keeps and castles throughout the land to secure his realm from those who wish him ill. Duke Robert in Normandy plots to regain his dukedom, which is still in pawn to Henry his brother our King, and he has plans afoot to try to wrest this kingdom from him.

This keep may yet be put to the test, though Duke Robert still has to cross the seas and raise support here. There are some who would side with Robert against Henry. My lands, which stretch from Exeter in the west as far as Carisbroke on Vectis Isle, are pledged in Henry's support. A keep is no use unless it has men to defend it. You have men to defend your walls and they will now have the keep as a sure place of refuge in case of attack, but there is need for one to command the defence. I have consulted with the wisest heads in the burgh and they agree with me that this is the man."

De Redvers placed his hand on Belesme's shoulder and looked about the crowd for their approval. Most nodded and murmured their assent, but a voice rose the crowd.

"What need have we of that old greybeard? We have done well enough in the past and I doubt if he could wield a sword to much effect now. Why not choose a younger man? What about Tovi or Brand? They are young and strong. I would fight beside them any day."

The crowd began to murmur, some agreeing and others showing dissent with this suggestion. De Redvers' brow clouded, not liking his words to be questioned. He held up his hands for silence.

"Greybeard he may be, but I warrant he has seen more service than the rest of you put together. Why, he fought at Senlac Field, and knows how Normans fight. He also knows the strength of Saxon arms. He tells me he respects them too, for his helm and shield which he still keeps bear the marks of Saxon axes to this day."

This brought a laugh from many, for Belesme was well liked.

"He fought in many other campaigns with Duke William when he was

King, and was near him at Mantes when he received his death wound, so do not say that he knows not how to fight. I'll warrant that for all his years, and he tells me that he has two score and ten, there are few here who could face him with sword and shield with much hope of success. More important, he knows much of the art of war - how to defend, and how and when to make an assault; when to use archers, and when to make a feint. I could have sent you another who had like skills to be constable of this keep, but I thought to choose one of your own number whom you know and can trust. You will not find him wanting, I'll warrant."

There was a general murmur of approval and several voices were raised in Belesme's favour, while others denounced those who had put forward Tovi and Brand. They for their part had sense enough to shout their support for Belesme, which quickly settled the matter. Belesme looked pleased, but kept his counsel as de Redvers continued.

"I have spoken to Thurstan, and have given orders for a place to be built near to the keep where Belesme can live, for his present cott is too distant. In time, when this great church is complete and the land where we now stand is no longer needed, it will be fenced about to form the bailey, and a ditch dug about it too. For now, the keep will be enough to deter those who may wish the King ill. Belesme will train you in the arts of war as he thinks fit, in the use of both sword and bow. A strong place is soon known, and those of evil intent will go elsewhere. I give you now your constable, Belesme of St Lo. Mark well his words, and you will find that he serves you well."

A cheer went up then, and several men pressed forward to shake Belesme's hand. De Redvers called again for silence.

"One final matter I have for you. Before the winter is out, there will be several more priests among you to care for your souls and say Masses for the dead as in the past. One of them will be appointed dean of this new church in place of Flambard. I bid you all, pray for those who are to come among you. Now, go about your business in peace."

He turned to Alwin, who stood at the foot of the motte.

"Where is my horse? I must leave you now and ride towards Winchester to see if Walter Giffard, the bishop, has yet found a man to be your dean. Then I must go to London, to the King to tell him of my many acts to secure my lands for his support."

"Will you not stay a while and eat once more with us before you depart? There is time to reach Brockenhurst before nightfall and you can rest there before continuing to Winchester tomorrow."

"It is hard to refuse you," de Redvers said, "for your wife Mary sets such delicacies before me that I am sorely tempted. So be it, but bid her not to place too many of her pigeon pasties and honey cakes before me or I shall not be able to fasten my sword belt."

Clapping Alwin on the back, they set off together towards Alwin's hall.

Meanwhile, I searched out where Isabel was standing. As I approached her and the children, I could see the look of pleasure on her face that I had been chosen as a tithing man.

"You must take heed of what your father says, children, for he is a man of note in the burgh now, as is your uncle Alric."

"Put not such ideas into their heads, my love. I am still the same person, and have only to see to ten men and they will be little trouble, being all honest folk. Now we must find Belesme. He is a far more important man here now, and I am glad of it, for his counsel has always been wise. Should things go ill, we could have no better man to lead our defence."

"Pray God that his skill will not be needed. I wonder where his cott is to be built. It will be good to have him near at hand and Ediva and her children too. She is a good friend to me and their children play well with ours and Alric's."

We found Belesme in the midst of a throng of young men who were questioning him about sword-play and other matters, which he parried good-humouredly.

"Have done lads. We are not on Senlac Field now, and pray God we never see the like again. Your Saxon house-carls were almost more than a match for us that day, and had it not been that your Fyrd left the hill to follow our retreating foot soldiers, we might well have lost the day. Believe me, I never wish to face one of your battleaxes again. I saw them cleave right through man and horse, and still strike hard on the ground below. Seek not war lad, for it is a terrible thing and men do things in the heat of battle that afterwards they regret for many a year. Booty there may be for some, but for each one who gains, there are four who lose. What of your wives and children? Would you wish them to suffer rape and pillage, and to see your children skewered on a spear? No. This keep is to prevent such as that. I mean this burgh to be known for its strong defences and well-trained men, so that any who might wish us ill, will turn away and try elsewhere and leave us to live in peace. Simple folk prosper more in peace than in war."

Seeing us approaching, Belesme shouldered his way through the throng, and he and I praised each other in our new roles, though his was by far the greater. I could see that he was pleased that he had been chosen for it.

"Our new Lord has placed the defence of the burgh in your hands then," I said. "He could not have chosen better. You are well liked and have often given sound advice which men heed - even if you are a Norman!"

I clasped him on both shoulders and grinned at him.

"That is the only thing I fear," he said, looking solemn, "that men will not follow me because I am not Saxon born, even though I now speak your tongue. I can do the job, but if men heed me not then all would be lost."

"Put your mind at rest on that score. You may not be Saxon born, but you have wed a good Saxon maid and have taken to our ways and you farm our land as well as any now. You heard what de Redvers said, that he had spoken to men like Alwin, Geoffrey and Father. They would not have backed you if they had any doubts. The only ones who spoke against you were a few hot- heads who wanted to wield power themselves and order others about. They would have failed at the first test, and Tovi and Brand had sense enough to see that. Have no fear, the burgh will be behind you, and Alric and I will see that you have the support you need too."

After Sext, when de Redvers had eaten, all of us assembled at the bridge, to send our new lord on his way towards Winchester. He had scarce gone half the distance towards Pure Well, when a horseman was seen approaching him. We watched to see what it might mean, and after a short space, de Redvers turned his horse and galloped back to where we stood. Without dismounting, he called out to Alwin.

"Here is news indeed. Word had just come to me that Henry Beauclerc has taken to wife Mathilda, the daughter of King Malcolm of Scotland and his Queen Margaret, who is your old King Edward's kinswoman. She has herself good claim to the crown of this realm. This will greatly strengthen Henry's hand, besides bringing peace to his northern border. It seems that the folk of London did them both great honour, and many who thought to support Duke Robert have not now done so. He is cut down to size it seems. Well is he called 'Curt-hose'," and he laughed to himself. "I must ride to London with all haste and do homage to our new Queen and pledge my support to Henry again. Now fare-you-well, and spread this good news as you can."

He spun his horse round where it stood and, spurring it, was away in a dust cloud to rejoin his party while we went to spread this news.

The feast of the birth of the Christ-child came and went, and the feast of the visit of the Wise Men was but a day off when a group of priests came to the burgh. Ten of them there were, and they went straight to seek out their few fellows who still laboured in the church. Rumour was rife that these were the men promised by de Redvers, so the church was unusually full for the Epiphany Mass. One of the new priests - a tall man with a thin but saintly face - elevated the Host before us, and when all had taken of the Mass, he spoke.

"Good people, I am called Gilbert de Dousgunels. I have been sent amongst you with these nine others to take the place of those priests who have died these many years past. Your lord, Richard de Redvers, knowing your plight, has spoken to Walter Giffard at Winchester and he has sent us to you. Having no dean, since Ranulf called Flambard was stripped of that office with all his others, Walter has appointed me in his stead. As dean, I have been granted by Richard de Redvers the lands that belonged in the past to this church and which the King had given to him to use for its building and welfare.

The church and its lands are granted in Frank Almagne, so that our dues are those of Divine Service only. The alms and altar offerings which have heretofore been given to the canons will continue to be theirs, that they may continue to serve the folk here. The wealth and lands belonging to the church I shall devote with all speed to the completion to the great church you are building. See, it is all written in this parchment."

He held up a scroll and unrolled it so that those nearest could see the seals that hung from its base.

"Here is the seal of Richard de Redvers, your lord, who sends you greetings by me for your prosperity. Let me read you what he says."

As news of what he said spread to those who stood outside, many pressed forward to hear. When at last no more could enter, a great hush fell on all as Gilbert de Dousgunels began to read. It was even as he had said. When he had finished, there was an excited murmur as he handed the parchment to Rodric, who as the teacher, could read better than the other canons. Rodric held up his hands for silence.

"Brethren, this is indeed great news. Gilbert de Dousgunels, we bid you and your brother priests a hearty welcome. Long we have waited for this day and lived in hope that it would come, though in recent years I must confess our faith grew dim. Now you have come, you have given us all new hope. Six years we have toiled to build this new church thus far, and without the support of Edward and Thurstan who have constantly sought to push the work forward we could not have built as much as we have. Now you have brought us the help we need. The silver and crops from the lands which our new lord has given back to this place will let us buy what is needed to complete the work of building. Once more we may hope that pilgrims will come here, and perhaps miracles may once more occur as in the past. This is the day when we celebrate the showing of the Christ-child to the Gentiles. Let it also be that after this day, once more we may have hope that this place and what it stands for may soon be shown to the world too."

There was a general murmur of assent and Gilbert again raised his hands for silence.

"I and my fellow priests will strive to bring your wish to pass."

Then, making the sign of the Cross over all of us, he concluded, "Now, the Mass is finished. Pax Vobiscum."

We all knelt, replying as we did so, "Et cum spiritu tuo," before rising to leave the church.

What excitement there was in the burgh that day! Though winter was upon us, there was a great willingness to press forward with the work of building while the frosts were clear of the ground.

Before returning to our cott, Isabel and I walked round the outside of the new church to view the extent of the work already completed. As we rounded the turret which stands at the east side of the north transept, we came upon Alnoth, who was gazing up at the turret, which at that point stood lower than the rest of the wall and only about the height of two men. The wall on this part had been most cunningly made, with interleaved arches, each with a slender column decorated in a different design, so that although the wall behind the columns was solid, it gave the impression of being hollow. Alnoth did not hear our approach, for he was wrapped in thought, so we went to stand beside him. At length, he gave a start and, passing his hand across his eyes, mumbled apologies.

"Why little brother," said Isabel linking her arm through his, "your thoughts must have been far away that you did not hear us approach. Will you share them with us or do you have some dark secret?"

"I was looking at this wall that we have built. Do you see how these arches interleave? When we build an arch, it is rounded, but where they cross as these do, they form a point. The round arch that we build can be weak if too much weight is put upon it, for the wall above it forces down on the top and pushes out the walls on each side. That is why Odo's plan for the church has the side aisles, for they are to support the tall pillars below the arches of the nave and take the great thrust of the roof. I think that this pointed arch will overcome that, but I must speak to Edward about it to see if he agrees. He has more knowledge of these matters than me."

He moved away from us to look at another part of the wall.

"Look at the walls of this transept. Something has gone awry, I think. Come round and look at the west side. There is to be only one small window in the wall, which you can see part-built. Then the corner has this five- column pillar rising on two sides. That is well done, for three of the columns are rounded, but the second and fourth come forward to a sharp angle. That gives the pillar interest and carries the eye upwards for its full height.

Now see the end wall. That has three windows beginning, and see how beneath the middle one there is a double column rising which will continue above it to the top of the wall. Then look left again to the turret, which has a single column rising beside it. Now see the turret itself. It is plain and dull and continues so until you come to the windows on the apse on the east side. To have plain stone above those interleaved arches, which run for all three sides of the transept, does not look right to me. What can be done to make it catch the eye? It is dull as it is."

Alnoth scratched his chin in puzzlement while I looked at the walls, trying to understand what he meant. Certainly, the effect seemed to jar, but I could not explain why. Isabel, meanwhile, was wandering about looking at all three sides of the transept, putting her head on one side and holding out her arms in front of her with one finger extended.

"There should be some carving, pillars perhaps, on this turret," Alnoth said at length, "but not the same interleaved ones there are below. Do you think simple arches would look right?"

Isabel and I looked at the turret again, trying to imagine what it would look like with arches against the stone. She stretched out her arms before her again, this time with two fingers together on each hand, squinting her eyes along them as she did so.

"Alnoth," she said quietly, "I know little of stonework, but could you have twin columns, like my two fingers, with a double line of arch above it? The columns would need to be thin I think, no thicker than a hand's breadth, so that the two of them would be the same size as the single column below. Would not that carry your eye upwards? The upper columns could stand on that line of carved stone above the fish scales carved on the stone over the lower arches. I think that might make it seem as if the windows on the end wall were continued round the turret and so join the whole transept into one. Look, Alnoth, hold up your fingers like mine and imagine they are the two slender columns. What do you think?"

The pair of them stood with their fingers outstretched, then walked slowly round the three sides of the transept while I followed behind trying to understand their thoughts. As we came to the western wall, Alnoth stopped and hurried back to look again at the south wall and the turret, his eyes bright with excitement.

"Yes, Isabel, you have found the answer. We can do the same on this west side too, and put a blind window in the blank space which forms the thickness of the wall between the single window and the five-fold pillar, with the same twin columns. That will link it all together. It will make this part of the church far better. It is the only place where such a thing can be done to the full height of the church. On the southern side there is to be a cloister, so the wall would not be seen as it is here, and the aisles on the sides stop short of the full height of the walls. I could carve intricate capitals for each pillar if Edward would let me. I have done some simple ones already. Look at this one, and this."

He darted forward and pointed out two of the carved capitals already in place below the arches on the turret.

"I can do better than those with practice and I want to carve leaves and flowers on them. I must see Edward as soon as maybe and see if he will agree. I am sure he will. I shall tell him that it was your idea."

"Give me no praise, I beg you. It was you who saw the need to decorate the turret. I only added a simple thought to it."

The three of us continued round the building till we came to where two paths met. Here Alnoth left us to go to his cott where his Matilda awaited him, while we returned to ours.

Edward seemingly liked Alnoth's plan, for he set him to carve the twin slender pillars straight away, ready for them to be raised against the wall of the turret once spring came again. He also spent much time in the evenings drawing designs for the capitals which would be placed over them, cunningly working in the shapes of leaves. We never ceased to wonder at the skill he seemed to have in his hands and how he could draw out such beauty from a rough piece of stone. Some of his fellow masons scoffed at him for spending so much time at his work, when they were off drinking in the ale-houses after the day's labour had ended.

"I do this work not for myself, though I confess it gives me pleasure," he would say. "I am helping to build this church and so must do the best I can to make it a place of beauty in the hope that it will be acceptable."

Meantime, Belesme had not been idle, for he used the winter months to have his new cott built on a piece of open ground beside the new keep. Like us, he had an upper chamber built, where Ediva could retire when the men wished to carouse, and which served also as a bed-chamber. Belesme also put his chest there, against the eaves of the roof and away from prying eyes, for he was amassing a goodly bag of silver and wished to keep it close. As there was loose stone to hand, at Edward's suggestion he had a stone hearth set in one end wall with the stone rising to the pitch of the roof and above it, forming a hollow pipe. This design was something that Edward had seen in one or two of the great halls being built for the Norman Eorls.

"It helps to draw up the smoke from the fire, and so keep the hall fresh. Richard de Redvers told me that he is thinking of adding one such to his hall at Exeter, so I thought to try out the same idea here to see if it works. If it fails there will be little lost, for we can easily change the end wall of your cott, though I am hopeful that it will be a great advantage. Besides, the stone end will give greater strength to the cott."

"Such new ideas may be all right for these who can afford to pay for them, but what of me?" was Belesme's reply. "Stone is costly, and the smoke hole we use at present works well enough and lets us cure our sides of hogs by hanging them from the roof trusses."

"You can cure your meat better by hanging it within the chimney, for it will receive all the smoke rather than part if it. Think of Ediva, she suffers much from redness of her eyes in winter, and even with much washing in pure water they pain her when she spends all day in the cott. At least let us try the idea, and if it fails I will rebuild the end wall myself."

Edward did as he wished, and it proved to be even better than he had hoped, so that Belesme's cott became known as the one where hogs were smoked best and lasted longest. Ediva's eyes greatly improved from the lack of smoke, so that he had grudgingly to admit that Edward's plan was good.

Lent was but a week away and the new priests were already starting to prepare us for the fast-time that was to come, when one of Richard de Redvers' esquires, Roland by name, came to the burgh, breaking his journey westwards to Exeter. He brought news of his lord, and also of events far afield and from across the water in the Norman dukedom. Many gathered in Alwin's hall to hear what he had to tell. He brought news of Ranulf Flambard too.

"He may have been bishop of a great see, and they say that Durham is perhaps the richest in the land after London, but he could not claim ecclesiastical rights, and so had to suffer imprisonment in the King's tower in London. Life was not hard for him, for though he has been stripped of all his honours, yet he was allowed two shillings a day on which to live. That is almost as much as I have for a fortnight."

Roland dusted a few crumbs of meat from the threadbare sleeve of his jerkin and took another pull from his ale mug and shook his head in suppressed anger.

"Anyway, Flambard was able to entertain his friends in his prison cell, and with their aid, persuaded Magnaville, the chief jailer of the Tower, to join them on many occasions, seemingly befriending him, and plying him with the best food and wines. It must have been a well-laid plan which needed the help of more friends than I thought he had. It seems that amongst the food and wine that Flambard had sent in for his feasting, was a rope hidden in a wine cask.

The carousing went on for some hours and those in nearby cells cursed him for the row they made. This Magnaville and the other jailers who were all invited to join in the feasting on that day made the most of the fare that was offered them, and before midnight they were all dead drunk and snoring like the hogs they were. The noise suited Flambard's purpose well, for as soon as he was sure that none would rouse, he fetched the rope from where it was hidden in the wine cask and fastened it to the column that divided the large window of his cell. Then he managed to squeeze his body through the opening."

"You mean that he has escaped from the Tower of London? No-one has ever managed to to that before. It is far too strongly built."

"That I do. He fled to France with his old witch of a mother, it seems. I wish I had been there to see it, for it must have been a comic sight. Let me continue and tell you what I heard from one of those who aided him. How he managed to squeeze through the half opening of the window, I do not know, for he is well covered. Like as not it was a good thing that his jailers were snoring so loud or his grunts and groans would have raised the alarm. He must have torn his bishop's robes in his efforts, for they say that shreds of cloth were found on the sill of the window. He took his staff with him too, fearing that without it he might not be given the dignity he thought was his due. Fool that he was, he left his bishop's gloves behind, thinking that none would be ready to kiss his hand in any case. But they would have served him better than his staff, for not being used to such playful activities as the use of a rope, he slid down fast, no doubt eager to make good his escape, and stripped the skin clean off his soft hands in doing so, and landed with a thud on his arse."

Tears of mirth sprang from Roland's eyes at the thought, and it was some minutes before he could compose himself enough to continue. The rest of us joined in his laughter, for it must have been a comical sight to see so mighty a one as Flambard reduced to such a plight. At length, when he had refreshed himself once more from his ale mug, Roland continued.

"It was lucky for Flambard that his friends were waiting for him at the foot of the wall or his escape might have been thwarted. As it was, they had to lift him bodily and carry him, for he would not help himself, groaning and complaining of his hurts and begging them to leave him be until he had somewhat recovered. This his friends wisely refused to do, fearing at any moment to have been surprised by guards at the Tower. In the end they had to stuff a cloth into Flambard's mouth to quieten him while they made good their escape past the great gate. Would that I had witnessed it. Four men, all closely wrapped in dark cloaks, hurrying along with their ungainly burden grunting and groaning like a sow in labour."

Roland paused again to revel once more in the picture in his mind, while we waited breathless to hear how it ended.

"They hurried him to a waiting boat which was already tied to the bank, and bundled him in. Then, oars muffled and rowing with the tide, they set off silently into midstream to make good their flight down the darkened river. It seems that his mother had been collecting such of Flambard's wealth as she could lay her hands on, and this was secreted in a place by the river called Greenwich, where ships often tie up to unload. Once there, Flambard was hidden secretly for a few days until the hue and cry that had been raised died down, for as you can imagine the King's anger was terrible to perceive when he heard of the escape.

"One told me that Henry stormed into his Tower, and having upbraided Magnaville for failing in his duty, ordered his eyes to be put out, saying that if he could not look to his prisoners, he did not need eyes. Then he commanded his tongue to be severed, for with no tongue he would not be tempted to feast when he should be on duty. It seems that he would have had Magnaville, thus mutilated, thrust through the same window that Flambard had used for his escape, but those with him restrained him, fearing that he would have broken his neck in the fall."

Roland picked up his ale-mug again to slake his thirst, while the rest of us sat dumbstruck at his tale, half doubting that it could be true.

"Only the fear of being branded a murderer should Magnaville have died, caused Henry to hold his hand. He had the whole countryside searched and all ships boarded to see if Flambard were hidden on one of them. Luck was with him, however, for he was not discovered, and within a week he was able to slip aboard his vessel with all the chests of treasure his witch-mother had collected, and with a favourable wind set sail at night and so reached the Norman dukedom in safety. Once there, he took horse straight to where Robert Curt-Hose had his Court, leaving his mother to follow at leisure with his treasure, guarded by those friends who had fled with him. All this news I had from one who had early returned from Normandy, and who passed through London and the King's Court."

We all shuddered to hear of such cruelty. Such happenings had been common enough under William, although so far things had been better with Henry as King. Alwin spoke what was in all our minds. "Are we to return to the habits of the two Williams then?"

"Who can tell?" said Roland. "Until this deed, Henry has been milder in his dealings with all men, and such laws as he has made have been for the good of common folk. Those who wield power and cross his path have had to suffer his tongue but not mutilation until this time. Perhaps there is some other cause for his rage."

Silence again fell upon us, to be broken once more by Alwin.

"Maybe he fears what Flambard will do in the Norman dukedom. He knows too much of the ways of the English, who will hold to the King and who may turn to Robert if the price is high enough. Robert has not given up hope of being a king rather than a mere duke. His wife brings dowry enough for him to redeem his dukedom and pay for soldiers to try for this land too. Henry could well fear what Robert could do with Flambard's aid. God grant that the likes of Richard de Redvers stand by the King, should it come to a trial of strength, and that wise counsels may prevail."

Matters rested thus, and we continued to go about our daily lives, troubled little by the events of the outside world. Men had sufficient to occupy their minds and bodies, tending their crops, going about their lawful business and caring for their families.

Spring warmed into summer, and the building of the church continued with renewed speed. Isabel and I went regularly to see how the north turret and transept progressed with Alnoth's slender columns. As the stonework rose, it became a matter of general marvel that there could be such beauty carved from stone, and all who passed through the burgh came to look at it.

There were also rumours from afar that Robert was raising an army in his dukedom, though they concerned us little. Belesme took his new office seriously and spent many hours after work was done teaching the more active men and boys to use the bow, and sometimes the sword. Though there were grumbles sometimes, when they found they could bring home food with their more accurate shooting they began to see the reason of it.

July was fast coming to an end, when a carter, who had been taking goods to Winchester, returned with the news that Duke Robert had landed at Portsmouth with a large force of both horse and foot soldiers and had been joined by some of the more discontented Norman barons who had settled in this realm. Hearing the news, Belesme and Alwin called the burgh together.

"We do not know whether Robert will march on Winchester or London," said Belesme. "Henry is holding Court at St Albans, so could reach London first. Robert may well decide on Winchester to secure the Treasury there, before turning to meet Henry in battle, for such there will surely be. Once he has Winchester, Robert may decide to secure Wessex at his back so that he may come here, since this burgh controls the trade routes to Sarum and beyond, with all its rich lands. It seems Robert tricked Henry who expected him to land at Pevensey as Duke William did before he fought Senlac Field. We must therefore, make ready to hold him at bay should he come this way."

"Why not march to fight him first?" asked one in the crowd.

Nay, lad. We bide here and let him come to us if he dares. It is for such a time that I have been training you, but it would be well to set a watch on Hengist's headland to give us warning should he come by sea round Vectis Isle. He must come past Catherine's Point and the white Needle rocks, so we shall have timely warning of his coming. He cannot come through the narrows by Hurst Point except when the tide runs with him, for the winds are contrary and the current strong, as your fisherfolk know. That would give us plenty of time, for he would have to wait for the next rising of the tide before he could enter this harbour - and even then without pilots he would probably go aground on the sand-bars. Let the watch on Hengist's headland build a signal fire to be lit if a fleet approaches. It can be seen from the keep, which can then raise the alarm."

"What of the folk who live in Stanpit, Huborne and other hamlets? Will they be safe?"

Alwin stepped forward to reply. "It were best that all who live in outlying places drive their stock within these walls, and bring such corn as they have left and any possessions they can carry with them."

"They can shelter within the walls of the church," said Gilbert. "Is it not said in the Scriptures: 'Come unto me all ye that are heavy laden, and I will give you rest,'? They will be safe enough there, even though the church is not yet roofed, for we can fix temporary shelters to keep folk dry should it rain. We can withstand a long siege if need be, for we have water and fish besides grain, and Ranulf of the guest-house can see to the feeding."

"Thank you, Gilbert, your offer is gladly accepted, and the beasts can graze on the fallow land of the demesne and also on the pastures by the river. They will be close at hand to drive into the burgh should the alarm be raised. It may come to nothing if Robert turns towards London, but this is the best plan for our safety. Belesme will take charge and organise the watches. We can continue to work in the fields, but I shall post a watch on horseback on the edge of Andret forest. Should any approach that way from Winchester, he will ride for the burgh, warning those in the fields as he goes. That should give time for all to reach the walls in safety, for troops move slowly. Have no fear. Belesme and I have discussed this long since, so we are well prepared."

We sent up a ragged cheer then, more to give ourselves courage than from any feeling of confidence. Too many were the tales of pillage and rape for any to be easy in their minds.

The anxious weeks passed, until at last one of Richard de Redvers' knights brought us good tidings.

"I was with Henry at St Albans, and travelled with him when he went to face Duke Robert. As soon as he heard that his brother had landed, he sent for his clerks, bidding them write to all the greatest in the land re-affirming what he had promised at his coronation, and bidding them come to his aid to defend the realm against the treacherous Robert. Anselm of Canterbury stood by the King too, and called on the other bishops to do likewise. He reminded those that might waver, that Flambard, who had joined himself to Robert, had been dispossessed of all his lands, and also the see of Durham."

This seemed to cause the knight some amusement, for he smiled to himself, perhaps because he had suffered at the hands of one of the more rapacious bishops.

"Then," he continued, "Henry called out the Fyrd and marched direct to meet Robert, whom he faced at Alton. It was a brave course to take, for Robert had the larger army. However, Henry knew his brother lacked the stomach for a fight. He has a new wife to please and prefers an easy life if he can get it. The two brothers parleyed, and all the while Henry's force grew in strength. In the end Robert caved in, gave up his claim to the throne here, and accepted a yearly payment of three thousand marks, no doubt converting it in his mind into wine and food. In return Henry gave up all his estates in the Norman dukedom except for his castle at Domfort, and promised to help Robert recapture Maine. All those who had joined Robert were pardoned if they would swear allegiance to Henry again. Thus the pact was sealed, and the two brothers went off seemingly the best of friends, for they also agreed that whichever brother should outlive the other should have have both the Norman dukedom and the English throne."

"Do you believe that such an agreement will hold?" asked Alwin.

The knight said nothing, but only raised his eyes skywards. "Who am I to read the mind of kings?" he asked with a smile. "But be sure of this, some there be who will soon be deprived of their lands and will have to buy them back. There are other ways beside taxes to raise three thousand marks - ways that will please most folk and yet keep the trouble-makers in check."

"Then Henry may prove to be more cunning than his brothers. At least we have peace and it may well last, for Robert will not try to use force again. Henry will see to that by keeping him close guarded, though it may be in the guise of entertaining him and his new wife."

"Peace in this country, yes, but I cannot think that Henry will willingly wait till Robert dies to claim the dukedom he has always coveted. He may find some excuse yet to wrest it from Robert, for he placed little store by it when he put it in pawn to red-faced William so that he could go crusading."

I felt that this knight was well informed of all that occurred at Court, and had the ear of his master, de Redvers, too. Before he took to horse again next day, Alwin, Belesme and Gilbert spoke to him.

"Tell our liege lord, Richard, that we stood ready to hold this burgh for him and to support the King," they said. "Plans were laid to bring all the folk from the outlying hamlets with their beasts and goods within these walls and shelter them in the church. The defence of the burgh and its new keep was in the hands of his constable and we had food enough to withstand a siege. Tell him that we could deny much of Wessex to any who wish harm to the King, for we control the rivers and trade routes from Sarum and its rich lands."

"Richard and the King will be glad to hear of your support and I will deliver your message faithfully," he said. With that he departed.

The harvest was gathered in peace and plenty, and it was not till Pentecost was some weeks past in the following year that Richard de Redvers once more visited the burgh. We received him with honour as was his due, and after Alwin had given an account of his stewardship, which all came to hear, Richard gave us news of the world beyond our sight.

"Henry has most of his realm at peace, and has forgiven those who sought to rise against him - at a price. I also have news of your previous dean, Flambard. He too has made his peace with Henry, and even Anselm of Canterbury has forgiven him. I heard read out many of the charters that restore to him most of his old lands and offices, including the see of Durham, though I did not put my hand to any of them."

Gilbert looked startled. "Is this church to be returned to Flambard then? Things would go ill for us if it were."

"Have no fear on that score. I saw to it that this burgh remains mine, and the church is likewise secure with you, Gilbert. The word you sent me that you had made ready to hold the burgh for me and the King, I passed to Henry straightaway. It heartened him to have the news in his hour of need, and I reminded him of it when Flambard's lands were being restored. The King saw that he would be better served with matters left as they are - and it suits me better too," de Redvers said with a grin.

"As thanks, and that you may pray for my soul, I am now giving to this church some lands at Ningweda on Vectis Isle. One, by name Absa, who owes me service, has also agreed to give you a parcel of land, so that the work of building may go forward faster."

Gilbert bowed low to Richard. "You do us much honour by your gifts. We will pray daily for your soul and for those of your family. I had feared the return of Flambard as dean, not because I would be displaced, that might be the will of God, but because he hindered the work of building by taking much of our wealth to himself."

"Your fears were well founded but, I think, groundless, for even though the King and Anselm have restored him to favour, Pope Paschal has not. Flambard was summoned to Rome to answer serious charges which, if found to be true, would have led to him forfeiting his rich see of Durham and being unfrocked as a priest. Flambard was able to buy friendship, however, for he found the six bishops necessary to support him in his defence and clear his name. You are not likely to see Flambard any more in these parts. Last year, his brother Fulcher was appointed Bishop of Lisieux, and when he suddenly died, Duke Robert agreed to appoint Flambard's own son Thomas, scarce twelve years old, to the see, agreeing that Flambard himself should administer it. He will be too busy running between Durham and Lisieux and keeping friends with Robert and Henry to his own advantage to concern himself with this place."

"Then we can continue building with an easy mind," said Gilbert. "I mean to press forward with the eastern part of the church and have it roofed as soon as maybe so that Mass can be held there, even though the rest is still being built. The crypt of the old church below the eastern end is too small for the growing numbers here now. We must also complete the dwellings for the new priests and see to the housing of a school for the children, for there is nowhere suitable where Rodric can teach them."

"See to that too, for I would not have any here ignorant of the teachings of Christ," said de Redvers.

"Let those that can be apprenticed to the masons and carpenters too, for unless they are properly instructed there will be no-one skilled to continue the many crafts that are needed. I have seen some of the carving in stone that your masons have done, and also fine work in wood. Such skills must be fostered. See to it also that the youths are taught the use of the bow and quarter staff. I would not have you prepare an army, but should you be called upon to defend the burgh, it were best you were prepared. Such preparations will not come amiss, and I will spread the tale that this is a strong place to discourage any who might be tempted to take it."

With those words, he rose to depart. We were sorry to see him leave, for his words gave us strength and hope. Under the protection of the King, as we had been in the past, we had little to fear. Many were the tales of those who found themselves with new overlords being called out to do battle against their neighbours with whom they had no quarrel, for the advantage of their lord alone. We were fortunate in Richard de Redvers, who, staying loyal to the King, sought prosperity for himself as well as us through peaceful conduct.

Chapter 16 1102–1120

Seventeen years have passed since Duke Robert landed his army at Portsmouth, spreading fear throughout the burgh that he might attack us to secure his back by holding Wessex and its trade. All were thankful that Henry was able to make peace with him; a peace that has lasted in this realm, if not in Normandy. As many suspected, Henry would not lightly let the dukedom go, and it was in '06 that he raised a strong force of hired soldiers and left for Normandy to settle the score once and for all with Robert. As usual, it fell on the ordinary folk to pay for the soldiers by a tax on each hide of land, which caused some discontent.

Whether by accident or design is not known, but the brothers met in battle at Tinchebrai on 28th September, the same day that their father, Duke William, defeated our ancestors at Senlac Field, and so took this realm to himself. It may have crossed Henry's mind to complete the reverse process and finally take the Norman dukedom to himself that day. Whatever he thought, that is what he did, but with far greater ease, for within one hour Henry overcame Robert's force, which was largely dismounted, by the combined use of foot-soldiers and a great cavalry charge.

Though Henry's losses were few, Duke Robert's force was all either killed or captured. Robert himself was captured along with many of his noble followers whom Henry then brought back to this realm and kept under secure guard. Some have since been let go - at a price - but Robert remains close guarded, though living in some comfort. We heard all this from Richard de Redvers and after his death in '07 from his son Baldwin, who was soon raised to be Eorl of Devon for the support he had given Henry.

We in Twynham and the rest of the realm remained at peace, though not without our troubles. With Gilbert as dean the building of the church at first progressed apace. However, within a couple of years or so, he felt he had to journey to Rome to receive from Pope Pashcal his blessing and authority to establish a monastic order here. Such were the trials of a journey of so great a distance that Gilbert died before he could again reach these shores.

When the sad news was brought to him, de Redvers appointed Peter de

Oglander, who had been his chaplain in Caen, as dean. Coming with such a recommendation, we had high hopes that we would be well served, but it was not to be. Within a short space of time this Peter appointed all his own friends to those prebends and chapels that were vacant, and they began to take all the revenues and gifts to the church for themselves, so that there was soon nothing left to pay for the building work. Thus it effectively came to a halt, in spite of all the efforts of Edward and Thurstan. We saw little more of Odo, for there were other and greater buildings that he had to see to, and within a few years he too had died, so Edward had to manage as best he could.

Ranulf Flambard we never saw, which caused no-one any sorrow. We heard that, having made his peace with Henry after Tinchebrai though not regaining his confidence, Flambard spent most of his time, when not at Durham, close to the King, travelling with him round this realm, and later in the Norman dukedom, picking up not inconsiderable crumbs of wealth and land. Some said that he had his eyes set on Canterbury to replace the ageing Anselm, but he was forestalled by Ralph d'Escures who, being at Rochester, was close to the King's friends and had only a few miles to move.

Not to be outdone, Flambard sided with Thomas, who as the other archbishop in York, and Flambard's neighbour at Durham, was striving to be considered Canterbury's equal. Some said that he even offered Henry a thousand marks of silver if he would take York's side in a Canonical Judgement, but Henry would have none of it, fearing perhaps the Pope's anger if he interfered in ecclesiastical matters. When Thomas of York died soon after, Henry gave that archbishopric to his own chaplain, Thurstan, so that once more Flambard was thwarted in his quest for the highest offices. Whenever news came of a new bishop being consecrated, Flambard's name always seemed to be mentioned, either in the choosing or at the consecration.

It seemed that he still wielded power and influence, for besides Henry, his Queen Matilda also saw to it that lands were added to him, thereby creating much wealth for himself but not always for the church he was supposed to serve. Since he was also allowed to protect his forests for hunting, much as the King controlled Andret, we were glad that he was so far distant. Nor did he forsake his family, for it was commonly known that there was not a member of it that did not hold some lucrative office. Glad we were that the building of our church was no longer under his control, even if Peter de Oglander did little to assist us.

Death took its toll on those who lived in the burgh. Belesme was the first of those I counted as close friends to die. It must have been the year that Baldwin succeeded his father, Richard, and was made Eorl of Devon. Belesme had found the task of constable not really to his liking.

"I thought to have done with fighting and wars," he said one day when I was sitting with him beside the stone chimney which Edward had built in his cott beside the keep.

"I came here to live out my days in peace, caring for my land and in the bosom of my family. You made me welcome, Hugh, when first I came, and it was partly because of you and the lands you showed me that made me decide all those years ago that this was where I should end my days. When Richard de Redvers asked me to be constable here, I could not refuse for the honour it brought me and as a way to repay the debt I feel I owe to the burgh. It has been a sore trial to me at times and I shall be glad to lay it down, for these bones of mine are weary."

A fit of coughing wracked his ageing body and he took a pull at his ale-mug to ease his throat.

"Goodwife Adeline's draughts no longer seem to ease my pains, for I am beyond even her cures now. I have had a full life and would not have led it otherwise, though I have sinned often enough and not repented as often as I should. I think it is time I was shriven. Do you remember when Walter Tirell came to my old cott by the forest, that day when red-faced William was killed while hunting, and how Godwine came to shrive him? Walter told me that he took great comfort from the size of the man and his quiet bearing. He said he felt that his sins were so great that no ordinary priest could bear to hear them, but that he could safely lay them on the shoulders of such a man as Godwine. Do you remember how he helped us with the moving of the stone from Catherine's hill?"

He chuckled at the thought of our secret which still none knew but those who had taken part.

"Would you bid Godwine come to me when he can, that I may prepare my soul."

I chided Belesme gently, but could see that he was nearing his end. He would not see the summer out, I knew, so I went to find Godwine in his cott at Stanpit. He came straightaway, as was his wont, walking with his great staff that would have looked like a young tree beside any other man. He too was ageing, and no longer walked with a spring in his step as of old. There was something about him which still drew young and old to him, so that he was seldom alone and those who spoke with him were the happier for it. He came into Belesme's cott and sat down beside him. I left them then, two friends as well as man and priest.

Ediva told me next day that they had sat far into the night going over old happenings, while she retired to her bed-chamber. When Ediva called me to come to Belesme some days later, I found him content and ready for the death that he knew could not be long delayed.

"See to Ediva for me, Hugh," he asked. "She can return to my old cott near the forest, and the children can manage my lands with her guidance, but I would like to know that you kept an eye on them too. Will you do that for me please?"

"Gladly," I replied. "You have done much for me that I have never been able to repay, and for friendship's sake what you ask is the least I can do for you."

He took my hands in his then, and pressed them thankfully.

"As Godwine would say, 'God's blessings be upon you'. As we older folk go to our rest, the life of this burgh will be in the hands of the likes of you and Isabel, and Alric and Emma. You have already proved your worth, and when Alwin is no more, I think it will fall to Alric to be bailiff for Baldwin's demesne. Ediva has often said how Isabel and Emma are well loved for their kindness and the help they give to the poor and widows."

"They do only what they think seems needful," I told him, "though since the priests have been caring less for the sick, it is true that they have been more active."

We sat a while longer. When Ediva came in, I rose to leave, saying that I would see him again in a few days. However that was not to be, for Belesme died that night and the whole burgh grieved at his passing, for he was well liked, few remembering that he had come here as a Norman.

When Baldwin heard the news, he made haste to appoint one of his young knights, Gerald of Sarum, as the new constable. His prancing horse and dashing ways caused some ill-will at first. Not for him a wooden keep. Within a year, the timbers had been torn down and a stout stone castle began to rise in its place with walls more than three arm's lengths thick. Much of the stone came from the shores of Hengist's headland, for it was hard. Edward had little to do with the building except that he provided some of the other stone from his quarries on Vectis Isle. He kept his counsel close on the quality of building, though Isabel heard from Alnoth that he would never allow such poorly finished stone to be used for the church. Indeed the walls seemed rough hewn, but as Gerald said, the keep was meant to repel enemies, not be a bower for a fine lady.

No sooner was the stone keep complete - and it stood as high as the church with room enough to house a fair-sized body of men - than Gerald set about building a stone hall for himself beside the mill-stream. He put it about that it was to house Baldwin when he visited the burgh.

"An English Eorl whose lands stretch from Devon to Vectis Isle should not be expected to sleep in a timber cott. These days all men of substance live only in stone-built halls."

There were many who found such talk hard to believe, but since they were paid to do the building, they were not eager to complain too openly. Many wondered at the sighting of the hall, for it was built in front of the keep so that it blocked the clear view to the mill-stream, obstructing a bow-shot at any who might seek to attack from that quarter. He built also a garderobe over the mill-stream, so that the stinking ordure was washed away down towards our mill. He had built a chimney too, for he had seen how clear the air was in Belesme's new cott, and it became a point of much interest to those who visited the burgh, for as yet there were few such things built.

Gerald sought to enclose the outer bailey with a ditch, taking water from the mill-stream, but it held little, since the ground rose towards the keep and the ditch was little more than a boggy stretch outside the timber palisade that enclosed the bailey. Though it would slow any who attacked, it would not prevent their coming. Thus Gerald lived in some comfort. There were many in the burgh who worked on his lands and in his household and we all prospered more than we might have done otherwise. Whenever Baldwin de Redvers came with his retinue, there was great feasting and merry-making, for Gerald had ambitions and wished to please his lord.

During these years there were some poor harvests, and sometimes there was a murrain on the flocks, but for the most part the harvests were rich and the flocks increased and fattened well. Sheep became more plentiful, for there was a great need of wool, not only in our own realm but also in Normandy and beyond. We cleared more land beside our assart and kept some sheep too, grazing them when we could on the common pastures. Since others were doing likewise, the hayward had to call a meeting to decide how best the grazing could be shared, for there was not enough for all. By general agreement, more land was cleared outside the walls and this was added to the pastures. Many were the folk who benefited thereby.

Martha and Ruth were kept busy at their spinning when they were not tending the vegetables and fowls in our garden, for Isabel took to weaving more cloth since there seemed to be a never-ending demand for it. Ships called regularly at the quay to collect great sacks of wool that had been brought down from the rich pastures round Sarum, and also such bolts of cloth as they had made there too. Whenever Isabel had cloth ready, she sold it for a good price; the more so as she had devised new colours aided by Goodwife Adeline who showed her different herbs and roots to use.

Simon and Oswald helped both in the mill and on our land, for I wished them to learn both skills. Both were growing into strong lads who could lift a near full sack of grain, though not with such ease as I liked to think I could have done at their age. When I talked of this to Isabel she told me not to be swollen-headed, teasing me by saying that she was sure that they were far stronger than I. We did not put it to the test, lest she be proved right. Osbern, who had always been clever with his hands and never liked them to be idle, began to spend his evenings when it was too dark to carve in wood, weaving baskets out of rushes from the river. They had long been used for that purpose and there was a ready supply of them, particularly along the banks of the Stour which ran near the mill, and towards Catherine's hill. He showed young Oswald and Simon the art, and before long both of them were making passable baskets too. They had many uses, for they were sturdy and could hold a fair weight. Indeed, Edward found he had need of a constant supply to carry mortar and building rubble to fill the space between the smooth outer faces of the stone walls and pillars.

When closely woven they would almost hold water, so that even flour could be stored in them. We therefore found them useful at the mill, and Ranulf of the guest-house was always calling for them. It was not long before we found that such baskets would fetch a good price in markets where there was no river near to hand. We also found ourselves selling them to ship's captains who came to collect the wool and grain from further inland.

For some weeks before and after Lammas, Oswald and Simon would leave their work in the mill to Father and I and take our boat up the Stour to cut the long rushes. When there was little grinding to be done, I would leave Father at the mill and join them. It was hard work and needed two of us working together.

You had to cut the rushes from downstream, or the boat would crush into the place where you were cutting. While one held the boat against a long pole sunk into the river bed, the other gathered an armful of rushes and then cut them off at the bed of the river with a sickle on the end of a pole, for they stood in almost an arm's length of water. They then had to be lifted and laid on a hurdle placed across the boat, which needed all the strength we had, for they were heavy with water. When the boat was full, we made for the bank where we would lay out the rushes in circles, the heads to the centre and the thick white ends of the stems outwards.

There they remained drying in the sun for several days before we could bundle them up and then stand them on end, as we would do with the sheaves of corn. Nor were they easy to handle even then, for the best were three arm's lengths and more long, but they were safe enough till we had gathered in our other harvest.

Then we could bring the bundles of reeds back to be stored against the winter evenings, when those who would otherwise have had idle hands set to work to weave the soft pithy stems into baskets, horse panniers and other containers. Some of the longest rushes we wove into floor-coverings, for they could be lifted and shaken clean and reused. Others were made into hangings to shield off part of the cott and keep out the chill winter winds. Since they gave off a pleasant odour, they were well liked. Those that were less good were used for thatching. By this means Oswald and Simon soon found that they had a ready market for their labours, and silver pence began to flow into their hands too.

Thus for some years our own wealth and that of the burgh increased, in spite of the taxes that were raised by the King. Such times could not last for ever. The year after Ralph of Rochester became Canterbury's Archbishop - '15 I think it must have been - the winter was so harsh that few could remember the like of it. Snow lay thick upon the ground for many weeks, and the harbour was once again frozen right across and the rivers almost ceased to flow. No grinding could be done at the mill, for the stream was solid ice and great was the loss of beasts of all sorts.

That year also, Father died. He had been ailing for some time, troubled by a dry cough that often took millers. In the bitter cold he found it hard to breathe and it near broke Mother's heart to hear his rasping breath as he struggled to take the ice-laden air into his shrunken body. Nor could he find ease beside the fire, for the smoke from it only brought on another fit of coughing. Though Goodwife Adeline's syrups soothed his chest for a time, they brought only temporary relief. Isabel would sit with him when she could, and Emma too, when Mother grew weary for lack of sleep at nights, for he needed tending more then as he gasped for breath in the frightening dark. As I sat with him one evening in the week before the festival of the birth of the Christ-child, he put his hand on mine.

"Hugh, my son," he said, "the mill will soon be yours. Treat it well as we have always done, and it will serve you and your sons as it has served me and my father. I have taught you all I know long since, and like me, you have always given honest measure. That I learnt from my father. It is the only way. Some scheme to short-change those who bring corn to be ground, or take more than their fair due in flour. Though they may gain a few silver pence in this world, they lose a kingdom in the next; and those that can will find another miller, so their profit here is short-lived. Our mill is well known for its good flour, and may it continue so with you."

His breath became more laboured, and he had to wait a while before he could continue. It grieved me to see him thus reduced from the fine figure he had been.

"Be sure to bring up Simon and young Oswald in the same way, for I would not have one who bears my name do otherwise. Care for your mother when I go, for she has been a loyal wife to me since we wed and she will grieve when I am gone. If she will, let Isabel comfort her, for she has a gentle way with her."

Again he was seized by a fit of coughing, and his withered hand felt for mine, seeking comfort from the touch.

"Now I would make my peace with God," he said finally. "Would that Godric were with us still, for he was wise and strong beyond belief. Godwine still remains, though even his great strength is failing now. Send for him if you will, that I may confess and be shriven, for my end is near I think. Nay, it is so, I know."

Rising, I left him then and went to fetch Godwine, who came with such haste as he could still muster, still a figure of respect. Leaving the two of them together, I sat with Mother in her bed-chamber while she talked over old times she and Father had passed happily together. After a while, Emma and Osbern came in and sat with us too.

At length, Godwine called to us to say that he was going. As we gathered round Father, I saw that he smiled contentedly.

"Godwine has confessed and shriven me and I am at peace. Soon I will join those of our family who have gone before, including your little Hugh. Come, Maud and all of you, kneel beside me that Godwine may bless us all this last time."

That done, Godwine left us then, and there was a tear in his eye I think. As I bade him farewell, I saw him take the path towards the church, where I thought he went to pray for Father's soul. We left Mother with him then, promising to come early next day to see how Father fared.

When I came to the cott next day I found him already dead, with Mother sitting peacefully beside him, his hand in hers.

We could not bury him, to our great sorrow, for the ground was too hard to dig the grave. Like so many others, he had to lie without the burgh wall until the thaw finally came. As a thank-offering for Father's life, Oswald, Simon and I gave a full day's grinding of our best flour to the church to feed the poor, who were suffering much in the harsh weather.

Though we tried to care for Mother, she would not be comforted, saying that she had been so long with Father that she could not live without him. Isabel persuaded her to come to live with us for a time, and spent long hours with her, as did Emma, but it was her wish to return to her cott where she had spent so many years, and she would not be persuaded otherwise.

Thus it was that before the thaw finally came, we found her one morning lying cold, but with a peaceful smile upon her face, having breathed her last during the night. When I went later to the church, to light a candle for her soul, I found Godwine saying his Office. Hearing my news, he crossed himself.

"Requiescat in pace," he said. "I feared her end was near when I saw her yesterday. I confessed her then as I did your father, and she was shriven, though both had little of which to be ashamed in their lives. The burgh is the poorer for their passing, for they lived their lives for others and will be sorely missed. It is for you and Isabel to take on their role now, Hugh, as I am sure you can. Life goes on. There is much evil in this world, but much good also, and it is for that good that we build this great church."

Thus comforted, we gave of our milling another day's labour to the church, in gladness and in sorrow. When the thaw finally came, we were able to lay Father and Mother to rest, side by side in one grave as they would have wished.

I then entered into the mill in my own right, and did homage and paid the Death Fee for it from Father's hoard of silver. The work continued much as before, though it was strange and sad not to have Father's advice when problems arose. Oswald and Simon had both mastered the art of milling, and we made out well enough when we could start the mill working after the water began to flow once again.

However, there was little enough work to be done after the poor harvest, and much less the next year. The rains came before Lammas-tide and did not cease till after Candlemas. Most of the grain lay rotten and beaten down in the fields, sprouting in the ear, and could not be harvested. Such grain as was gathered was poor and mouldy and could not be dried and there was famine once more. The King also raised yet another aid on all the land, which fell heavily on all folk, but particularly the poor who had no silver with which to pay and no grain to offer instead. The King never knew of our plight, for he was in his dukedom of Normandy, and there were none who cared to tell him how ill we fared.

It was during that winter that Alwin met with disaster. He had journeyed to Sopley and beyond to see to matters for the demesne. The weather was so foul that Mary had begged him not to go, for the way was said to be impassable with the rain and the flooding of the rivers. He said that needs must and departed early, promising to return before darkness fell, so that he could still clearly see the way.

Vespers had begun, when Alwin's horse was seen limping in through the Bar Gate, all muddied and with a torn saddle. News was taken at once to Mary, who sent Alric and any others who could be quickly found to see what had befallen Alwin. It was three hours before they returned to Mary who was waiting anxiously with Isabel and Alnoth beside her, bearing Alwin's body.

"He must have been thrown from his horse when trying to leap a flooded ditch," Alric said. "We marked the place to one side of where the road should be, but is now beneath the flooded river. His horse had tried to leap a ditch, but lost its footing and fell, trapping Father beneath, crushing his ribs and breaking his right leg. It was thus we found him, still breathing but in great pain. I cradled him in my arms, and with great difficulty he spoke a few words to me. Knowing that death was near, he committed you to my care, Mother, saying that you had given him great happiness in his life, and that he could not have done without you. He bade you not to grieve, but to pray for his soul. It seems he had confessed his sins before Mass last Sunday, and he bade me ask Peter, the dean, to light a candle for him for anything he might have done amiss since then.

"Father told me that he had tried to do right by all men, and if at the Last Judgement it was found that in his life he had given more than he had taken, then he should be content. I told him then that I thought it would be so, and he smiled. I made the sign of the Cross over him, and as he breathed his last, I committed his soul to God in the hope that he may not go unshriven."

All this Isabel told me later when she returned, grief-stricken, for she had loved her father dearly. I comforted her as best I could, but her concern was more for her mother, with whom she spent much time trying to ease her grief.

As Isabel said to me one evening some months later, when we were sitting by our hearth, "Though death comes to all of us, taking some early and some late, some peacefully and some in pain and anguish, whenever it comes it brings sorrow. Only later, when the sharp pain of grief begins to ease, do the memories of past happiness begin to shine through. Then we can draw comfort and strength from the good things that we remember of the life of the one who is gone and try to copy them in our own lives. In that way the example of those that die is not in vain."

The dark years continued and the weather remained foul, with little but rain, hail, lightning and thunder, and great winds. Once more crops lay ruined in the fields. At the beginning of the year there was a great shaking of the earth. Many stout stone buildings fell in other parts of King Henry's lands, though the greater part were in the dukedom rather than this realm. Famine increased, and the taxes that the King raised to pay for his wars to hold his lands in Normandy and beyond, fell heavily on all men.

Many there were that died during those years. Mary did not long survive Alwin, for she was of a great age, and as she said, there was little left for her to live for. Her passing caused Isabel much sorrow. Then young Oswald's wife, Elizabeth, the daughter of the miller at Sopley, a much-loved lass whom he had wed not a year before, died in child-bed, the babe living but two days longer than her.

It seemed that there was wrath in Heaven at men's misdeeds, for all men seemed to be suffering. That year we heard that Pope Paschal died, and when John of Gaeta received the three-fold crown as Pope Gelasius, he too died within a few months. Many of King Henry's eorls and other nobles were killed in battle or died afterwards. However, by wedding his son, William, to the daughter of the Eorl of Anjou, he gained much land south of his Norman holdings. Little good did such conquests do us, for the lands were so far distant that no-one in the burgh had ever been there. Yet it cost us dear, for the aids the King raised yearly to pay for holding these new lands had to be found by us.

It was not till '20 that it seemed that matters might once more become better, for then Henry made peace with the French King. He greatly increased his lands in France, with Anjou added to Normandy, and Maine, which lay between them, under his protection too. That year the taxes were much reduced, to the relief of all men but particularly common folk like us. When the rain ceased and the crops once more grew in the fields and could be harvested, hope returned to the land.

It was after four years' strife that news came from a sea captain who brought goods from Barfleur to our quay. Henry had decided to return from his dukedom to this realm before the winter gales set in once more. Baldwin, our lord, had spent much time with the King, so it seemed that we should see more of him in the future than we had these past years. There was much activity in the burgh, particularly by Gerald of Sarum the constable, for he wished the keep and his house to be well presented when next Baldwin, the Eorl of Devon, came.

When Eorl Baldwin did come, it was with a sad countenance, for tragedy and disaster had struck the King's family. It was Gerald who gave us the sad news after Baldwin stayed for one night only, before leaving for his castle in Exeter. Alric, as bailiff now, called some of us together to hear Gerald's tale.

"It was late in November, the 25th I think, when the King finally gave orders for the fleet to sail. We had ridden at anchor for some days while Henry made merry with his Norman friends, for he did not mean to return to his dukedom for some time and wished to leave his friends in good humour. To please his son William, now wedded and master of Anjou and who felt himself to be a King in all but name, though he was but seventeen years old, the King gave him command of one of his best and finest ships.

"It was painted all gleaming white, and with new sails dazzling white in the sun. Henry for his part went on board his own ship with a few of the older Eorls including Baldwin, taking William's young bride with him, for he did not wish to leave the young lass to the rough carousing of William and his friends. Henry sailed with the rest of the fleet, and as he passed William's White Ship, the lad called out, waving a jewelled goblet full of wine, that he would sail soon himself but still awaited a few friends who were delayed on shore. Besides, the wine was good and they would finish that first. I was standing within earshot of the King, and heard him call out to William not to delay too long, for the tide was already on the ebb, and the passage was dangerous once darkness fell."

"That was wise counsel by the King," said Alric. "I would not enter this harbour when it is dark for fear of the sand-bars, and I know the entrance well, though it is constantly changing."

"Then you have a wise head on your shoulders now, which perhaps was not always so. Did you never enter by night when you were a lad?"

Alric replied, "Once, yes, and stuck fast on the bar for half the night till the tide rose again. Luckily, there was little sea running, but it was chill and I learnt my lesson, besides having to endure Father's wrath."

"You never told me that," I said.

"Would you have bragged about such folly?" Alric asked, with a sly grin. "But continue, Gerald. What happened next?"

"I heard the young Prince call out to the King that he had good pilots and would not be long delayed. With the speed of his new ship he would reach England first and show his father how to sail. Then, putting his arm round his half-sister, the Countess of Perche, he cried out that they both sent their love to his bride and would join her in a dance next evening.

With that, we sailed out of earshot and I stood watching the young Prince and those with him drinking to a fast passage. We sailed on, and though the winds were fierce we missed the worst of the storm and made safe passage to our landfall. There we waited for sight of the Prince's 'White Ship'. All that day we waited, and the next, until the King, growing anxious, sent out three vessels, one east, one west and one back to Barfleur seeking news."

Gerald paused, looking grim and sad as if he did not wish to continue. "What had happened?" I asked, at length.

"It was some days before certain news came, and then it was only from one who was seemingly a butcher, who was sailing with them to prepare the meats for the great number of those on board - three hundred souls all told he said. It seems William delayed too long his leaving and the tide was ebbing fast. Besides, it grew dark, so that the pilots could not clearly see their line of sailing even if they had been sober.

"The butcher knows not exactly what befell, but, from the noise of shouting and laughter it seems that there were few if any of the crew who were sober enough to sail the ship properly, for the whole ship was enjoying the wine that Prince William so liberally handed out. Certain it was that the ship sailed fast, for the butcher said he could hear the wind howling in the rigging and the spray came high over the prow. The next thing he remembers was a great grinding shock and the ship rose up at the bow before crashing down with a horrible rending sound as timbers split and shattered. Then water seemed to be everywhere."

"They must have hit a rock," said Alric, "for nothing else could cause such damage. I do not know the harbour, but are there rocks known there?"

"As we sailed out," replied Gerald, "our pilot pointed to a patch of foaming water. I told the Prince's pilot to be sure to sail well clear of that place and keep to the course that we followed. That foam hides the rock called Quilleboeuf which has wrecked many unwary ships. At low tide it is clearly seen above the water, but it is more dangerous when the tide is on the ebb as then it is hidden. I thought nothing of it at the time, for the pilot that the King had placed on the Prince's ship was greatly experienced."

Gerald covered his face with his hands to hide his grief, too overcome by the thought of what he had to tell. It was some time before he was sufficiently calm to be able to continue.

"Maybe it is even as you have said, that they foundered on that rock. Anyway, all on the ship were suddenly sobered, and worked to save all they could. Those of the crew who had been in the rigging setting the sails were thrown overboard and lost in the storm-tossed seas or dashed against the rocks. While the young nobles and such crew as remained worked to try to save the ship, one or two small boats, such as are always carried on board, were finally launched, and Prince William and the most noble of those on board were cast adrift to try to row to the shore, for all wished to save the King's son and heir and to summon help if that could be done.

The butcher saw them row clear while he was struggling with the others still on board to save the ship. Then the Prince's half-sister was seen to run to the ship's side, waving frantically and crying out to William to save her. Her voice seemingly carried over the water above the noise of the crashing waves, for suddenly the butcher says that he saw the boat with the Prince on board turn round and start to row back towards the stricken ship. Those with him tried to stop him, for they could be seen waving their arms at the Prince, but he would have none of it, taking an oar himself, and rowing like a mad thing back to the ship and his sister."

"That was a most brave thing to do," I said. "He was surely risking his own life. Did they succeed in rescuing the young Countess?"

"They reached the ship again. As they tried to make fast, so that the young girl could be lowered in safety to them, many of those still on board leapt in panic into the small boat, so that it wallowed and sank beneath their weight. All in it were lost; some dashed to pieces against the ship, others drowned in the turbulent waters. Those who had already rowed away, seeing the Prince's boat overturn and smash against the ship, hesitated in their flight to safety. While those at the oars argued as to what to do, they were swept onto the rocks themselves and perished likewise."

Gerald paused and once more put his hands to his eyes, as if trying to blot out the sight of what must have happened. After a while, when he had composed himself again, he continued.

"Meanwhile, those still on the ship were trying to break off pieces of timber.

These they threw into the sea, and then committed themselves likewise to the mercy of the waves, hoping to reach the shore supported by anything that would bear them up, for few could swim. The butcher was amongst these, and it seems that he was the only one who succeeded in reaching dry land in safety, for he lashed himself to a spar before leaping into the waters.

"He knew not exactly where he landed or when, for he was himself near drowned in the turbulent waves. He must have been thrown up onto the shore in a sandy inlet, for it was there that he was found next day by one who gathered mussels by the shore, battered and half out of his wits and still lashed to his spar."

"Were any others saved? Some others must surely have reached safety, for it cannot be that all were drowned save the butcher?"

"None; all perished save him. The butcher said that the Prince and all in his boat would have reached the shore in safety had they continued rowing as they were, for they were well clear of the rocks, but when William heard his sister's cries he could not forsake her, and in trying to save her sealed his own death."

There was a long silence then as all of us tried to take in the awful tragedy.

At length, I was moved to say, "Is it not said in the Gospels 'Greater love hath no man than this, that he lay down his life for his friend'? Though he may have been headstrong and wild in his life, in his death the Prince redeemed himself and so surely earned his place with the angels."

"Amen to that," added Alric, and all those who sat listening crossed themselves.

"What of the King? Who was brave enough to break the news to him, and how was he affected by it?"

"That I know not, but it is said that when he heard the news he fell down in a faint, and for many days spoke to no-one in his grief. Besides William whom the King had named as heir to his throne, Richard, another of his sons, Richard Eorl of Chester and his brother and many more of the younger nobles of the Court were lost so that the King is now without many of his most trusted friends, having only greybeards left. It was the young nobles who sailed with William, while the few sages were on the King's ship."

"How many were there lost all told?"

"It is said that the ship was overloaded, for the final tally is three hundred souls, but of that number very few have yet been washed ashore. Of all that great number, one only has lived to tell the tale."

Again we all fell silent as we tried to comprehend such a great loss of life.

"Why," I said at length, "that is more than all the souls that live in the burgh."

Peter the dean nodded gravely. "True," he said, "we should pray for their souls, for like all men who are drowned, they die unshriven. I will light a candle for them and we will pray daily for a month that their souls may not be kept in torment."

"We should perhaps redouble out efforts to complete the church with all speed so that we can offer our prayers in a more fitting place," said Edward.

Others nodded their agreement, but Peter looked at him sharply then, knowing that it was because of him that the work of building was so long delayed.

"I will see if money can be found, but as you know, these past few years there has been little enough produced on the church's lands, or any other land for that matter."

It was a lame excuse, as Peter and all of us knew, and the shaft had struck home. I had little hope that the work on the church might soon begin again in earnest, for it was well known that Peter and his brother priests took most of what the church lands produced to themselves. Even the tithes which we all paid seemed to disappear into the bottomless pit of their greed. Catching Alric and Edward's eye, I could see that their thoughts were as mine.

Alric bent forward and whispered in my ear for a while. To the questioning look he gave me, I nodded my agreement. Alric turned then to Gerald.

"When next you speak with Baldwin de Redvers, will you pray him to give our humble duty to the King. Beg him say that we grieve with the King at his great loss. Let him say that living by the sea as we do, we understand what it means to lose one by drowning and that our dean, Peter, has ordered that prayers should be said for a month for Prince William and all those who perished with him. Let him also say that these prayers are offered because this was a Royal burgh in the time of William his royal father and King Edward before him. Though now the burgh belongs to Baldwin de Redvers, whom we gladly serve, yet we remember our royal links, and again pledge our loyalty to the King. Let him also say that soon we hope to have this great church finished, when we will be able to offer our prayers in a more fitting place."

"I will deliver your message in a few days, for I must speak with Baldwin on other matters soon. The King will surely be glad to have your condolences, for to lose a son is a terrible thing for any man. To lose the heir to one's kingdom, must be a double blow, for it may threaten the peace of the realm."

I could see that Peter was not pleased that Alric had spoken thus, nor at Gerald's response, thinking perhaps that he should have spoken. The rest of us, however, were well pleased with Alric, and felt that nothing but good could come of it.

Solemnly we rose, and went to our cotts.

Next day everyone was summoned to hear the dreadful news and a Requiem Mass was said for the souls of the departed. Though living by the sea we were accustomed to men being drowned, yet so great a number, and the King's heir besides, caused us great sadness.

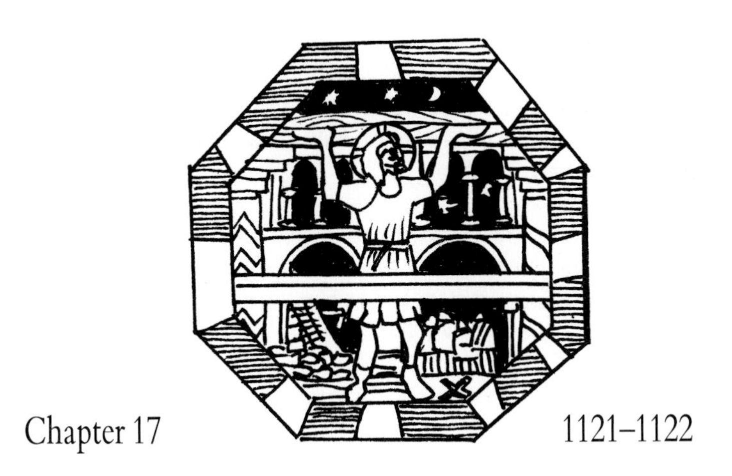

Chapter 17 1121–1122

Not many months later, Baldwin de Redvers again visited us, bringing messages from the King. Baldwin bade Alric summon all the folk so that they could hear what he had to tell them.

"The message of condolence that you asked me to give to King Henry was most kindly received. Many of those near to him tried to offer him comfort in his sorrow, but the King was moved by the thought that a whole burgh should offer their prayers for him and the soul of his son. He spoke to me of it several times, saying that if his people felt that way towards him then he need have no fear of their loyalty. He bade me also see to it that the church you are building is hastened forward with all speed. This message I give to you, Peter de Oglander, in particular, commanding you as dean of this place to use such gifts, tithes and other revenues as you have for the work. Because this is now my burgh, I will myself help the work forward by granting to the church the fees from certain other messuages which have recently been built near the castle ditch and stretching towards the Avon river and others also which are near the Stour and near the churchyard. I shall also give to the church the tithe of tolls that are taken on my ferry across the River Stour, and also the tithe of salmon and all other fish that are taken from the rivers of my demesne."

Baldwin paused then, to let folk hear and understand what he had said. Then he turned to Peter. "All these fees and rights are to be used for the building of this church, that it may go forward more quickly."

Baldwin looked round him and, seeing how many children there were amongst the crowd, turned to Peter again.

"Tell me, Peter, is there a school here where the children may learn the Gospels and teachings of the church?"

"There is no proper school, my Lord, but Rodric, one of our priests, spends such time as he can spare instructing the children. He teaches them their 'Pater Noster' and 'Ave' and some of the teachings of Christ, to their great benefit, but there are many other tasks that Rodric has to perform. Besides, parents are loath to release their children to him even for a short time, since even small hands have their uses."

"Send for Rodric that I may speak with him."

There was a movement in the crowd and Rodric pushed his way to the front and came to stand before Baldwin.

"I am Rodric, my Lord."

"Tell me truthfully, do the children learn well from you?"

"Who am I to answer that, my Lord? Some come readily enough when they know I shall be in the church porch to instruct them. I confess that it gives me pleasure to try to teach them, though it may be a sin of indulgence to admit such a thing."

Isabel spoke out then. "My Lord, Rodric has been a good teacher to my children and many others." There was a general murmur of approval and nodding of heads, for Rodric kept many of the more unruly children in check and was well liked for it.

"From now on, Peter," said Baldwin, "Rodric shall spend all his time teaching the children. I will see that he receives full payment for the task. If they are anything like me when I was a lad, then he will earn every silver penny of it."

His wry smile brought laughter from those standing near, who were glad to hear such a confession come from Baldwin's lips.

"Nor shall he continue to teach in the church porch. A place shall be found on the south side where the cloisters are to be built. There shall be built a proper place where he will teach the children. Edward, Peter, speak to me about this later, and, Peter, because I am granting you these things, continue to pray for the soul of the King and his dead son, and also my soul and those of my family."

Peter bowed low to hide his face. Though he was no doubt pleased that the church was to have added tithes and other fees and benefits, it was clear that he little liked the fact that he would now have to devote so much of his revenues to building the church rather than keeping them for himself and his friends. By the expressions on many of the priests' faces, they thought the same too.

There was general rejoicing this turn of events, for it meant that more men would be needed to work on the church. Not all the children were as pleased though but Rodric soon won them over by taking them into the fields and beside the river, to show them about animals and birds and how to treat them.

A few weeks later when Peter returned from a visit he had made to Winchester to see the Bishop he called some of us together.

"The news is that Henry has taken a new wife. It is hoped that she will comfort him in his distress, for he is still in sombre mood and it is hard to rouse him. Besides, he needs to produce another heir if the realm is not to sink into anarchy when he dies, though pray Heaven that such an event is many years distant yet."

"What is she like, this new Queen? Is she of royal blood like the last one?" Alric asked.

"No. Nor did I see her, for she is still at Windsor. They say she is a most fair maid, Adelicia by name, from Brabant, though I do not know where that is. Some said that it was to the east of the French King's lands, near Flanders, so it will not be easy for Henry to visit any lands she may bring as dowry. I heard also that there was trouble at the marriage service."

"How so?" I asked. "Did some of the English Eorls think that he should have wed one of their number? It could be risky surely, for it would increase the power of one at the expense of the others, and thus cause jealousy."

"Not that; it was the bishops this time. Archbishop Ralph of Canterbury, recently come from Rochester, thought to perform the marriage service, as Primate of the church, but he had not reckoned with Roger le Poer of Sarum. As Chancellor for many years, and now the Chief Justiciar, he has ruled the realm for the King during his long absences abroad, and with such power and influence most men rank him next to the King himself. He took it into his head that he had the greater claim to unite the royal couple."

Peter smiled to himself, as if at some private joke, before he continued.

"William of Winchester was present at the time with many other bishops including Flambard, all gathered in the Chapter House before entering the church. He told me that the contest between the two was so great that they were like to have come to blows. William told me that he had to step between them to calm them and cause reason to prevail. In this he succeeded, and Roger of Sarum backed down, though with some ill-grace, having to be content only to add some prayers after the pair had been united as man and wife. There was much jostling for position in the procession too, with Roger elbowing out Flambard into the second row beside William, so that he could stand at the head beside Ralph. William told me this with some glee, for Winchester has little love for Durham, both bishops seeking to gain influence and power, one in the north and the other in the south."

"Why do men worry about who stands first?" I asked. "Is it really such an important matter?"

"It would seem so," Peter replied, "though it would be better if they gave more thought to the cure of souls than to their own advancement."

"At least such things do not worry us," Alric said. "Now that Flambard is no longer here to build our church to his glory we can concentrate on its true purpose. It is good that work is now progressing apace again. Edward, when do you think you will start to raise the first timbers for the roof?"

Edward thought for a few moments, and counted on his fingers before replying.

"Next year, if all goes smoothly. The arches over the triforium at the eastern end are almost complete now. I would not wish to raise the first roof timbers until we have the crossing and the transepts complete. How think you, Thurstan, is not that your plan too?"

"Indeed it is, and perhaps the first two arches past the crossing too. I have timbers being roughly prepared now to bridge the main span, and also the slightly shorter span across the transepts. It has been hard to find trees long and straight enough, but we have almost enough now and they are seasoning ready for when they will be needed. There is much work to be done on them yet to square them up before I can set my most expert carpenters to work to cut the joints in them where other timbers are to be fixed. I have been watching closely those that may be best fitted for the work and I have found two or three who may well have mastered their craft sufficiently."

Thurstan looked down at his hands with a thoughtful frown on his face, and said nothing for some time. Eventually he looked up, but his eyes were seeing something far distant.

"One man in particular I have noticed, but do not know his name. He works quietly, away from the rest, and his work is always clean and well finished. I must seek him out when the time comes. Your brother Osbern may be another, Hugh, but say nothing to him yet for I have not decided. There will be need to make strong pulleys and winches to raise the great weight of the timbers too. I must journey to Sarum to see what they have done, for they have a similar problem."

"You will need tall scaffolds between the pillars too, I think," said Edward. "A stone can be raised to the top of the walls in a basket by a simple pulley, for each stone is no more than one man can lift and can be rested on the top of the wall while it is being fixed in place. Your timbers will need supporting while they are swung into position, for they will be of massive weight. I would come with you to Sarum, Thurstan, so that I, too, can see how they manage these things there."

The two of them departed shortly after for Sarum, while we continued with our labours. The work of completing the walls progressed with greater speed than it had for some years. On their return from Sarum, Thurstan began to assemble the scaffolds between the pillars, ready for when the timbers should be raised.

One evening, when Isabel and I were sitting by our hearth with the family round us, Osbern came by with his wife Adela, as he often did, and joined us to share such news as we had.

"I have been working near one the carpenters recently. He seems not like the others," he said, with a puzzled look on his face. "His work is more finely finished than any I have seen elsewhere, and by watching him I have learnt several skills to make my own work better. Though I have tried to draw him out, he says little. I asked him from which master he learnt his trade. All he would say was that he learnt his craft from his earthly father, one Joseph by name, which struck me as an odd way to put it. He would not say in which place he had lived. By the looks of him, he does not come from these parts, for he does not have the complexion of us Saxons or even the Normans. I have heard some say, who have been crusading, that he resembles those who live in those eastern lands. That is hard to believe. What reason could one have to journey all that way to come here to practise his trade? All he will say is that he does indeed come from a distant land. Nor can I find his name, for none seem to know. Those who speak to him call him Joseph's son. There is something compelling about his voice that those who hear it find it hard to forget. I can hear his voice in my head now. It is deep and resonant, and somehow strong. I cannot put a name to it, but when he does speak, you find you have to listen."

Osbern sat staring at the hearth for some time with a puzzled look on his brow.

"I wish I knew more of the man, for I am sure he has much to tell and I would surely listen. He seems to have a way with children too, for twice I have seen him sitting in a group of them telling them stories, while they listened with rapt attention."

"He sounds an interesting fellow," I said, "and if he can hold the children then no doubt he will be a friend of Rodric. Next time I see him, I will ask him what he knows of the man. You say he is a fine carpenter? Then Thurstan will need him for the roof, no doubt."

Osbern looked at us excitedly, trying at the same time to hide his pleasure.

"I think Thurstan has in mind that each master carpenter should make a complete roof truss, with its tie beam, collar beam, king post and two queen posts, and principal rafters. Each man will then be responsible for seeing that the joints fit securely and firmly together, so that the whole will stand solid when it is raised. It is a great thing to be given such a responsibility; I must not let him down." Osbern added, nodding gravely.

"Have no fear, Osbern, you too are a master carpenter now. Thurstan would not have chosen you for the work if he did not think that your work was of high enough quality, is that not so Isabel?"

"Surely. Thurstan is careful in everything that he does, and if he has chosen you to form the timbers, then you may be sure he is satisfied that you can do the work well. Tell me Osbern, is this man you spoke of to make one of the roof trusses too?"

"Yes indeed, and I mean to follow his work closely, if I am to make mine as well as possible. His jointing is always so smooth and tight that when he puts two timbers together they seem as if they have grown as one in the tree. I think I shall see if I can move my bench next to his so that I can follow his work more closely and learn from him. It is something wonderful to handle, two well-jointed timbers and feel them to be solid as though they had grown as one. Once or twice I have managed it myself and it is hard to describe the pleasure it gives."

I glanced across at Isabel and caught her eye, and we both smiled, for it seemed that in speaking thus, Osbern was showing the nature of a true craftsman. I thought back to the day when he had brought us the cradle he had made for our first-born those many years ago. Our Martha was the first to have lain in it, and it had been used by our four other children since, including poor little Hugh who had died so young. It was the first fine piece of work Osbern had made. He had poured all his loving care into it and it was one of our most treasured possessions. It was still as solid as the day he made it, and the carvings as clear. Perhaps soon, if I read our Martha's feelings aright, she might need a cradle for a babe of her own, for she had eyes for none but Ernwi,the son of Roger the hayward. He seemed to be spending all his spare moments in her company. It would be a good match, and there would be a virgate of land and more to come to the marriage. My thoughts were wandering from Osbern and his craft. I must seek out Thurstan and find out more of this son of Joseph whose work so drew Osbern.

I passed through the churchyard a few days later and found Osbern busy with his timbers, cutting them to shape. He was so intent on his work that he did not hear me approach and it was not until I spoke to him that he looked up with a start.

"Why, Hugh," he said, "I did not hear you coming. I was busy with this joint here. It is for the king post which goes in the centre of the collar beam. You can give me a hand with it, if you have a moment, so that I can see if it fits as it should."

Together we lifted the heavy timber with its projecting tongue and gently lowered it into the slot that Osbern had cut in the centre of the collar beam.

"Hold it upright or it will not slide in," Osbern said. "Move it a little to the right, now a bit towards me - too far - back a bit. There, that should do it. Now ease it downwards into the slot I have cut. Do not wriggle it from side to side or you will make it bigger at the top and it will not hold firm. If it is made rightly, the tenon will exactly fit the mortise. Gently now, I think it is going in. Now pull down on the post to make sure it is fully home in its place. There, I think that should do it. Let me look."

He bent down to examine the joint carefully, squinting his eye to see if there was any light showing between the two timbers where the one rested on the other. At last he seemed satisfied, and he straightened up. Then he took hold of the king post with both hands and tried to move it from side to side before standing back and putting his hands on his hips and smiling.

"There; firm as a rock, as it should be. Try it," he said, turning to me. "See if you can move it."

I took hold of the post as he had done and tried to move it in the socket but there was no movement either from side to side or from back to front. All I succeeded in doing was rocking the two timbers back and forward as if they were a solid tree with one huge branch sticking out of it.

"Why, it seems as if it is one solid piece, Osbern. Is that how it should be?"

"That is what I have been trying to do for some time, and at last I think I have found the right way. It was the man Joseph's son who showed me the knack. I could not have done it without his help and guidance. He is truly a wonderful craftsman, but I think he has had to learn the hard way, as we all seem to do, for he has an odd scar in the centre of each palm, and on the backs of his hands too. Perhaps he had some accident when he was younger, though I do not like to ask him about it. His hands are strong and steady enough, whatever happened to them. You should see him when he is using a chisel, how he can shave off the finest sliver of wood so that his joints may fit exactly. All his joints are like this one which is why I have wanted to do one the same. If he could do it, then I knew it was possible, though none of the other master craftsmen so far have been able to make so tight a joint."

Osbern stood back with his head on one side and looked critically at the joint he had made. Then he walked round and inspected it from the other side.

"I must ask him to examine this next time I see him, to see if he thinks it is good enough. I hope it is, but I must be sure before I bore the hole through the collar beam to take the peg which will hold the two timbers together so that they can never come apart. That is the final piece of the joint, and can only be done when the whole roof truss is assembled. Now, help me lay the two timbers down on the ground before they fall over. That is the only thing that can damage the joint and perhaps break off the tenon in the mortise, in which case all the work will have been wasted."

Working together, we gently lowered the upright king post and made sure that it was well settled on the flat ground. It was good to see Osbern take such a pride in his work, much as Isabel's younger brother Alnoth did in his stone work.

I went on my way thinking that it must be the same for every craft. I took a like pride in setting the millstones so that they ground the flour as finely as possible. Each man must use his talents as well as he can, though I felt that some tasks needed far more skill than others.

The year progressed, and Osbern told us how the roofing timbers were all taking shape. Meantime, Edward set many men to the task of making long lengths of rope by which the timbers could be hauled up to the tops of the arches through a system of pulleys which he and Thurstan had brought back with them from their visit to Sarum. They explained that by running the rope up and down through the pulleys, the weight of the timbers would be much reduced for those who had to raise them. Without such a system it would not have been possible to lift the timbers, since each one weighed much more than all the men set to pull on the rope.

Harvest was gathered in once more before Thurstan and Edward agreed that all was now ready to raise the huge roof timbers into place at the east end of the church, and also the crossing. First came the roof plates, which ran the whole length of the top of the arches which were supported by the massive pillars. These were laid end to end, set well back from the inner edge of the arch. They were joined by what Osbern called a half-lap joint, so that the end of each timber was cut to half its thickness and then laid one on top of the other to form one continuous run of timber. Where they joined, they were fixed together with wooden pegs to hold the two halves together. At the centre of each pillar, the wall plates were deeply notched, so that the great tie beams - the biggest timbers to be used - could rest securely in place, their ends similarly notched so that they could not move apart. These would then be securely pegged together.

The first three arches of the east end of the church were tackled together. The tie beams were raised and fixed to the wall plates to span the great space between the pillars. Then the three collar beams, each with its king post and two queen posts, were put together on the ground inside the church, near where they were to be raised, and the smaller upper collar beam set on top of it all.

This framework was then securely pegged before each one could be raised with much effort and supported by a scaffold on top of the massive tie beam. There it had to be held firm, while the principal rafters were raised. This called for great skill and accurate movement, for the rafters had to be raised high over the collar frames and then slowly lowered so that the mortises cut into the rafters would fit over the tenons which stuck out from the end of the collar beams.

I looked thoughtfully at all the pieces of timber, each one of which had its rightful place in the whole. It crossed my mind that such a structure was much like our own lives, where each man looked to his neighbour for support. Alone, one was puny, but acting together, almost anything could be accomplished.

When the day came to raise the first three collar beams and their rafters, Alric declared a boon-day for men on the demesne. All of them were to come to the church to help with the raising, for many hands were needed. I made sure that I was put to help on the beam that Osbern had been working on, for I felt a certain pride that my brother should have a part in such magnificent work. As we heaved away at the ropes to lift the massive structure, I think we all felt that we were part of a common purpose, joined in the noble work of completing the church that we would soon be able to use.

There was much shouting and heaving as we strained together to lift the massive timber frames, while Osbern stood on top of the scaffold, directing the positioning of the timbers above the tie beam. He checked that it was vertically above the beam by using a plumb bob which he dropped from the collar beam and gently adjusted it until it just touched the tie beam below it. Then he hammered in wedges to hold the frame in place, while we relaxed the rope which had been holding the frame, and took what I felt was a well-earned rest.

Others, meanwhile, had been securing the first of the principal rafters to other ropes, and we were called upon to raise that too. Though it was but half the weight of the frame, it still took almost as much effort to raise since it was held at both ends so that the top could be raised higher than the foot. Under Osbern's directions we gradually lifted the rafter as it came towards the side of the collar frame.

Osbern scrambled about on the frame examining the joints carefully. Then we saw him feel in his apron and bring out a hammer and a wooden peg which he fed into the hole already drilled at the joint. Tapping it gently at first, he finally drove the oak peg firmly home to secure the joint solid. Next, he moved to the other joints and hammered more oak pegs in to hold them likewise until the whole rafter was firmly fixed in place. When he was satisfied, he called down to us.

"Now raise the other rafter on the other side and we will fix that one too. It will be the same task, but there is one extra point to watch. We have to make sure that the two rafters meet at the top so that they can be fixed firmly together. When you are ready, start raising the timber."

We took up the rope again. Gradually the great balk of wood rose in the air, to be steadied and moved into place by Osbern's guiding hand, with Ralf and Swein helping him as he directed. At last, the rafter slid into place. There was a cry from Swein who was perched high up on the top of the first rafter.

"It fits exactly Osbern! It is a marvel. I can see no light between the two timbers. It is a perfect fit. Shall I hammer in the peg to hold it?"

"Let me come up and see first, Swein. Wait till I have checked the other joints to see that all is as it should be."

Those of us who were on the ground hauling on the ropes waited with baited breath. This was the final moment, when we should know if the master carpenter would prove his worth and the whole roof truss would finally come together as one piece. As Osbern clambered about on the timbers high above us, examining first one joint and then another, I sent up a silent prayer that all would be as he hoped. Looking round at those who held the ropes with me, it seemed that others did the same, for we all knew that if anything should be wrong then there would be a great delay while the work was redone.

At length, he called out, "Hammer away, Swein! It all fits as it should."

A great cheer rose from those of us on the ground.

"Now send up the wind-braces," cried Osbern.

We were brought back to our senses, for the work was not yet finished.

"We need to fix the first ones to the wall plates to support the rafters and prevent them swaying in the wind. Once we have the second rafter in place, we can attach the main purlins to the two frames and then it will be solid."

A few of us set to work again to lift the curved wind-braces, which needed the strength of two men only to raise. Quickly they were set in position and then pegged firm. Then Osbern made a final inspection before calling for Thurstan to come up and examine it for himself. Those of us on the ropes took the chance to relax for a while as Thurstan clambered up to inspect the whole structure. For my part, I kept an eye on Thurstan to see if he would be satisfied, for much depended on what he found. I could see him nodding with approval as he went from joint to joint, until at last he called down to us.

"It is all well made and firmly fixed. This is good work indeed. Well done Osbern! This is the work of a true master carpenter."

A cheer went up again from those of us below and I felt my heart swell with pride. We were all glad to see the start of the roof and knew that it would not be long before we could use at least part of the church in the dry.

Thus the work continued, and before the day was ended we had raised the second roof truss, under the guidance of Joseph's son who had made it, and fixed it firm. I too was struck by his calm and confident voice which Osbern had remarked upon. When Thurstan came to inspect that second roof truss before the fixing pegs were hammered home, he said it was all unblemished and the finest work he had ever seen. I called to mind what Osbern had said about the skill of the one who had made it, and pondered on it later, for it seemed to hold the key to much that puzzled me at the time.

Before we finished that day, we also hauled up the first pair of the main purlins, and they too were fixed into position, so that the two trusses were firmly fixed together. We went weary to our beds that night, but content with what we had done.

By the end of the week, the remaining trusses for the eastern end of the church were all in position. The main roof structure from the east end as far as the walls of the crossing which would hold the central tower was in position, and the trusses held by their purlins and wind-braces. All was now set to raise the main tie beams at the crossing and the transepts.

The next Sunday, as Isabel and I were returning through the churchyard after Mass with Osbern and Adela and also Emma and Alric, we came across a group of the craftsmen who were engaged on the building work, seemingly arguing, for we heard raised voices.

"I do not mind helping a neighbour, or one whom I know, if he is in difficulty," one voice was heard to say, "because I would expect him to do the same for me. But why should I go to the aid of a stranger whom I shall probably never see again?"

There were a few murmurs of agreement at this. Then came a deep rich voice which I thought I recognised.

"But who is your neighbour, my friend? Let me tell you a story."

Osbern tugged at my sleeve and whispered. "Let us stay and listen. You know who is speaking, don't you?"

I looked at Osbern and saw his eyes bright with excitement, and I knew whom he meant. The six of us moved closer to the group and settled ourselves on the ground to listen to the speaker as he began his tale.

"A merchant was journeying from Winchester to the Abbey at Beaulieu recently, and as he travelled through the King's forest of Andret, he was set upon by thieves, beaten up and robbed of all he had on him."

"More fool him for journeying alone," one of the group said. "The King may say his roads are safe, but there are plenty of vagabonds who still prey on unwary travellers, and besides, the merchant could probably afford it."

"That may not always be so, Wolfric, but let us hear the rest of the story."

"Thank you, my friend. As I was saying, the merchant was left robbed and bleeding at the side of the road. Before long, a monk came by, telling his beads, and also on his way to Beaulieu. When he heard groaning coming from the ditch beside the road, he went over to see what it was all about. Seeing the injured merchant and the state that he was in, he turned away and carried on towards Beaulieu, still telling his beads, adding an extra prayer for the injured man. Some time later, by which time the merchant had succeeded in dragging himself out of the ditch to the side of the road, a knight on horseback rode up. When he saw the body at the side of the road, he reined in his horse so that he could take a closer look. The merchant, who was far gone by then, managed to raise one hand in supplication, begging aid. The knight, who was gallantly dressed, fearing that his clothes might become soiled, turned his horse back onto the highway and continued on his way. He quickly put the merchant out of his mind, for it seems he had more important things to think about."

The speaker paused for a while, and some of us shifted our positions to make ourselves more comfortable. Then, looking round at all of us, he continued.

"Finally, a Jew came by riding on a donkey. He was deep in thought about a loan he was hoping to make to a needy noble whom he was hurrying to see, when his thoughts were suddenly interrupted by a faint cry from the side of the road. Looking round, the Jew saw the wretched figure of the merchant, whose hand still moved feebly. Stopping his donkey at once, he jumped down and hastened to the figure on the ground and, lifting the merchant's head gently, began to comfort him, asking what had happened, at the same time trying to find out the extent of the poor man's injuries. The Jew tended him there beside the road, giving him something to drink to revive him. He then bound up his injuries as best he could and staunched the bleeding."

There were a few surprised murmurs from some of those who sat round, for many cared not for the Jews, despising them for the usury they exact, though they were willing enough to accept their loans of silver.

"When he had done as much as he could to keep the merchant alive, he helped him up and sat him on his donkey and walked, thus supporting him, till they came to the abbey at Beaulieu. There he knocked at the gate and asked for the infirmarer, to deliver the injured man into his care. At first, the monk who came to the gate was unwilling to let a Jew into the abbey, saying that he would see to the injured merchant himself. The Jew insisted, and together they went to the infirmarer, who treated the poor merchant's injuries and added that if he had been delayed but an hour longer, he would surely have died.

All this while, the Jew stayed with the merchant, helping the infirmarer as much as he could, and insisting that he sleep beside the man in case he needed anything during the night. When next day the Jew came to leave, he pressed two silver pence into the infirmarer's hands, telling him to care for the merchant as long as was needful, and that if he needed more silver for medicines, he would pay for them next time he passed that way."

The speaker paused again, and we all sat silent, waiting for him to continue the story. At length, he spoke again, and looking at the man who had first spoken, he asked him in a quiet voice, "Tell me, my friend, which of those three men do you think was the neighbour to the merchant?"

"Why, the one who looked after him, I suppose."

"Then do you not think that we should try to do the same to all men?"

There was silence again for some time, while all there pondered upon what had been said. At length, Isabel rose and we took our leave.

As we went, each to our own homes, Isabel said quietly to me, "That tale reminds me of one I have heard before, though I think it was from another land, but the message is clear wheresoever it was."

I looked into her serious eyes then, and I think we both knew to what she was referring. There was something compelling too about the teller of the tale which had struck both our hearts.

The work on the roof of the church continued all the next week, and the shorter tie beams for the transepts were raised and fixed to their wall plates.

It was near the end of the day when the time came to raise the massive beam which would span the walls of the crossing where the east and west ends of the church came together to meet the transepts. Once more, many of us were called upon to help raise the huge timber into its position, high up on top of the walls where the tower would eventually rise. It was a beautifully cut timber, smooth and straight, for it would be in a commanding position in the centre of the crossing.

While we waited for the order to start raising the beam on the ropes, I ran my hand over its surface. I felt its smoothness and strength, and wondered how many hundreds of years it had been in the growing. It must have come from a mighty tree in Andret Forest.

At length, a cry came from above and we started to haul on the ropes. Slowly, and with much effort, the beam rose in the air until it was at the right height. Then those who were to place it began to swing it into position across the wide gap that it had to bridge. It seemed that we held the ropes steady for a long time and we began to grow restless. Usually, it was a simple matter to place the tie beams on the wall plates, so as we still strained to hold the beam aloft, some of us began to look upwards to see if anything was amiss. Then a cry went up for Thurstan to come and look.

Others shouted down to us, "Tie the ropes off as best you may, and secure the beam so that it does not fall. There is something amiss. Thurstan is coming up to look."

We made fast the ends of the ropes to the scaffold and eased our aching limbs, then sat around and gazed upwards, trying to find out what was wrong. After a time, Thurstan came slowly down, his face grim.

"Something terrible has happened," he said. "This beam, which I had been keeping especially to bridge the centre of the crossing, has been cut too short. It will not span the distance between the two walls by the length of my foot. How can this have happened? I thought I had been so careful in choosing the trees for the tie beams and I had them all stacked on one side for this especial purpose, with strict orders that none were to be used except as I directed. Can I have counted or measured wrongly? What are we to do, for there are no more trees that are long enough? The crossing is ruined."

Thurstan groaned aloud in his dismay. He turned to those who had been on the ropes.

"It seems that there is a problem and that the beam is too short. I do not understand why at the moment, so we will have to lower the beam to the ground again now. In the morning I will see if I can find the answer. I am truly sorry, for you have worked so well and given freely of your time to help in this work, and now it seems that I have let you all down."

He looked abashed, and there were one or two grumbles at the wasted effort. Others soon silenced them, for Thurstan was held in great respect as a fine craftsman and a kindly employer. We let the ropes loose again and gently lowered the massive beam to the ground, resting it on several logs of wood so that it could be the more easily handled next day. Then, with saddened spirits at the disaster that had halted the work, we trudged wearily to our homes.

While we were eating our evening meal, Osbern came in with a troubled brow and sat down with us.

"I do not understand it," he said. "I was with Thurstan when he measured that beam and we both checked its length. I am sure it was long enough. I blame myself, for I am sure Thurstan could not make a simple mistake like that. It must have been me."

"Thurstan said nothing about you in my hearing," I said. "He took all the blame on himself."

"How like the man. I have worked with him now many years and he never seeks to blame others but only himself for whatever faults there may be. That is one of the reasons why men work so well for him, because they feel badly when he takes the blame for their mistakes. Their pride is hurt then, so that they feel they have to make amends and do better, for others know full well where the blame really lies."

"That may be so in some cases," murmured Isabel, but not in this case I fancy. If something is wrong, it will not be laid either at your door or his. There is some other reason I feel sure. Why do you not seek out Joseph's son and ask him? He is a master carpenter too and you greatly respect him. He may be able to give the answer."

"Yes indeed. I will ask him first thing in the morning before I start work. If we have made an error, I am sure he will be able to tell us what it is, but at the moment it baffles me completely."

We let the matter rest there for the night, and soon after Osbern rose to leave us and return to Adela in his cott.

The next day dawned fine and bright. The sun shone warm on my face as I made my way to the church to see if the problem had been solved and we could raise the beam to its rightful place. As I drew near, I could hear the sound of many voices coming from the church. They seemed to be excited too. Entering by the west end, and passing down the yet-to-be-completed arches there, I became aware that those in the church were all gathered under the crossing, gazing upwards and pointing. My curiosity aroused, I quickened my pace to join them, before taking my place on the rope I had held yesterday. As I neared the crossing, Osbern came running up to me in great excitement.

"Come and see," he said. "The beam is up in its place! Look, there it is! Spanning the crossing as it should be. Thurstan has just been up there. When we came in early this morning to have another look at it, we were surprised to see that it was no longer on the ground where we left it last night. You remember we had set it on several logs so that it would be easier to move today? Well, the logs are still there where we put them. Look, there they are, but the beam had gone. We could not think what had happened. It is far too heavy for anyone to move and as Thurstan said to me why should anyone wish to move it? We both looked round the crossing to see if it had somehow been moved to one side, but the space is clear as you can see except for the people standing here. Then I happened to glance upwards. I cannot think why. Perhaps I was seeking inspiration from Heaven, I don't know. Then I saw it. Right up where it should be. Look!"

He pointed up to the top of the walls again. I followed his pointing finger and saw that what he said was true. The huge beam spanned the crossing as it should. Amazed, I looked at Osbern for some explanation.

"The beam lies there in place. I had to blink twice to make sure my eyes were not playing tricks on me, but it was true. I looked again to make sure, and then called to Thurstan. He came over to where I was standing. I pointed upwards, for I was too amazed to speak. He looked up too, and his jaw fell open and he blanched, and blinked as I had done. Then he rubbed his eyes and looked again to make sure. The beam was there.

He said to me, 'Wait here. I am going up to look. Don't tell anyone till I have been up to see and made sure that what we are looking at is real.' He clambered up the scaffolding and almost ran along the top of the wall to where the beam was. Then he slowly bent down and stretched out his hand to touch it, unwilling to believe that it was real, but it was. Solid oak, and well set. I could see him as he ran his hands over it lovingly, for that beam had been his pride. He had kept it on one side especially for the crossing. That was why he was so upset when it seemed too short last night. Isn't it wonderful? I am so pleased for Thurstan."

Osbern grinned happily, then dashed off to tell some of the others. As for me, I made my way to where Thurstan was standing, still looking dazed by the events of the morning. He looked towards me as I approached.

"I still cannot understand it," he said. "You saw the beam where we left it last night, didn't you?"

"Yes, indeed. I helped settle it on the logs here after we had lowered it. It was too short. We could all see that from the ground. I felt so sorry for you when you had to tell us."

"Well, look at it now," he said. "There it is, up in its place, and as firm as a rock, and there is almost an arm's length of timber resting on the top of each wall as there should be. I cannot understand it. I have been up there to look at it, and it is true. Yet how was it raised? It needs many men to lift it, and no-one seems to know anything about it. It is a mystery," and he turned away scratching his head.

I looked for Osbern again, for I had a question I wanted to ask him alone. Finding him in a group of carpenters, I drew him eventually to one side.

"Have you had a chance to speak to Joseph's son yet?"

He looked puzzled. "No. I could not find him this morning when I came to my bench. I work next to him as you know. I have been looking for him on and off ever since, but he is nowhere to be seen. Those I have asked so far have not seen him either."

"Then let us go and seek him out now," I said, "and see if he can throw any light on this mystery."

We left the church and went to where Osbern worked, asking any we passed if they had seen the man we sought, but none had. As we neared Osbern's work-bench, he suddenly stopped and pointed.

"Look, his bench is clear. He always keeps his tools below the bench but they are gone, and the bench is swept clean as if it has never been used."

He passed his hand over the surface of the bench and, raising his palm towards me, he showed it to me.

"Look, there is not even any dust upon it. I could be forgiven for thinking that no-one had used this bench if I did not know otherwise."

Though we sought him for the rest of that day and asked others too, it seemed that no-one had seen him since the previous day. Nor was there any trace that he had ever lived amongst us. Many could tell of a kindness he had done to them, and others too remembered some of the stories he had told. Had not Isabel and I and the others heard one only the previous Sunday after Mass? Rodric had good cause to remember him too, for oft-times he had found him sitting in the middle of a group children, telling them tales, which they always seemed to enjoy and remember afterwards. Rodric said that he had at first tried to shoo the children away, fearing that they might be hindering the man from doing his rightful work as a carpenter. He rebuked him, it seems, saying that children were part of the Kingdom of Heaven, which brought a smile to Rodric's lips when he saw who some of the children were. He let them stay afterwards, for the man seemed content enough to have them round him, and the children were happy too.

The mystery increased as the days passed, for it seemed that this man had never appeared at the pay table to receive his wages. Neither Osbern nor Thurstan could explain how this could have come about, but it seemed to be true nonetheless.

As time went by, some began to forget that he had ever been amongst us, though whenever I went into the church and saw the huge beam up in its rightful place I could not forget. Nor could Osbern, who acknowledged how much he had learnt of his trade from the man. Likewise Thurstan; though he could not explain how the beam came to be positioned where it was, yet he was certain that the man had been with us. He felt sure too, that somehow the man had had a hand in the strange events that had occurred. Isabel and I, Osbern, Emma, Alric and the others, discussed the matter often. I am sure we all felt that some Power, far greater than any on this earth, had been at work amongst us.

As the months passed, the roof progressed, and before winter set in the whole of the eastern end was covered in, with the transepts and the crossing too, and the first bay of the western end of the church. The aisles on each side of the eastern end had also been covered with a sloping roof as far as the crossing and transepts. More than half the church had now been roofed over, and Peter, our dean, agreed that it would be possible now to hold Mass in that part of the new church rather than in the crypts as we had done for so many years. Great was the joy in the whole burgh when we heard this news, for at last it seemed that all the years of effort were bearing fruit. As the season of Advent was already upon us, what better day could be chosen for the first Mass than the festival of the birth of the Christ-child?

Thus it was, when the festival of Christ's birth came, that we held the High Mass in the eastern end of the new church itself, secure and dry with the roof above us. The floor had been swept clean, all the building rubble cleared out, and everywhere decked out with branches of fir and holly, which was bright with red berries. First, there was a great procession round the new building with much singing of the 'Jubilate Deo' and other anthems. Then we entered the church from the western end, following Peter and all the priests in their finest robes as they made their way towards the newly raised altar in the apse at the eastern end, where they would celebrate the Mass.

As I passed under the crossing, with Isabel on my arm, we both looked upwards to that massive beam, solid and firm, and we wondered.

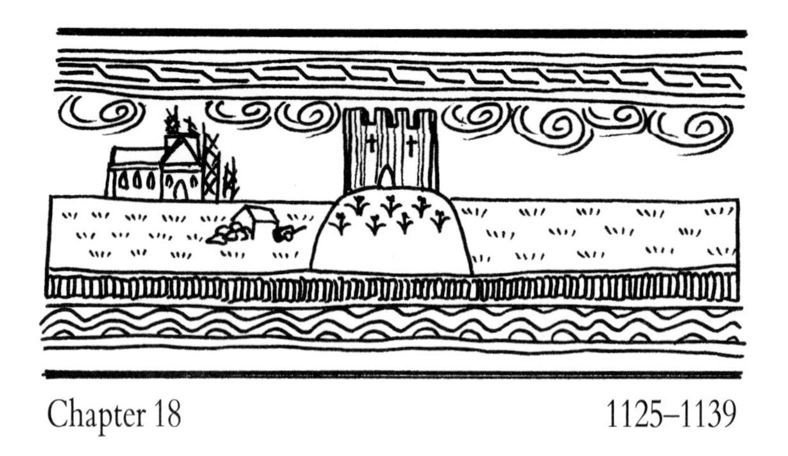

Chapter 18 1125–1139

There was a general feeling of satisfaction amongst those who lived and worked in the burgh, now that the eastern part of the church was completed and in use for Mass and the other Offices. Much of what we had been toiling to achieve for so many years was at last coming to fruition. With it, however, came a slackening of effort, so that the work on the remainder of the building slowed down noticeably. The troubles in the land added to this slowing of the work too, for the King went over to his lands in Normandy and elsewhere, since there was much warring in those parts.

Before he went, Henry placed the care of the realm in the hands of his friend and adviser, Roger le Poer, Sarum's Bishop, who was already Chancellor and Chief Justiciar. To him, aided by his two nephews, the Bishops of Ely and Lincoln, the King committed the good governing of the realm, and in particular, orders to raise such taxes and other levies as might be needed to pay for the men the King needed for his armies.

Though Roger of Sarum did right in most things and the laws of the land were upheld, the taxes he raised bore heavily on all folk. Men found them harder to bear than in earlier times, for the weather was foul for several years, so that the crops were once more thin in the fields. The price of grain was so high that an acre's seed of wheat or barley sold for six shillings. Such a thing had not been known before.

Matters were made worse, for the moneyers, who alone had the right to strike the silver pennies, began to make poor money. With each succeeding minting it was found that a silver penny held less and less silver until at last it was found that a penny held no more than fourteen grains of silver instead of the twenty-two grains that it was supposed to have. It was told to the King that a man who had a pound of the poor coins could only buy twelve pence worth of goods with it.

Thereupon the King commanded Roger of Sarum to call all the moneyers in the land to Winchester at the time of the feast of Christ's birth. There, before the festival of the Epiphany at the start of '25, the King ordered that the right hand be struck off every one of them, and that they be so mutilated below that they could no longer sire a child. This he did because the moneyers had so ruined the land with their fraud that men would no longer accept the King's coins, but traded by barter if they could, or not at all.

We had no moneyer in the burgh, for we used the silver pennies struck in Winchester. Some who travelled there saw the moneyer after he had suffered the King's wrath. They said that he was a sorry sight, scarce able to walk from his injuries and the shame of them, and his right arm but a raw stump. Such cruelty I found hard to accept, but then most of my trade at the mill was for goods, not silver, and so the poor coins did not affect us much . Others said that such barbarity was needed in harsh times to cure a great evil. Many felt that the King had sunk to less than human action, and that other ways could have been found, even though men knew that the loss of a hand was the punishment for taking deer in the King's forest of Andret.

More serious to us were the floods that covered much of the land on St Lawrence's Day, and which swept away the bridges that crossed the River Avon on the edge of the burgh. Many folk and beasts in the fields were drowned and we were cut off until the bridges could be replaced. Nor was that the end of our troubles, for yet again the crops lay rotting in the fields and could not be harvested, and famine and disease struck down both men and beasts.

That year, I had less corn to grind than I could ever remember. The lands of the church produced so little that there was scarce enough to feed those who were starving, and none left to sell, nor was there money to pay for the building works. As new pence were struck, men once more began to trade freely, and when the next year the harvest was good, our troubles seemed to be over for a while.

It was after another harvest had been gathered in towards the end of 1128 that a monk travelling towards the west came, bringing us important news. He had journeyed from the far north where he had been on a pilgrimage to pray over the incorruptible body of St Cuthbert in his tomb in the great church at Durham. While he was there, he said, Ranulf Flambard, their bishop, had died. Though many had forgotten all about the man, and there were many who had never known him, for he had not been near the burgh for several years, the older folk had cause to remember him well enough. Our dean, Peter de Oglander, called us all together to hear the news, and what the monk could tell of the man who had started the building of our church.

"It cannot be denied that Flambard was a great and powerful man," the monk said. "Many are the stories told of him in the north. How he tried to have York's Archbishop Thurstan, whom Flambard had himself ordained some years before, accepted as superior to Canterbury. He even offered to give King Henry a thousand marks, with another hundred for the Queen, if he would agree, but the King knew which side could bid the higher, so he would not agree. Flambard's bid to have control over all the church in the realm failed, though his power in the north was formidable. Nor did he fare well with his monks in his early years, though he came to terms with them later and gave them land on which he built at his own expense a church, hermitage, and hospital for the poor and endowed them all, so that it cannot be said, as some hold, that he was impious."

"We saw little of his piety here," Alric said. "The church he first wished to build here was to have been more for his own glory than to the glory of God."

"It seemed that this was not acceptable, for the man could not build as he wished," I added. "We should give Flambard some credit for having started us on the way we have now gone, by agreeing that our church should be built here in the burgh. Though I cared little for his bullying methods, he could be mastered if one stood up to him. Isabel, do you remember when he nearly trampled old Meg under his horse's hooves? I have seldom seen a man more put out. It taught him a lesson I think."

"Do not remind me of it. I shiver every time I call it to mind. I was so angry with him, I could not help myself."

Isabel shook her head and frowned as she spoke, and I felt constrained to lay my hand on her arm to soothe her.

" Great wealth he certainly had, and vast lands all over the north of the realm, which he had persuaded the King to give him at different times," the monk continued. "The monks of Durham also told me that all the lands that had once belonged to the church there were restored at some time to him, and he profited greatly thereby. He cared for the great church he was building too, though at the time many hated him for what he did."

"How so?" I asked. "Can men hate what benefits the church?"

"If it harms them, yes. Flambard made many enemies when he cleared the land round his church and the castle of all the miserable dwelling places that had been built in its shadow. The church was being soiled by all their filth and imperilled by their fires. To clear them away was a benefit, for it made a space where men could take their ease and gaze upon the magnificent building and derive inspiration from it and learn of the greatness of God."

"It is for the same reason," said Edward gravely, "that I do not wish any dwellings to be built near to the church here either."

We all nodded in agreement, for to build close to the church would hide much of its splendour.

"He saw to the needs of his son too," continued the monk. "Much was added to the lands of the church in Lincoln, which Flambard's son Elias held until his death. But these lands then returned once more to Flambard. I heard say in Durham that those same lands would now fall free and quit to God, St Mary and the church of Lincoln and its bishop - and surely this is right. Some say that it was Flambard who brought the beautiful illuminated Gospel of St John to Durham, which I have seen with my own eyes, but I cannot say for certain. I have never set eyes on a more beautiful work. Reading some of the chapters, I found myself transported to the Holy Places, as I looked at the lovely pictures that form so much of the work."

"There is a book at Winchester which I saw once," Peter said. "That too had most cunningly drawn pictures of the saints, but I have not seen the one you speak of."

"I met Flambard once," continued the monk. "When I bent to kiss his hand, my eyes were dazzled by the massive ring of gold on his finger, set with a single uncut sapphire, the size of which I am never likely to see again, not even on the King's hand."

He held out his hand and showed us the size of the stone, which would have hidden more than the width of his finger. Such a jewel I found hard to imagine.

"When they placed his body before the altar in the church, his coffin was draped with his two copes, one at each end. At the head, was his green cope embroidered with large griffons which he had himself used to cover the coffin of St Cuthbert when he brought the saint's body for burial in the church. At the foot was his other cope set with a myriad of small pearls, which shone like the rippling sea. They buried him with great pomp, such as would have pleased his arrogant spirit, though it contrasted strangely with the poverty of the habits of many of the monks who attended him that day. It might have done his soul much good had he been able to gaze out of his coffin to see them, and to know that for all his wealth he would be reduced to their poverty at the last. Is it not truly said that we bring nothing into this world, and assuredly can carry nothing out of it when we leave?"

There was a long silence when the monk had finished, while all present pondered his words. At length, Peter spoke.

"Next Sunday we shall celebrate a solemn Mass for the soul of the departed Ranulf called Flambard. A fiery torch he was, and many were burnt who came too near to him. Yet he had great vision, and for that we must give thanks."

On that day, those of us who could remember the man had mixed feelings. For my part, I was content to leave the verdict to the Day of Judgement, when all men's deeds will be laid bare and weighed in the balance before the Throne of Grace.

Other events, which were probably of more importance to the mighty, but which at the time had scarcely reached our ears, had been taking place. At the feast of Christ's birth at the end of '26, when we in the burgh were concerned more with keeping alive because of the famine that plagued the land, the King summoned all the great nobles of the land to his Court at Windsor. There he told them that since his son William had been so tragically drowned he now named his only remaining child, Maud, the recently widowed wife of Henry, the Holy Roman Emperor, as his heir to succeed him. Chief amongst those present who swore allegiance to Maud, were her uncle David, the Scots King, her half-brother Robert, Eorl of Gloucester, and her two cousins, Count Stephen and Henry of Blois, Abbot of Glastonbury. There were also many bishops led by William, the Archbishop of Canterbury.

News of these events was sparse, since it seems that Maud herself was soon despatched across the sea to France to wed Geoffrey, son of the Count of Anjou. Henry thus secured those lands as an ally to his cause in his French domains. It was rumoured that Count Stephen was angered that he was not himself named to succeed, for he had a good claim. Others said that there had never before been a Lady as ruler of this realm, and liked not the thought. Such matters, however, seemed of little consequence to us at the time.

It must have been a couple of years afterwards when we heard that the King agreed that William of Canterbury should call all the chief clergy together to persuade them that they should no longer keep their wives. The Archbishop said that what they did was against the laws of the church, and that they risked losing their churches and houses. However the move came to naught, for the King allowed all the clergy to return home as they were, which pleased them greatly, so that they were more willing to do the King's bidding thereafter.

The same year, Peter, our dean, brought us news that Bishop William Giffard of Winchester had died towards the end of January, and that the King had appointed his nephew, Henry of Blois, the Abbot of Glastonbury, to the see in his stead. With his friend Roger of Sarum as his Chief Justiciar it seemed to many that the King was gaining close control over the church in the realm.

When Pope Honorius died the same year, and there were two rival Popes elected in his stead, Dean Peter said that there was no-one to lead the church, and heresy thrived as never before. Whether God was angry in his Heaven over these events I know not, but on the eve of St Nicholas there was a great earthquake, the like of which none could remember, and the following year near Epiphany-tide, just before men went to their rest, the whole heavens towards the north were seen to be burning with a great fire, though it did not touch the earth and nothing was destroyed by it. Peter said it brought to his mind the Book of Daniel, where it is recounted how King Belshazzar of the Chaldeans saw on the walls of his palace the fiery writings, the night he was slain, and his kingdom destroyed by Darius King of the Medes.

Many folk feared what might befall us with such evil portents. When more men were called for to continue with the building of the remainder of the church, there was no shortage of volunteers, for men hoped to earn a place for themselves in Heaven thereby.

Nor did our troubles cease then. That same year, a murrain struck the beasts in the field, so that there were scarce enough to pull one plough in the whole burgh and men had to harness themselves to the plough to till their land. Our assart was scarce half tilled, and then only because Alric was able to lend us one of the three beasts he had left on Lord de Redvers' demesne. The swine suffered likewise and died where they stood, seized by some fell plague, their flesh rotting quickly so that it could not be eaten. All ours were lost, even the two we kept at the end of our land by the wall, which caused Isabel much grief, for she fed them by hand herself.

Furthermore within a month another pest took the fowls over all the realm. They were to be seen lying everywhere, limp upon the ground where they had fallen from their perches. Isabel saved but three of ours besides the cock-bird, but there were no eggs to be had until the next year when the new chicks had been hatched and grown.

Those that came from far afield told of the same disasters, and that famine once more stared many in the face. Because we had killed and cured some of our swine before they were struck down, we were able to eat and help others that were less fortunate than us. We also had fish to eat in plenty, and these we caught as often as we could, selling them to vills inland who were not blessed with rivers as we were. In this way we survived, and those who worked on the church were able to continue, if slowly, for there were none who did not feel the pangs of hunger. Rightly did Peter tell us that all this was God's punishment of men who had turned from Him with their quarrels and self-seeking.

The evil times eventually passed, the crops grew once more, beasts and fowls flourished in the field again and work continued on the church. On the south side, the walls rose higher towards the west end, and the beginnings of the cloisters began to take shape. The first part of this was set apart to be used as the school where the children could be taught. Being the sunniest part of the building, it was well favoured, and many of the priests began to use it too for their study and for copying their books. The result was that one or two of the older boys began to take an interest in what the priests were doing and to attach themselves to a particular priest so that they could learn their art.

One of these was our Martha's first child, whom she had named Hugh after me, and after our own lost son. It gave Isabel much pleasure to see our eldest grandchild drawn towards this difficult art. It seemed that he had the skill to draw too, for though he could not yet illuminate and colour the first letter of a passage, yet he could draw with great skill the designs round the edge of the pages, filling them with intricate patterns of foliage and animals, ready for others to colour when the time was ripe. Some of the ideas for his designs came from Isabel, who encouraged him to produce these beautiful things.

The best designs he copied from the magnificently illuminated Benedictional of Saint Ethelwold which had been kept in the Chapter House of the church at Winchester these last hundred and fifty years, and which Dean Peter said was the most beautiful thing he had ever seen. He took young Hugh and some of the other scribes to see it when he went to Winchester to buy cloth for the priests' habits at the annual fair of St Giles during the first weeks of September. When Hugh came back, he could not contain his excitement at the beauty of the book, and spent many hours telling us about it and drawing the creatures and flowers that it showed. Isabel particularly paid him close heed and tried to copy them herself, for she had some skill with a pen and inks.

As for me, I could only look on in wonder. I have no such skill in my fingers, though it is said that I can still cut and set a millstone as well as any within twenty leagues of the burgh.

It must have been on Trinity Sunday the next year that we heard that a large piece of land had been given to our church. As happened every year on that day, those who wished to make an offering to the church brought it to High Mass, where it was presented to Peter, who then placed it on the altar that it might be dedicated in charity to God's service.

Amongst those who came that year were Witro the falconer and his wife Adeline. Most of the gifts were in kind, such as sacks of grain, or small fowls or beasts, or sometimes a purse of silver. We brought nothing that year, for we had given thank-offerings for the safe delivery of each of our children and grandchildren in years past and there was nothing, other than our continued health and the success of our mill, of special note for which we wished to give thanks.

Several people had brought their offerings to Peter, and these already lay on or around the altar, when Witro the falconer with Adeline his wife, approached with a parchment which they laid in Peter's hands. We saw Peter bend forward to catch what they whispered to him as they handed him the roll.

We saw him start with surprise as he took it. He then quickly unrolled the scroll and cast his eye over what was written therein. When he came to the end, he allowed the scroll to roll up again and, bending forward, took the hands of each of them in turn. Then, still holding the scroll, we saw him ask them to kneel, which they humbly did, while Peter blessed them both,making the sign of the Cross over them as he did so. As they rose to go, Peter turned towards the altar and raised the parchment high above his head before placing it with all reverence in the centre of the altar. Isabel and I exchanged glances at this, each of us wondering what the gift could be, for by Peter's actions, it was no ordinary offering.

We fell in with Witro and Adeline as we left the church, for Isabel wished to speak to her about some simples that she needed for the grandchildren who were suffering the usual children's ailments. As we walked with them towards Stanpit, Goodwife Adeline confided in us.

"We are no longer young and have no children of our own, as you know. Witro and I have always meant that our land should go to the church when we die, that Masses may be said for our souls and the work of healing may continue. This last year, I have been telling Simon the infirmarer all that I know of remedies and cures and showing him how I make my infusions and decoctions. There is little more that I can show him now, for he is a quick learner and has understood all that I have told him."

She cast a questioning glance then at Witro, who nodded, before she continued.

"Witro and I decided that today it was time to give the church all our lands. We have a hide and a virgate between us and we find it hard to work the soil now at our age. This morning after Mass, we gave Peter the parchment we have had drawn up so that the land will now belong to the church. We will continue to live in our cott until we die, and such food as we require from our land we can have, but the priests will now work the land for the benefit of the church. Most of the land I had as a dowry from my father, Alwric the Small, though it was held under a mortgage made to Father by Godric the priest, which was transferred to Peter when he became dean. Now we have cancelled all the debt and he will no longer have to pay me for the land, and can use it how he will. We are happy to have done this, aren't we Witro?"

Isabel and I marvelled at such generosity. It was so like Goodwife Adeline, who had spent all her life healing and caring for others.

About this time too, we heard that Bishop Henry had given some hides of land to a small church in the vill of Sparkford, a mile or so this side of Winchester, so that a hospital, which was to be named Saint Cross, could be established to care for thirteen poor men who were too feeble to fend for themselves. In addition, there should be daily provided a dole of bread, ale and a pottage, for one hundred other poor men, who had only to come and knock at the door and ask, and they would be fed. Bishop Henry also gave this hospital of Saint Cross, as it soon became widely known, the tithes of several churches, including those of Twyford and Fareham, so the Hospital should never lack the means to continue its work. Dean Peter told us that Bishop Henry had written to Pope Innocent in Rome asking for his blessing on the venture, which he gladly gave.

Those who had cause to travel to Winchester and who had no money of their own, particularly the priests, would often thereafter call at the hospital and ask for the dole, which was always freely given, to their great comfort. Dean Peter said that he knew of no other place that fed so many freely. The fame of Saint Cross spread far and wide, so that there were many who heaped blessings on the head of

Henry of Blois for his charity. Though the church in our burgh and in many other vills never turned away any traveller or pilgrim who was in need, we had not the means to feed so many as Saint Cross.

Then at Lammas-tide in '35 there came a day when the sun was so darkened in the sky at midday that it seemed like a three-day-old moon. Stars were seen to be shining round the sun which had never before been seen at noon-time. No-one could give a reason for such an occurrence, but all men feared some dreadful calamity. Many, who had not been to a priest for longer than they could remember, confessed, fearing for their souls.

It was a few days after the feast of St Andrew that same year, when a ship came into the harbour bringing wines from Normandy, and also the sad news that Henry the King was dead. Great was our sorrow, for though he had spent much time in recent years out of this realm in his lands in France, his law had been good. Those whom he had left to rule the land, like Roger of Sarum and Henry of Winchester, of whom we heard much from Dean Peter, had done the King's bidding, for all were in awe of him and none dared disobey his commands for fear of retribution. Though some, like the fraudulent moneyers and certain of the great barons, had much to fear from his harsh punishments, ordinary folk like us had much to be thankful for, since men could live and work in peace without fear that their goods and beasts would be taken from them. It was also said that those who travelled could do so in safety even if their purse were full of gold.

Peter said a Mass for the soul of King Henry and prayed for the Empress Maud, whom now we should have as our Queen.

"She will have need of our prayers," he said, "for there has never been a lady set to rule over this land before. There is like to be trouble from some of the great men of the land, who care more for their own power than the peace of the realm."

"Amen to that," said Alric. "Baldwin de Redvers has sworn fealty to Maud so that we should have little to fear here. From what I have heard when I have been in Winchester, there are those who would back Count Stephen if he should lay claim to the crown. You rightly say that some do not like the idea of a woman ruling the land, and others would back Stephen merely to cause trouble, hoping thereby to gain from the confusion that would follow. Pray Heaven that we do not have wars such as have torn the King's French lands since the time Duke William came here."

Isabel, who was sitting with us, put her hand to her face in anguish.

"Is this really possible? We have lived in peace for as long as I can remember. We have had our share of famine and hardship and some of our folk have not returned from the fighting that they chose to seek, yet we have been spared the cruelty of war in these parts."

"Calm yourself, my love," I said, taking her hands in mine. "Let us hope that peace will continue."

However it seemed that this was not to be, for within a fortnight a merchant who had been in Winchester brought us grave news.

"Count Stephen of Blois has crossed from his lands in France, and ridden to London where the folk of that city have proclaimed him King."

We were struck dumb by such news, unsure if we could believe it and fearing what it might herald.

"How can that be?" I asked on hearing his news. "Surely they cannot go against the oaths taken by all the great men of the land who have sworn to accept Maud as the Lady of this realm?"

"Since London is the capital of the realm, they say that they can claim this right, but it means trouble for sure. I hear that there are many who will side with Stephen against Maud. At all events, he rode straight from London to Winchester, where I saw him. I heard that his brother Bishop Henry, and also Roger of Sarum, the dead King's Chief Justiciar, both welcomed him and did him homage as their King. I was told too that William de Pont de l'Arche, the Treasurer, handed to Stephen the dead King Henry's treasure chests, doing him homage likewise. Stephen is now fairly set to rule the realm - at least till Maud comes to try to take it from him - which she will have to do by force."

"I feared as much," said Isabel, turning to me with an anxious brow. "How safe is this burgh, do you think?"

"It should be secure enough with its walls and castle," replied Alric. "Baldwin de Redvers has sworn fealty to Maud and will withstand Count Stephen, I have no doubt, and will send men to help defend the burgh should the need arise. I think this place will be of little consequence to Stephen, since it is on the far side of the forest of Andret, though it does control the route from the sea to Sarum. We must look to our defences, I think. Do not be alarmed Isabel. It may all be smoothed over yet."

"I pray so for all our sakes," she murmured, and I saw that she offered up a prayer and crossed herself, so I put my arm round her to reassure her.

"De Redvers you say?" said the merchant. "Now there is one who seeks his own good. Though he has sworn allegiance to Maud, as you say, he has been prepared to put his own advantage above the oath he swore to the Lady Maud. I heard tell at Winchester that Count Stephen sought his support, for he has great lands in Wessex. Baldwin de Redvers was loath to break his oath to the Lady Maud, so he thought to bargain with Stephen. If Stephen would confirm Baldwin in all his lands, then he would support him in his claim to the crown."

"That seemed a reasonable offer," said Alric, scratching his chin. "He had much to lose which ever way he decided, and it makes sense to consolidate your position one way or the other."

"True enough, but did Count Stephen accept the conditions?" I asked.

"Not so. It seems he felt strong enough with the support he already had, not to have to bargain with de Redvers, so he turned down the offer, foolishly some said. This put de Redvers in a tight corner. Wisely he left Winchester before Stephen could make up his mind what to do with such a slippery fish, and rode fast towards his castle at Exeter. He is presumably holed up there now, waiting the outcome of events. As I came through the gate leaving Winchester, I heard rumours that Stephen was mustering a large troop of horse and men and intended to follow de Redvers to Exeter and lay siege to him there and take his lands by force."

"At least they are not coming here," I said. "If Stephen does overcome de Redvers at Exeter, no doubt he will take all his lands from him, and that will include this burgh too. Alric, will that make any difference to us do you think?"

"I doubt it. In Father's day, this burgh belonged to the King, so it may well do so again. We still have to pay the taxes and also find our tithes whoever is our overlord. More important is the character of the man, and whether he will treat us well or try to take more than his due. At least if the King is our lord, we can seek justice in his royal courts. As I see it, the greater danger lies in whether the Lady Maud and Count Stephen decide to settle their rival claims by battle. If that were to happen, who can tell if anywhere in the land will be safe. I pray that it does not come to that."

"So do we all," replied the merchant. "There was much unease in Winchester amongst the merchants and other folk whose livelihood depends on peace. It is all very well for great lords to posture and call out their men to fight. They make sure that the damage is done to other men's land. We are the ones who suffer loss and are killed. They have armour to protect them, and if they have the misfortune to be captured, they are worth more alive than dead, and so pay the ransom asked - which means we have to pay."

The rest of us nodded gravely as we took in this unwelcome prospect. At least we might escape attack since we were somewhat apart from the centre of power. Though we often cursed the forest of Andret with its harsh laws, and because it held little good land that could have been profitably farmed, it did offer us protection, for no baron was likely to try to claim it since it was the King's forest. To take it would bring down the full fury of the royal displeasure for little purpose, for most of the land was poor scrub, such as deer liked.

The weeks passed as we awaited the outcome of events. Gerald, the constable, had all the able-bodied men in the burgh practise with bow and sword and made a thorough inspection of the walls to see that they were in good repair. When he came to the section that I still had the care of in payment for our cott and land, he looked pleased.

"Would that we had more here like you, Hugh. This is the strongest part of the wall. I knew it would be good because you have always taken your duties seriously. I only wish that you had the care of the wall on the other side of the burgh, for it is from the east that any attack that may come will be launched. We have the castle to protect the gates by the bridges, and a bow-shot can cover much of the area, but the walls are not strong there. It would be better if they were stone-faced, for then it would be harder to scale them. Once the walls are scaled, the only defence is the castle. Set on its mound, it can command the ground beneath it and protect those within. The rest of the folk would be defenceless, for they cannot all take shelter within the castle: there is no room. Nor could we feed them.

Gerald stood silent for a while, then turned to face me.

"Hugh, I know that you work little in the mill nowadays, leaving it largely to your sons, Oswald and Simon. I have my hands full training men to use the bow and sword. If I gave you five men, could you see to the strengthening of the wall on the east side? I have spoken to Alnoth, and he will spare me five young masons who will do the work. You know how a wall should be built. Will you oversee facing the wall with stone for me? The masons will do the work, but they need a watchful eye kept on them. The safety of the burgh may be at stake, and I would like to know that I can trust the work will be well done."

I looked at Gerald in surprise. "You have more than a little fear that we may be attacked then."

"I had news this morning from Exeter that de Redvers is besieged and likely to have to surrender soon, for they have little water left. When that happens, if Henry of Blois has his way, even though he is a Bishop and so should be against taking life, de Redvers' life will surely be forfeit. Who can tell then what will happen to us?"

"I am no builder, as you know, but if I can help in the way you ask, then gladly will I do so. I am too old to do much work now, though I can still draw a bow and will help man the walls if need be. Perhaps, as you say, my most useful task now is to watch over others, to see that they work as they should. I would prefer to do the work myself rather than tell others what to do, the more so as they probably know more of the work that I do, but if that is what will help you most, then so be it."

He clapped me on the shoulder.

"I knew I could count on you, Hugh. It is you older folk who must set the example, and keep the others busy and calm. Isabel and your sister Emma are organising the women to tend the fields so far as they can, while the men are seeing to the strengthening of our defences. I do not mean this place to fall without a fight. If we can be seen to be strong, we may well survive, and those who would seek to take us may be persuaded to look elsewhere for easier pickings."

I took on the task I had been allotted, and Alnoth helped me when he could by visiting the walls. He would stand by me sometimes, whispering to me what he thought should be done, so that I seemed to speak with authority. Alric had charge of the gate-houses and with Osbern to help him, caused them to be be strengthened likewise. After a few weeks, the burgh took on the appearance of a well fortified place, such as we hoped might deter all but the most determined attackers. In this manner we hoped that we might be left in peace.

It was the next year before we heard news of Baldwin de Redvers again, for men travelled as little as possible during those troubled times. A ship struggled into the harbour and came with difficulty to the quay. The captain sought aid from the infirmarer for two of his crew who had arrow wounds.

"We were attacked by a ship manned by Baldwin de Redvers' men. They waylay all who try to pass between Vectis Isle and the mainland to the east. Little trade enters Portsmouth or Southampton these days and Count Stephen is being hard-pressed to gain supplies for Winchester."

"We thought de Redvers was holed up in Exeter and about to surrender, and that even his life might be forfeit," exclaimed Alwin, who was standing near.

The captain laughed. "So one might have thought, and so it would have been if Henry of Blois had had his way, but Count Stephen, it seems, is easily persuaded to change his mind. A sign of weakness if you ask me. I have little use for the Lady Maud, who by all accounts is high-handed and rude in her dealings with all men, but Stephen is little better, being of a weaker temperament. When de Redvers surrendered, as he was forced to do, being without water, Count Stephen allowed his men to march out of Exeter with their arms and join whomsoever they wished. Such foolishness is hard to imagine. As for de Redvers himself, he fled, pursued by Stephen, with all speed to Vectis Isle where he has great lands, as you know. He made good his escape and has for the last few months been preying on all ships plying their trade east of Vectis, since he assumes that they will be trying to succour Stephen."

The captain looked for signs of damage such as might have been received in a fight. Then he cast his eye towards the infirmary, seeking his two injured men.

"I had thought to enter Southampton by the western channel, and thought I had rounded the white Needle Rocks safely, when I found one of de Redvers' ships lying in wait for me. I could not flee north because of the shingle bank that blocks the way, so I had to cut and run westwards. Unfortunately, two of my crew were hit by their arrows, so rather than continue on to Poole, I sought refuge in this harbour. I took a gamble that de Redvers' ship would not know the channel here as well as I do and I was proved right."

"We have heard tell of attacks on ships round Vectis, but did not know who manned them. There are better pickings to the east, which is why they do not attack what tries to come in here. Ships heading for Poole keep well to the west so are safe enough too. Ah! Here come your men. They seem in good heart now. How go your wounds, men? Has our infirmarer tended them well?"

The sailors came forward with Simon the infirmarer between them. They looked pleased enough, for they were grinning broadly.

"I have never before had such treatment for my wounds," cried the elder of the two. "Before Simon here drew out the arrow, he gave me a draught. Afterwards he bathed the wound and covered it with a soothing ointment given him by a local healer. I wish I had known of her before today. It would have saved me much grief and pain that I had from earlier wounds. How about you, Martin? How does your wound feel? It is your first, I think."

The younger of the two sailors, who was little more than a lad with hardly a hair yet upon his chin, tried to look brave.

"I do as well as you, I think, though I can still feel where the arrow entered my shoulder. I am glad that it is no longer there, for it pained me sorely till it was drawn."

"You looked like half an angel with the arrow sticking out of your back," laughed the captain. "You only needed one in the other shoulder and, with your hairless chin, you could have joined the Heavenly choir if we could have found you a harp."

We all laughed, and Martin, looking a little sheepish at first, took it in good part.

"At least I would have been in better company there than joining you stoking the flames of Hell."

"Well said," cried the captain. "We'll make a sailor of you yet. Tell me, Master Simon, what is this balm you have used on these men's hurts? Is it some secret decoction, or may we learn its properties?"

"No doubt it is one of Goodwife Adeline's balms," I said. "Is that not so, Simon? I hear she has been teaching you how to use her remedies."

"Very true, Hugh. The draught I gave them was one of hers too. It dulls the pain wonderfully for a while, but does no lasting harm if taken rarely and only when the pain is likely to be severe."

Simon turned to the captain before continuing.

"I will give you a phial of the draught, but be warned: used wrongly, it can dull the brain and cause most hellish dreams, such as I would wish on no man. Put no more than ten drops in a beaker of water and use it only twice: once when you draw the shaft or set the bone, and once a day later. That way no harm can come and the worst pain will be eased. I will give you some of the balm I used to dress the wounds too, for it will help to keep them sweet. Be sure to keep the wounds covered for a week that the healing may do its work, and use the limb as little as possible during that time. That way you will be returned to full vigour much sooner."

"What, are we to be cosseted and treated like weaklings for a week? Well, Martin, if that is our fate, let us make the most of it. Come sit here by me, and let this good priest bring us his best ale and meat. I am sure such things will help our wounds to heal wonderfully."

The older sailor burst into a huge grin and, putting his good arm round young Martin, who entered readily into the spirit of the game, he sat him down on the ground beside him and looked expectantly round at the rest of us. The captain roared with laughter.

"Why, you rogue! Did you think that I would let you get away with such idleness, and after these good people have treated us with such kindness? On your knees, man, and grovel before the priest here and beg his forgiveness. If he does not give you a score of 'Pater Nosters' as penance for your sins I will order them myself. How say you, Master Simon, is that not a just punishment for his sins?"

Simon looked taken aback at first, not knowing whether the captain jested or was in earnest. Then he saw his grinning face.

"It would be just, but he has suffered enough pain with his wound to pay the price of his sins, so I will grant him absolution this time. Come here then and kneel, that I may absolve you."

Realising that the priest had got the better of him, the sailor knelt before Simon, who made the sign of the Cross over his bowed head. As he rose, he took the priest's hand.

"You are a good man, Master Simon, and I would not insult your cloth, for you have treated us both most kindly and we are much in your debt. I beg you pray for us when the storms blow, that we may be brought safely to land. When I come again, I will hope to offer silver at your altar that your hands may continue to heal others as they have me."

"Thank you. I will pray for your ship and all who sail in her, that God may hold you in His hand that you come to no harm. I would not have given you absolution had I not known you spoke only in jest. Now I must go and prepare a phial of the draught and a pot of the balm as I promised, though I pray that you may not have cause to use them. Pax Vobiscum," Simon added as he turned to go to his infirmary.

"There goes a good man," remarked the captain.

Alric nodded. "We are blessed with some good priests here. With the wonderful simples and balms that Goodwife Adeline has shown Simon how to prepare, we find that we have less sickness than one might expect. Now that your men have been attended to, will you eat with us? You cannot set sail till the tide rises again, for your ship will never cross the bar. Besides, I would see what you have on board. Perhaps we can trade with you."

We all repaired to Alric's hall, and before the ship departed the next day, there was much exchange of goods to our mutual profit. As we stood at the quay watching the sailors make ready the sails, the captain came ashore once more.

"When next I pass this way, I will call again and bring with me such things as I know you will want. Till then, farewell, and let us hope for all our sakes, that peace may soon return to the land - and to the seas."

The ship departed and life continued much as before, though with the ever-present threat of an attack by the supporters of either Count Stephen or the Lady Maud. Alric and I agreed that it was good we had such a constable as Gerald to make sure the burgh was well fortified. The more so as rumours began to reach us that there had been uprisings in various parts of Wessex. Such few travellers as passed through brought tales of attacks on Dorchester, Corfe's great castle, and Wareham, with its little port.

As we sat by Alric's hearth one evening, he looked gloomy.

"It seems, Hugh, that the Lady Maud is bent on making as much trouble for Count Stephen as she can. Any baron who thinks that he may benefit from unrest, seems to be taking her part, hoping, no doubt, to gain lands as a result."

"If you want my opinion," I replied, "it was a pity that Count Stephen did not accept Baldwin de Redvers' conditions for supporting his claim and confirm him in his lands. I know too little of the rival claims and arguments to know who has the better claim to the crown of this realm. It is peace that we need, and a strong ruler, such as Henry was. He may have been harsh, but he was just."

"True enough. By all accounts the choice lies now between a weak King, who changes his mind depending on whom he spoke to last, and an arrogant and haughty Queen, who still thinks she is an Empress, though she has been widowed some years now, and who insults those to whom she should be looking for most help. The Lady Maud may have been named by Henry to succeed him, and those who swore an oath to her should be bound by it, but she has brought the troubles on her own head by not being here when she was needed, and by her treatment of those who thought to support her. Nor will she find it easy to persuade Englishmen to accept her as Queen. It is not in our nature to be ruled by a woman. Has ever a Queen ruled this land, Hugh?"

I scratched my head and thought, and looked at the others, for I could not remember hearing of such a thing.

"If what you say of Lady Maud is true, then she will find it hard to draw any great following to her banner. We are not used to Queens here."

"Agreed," mused Alric. "I suppose Henry, knowing Count Stephen's weaknesses, thought he had made her claim such by the oaths he extracted from those around him. A pious hope it seems now, and we are left to suffer its results. We should be more than ever thankful that the forest of Andret separates us from Winchester and that seat of power."

There was a knock at the door and Dean Peter entered, looking worried.

"What brings you here at this time?" asked Alric. "Come, sit beside me and take a horn of ale. By the look on your face, you have need of one."

"My thanks to you. Yes indeed. More troubles seem to be mounting about our heads, and though they affect the church most, yet I think they will have wider consequences."

"Why, what has happened now?" I asked.

Dean Peter took a long draught from the beaker that Alric had handed to him and sighed.

"You know that Henry of Blois was hoping, no - expecting - to be elected Archbishop of Canterbury to fill the see left empty for almost three years. I have now heard that not he, but Theobald, who was Abbot of Bec in France, has been given the see with Count Stephen's agreement, supported by the rival Beaumont family. To make matters worse, Pope Innocent has made Henry of Blois his Legate, so that Canterbury has to take orders from him. No-one has sole charge of the church now."

Peter put his hand on his tonsure and stroked it. A worried look crossed his face as he looked round the table.

"Worse still, a priest has just arrived from Winchester to say that Count Stephen has arrested Bishop Roger of Sarum also Alexander of Lincoln, and would have taken Nigel of Ely too, had he not managed to escape. These are the men who controlled the realm in Henry's day when he was away dealing with his lands in France, and who have continued to do so for Count Stephen. Though their loyalty may have been suspect, yet to act as Stephen has done must surely weaken his position. It is bound to turn many of the strongest in the land against him and probably throw them into the Lady Maud's lap. Worse still for Stephen, Henry of Blois, his own brother, has been turned against him."

There was a shocked silence as we heard this news.

"When did all this happen?" I asked.

"It seems it has been unfolding these last months but news has only just reached me," Peter said. "Few venture abroad these days if they do not have to, preferring to keep within the safety of their walls. Even priests do not travel if they can avoid it, for they risk being taken as spies, even though they be about God's business. Men do not trust those they do not know, and even those they know may not be safe, as the bishops are learning to their cost. The priest also brought a rumour that the Lady Maud is expected to come to these shores soon with an army."

"That will mean war in the land," cried Emma, who had been growing increasingly agitated. "Will any be safe?"

Alric put his hand on her arm to quieten her.

"Have no fear, my love. We are secure enough here."

He turned towards me, and I could see that there was something on his mind.

"Do you think we should make plans to move some of the stock, and perhaps those least able to help themselves over to Hengist's headland? The land is well defended by the double ditches, and is not likely to be attacked since it has no military advantage these days. It would be a safe haven for those who shelter there. Besides, it would free the burgh of the worry of protecting them should there be an attack. What think you?"

All eyes turned towards me then as I considered this new plan of Alric's.

"Let us keep this close for the moment till we have put the matter to Gerald and seen what he thinks. I am inclined to think that there is sense in the suggestion." I sat silent for a while as an idea began to take shape in my head.

"Should the town be attacked and fall, which Heaven forbid, then no doubt everything would either be put to the torch or stolen. Those who escaped with their lives would be hard put to it if they had lost all their beasts too. Yes, I would be in favour of making plans to move the best beasts, and perhaps some of the seed corn, to safety on Hengist's headland. It could be well hidden there, for there is plenty of woodland to use to make pens to keep in the stock. Only a few men would be needed to tend the animals. That way, at least we would be able to rebuild our livestock. As for the sick and weak and the children, would they not be safer in the church, Peter? They could seek sanctuary there surely? No man would dare touch them there."

Peter looked round at the rest of us.

"The church is open to all men at all times, but I will not have it made into a fortress to be defended with sword and bow. Besides, it is still open at the west end where the wall is not yet built and would offer little if any protection against attackers."

Alric looked startled.

"Are you then saying that you would not grant shelter to those who might seek a refuge if the burgh is being taken? What will the priests do?"

"You misunderstand me, Alric. The church is open to any who seek to enter it and will always give sanctuary to those who are fleeing from their enemies. If they are felons, then we priests would try to persuade them to give themselves up to be tried according to the laws of the land. If they are fleeing persecution, then we priests would try to bar the way to those who wish to maltreat them. Remember that the church has the power in dire cases to excommunicate those who flout its teachings. To answer your question, yes, we would give sanctuary to the the sick, the old and the children, and any who come to us in peace."

Peter turned to the constable and looked severely at him.

"Do not think that you can use the church as a last place of resistance, Gerald, if the walls be breached and the bailey falls. The church is a House of Prayer not a place of war."

"I understand," replied Gerald. "Would you not have a better chance of sheltering those who might seek refuge in the church if you completed the west wall? It has been long since any work was done on the building now. I wonder that you have not made greater efforts to complete it. One would have thought you would have stood a better chance of protecting your flock if the only entrance to your sheep-fold were by the door. At the moment you would be hard put to it to keep out the wolves, I think. To my mind, a stout wall is a better protection than an overfed priest, even though he may threaten excommunication. Besides, would such a threat carry any weight these days when Canterbury and the Papal Legate support opposite sides? I think not."

Peter looked shocked at this outburst, and we could all see that the shaft had gone home. Indeed there had been little work done on the church for some years, and it was a fact that the west end was still quite open, so that the wind and rain swept in at will. Many folk had long been grumbling that they had to stand in the cold and wet at Mass, while the priests, who stood at the eastern end, were well protected from the elements. Though Peter countered these complaints with excuses that there was no stone, or else he could not afford to pay the builders, it was generally supposed that most of the money that should have been used for the building had gone into the bellies and pockets of him and his fellow priests in recent years.

Many of them lived far too well, skimped their Offices and took little care of our souls and, apart from Simon, ignored the sick. Though Alric and I and some of the other elders in the burgh had thought of making a protest to Henry of Blois at Winchester, for he was our Bishop, by common consent we agreed that there was little purpose in doing so in these troubled times. I shot a glance at Alric, and could see that he thought as I did, for he took up the same argument.

"Gerald is right, Peter. I agree that you are here to do God's work. Surely you could do it more effectively in a complete church. It is written in the Gospels surely: 'Suffer the little children to come unto me and forbid them not', but you would do them no kindness if by gathering them into your church you only made it easier for them all to be abused and slaughtered."

There was a stunned silence as Alric let his words sink in. No-one broke the silence, least of all Peter who looked thoroughly abashed. After a while, Alric turned to me.

"We are right to suggest Hengist's headland as a safe refuge. For the moment it must be so for both men and beasts, since as Gerald says, the church offers no protection in its present form, despite Peter's protestations. We must tell folk so when we explain our plans for their defence. Heaven grant that no attack comes before we have made our preparations. As for you, Peter, it seems to me that the best place for you and your priests is on your knees before the altar to pray for our souls, for you offer us no other help."

Peter raised his hands to try to quieten the rest of us, for he could see that tempers were rising.

"Alric, Alric, be not over-hasty. You do not know the difficulties that we priests have to face. Money is short and stone hard to come by, particularly now that Baldwin de Redvers controls the sea passage from Vectis Isle and our quarries. Be assured, we will do our best to complete the west end as soon as we can."

"Have you not recently received a hide and a virgate of land from Witro and Adeline?" I asked, pressing home the advantage we had gained. "Why should Baldwin's raiders attack a ship carrying stone? They would have no use for it, and could use their time to better advantage attacking merchant vessels. Such arguments carry no weight."

I turned to Gerald.

"Do you not think that you and Alric and I should take a boat to Hengist's headland tomorrow to scout out the best place to build a pen for the stock? We must look to see where best we can have shelters built for the sick and elderly, where they will be hidden. You are surely right, they will be safer there than in the church as it now is. There will be plenty of grumbling amongst those who will have to take shelter on the headland, but better that than being slaughtered. Perhaps later, if Peter can complete the west walls, we may be able to revise the plans, but I think it will be best if we say nothing to anyone until we have our plan fully worked out."

I rose then.

"Come Isabel, it is time for us to leave. Gerald and Alric, shall we meet by the mill tomorrow at sun-up and take my boat across to the headland? We shall need a full morning to find the best places and to mark them out for the stock pens and where the shelters are to be built."

I winked at them both, and as we left I put my arm round Isabel and gave her a squeeze. She smiled at my cunning. As I passed Emma, I saw her eyes twinkle with amusement, for she well knew what we were trying to do.

Next day we met as arranged. We were kept waiting for some time for Gerald to arrive. When at last he approached the boat, which was tied up beside the mill, I saw by his grin that he had something to tell us.

"What kept you?" asked Alric. "We have been waiting for you this past half hour."

"A worthwhile meeting I think. Just as I was leaving, Peter hurried up, anxious to speak privately with me. You caught him on the raw last night, for he was full of excuses this morning and promises too. He has undertaken to hire as many men as will be needed to complete the west wall as quickly as possible. It seems that he has suddenly found money to buy stone and other materials and also to hire ships to bring it from Vectis. It was only with difficulty that I kept a straight face and congratulated him on his good fortune. He begged me not to tell anyone of our plans to make a safe haven on the headland for he was sure he could complete the wall long before any attack might come."

"He has changed his tune then. What did you reply to that?" I asked.

"I told him that we were going as we had agreed to scout out the land this morning, but need not make our plans public yet. After all, as I told him, it would be better if we kept the plans secret for a while, lest some spy learn of them and so render them useless. This seemed to satisfy him. I took a promise from him also that work would start this day using what stone is already lying about."

"The foundations have been dug out and filled with stone these many years, so that all is ready to raise the walls," said Alric. "There has been no excuse for his idleness in progressing the work, other than his greed and easy living."

The morning passed quickly enough as we wandered over the lower parts of the headland. There were good sheltered places where stock could be penned and yet not be seen from across the harbour. There was grass in plenty too. If we needed to drive the beasts over there, they could remain for some weeks and still be well fed. We also found sheltered places where huts could be built if need be, and marked them out. Thus satisfied, we re-crossed the harbour.

As we neared the quay by the mill, Alric looked at Gerald and me.

"This matter should be kept secret for the moment, for two reasons. First, if folk came to hear of it they might take fright and flee from a danger that is not yet upon us. Second, as you have rightly said, Hugh, if our plan became known outside, any ill-willed attacker might well go first to the headland and seize the cattle and other livestock that we have hidden there, before settling down to besiege the burgh with well-filled bellies. Gerald, have you two men whom you can trust absolutely to keep silent, who can help the three of us build the stock pens? I think Hugh and I can speak for our brothers Alnoth and Osbern to help too, and no word of all this would pass any of our lips. How long do we need to complete the work, Hugh? Two weeks, do you think?"

I thought for a while, weighing up what needed to be done. First, to cut down suitable small trees to make the fence posts and fix them into the ground. Then, set branches to them to make a secure enclosure that cattle would not break down. Finally, to built simple shelters for those who would tend the beasts, where they could be dry and warm, perhaps for some weeks.

"We must build a small storehouse too, for grain and other food that those in charge of the beasts will need. Should we not also make a store for some seed corn? If the burgh be put to the torch - which Heaven forbid - we may need seed to sow the fields again. Yes, I think two weeks should suffice. We have to remember that if we all are seen going daily across the harbour, questions will be asked by those whose eyes are open. We shall have to be seen about our usual business, too."

Gerald nodded approvingly.

"You seem to think of everything. It were best to allow two weeks as you say, Hugh. I will undertake to find two men I know I can trust. They will keep silent, for it is the safety of their own families that will be at stake too."

"This brings to mind the time, many years ago, and long before you came here Gerald, when Flambard wished to build our great church on the top of Catherine's hill. You have heard the story, I am sure, how the stone that had been laboriously carted up the hill during the day was found back on the present site the next morning." Alric smiled then. "Have you never questioned, Gerald, how this came about?"

"I had always supposed it to be some miracle. Certainly that is what folk here have always told me. Do you know otherwise?"

I shot a glance at Alric, and we both smiled, for none had ever revealed the secret of what really happened.

"I remember old Godric saying once that God liked to work his miracles with man's aid."

Gerald looked at us closely then, and a slow smile spread across his face.

"Who am I to gainsay what the priest has said? One thing I do know, it would have been a disaster if the church had been built on top of that hill. The burgh would have died long since, and any new one built on that hill would not have held more than a few days, for it would have had no water. Where the church stands now adds strength to the burgh and offers a safe refuge in time of danger - or it will do, when Peter finally bestirs himself."

"So be it then. Hugh and I will start to make the enclosure for the beasts tomorrow, with Alnoth and Osbern joining us as soon as they are able. Bring your two men as soon as maybe. It were better if you came by land, over the ford at Iford. It would not do for too many of us to be seen taking the same route."

This we did, and, in a little over the two weeks I had thought, the work was completed to our satisfaction. We felt that we could sleep easier in our beds, knowing that we had done all we could to safeguard the continued life of the burgh.

Meantime, Peter had bestirred himself to such effect that there was now a large host of men busily working on the walls at the west end of the church. Nor was Alnoth able to give us much help, for he was needed, as master mason, to set the stones on the facing of the wall. This was to our advantage, for all talk was now on the progress of the church, and no-one noticed when we were absent on the headland.

In six months the walls had progressed so far that it was possible to fix the arch over the western door. The doorway that gave onto the churchyard at the western end of the north wall was also completed. Osbern, meanwhile, had been busy with his carpenters making the doors that would be fixed at both entrances, so that before work had to cease when the weather became frosty and foul the church was secure, with solid doors at all its entrances.

At Mass on the Sunday after the doors had been hung, Peter stood up and addressed the congregation.

"You know that we live in troubled times, and that many places have suffered attack from evil men who seek their own ends rather than the good of the realm. This place is well protected, with its walls and castle set high on its motte. Gerald has trained you to protect yourselves too, should an attack be made against us. Many had thought to seek refuge within the church, should calamity strike and the walls fall, although until now the church could have offered little protection, for the west wall was not built. Now, as you can see, we are secure, and the doors are set, so that all who enter may feel safe. I have hastened the work forward as fast as possible because of the danger that may threaten us. The west wall will continue to rise until it is at the full height to take the rest of the roof, but remember, this is a church not a fortress. Men may seek refuge here, but not fight from it. Holy church will protect those who come for succour, but will not act as a bastion from which to attack a foe. Now go in peace, and may Heaven protect us all from our enemies."

Men were heartened by this, and felt more secure, though Alric and I could only hope that their faith would not be ill-founded.

Chapter 19 1140–1148

The start of the new decade brought news of several deaths, most of which affected us in the burgh only indirectly. Roger of Sarum died and Count Stephen took control of the see himself. We heard too that Thurstan, who held the archbishopric of York, had also died, which led to a dispute as to who should succeed there too.

More important to us were the deaths of Dean Peter, and Goodwife Adeline and her husband Witro the falconer. Witro was renowned for his skill at training birds for the chase and had in his day provided falcons for the King. There was universal mourning at the passing of Adeline, for there were few in the area whose lives she had not touched, either with her healing balms or by kindly words. Isabel and I particularly owed her a great debt, for she had often helped us over our family's ailments and had been present at most of their births.

There were few however, who mourned Peter's passing. Once he had raised the walls at the west end of the church to the height of the door archways and made the whole building secure from attack, money for any further work dried up, and it was noticed that the priests reverted to their old idle habits once more. There seemed little that we could do to restart the building work. Alric tried without success to see Henry of Blois at Winchester. Gerald, as constable, failed likewise to see Baldwin de Redvers, who was still close-kept in his castle on Vectis, hampering Count Stephen were he could while adding little if any support to the Lady Maud.

After Peter had been buried, most of the priests became even more idle, often even ceasing to say their Offices. Only Simon, who cared for the sick as far as he was able, and Robert, whom Henry of Blois had appointed as the first vicar of the church a few years previously, seemed to have any interest in the souls of the folk who lived in Twynham and the small vills round about to which they were supposed to minister. These two finally asked Alric to call a meeting of the older folk, to see what could be done. There it was decided that Robert, Alric, Gerald and I should journey to Winchester to see Henry of Blois and beg him to appoint a new dean who would once more take charge of the church, to complete it, and perhaps more importantly, rouse the priests from their lethargy to fulfil their Offices as they should.

The four of us made the journey, not without some trepidation. Rumour was rife of bands of marauding soldiers who supposedly supported Count Stephen or the Lady Maud, but who, if the truth be known, sought only their own advantage. We were glad enough to be able to rest at the Hospital of Saint Cross a mile outside the gates of Winchester during the the weeks that we had to wait before we could gain an audience with Henry of Blois. Though we paid for our lodging at first, in the last few days our silver ran out, and we were not too proud to seek the dole of bread, ale and a bowl of pottage, which was freely given to all who asked. Amongst those who were fed, we met several who had once been rich, but who had lost all, either in the famine of recent years, or in the fighting. Their state was in many cases most pitiful.

As we finally left the hospital, I spoke to the Master, one Robert of Limesia, who devoted his life tirelessly to feeding the many starving folk.

"You have cared for the four of us with the utmost Christian charity, never questioning us to know if we were vagabonds or truly destitute, and we all thank you for it."

"I know your errand, how you are waiting to see Henry of Blois so that you may further God's work in your burgh. I have only been playing my part in the scheme of things by feeding you. I would have done so even if you had been sturdy beggars, for by our foundation I can turn none away who come and ask for food."

"When next one of us passes this way, we promise to bring a purse of silver as recompense for the hospitality you have given us, for there are many in greater need than us who will make calls on your charity and we would like to further your work."

Robert of Limesia smiled and bade us go with him into his small study. There he found parchment and a quill, and began to write. When he had finished, he sealed it, and handed it to Robert, our vicar.

"Take this with you, and give it to Henry of Blois when you see him. He founded this hospital and I have told him in this parchment of your errand and your promised gift to this place. Is it not written 'Cast your bread upon the waters and it shall return to you a hundred fold'? You have only the interests of your burgh and its church at heart. May your efforts receive the success they deserve. Pax Vobiscum", he said, and made the sign of the Cross over the four of us as we rose to leave.

At last Henry of Blois gave us audience. He read the parchment that we brought from Master Robert of Limesia, and listened to what we had to say before turning to me first.

"You are Hugh, the miller of the church mill, I take it? It was you whom Robert, my Hospital Master, says gave him thanks for his hospitality and offered a purse of silver to further my work there."

"True, my Lord, but I was only the spokesman for the four of us. We all felt the same and will help to fill the purse we promised."

"Quite so," the Bishop replied, "and likewise I take it that you are all four concerned for the welfare of your burgh and its church. At least that is what my

Hospital Master reports, for he has listened to you over this last three weeks while you have been waiting for this audience and has noted your genuine concern."

We all started, fearful of what might have been reported about us.

"Have no fear," said Henry, "Robert of Limesia is no spy. He commends you all to me, and hopes that I can find a good man to be your dean. I have had tales brought to me of Peter's idleness, but other matters were of more importance than that at the time. Now he is gone, I will see what I can do. You have a noble building in your burgh and it deserves to be finished quickly. Tell me. I have heard tell that you have some among you that can illuminate a manuscript well. Is this so?"

"Rodric, who teaches the children, is skilled at the art," said Robert. "He is passing on his skills to some who have the talent. There is one lad in particular, Hugh by name, the grandson of Hugh the miller here who has such skill in his fingers that it makes us all wonder at the beauty of his drawing. Is that not so, Hugh?" Robert turned to me as he spoke.

"My Lord, such talent as he possesses does not come from me for sure, but from my wife Isabel, who can draw most lifelike birds and beasts. She has passed on her skills to young Hugh, who seems to have further improved them. He drew his inspiration to attempt such work after seeing the beautiful 'Benedictional Of Saint Ethelwold' in the Chapter House here."

"Ah, yes," replied Henry of Blois, nodding with satisfaction. "I doubt there is a finer book anywhere in the land, except perhaps the beautiful Saint John's Gospels in Durham which Ranulf Flambard showed me once. You say your grandson tries to copy such works? He must be very skilled then."

"I can vouch for that," added Alric, "and from where his cunning comes. Hugh's wife Isabel is my sister, and I have always known her to be gifted in such things."

"Then you must both encourage the lad in his work, for it is to the greater glory of God, is it not?"

Henry of Blois paused a while, looking at the parchment that he still held before addressing us again.

"I have someone in mind who could be your dean. But tell me first, and be truthful mind, whom do you support in these present troubles: my brother Count Stephen, or the Lady Maud?"

We had not thought to be asked such a question, and I for one was taken aback by it. Alric was the first to recover.

"My Lord, for longer than any can remember, Twynham has been a Royal burgh, or else part of the lands of one who supported the King. The great Book of Domesday records that the burgh belonged to the blessed Edward, before Alfred the Saxon became King. Then Duke William was our lord, and after him his two brothers, William and Henry. King Henry gave the burgh to our present lord's father, Richard de Redvers, and through him we owed allegiance to the King. These present troubles have so far passed us by, though we have made sure that the burgh is well protected to withstand any who may think to attack us. We owe allegiance to Baldwin de Redvers as our lord, but have not seen him for many years and do not know which side he presently supports. First, though, we must be loyal to the ruler of the whole realm, and in the last resort must do his bidding unless force prevents us."

"This is true, my Lord," added Gerald. "As Constable of the Keep, I swear that I will hold the burgh for so long as I am able against all attack. Since we do not know the Lady Maud, who has not been seen in the realm until recently, and since Baldwin de Redvers has been driven out to Vectis Isle and seems to be harrying our coast causing us all harm, it would seem that we should support Count Stephen."

"Wisely said."

Henry of Blois twisted his bishop's ring round his finger thoughtfully before he spoke again.

"De Redvers is likely to find his lands forfeit if he continues to hinder my brother."

He paused again, looking closely at us through half-closed eyes.

"I can count on you to hold Twynham for Stephen then, should the Lady Maud try to take it? Not that I think such a thing is likely, for her forces have not come this far south yet."

The four of us exchanged glances, and each of us nodded our agreement before Alric spoke for all.

"My Lord, these matters are beyond our understanding. Twynham is a small burgh, and we only wish to live our lives in peace, farm our lands, and trade as we may. Most news of the events of which you speak come to us at secondhand from ships that enter our harbour or from travellers who pass through. As bailiff of my lord's demesne, I see to it that his crops are gathered and his rivers yield the fish they should. The dues from the weekly market recently granted to Eorl de Redvers I gather and hold till I can render an account to him. Goods which come down by the gentle River Avon from Sarum and beyond we hold in the burgh until they can be shipped away. Likewise, what is brought in from across the seas we hold till the merchants to whom they belong can arrange for their collection. Often goods were passed back up the meandering Avon for your late brother Prelate, Roger at Sarum. The Stour stream, though it joins the Avon not a bow-shot from the mill, flows too swiftly for two-way trade. Thus we trade and live our lives in peace with one another."

Alric ceased speaking, and looked carefully at Henry of Blois. His hooded eyes gave nothing away, though he did not seem displeased by what he heard. Before he continued, Alric looked questioningly at Robert and me, and we both nodded our agreement.

"Those who offend against the King's laws, we punish according to the laws which King Henry and those before him laid down. We take a View of Frankpledge as we should, and I can record that the stocks, pillory and ducking stool are rarely used, for most men would rather live their lives peaceably. The reeve and hayward see to it that the fields are properly tilled, and our beasts are turned out into the pasture at the proper seasons to graze and dung the land. Great matters of state we know little of, preferring to leave them to those who understand those things. As I have said, as a Royal burgh, Twynham has always been loyal to our sovereign. Count Stephen has been crowned as King, so we will support him, as we hope Baldwin de Redvers will too."

Alric held Henry of Blois' eye while he spoke, and when he had finished, he continued to face him as a equal, great man though he was. The bishop averted his eyes first and, by the smile that twitched the corner of his lips, he seemed content with what he had heard. At length, he turned to Robert, who, as a humble vicar, had remained silent in the presence of so great a churchman.

"Now, Robert, you have heard what has been said, what have you to add?"

"My Lord, everything that has been said is true. Great matters of state are beyond us, and though we hear of wars and rumours of wars, so far they have not come too close as to cause us any great concern. For my part, I have enough to do caring for the souls of those in the burgh, saying my Offices, and doing what I can to further the building of our great church, though I have little enough support from my brother priests."

"Ah, yes: tell me about that, and how the building progresses."

"By fits and starts, I fear, my Lord. For many years it progressed well enough. I would not speak evil of the dead, but during the time of Peter little enough was done, until with the threat of attack he found himself forced to complete the walls at the west end, at least to the height of the door arches, so that the building could become a sanctuary should the burgh be attacked. Since then nothing further has been done and men grow restless, feeling that all their labour over the years is being counted as of little worth. It is not so, my Lord. It is a fine building and, when complete, will compare well with the beautiful church here in Winchester, though it is not as large."

This brought a fresh smile to Henry of Blois' lips.

"What, Priest, would you compare your church to ours? It seems that all you Twynham folk have an over-large opinion of yourselves."

Robert blushed deeply.

"I did not mean to decry your fine church, my Lord," he stammered. "I shall do penance for my sin of arrogance."

He hung his head in shame and fear lest he had spoilt our chances of finding the new dean we so sorely needed.

"Take it not so hard, Robert. I do not blame you for wishing to further your great enterprise, and I hear it is indeed going to be truly magnificent. Believe me, I am as keen as you for it to be finished so that God's work may be the better furthered. Tell me, did I not hear that something miraculous occurred when the roof was being raised?"

"I believe so, but that was before I came to Twynham, my Lord. Alric and Hugh can tell you more accurately than I what took place."

Henry turned a questioning glance to us, so we told him how one particular beam had been found to be too short when it was first raised, and how the next day it was seen to be firmly fixed in its rightful place. I also told him how my brother Osbern had shown me where the Carpenter, who had so impressed Thurstan with his workmanship, had worked at the bench beside him, and how on the day that beam was found to be raised, the Carpenter was not to be found and was never seen again.

"Most interesting," Henry mused, stroking his chin. "It confirms the tale I had heard, but you have added more detail, for which I thank you. Can you offer any explanation?"

"My Lord, we cannot," I replied. "I questioned Osbern closely many times about that beam, for he is a master carpenter, and told me that he had often spoken with that other Carpenter. Indeed, I heard Him speak myself once. The tale He told reminded Isabel my wife of a story from the Gospels. What struck me most was His voice, which compelled one to listen. Never have I heard the like of it for strength and conviction."

Once more Henry nodded, seeming to be deeply interested in what we told him.

"What of your works of healing? I have heard tell that many people come to your burgh with sickness and leave made whole again. Is this true?"

"We are blessed with a wonderful spring of water, which seems to cure ailments of the eyes," said Alric. "Indeed, when Hugh and I were lads, at the time the Domesday Record was being made, we sent three flagons of the water back to Walkelin, who held this see before you. For Gilbert the Clerk, who was compiling the record, said that he suffered from his eyes. We never heard if it was successful."

"So that is where the water came from. Yes, it worked well, and Walkelin was well pleased. When Walter Giffard, who succeeded him, asked about the source of the water, none could remember. I am glad to know of it. You must tell me where this spring is. I have heard of other cures being done in your burgh too. Some say they are miraculous. Is this so?"

"That I cannot say, my Lord, but there was an old goodwife who lived about a mile outside the burgh near to the well where the pure water is. Sadly, she died last year, and is sorely missed. She had some wonderful decoctions and infusions which seem to cure most ills. In her old age, she had been instructing Simon, our infirmarer, in her remedies so that they will not be lost. He says they are truly wonderful in their effect, and their fame has spread far and wide. I have good reason to be thankful to her, for it was she who, when I was just a lad, first saw my love for Isabel who later became my wife. She bade me tend her as I would a budding flower. This I have tried to do, and she has bloomed to such glory that I still wonder at it."

I blushed and hung my head in confusion as I spoke, for these were more rightly matters kept as between a man and wife alone. It seemed that Henry of Blois drew all the truth from us that day.

At length, he rose and called for a clerk to bring parchment and a quill. While he was coming, he turned to us again.

"You have all impressed me by your frankness and told me much that is of great interest. Your honesty and loyalty shall be rewarded. Like you, I pray that these troubled times may soon be over and that the peace we had in King Henry's time may be restored. Like you, I pray too that your burgh may be left in peace so that you may live your lives without fear, and complete your fine church soon."

He picked up the quill which the clerk had brought and began to write on the parchment.

"Your burgh deserves a better dean than you have had in recent years. I have had in mind one of my chaplains to be your dean. His name is Hilary. He has my trust and he is honourable. Besides being a man very learned in the law, he also has the ear of Pope Innocent in Rome. He will serve you and your cause well. Now leave me and I will see to his appointment. With Hilary as your dean, I trust your church will soon be completely finished, and the care of the souls in the burgh will be in good hands. Pax Vobiscum."

We knelt before him then as he made the sign of the Cross over the four of us. Then he turned on his heel and went out with his clerk, leaving us to make our way back with our good news.

As we passed by the Hospital of Saint Cross, we broke our journey to tell Robert of Limesia how we had fared and to thank him for the message he had sent on our behalf to Henry of Blois.

On our return, we called the folk together to tell them of our success. We put together the purse of silver we had promised to Robert for the feeding of the poor at the hospital. This Alric sent by horseman the next day, and he returned, bringing a blessing from the Master, Robert.

Two months later, Hilary arrived, accompanied by four priests. He immediately summoned all the burgh to the church to read to them the charter telling of his appointment as dean.

"People of Twynham," he said. "I have been appointed your dean by Bishop Henry of Winchester. He is brother to Count Stephen of Blois, your rightful King. I know that for some years now the cure of souls and work of building the church here have both been sadly neglected. From today, it is my intention that things should be different, and I bring with me four new priests to help me in the work. There is sore trouble in the land at present, but God's work must continue and is even more important than in more settled times. I look to all of you to help press forward the completion of the church, while I and my brother priests care for your souls. Some of our Offices have been sadly neglected, but that will be remedied. Those of you who have not been to Confession since Easter should do so within the next week. For who can tell when any one of us may die, and I would not have any of you go unshriven for the sake of your immortal souls. Remember that absolution awaits all who are truly penitent. Now go in peace, and be about your business."

Thus Hilary came among us and brought great comfort to many. At first, there was much grumbling amongst the more idle priests, but they were soon put to shame by the others. One, by name Sylvester, who had some training as an infirmarer, attached himself to Simon and quickly won the hearts and minds of many in the burgh. He knew of some remedies that were new to us and which proved to be most effective. These, coupled with the cures that Simon already had from Goodwife Adeline, and the use of the water from the pure well at Stanpit, caused our fame to spread wider than it had before. We soon found that even in those troubled times people came in increasing numbers to find cures for their ailments.

As for the building work, this was resumed with great vigour. Stone seemed to be more readily available than for many years past and boats came constantly into the harbour bringing fresh supplies from Vectis. Nor did any of them suffer attack from de Redvers' ships. Whether this was because they knew they carried supplies for his land, or because there was no profit in attacking such a cargo, I know not. It is likely also that Henry of Blois, who wielded great power in the land as the brother of Count Stephen, had sent word out that the boats carrying stone for the church were not to be stopped. Sailors rightly feared the wrath of the church, for they felt that they were in the hands of God, who alone could preserve them in times of storm. Once more the walls began to rise again so that the western windows began to take shape. and men took heart as the end of the task of building the church itself seemed to be almost within sight.

It was not long before Hilary began to draw up plans to add the conventual buildings to the church. Cloisters had long been foreshadowed, and their beginnings already stood against the south wall of the church itself. It was here that the school was held, though it had to be carried on in little more than a timber shelter. However Hilary had greater plans.

"A church of this size should be part of an abbey, with a body of Regular Canons under the control of a prior, such as happens in the monastic orders at Bec and Caen and such places in France. We must work towards that end and so build, that when at last we are able to make our plea to the Holy Father in Rome, he may look with sympathy on us." Thus he spoke one evening when the elders of the burgh were meeting in Alric's hall.

"Then there will be many more years of building yet to come," said Alnoth. "The church is rising fast now at the western end and may be ready to receive its roof next year if all goes well. How many years shall we be building if we are to complete what you have planned?"

"Who can tell?" Hilary spread his hands wide, as though seeking the answer from all of us.

"Perhaps, like Mother church herself, the building will never be finished, but will grow and be changed to suit the needs of each succeeding generation. We must leave that to those who come after us."

Thus matters rested, and the work continued, both on the western walls and on the plans that Hilary was forming for the rest of the buildings.

Spring had warmed into summer the next year before any hard news reached us of the continued conflict between Stephen and the Lady Maud. It was only then that we heard that Maud had surrounded Winchester, causing Henry of Blois to flee, though she suffered grave losses in the fight to take the city.

It seems that earlier Maud had had greater success than we thought possible, for she had taken Count Stephen captive at Lincoln. Ill-luck dogged him that day; it was Candlemas at the start of February. The taper he was offering before Mass broke, and the pix, containing the body of Our Lord, fell upon the altar when its chain broke too. Those present, including Stephen, took these as ill omens. Though some men fought bravely, they were disheartened and were defeated, fleeing as they could. As for Stephen, he kept his ground like a lion, standing alone and wielding his battleaxe so fiercely that for a long time all who tried to take him were repelled. When at last he was overpowered, Maud sent him in chains to her castle in Bristol. Those who heard of it were shocked at such treatment, not only of an anointed King, but of one who had fought so bravely.

About the same time, news was also brought to us that some months earlier Maud had been welcomed by the citizens of London. However, she made such high-handed demands of them that they quickly turned against her and, swarming out of London like a hoard of angry wasps marched on the vill of Westminster where the Lady Maud was just about to sit down to a sumptuous banquet. Taken completely by surprise, she left the table before she had touched any food and fled with a few followers to Oxford. Many of those who had formed her Court remained in Westminster and switched their support to Count Stephen.

When the Lady Maud came south and took Winchester, she found little support there, the more so when Stephen's Queen, Matilda, came with an army to surround her and demand the release of her husband. This she achieved, and we heard later that Stephen had taken the castle at Wareham, though he was himself almost recaptured at Wilton, outside Sarum.

All this brought constant fear to us, for the opposing forces were far too near for comfort. Once more we were thankful to have the great forest of Andret and the barren heathlands towards Poole harbour between us and the opposing forces. Most men tilled only those fields which were near to the burgh, within whose walls they could safely flee at the first sign of danger. Our assart towards the forest edge we had ploughed and sown in hope. We risked gathering a quick harvest of some of the corn when a merchant, who happened to pass through, said that his latest news was that both factions were once again away to the north, near Oxford.

Matters continued thus for several years, with new rumours reaching us every few months.

Baldwin de Redvers finally threw in his lot once more with Count Stephen. When at the same time the burgh was returned to him, we felt that, with such a powerful lord to protect us, we might be safer from attack. About the season of Advent in 1147, Hilary was consecrated to the see of Chichester. We remained under his charge, though we saw little of him thereafter.

At the same time, there came from Winchester, Baldwin de Redvers' steward bringing a fresh charter for our church. Since Hilary was no longer in the burgh, Robert the vicar read it out to all of us after Mass.

"Hear what our Lord Baldwin now bestows upon this church," he said. "Not only does he confirm Hilary as dean with all the churches round about, including their tithes, church-scots, lands, rents, and villein fees which have been the church's due in the past, he also confirms our right to hold our school and further the teaching that we have done these past years. The Church Court, which Eorl Baldwin's father Richard established, but which has been little used, is now recognised, with sac and soc, toll and team, and infangenethef. There are listed here the lands and messuages in the burgh between the Avon and the Stour, some of which are new and some you know of, which are also confirmed as belonging to the church and whose profit shall be for the use of the canons and the work of building."

Here he paused, casting his eye down the charter to summarise the lands, before speaking again.

"There is land next to the cemetery and land between the cemetery and the Avon, Gamelin's messuage above the moat, and another, and then all the lands that belonged to Alnod and Alsi, those two greatly loved priests who died many years ago."

Isabel and I exchanged glances, for we well remembered those two when we were children.

"Baldwin has also granted us new land at Hengist's headland, and confirmed our holding of lands at Stanpit, Bashley, and elsewhere, and also on Vectis Isle at

Ningweda. There are other lands which he now gives us further distant, which we shall have to go and see. Some of these are near Southampton, so that they may have to wait for more peaceful times, though the value of them can be called to our use. There are other new benefits too. Listen to them."

Robert paused again to make sure that he had the attention of all who were present.

"Eorl Baldwin has granted the church the tithe of the annual fair, and also the tithe of wreck which occurs in his fee on lands which the church controls. If any great fish is landed, then the church is to have half, besides the first salmon caught each year, and a tithe of all other fish including salmon. All new lands which the Eorl has, both within and without the vill, shall render a tithe of standing crops only to the church. For the comfort of the priests and those for whom they care, Eorl Baldwin's lands shall send two loads of heath daily and one hundred loads of turf a year, so that their fires may be kept burning in all weathers. The priests are also now to be free of all tolls on the Eorl's lands, whether they buy or sell, and, when Eorl Baldwin is absent from the burgh, the church may buy first any goods that are brought in."

He turned to Alric then.

"This matter concerns you as bailiff. Eorl Baldwin states that when he is not in the burgh his servants are neither to profit from selling goods to the church nor to exact a toll on goods sold to them. He bids you see to it that this is obeyed, for he wishes all such profit to go to the church for its benefit. For my part, I shall ensure that the monies are put to good and proper use."

This brought a general murmur of approval, for most could remember all too well how Peter had abused the wealth that used to come to the church. As Robert began to roll up the parchment, he broke into a smile.

"There is one more thing that has been granted us. The priests and all servants of the church may fish at will below where the Stour and Avon join, a bow-shot below the mill, for all fish except the salmon. It seems that our Lord Baldwin does not wish us to go hungry, for which we shall give him thanks in times of dearth."

There was much nodding of heads amongst those present, for it was a most generous charter, with many new benefits. Two voices in the crowd were raised in protest.

"You priests will have food enough in time of famine, but what about us poor serfs? Are we to continue to starve because our land yields no crops?"

"Yes, and shall we have to die of cold too, for lack of turves for our fires?"

I looked round to see who spoke and was not surprised to see that it was two renowned wastrels whose few strips of land were known more for their weeds than crops. Their neighbours constantly complained to the reeve that the seeds of tares and other weeds blew onto their lands to spoil their crops, but those two cared little for the constant rebukes, as Robert well knew.

"Have no fear, Swein, nor you Ernwi. No man who works his land shall go hungry when their crops fail. The goods that are given to the church will be used for the benefit of those who fall on hard times through no fault of their own. Whether it be corn or fish or fuel, it shall be given them. Do not think that you can be idle and then come to us for succour. Remember the parable of the talents. 'He that works shall be rewarded, but from him that does no work shall be taken even what he has.' Look to your strips, men, and help yourselves first if you wish to secure yourself in times of hardship."

They looked abashed at this, knowing that the rebuke was just, though they cared not to receive it so publicly. Some started to mock the two of them, but Alric quickly silenced them.

"Have a care how you speak," he said, "for there are few who can claim never to have been idle."

Robert raised a warning finger.

"The bailiff is right. Remember the words of our Saviour: 'let him who is without sin cast the first stone'."

As Isabel, Emma, Alric and I talked over the contents of this new charter that evening, it crossed my mind that Hilary and Henry of Blois had both had a hand in its drafting, for de Redvers was giving to the church much more than it had held before. Perhaps this was meant to be as penance for his past changes of loyalty. Whatever the reason, it meant far greater riches for the church, which would be for our benefit too.

"With such added wealth, perhaps we shall see the church and all its buildings finished in our lifetime."

"Perhaps, Hugh," said Alric, "though neither of us have many years left on this earth, I think. My bones remind me of this every day."

"You feel that too?" I replied. "I would like to live to see the church finally complete, and perhaps the monastery at least established."

"That must be in the hands of God," said Isabel. "Come let us go home so that I may rub your joints with one of Goodwife Adeline's ointments. You know they ease your aching limbs."

We left Emma and Alric and made our slow way back to our cott.

All four of us were feeling our age. Our eyes were beginning to dim a little and my arms had not the strength of former years. For me, it was my pride that kept me going, I think - though sometimes I felt inwardly that the young looked on me as a doddering fool. I longed to be young again and lift a full sack of grain in each hand as I had done in my prime.

Thus life continued, and the roof was finally completed over the west end of the church. Great was the joy of the whole burgh when the last timber was put into place, and we sent word to Hilary at his see in Chichester. He would not let us rest, however. He sent his blessing, and also plans for a short tower to be raised over the crossing in the centre of the church - that place where the great beam stood - and with the plans he sent a bell. It was his plan that within this tower, which would rise to a point above an open arch on each side, should hang a bell which would summon all to Mass, and remind those who worked in the fields of the time for evening prayer, when the angelus was sounded. Osbern looked at the plan, and after making a few changes to its structure, he nodded his approval.

"It would not have held a swinging bell for long if we had built as Hilary had shown it. I have strengthened the timbers so that when the bell is raised and swung full circle it will bear the strain and weight. Who knows, we may have need of such a bell to call the folk to arms should we be attacked in these evil times. Better it were strong enough to take a mighty pull than have it come crashing down about our heads."

Alric shook his head in sorrow.

"It is a sorry world that we live in if we should have to use a bell which is meant to call folk to prayer to summon them to arms. You are right, Osbern. It is better to be prepared than sorry later."

The tower was built during the following months, and the bell hung. Before the Lenten fast began, we rang the bell for the first time and it proved a great blessing. All could now know the hours, for the bell was sounded before each daytime Office. Men could also hear the angelus when they were in their fields, and so make their way homeward, before the gates were closed.

Chapter 20 1148

Osbern's words proved to be more prophetic than he knew. Not many weeks later, when the crops were starting to ripen in the fields, anxious news was brought to us by a rider sent by Baldwin de Redvers. Dust covered, he rode with all haste into the burgh, asking for the constable by name. When Gerald heard his news, he summoned those of the elders who could quickly be found, and also Robert the vicar, to gather in the keep.

"This is Ailmer, one of Eorl Baldwin's esquires. It were best that he give you his news himself, and we can then question him so that we may plan how best we may act. We must act fast, so do not question him on matters that are of no importance. Now, Ailmer, speak up."

Still travel-worn, for he had had no time to refresh himself from his ride, Ailmer looked round at us all.

"Eorl Baldwin has sent me to warn you of the approach of a large force of horse and foot. It is commanded by one Walter de Pinkney, who has escaped Count Stephen's watching army near Bristol and has already moved past Wilton to the west of Sarum. At first it was thought that they would attack Sarum itself before moving on towards Winchester, for which reason Count Stephen sent a force to hold Sarum and bar his way across the river Avon. Instead, they turned south, following the western bank of the river and using it to protect their flank from any surprise attack by Stephen's force. When I set off, they were nearing the small vill of Fordingbridge where there is an easy crossing of the river. They still kept to the west of the Avon river, shadowed by Stephen's men on the eastern bank, so that it seemed that the threat was not to Winchester after all."

A worried frown crossed Gerald's brow as he listened with alarm.

"What are his plans then, and where does he mean to attack? Is anything known?"

"One who had managed to enter de Pinkney's lines, passing himself off as a trader, overheard de Pinkney say that he intends to sweep south along the edge of the heathland that rises to the west of the Avon, taking Ringwood first, before coming to the coast to take this burgh of Twynham. Then he means to turn westwards again to take the vill of Poole and capture its harbour before continuing his sweep through to take the castle of Wareham. Then he means to seize the other castle at Corfe, which holds the gap in the hills that commands the whole of Purbeck. It seems that the Lady Maud plans to make a strong base in this area, guarded by the castles from which she can mount a great attack on Winchester and Sarum."

"Has she forces enough for such a plan?" Gerald asked.

"She will succour her forces with aid from France, through the harbour here at Twynham and the ports of Poole and Wareham. Bristol is too distant to form a base for such a campaign, for ships would have to pass right round the Cornish coast to reach it. Talk was, that with a firm base here, the Lady Maud could mount a new assault on Count Stephen from this coast, and drive him north out of his base at Winchester and Sarum. Eorl Baldwin commands you to hold this burgh at all costs. If Twynham holds, then he thinks Poole and Wareham will not fall, for de Pinkney has not force enough to attack them while this place still threatens his back."

There was a stunned silence. None dared speak till the full importance of Ailmer's words had sunk in. Alric broke the silence at last.

"Then we are to be attacked at last. I have feared this day's arrival for many years. At least we have made our plans and our walls are as strong as we can make them. What sort of man is this Walter de Pinkney? Have you seen him, Ailmer?"

"No, but his reputation goes before him. If what is said is true, then I have no desire to do so. He gives no quarter, nor asks for any. Those whom he captures are like to be mutilated so that they can fight no more. If they are women, it were better that they were dead before he lays his evil hands on them. Young or old, he takes his pick first, before handing the rest over to his men to abuse as they will."

Ailmer's face twisted into a grimace. "I will not soil my mouth by telling you of the tales of rape and mayhem that I have heard. No woman is safe within a mile of him, and he is never satisfied with however many he takes for what he calls his pleasure. I have seen two poor wretches he had taken, and they were driven out of their minds by what they had suffered. I cannot speak more of it."

A shiver ran through Ailmer's frame as he spoke, and he screwed his eyes tight shut as if to keep out the dreadful sights of which he spoke .

"Then we must keep all our womenfolk safe, and the children too. Robert, they must surely all seek sanctuary in the church if the burgh walls are breached."

Alric looked towards Robert, who, recovering from the shock of what he had just heard, nodded his assent.

"It is good that we made the stockade for the beasts on Hengist's headland, for they will be needed now. How think you? Shall we muster all the beasts we can from around the burgh and drive them all to the headland and pen them there? All the food that can be gathered in time, must be brought here, so that de Pinkney will have little on which to feed his force."

"How long do you think we have before de Pinkney reaches us here?" Gerald asked. Should not Robert have the church bell rung to sound the alarm and warn all the folk in the fields?"

Edric the reeve shook his head.

"That would bring all hurrying, and the beasts left in the fields to be taken by this man de Pinkney, giving him the very food we mean to deny him. Rather let us send riders through the fields and to all the surrounding cotts telling the folk to gather all they can together onto such carts as they can lay their hands and make all haste here. Those living to the north at Winkton, Sopley and Herne, and to the west at Holdenhurst, and who have beasts, should drive them across the ford at Iford and make for Hengist's headland. Those at Stanpit and near the pure well can do likewise, leaving their womenfolk and children here the while. I will tell the riders to make their own way to the headland as soon as they have warned the folk, so that the pens may be prepared for the cattle and other beasts. Alric, have we a boat that can go to the headland to bring the riders back by water? I think it best that at least some of the horses be left in safety on the headland so that, should the burgh fall, not everything will be taken."

Alric nodded in agreement. "Wisely said, Edric. How much time do we have, Ailmer?"

"I doubt they will be here before tomorrow. De Pinkney is moving slowly, taking his pleasure of those he captures, so I fear that he will be fully occupied this night at least."

"Well, that gives us a few hours," said Gerald. "Edric, find six riders and send them off at once to warn the folk. Tell them to make all haste and to be within the walls before the angelus sounds. That will give them a few hours to gather their goods together. Have all the men bring any weapons they may have and all such things as scythes and knives which could be used as weapons. It were better that they were with us than be allowed to fall into de Pinkney's hands and used against us. I will send a boat to the headland to bring back the six riders. They must leave their horses there. What think you Alric? Should we send six of the older men over in the boat to take charge of the beasts? We cannot spare young men from the walls for such a task."

"Wise counsel Gerald."

There was a worried silence for a few moments before Alric spoke once more.

"Six steady heads and hearts will be enough to control the beasts, and keep them out of sight. We must seek volunteers for the task, for should de Pinkney's men find them they will have no chance to defend themselves. Their lives will depend on their remaining unseen, and they may well have to fend for themselves for some weeks. There is some food already stored over there, but it were as well that a cart-load of flour and some dried meat be sent there too."

Alric's brow clouded, as he thought for a moment. there was so much he needed to see to.

" Fresh water they have in plenty from the river, provided they remember to take it at the end of the ebb tide when the sea water has been washed out, or it will taste salt. They will not lack for fish. They must watch their fires and light them only on the seaward side of the headland so that the smoke is not seen. Nor must they show lights at night or they will give themselves away. Yes, six will be enough, but I would prefer five men and one goodwife who can cook and care for them."

This brought a smile to Gerald's face.

"Alric, you always think of men's comfort. You are right. The men will have trouble enough fending for themselves and controlling the beasts, so it is right that they should not have to worry about where their next meal is coming from. Will you see to it then? Have them ready to sail within the hour, if possible, with cooking pots and bedding and all such things as they may need. Now we must act. Edric, get the men to horse now and warn the folk."

Edric rose and left quickly, pleased to be able to act. As he went out, Gerald looked at Ailmer again.

"You said that Count Stephen commands us to hold the burgh at all costs. Does he mean to send men to help us? You said he had a force shadowing de Pinkney on the east bank of the Avon. Where are they now, and what will they do? We could use any that he can spare, for we have few enough to hold the walls against a determined attack."

"Their orders were to shadow de Pinkney until it was clear that he did not mean to turn against Winchester, and then return there. Count Stephen does not dare denude the heart of his defence, lest the Lady Maud makes a sudden attack on it and captures his Treasury, for then all would be lost."

"Does he not realise that if he allows this place to fall, and Poole and Wareham likewise, the very threat he fears may well come to pass? Surely it would be better to send us help so that, as he himself says, if Twynham holds, all will remain secure?"

Ailmer nodded. "What you say would seem to make sense. All I can suggest is that you send a rider to Winchester seeking such aid as Stephen feels he can send, putting your reasons to him as you have to me. As you say, even twenty well-armed and trained men here would make all the difference."

He sighed, and shook his head despondently, for there was little comfort he could give us.

"I do not hold out much hope for you. Stephen has so many demands made on his armed men that it largely depends on who speaks to him last whether you win the support you need or not. He is like a man trying to put out a stubble fire. He rushes about from one spark to the next, stamping on each in a desperate attempt to keep all under control instead of dealing with the heart of the blaze. From what I can hear, that centre is most likely soon to be here. You have not the force to go out and meet de Pinkney in battle, which would probably be the best answer."

Alric and Gerald exchanged worried glances.

"We will hold out as long as we can," said Gerald, "but it may not be long enough. What say you, Alric, should we not send a rider on a fast horse to Winchester to beg for help?"

"I agree, but by the time help comes we shall already be besieged and they would not be able to fight their way in to help us. It were best that any help that is sent comes by sea. De Pinkney would be unable to prevent them entering the harbour, and they could sail right up to the quay in safety. They would be fresh too and not wearied from a long march. Besides, they could load the ship with more arms to help our defence."

Gerald's eyes brightened at this new thought. He turned to Ailmer.

"Where is Stephen's shadowing force now, do you think?"

"I doubt if they would have come any further south than Ringwood. After that they would turn back through the forest of Andret and make their way back to Winchester, feeling that the threat had passed."

"Then let us send a man to intercept them and see if part of the force can be persuaded to turn south and come to our aid. They could easily take ship at Beaulieu and reach us with greater ease than coming by foot." The rest of us nodded in agreement with this plan which seemed to offer our best hope.

"Now, Ailmer, what will you do?" asked Gerald. "Will you stay with us and help to defend the burgh? We can use your skill at arms, I have no doubt."

"I would willingly do so, but I must ride to Poole and then Wareham to warn them of de Pinkney's coming. Another esquire was sent there at the same time as I came to you, but I do not know if he has made the journey safely. It were best that I rode there first to make sure that they have been warned and are putting their defences in readiness. If I can, I will return to help you."

"You will need a fresh horse then. Come with me," said Alric, rising. " I must first send the rider on his way to seek help from Stephen's men, then I will provide the fastest horse I have. While it is being saddled, come and eat with us so that you may be on your way refreshed."

The two of them went out, Ailmer a little stiffly, I thought, for he had ridden far and fast already.

Gerald turned to Robert.

"We must prepare to house the women and children and those who are too old to fight. They can sleep within the bailey for the moment, but if de Pinkney's force attacks too strongly then it were best that they seek shelter in the church. Can you house them all, Robert?"

Robert looked solemn, for this was something he had never had to face before.

"The church is always open to all who seek comfort and shelter. Is it not written in the Scriptures: 'Come unto me all ye who are heavy laden and I will give you rest'? We can house all who come, and the walls will provide a defence against any attack. I trust that even this Walter de Pinkney would not think to commit such sacrilege as to force his way into a church to pillage it and ravage those who shelter within its walls. We have food in plenty for some time, but it is in store some distance from the church, so that if the burgh were to fall those sheltering within would quickly starve."

I had held my peace so far, for these matters were better solved by those who understood them better than I. Where bread was concerned, I felt that I could rightly speak.

"Can you not move some of the milled flour into the church itself? I have strong sons and grandsons working in our mill who will gladly help. If you think you may be short of flour, then I will see to it that we grind as much as possible until the need is satisfied. The mill can be kept grinding all night if need be. I may be old now, but I can still lift a sack of corn. At such a time, all must play their part, and it will not harm me to lose a night or two's sleep."

Robert raised a hand in blessing.

"Hugh, you are ever thoughtful. If you can do as you say, then we should be able to keep all fed. Have them bring the sacks of flour into the south transept and store it there. The door to the cloister opens near, and so long as we can use the kitchens which stand to that side, we shall have no difficulty. I will send John, who is in charge of the guest-house, to your mill so that you can make arrangements with him. You can use our carts to bring the sacks of flour to the church. I will have barrels filled with water too and small beer, or those we feed may die of thirst. Straw we shall need too, for bedding. I must away and see to it all."

Robert rose and hastened out to see to his tasks, and the rest of us went our separate ways, each to see that whatever could be done for our defence and the security of his family. Before reaching our mill, I called first at our cott. I warned Isabel to send word to all our family of what was afoot, bidding her not to alarm them but to tell them that they should make ready to move at a moment's notice should the need arise. It was our grandchildren's babes I feared for most, for two of them were still at the breast, the youngest of all, our granddaughter Mary's babe, being scarcely a month old. Mary had wed Roger the woodman, whose cott was by the Bar Gate. He would not be back till evening time, for he was tending the trees by Catherine's hill and would see no-one all day like as not.

I had no fears for Roger, for he was a huge man and carried an axe which he had made himself. No-one else in the burgh could wield it for its weight and size. It was his pride and joy, and its edge he kept so keen that he had often-times used it to shave his beard.

Before I went on to the mill, I warned Isabel once more.

"Be sure that Mary comes to our cott with her babes as soon as she can. Let her not wait for Roger to return, for he will be safe enough working in the woods and can take care of himself. I would not be happy to think of Mary so close to the Bar Gate which may be the first place to be attacked."

"You are right, Hugh," she replied, "but you know what a stubborn creature Mary is; she will not lightly leave her cott without knowing that Roger is safely within the walls. I will do my best, but do not count on it."

Satisfied that I had done what I could to secure the safety of the family, I hurried on to the mill. There I found them all fully busy. Calling all who were working there together, I quickly outlined what was to be done. Between us, we loaded onto carts all the milled flour that was waiting to be collected, and took it with all speed up to the church and in by the southern door. There, John of the guest-house was waiting for us to show us where the sacks should be piled.

"I am keeping back four sacks to send over to Hengist's headland for those who will care for the beasts," I told him. "We are still grinding at the mill and will do so all night if need be, to make sure that all the corn we have is prepared in case of need. Who knows how long we may have to last."

John nodded hastily as he busied himself seeing to other foods that were being brought into the church for safe storage. Then he hurried away to supervise the barrels which were coming in and which he would have filled with water. Others that held small ale were already stacked against the wall on the opposite side of the transept. As I returned to our mill I met a cart loaded with straw for bedding coming from Alric's barn. Another, loaded with timber for firing, was crossing the market square. Everywhere folk hastily made ready such things as they thought most needful for instant flight into the safety of the church.

Having seen that all was well with the milling and that the boards were well set in the mill-race, I went to the quay to see if the boat was being made ready to go to the headland. Alric met me with a worried look on his face.

"Hugh, we shall never put six people and all their food into one boat. Can you make yours ready too? I would like to send the first away to the headland as soon as possible, so that at least some of the party will be ready when the first of the beasts arrive."

"Leave it with me, Alric. I have kept back four sacks of flour to send to the headland and will bring them to our boat now and make all ready. Tell those that are ready to go now, to come to the mill straight away. They can leave as soon as the boat is loaded."

I hurried away to make ready our boat, which lay as usual tied up by the outflow of the mill-race. Hardly had I put the four sacks into the boat, before the first two who were to care for the beasts arrived. Quickly they stowed their belongings into the boat, and climbing aboard themselves, I made ready to cast them off.

"Keep the boat with you on the headland," I said. "Make sure it is well hidden in the reeds so that it cannot be found. It may well prove useful if you wish to reach us at any time, though it were best you came at night. If you do come, tie the boat up here where I normally keep it; and have a password, so that we do not think you are de Pinkney's men."

I thought for a moment, seeking a word that would serve.

"Let the word be 'Flambard'. Those of us who are here will be told, and it is not a word that others would think of. The other boat that is bringing the rest of your party can bring back the horsemen when they come. Now go quickly, and may God be with you."

I untied the rope that held the boat and shoved them out into the stream, where they quickly gathered pace as the current took hold. Setting their oars, they rapidly moved out of sight across the Clay Pool to where the Avon joins the swift Stour, and were soon hidden by the reeds, and so safe from prying eyes and gossiping tongues. I then returned to the mill to see that everything was being pressed forward with all speed.

Isabel came hurrying in soon after, outwardly calm so as not to awaken the fears of others.

"I have warned them all, and they are making ready," she said. "Martha and Ruth have gone to see Simon the infirmarer to offer their aid to any who may be wounded in the attack. I have already told him that he must have my store of simples and balms to add to his, for if there is to be fighting, we may well need all that we have."

I smiled at her for her thoughtfulness, but saw a cloud cross her brow.

"What is it that troubles you, my love?"

"It is young Mary," she replied. "As I feared, she will not leave the Bar Gate until Roger is returned. I was scarce able to restrain her from rushing out into the wilds to find him. I persuaded her in the end by saying that she could not take her babe with her and there would be no-one to care for little Osric who would be frightened out of his wits if he were left alone, and him not yet three years old. She saw reason in the end, but insists on staying by the gate until Roger is safely returned."

"Should I go and find him in the woods, do you think, to put her mind at rest?"

Isabel took me by the arm, and I saw a look of fear in her eyes.

"There is nothing you could do, for you do not know which part of the wood he is in. You are too old for such foolish bravery. Besides, the rider who set out towards Holdenhurst knows that Roger is cutting on Catherine's hill and will be sure to send word to him by one of those he meets along the way."

Putting on a brave smile, she added with a sigh, "I shall be glad when he is safely within the walls."

I looked quickly round the mill to satisfy myself that all was well.

"There is nothing more I can do here for the moment, I will go and be with Mary for a while and try to ease her fears. I must see Gerald too, for I have a message for him. Go back to our cott and see to our own preparations, for we must be ready too, so that we can give aid to others if the need arise."

Isabel returned to our cott, and I went in search of Gerald, whom I found supervising the young men, telling them where they should stand in defence of the walls when an attack came. Drawing him to one side, I told him of the password I had arranged.

"Well done," he said. "I will leave you to keep guard over that part of the wall with your family. Make sure that one is always near the mill to warn us of any surprise attack from that quarter. I do not think de Pinkney is likely to try to enter the burgh by the river for he has no boats, and I have given orders that none are to be left where he can capture them. That way we should be safe from a seaborne attack."

As I neared the Bar Gate, I could see Mary standing outside it, clutching her babe to her breast and holding little Osric's hand in hers. It plucked at my heart strings to see her thus anxious, though I knew my feelings would be the same had it been Isabel who was awaited. Holding out my arms, little Osric came running to me, and I gathered him up, making a fuss of him to distract his attention. Mary forced a smile to her face as I put my free arm round her shoulder, drawing her near to me to give her comfort and, I hoped, strength.

"Do not be over-anxious Mary. There are some hours before anything can happen, and Roger will be safely back well before that. He is always home before the angelus sounds, which is the time we have said that folk should be within the walls."

"Do you think that we shall really be attacked?" she said, wiping a tear from her eye.

"I fear so, but we cannot say exactly when. It may be tomorrow, or it may not be for a day or two. No-one can say. Cheer up: we are well defended, and our walls are strong. Besides, we have sent a rider to Count Stephen asking for reinforcements. We mean to drive off this man de Pinkney and not just sit inside our walls while he lords it over the countryside all round. He is a foreigner after all and a bully too, and like all bullies a coward when put to the test. Those with him are mostly only looking for booty. Remember we are all good Saxon stock, and we have held this place against all comers from well before the Normans came so I see no reason why we should let some upstart Norman take it from us now. Isn't that right, Osric?" and I gave a growl and hugged him as he sat on my hip.

Mary laughed then. "Oh Grandfather, I do believe you would see them off single-handed given half a chance."

I looked away out of the gate again, feeling that the strain was easing, and saw the unmistakable figure of Roger in the distance.

"Well, it looks as if he is going to be early this evening, too."

Mary gave a start and turned to look. With a cry of delight, she began to run towards him.

"Wait for me," I cried, wishing to restrain her from rushing out of the safety of the gates. "I am carrying Osric, and I am not as young as I was."

When Roger was within twenty yards of the gate I set little Osric on the ground so that he could run to his father. The huge man came to his wife with measured tread and folded her in his arms as was his custom, before planting a gentle kiss on the forehead of his tiny babe. Then we all turned and made our way back to their cott.

Once inside the door, I drew Roger aside and told him all that I knew. He looked grave.

"Mary and the children will be safe enough in the cott so long as we can hold the walls. I shall speak to Gerald and see if he will allow me to guard this gate. I would be happier if I knew that I was close to Mary and could protect her if anything should go wrong. I am not a fighting man, God knows, but in such times as these a man must see to his family if he is to be able to hold up his head."

Roger lifted his great axe and fingered its edge.

"The smith fashioned this blade to my design, and I cut the shaft myself when first I started working in the woods. There is none other that can wield this axe. I thought to use it for nothing but keeping the forest and woodland in good heart. Pray God I never have to use it to draw blood."

"Amen to that," I added, and I clapped him on the arm, for I felt as he did.

"Though I know you would wish to keep them all close by you, when you think the time is ripe Roger, send Mary and the babes to us. They will be safer by the mill, and it is close to the church, which is to be our final refuge should the worst come to pass. Isabel will see that they come to no harm, for she will be working closely with Simon the infirmarer. As for me, I shall do whatever Gerald asks of me. Let us hope that the re-enforcements that we have sent for arrive in time. We should be able to hold the walls, but without help we cannot break out and give de Pinkney battle and so drive him off. He is a bully and a braggart from what I hear, so that if we could get him on his own we might see his real colour and find it to be very different from what he would have us think."

"We shall manage, I have no doubt." mused Roger. "When men have to fight for what they believe in and love they find an inner strength. Certainly we could do with more men to be sure of holding the burgh. I must away and find Gerald, and see what use he can make of me."

He slipped out then, while I stayed a while to see that Mary was calm and was making such preparations as she could to come to us with the babes. I helped her load a hand-cart with such possessions as they had, and between us we took them to our cott. From there, they could be quickly moved into the church with our belongings, if need be.

As the rest of the day passed, some folk busied themselves burying their hoards of silver, others made space to receive their kin who were coming in from outlying dwellings to shelter within the walls. Those who had no kin and no friends who could take them in were found shelter within the bailey of the keep. Though many beasts were driven across the rivers and hidden on Hengist's headland, there were still plenty that were brought for shelter within the walls. Such as could be housed were taken to Alric, who put them with the demesne stock where they could be fed and watered. Many were the fowls and pigs that ran squawking and squealing through the streets as their owners tried vainly to keep them tethered.

Sleep was late coming to many that night. Eventually, peace and quiet returned, though all night long there could be heard the soft tread of feet, as those who patrolled the walls kept close look-out for the feared approach of Walter de Pinkney and his force. I stayed in the mill all night, grinding such corn as I could. The other men of the family I had sent to take their rest, for they would need it more than I if we were to face an attack. They would be the ones who would have to repel it, so that my best service would be to see that the burgh was well supplied with bread. Twice during the night Isabel brought me food and drink, and would have stopped with me all night had I not insisted that she get some sleep herself. Her aid with the wounded would be needed soon enough if things went badly.

An hour after dawn, when I went to the bailey where all the men were summoned to gather, there was an air of keen expectancy. Men were standing about in groups bragging to each other about how many of de Pinkney's men they proposed to skewer on the end of their swords. They had had little enough training and their talk was as much to keep up their own spirits as to impress their fellows. I could not help regretting that we no longer had Belesme of St Lo as constable, with all his experience in wars, fighting at the side of Duke William though he had been dead many years now, I still missed my old friend. Soon enough Gerald appeared from the keep. He looked confident enough, dressed as he was in his full armour of chain-mail, with a sword hanging from his side and his bow slung across his back. The men gathered in the bailey sent up a cheer when he appeared, and he smiled at them and raised his arms for silence.

"Men of Twynham, I have trained you in the arts of war and you know well how to handle your weapons. Use them as you have been taught and they will serve you well. Our walls are strong and this keep behind me overlooks the bridges that lead to the gate on this side. Should Walter de Pinkney's men try to storm the burgh from here, the archers in the keep will drive them off as they crowd the bridge or try to ford the river and mill-stream. More likely they will try to take the Bar Gate, but the land lies open there, so that once more our archers can bring down any who try that side. To the west as you know, the land becomes marshy once you pass the Canons' Gate, so that any who try to reach the walls there will be forced to move slowly and become easy targets for us. Our strength lies first in our walls and your bow-strings. Use them both to best advantage. Keep within the walls and use their shelter to protect your bodies." Gerald unhitched his bow from his shoulder and put its end on the ground. Then he set the bow-string and tested it, nodding with satisfaction as he did so.

"It will serve no purpose to dash out and try by cut and thrust to drive this man away, though he will no doubt tempt you to do so by false retreats. I have talked with those who fought long years ago at Senlac Field, and have heard how Duke William won that day against your brave Saxon housecarls by that trick. Learn from their deaths, and keep yourselves alive. Do not think that you are alone. I have sent to Count Stephen and he will surely send armed men to succour us in a few days. Shoot straight and acquit yourselves like the hardy Saxons that you are, and there will not be many of de Pinkney's men left for Stephen's men to round up. Then we shall see the colour of the man. Though he bullies his men and boasts about the strength of his own sword arm, I hear he is a craven coward like all bullies when cornered. Strike him down, and his force will melt away, so look to your bow-strings when you sight him. Remember at all costs, stay within the walls. Taunt them to approach, so that you may easily shoot them down. Now, form yourselves into your three companies, and those who have no place allotted them stand before me here."

There was a general movement as all moved to the place where their own company paraded in the bailey. Those who lived in outlying cotts and were not in one of the burgh's tithings, gathered to one side. They looked a motley crew, armed as they were with axes or scythe blades, or long knives fixed to the ends of poles. Some carried bows and hunting knives, but all looked determined to play their part. These men Gerald divided into three parts and sent each to one of the three companies. When all were once more settled and quiet, he addressed us all again.

"The three companies will each take one side of the walls. I will command the company that faces the mill-stream, so that I can also command the keep. Edric the reeve will guard the Bar Gate and the wall at that side. Remember you have amongst you Roger the woodman. I feel sorry for any who comes within reach of his great axe."

"The wall with the Canons' Gate will be commanded by Alric the bailiff of our Lord Baldwin de Redvers. His family and Hugh the miller's family have for long kept that wall in good repair, so it seems right that they should have the task of keeping this wretch de Pinkney's men from harming it." Looking towards where we stood, Gerald grinned, "I know how it would grieve you all if any tried to damage that wall."

Gerald turned to address us all again.

"We do not know how soon de Pinkney and his men will reach us, but it may well be within the next few hours. Until they are sighted, be about your tasks and put yourselves in readiness. Your commanders will post sentries at each gate, and I shall have a watch upon the top of the keep to give us warning of their approach. Whoever sights them first will send word to me here, so that if need be I may sound the alarm. When that sounds, let each man go to his post and await further orders.

Keep your wives and children within doors where they will be safe. Before you disperse, Robert the vicar will bless us all and commend our cause to God. Let any who has sins to confess make his peace with his Maker and be shriven by the priests who will be standing ready within the church to hear their confessions. May God be with us this day, and guard us till this danger passes."

There was a great silence then, as first Gerald and then all the rest of us dropped quietly to our knees and bowed our heads to receive absolution and blessing from Robert. As his voice came clearly over the still air of the bailey, I could not help wondering how many of us would see dawn rise in a week's time.

Even after Robert had ended his blessing and dismissed us and we had answered his "Pax vobiscum" with our "Et cum spiritu tuo", many stayed with bowed heads, deep in their own personal thoughts and prayers. Though all had heard many tales of slaughter and maiming in battles, none of us as yet had met such things face to face.

That at last we were to experience such things came as a sobering shock to all of us. Gerald was right to make us face the prospect first, so that we could prepare ourselves for the as yet unknown horrors of war. He left us communing with our souls until gradually the first few began to rise soberly to their feet. He turned on his heel and, calling to his lieutenants, marched smartly back towards the keep. The rest of us took our cue from him and rose, dusted down our jerkins, straightened our shoulders, and with as brave a heart as we could muster, set off to our posts.

When I reached the Canons' Gate, I found most of our family already there, standing facing Alric, who was surrounded by all his menfolk and those who were serfs on the demesne. Calling for silence, Alric gave his orders, dividing the men into watches of two hours each.

"There is no need yet for all men to be standing at their posts. All the gates are closed and barred. Provided we keep an active watch from the top of the gate-house which has a clear view of all the wall from Hugh's mill by the quay up to the corner where the wall turns towards the Bar Gate, we shall have warning enough of any attack and shall not be taken by surprise. Either I or one of our tithing men will be in the gate-house at all times. As soon as anyone is seen approaching the wall on this side, call me. If they look like Walter de Pinkney's men approaching, then I will sound the alarm on my horn by two rising notes repeated three times."

He put his horn to his lips and blew it quietly so that all might know the sound he meant.

"When you hear that call, all of you come running and assemble here before the gate, so that I may place you where the danger seems likely to strike. The other companies have their own alarm calls, so do not come unless you hear mine. If there is a general alarm, the bell will be constantly rung at the church. Then we shall all muster at our posts. Your families are safe enough while the walls hold, and remember that the church will give sanctuary to any who seek it. Now, go about your business. See to your weapons and look to your families and keep them calm."

When the watch had been set, I made my way to Alric's side.

"Let me command a watch with the tithing men so that you may be free to see to other matters. Send me as much corn as you have stored so that we may grind it and store it in the church. When my sons and grandsons are not on watch, they will continue at the mill, and I can take my turn there as well. That way we will make all preparation that we can."

Alric put his hand on my arm.

"I always rely on you, Hugh. Thanks for your help. Will you take the second watch so that I can do the rounds of the burgh and confer with Gerald? Emma has gone to see Isabel, and between them they are organising the older women to care for any who may be injured in the fighting. The younger women will have enough to do caring for their menfolk and children, and keeping them amused and out of harm's way."

With that, we parted. Like everyone else that day, I found plenty to occupy my mind, so that it was with surprise that I found Isabel coming to find me with a basket containing bread and cheese and a flagon of small ale.

"What hour is it, my love?"

"Well past noon, Hugh. I guessed you would be preoccupied with matters and so give no thought to your food, so I have brought some for you. How goes it do you think? There is no sign of de Pinkney's men yet. Do you think they have decided to turn away and perhaps make for Poole and Wareham only?"

I shrugged my shoulders, for my mouth was full of the victuals Isabel had brought.

"Who can say? But I fear they will come sooner or later. The plan Ailmer told us makes good sense. Perhaps Stephen's men have decided to give him battle to the north. If he defeats them, then we will be saved a siege, otherwise I fear it is only a matter of time."

Isabel stayed with me while I ate, and it was a comfort to have her by me.

"I have taken my harp into the church for safety. Besides, that is where I am most likely to need it if we are attacked. At least I can use it to sing to those who take refuge there and help to calm them. I fear greatly for the children. Why must they be frightened so?"

It was half-way through the afternoon that the first report came. Those watching from the Bar Gate saw smoke rising about two miles distant. From their position it seemed that it was the cotts at Sopley that had been fired and probably the mill too. I felt my mouth go dry when I heard the news; so, de Pinkney was determined to attack us.

Gerald toured the walls shortly after, to reassure us and tell us all he knew.

"I do not think they will reach here before tomorrow. They will feast on what they can plunder from Sopley tonight and march here tomorrow. Set a good watch and the rest of you get what sleep you can. You will need to be fresh tomorrow."

Many were the anxious hearts that night, though men put on brave faces to their fellows and tried to make light of their fears.

At mid-morning next day, the alarm sounded from the Bar Gate. We stopped in our tracks at its sound but then continued with our normal tasks, as we had been ordered, waiting for our summons to arms. There was much shouting from that end of the burgh, but after half an hour all was quiet again. Later Gerald came to our gate with news. He looked pleased.

"First blood to us," he said. "A body of de Pinkney's men tried to storm the gate, but were driven off with their tails between their legs. Three of them were shot and killed, and seven more were wounded and had to be carried away by their fellows. From what I heard, our arrows were well aimed, and some of the wounded may not live. None of our men were hit, though arrows were flying thick. We have given de Pinkney something to think about. He will try another point next time, and perhaps different tactics."

True enough, this happened before darkness fell. This time they came in greater force at the gate by the keep. Once more they were repelled, driven back by well-aimed arrows from the top, as well as from the walls and gate-house. Some, braver, than the rest, managed to rush the bridge, and set a ladder against the gate-house. This they scaled, and it was only after some hand-to-hand combat that the ladder was finally dislodged, and those upon it slashed down and sent packing. Gerald himself was in the forefront of those who held the gate-house, driving his sword into those who tried to scale the top of the gate, killing two of them and so wounding three others so that they would fight no more.

This was not done without loss. Ralf, who kept the ale-house by the gate, was pierced through the lung by a sword and died later that night in a welter of blood. Two serfs, who had fought like wild beasts and done great harm to several of de Pinkney's men, themselves suffered wounds which would put them out of the fray for some time.

Once more Gerald toured the walls to encourage us all. The sight of his bloodied shirt of chain-mail and stained and dented sword brought home to us the stark reality of our situation, though, as yet, there had been no attack on our side of the burgh.

"We have fought them off twice and sent them bloodied away. By my reckoning we have killed eight so far and wounded twice as many though we have one man killed and two wounded. He will not attack again this night, I think, so we must wait and see what tomorrow brings. We shall be ready for him whatever he decides to do. Take your rest now, and set a sharp guard. We are holding well and I am sure can do so till Stephen sends us help."

With that he left us, and we made ready to pass another night watching.

Matters continued thus for several days. Each day brought fresh attacks on the walls as de Pinkney tried to find out a weak place in our defence. Each time they were driven off with loss. Though our folk suffered too, they fared far better than those who attacked us. Of the five who died defending our walls, three had foolishly exposed themselves high above the walls in bravado, and earned an arrow through the heart for their pains. The injured were tended by Simon, with Isabel and Emma assisting as they could. Several times Simon had to draw out arrows, but they were mostly flesh wounds which Goodwife Adeline's balms soon helped to heal. More serious were the sword thrusts and slashes which left gaping wounds. These were bound up and sometimes sewn with fine thread, while the broken bones were set and splinted.

We had held the burgh for a week when I happened to pass through the infirmary on my way to see Rodric the priest, who was doing valiant work keeping the children amused and out of harm's way. Their mothers were fully occupied helping their menfolk at the walls. I saw Isabel sitting beside the bed of one man who had been grievously wounded the day before.

His right arm had been shorn clean off, and besides an ugly head wound, he had suffered a deep sword thrust in his chest. I could hear his laboured breathing as I approached. Isabel, who was softly plucking at the strings of her harp and singing gently to him, turned her head as I approached and shook her head.

The man coughed painfully and blood seeped from his mouth. Isabel wiped it away gently and murmured a few words to comfort him in his pain, and a faint smile crossed his lips. She lifted his head then and helped him to drink a little from the beaker that stood beside her. As she lowered his head again, he sighed, opened his eyes and murmured what I took to be his thanks. Then he closed his eyes again and a shaft of pain crossed his face. Isabel took up her harp once more and continued to sing softly, which seemed to bring ease to the man. After a while, he drifted off into a fitful sleep, and Isabel, quietly laying down her harp, rose stiffly to her feet.

"He fought bravely at the gate by the keep. But for him and Gerald, I hear, it might well have gone ill for us. We have done what we can for him, but his wounds are too grave I fear. He has a wife and three children, the eldest not more than eight years old. How will they fare now? She has been here most of the day, but I sent her away to see to her children and try to get some rest, for she was near dead on her feet with fatigue. I promised her if the end were near that I would send for her. Robert has heard his confession and shriven him, so that he will die in peace."

She looked at the man, who lay breathing shallowly.

"He will not last the hour, I think. Would you go to his cott and tell his wife for me. I cannot leave him now. Stay with his children and tell them of their father's bravery. It may help them in their grief."

Isabel went to sit beside the man again and I left to seek out the poor girl so soon to be made a widow. I found her sitting at the hearth of her mean cott with her three children round her, trying to keep them amused while they kept asking when their father would be coming back to eat his evening meal. As I entered, she looked towards me with anguished eyes, fearing the tidings that I probably brought. Motioning to her with my hands to stay calm, I came to sit beside her, while she sent the children to another part of the cott on some errand. Taking her hands, I held her eyes with mine.

"I have been sitting with your man and hearing from my wife how he fought bravely and perhaps saved the day for the burgh. Would that we had more like him, for then we should have nothing to fear. You should be proud of him. Go to him now and hold your head high, for be assured the whole burgh is in your debt for his valour at the wall this day." She rose, and telling the children to stay with me while she was gone, went out with as firm a step as she could muster. I kept the three children amused as best I could until I heard footsteps outside, and Isabel entered with her, closely followed by Gerald the constable. The children ran to their mother as soon as she came in, and she hugged them to her, trying to hide her tears. Gently, Gerald put his hands on the shoulders of the elder two, while their mother held the youngest to her.

"You will have to be very brave now, and care for your mother, for your father has been taken from us. Listen while I tell you of his courage. They were attacking the gate-house by the keep, trying to scale its walls. Your father saw a man appear at the top of their ladder and rushed at him, cutting him down with his knife. As he fell, the man struck your father a savage blow to his head, half blinding him. Your father took no notice of his wound, but seized the ladder and thrust it away from the wall.

I was driving off another who had already scaled the wall, so could not go to his aid. I could see a third man reach the top of the ladder and thrust his sword at your father, piercing him in the chest. Even then your father clung to the ladder and, with a mighty effort, he hurled it sideways so that it fell to the ground with those who still clung to it. As he fell, the man who had already wounded your father swung his sword again with such force that it near severed your father's arm."

Gerald then took a hand of each child in his and gravely smiled at them.

"But your father had saved the gate-house and also, I think, the burgh. We all owe him our lives. Do you remember what it says in the Scriptures? 'Greater love has no man than this, that he lay down his life for his friends?' This your father has done, and we shall honour him for his courage and love. You should be proud of him and try to help your mother in her sadness."

The eldest boy fought back his tears and thrust out his chest and turned to his mother.

"When I grow up, I shall try to be as brave as Father. Let me be a man now, so that I can help you till our fields." His younger brother nodded agreement through his tears. Again Gerald smiled at both of them and patted their shoulders.

"Good man," he said. "Have no fear, there will be willing hands to help with your harvest and ploughing."

"Come to me in your sadness when you wish," said Isabel. "I too have lost loved ones and would share your grief if you will let me".

As we rose to leave, the boys' mother looked gratefully up at us, trying to force a smile. We left her then to be with her own and come to terms with her grief.

As we neared the keep where we would part, I spoke to Gerald. "What news of King Stephen? Is any help coming from him?"

Gerald shook his head. "The messenger we sent has not returned, nor is there any news of those we hope will come to aid us. We can hold out for some time yet, and we have inflicted more hurt on them than they on us. Some of the serfs are growing restless and there are mutterings amongst them that it is not their fight and they see no reason why they should suffer for it. I do what I can to stiffen their resolve, but it is not easy."

"I will speak to any I see and try to encourage them. Better the devil you know than the devil you don't, and by all accounts this de Pinkney would turn out to be the worst of the lot."

"Very true, and my thanks for your support."

We parted, and I could see the burden lay heavy on Gerald's shoulders. He had fought most bravely himself, giving a magnificent example to all of us, though he laughed it off when any mentioned it.

When I had completed my watch at the Canons' gate-house two hours after midnight, I fell exhausted on my bed and into a sleep troubled by horrid dreams.

I was roughly woken by the urgent clanging of the church bell followed by distant shouting. Horrified, I realised that it was the general alarm.

"Quick, Isabel, gather your things. You must make for the church. I fear some disaster has happened. I must go to the Canons' Gate and see if there is anything I can do."

Within seconds we were out of the door. From the direction of the keep rose a great column of smoke. We had not gone fifty paces before we were met by figures fleeing to the safety of the church.

"The gate by the bridges has been betrayed and is taken," cried one man,, "and the keep has been fired. Those within have fled its safety, or are fighting in the streets. De Pinkney's men are putting everything to the torch. No one is safe. The burgh is bound to fall."

He rushed headlong towards the church door to join the jostling crowd of women clutching children and pathetic bundles of belongings. I looked anxiously at Isabel.

"Go," I said. "You can serve us best by calming those who are seeking sanctuary. If you can assemble the family in one place, do so, that we may know they are all safe. I must go to the gate-house first to see if I can help, but will join you when I can in the church. God be with you."

I kissed her hurriedly, not knowing if I would see her again, and hurried as fast as I could to the Canons' Gate.

I did not reach it, for the young men who formed its guard came running with drawn swords, heading towards the keep. Their leader shouted to me, "Go to the church. It is hand-to-hand fighting only now. Gather such women and children as you can on the way, and go and help the priests quell the panic of those who have sought sanctuary."

This I did, opening doors of cotts to see that none were still left hiding in terror. When it seemed that all were safe, I looked hurriedly round me. There was no-one in sight and the hubbub came only from towards the keep. I hastened once more to our cott to gather up such things of value that I could carry and, thus burdened, made my way panting to the church. It took but a few moments to find one of the family who was waiting to lead me to where they were all assembling.

"Are we all here?" I asked, trying desperately to count those I could see.

"Mother is tending the wounded," answered Martha." The men are all at the keep, trying to drive back de Pinkney's men. Only Mary is missing with Osric and her babe. They have furthest to come from the Bar Gate, but there is no sign of them yet. They could not come by the High Street, for some of the cotts in the market square have been put to the torch. They will try to make it round by the wall and the Canons' Gate, I expect."

Followed by Martha, I made my way back towards the door on the north side, where two priests stood directing those who came hurrying in to places of refuge.

"I must go and find them. Mary will be slowed by the two children, and I could carry one of them."

"Let me go, Father, I can run faster than you."

"No, Martha. You do not know what de Pinkney does to women who fall into his grasp."

One of the priests who stood by the door barred our way with his arm.

"Neither of you will go," he said. "Robert has given orders that none who enter the church for sanctuary shall leave lest they be taken by Walter de Pinkney's men. We priests may go and seek those who are missing, for Mother church and the Cross protect us."

He took hold of the crucifix that hung from his girdle then, and raised it between us.

"It is young Mary and her two little ones who are missing, you say? They live by the Bar Gate, don't they? I know the place."

With that he made to pass out through the door, but Martha gave a quick cry.

"Look, there they are! They have just come into the churchyard."

We all turned to where Martha was pointing and saw Mary struggling along, holding her babe to her breast, while she pulled the frightened Osric along with her other hand. She had scarcely crossed half the distance to the church when from behind another dwelling there appeared a huge pot-bellied ruffian clad in chain-mail, closely followed by two other burly louts. Each held a sword that dripped blood.

"It is de Pinkney himself," gasped the priest, "with two of his henchmen. Heaven help Mary if he takes her."

Before the priest could make a move, de Pinkney had seen Mary. With an ugly laugh, he fumbled to loose his breeches.

"Seize that wench for me," he bellowed, "and spread her out that I may take her."

At once the two louts ran to her. The first, gripping her shoulder with one hand, struck her back-handed across the face and threw her to the ground. The other, grabbing the babe she clutched, launched a savage kick at its tiny body and watched it fly into the air and fall in a limp heap. Little Osric, meanwhile, loosed from his mother's hand, had set off screaming towards the safety of the church door. De Pinkney strode to the prostrate Mary and, gripping her robe, tore it bodily from her laying her pale flesh bare from breast to thigh.

Standing in the church door, we were all frozen to the spot with horror. Edward the young priest was the first to recover his senses. Elbowing the rest of us aside, he dashed towards the prostrate Mary, raising his crucifix high above his head as he did so.

"In the name of God, leave her!" he cried.

The priest's cry stopped Walter de Pinkney and his two henchmen in their tracks; all three looking in astonishment at the rapidly approaching figure of Edward with his flying robes and outstretched crucifix.

None of us had seen another figure that had emerged from the direction of the Canons' Gate and now charged towards the group still standing motionless in the churchyard. It was Mary's husband, Roger.

With a great roar, he crossed the intervening space in a few bounds and with one mighty sideways swing of his massive axe caught the two louts whose backs were turned towards him, near severing them both in two, so that they fell, a twisted mass of blood and flesh, without even uttering a cry.

De Pinkney turned, and saw the awesome figure of Roger towering above him. Realising his plight, he blanched, terrified, and clasped his hands in supplication.

"Spare me, spare me!" he jibbered.

Roger, who had seen what was about to happen to his precious Mary, was deaf to all cries and devoid of pity.

"Never!" he roared.

Raising his axe above his head, he brought it crashing down on the cowering figure that knelt at his feet, cleaving him through chain-mail and body from shoulder to navel, splattering himself with the tyrant's blood as the body fell lifeless at his feet.

Edward was the first to reach Mary, who still lay unconscious where she had been thrown. Covering her nakedness and gathering her in his arms, he staggered back towards the church, where by this time Martha and I had sufficiently recovered ourselves to rush to his aid. As we all made our way back towards the church with the limp figure of Mary cradled in our arms, we heard other shouts behind us.

Turning, I saw that two groups of armed men had entered from opposite sides of the churchyard. From the direction of the still-burning keep came a large group of de Pinkney's men, while from the Canons' Gate came a body of men from the burgh, led by Edric the reeve. Seeing each other, they both started to charge, only to be stopped short by another great bellow from Roger. Turning towards him, they saw that he stood astride the two mangled corpses of de Pinkney's henchmen, while he held up the limp and twisted body of Walter de Pinkney in one hand, and in the other he brandished his great axe above his head. A gasp went up from de Pinkney's men, and they hesitated in their headlong forward rush.

"Walter is dead," one of them cried, " and his two squires with him. We are lost. Flee for your lives men. We cannot stand against that giant. It is the Devil himself."

Some turned tail then and fled, spreading their dreadful news. Others threw down their arms in panic and rushed headlong towards the gate, trying to make good their escape. Seeing the confusion, Edric urged on his men in hot pursuit, cutting and slashing at any who tried to stand against them. In no time, the shouts and cries from the keep grew into cheers as Edric's men met with Gerald's force, who had been still valiantly trying to hold the bailey. Between them they finally drove the remnant of de Pinkney's men out of the burgh, leaving a trail of dead and wounded behind.

I left Mary in the tender care of Martha and Edward the priest while I went in search of the babe. The limp body lay in a hollow of the ground, so I bent to gather it gently into my arms, fearing for what I would find. The child lay motionless, but blood seeped from its mouth and there was no sign of life. Sorrowing, I began to make my slow way back towards the church. As I neared Roger, who still stood where he was, surrounded by the three grisly corpses, he turned unseeing eyes towards me.

"Come Roger," I said, "we must go to Mary. She is bruised but safe from harm and untouched," and I took his arm.

He came unresisting, trailing his great axe behind him, still overcome by the destruction he had wrought.

As we neared the church door, willing hands came to help us. I found Isabel was by my side, and into her hands I delivered the limp bundle I still held, shaking my head to her anxious glance. She nodded silently and moved quietly away, while I took Roger to where Mary had been lain and was now recovering. Seeing her sitting up, and taking a soothing draught, Roger let out a strangled cry and rushed to her side, pressing kisses on her hands, for her face was bandaged where she had been struck. They were safe enough together now, and each would be the best healing medicine for the other.

I sought out Isabel, and found her with Martha and our other daughter Ruth, gathered round the dead babe. Edward the priest knelt between them, as he murmured the words of absolution and committed the soul of the hapless child to God.

"Does Roger know?" Isabel asked.

"Yes, but he has not taken it in yet. Though I was carrying the babe with me as I led him to the church, his eyes were unseeing. The shock of what he has done to those three brutes and what so nearly happened to Mary has been too great for him. I would not wish to add to his anguish till he is calmer. How is Mary? Does she know yet?"

"No. I have not thought fit to tell her till she has recovered a little from her hurts. Let her be with Roger for a while, that they may comfort each other first."

We left them together, till Gerald and Edric came from the keep seeking Roger, whose great feat of slaying Walter de Pinkney had turned the day into victory. Telling them all that I had seen, I begged them to go gently with Roger, for though he was a hero, he would be inconsolable in his loss and I feared for Mary too.

Only time, that great healer, would mend their wounds, which, as Isabel and I knew full well, would go deep. With so much destroyed, I wondered if life would ever be the same again.

Chapter 21 1148–1150

Several days passed before Roger could reconcile himself to having killed the three men. "They have killed my child and would have violated my wife," he moaned, "but is that reason enough for me, who have never killed an animal willingly, to kill three men in my rage? I shall have their deaths on my conscience for ever, may God forgive me."

Both Edward, the young priest who had seen all that had occurred, and also Robert the vicar, talked to Roger earnestly, persuading him that no man living would have done otherwise, for the love he bore his family.

Meantime, Isabel went to stay with Roger and Mary to care for them and young Osric, who could not understand why his little brother was no longer there. Most of the time, they sat talking over the happy times they had had together, while Isabel encouraged them to remember the joy the babe had given them. Isabel helped them greatly by sharing her own grief at the loss of our little Hugh, so many years ago. She had with her, her harp, and with it sang them many of the old songs of love and sacrifice of our Saxon forbears, soothing them with the melodies and words.

We were not alone in our grief. There was hardly a family that had not suffered in the attack on the burgh. Alric's son, John, had been sorely wounded in the thigh and chest, and though he lingered for some days there was little anyone could do to heal his deep hurts and the loss of blood he had suffered. He finally expired a week later, with Alric and Emma at his bedside. As for Alric, he had been seriously burnt as he tried to pull the thatch from a burning cott after it had been put to the torch. At his age, I doubted that he would last the year, nor Emma either, for she had been ailing for some time, and the loss of their son affected them deeply.

The fire that had destroyed the roof of the keep, and the remaining fires in the burgh, had been put out. Over the days that followed, those that were unhurt or only lightly injured secured the walls and once more firmly barred the gates. As for de Pinkney's force, what was left of it slunk off and melted into the woods and heathlands of the surrounding country and we were left in peace once more, to bury our dead and heal our wounds.

I did what I could to help organise the rebuilding of the many homes that had been destroyed. Though I was much enfeebled with my age, I could give counsel and encouragement to those whose lives had been so rudely shattered. I also saw that none went hungry, by seeing that all had flour to make their bread. The beasts we had so prudently sent to Hengist's headland for safety were brought back again and put once more to use.

Finally, a messenger came with news that the force which King Stephen had at last sent to come to our aid had met with the remnants of Walter de Pinkney's men, and either killed or captured those few who had not been able to make good their escape. We knew then that the threat to the burgh was finally lifted.

We also learnt how we had been betrayed. It seems that the two serfs, Swein and Ernwi, who had always been idle and troublesome, had grown fearful of the continued attacks by Walter de Pinkney's men on the gate by the keep, where they formed part of the guard. One of them had secretly slipped out and offered to open the gate at night and betray the burgh in return for a bag of silver and a safe passage.

"Thirty pieces of silver," was Gerald's comment, when he reported these findings.

"The two of them had tried to persuade the third member of their watch to join their scheme," continued Gerald. "He, stout fellow that he was, would have none of it, telling them that he would not trust Walter de Pinkney's promise further than he could spit. Foolishly, he threatened to tell me of their plot next day. This only earned him a blow on the back of the head, which laid him out senseless on the top of the gate-house. When he came to himself again, the gate was taken and there was fighting all around him. Drawing his sword, he joined in the general melee and managed to cut down two of those who had broken in before he was himself wounded in the thigh and arm."

"He fought bravely then," I said. "Is it known what happened to Swein and Ernwi?"

Gerald grinned. "They were both found face down in the mill-stream. Both had dagger wounds in the back which had pierced their hearts. When first I heard this, I wondered, but when Wolstan, who had been the third member of the guard, told me his tale when I visited him two days later as he recovered from his wounds, all became clear. He had been right not to trust de Pinkney, for the promised purse of silver turned out to be a shaft of steel."

"They got their just desserts," I replied, "and died unshriven too. No doubt their torment will be to contemplate the souls of those whose deaths they caused."

After a week or so, Isabel persuaded Mary and Roger to come with us over to Hengist's headland to the place where the two of us had agreed to wed, and where Isabel had poured out her heart after the loss of our Hugh. There in the peace of the land around us, and the view of the distant white cliffs of Vectis Isle and Alban's headland, the four of us quietly sat, soothed by the soft breeze and the murmur of the waves breaking on the beach. While the sea-birds circled overhead, we talked over the loss each had suffered.

Isabel told them how she and I always came to that spot in times of greatest stress to resolve our problems and renew our spirits. She told them of the day when I had snatched her from the waves that had tried to claim her, and that it was here that I had brought her to calm her; how it was here, soon after, that we had pledged ourselves to each other; and how it was to this same spot that we had come, after our own babe was taken from us. As we stood, gazing out over the sunlit water, I sensed that Mary and Roger both relaxed at last. With a deep sigh, Roger turned to me and grasped my hand.

"You have renewed my spirit, Hugh, and shown me that life must go on. There is much still for us to do in the burgh and elsewhere, and, with your help, I know now that Mary and I can play the part that is set for us."

Mary stood beside her grandmother, and turning to her, hugged her close.

"You have shared your grief with me, which must have pained you greatly, even after all these years. The only way I know to thank you is to try to live my life as you have done. Like you, we shall have other children to replace the babe we have lost. Until today I did not think that we would, but I know now that we shall. Is that not so, Roger?" she said turning to him. "May they be as good woodmen as you."

She held out her hand to Roger and the four of us moved close together. A smile lit up Mary's face, as she looked at the three of us.

"There is no sadness that can overcome us if we are united as a family. Mother and Father have stood by us in our grief too, but did not have a loss like yours to share with us."

She turned and faced the sea and spread her arms wide above her head in a gesture that I had seen Isabel use so often when we were young.

"Come" she said, "I can face life again now for you have shown me how it must be done. We must return to the burgh. There is much to do, for others have suffered even more grievously than us and need our help."

She turned towards Roger and buried her head in his chest.

"My love, you and I have our lives before us. It is for us and those of our generation who have survived these last weeks to see that the burgh rises again as it should."

She took Roger by the hand then, and ran lightly down the slope towards where we had left the boat, dragging the smiling Roger behind her. I looked at Isabel as I felt the pressure of her arm about my waist.

"They will be all right now," she said.

"Because you showed them the way," I replied.

Over the months that followed, there was a great feeling of community in the burgh. When Alric died, for he did not recover from his burns and the loss of his son, everyone came to his burial. He had been a well-loved bailiff who had dealt justly with all men and was respected for it. Isabel mourned the loss of a much loved brother and I had lost my closest friend in all my life.

Thus it was that by common accord everyone helped his neighbour to re-build what had been destroyed. New cotts rose with astonishing speed and it had to be admitted that they were better built and more comfortable than many of those that had been destroyed. This was largely because master carpenters like my brother Osbern showed them how to build the wooden house frames stronger and how to make upper rooms for sleeping. A few even built stone chimneys at one end to help clear the smoke from the hearth and make the air within the cott clearer, to the comfort of all who lived within.

Baldwin de Redvers visited us a month or so later, and when he saw how the keep had been damaged by fire, he gave orders that it should be well repaired and the gate-houses and walls strengthened with stone. Such a task would take some months, we knew, and those who had skills that could be used on it were grateful for the work, for there had been little done on the church during the troubles. When he had set these things in train, Baldwin called the whole burgh together and addressed us.

"Men of Twynham, you fought bravely to save this burgh, and fought better than you knew. By your courage, you not only saved this place, but also prevented the Lady Maud from establishing a base from which to mount an attack on King Stephen and perhaps drive him from this realm. You suffered greatly for your bravery, but I will not have it go unrewarded. As you know, Alric my bailiff has recently died, and I grieve with you at your loss, for he was one who has served both me and you well. Now I shall appoint a new one in his stead."

He looked round the assembled crowd for the man he wanted, while the rest of us waited to hear whom he had chosen.

"It is Alfred, who is Alric's grandson. He has been well taught in his duties I know, and if he serves me and you as well as Alric, then we shall all be well pleased."

He beckoned to Alfred, to come and stand beside him. Putting his arm round Alfred's shoulders, he turned to him.

"You are some years younger than your grandfather was when he became bailiff here, but you have worked with him for many years, and so you know what should be done. I trust you, as I trusted him, and I know that you will not let me down."

Alfred blushed at this show of confidence in him.

"I will do my best, my Lord."

"No man can do more than that, and I think your best will, in time, be as good as Alric's."

I looked at Emma, who stood close to us. Though she looked drawn with grief from the loss of Alric, I saw her glow with pride for her grandson.

"Alfred, your first duty will be to see to the ease and comfort of those families who lost their menfolk in the recent fighting. From my store, you are to distribute corn to them all, so that they do not go hungry. Further, I decree that at plough-time and harvest, each man who owes me boon work is to do one day's labour, not in my fields, but on these families' strips, so that they may have crops to eat. The strips that belonged to those traitors Swein and Ernwi are to be divided amongst the families who have lost a man, so that they may have more land of their own by which they may live. You are to see to this Alfred, with Edric the reeve."

He ceased speaking, while he looked over the crowd as if searching for someone. At length, he continued.

"I also give to Roger the woodman, who turned what would have been a defeat into our victory, a virgate of land towards Catherine's hill, between the two rivers. His courage in slaying Walter de Pinkney and his two esquires must not go unrewarded, for all of us owe him a great debt. Like many of you, he and Mary have suffered a loss too."

There was a murmur of approval at this generosity, tinged with sadness, for all knew of the fate of their babe. As for Roger, he moved forward with his usual slow pace, and, kneeling before Baldwin, placed his hands between those of Baldwin in homage. Mary, with Osric beside her also hastened forward, tears in her eyes, to thank Baldwin and bless him. Smiling, Baldwin then bent to lift Osric into his arms.

"What do you want to be when you are a man?" he asked.

"A great lord like you." Then catching sight of me where we stood close by, he added, "Or perhaps a miller."

Baldwin gave a roar of laughter.

"Well, perhaps there is less difference between the two than you suppose,"

He fumbled in his scrip and took out a gold piece which he put it into Osric's small hand.

"Here lad, millers and lords both need gold. Whichever you turn out to be, here is something to start you on your way."

He bent down then to set Osric on his feet again, before handing him back to Mary.

"You have a fine son there, and may you be blessed with many more."

A crowd began to gather round Osric to see the gold piece he held in his hand, for they were not commonly seen amongst us. Baldwin had not finished however, and he raised his hands to command silence again.

"Finally, in gratitude for the help and succour that Robert the vicar, Simon and Edward and all the other canons of this church gave to the folk of the burgh, and the shelter they offered you all when Walter de Pinkney broke in and would have put to the sword all whom he did not ravish, I give to the church a virgate of land at Hoburne, beside the land they already hold at Stanpit, and I command that the fruits of this land are to be used to feed and succour the hungry here and any travellers who may come."

A great cheer went up from everyone who was gathered there. It is not often that a great lord shows such generosity.

As we moved away from the bailey where we had been gathered, we joined Emma, still bursting with pride, and Mary, Roger and Osric, who insisted on holding on to his gold piece in his hot little hand. Together, we returned to the bailiff's hall, where Emma still lived and into which Alfred and his family would now move.

"Alfred will be a fine bailiff, Emma," I said. "He will the have support of most folk, for he is well liked and knows the job. You will be able to guide him sometimes, and if I can be of help, he has only to ask."

She smiled. "He may have to look to you more than me, for I do not think I am long for this world. Since the burgh was burnt, my breath has come hard. I was with Alric as he tried to put out the fires and I took in so much smoke that it scorched me inside, and sometimes I can scarcely breathe." She gasped for breath as she spoke and was seized by a fit of coughing.

"I will speak to Simon," said Isabel. "He has all my balms and simples now, and I think he may be able to make you a soothing draught."

"It is kind of you, but I have little enough to live for now that Alric is gone. After so many good years together, to be without him is like losing half oneself. Besides, I am weary and will gladly join him whenever it pleases God to call me."

"That does not sound like my sister who used to play with us boys when we were young, and outrun us as often as not."

Emma sighed again. "Those days are long gone, but they were good times were they not? It is years since I have run like that."

"My brother Alnoth would agree with you Emma," said Isabel. "He seldom leaves his cott now, for his breath comes rasping. They say that it is the stone dust from his work as a mason that has affected him. Many of those who worked on the stone, carving it into beautiful shapes, have suffered likewise. I have given him soothing cordials to drink which give him some ease, but there is little I can do now, I fear."

It was as she said. It was some years since Alnoth had been able to work as a stone carver, but every time I went into the church I marvelled at some of his work. The beautiful arches and crossed stone-work he had carved on the north turret were a source of wonder to all who saw them. For those who knew where to look, there were the faces of several folk which looked down on the rest of us below. There was Edward the master mason, who had taught him all he knew, and Thurstan, the master carpenter, and Godric who had been priest when the great Domesday survey was made; others too whom I could not name. I liked to think of them watching over the rest of us from their places high up on the walls or on the capitals of some of the pillars, seeing that all was well.

The harvest had not been gathered before both Emma and Alnoth were taken from us within a week. It was all the more sad because, had they lived for another week, they would have heard the news that Baldwin de Redvers brought to Robert and the other canons. Tidings that would have pleased them both, as it did us. Baldwin de Redvers, passing through on his way to his great castle at Exeter, called together Alfred his new bailiff, Robert the vicar, and the rest of the elders in the burgh.

"It seems we shall have peace at last," he said. "King Stephen and the Lady Maud are seeking to make an agreement as to who shall rule this realm. After so many years of warfare, from which only the greedy barons have prospered, they both know that neither of them can hope to defeat the other and still have a land to rule. The Lady Maud's son, Henry, has been driven back into Devon, and though he has taken Bridport, I can hold him there so that he can make no further attack upon us."

Baldwin sat with his hands on his knees, looking from one to the other of those who were seated at the table. He seemed content with what he was to tell us.

"The plan is that Stephen should remain king of this realm for so long as he lives. The Lady Maud's son, young Henry, who is no more than sixteen years old yet, though he has already proved himself in battle, should become Duke of Normandy and, when King Stephen dies, he will take the throne of this realm as Duke William did before him. Nothing is finally settled, but this seems to be the best chance we have of peace in this land and I and many others have pressed Stephen to agree. The Lady Maud is satisfied, for by this means she will secure a kingdom for her son which she has little chance of gaining for herself, and that without a fight. Besides, she would rather live across the seas and give herself the airs of an ex-Empress - much good may that do her! We have seen how she upbraids and insults the greatest in this land, and there are few who will not be glad to see the back of her."

As this new turn of events began to sink in, I could not help feeling how pointless the many years of warfare had been if the pact that was proposed came to pass.

"For what purpose have crops been burnt then, burghs like ours put to the torch and men slaughtered these many years past?" I asked. "Great matters of state concern ordinary folk like us little. We only wish to till our land, complete our church and raise our families in peace."

Baldwin nodded gravely, and passed one hand across his careworn brow.

"You speak the truth. Though I would not agree with those who accuse me of it, some say that I myself have been guilty of such conduct in the past. I had good reason not to fall in with King Stephen's wishes at first, for I had no means of knowing if he would honour the old King Henry's charters by which I held my large estates. When Stephen would not give me his word, I felt I had little choice but to flee his presence and secure my position. Many others felt the same, because none knew if Stephen would stand by his word. Events proved us right for some years.

He scratched his chin for a while, wrapped in his own thoughts on matters which were outside our knowledge.

"I still say that he brought much of the trouble himself, though he was in a difficult position, as we were too, with so many of the great men having sworn allegiance to the Lady Maud as the next Queen. Nevertheless he was here and a man, and she was a lady and absent. However, I think we can put all that behind us now and once more live in peace."

"Pray Heaven that may be so," said Alfred. "Even with Edric the reeve to help me , my task as bailiff is hard enough without having to worry whether we are to be attacked or not. We lost a full plough team of oxen when they burnt the burgh, besides many sheep, goats and pigs, and two full barns of corn that were put to the torch. It was fortunate that we had hidden so many of the best beasts and other stock on Hengist's headland or we should be in a sorry plight. With the men who were killed or wounded, and some still not able to work from their hurts, we shall be hard-pressed to gather in the harvest, which will be small in any case this year."

"That is true enough," I added. "We have not had a full day's grinding at our mill since we drove off de Pinkney's men."

"I know how it is," de Redvers sympathised. "You can only do your best. Your first task is to see that those brave men who held the burgh, and the families of those who were killed, are fed and cared for. Without them I should have nothing from my estates here - nor would the church I think" he added looking at Robert, who nodded sadly in agreement.

It was a sorry gathering to be sure, which even the news of more peaceful times to come did little to cheer. But life had to continue, and there was no good to be had from being miserable.

After Baldwin had gone on his way, by common consent we all buckled down to the task of doing the best we could to rebuild our shattered lives. At our age, Isabel and I could do little to help other than try to encourage the younger men to look on the bright side and to the future.

About a month after Lammas-tide the following year, when the cotts had been rebuilt and the fields were once more growing good crops and the younger beasts that were left had been put to work at the plough, Robert received a visit from Bishop Henry of Blois. Such a visitation created much excitement,and a special Mass was celebrated by the noble bishop, which the whole burgh came to witness. After the Mass was finished, Henry of Blois addressed us.

"I have watched the building of this church, dedicated to the Holy Trinity, and like so many others, have marvelled at its glory. Though it is not as large as my church at Winchester, it is a noble place. The cloisters and other buildings for the convent that is to stand beside it are once again rising and will soon be able to house the priests for which they are being built. I must tell you now, that I have written to Eugenius, the Bishop of Rome, who has authority over all these matters, asking him in his wisdom, to allow me to establish here a House of Canons Regular of the Augustinian Order. I have now heard from Rome that my wish has been granted and that such a House is shortly to be set up."

A general murmur of wonder rippled through the crowd, so that Henry of Blois could not continue for some time. He waited for quiet once more to be restored.

"Have no fear, your present vicar, Robert, will continue to serve amongst you, and those priests whom you have will also remain here to continue their good work. Some, I know, have taken wives, as they are permitted to do, but the new canons will be bound by the rules of Saint Augustine which are more strict, and none will be permitted to take a wife. The prior has not yet been named, but when he is, I will tell you."

Again a buzz of wonder and surprise spread through those who listened.

"Many other changes will come about in due course, but they will be for the better and mean that this place will grow in fame as its learning increases, and the miracles, for which it is already famous, become more numerous. The lands which the church now holds it will continue to hold, as will the lands held by your priests. My brother, King Stephen, has agreed to this, and so have your lord Eorl Baldwin de Redvers and your Dean Hilary, who is now Bishop of Chichester. This will be confirmed to you in due course in new charters. I am also granting you silver to buy the stone needed to complete the buildings. The stone will come from Vectis as it did for the church, and the ships carrying it will start to arrive within the month. I mean this priory to take its place amongst the greatest in Christendom. Now go in peace, and be about your business."

There was an awed silence when Henry of Blois had finished speaking. Gradually the importance of his words sank in, and folk began to move away and leave the church by its two great doors, the one to the north and the other to the west. The priests, as was their custom, left by the south door, which led to their quarters. Isabel and I walked slowly back to our cott. As we stood by our door, Isabel turned and looked back at the massive church standing on its slight rise to the east.

"Who would have thought, when Ranulf Flambard first said that he wished to build a church here, that it would become so great and famous."

"Do you remember how his attempts to build it in the wrong place were frustrated?"

"Though you and Alric and our fathers, and Godwine and the other priests helped move the stone back to where we felt it should rightfully be, I am still sure that what we did was meant to happen," she said. I could not help agreeing with her.

Henry of Blois was as good as his word, and the stone for the conventual buildings soon began to arrive at the quay. There was great activity once more round the church. Masons were hard at work again, and carpenters, and plumbers working on the lead needed to make the buildings watertight. The work continued all the rest of that year and into the next, which saw the beginning of another new decade.

It was good to see how the burgh had recovered from the attack upon it, and that all traces of the fire seemed to have gone. Most of those who had been wounded had recovered sufficiently to be at work again, and even those who had lost limbs had found ways of managing their land. A man with one hand can find ways to dig and hoe, and even hold a plough if he has to, particularly if the alternative is to starve. Those who did their best found willing helpers amongst their neighbours, for when we had all suffered, we became more thoughtful for the needs of others. In this we were encouraged by Robert, who, at Mass, retold for us the parable of the sheep and goats from the Gospels, explaining how Christ told us that those who helped their neighbours would be gladly received into His Kingdom.

Thus we all began once more to prosper, and ships came freely into the harbour bringing goods that could be traded inland as far as Sarum. From the burgh, we sent out wool and often cloth, reeds for thatching, and corn and flour when we had it to spare, for there was great demand for these things in Winchester and other places.

Travellers came again in increasing numbers, for we were well known for our cures of certain sicknesses, which some thought to be miraculous. Under the guidance of Rodric, some of the young men were once more becoming proficient at copying the old books. Amongst the best was Hugh, our daughter Martha's son, a man of thirty summers now, whose skill with a quill and small brush produced some beautiful illuminations to the manuscripts.

That summer, Isabel and I often sat outside our door in the warm evenings, thinking back over all that had happened in our long lives, thankful that at last peace seemed to have returned to the realm.

It was the week before the feast of the Holy Trinity that the first eight of the new Canons Regular arrived from Winchester, clad in their black robes. Young Osric, our great grandson, brought us news of their approach. He had seen the little group of black-clad figures approaching along the road from Stanpit and ran to tell us. I hobbled slowly to the bridge by the gate to watch and stand beside Alfred our new bailiff, with Isabel on my arm, for we were both full of aches and pains these days. I thought back to the day so long ago when I had stood in the same place, with Isabel close beside me, to watch Gilbert the clerk, accompanied by Belesme of St Lo, come to make the great Domesday record. How long ago that seemed now. Isabel and I were about the only ones left who could remember that day.

As the black-clad figures approached, I looked at the one who seemed to be their leader. A tall, spare man, with a fine face and a piercing eye, though the corners of his mouth seemed ready enough to turn into a kindly smile. Reaching the bridge, he stopped upon it while the others stood grouped behind him. Then he felt at his waist with his left hand and raised the crucifix that hung there from a cord. Raising his right hand in benediction, he spoke clearly in a firm voice. "Peace be upon this place, and all who dwell therein. I am called Reginald, and have been sent with these others by Henry of Blois, and with the blessing of Eugenius, the Bishop of Rome and Holy Father of the church, to establish here a House of Canons, that God's work may prosper in this great church of yours."

Robert, who was standing with the rest of us in the gateway, stepped forward then, and knelt humbly before this tall black-clad priest, expecting to receive his blessing. Instead, Reginald bent down and, taking him by the arm, lifted him to his feet. Then embracing him, he gave him the kiss of peace.

"You should not kneel to me, Robert, for I do not mean to supplant you, but to work with you towards this end. Let us go first as we should, into your church, that we may give thanks and ask for God's blessing on the work we are sent to do. By our efforts alone we can accomplish nothing."

We all made our way into the church where Robert and Reginald, accompanied by all the priests and the new Black Canons, said a solemn Mass. There was much interest in their strange new garb, for all our priests had until that time worn the brown habit. By the time the Mass was finished, most of the folk in the burgh had crowded into the church, curious to see these new strange figures.

When Reginald had finished saying Mass, he turned to face us all, spreading wide his arms in welcome.

"Brethren, we are to be amongst you at the wish of the Holy Father, Eugenius, in Rome, as well as your Bishop Henry of Blois. We are to serve this place, and establish here a House of Augustinian Canons Regular, of which I, Reginald, have been appointed the first prior. Hear the charter of your Bishop Henry confirming this."

He felt in the pocket of his habit and drew out a scroll of parchment, from which hung several seals of red wax. Carefully unrolling this, he held it aloft so that all might see. Then in a clear voice he spoke.

"This year of our Lord 1150, Stephen being King, and on the petition of Baldwin Eorl of Devon, and his son Richard, Hilary being your dean and Lord Henry of Blois, your bishop at Winchester: to all their tenants and men, French and English, greetings. We make known to you, beloved, that whereas God inspired us that the Order of Canons Regular should be instituted for the honour of God and for the health of our souls and those of our ancestors, in the church of Christ of Twynham, we have granted and given to the same Canons Regular and to their successors there serving God, and to serve God, to possess freely and quietly and undisturbedly whatever the aforesaid church held on the day on which King Henry gave it to the elder Richard de Redvers, our predecessor, as well in ecclesiastical benefices as in lands or in rents whatsoever, to wit the church of Boldre with its chapels of Brockenhurst and of Lymington, the church of Hordle, and the church of Milford, the church of Stoppole, the church of Piddleton, and the chapel of Holdenhurst. All these churches and chapels we have confirmed to the aforesaid Canons with all their appurtenances and liberties. In the island called Vectis, the town which is called Ningweda with all its lands and rents, the land of Apsa with all its appurtenances, the land of Presteton, which is in the same island, the town of Herne with all its appurtenances, the land of Gorstell and a virgate of land next to the bridge of Huver, and another virgate of land which Ailmer the priest held, the land of Presteton, the land of Huborne, a hide of land and a virgate at Swinford, one land at Hampton, which belongs to the Manor of Ningweda. This is witnessed by Lucy the Countess, Henry de Redvers, and William his brother, and many others."

Here Reginald held aloft the parchment with its seals hanging from it for all to see. Many craned their necks to catch a glimpse of such an important document, coming from so great a set of nobles, the likes of which none had ever seen before.

However Prior Reginald had not finished. "Hear me again, for there is more. Though I have been placed as prior of this church, your present priests will still remain to work amongst you and to pray for you."

Feeling in the pocket of his habit again, he withdrew a second parchment, which he held aloft likewise.

"Hear what Henry of Blois, your bishop, has ordained," Prior Reginald said, waving the parchment above his head for all to see before he read it.

"The Secular Canons who now say Mass and have the cure of your souls shall continue to enjoy their prebends as long as they work in obedience to the prior, whether it be me or whoever comes after me. Those that serve the churches and chapels of this priory shall continue to do so, but as they die, the prebends, churches, and their profits shall go to the newly established Canons Regular. They will, in future, appoint all new incumbents, subject to the rights of the bishop. Bishop Henry also ordains that all past and future benefactions to the church by the faithful shall be inviolate, and in particular those already listed in the charter that I have just read to you."

Reginald carefully rolled up the parchment he had just finished reading, before putting it away in the pocket of his habit and drawing out yet another small parchment, from which hung a heavy red seal.

"Lastly, Lord Henry of Blois, your Bishop, wishes to inform the clergy and people of his diocese that in response to a supplication and presentation by me, Reginald, newly appointed as prior and the other Canons Regular of this church of the Holy Trinity of Twynham, that he has admitted and duly instituted Robert the Chaplain to the perpetual vicarage of this church, on the understanding that he shall receive daily the corrody of one Canon and one attendant, ten shillings a year, offerings at Confessions, and mortuary fees up to six pence, halving anything above that with the Canons, and Mass-pence which Hutgredus his predecessor had. Also four baskets of oats for his horse, and a third share of Langeneya meadow."

Rolling up this last parchment, he beckoned to Robert, who stepped forward and stood before him. Prior Reginald then placed this last parchment into Robert's ready hands, smiling as he did so. He seemed anxious for all to know that

Robert's kindly work amongst us was fully recognised. Then he waited, to allow those in the church to take in what he had said, for there was a great deal that he had told us which many were finding hard to understand. Eventually, he looked round on all of us and smiled.

"You see, we shall all be working together to try to bring about God's Kingdom on this earth. Good people of Twynham, go about your business now, and if any are in doubt about what I have said, let him come to me. I mean to sit daily in the door of the church on the north side for an hour after the angelus has sounded. Let any man come to me then, and I will hear his complaints. In this way we shall help the burgh to prosper. Go now in peace, and serve the Lord."

He raised his hand in blessing, while we crossed ourselves, and murmured "Et cum spiritu tuo" before turning to make our several ways back to our homes.

As Isabel and I sat by our hearth that evening, all our family gradually came to gather round us to consider the events the day had brought. By common consent, we agreed that great things had happened that day. I sat little Osric on my knee and looked with my dimming eyes at all our family.

"This day has called to my mind another great day that few besides Isabel and I remember," I said.

I told them of the coming of Gilbert the clerk and Belesme of St Lo who had become my friend, and the making of the great Domesday Book. I told them too how Isabel and I had served Gilbert and Belesme at table that day, and how at her suggestion we had brought water from the pure well near Stanpit to clear Gilbert's painful eyes. I told them many things of our early life together, and of the love, joys and sorrows Isabel and I had shared. Taking her hand in mine, I told them how she had supported and strengthened me through the years.

"Alone I could not have managed," I said, "but with such a wife as my Isabel, nothing seemed too hard for us together to surmount. We have always tried to think of each other and never to go to sleep at the end of the day with a quarrel unresolved, for the fault would lie always in part with both of us. We have shared our joys and sorrows, and each of us has tried to give to the other more than we have taken. That I believe is the secret of a happy marriage."

We were all silent for a long time, each husband and wife thinking over what I had said. At length, one by one they rose and bid us good-night and safe repose.

Alone finally, I turned to Isabel and, taking her hands in mine, bent and kissed her.

"I am glad to have lived to see this day," I said. "We have seen great things in our lives and played some small part in shaping this burgh. With the new order of Augustine's Canons, this great church we have watched being built will become known throughout the realm. Who can tell what part it will play in the wider scheme of things? As for us, thank you for making me so happy all these years."

We sat silent for some time, content to be together with our memories.

"From the first," I said, "I knew that I could not live without you. I can ask for no more for our children and their children than that they may be as happy as we have been."

Isabel smiled, and kissed me. Then leaning her head on my shoulder, she whispered "My Love and my Life."

Epilogue

Nineteen summers have passed since Prior Reginald and his brother monks first came to Twynham and established the Order of Augustinian Canons Regular here. Looking back on that summer of 1150, it seems that it marked the end of one era for our family, as well as for the burgh, and the start of another.

My husband Roger had taken on the tilling of the virgate of land that Baldwin de Redvers had given him for his bravery when the burgh was burnt by Walter de Pinkney two years earlier. He is still a woodman, for he loves his trees, but we have been able to gather good crops from our own land and thus pay for a serf who helps with the ploughing and harvesting.

It was some time before Roger was able to tell me all that had befallen that fateful day, for I had thankfully no memory of it. Roger's memory was faulty too. The shock of what he saw about to happen to me, and his rage, which caused him to slay all three of them with his great axe, had driven all recollection of the events from his mind. He had only pieced it together afterwards with the careful help of Edward, the young priest who had tried to rush to our aid. Osric, our son, was luckily too young to understand what happened that day, though ever since he has had a great fear of blood.

He, like the rest of the family, still treasures the memory of that evening in 1150 when we all sat in Grandfather Hugh's cott - he holding Grandmother Isabel's hand - as he told us of events long past and their happy life together. During the days that followed I spent much time with them listening to the tales he had to tell.

It was barely a month later that Grandfather Hugh died. He had been ailing all year, so that it was no surprise when I went to his cott one morning early to find Grandmother Isabel sitting beside the bed where he lay, quietly holding his hand.

"He slipped away from me during the night," she said. "Though I do not know what I shall do without him, I cannot grieve for him, for he has now joined so many of our family and friends. Pray Heaven that I may soon join him too."

When, sorrowing, I told Roger, he first crossed himself and offered a prayer for Grandfather's soul. Then he held me close.

"Mary, my love," he said, "be happy for him, for he is with the angels now. He will be welcomed by his own babe and ours too."

Grandmother Isabel was greatly comforted that so many in the burgh came to the Requiem Mass that Prior Reginald said for his soul, for Grandfather Hugh had been well liked.

Though Grandmother bore her loss as well as her frailty would allow, it was clear that she was waiting for the time when she too could join him.

Roger and I, with our family, moved into Grandfather Hugh's cott to care for Grandmother, for she could not manage on her own and would not move in with us. She had known no other home since their marriage, she said, for she and Grandfather Hugh had built the cott. It was full of memories of their long life together.

Pentecost was barely past when Roger and I found her one evening, sitting by her hearth, her hands resting on her harp which lay across her knees. By the expression on her face, she also had gone peacefully.

Many came to her Requiem Mass too, for she had been greatly loved. We buried Grandmother Isabel beside Grandfather Hugh, where she wished to lie.

The whole family gathered enough silver to have a silver candlestick made to stand on one of the side altars in their memory. It matched the one already provided in memory of Alric and Emma. We also paid for a Mass to be said for their souls every year on the day that each had died.

After Grandmother Isabel died, it was agreed that we should remain there on the same terms, keeping the burgh wall in good repair. It is a fine cott with its upper rooms, much larger than ours by the Bar Gate, and with plenty of land for vegetables and a pig or two and some fowls, so that I have been able to feed all the family better and also sell what was spare in the market each week.

Osric, who is now seeing his twenty-fourth summer, joined others of the family in the Priory Mill. He seems to have the same skills as Grandfather Hugh, for it is said that the millstones are as finely set as they were in his day. The flour is much sought after, selling for more than that from other mills. The fact that the seed corn used on the Priory lands is the best that can be had, as it was in the days of old Alsi the priest, back in the time that the great Domesday record was made, no doubt helps.

Roger and I were glad when last year Osric took to wife Elfrida, the pretty daughter of Edric the reeve. Osric used the gold piece that Baldwin de Redvers had given him that day he gave Roger his virgate of land, to pay for the cott he built on a parcel of land near the mill. There he now lives with Elfrida. She is expecting their first child before the end of the year. I am pleased for them both, for our family will now continue and still work the mill.

Much has happened in the burgh since Prior Reginald came in 1150. Such is the fame of the Priory now, that folk often talk of the burgh and church as though they were one, speaking of "Christchurch-Twynham". Many miracles are said to have been performed here, and after visiting the infirmarer, pilgrims frequently come to pray at the altars of our church, hoping to be cured of their ills.

The fame of the school has spread too, and several sons of lesser nobles have been sent to sit at the feet of our precentor, who, besides leading the singing at the services from his place at the right of the choir, acts also as librarian of the ever-growing stock of books. Aided by his assistant, the succentor, he spends much time instructing the young nobles and the lads of the burgh in Holy Writ, besides teaching them to write and calculate. Those that have the skill also learn the arts of copying and illuminating the precious manuscripts held in the library, some of which are a wonder to behold.

Some years ago a sacrist was appointed from amongst the canons to take charge of the fabric of the Priory. The cellarer, whose task it is to run the ever-growing estates held by the church, is finding that there is almost more than one man can manage. When I was a child, the sub-cellarer was little more than the head cook for the canons. Now he has to oversee the extensive gardens which provide the vegetables necessary to feed so large a company. He also sees that the kitchener and his under-cooks prepare and provide the large number of meals required daily for the Priory household. Pilgrims and travellers constantly call, and are cared for by the hosteller and almoner, who find that many have need of guidance as well as food and shelter. It is a large and busy community now, such as my Grandfather Hugh would scarcely recognise.

The same year, 1150, or it may have been the year after, I cannot rightly remember, Bishop Henry came with a general ordinance he had issued concerning all the vicarages in his see. This he read out to us after High Mass one feast day. He made an impressive figure as he stood before the high altar in his cope and mitre, with his chaplains standing on either side of him.

"Since it is a bishops's duty to foster the temporalities of his flock when they are vowed to religion and hospitality as this priory is," he said, "so that you may be the more fervent in worship, the more ready to entertain, and the more disposed to works of mercy, I, Henry of Blois, and Bishop of Winchester, make known to the faithful that not only have I granted to the Canons Regular of Christchurch at Twynham that they should enjoy the revenues of all their beneficies, but also that in the instance of Reginald the Prior and the canons, and so that I may remove all causes for litigation by the malevolent, I have named these vicarages which are sufficiently taxed. Thus to the Vicarage of Christchurch belongs a corrody of one canon and one attendant, confession offerings, Mass-pence to the sum of ten shillings a year, mortuary payments up to six pence and the halving with the canons of aught above that, a third of Langheneya mead, and four baskets of oats, all of which Hutredus the priest had before Robert his successor, who had been duly instituted to the vicarage here. To Sopley vicarage belong all except corn-sheaves, but the chaplain shall account for all and shall minister to Winkton chapel, paying five shillings a year to the Priory for his tenure of a virgate of land."

Henry of Blois paused a while, and looked round at all of us. Then he scanned the parchment he held before looking up again.

"There follow several other items which do not concern this place, which I shall pass over. To continue with what does concern this priory."

He cast his eyes down the parchment once more, murmuring to himself till he came to the place he sought.

"Yes, here we are. There are two salterns which are held by the Rector of Milford, but which belong to this priory. Also, from the priest who holds the vicarage of Boldre is due a pension of four silver marks which he is due to pay on the altar of the Holy Trinity in this priory. I further confirm that the canons here are free to confirm or dismiss their chaplains at will, saving a just livelihood for them, but when rectors resign, I agree to institute without question those whom the canons present as fit successors."

Henry of Blois ceased reading then, and held aloft the parchment he had in his hands. "See: it is all written here and witnessed by Selida, Abbot of Hyde, Ralph, Archdeacon of Winchester, and Master Jordan."

There was a general murmur of approval, for it seemed that Henry of Blois was giving greater freedom to the prior and his canons than might have been expected. Perhaps he trusted them to do right more than some. Who can tell? Certainly we prospered under their guidance, and the fame of the Priory grew with each succeeding year.

The bishop then handed the parchment to one of his chaplains, and took another from him. This he held aloft, and I saw that it had a heavy seal at its foot.

"This is from the Holy Father Eugenius himself, and has been sent to me from Rome. It is, as you can see, sealed with the leaden bulla that all such ordinances have. In it the Holy Father confirms the appointment of your Prior Reginald and his Secular Canons, and much else which I have already told you. He also states that the canons themselves should elect all future priors. This I give to Reginald, for it is by this authority that he will act."

Reginald stepped forward, and received the weighty parchment from the bishop with a bow. Turning, he showed it to the other canons, who had crowded round.

Many of us wondered that so small a burgh as Twynham should have come to the notice of so great a man as the Pope.

It was probably the year after, that Eorl Baldwin came once more to the burgh, bringing with him another large parchment. As was his custom, he stood in the porch of the Priory after Mass, with his clerks and seneschals round him, for this was the best time and place to have the whole burgh gathered together.

Holding the parchment aloft he said, "Good people of Christchurch-Twynham, I know that the Holy Father in Rome and my Lord Henry of Blois, your bishop, have both decreed how this priory is to be governed and what lands it holds for Mother church. As your temporal Lord, I now wish to confirm certain rights and land holdings which I and my father before me have given to you."

Eorl Baldwin unrolled the parchment he was holding, then addressed us in his clear voice. "I too confirm to the Canons Regular of this Priory of Christchurch at Twynham, the right to elect their own prior, and also to have the benefit of the church tithes, church-scot, men, lands, and holdings, with the right to acquire from the Secular Canons as they die, whatever they had on their fee, namely the manors of Ningwood and Prestaton and the church at Thornley, all on Vectis Isle, the lands of Hamstede, and the land in Hamton. Also the church at Piddleton and its chapels granted by my father Richard, and the ancient prebend there; the tithes at Herne on the demesne of Alured de Brockelia, and the manor of Apse on Vectis which were granted by Roger de Hestro; also lands close to this burgh at Huborn, Sopley, Grove, the two lands at Herne, with half a hide at Bosley, which was once held by William Closeward; also the two virgates by the Holdenhurst bridge, sometimes called Iford.."

As Eorl Baldwin waited for a few moments so that we could reckon up these lands, Roger pulled at my sleeve to attract my attention.

"Why Mary, it seems to me that the Priory owns half the land hereabouts. No wonder there is food enough to feed all who come, and to spare, and also to pay for raising new buildings."

"True enough, and it is fortunate for us that the Prior is honest and uses his revenues as he should. I hear that it is not always so elsewhere."

Our attention was once more drawn to Eorl Baldwin, who was about to continue.

"I also confirm in my fee to the Regular Canons, all other rights that were before-times enjoyed by the Secular Canons, namely the tithes of tolls at Christchurch-Twynham, the tithes of wreck within the parish, except that they are only to have the left-hand side of any great fish that shall be beached; the first salmon to be caught each year, tithes of all other salmon, and a tithe from all newly ploughed land in and around the burgh. Next I confirm that the Regular Canons are to have the same privileges and dues as the Secular Canons had, namely the right to trade toll-free on all my lands, with freedom from services, gifts and aids. I also grant all men of the church the right to come before no Hundred or other court save for murder or homicide, but if they owe forfeit to me or my men, then the jurisdiction is to be mine, but the compensation shall go to the Priory. If the men of the church be arrested for felony, they shall have their court as under the Secular Deans, to wit, free of shire or other such courts, so that they may be tried by my bailiffs."

Eorl Baldwin looked round smiling at all those who were gathered before him. He held up the parchment, with its waxen seals hanging below it, for all to see.

"It is all written down here even as I have said, and it is witnessed by my son Richard, who is heir to all my lands. He will continue the rights and privileges that I have granted to you after I am dead. It is also witnessed by Hubert de Fals, Hugh Peverel, and Geoffrey de Insula."

In the general hubbub of conversation that followed the reading, those nearest to Eorl Baldwin strained forward to see the parchment and its seals, though none of them could read what was written. Prior Reginald, who was standing beside him, raised his hands for silence.

"Have no fear good people, I have read this parchment, and it is even as my lord says. By his generosity this priory is greatly enriched, and be assured that all the goods and silver that are received shall be used for God's purposes."

I felt Roger squeeze my elbow as he bent to whisper in my ear.

"It is good to hear Reginald say that, Mary. I have heard that some abbeys and priories have grown lazy with over-much wealth, so that their priests neglect the cure of men's souls and think only of their own comfort. I am not sure what is to happen when any man of the church commits some crime. It seems that they are to be judged not in the usual courts, but perhaps by the church itself. There are plenty who would claim such a benefit, for the church's punishment is less than that of the King's courts. Who would not say a penance daily, or even give silver to the church rather than lose a hand?"

"I trust such things will not happen here," I replied. "With Prior Reginald to watch over our affairs, and Henry of Blois near, besides Eorl Baldwin, it does not seem likely. What happens afterwards, when they are gone? What then?"

Roger nodded thoughtfully.

"Much may depend on King Stephen, who gives us little enough encouragement to hope for a peaceful life. He may have agreed with the Lady Maud that he is to remain King till his death, and that her son, Duke Henry will reign after him - and no doubt she intends to call the tune for him - but all can still be overturned if the barons decide to take the law into their own hands. We can only live in hope."

He sighed heavily, and I knew how troubled he felt, for the same thoughts were passing through my mind too.

Not long afterwards we heard that the young Prince Henry had gone to pay homage to his overlord, King Louis of France. It was said that he was more a monk than a king, for he spent his time at prayer rather than enjoying himself in a luxurious court. Things moved apace it seems, and the French King's Court was amazed when, within months, Henry had persuaded the Pope that King Louis' marriage to his Queen Eleanor was void, and promptly married her himself. Though we in the burgh do not fully understand these things, it seems that Queen Eleanor brought with her as dowry all Aquitaine, and much else of the western side of France, so that the young Henry's lands far outstretched those held by King Louis, or our own King Stephen.

At the time it meant little to us, though Baldwin de Redvers, who passed through the burgh some months later, said it showed how powerful the next king of England would be. He said it would keep the French in check, for their nobility were a grabbing self-interested bunch. We had no knowledge of such things, but it did cross my mind that the world had turned full circle, since William Duke of Normandy had come to conquer this land. Now our next king would take over most of France besides the Norman dukedom.

I was more interested in Queen Eleanor, who, it seemed, could change husbands to suit her own advantage. When King Stephen died in 1154, the young Henry, still in his twenty-first year, and his queen came over to be crowned in London. She took its people to her heart, but could not stand the weather. She complained that it rained too much and it was far colder than she was used to in southern France. Prior Reginald, who had travelled as far as Rome, said she was right in this.

Reginald, who had been at the coronation, said that the crowning itself was a magnificent affair. All the nobility of this land, from the Queen's lands in Aquitaine, and those from Henry's lands in Normandy and Anjou and elsewhere were there, dressed in their finest clothes of gold and silken thread such as he had never seen before, with jewels sparkling from every finger and breast.

"It grieved me to see the state of the great abbey at Westminster where the crowning was held," Reginald said. "The stonework was in decay, with weeds growing from its walls. All around, its buildings were in disrepair for lack of money to keep them maintained. Much of the great lands that the abbey holds were stolen and ravaged during the troubles, so that the coffers were empty and the works not done."

Shortly afterwards the royal couple came to Winchester to hold court there. Roger and I decided to make the journey to see them, for they were said to make a handsome pair. We watched them pass by on horseback through the crowded street. As they drew near, Roger tugged at my arm.

"Did you ever see such a handsome woman, Mary? No wonder King Henry fell in love with her. See her shapely figure and winning manner and how she smiles on all around her. Ah, and her brown eyes and dark flowing hair! See how it is held in four long plaits that reach almost to her waist, and how it shows off her skin. Why, it is clear as alabaster! No wonder she found the French King Louis dull and craved for a real man like our King Henry."

Roger bent his head, and whispered in my ear.

"It is rumoured that Louis seldom bedded her, spending all his nights on his knees in prayer, and they do say that she seldom slept alone. I doubt she will find fault with Henry on that score."

Roger nudged me in the ribs as he spoke, but I scolded him for his idle prattle.

"It is not seemly to speak so of your King or his Lady. She has born him one son already, and it seems that she may be carrying another now, so that she is doing her duty by this realm. What a fine figure he cuts! Look at his broad shoulders and massive chest and bulging muscles. There is power and restless energy in that frame. No wonder he needs a stout horse, for I think he could ride all day and never tire. I hear he is bandy-legged from constant riding, though few would hold that against him. That red hair is true Norman for sure, just like the first and second Williams they say. If his temper is as fiery, it would be a brave man who dared to cross him."

At that moment Henry passed beside us and turning towards where we stood, looked straight at me. I gripped Roger's arm in my excitement.

"Look at his eyes! Did you ever see such grey eyes, and how they seem to bore right into your innermost thoughts. Nothing can be hid from such a man, I think. It makes my bones melt to look at him."

"Do you fancy him yourself, Mary?" Roger asked with a twinkle in his eye.

I slapped his hand in mock anger, for I knew he only teased.

It did seem to me that this handsome young giant, with his boundless energy who was said to have a wise head on his shoulders, had the makings of a noble king who would put right many of the ills that had befallen the realm in the past.

"If anyone can bring lasting peace to the land, it will be him," I said.

" Pray Heaven that his sons be cast in a like mould too," Roger answered.

As the years passed, it seemed that my hopes were to be fulfilled. Peace did continue, and the laws of the land were firmly enforced, so that men felt once more that justice was done to them. It was said, though with what truth I know not, that those whom Henry could not tame with his tongue and penetrating eye, the Queen won over with other favours. Certainly, it was common knowledge that she was never short of fawning companions at the royal Court; but peace there was and the whole realm prospered.

True, we in the realm saw little of our King, for he spent most of his time in his far greater lands in France, often in conflict with other French nobles who supported the French King Louis against him. Such matters troubled us little, however.

News of them came to us mainly from ships bringing goods from across the water, so that we listened but took little note. Only occasionally did such things touch our lives, like the time when Gundulf, the son of Gunric the new reeve, who had gone to fight in King Henry's army in France, was killed in a siege of some French castle. We mourned his death, and I did what I could to comfort Gunric's wife Mildred, who had been my friend since childhood.

During all this time life in the burgh continued and folk began to prosper again with the crops growing well when the weather was fine, for there was much good land. Those who had suffered during the troubles gradually learnt to put the memories of those evil days behind them. I counted Roger and myself amongst them.

More cotts were built as families grew, and several more assarts were carved out of the wild land towards the great forest of Andret. Baldwin de Redvers took care that the stone keep was maintained in good repair and well stocked with swords and arrows. Some said that they could not see the need for such a strong place now that there was once more peace in the land. Others felt that it was a comfort to know that there was a stronghold to defend the burgh, should the need ever arise again. When Baldwin came, he would lodge with his noble friends in his fine hall, with its huge storerooms beneath and several spacious rooms above. At one end was one of the new chimneys, which allowed the smoke from the fire to escape into the air above and so keep the room fresh. We heard tell that several of Eorl Baldwin's friends went away determined to copy his idea, and build chimneys in their halls.

Some years later, by which time Henry had persuaded the Pope - a new one called Alexander - to appoint Thomas Becket to the see at Canterbury, our fears that men of the church might suffer too light a punishment for their crimes seemed to come true. There seemed to be many more felonies committed and men grumbled that it was no longer as safe to travel the roads as it had been in the past. Robbers abounded, and it became increasingly common for men to claim that they held some minor church office, though exactly what often seemed in some doubt.

For this reason, King Henry called all his bishops together at his hunting lodge at Clarendon, outside Sarum. We heard that he bullied them into agreeing that the worst of the abuses should cease. There was uproar, but in the end Thomas Becket agreed, though he changed his mind soon afterwards, to the King's anger. The two did not speak for years afterwards, though Henry was mostly in France, but at least more men were brought before the proper courts and received their due punishment.

Then this year, 1169, just after Pentecost, Henry of Blois came once more to the burgh, this time with another parchment, bearing the great lead bulla of Pope Alexander. He spent some time that day with Prior Reginald, before he finally called the whole burgh together to hear what the Holy Father had decreed. As was his usual custom, he stood on the steps before the high altar with his chaplains, and with Prior Reginald on one side, and Robert the vicar on the other. When all were quiet with expectation, he called his scribe forward to bring him the Papal parchment, which he carefully unrolled so that the heavy lead seal hung down from its lower edge.

"Pax vobiscum, good people of this priory and burgh of Christchurch at

Twynham. Hear the words of the Holy Father, Alexander, who has answered the petitions of your Prior."

He cleared his throat, and adjusted his hold on the heavy parchment, before starting to read.

"His Holiness writes to the Prior of the church of the Holy Trinity at Twynham and his brethren vowed to the Regular Order of Saint Augustine, that since he is bound to grant just petitions, he has followed the example of Pope Eugenius in taking this church under the protection of the Holy see by this charter."

There was a subdued murmur of awe, for many wondered that such a mighty man as the Pope himself should continue to take such interest in our church, which was so far distant from Rome.

"First," declared the Bishop "the Holy Father decrees the perpetual establishment here of the Augustinian Canons, and that their goods and possessions, both present and future, whether grants of popes, princes, or others, shall be theirs for ever, and in particular the following."

Here he listed all the lands of which we had already heard, but added others of which we knew nothing: lands in Wiltshire, a virgate in Bulnore, land in Debourne granted by Richard Mascharell with the assent of Eorl Baldwin and his son Richard; land held by Roger Long, and some more held by two peasants, Odd and Geoffrey, opposite the Canons' Gate; some lands at Milford, and Piddleton, and also of Bleakdown on Vectis Isle.

As we listened to the long recital of lands belonging to the church, we noted that once more new lands had been added, which men had given in the hope of attaining salvation. Then Henry of Blois continued.

"Let no man exact tithes of the canons on lands tilled by their labour or at their cost, or for the increase of their flocks. Let them have complete freedom to admit to their community any man, lay or cleric, seeking refuge from the world, but those so received shall not leave the canons' cloister save with written permission and to join a stricter Order. At times of general interdict, after locking out any interdicted or excommunicated persons, they may hold services with lowered voices. Take note also that the right of burial is to be open to all seeking interment at Christchurch-Twynham unless they be excommunicate or under interdict. On the Prior's death, there shall be a fair election of whomsoever the brethren shall choose, according to their Rule. It is also decreed that no man shall damage, annex, withhold, diminish or encumber the said church or its property, which are to be preserved intact, saving the authority of the Apostolic See and the rights of the Diocesan Bishop."

Henry of Blois looked round on us all then, as if to impress upon us the importance of what he had just said. At length, he continued in as stern a voice as he could muster.

"God's judgement is invoked on all who refuse to atone for infringing this decree, but let those who uphold the Priory find peace everlasting. Granted at Beneventum by the hand of Gerard, Notary of the Holy church, Anno Domini 1169, in the tenth year of Alexander the third."

I still remember the long silence that followed when Bishop Henry finished speaking and I can still see him in my mind's eye, standing on the altar steps in his glittering cope, surrounded by all the other priests in their finest robes. Such a decree was not lightly made, and would not lightly be broken, for fear of everlasting damnation and Hell fire. Many who stood near Roger and I seemed to blanch at the thought, and I saw several lips tremble. It seemed to us that even greater power was being given to the church. It crossed my mind that things might go awry if ever there were to be a prior who was lax or self-indulgent.

That night, our whole family came together into our cott, which had once belonged to Grandfather Hugh. Long was the discussion we had. By common consent we agreed that our burgh, protected by its stone castle, and with its fine Priory church, famed not only for its size and magnificent carving but also for the many miracles associated with it, and the growing importance of the school as a centre of learning, would continue to be a place from which men would draw strength and inspiration to lead their lives according to the will of God. It would surely benefit all who came within its boundaries and far beyond.

There was not one of us that night who did not feel humble to be part of that great community, and perhaps somewhat over-awed by the duty it placed upon each of us to live up to the example which was set before us. We were members of Christ's church, and citizens of Twynham - names that would live on for ever.

The Norman Church

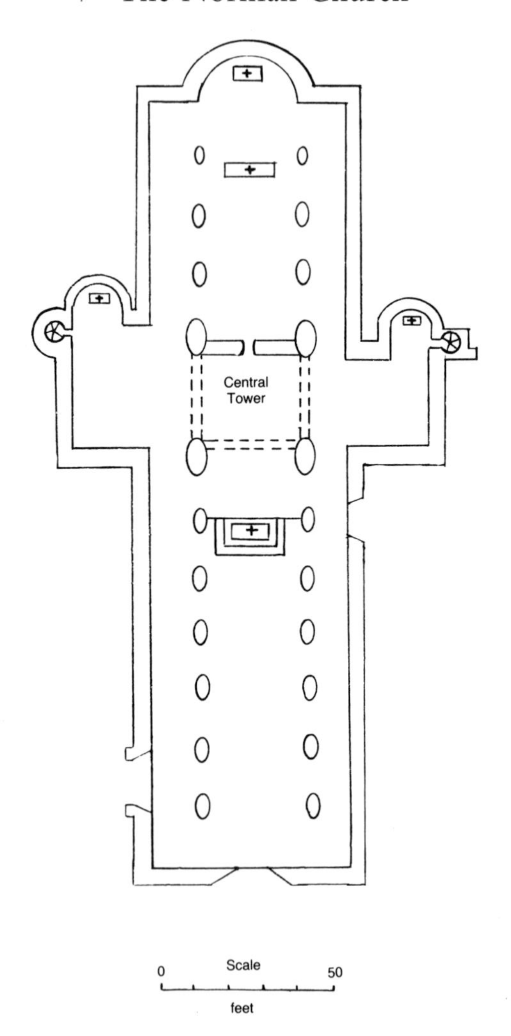

Main Characters in Hugh of Twynham

Oswald (the Miller)	– Hugh	b 1072	marries Isabel
Maud – his wife	Emma	b 1073	marries Alric
	Osbern	b 1077	marries Adela
Alwin (the Bailiff)	– Alric	b 1072	marries Emma
Mary – his wife	Isabel	b 1074	marries Hugh
	Alnoth	b 1076	marries Mathilds

Hugh — Isabel

Martha b 1095 | Hugh b&d 1096 | Ruth b 1097 | Oswald b 1098 | Simon b 1100

(Martha b 1095:) Hugh b 1120 | Mary b 1121 – Roger the Woodman

(Mary and Roger the Woodman:) Osric b 1145 | baby b & d 1148 | Osbern 1150

Secular Canons:–	Alnod ‡	old priest with much land
	Alsi ‡	fat priest
	Godric ⋆	priest in charge
	Godwine ‡	the kindly giant of Stanpit
	Ranulf	of the guest house
	Roderic	the teacher
	Simon	the infirmerer
Other characters:–	Belesme of St. Lo	Norman soldier
	Gilbert	Domesday Commissioner
	Goodwife Adeline ⋆	the healer, wife of Witro
	Ranulf Flambard ⋆§	first Dean of Twynham
	Odo	Master Builder
	Edward	Master Mason
	Thurstan	Master Carpenter
	Witro ⋆	the falconer

⋆ named in the Christchurch Cartulary.
‡ named in Domesday records.
§ named in the Durham Charters.

The Medieval Monastic Day

The medieval day was ruled by the times of the seven services or Offices:– Matins, Lauds, Prime, Terce, Sext, Vespers, and Compline.

The daily time-table was much as follows, though there were local differences. The times varied somewhat in winter, which for the priests started on September 13th, and ended on Ash Wednesday, the start of Lent, 46 days before Easter. This is a movable feast, fixed by the date of the Jewish Passover, which is itself fixed by the lunar calendar.

2 a.m.	The priests were roused, to say Matins.
5 a.m.	Lauds, after which they returned to bed until Prime.
8 a.m.	Prime, after which they returned to the dormitory to wash then they returned to the chapel to say Terce or Morrow-Mass, which was followed by breakfast, taken standing in the refectory.
10 a.m.–12 noon	Work at their allotted tasks.
12.30 p.m.	Sext.
2 p.m.	Main meal of the day, taken seated in the refectory, usually in silence, while one of their number read to them from a religious book.
3–5 p.m.	Reading or study, usually of a religious subject.
5 p.m.	Vespers, after which the priests put on their night shoes and returned to the refectory for a light meal.
6 p.m.	The angelus bell was sounded, heralding Compline, the last Office of the day. This bell would be heard by those working in the fields near the burgh. Many would say their own prayers then, giving thanks for the day's work, and perhaps asking some boon of God.
6 p.m.	Compline.
6.30–7 p.m.	The priests retired to bed, to sleep until they were roused at 2 a.m. next morning for Matins once more.

Glossary

Acre. Area of land, of any shape, but conventionally 220 yards long by 22 yards wide. This formed a "strip", of which each villein had on average 30, ten in each of the three main fields of the manor estate. Strips would be separated by an earth bank. An acre strip was as much land as a yoke of oxen could plough in one day; a distance of ploughing of about four miles.

"Agnus dei qui tollis peccata mundi, miserere nobis, et dona nobis pacem". "Oh Lamb of God, that takest away the sins of the world, have mercy upon us, and grant us thy peace." Part of the Mass, frequently used as a prayer.

Aid. A subsidy or tax paid to the king for a special purpose, such as a war; theoretically a loan but very seldom repaid.

Angelus. A bell rung at morning, noon and sunset, calling people to prayer - usually to the sunset bell.

Appurtenance. All the outbuildings belonging to a property.

Ard. Anglo-Saxon wooden plough, still used in Norman times. Later models had a metal tip or were fixed with a spade-shaped under-blade which helped to turn the soil over for better cultivation. Ards were normally pulled by eight oxen or cattle.

Alod. Freehold land derived from primitive hereditary occupation, which was quite rare. Most land was held from a superior land lord - quite often the King himself - to whom various types of service or rent was due.

Assart. Land which had been cleared by grubbing out trees and bushes from forest land to make it arable (though not, of course, the king's designated forests). As all land belonged to the King it was technically an offence but many ordinary folk acquired land in this way.

Bailey. External wall, sometimes of stakes only, but often of stakes surmounting an earth bank, enclosing the outer courtyard forming the first line of defence of feudal castles.

Bailiff. The King's officer or representative in a hundred or **burgh** who was responsible for the efficient running of the estate and sometimes also its defence if there was no constable.

Bordar. A villein who held his hut at his lord's pleasure.

Brock. Old name for a badger.

Burgh. Ancient township, having a charter from the King. In Saxon times it was usually defended by a stout wall.

Collibert. A freed-man, holding land and freed from strict serfdom but still bound to render certain dues and services to his overlord.

Coney. Old name for a rabbit. The Normans greatly increased their numbers as a source of food, keeping them in warrens within many castles for eating in time of siege.

Cott. A small dwelling or cottage as used by the majority of people, consisting originally of one room, perhaps with a section partitioned off for sleeping. In time they became larger and had more rooms.

Demesne. Property of a lord (derived from 'domain'); defined area of private property under someone's influence or control.

Doxy. Unmarried mistress or beggar's wench, usually regarded as a prostitute.

Eorl. Now obsolete word for Earl: a man of noble rank, as distinguished from a **ceorl/churl** or ordinary **freeman**. The Saxon equivalent was Governor; by Norman times it was the equivalent of a Count.

Frankpledge. System whereby every member of a **tithing** was answerable for the good conduct of, or damage by, any one of the other members.

View of Frankpledge. Court held periodically in the burgh, when all members of each tithing had to be present and answer to the lord or his **reeve** for their good behaviour; sometimes called the **Court Leet.**

Freeman. A man who is free or enjoys liberty; one who holds a particular franchise or privilege.

Fyrd. Military array of the whole country before the Norman Conquest, also the obligation of military service. It was still used loosely in Norman times.

Gambeson. Military tunic of leather, often padded for further protection; sometimes thick cloth only.

Garderobe. Locked chamber for storing clothes and by extension a private room ('privy') or lavatory.

Gavel. Mason's setting maul.

Gavel Tax. Payment of tax to a superior; tribute.

Geld. A tax on land.

Goodwife. Mistress of the house. As a prefix to a name it equates with 'Mrs.', a polite form of address.

Hauberk. Piece of defensive armour originally for neck and shoulders but soon became a long coat of chain mail which adapted itself readily to the movements of the body; more effective against sword thrusts and arrows than the leather **gambeson.**

Homage. Formal recognition of allegiance to a superior, whereby you bound yourself to serve your master or overlord.

Housecarl. King's men or bodyguard; household troops of Danish and Saxon kings, such as Harold.

Hue and Cry. This was raised by other members of a **tithing** to pursue and bring to justice one of their number who had committed some crime. If they failed to catch him and bring him to justice they were liable themselves for his fine.

Hide. An area of land sufficient to support a family with all its dependants (approximately 120 acres). This was the amount of land that could be cultivated by one plough team in a year.

Infirmarer. The priest whose task it was to care for the sick in the monastery. He was also the main, or only, doctor in the area and used ancient herbal medicines.

Infangenthief. The right of the Lord of the Manor to try and fine one of his own men caught thieving on the lord's lands. This could be a valuable source of income, and was open to abuse.

Justiciar. The chief political and judicial officer under Norman and Plantagenet kings. He acted as regent in the King's absence, represented the King in all relations of state, and was the royal deputy in the King's presence. Probably equivalent today of the Lord Chief Justice, Prime Minister, Foreign Secretary and Chancellor of the Exchequer rolled into one.

Mainprize. To take someone in hand, and make oneself legally responsible for his actions; giving a surety to get someone released from gaol.

Mark. A sum of money, 13 shillings and 4 pence, or two thirds of a pound. The fine for breaching bail and not surrendering as required could be half a mark. The average wage was about one penny a day.

Messuage. Area of land intended to be occupied by a house or cott and its appurtenances and its garden.

Motte. A castle mound, or the castle built on the mound.

Murrain. Plagues or pestilences usually referring to animals and regarded as fatal.

Parage. Parity or equality of condition; usually refers to land held equally with another(often a brother or sister) without any duty of **homage** or service.

"Pax vobiscum ... Et cum spiritu tuo". Conventional greeting by a priest, and its response. "Peace be with you" ... "And with thy spirit".

Pix. Vessel in which the consecrated host, or bread of the sacrament, is reserved in church.

Plastron. Breast plate of steel formally worn beneath the **hauberk**; could sometimes be leather.

Plough. Team of eight oxen, or cattle, harnessed to pull an **ard**.

Precentor. A senior priest whose duties included looking after the singing in church and training the choir etc.

Quern. Simple apparatus for grinding corn; usually two stones, one on top of the other. The top one was either rubbed back and forth, or rotated on the lower stone to grind the grain placed between them. Querns were discouraged by Lords of Manors who owned mills because it deprived them of income.

Radknight. A Saxon or Norman tenant holding land on condition of performing military service on horseback.

Receipt. Old word for recipe.

Reeve. The Saxon or Norman official having local jurisdiction under the King. He acted as the local magistrate and was also responsible for the administration of the burgh, acting as overseer of the tenants and other workmen. He worked closely with the hayward, swine-herd, and other local officials in the **burgh**.

Rod. A unit of measurement about 5 yards. It was the standard width of a cott. Ten rods was often the length of a garden. An acre was conventionally 4 rods by 40 rods, 4 rods making a furlong (or furrow-long).

Sac and Soc. Certain rights of jurisdiction which by custom from the times of the Danes (King Cnut) belonged to the Lord of the Manor, and were included in the grant of the manor by the King. It gave the ability to fine in certain cases, and was therefore valuable.

Sacrist. church official charged with the custody of sacred vessels, relics and vestments.

Scrip. Small purse or satchel used to hold personal belongings and coins; used before clothes had pockets.

Scullion. A mean or despicable person; a servant who has the dirtiest household jobs.

Shrive/shriven. To impose a penance; hence to hear confession from, and administer absolution to, a person.

Succentor. One who takes up the chant in church singing after the **precentor** has set the tune. Usually presided over the left side of the choir, where the precentor presided over the right side.

Toll. The right to tax goods coming into the Lord's land or the **burgh**; the proportion of grain taken by the miller as payment for grinding; the rent paid for a mill or a house in kind rather than cash.

Team. Anglo-Saxon law, usually coupled with **Toll**. Suit for the recovery of goods allegedly stolen; a method of vouching to the warranty of ownership of goods.

Tithe. Payment of one tenth of one's crops to the church for the maintenance of the church and the priests. Tithe barns were later built to hold the considerable produce.

Tithing. A group of men, usually ten, bound to be responsible for each other under the system of **Frankpledge**.

Triforium. Gallery or arcade in the wall over the arches at the sides of the nave and choir in a large church.

Vill. The Norman equivalent of the **burgh**.

Villein. A feudal tennant with few rights. He was allocated a portion of land by the lord of the manor in exchange for certain feudal duties.

Virgate. Area of land commonly a quarter of a hide or about 30 acres. A man could scratch a living off a virgate if he was lucky.

Yard. A unit of length taken from the nose to the end of a man's clenched fist held horizontally sideways or roughly three times the length of a man's foot.